# ISAAC ASIMOV
## PRESENTS

# THE GOLDEN YEARS OF SCIENCE FICTION

**EDITED BY ISAAC ASIMOV
AND MARTIN H. GREENBERG**

**BONANZA BOOKS
NEW YORK**

This 1983 edition is published by Bonanza Books,
distributed by Crown Publishers, Inc. by arrangement with
Daw Books, Inc.

This book was previously published as two separate works entitled
Isaac Asimov Presents The Great SF Stories, I, 1939 and
Isaac Asimov Presents The Great SF Stories, II, 1940

Manufactured in the United States of America

**Library of Congress Cataloging in Publication Data**

Main entry under title:

Isaac Asimov presents the golden years of science fiction.

   Originally published in 2 v.
   1. Science fiction, American.   2. Science fiction,
English.   I. Asimov, Isaac, 1920-      .   II. Greenberg,
Martin Harry.
PS648.S3I79      1983        813'.0876'08        82-19720

ISBN: 0-517-401479

h g f e d c b a

# FOREWORD

It is rare when we can say that in a single volume can be found virtually many of the foundation stones of a branch of literature.

Yet in this anthology combining the pivotal years 1939 and 1940, which appeared originally in separate volumes, will be found thirty-six stories by the writers who changed science fiction from quick and easy pulp action to the branch of literature that commanded respect and came close to the realities of the space age.

Thus it is appropriate that this be the first collection that Isaac Asimov designed to be a definitive series of SF anthologies covering year by year the truly memorable stories. These now classic tales forecasted and helped inspire such developments as nuclear power, satellite technology, microminiaturization, men on the moon, exploration devices on Mars and Venus, as well as providing source material for such movie box-office successes as *Star Wars, E.T., Star Trek* and many others.

—JHR

# ISAAC ASIMOV
## PRESENTS

# THE GOLDEN YEARS OF SCIENCE FICTION

## Volume 1

# ACKNOWLEDGMENTS

# CONTENTS

# Introduction

In the world outside reality, it was a very bad year indeed. On March 28 Madrid fell to the forces of Francisco Franco, ending the Spanish Civil War. On April 15, President Roosevelt sought assurances from Hitler and Mussolini that they would not attack a long list of nation states (they said they would consider the request). On May 4 Vyacheslav Molotov (not yet named for the cocktail) replaced Maxim Litvinov as Soviet Foreign Minister, paving the way for the Hitler-Stalin Pact a few months later. On May 22 Hitler and Mussolini signed the "Pact of Steel."

On September 1 Germany grew tired of conquering without war and invaded Poland. On the 3rd Britain and France reluctantly declared war on the Third Reich. On September 17 the U.S.S.R. invaded Poland from the East—by September 30 Germany and the Soviet Union had agreed on the partition of Poland between them, and Hitler's master plan had passed another hurdle triumphantly.

On October 10 the deportation of Polish Jews to "reserves" began, and the Soviet Union invaded Finland on November 30, while Great Britain and France maintained a firm inactivity and the United States pretended it was on another planet.

During 1939 D.D.T. was invented. Pan American began "Clipper" flights between the United States and Europe. John Dewey's CULTURE AND FREEDOM was published. Texas A. & M. was the National Collegiate Football Champion. Picasso painted "Night Fishing at Antibes." The record for the mile run was still the 4:06.4 set in 1937 by Sydney Wooderson of Great Britain. "Grandma" Moses became famous. Bobby Riggs became the USTA Champion by defeating S. Welby Van Horn (Billy Jean King was not yet born). Jacob Epstein created "Adam" out of marble. Alice Marble was the National Women's Singles Champion. William Walton wrote his *Violin Concerto*. Byron Nelson won the U. S. Open. Robert Graves published THE LONG WEEK-END. Ralph Guldahl won the Masters Tournament. John Steinbeck published THE GRAPES OF WRATH. Johnstown won the Kentucky Derby. THE MAN WHO CAME TO DINNER by George S. Kaufman and Moss Hart made it big on Broadway, as did William Saroyan's THE TIME OF YOUR LIFE. Oregon won the NCAA Basketball Championship. GONE WITH THE WIND and GOODBYE MR. CHIPS were the movies of the year. Joe DiMaggio led the majors with a .381 average before he turned to selling coffee-makers. "Roll Out the Barrel," the prophetic "The Last Time I Saw Paris," and "Hang Out the Washing on the Siegfreid Line" were hit songs. New York defeated Cincinnati four games to none to take the World Series. Joe Louis beat a bunch of turkeys to retain his heavyweight boxing championship.

And the distant knell of doom went unheard as in Germany Hahn and Strasseman discovered uranium fission, Lise Meitner in Sweden let the cat out of the bag, and Niels Bohr carried the news to the United States.

Death took Zane Grey, William Butler Yeats, Ford Maddox Ford, and the recently exiled Sigmund Freud.

Mel Brooks was still Melvin Kaminsky.

But in the real world it was a very good and important year.

In the real world the very first World Science Fiction Convention was held in New York as Sam Moskowitz and Don Wollheim fought for control of The Movement. In the real world UNKNOWN was published as a fantasy companion to ASTOUNDING: STARTLING STORIES; SCIENCE FICTION; FANTASTIC ADVENTURES; FUTURE FICTION; FAMOUS FANTASIC MYSTERIES; and PLANET STORIES all saw the light of day for the first time.

In the real world, John Campbell spent his first full year as editor of ASTOUNDING and the "Golden Age" was born with a flurry of writers Campbell was either to conceive or develop. Important people made their maiden flights into reality: in March—Isaac Asimov with MAROONED OFF VESTA; in April—Alfred Bester with THE BROKEN AXIOM; in July—A. E. van Vogt with BLACK DESTROYER; in August—Robert A. Heinlein with LIFE LINE and Fritz Leiber with TWO SOUGHT ADVENTURE; and in September—Theodore Sturgeon with ETHER BREATHER.

More wondrous things occurred in the real world: SINISTER BARRIER by Eric Frank Russell and LEST DARKNESS FALL by L. Sprague de Camp were published in UNKNOWN. ONE AGAINST THE LEGION by Jack Williamson and GREY LENSMAN by Doc Smith were serialized in ASTOUNDING (the last installment of the latter appearing in 1940). WAR WITH THE NEWTS by Karel Capek and THE OUTSIDER AND OTHERS by H. P. Lovecraft appeared in hard covers, as did the late Stanley Weinbaum's THE NEW ADAM.

The New York World's Fair influenced a generation of New York (and a few others) sf fans, editors, and writers-to-be. HARPER'S published an attack on science fiction—"Doom Beyond Jupiter" by one Bernard De Voto—no one cared.

And distant wings were beating as Barry N. Malzberg, Michael Moorcock, and Peter Nicholls were born (the last to a critical reception).

Let us travel back to that honored year of 1939 and enjoy the best stories that the real world bequeathed to us.

# I, ROBOT

*Amazing Stories*, January

# by Eando Binder (1911–1975)

*"Eando Binder" was the name used by the brothers Otto and Earl Binder on a number of science fiction stories, although after 1940 Otto worked alone. The Binder brothers are best known for three series published from the late thirties to the early forties—"Anton York," an immortal man, stories collected as ANTON YORK, IMMORTAL (1965); the "Via" stories under the name "Gordon A. Giles," all appearing in* Thrilling Wonder Stories; *and the "Adam Link" stories about a robot, collected as ADAM LINK—ROBOT (1965).*

*I, ROBOT was the first of the tales, most interesting because it was one of the very few science fiction stories told from the point of view of a non-human. Adam Link captured the imagination of the readers of* Amazing Stories *with adventures like this one.*

*(It certainly caught my attention. Two months after I read it, I began "Robbie", about a sympathetic robot, and that was the start of my positronic robot series. Eleven years later, when nine of my robot stories were collected into a book, the publisher named the collection I, ROBOT over my objections. My book is now the more famous, but Otto's story was there first. IA)*

*My Creation*

Much of what has occurred puzzles me. But I think I am beginning to understand now. You call me a monster, but you are wrong. Utterly wrong!

I will try to prove it to you, in writing. I hope I have time to finish. . . .

I will begin at the beginning. I was born, or created, six months ago, on November 3 of last year. I am a true robot. So many of you seem to have doubts. I am made of wires and wheels, not flesh and blood.

My first recollection of consciousness was a feeling of being chained, and I was. For three days before that, I had been seeing and hearing, but all in a jumble. Now, I had the urge to arise and peer more closely at the strange, moving form that I had seen so many times before me, making sounds.

The moving form was Dr. Link, my creator. He was the only thing that moved, of all the objects within my sight. He and one other object—his dog Terry. Therefore these two objects held my interest more. I hadn't yet learned to associate movement with life.

But on this fourth day, I wanted to approach the two moving shapes and make noises at them—particularly at the smaller one. His noises were challenging, stirring. They made me want to rise and quiet them. But I was chained. I was held down by them so that, in my blank state of mind, I wouldn't wander off and bring myself to an untimely end, or harm someone unknowingly.

These things, of course, Dr. Link explained to me later, when I could dissociate my thoughts and understand. I was just like a baby for those three days—a human baby. I am not as other so-called robots were—mere automatized machines designed to obey certain commands or arranged stimuli.

No, I was equipped with a pseudo-brain that could receive *all* stimuli that human brains could. And with possibilities of eventually learning to rationalize for itself.

But for three days Dr. Link was very anxious about my brain. I was like a human baby and yet I was also like a sensitive, but unorganized, machine, subject to the whim of mechanical chance. My eyes turned when a bit of paper fluttered to the floor. But photoelectric cells had been made before capable of doing the same. My mechanical ears turned to receive sounds best from a certain direction, but any scientist could duplicate that trick with sonic relays.

The question was—did my brain, to which the eyes and

ears were connected, hold on to these various impressions for future use? Did I have, in short—*memory?*

Three days I was like a newborn baby. And Dr. Link was like a worried father, wondering if his child had been born a hopeless idiot. But on the fourth day, he feared I was a wild animal. I began to make rasping sounds with my vocal apparatus, in answer to the sharp little noises Terry the dog made. I shook my swivel head at the same time and strained against my bonds.

For a while, as Dr. Link told me, he was frightened of me. I seemed like nothing so much as an enraged jungle creature, ready to go berserk. He had more than half a mind to destroy me on the spot.

But one thing changed his mind and saved me.

The little animal, Terry, barking angrily, rushed forward suddenly. It probably wanted to bite me. Dr. Link tried to call it back, but too late. Finding my smooth metal legs adamant, the dog leaped with foolish bravery in my lap, to come at my throat. One of my hands grasped it by the middle, held it up. My metal fingers squeezed too hard, and the dog gave out a pained squeal.

*Instantaneously, my hand opened to let the creature escape!* Instantaneously. My brain had interpreted the sound for what it was. A long chain of memory-association had worked. Three days before, when I had first been brought to life, Dr. Link had stepped on Terry's foot accidentally. The dog had squealed its pain. I had seen Dr. Link, at risk of losing his balance, instantly jerk up his foot. Terry had stopped squealing.

Terry squealed when my hand tightened. He would stop when I untightened. Memory-association. The thing psychologists call reflexive reaction. A sign of a living brain.

Dr. Link tells me he let out a cry of pure triumph. He knew at a stroke I had memory. He knew I was not a wanton monster. He knew I had a thinking organ, and a first-class one. Why? Because I had reacted *instantaneously*. You will realize what that means later.

I learned to walk in three hours. Dr. Link was still taking somewhat of a chance, unbinding my chains. He had no assurance that I would not just blunder away like a witless machine. But he knew he had to teach me to walk before I could learn to talk. The same as he knew he must bring my brain alive fully connected to the appendages and pseudo-organs it was later to use.

If he had simply disconnected my legs and arms for those first three days, my awakening brain would never have been able to use them when connected later. Do you think, if you were suddenly endowed with a third arm, that you could ever use it? Why does it take a cured paralytic so long to regain the use of his natural limbs? Mental blind spots in the brain. Dr. Link had all those strange psychological twists figured out.

Walk first. Talk next. That is the tried-and-true rule used among humans since the dawn of their species. Human babies learn best and fastest that way. And I was a human baby in mind, if not body.

Dr. Link held his breath when I first essayed to rise. I did, slowly, swaying on my metal legs. Up in my head, I had a three-directional spirit-level electrically contacting my brain. It told me automatically what was horizontal, vertical, and oblique. My first tentative step, however, wasn't a success. My knee joints flexed in reverse order. I clattered to my knees, which fortunately were knobbed with thick protective plates so that the more delicate swiveling mechanisms behind weren't harmed.

Dr. Link says I looked up at him like a startled child might. Then I promptly began walking along on my knees, finding this easy. Children would do this more only that it hurts them. I know no hurt.

After I had roved up and down the aisles of his workshop for an hour, nicking up his furniture terribly, walking on my knees seemed completely natural. Dr. Link was in a quandary how to get me up to my full height. He tried grasping my arm and pulling me up, but my 300 pounds of weight were too much for him.

My own rapidly increasing curiosity solved the problem. Like a child discovering the thrill of added height with stilts, my next attempt to rise to my full height pleased me. I tried staying up. I finally mastered the technique of alternate use of limbs and shift of weight forward.

In a couple of hours Dr. Link was leading me up and down the gravel walk around his laboratory. On my legs, it was quite easy for him to pull me along and thus guide me. Little Terry gamboled along at our heels, barking joyfully. The dog had accepted me as a friend.

I was by this time quite docile to Dr. Link's guidance. My

impressionable mind had quietly accepted him as a necessary rein and check. I did, he told me later, make tentative movements in odd directions off the path, motivated by vague stimuli, but his firm arm pulling me back served instantly to keep me in line. He paraded up and down with me as one might with an irresponsible oaf.

I would have kept on walking tirelessly for hours, but Dr. Link's burden of years quickly fatigued him and he led me inside. When he had safely gotten me seated in my metal chair, he clicked the switch on my chest that broke the electric current giving me life. And for the fourth time I knew that dreamless non-being which corresponded to my creator's periods of sleep.

### My Education

In three days I learned to talk reasonably well.

I give Dr. Link as much credit as myself. In those three days he pointed out the names of all objects in the laboratory and around. This fund of two hundred or so nouns he supplemented with as many verbs of action as he could demonstrate. Once heard and learned, a word never again was forgotten or obscured to me. Instantaneous comprehension. Photographic memory. Those things I had.

It is difficult to explain. Machinery is precise, unvarying. I am a machine. Electrons perform their tasks instantaneously. Electrons motivate my metallic brain.

Thus, with the intelligence of a child of five at the end of those three days, I was taught to read by Dr. Link. My photoelectric eyes instantly grasped the connection between speech and letter, as my mentor pointed them out. Thought-association filled in the gaps of understanding. I perceived without delay that the word "lion," for instance, pronounced in its peculiar way, represented a live animal crudely pictured in the book. I have never seen a lion. But I would know one the instant I did.

From primers and first-readers I graduated in less than a week to adult books. Dr. Link laid out an extensive reading course for me in his large library. It included fiction as well as factual matter. Into my receptive, retentive brain began to be poured a fund of information and knowledge never before equaled in that short period of time.

There are other things to consider besides my "birth" and "education." First of all the housekeeper. She came in once a week to clean up the house for Dr. Link. He was a recluse, lived by himself, cooked for himself—retired on an annuity from an invention years before.

The housekeeper had seen me in the process of construction in the past years, but only as an inanimate caricature of a human body. Dr. Link should have known better. When the first Saturday of my life came around, he forgot it was the day she came. He was absorbedly pointing out to me that "to run" meant to go faster than "to walk."

"Demonstrate," Dr. Link asked as I claimed understanding.

Obediently, I took a few slow steps before him. "Walking," I said. Then I retreated a ways and lumbered forward again, running for a few steps. The stone floor clattered under my metallic feet.

"Was—that—right?" I asked in my rather stentorian voice.

At that moment a terrified shriek sounded from the doorway. The housekeeper came up just in time to see me perform.

She screamed, making more noise than even I. "It's the Devil himself! Run, Dr. Link—run! Police—help—"

She fainted dead away. He revived her and talked soothingly to her, trying to explain what I was, but he had to get a new housekeeper. After this he contrived to remember when Saturday came, and on that day he kept me hidden in a storeroom reading books.

A trivial incident in itself, perhaps, but very significant, as you who will read this will agree.

Two months after my awakening to life, Dr. Link one day spoke to me in a fashion other than as teacher to pupil; spoke to me as man to—man.

"You are the result of twenty years of effort," he said, "and my success amazes even me. You are little short of being a human in mind. You are a monster, a creation, but you are basically human. You have no heredity. Your environment is molding you. You are the proof that mind is an electrical phenomenon, molded by environment. In human beings, their bodies—called heredity—are environment. But out of you I will make a mental wonder!"

His eyes seemed to burn with a strange fire, but this softened as he went on.

"I knew I had something unprecedented and vital twenty years ago when I perfected an iridium sponge sensitive to the impact of a single electron. It was the sensitivity of thought! Mental currents in the human brain are of this micro-magnitude. I had the means now of duplicating mind currents in an artificial medium. From that day to this I worked on the problem.

"It was not long ago that I completed your 'brain'—an intricate complex of iridium-sponge cells. Before I brought it to life, I had your body built by skilled artisans. I wanted you to begin life equipped to live and move in it as nearly in the human way as possible. How eagerly I awaited your debut into the world!"

His eyes shone.

"You surpassed my expectations. You are not merely a thinking robot. A metal man. You are—life! A new kind of life. You can be trained to think, to reason, to perform. In the future, your kind can be of inestimable aid to man, and his civilization. You are the first of your kind."

The days and weeks slipped by. My mind matured and gathered knowledge steadily from Dr. Link's library. I was able, in time, to scan and absorb a page at a time of reading matter, as readily as human eyes scan lines. You know of the television principle—a pencil of light moving hundreds of times a second over the object to be transmitted. My eyes, triggered with speedy electrons, could do the same. What I read was absorbed—memorized—instantly. From then on it was part of my knowledge.

Scientific subjects particularly claimed my attention. There was always something indefinable about human things, something I could not quite grasp, but science digested easily in my science-compounded brain. It was not long before I knew all about myself and why I "ticked," much more fully than most humans know why they live, think, and move.

Mechanical principles became starkly simple to me. I made suggestions for improvements in my own make-up that Dr. Link readily agreed upon correcting. We added little universals in my fingers, for example, that made them almost as supple as their human models.

Almost, I say. The human body is a marvelously perfected organic machine. No robot will ever equal it in sheer efficiency and adaptability. I realized my limitations.

Perhaps you will realize what I mean when I say that my eyes cannot see colors. Or rather, I see just one color, in the blue range. It would take an impossibly complex series of units, bigger than my whole body, to enable me to see all colors. Nature has packed all that in two globes the size of marbles, for *her* robots. She had a billion years to do it. Dr. Link only had twenty years.

But my brain—that was another matter. Equipped with only the two senses of one-color sight and limited sound, it was yet capable of garnishing a full experience. Smell and taste are gastronomic senses. I do not need them. Feeling is a device of Nature's to protect a fragile body. My body is not fragile.

Sight and sound are the only two cerebral senses. Einstein, color-blind, half-dead, and with deadened senses of taste, smell, and feeling, would still have been Einstein—mentally.

Sleep is only a word to me. When Dr. Link knew he could trust me to take care of myself, he dispensed with the nightly habit of "turning me off." While he slept, I spent the hours reading.

He taught me how to remove the depleted storage battery in the pelvic part of my metal frame when necessary and replace it with a fresh one. This had to be done every forty-eight hours. Electricity is my life and strength. It is my food. Without it I am so much metal junk.

But I have explained enough of myself. I suspect that ten thousand more pages of description would make no difference in your attitude, you who are even now—

An amusing thing happened one day, not long ago. Yes, I can be amused too. I cannot laugh, but my brain can appreciate the ridiculous. Dr. Link's perennial gardener came to the place, unannounced. Searching for the doctor to ask how he wanted the hedges cut, the man came upon us in the back, walking side by side for Dr. Link's daily light exercise.

The gardener's mouth began speaking and then ludicrously gaped open and stayed that way as he caught a full glimpse of me. But he did not faint in fright as the housekeeper had. He stood there, paralyzed.

"What's the matter, Charley?" queried Dr. Link sharply. He was so used to me that for the moment he had no idea why the gardener should be astonished.

"That—that thing!" gasped the man finally.

"Oh. Well, it's a robot," said Dr. Link. "Haven't you ever heard of them? An intelligent robot. Speak to him, he'll answer."

After some urging, the gardener sheepishly turned to me. "H-how do you do, Mr. Robot," he stammered.

"How do you do, Mr. Charley," I returned promptly,

seeing the amusement in Dr. Link's face. "Nice weather, isn't it?"

For a moment the man looked ready to shriek and run. But he squared his shoulders and curled his lip. "Trickery!" he scoffed. "That thing can't be intelligent. You've got a phonograph inside of it. How about the hedges?"

"I'm afraid," murmured Dr. Link with a chuckle, "that the robot is more intelligent than you, Charley!" But he said it so the man didn't hear and then directed how to trim the hedges. Charley didn't do a good job. He seemed to be nervous all day.

*My Fate*

One day Dr. Link stared at me proudly.

"You have now," he said, "the intellectual capacity of a man of many years. Soon I'll announce you to the world. You shall take your place in our world, as an independent entity—as a citizen!"

"Yes, Dr. Link," I returned. "Whatever you say. You are my creator—my master."

"Don't think of it that way," he admonished. "In the same sense, you are my son. But a father is not a son's master after his maturity. You have gained that status." He frowned thoughtfully. "You must have a name! Adam! Adam Link!"

He faced me and put a hand on my shiny chromium shoulder. "Adam Link, what is your choice of future life?"

"I want to serve you, Dr. Link."

"But you will outlive me! And you may outlive several other masters!"

"I will serve any master who will have me," I said slowly. I had been thinking about this before. "I have been created by man. I will serve man."

Perhaps he was testing me. I don't know. But my answers obviously pleased him. "Now," he said, "I will have no fears in announcing you!"

The next day he was dead.

That was three days ago. I was in the storeroom reading—it was housekeeper's day. I heard the noise. I ran up the steps, into the laboratory. Dr. Link lay with skull crushed. A loose angle-iron of a transformer hung on an insulated platform on the wall had slipped and crashed down on his head while he sat there before his workbench. I raised his head, slumped over the bench, to better see the wound. Death had been instantaneous.

These are the facts. I turned the angle-iron back myself. The blood on my fingers resulted when I raised his head, not knowing for the moment that he was stark dead. In a sense, I was responsible for the accident, for in my early days of walking I had once blundered against the transformer shelf and nearly torn it loose. We should have repaired it.

But that I am his *murderer*, as you all believe, is not true. The housekeeper had also heard the noise and came from the house to investigate. She took one look. She saw me bending over the doctor, his head torn and bloody—she fled, too frightened to make a sound.

It would be hard to describe my thoughts. The little dog Terry sniffed at the body, sensed the calamity, and went down on his belly, whimpering. He felt the loss of a master. So did I. I am not sure what your emotion of sorrow is. Perhaps I cannot feel that deeply. But I do know that the sunlight seemed suddenly faded to me.

My thoughts are rapid. I stood there only a minute, but in that time I made up my mind to leave. This again has been misinterpreted. You considered that an admission of guilt, the criminal escaping from the scene of his crime. In my case it was a full-fledged desire to go out into the world, find a place in it.

Dr. Link and my life with him were a closed book. No use now to stay and watch ceremonials. He had launched my life. He was gone. My place now must be somewhere out in the world I had never seen. No thought entered my mind of what you humans would decide about me. I thought all men were like Dr. Link.

First of all I took a fresh battery, replacing my half-depleted one. I would need another in forty-eight hours, but I was sure this would be taken care of by anyone to whom I made the request.

I left. Terry followed me. He has been with me all the time. I have heard a dog is man's best friend. Even a metal man's.

My conceptions of geography soon proved hazy at best. I had pictured earth as teeming with humans and cities, with not much space between. I had estimated that the city Dr. Link spoke of must be just over the hill from his secluded country home. Yet the wood I traversed seemed endless.

It was not till hours later that I met the little girl. She had been dangling her bare legs into a brook, sitting on a flat rock. I approached to ask where the city was. She turned when I was still thirty feet away My internal mechanisms do not run silently. They make a steady noise that Dr. Link always described as a handful of coins jingling together.

The little girl's face contorted as soon as she saw me. I must be a fearsome sight indeed in your eyes. Screaming her fear, she blindly jumped up, lost her balance, and fell into the stream.

I knew what drowning was. I knew I must save her. I knelt at the rock's edge and reached down for her. I managed to grasp one of her arms and pull her up. I could feel the bones of her thin little wrist crack. I had forgotten my strength.

I had to grasp her little leg with my other hand, to pull her up. The livid marks showed on her white flesh when I laid her on the grass. I can guess now what interpretation was put on all this. A terrible, raving monster, I had tried to drown her and break her little body in wanton savageness!

You others of her picnic party appeared then, in answer to her cries. You women screamed and fainted. You men snarled and threw rocks at me. But what strange bravery imbued the woman, probably the child's mother, who ran up under my very feet to snatch up her loved one? I admired her. The rest of you I despised for not listening to my attempts to explain. You drowned out my voice with your screams and shouts.

"Dr. Link's robot!—it's escaped and gone crazy!—h' shouldn't have made that monster!—get the police!—nearly killed poor Frances!—"

With these garbled shouts to one another, you withdrew. You didn't notice that Terry was barking angrily—at you. Can you fool a dog? We went on.

Now my thoughts really became puzzled. Here at last was something I could not rationalize. This was so different from the world I had learned about in books. What subtle things lay behind the printed words that I had read? What had happened to the sane and orderly world my mind had conjured for itself?

Night came. I had to stop and stay still in the dark. I leaned against a tree motionlessly. For a while I heard little Terry snooping around in the brush for something to eat. I heard him gnawing something. Then later he curled up at my feet and slept. The hours passed slowly. My thoughts would not come to a conclusion about the recent occurrence. Monster! Why had they believed that?

Once, in the still distance, I heard a murmur as of a crowd of people. I saw some lights. They had significance the next day. At dawn I nudged Terry with my toe and we walked on. The same murmur arose, approached. Then I saw you, a crowd of you, men with clubs, scythes, and guns. You spied me and a shout went up. You hung together as you advanced.

Then something struck my frontal plate with a sharp clang. One of you had shot.

"Stop! Wait!" I shouted, knowing I must talk to you, find out why I was being hunted like a wild beast. I had taken a step forward, hand upraised. But you would not listen. More shots rang out, denting my metal body. I turned and ran. A bullet in a vital spot would ruin me, as much as a human.

You came after me like a pack of hounds, but I outdistanced you, powered by steel muscles. Terry fell behind, lost. Then, as afternoon came, I realized I must get a newly charged battery. Already my limbs were moving sluggishly. In a few more hours, without a new source of current within me, I would fall on the spot and—die.

And I did not want to die.

I knew I must find a road to the city. I finally came upon a winding dirt road and followed it in hope. When I saw a car parked at the side of the road ahead of me, I knew I was saved, for Dr. Link's car had had the same sort of battery I used. There was no one around the car. Much as a starving man would take the first meal available, I raised the floorboards and in a short while had substituted batteries.

New strength coursed through my body. I straightened up just as two people came arm in arm from among the trees, a young man and woman. They caught sight of me. Incredulous shock came into their faces. The girl shrank into the boy's arms.

"Do not be alarmed," I said. "I will not harm you. I—"

There was no use going on, I saw that. The boy fainted dead away in the girl's arms and she began dragging him away, wailing hysterically.

I left. My thoughts from then on can best be described as brooding. I did not want to go to the city now. I began to realize I was an outcast in human eyes, from the first sight on.

Just as night fell and I stopped, I heard a most welcome sound. Terry's barking! He came up joyfully, wagging his stump of tail. I reached down to scratch his ears. All these hours he had faithfully searched for me. He had probably tracked me by a scent of oil. What can cause such blind devotion—and to a metal man!

Is it because, as Dr. Link once stated, that the body, human or otherwise, is only part of the environment of the mind? And that Terry recognized in me as much of mind as in humans, despite my alien body? If that is so, it is you who are passing judgment on me as a monster who are in the wrong. And I am convinced it is so!

I hear you now—shouting outside—*beware that you do not drive me to be the monster you call me!*

The next dawn precipitated you upon me again. Bullets flew. I ran. All that day it was the same. Your party, swelled by added recruits, split into groups, trying to ring me in. You tracked me by my heavy footprints. My speed saved me each time. Yet some of those bullets have done damage. One struck the joint of my right knee, so that my leg twisted as I ran. One smashed into the right side of my head and shattered the tympanum there, making me deaf on that side.

But the bullet that hurt me most was the one that killed Terry!

The shooter of that bullet was twenty yards away. I could have run to him, broken his every bone with my hard, powerful hands. Have you stopped to wonder why I didn't take revenge? *Perhaps I should!* . . .

I was hopelessly lost all that day. I went in circles through the endless woods and as often blundered into you as you into me. I was trying to get away from the vicinity, from your vengeance. Toward dusk I saw something familiar—Dr. Link's laboratory!

Hiding in a clump of bushes and waiting till it was utterly dark, I approached and broke the lock on the door. It was deserted. Dr. Link's body was gone, of course.

My birthplace! My six months of life here whirled through my mind with kaleidoscopic rapidity. I wonder if my emotion was akin to what yours would be, returning to a well-remembered place? Perhaps my emotion is far deeper than yours can be! Life may be all in the mind. Something gripped me there, throbbingly. The shadows made by a dim gas jet I lit seemed to dance around me like little Terry had danced. Then I found the book, *Frankenstein*, lying on the desk whose drawers had been emptied. Dr. Link's private desk. He had kept the book from me. Why? I read it now, in a half-hour, by my page-at-a-time scanning. And then I understood!

But it is the most stupid premise ever made: that a created man must turn against his creator, against humanity, lacking a soul. The book is all wrong.

*Or is it? . . . .*

As I finish writing this, here among blasted memories, with the spirit of Terry in the shadows, I wonder if I shouldn't. . .

It is close to dawn now. I know there is not hope for me. You have me surrounded, cut off. I can see the flares of your torches between the trees. In the light you will find me, rout me out. Your hatred lust is aroused. It will be sated only by my—death.

I have not been so badly damaged that I cannot still summon strength and power enough to ram through your lines and escape this fate. But it would only be at the cost of several of your lives. And that is the reason I have my hand on the switch that can blink out my life with one twist.

Ironic, isn't it, that I have the very feelings you are so sure I lack?

(signed) ADAM LINK

# THE STRANGE FLIGHT OF RICHARD CLAYTON

*Amazing Stories,*

March

## by Robert Bloch (1917–    )

*Robert Bloch has been around the science fiction world for a long time, being one of the members of the "Lovecraft Circle" in his youth. Although he is primarily a writer of the supernatural and macabre story, he also produced some excellent science fiction, most of which is available in his collections ATOMS AND EVIL (1962) and THE BEST OF ROBERT BLOCH (1978). His skill as an after-dinner speaker masks a real talent for the shocking and the unexpected, as his non-sf novel PSYCHO illustrates. He also had the unusual distinction of winning a Hugo Award for a work of fantasy, "That Hell-Bound Train" (1958, Award in 1959).*

*Space travel is science fiction for too many people, although the exploration of the great unknown of space has provided us with many wonderful stories—as has the voyages that take place between our ears.*

*(This story appeared in the magazine issue that contained my own first published story, "Marooned Off Vesta." Bob's story was the only one in that issue which, in my eyes, was better than mine. I was not unduly troubled with excessive modesty even then, you see. IA)*

25

Richard Clayton braced himself so that he stood like a diver waiting to plunge from a high board into the blue. In truth he was a diver. A silver spaceship was his board, and he meant to plunge not down, but up into the blue sky. Nor was it a matter of twenty or thirty feet he meant to go—instead, he was plunging millions of miles.

With a deep breath, the pudgy, goateed scientist raised his hands to the cold steel lever, closed his eyes, jerked. The switch moved downward.

For a moment nothing happened.

Then a sudden jerk threw Clayton to the floor. The *Future* was moving!

The pinions of a bird beating as it soars into the sky—the wings of a moth thrumming in flight—the quivering behind leaping muscles; of these things the shock was made.

The spaceship *Future* vibrated madly. It rocked from side to side, and a humming shook the steel walls. Richard Clayton lay dazed as a high-pitched droning arose within the vessel. He rose to his feet, rubbing a bruised forehead, and lurched to his tiny bunk. The ship was moving, yet the terrible vibration did not abate. He glanced at the controls and then swore softly.

"Good God! The panel is shattered!"

It was true. The instrument board had been broken by the shock. The cracked glass had fallen to the floor, and the dials swung aimlessly on the bare face of the panel.

Clayton sat there in despair. This was a major tragedy. His thoughts flashed back thirty years to the time when he, a boy of ten, had been inspired by Lindberg's flight. He recalled his studies; how he had utilized the money of his millionaire father to perfect a flying machine which would cross Space itself.

For years Richard Clayton had worked and dreamed and planned. He studied the Russians and their rockets, organized the Clayton Foundation and hired mechanics, mathematicians, astronomers, engineers to labor with him.

Then there had been the discovery of atomic propulsior and the building of the *Future*. The *Future* was a shell ^ steel and duraluminum, windowless and insulated ⊦

guarded process. In the tiny cabin were oxygen tanks, stores of food tablets, energizing chemicals, air-conditioning arrangements—and space for a man to walk six paces.

It was a small steel cell; but in it Richard Clayton meant to realize his ambitions. Aided in his soaring by rockets to get him past the gravitational pull of Earth, then flying by means of the atomic-discharge propulsion, Clayton meant to reach Mars and return.

It would take ten years to reach Mars; ten years to return, for the grounding of the vessel would set off additional rocket-discharges. A thousand miles an hour—not an imaginative "speed of light" journey, but a slow, grim voyage, scientifically accurate. The panels were set, and Clayton had no need to guide his vessel. It was automatic.

"But now what?" Clayton said, staring at the shattered glass. He had lost touch with the outer world. He would be unable to read his progress on the board, unable to judge time and distance and direction. He would sit here for ten, twenty years—all alone in a tiny cabin. There had been no room for books or paper or games to amuse him. He was a prisoner in the black void of Space.

The Earth had already faded far below him; soon it would be a ball of burning green fire smaller than the ball of red fire ahead—the fire of Mars.

Crowds had swarmed the field to watch him take off; his assistant Jerry Chase had controlled them. Clayton pictured them watching his shining steel cylinder emerging from the gaseous smoke of the rockets and rushing like a bullet into the sky. Then his cylinder would have faded away into the blue and the crowds would leave for home and forget.

But he remained, here in the ship—for ten, for twenty years.

Yes, he remained, but when would the vibration stop? The shuddering of the walls and floor about him was awful to endure; he and the experts had not counted on this problem. Tremors wrenched through his aching head. What if they didn't cease, if they endured through the entire voyage? How long could he keep from going mad?

He could think. Clayton lay on his bunk and remembered—reviewed every tiny detail of his life from birth to the present. And soon he had exhausted all memory in a pitifully short time. Then he felt the horrible throbbing all about him.

"I can exercise," he said aloud, and paced the floor; six steps forward, six back. And he tired of that. Sighing. Clayton went to the food-stores in the cabinet and downed his capsules. "I can't even spend any time eating," he wryly observed. "A swallow and it's over."

The throbbing erased the grin from his face. It was maddening. He lay down once more in the lurching bunk; switched on oxygen in the close air. He would sleep, then; sleep if this damned thrumming would permit. He endured the horrid clanking that groaned all through the silence; switching off the light. His thoughts turned to his strange position; a prisoner in Space. Outside the burning planets wheeled, and stars whizzed in the inky blackness of spatial Nothingness. Here he lay safe and snug in a vibrating chamber; safe from the freezing cold. If only the awful jarring would stop!

Still, it had its compensations. There would be no newspapers on the voyage to torment him with accounts of man's inhumanity to man; no silly radio or television programs to annoy him. Only this cursed, omnipresent vibration. . . .

Clayton slept, hurtling through Space.

It was not daylight when he awoke. There was no daylight and no night. There was simply himself and the ship in Space. And the vibration was steady, nerve-wracking in its insistent beating against the brain. Clatyon's legs trembled as he reached the cabinet and ate his pills.

Then, he sat down and began to endure. A terrific feeling of loneliness was beginning to assail him. He was so utterly detached here—cut off from everything. There was nothing to do. It was worse than being a prisoner in solitary confinement; at least they have larger cells, the sight of the sun, a breath of fresh air, and the glimpse of an occasional face.

Clayton had thought himself a misanthrope, a recluse. Now he longed for the sight of another's face. As the hours passed he got queer ideas. He wanted to see Life, in some form—he would have given a fortune for the company of even an insect in his soaring dungeon. The sound of a human voice would be heaven. He was so *alone*.

Nothing to do but endure the jerking, pace the floor, eat his pills, try to sleep. Nothing to think about. Clayton began to long for the time when his nails needed cutting; he could stretch out the task for hours.

He examined his clothes intently, stared for hours in the little mirror at his bearded face. He memorized his body, scrutinized every article in the cabin of the *Future*.

And still he was not tired enough to sleep again.

He had a throbbing headache constantly. At length he managed to close his eyes and drift off into another slumber, broken by shocks which startled him into waking.

When finally he arose and switched on the light, together with more oxygen, he made a horrible discovery.

*He had lost his time-sense.*

"Time is relative," they had always told him. Now he realized the truth. He had nothing to measure time by—no watch, no glimpse of the sun or moon or stars, and no regular activities. How long had he been on this voyage? Try as he might, he could not remember.

Had he eaten every six hours? Or every ten? Or every twenty? Had he slept once each day? Once every three or four days? How often had he walked the floor?

With no instruments to place himself he was at a total loss. He ate his pills in a bemused fashion, trying to think above the shuddering which filled his senses.

This was awful. If he lost track of Time he might soon lose consciousness of identity itself. He would go mad here in the spaceship as it plunged through the void to planets beyond. Alone, tormented in a tiny cell, he had to cling to something. What was Time?

He no longer wanted to think about it. He no longer wanted to think about anything. He had to forget the world he left, or memory would drive him frantic.

"I'm afraid," he whispered. "Afraid of being alone in the darkness. I may have passed the moon. I may be a million miles away from Earth by now—or ten million."

Then Clayton realized that he was talking to himself. That way was madness. But he couldn't stop, any more than he could stop the horrible jarring vibration all around him.

"I'm afraid," he whispered in a voice that sounded hollow in the tiny humming room. "I'm afraid. *What time is it?*"

He fell asleep, still whispering, and Time rushed on.

Clayton awoke with fresh courage. He had lost his grip, he reasoned. Outside pressure, however equalized, had affected his nerves. The oxygen might have made him giddy, and the pill diet was bad. But now the weakness had passed. He smiled, walked the floor.

Then the thoughts came again. What day was it? How many weeks since he had started? Maybe it was months already; a year, two years. Everything of Earth seemed far away; almost part of a dream. He now felt closer to Mars than to Earth; he began to anticipate now instead of looking back.

For a while everything had been mechanical. He switched light on and off when needed, ate pills by habit, paced the floor without thinking, unconsciously tended the air system, slept without knowing when or why.

Richard Clayton gradually forgot about his body and the surroundings. The lurching buzz in his brain became a part of him; an aching part which told that he was whizzing through Space in a silver bullet. But it meant nothing more, for Clayton no longer talked to himself. He forgot himself and dreamed only of Mars ahead. Every throb of the vessel hummed, "Mars—Mars—Mars."

A wonderful thing happened. He landed. The ship nosed down, trembling. It eased gently onto the gassy sward of the red planet. For a long time Clayton had felt the pull of alien gravity, knew that automatic adjustments of his vessel were diminishing the atomic discharges and using the natural gravitational pull of Mars itself.

Now the ship landed, and Clayton had opened the door. He broke the seals and stepped out. He bounded lightly to the purple grass. His body felt free, buoyant. There was fresh air, and the sunlight seemed stronger, more intense, although clouds veiled the glowing globe.

Far away stood the forests, the green forests with the purple growth on the lushly-rearing trees. Clayton left the ship and approached the cool grove. The first tree had boughs that bent to the ground in two limbs.

Limbs—limbs they were! Two green arms reached out. Clawing branches grasped him and lifted him upward. Cold coils, slimy as a serpent's, held him tightly as he was pressed against the dark tree-trunk. And now he was staring into the purple growth set in the leaves.

The purple growths were—*heads*.

Evil, purple faces stared at him with rotting eyes like dead toadstools. Each face was wrinkled like a purple cauliflower, but beneath the pulpy mass was a great mouth. Every purple face had a purple mouth and each purple mouth opened to drip blood. Now the tree-arms pressed him closer to the cold, writhing trunk, and one of the purple faces—a woman's face—was moving up to kiss him.

The kiss of a vampire! Blood shone scarlet on the moving sensuous lips that bore down on his own. He struggled, but the limbs held him fast and the kiss came, cold as death. The icy flame of it seared through his being and his senses drowned.

Then Clayton awoke, and knew it was a dream. His body was bathed with moisture. It made him aware of his body. He tottered to the mirror.

A single glance sent him reeling back in horror. Was this too a part of his dream?

Gazing into the mirror, Clayton saw reflected the face of an aging man. The features were heavily bearded, and they were lined and wrinkled, the once puffy cheeks were sunken. The eyes were the worst—Clayton did not recognize his own eyes any more. Red and deep-set in bony sockets, they burned out in a wild stare of horror. He touched his face, saw the blue-veined hand rise in the mirror and run through graying hair.

Partial time-sense returned. He had been here for years. Years! He was growing old!

Of course the unnatural life would age him more rapidly, but still a great interval must have passed. Clayton knew that he must soon reach the end of his journey. He wanted to reach it before he had any more dreams. From now on, sanity and physical reserve must battle against the unseen enemy of Time. He staggered back to his bunk, as trembling like a metallic flying monster, the *Future* rushed on in the blackness of interstellar Space.

They were hammering outside the vessel now; their iron arms were breaking in the door. The black metal monsters lumbered in with iron tread. Their stern, steel-cut faces were expressionless as they grasped Clayton on either side and pulled him out. Across the iron platform they dragged him, walking stiffly with clicking feet that clanged against the metal. The great still shafts rose in silvery spires all about, and into the iron tower they took him. Up the stairs—clang, clang, clang, pounded the great metal feet.

And the iron stairs wound round endlessly; yet still they toiled. Their faces were set, and iron does not sweat. They never tired, though Clayton was a panting wreck ere they reached the dome and threw him before the Presence in the tower room. The metallic voice buzzed, mechanically, like a broken phonograph record.

"We—found—him—in—a—bird—oh—Master."

"He—is—made—of—soft—ness."

"He—is—alive—in—some—strange—way."

"An—an—im—al."

And then the booming voice from the center of the tower floor.

"*I hunger.*"

Rising on an iron throne from the floor, the Master. Just a great iron trap, with steel jaws like those on a steam-shovel. The jaws clicked open, and the horrid teeth gleamed. A voice came from the depths.

"*Feed me.*"

They threw Clayton forward in iron arms, and he fell into the trap-jaws of the monster. The jaws closed, champing with relish on human flesh. . . .

Clayton woke screaming. The mirror gleamed as his trembling hands found the light-switch. He stared into the face of an aging man with almost white hair. Clayton was growing old. And he wondered if his brain would hold out.

Eat pills, walk cabin, listen to the throbbing, put on air, lie on bunk. That was all, now. And the rest—waiting. Waiting in a humming torture-chamber, for hours, days, years, centuries, untold eons.

In every eon, a dream. He landed on Mars and the ghosts came coiling out of a gray fog. They were shapes in the fog, like slimy ectoplasm, and he saw through them. But they coiled and came, and their voices were faint whispers in his soul.

"Here is Life," they whispered. "We, whose souls have crossed the Void in death, have waited for Life to feast on. Let us take our feasting now."

And they smothered him under gray blankets, and sucked with gray, prickling mouths at his blood. . . .

Again he landed on the planet and there was nothing. Absolutely nothing. The ground was bare and it stretched off into horizons of nothingness. There was no sky nor sun, merely the ground; endless in all directions.

He set foot on it, cautiously. He sank down into nothingness. The nothingness was throbbing now, like the ship throbbed, and it was engulfing him. He was falling into a deep pit without sides, and the oblivion closed all about him. . . .

Clayton dreamed this one standing up. He opened his eyes before the mirror. His legs were weak and he steadied himself with hands that shook with age. He looked at the face in the glass—the face of a man of seventy.

"God!" he muttered. It was his own voice—the first sound he had heard in how long? How many years? For how long had he heard nothing above the hellish vibrations of this ship? How far had the *Future* gone? He was old already.

A horrid thought bit into his brain. Perhaps something had gone wrong. Maybe the calculations were at fault and he was moving into Space too slowly. He might never reach Mars. Then again—and it was a dreadful possibility—he had passed Mars, missed the carefully charted orbit of the planet. Now he was plunging on into empty voids beyond.

He swallowed his pills and lay down in the bunk. He felt a little calmer now; he had to be. For the first time in ages he remembered Earth.

Suppose it had been destroyed? Invaded by war or pestilence or disease while he was gone? Or meteors had struck it, some dying star had flamed death upon it from maddened heavens. Ghastly notions assailed him—what if Invaders crossed Space to conquer Earth, just as he now crossed to Mars?

But no sense in worrying about *that*. The problem was reaching his own goal. Helpless, he had to wait; maintain life and sanity long enough to achieve his aims. In the vibrating horror of his cell, Clayton took a mighty resolve with all his waning strength. He *would* live and when he landed he would see Mars. Whether or not he died on the long voyage home, he would exist until his goal was reached. He would fight against dreams from this moment on. No means of telling Time—only a long daze, and the humming of this infernal spaceship. But he'd live.

There were voices coming now, from outside the ship. Ghosts howled, in the dark depths of Space. Visions of monsters and dreams of torment came, and Clayton repulsed them all. Every hour or day or year—he no longer knew which—Clayton managed to stagger to the mirror. And always it showed that he was aging rapidly. His snow-white hair and wrinkled countenance hinted at incredible senility. But Clayton lived. He was too old to think any longer, and too weary. He merely lived in the droning of the ship.

At first he didn't realize. He was lying on his bunk and his rheumy eyes were closed in stupor. Suddenly he became aware that the lurching had stopped. Clayton knew he must be dreaming again. He drew himself up painfully, rubbed his eyes. No—the *Future* was still. It had *landed!*

He was trembling uncontrollably. Years of vibration had done this; years of isolation with only his crazed thoughts for company. He could scarcely stand.

But this was the moment. This was what he had waited for ten long years. No, it must have been many more years. But he could see Mars. He had made it—done the impossible.

It was an inspiring thought. But somehow, Richard Clayton would have given it all up if he could only have learned what time it was, and heard it from a human voice.

He staggered to the door—the long-sealed door. There was a lever here.

His aged heart pumped with excitement as he pulled the lever upward. The door opened—sunlight crept through—air rushed in—the light made him blink and the air wheezed in his lungs—his feet were moving out—

Clayton fell forward into the arms of Jerry Chase.

Clayton didn't know it was Jerry Chase. He didn't know anything any longer. It had been too much.

Chase was staring down at the feeble body in his arms.

"Where's Mr. Clayton?" he murmured. "Who are you?" He stared at the aged, wrinkled face.

"Why—it's Clayton! he breathed. "Mr. Clayton, what's wrong, sir? The atomic discharges failed when you started the ship, and all that happened was that they kept blasting. The ship never left the Earth, but the violence of the discharges kept us from reaching you until now. We couldn't get to the *Future* until they stopped. Just a little while ago the ship finished shuddering, but we've been watching night and day. What happened to you, sir?"

The faded blue eyes of Richard Clayton opened. His mouth twitched as he faintly whispered.

"I—lost track of Time. How—how long was I in the *Future?*"

Jerry Chase's face was grave as he stared again at the old man and answered, softly.

*"Just one week."*

And as Richard Clayton's eyes glazed in death, the long voyage ended.

# TROUBLE WITH WATER

*Unknown, March*

## by H. L. Gold (1914–     )

*One of the most significant figures in the history of science fiction, Horace Leonard Gold was the founding editor of GALAXY SF, and under his direction it quickly became the leading magazine in the field during the Fifties.*

*Unfortunately, his fame as an editor has obscured his talent as a writer. Gold was an original, clever author, and a more than competent stylist. His best work was collected in 1955 as THE OLD DIE RICH AND OTHER SCIENCE FICTION, a book that strongly deserves reprinting.*

*"Trouble With Water" is arguably his best story—and* not *because the protagonist's name is Greenberg. Think about this one the next time you feel thirsty.*

*(This was the funniest fantasy I had ever read, in my opinion, at the time it appeared. It appeared in the maiden issue of UNKNOWN FANTASY FICTION, and though the lead novel was Eric Frank Russell's classic SINISTER BARRIER, Horace's story was my favorite in the issue. IA)*

Greenberg did not deserve his surroundings. He was the first fisherman of the season, which guaranteed him a fine catch; he sat in a dry boat—one without a single leak—far out on a lake that was ruffled only enough to agitate his artificial fly.

35

The sun was warm, the air was cool; he sat comfortably on a cushion; he had brought a hearty lunch; and two bottles of beer hung over the stern in the cold water.

Any other man would have been soaked with joy to be fishing on such a splendid day. Normally, Greenberg himself would have been ecstatic, but instead of relaxing and waiting for a nibble, he was plagued by worries.

This short, slightly gross, definitely bald, eminently respectable businessman lived a gypsy life. During the summer he lived in a hotel with kitchen privileges in Rockaway; winters he lived in a hotel with kitchen privileges in Florida; and in both places he operated concessions. For years now, rain had fallen on schedule every week end, and there had been storms and floods on Decoration Day, July 4th and Labor Day. He did not love his life, but it was a way of making a living.

He closed his eyes and groaned. If he had only had a son instead of his Rosie! Then things would have been mighty different—

For one thing, a son could run the hot dog and hamburger griddle, Esther could draw beer, and he would make soft drinks. There would be small difference in the profits, Greenberg admitted to himself; but at least those profits could be put aside for old age, instead of toward a dowry for his miserably ugly, dumpy, pitifully eager Rosie.

"All right—so what do I care if she don't get married?" he had cried to his wife a thousand times. "I'll support her. Other men can set up boys in candy stores with soda fountains that have only two spigots. Why should I have to give a boy a regular International Casino?"

"May your tongue rot in your head, you no-good piker!" she would scream. "It ain't right for a girl to be an old maid. If we have to die in the poor-house, I'll get my poor Rosie a husband. Every penny we don't need for living goes to her dowry!"

Greenberg did not hate his daughter, nor did he blame her for his misfortunes; yet, because of her, he was fishing with a broken rod that he had to tape together.

That morning his wife opened her eyes and saw him packing his equipment. She instantly came awake. "Go ahead!" she shrilled—speaking in a conversational tone was not one of her accomplishments—"Go fishing, you loafer! Leave me here alone. I can connect the beer pipes and the gas for soda water. I can buy ice cream, frankfurters, rolls, sirup, and watch the gas and electric men at the same time. Go ahead—go fishing!"

"I ordered everything," he mumbled soothingly. "The gas and electric won't be turned on today. I only wanted to go fishing—it's my last chance. Tomorrow we open the concession. Tell the truth, Esther, can I go fishing after we open?"

"I don't care about that. Am I your wife or ain't I, that you should go ordering everything without asking me—"

He defended his actions. It was a tactical mistake. While she was still in bed, he should have picked up his equipment and left. By the time the argument got around to Rosie's dowry, she stood facing him.

"For myself I don't care," she yelled. "What kind of a monster are you that you can go fishing while your daughter eats her heart out? And on a day like this yet! You should only have to make supper and dress Rosie up. A lot you care that a nice boy is coming to supper tonight and maybe take Rosie out, you no-good father, you!"

From that point it was only one hot protest and a shrill curse to find himself clutching half a broken rod, with the other half being flung at his head.

Now he sat in his beautifully dry boat on an excellent game lake far out on Long Island, desperately aware that any average fish might collapse his taped rod.

What else could he expect? He had missed his train; he had had to wait for the boathouse proprietor; his favorite dry fly was missing; and, since morning, not a fish struck at the bait. Not a single fish!

And it was getting late. He had no more patience. He ripped the cap off a bottle of beer and drank it, in order to gain courage to change his fly for a less sporting bloodworm. It hurt him, but he wanted a fish.

The hook and the squirming worm sank. Before it came to rest, he felt a nibble. He sucked in his breath exultantly and snapped the hook deep into the fish's mouth. Sometimes, he thought philosophically, they just won't take artificial bait. He reeled in slowly.

"Oh, Lord," he prayed, "a dollar for charity—just don't let the rod bend in half where I taped it!"

It was sagging dangerously. He looked at it unhappily and raised his ante to five dollars; even at that price it looked impossible. He dipped his rod into the water, parallel with the line, to remove the strain. He was glad no one could see him do it. The line reeled in without a fight.

"Have I—God forbid!—got an eel or something not ko-
sher?" he mumbled. "A plague on you—why don't you
fight?"

He did not really care what it was—even an eel—anything
at all.

He pulled in a long, pointed, brimless green hat.

For a moment he glared at it. His mouth hardened. Then,
viciously, he yanked the hat off the hook, threw it on the
floor and trampled on it. He rubbed his hands together in anguish.

"All day I fish," he wailed, "two dollars for train fare, a
dollar for a boat, a quarter for bait, a new rod I got to
buy—and a five-dollar-mortgage charity has got on me. For
what? For you, you hat, you!"

Out in the water an extremely civil voice asked politely:
"May I have my hat, please?"

Greenberg glowered up. He saw a little man come swimming vigorously through the water toward him: small arms
crossed with enormous dignity, vast ears on a pointed face
propelling him quite rapidly and efficiently. With serious determination he drove through the water, and, at the starboard
rail, his amazing ears kept him stationary while he looked
gravely at Greenberg.

"You are stamping on my hat," he pointed out without anger.

To Greenberg this was highly unimportant. "With the ears
you're swimming," he grinned in a superior way. "Do you
look funny!"

"How else could I swim?" the little man asked politely.

"With the arms and legs, like a regular human being, of
course."

"But I am not a human being. I am a water gnome, a
relative of the more common mining gnome. I cannot swim
with my arms, because they must be crossed to give an appearance of dignity suitable to a water gnome; and my feet
are used for writing and holding things. On the other hand,
my ears are perfectly adapted for propulsion in water. Consequently, I employ them for that purpose. But please, my
hat—there are several matters requiring my immediate attention, and I must not waste time."

Greenberg's unpleasant attitude toward the remarkably
civil gnome is easily understandable. He had found someone
he could feel superior to, and, by insulting him, his depressed

ego could expand. The water gnome certainly looked inoffensive enough, being only two feet tall.

"What you got that's so important to do, Big Ears?" he asked nastily.

Greenberg hoped the gnome would be offended. He was not, since his ears, to him, were perfectly normal, just as you would not be insulted if a member of a race of atrophied beings were to call you "Big Muscles." You might even feel flattered.

"I really must hurry," the gnome said, almost anxiously. "But if I have to answer your questions in order to get back my hat—we are engaged in restocking the Eastern waters with fish. Last year there was quite a drain. The bureau of fisheries is coöperating with us to some extend, but, of course, we cannot depend too much on them. Until the population rises to normal, every fish has instructions not to nibble."

Greenberg allowed himself a smile, an annoyingly skeptical smile.

"My main work," the gnome went on resignedly, "is control of the rainfall over the Eastern seaboard. Our fact-finding committee, which is scientifically situated in the meteorological center of the continent, coördinates the rainfall needs of the entire continent; and when they determine the amount of rain needed in particular spots of the East, I make it rain to that extent. Now may I have my hat, please?"

Greenberg laughed coarsely. "The first lie was big enough—about telling the fish not to bite. You make it rain like I'm President of the United States!" He bent toward the gnome slyly. "How's about proof?"

"Certainly, if you insist." The gnome raised his patient, triangular face toward a particularly clear blue spot in the sky, a trifle to one side of Greenberg. "Watch that bit of the sky."

Greenberg looked up humorously. Even when a small dark cloud rapidly formed in the previously clear spot, his grin remained broad. It could have been coincidental. But then large drops of undeniable rain fell over a twenty-foot circle; and Greenberg's mocking grin shrank and grew sour.

He glared hatred at the gnome, finally convinced. "So you're the dirty crook who makes it rain on week ends!"

"Usually on week ends during the summer," the gnome admitted. "Ninety-two percent of water consumption is on weekdays. Obviously we must replace that water. The week ends, of course, are the logical time."

"But, you thief!" Greenberg cried hysterically, "you murderer! What do you care what you do to my concession with your rain? It ain't bad enough business would be rotten even without rain, you got to make floods!"

"I'm sorry," the gnome replied, untouched by Greenberg's rhetoric. "We do not create rainfall for the benefit of men. We are here to protect the fish.

"Now please give me my hat. I have wasted enough time, when I should be preparing the extremely heavy rain needed for this coming week end."

Greenberg jumped to his feet in the unsteady boat. "Rain this week end—when I can maybe make a profit for a change! A lot you care if you ruin business. May you and your fish die a horrible, lingering death."

And he furiously ripped the green hat to pieces and hurled them at the gnome.

"I'm really sorry you did that," the little fellow said calmly, his huge ears treading water without the slightest increase of pace to indicate his anger. "We Little Folk have no tempers to lose. Nevertheless, occasionally we find it necessary to discipline certain of your people, in order to retain our dignity. I am not malignant; but, since you hate water and those who live in it, water and those who live in it will keep away from you."

With his arms still folded in great dignity, the tiny water gnome flipped his vast ears and disappeared in a neat surface dive.

Greenberg glowered at the spreading circles of waves. He did not grasp the gnome's final restraining order; he did not even attempt to interpret it. Instead he glared angrily out of the corner of his eye at the phenomenal circle of rain that fell from a perfectly clear sky. The gnome must have remembered it at length, for a moment later the rain stopped. Like shutting off a faucet, Greenberg unwillingly thought.

"Good-by, week-end business," he growled. "If Esther finds out I got into an argument with the guy who makes it rain—"

He made an underhand cast, hoping for just one fish. The line flew out over the water; then the hook arched upward and came to rest several inches above the surface, hanging quite steadily and without support in the air.

"Well, go down in the water, damn you!" Greenberg said

viciously, and he swished his rod back and forth to pull the hook down from its ridiculous levitation. It refused.

Muttering something incoherent about being hanged before he'd give in, Greenberg hurled his useless rod at the water. By this time he was not surprised when it hovered in the air above the lake. He merely glanced red-eyed at it, tossed out the remains of the gnome's hat, and snatched up the oars.

When he pulled back on them to row to land, they did not touch the water—naturally. Instead they flashed unimpeded through the air, and Greenberg tumbled into the bow.

"A-ha!" he grated. "Here's where the trouble begins." He bent over the side. As he had suspected, the keel floated a remarkable distance above the lake.

By rowing against the air, he moved with maddening slowness toward shore, like a medieval conception of a flying machine. His main concern was that no one should see him in his humiliating position.

At the hotel he tried to sneak past the kitchen to the bathroom. He knew that Esther waited to curse him for fishing the day before opening, but more especially on the very day that a nice boy was coming to see her Rosie. If he could dress in a hurry, she might have less to say—

"Oh, there you are, you good-for-nothing!"

He froze to a halt.

"Look at you!" she screamed shrilly. "Filthy—you stink from fish!"

"I didn't catch anything, darling," he protested timidly.

"You stink anyhow. Go take a bath, may you drown in it! Get dressed in two minutes or less, and entertain the boy when he gets here. Hurry!"

He locked himself in, happy to escape her voice, started the water in the tub, and stripped from the waist up. A hot bath, he hoped, would rid him of his depressed feeling.

First, no fish; now, rain on week ends! What would Esther say—if she knew, of course. And, of course, he would not tell her.

"Let myself in for a lifetime of curses!" he sneered. "Ha!"

He clamped a new blade into his razor, opened the tube of shaving cream, and stared objectively at the mirror. The dominant feature of the soft, chubby face that stared back was its ugly black stubble; but he set his stubborn chin and glowered. He really looked quite fierce and indomitable. Unfortunately, Esther never saw his face in that uncharacteristic pose, otherwise she would speak more softly.

"Herman Greenberg never gives in!" he whispered between savagely hardened lips. "Rain on week ends, no fish—anything he wants; a lot I care! Believe me, he'll come crawling to me before I go to him."

He gradually became aware that his shaving brush was not getting wet. When he looked down and saw the water dividing into streams that flowed around it, his determined face slipped and grew desperately anxious. He tried to trap the water—by catching it in his cupped hands, by creeping up on it from behind, as if it were some shy animal, and shoving his brush at it—but it broke and ran away from his touch. Then he jammed his palm against the faucet. Defeated, he heard it gurgle back down the pipe, probably as far as the main.

"What do I do now?" he groaned. "Will Esther give it to me if I don't take a shave! But how? . . . I can't shave without water."

Glumly, he shut off the bath, undressed and stepped into the tub. He lay down to soak. It took a moment of horrified stupor to realize that he was completely dry and that he lay in a waterless bathtub. The water, in one surge of revulsion, had swept out onto the floor.

"Herman, stop splashing!" his wife yelled. "I just washed that floor. If I find one little puddle I'll murder you!"

Greenberg surveyed the instep-deep pool over the bathroom floor. "Yes, my love," he croaked unhappily.

With an inadequate washrag he chased the elusive water, hoping to mop it all up before it could seep through to the apartment below. His washrag remained dry, however, and he knew that the ceiling underneath was dripping. The water was still on the floor.

In despair, he sat on the edge of the bathtub. For some time he sat in silence. Then his wife banged on the door, urging him to come out. He started and dressed moodily.

When he sneaked out and shut the bathroom door tightly on the flood inside, he was extremely dirty and his face *was* raw where he had experimentally attempted to shave with a dry razor.

"Rosie!" he called in a hoarse whisper. "Sh! Where's mamma?"

His daughter sat on the studio couch and applied nail-polish to her stubby fingers. "You look terrible," she said in a conversational tone. "Aren't you going to shave?"

He recoiled at the sound of her voice, which, to him, roared out like a siren. "Quiet, Rosie! Sh!" And for further emphasis, he shoved his lips out against a warning finger. He heard his wife striding heavily around the kitchen. "Rosie," he cooed, "I'll give you a dollar if you'll mop up the water I spilled in the bathroom."

"I can't papa," she stated firmly. "I'm all dressed."

"Two dollars, Rosie—all right, two and a half, you black-mailer."

He flinched when he heard her gasp in the bathroom; but, when she came out with soaked shoes, he fled downstairs. He wandered aimlessly toward the village.

Now he was in for it, he thought; screams from Esther, tears from Rosie—plus a new pair of shoes for Rosie and two and a half dollars. It would be worse, though, if he could not get rid of his whiskers—

Rubbing the tender spots where his dry razor had raked his face, he mused blankly at a drugstore window. He saw nothing to help him, but he went inside anyhow and stood hopefully at the drug counter. A face peered at him through a space scratched in the wall case mirror, and the druggist came out. A nice-looking, intelligent fellow, Greenberg saw at a glance.

"What you got for shaving that I can use without water?" he asked.

"Skin irritation, eh?" the pharmacist replied. "I got something very good for that."

"No. It's just— Well, I don't like to shave with water."

The druggist seemed disappointed. "Well, I got brushless shaving cream." Then he brightened. "But I got an electric razor—much better."

"How much?" Greenberg asked cautiously.

"Only fifteen dollars, and it lasts a lifetime."

"Give me the shaving cream," Greenberg said coldly.

With the tactical science of a military expert, he walked around until some time after dark. Only then did he go back to the hotel, to wait outside. It was after seven, he was getting hungry, and the people who entered the hotel he knew as permanent summer guests. At last a stranger passed him and ran up the stairs.

Greenberg hesitated for a moment. The stranger was scarcely a boy, as Esther had definitely termed him, but Greenberg reasoned that her term was merely wish-fulfillment, and he jauntily ran up behind him.

He allowed a few minutes to pass, for the man to introduce himself and let Esther and Rosie don their company manners. Then, secure in the knowledge that there would be no scene until the guest left, he entered.

He waded through a hostile atmosphere, urbanely shook hands with Sammie Katz, who was a doctor—probably, Greenberg thought shrewdly, in search of an office—and excused himself.

In the bathroom he carefully read the direction for using brushless shaving cream. He felt less confident when he realized that he had to wash his face thoroughly with soap and water, but without benefit of either, he spread the cream on, patted it, and waited for his beard to soften. It did not, as he discovered while shaving. He wiped his face dry. The towel was sticky and black, with whiskers suspended in paste, and, for that, he knew, there would be more hell to pay. He shrugged resignedly. He would have to spend fifteen dollars for an electric razor after all; this foolishness was costing him a fortune!

That they were waiting for him before beginning supper, was, he knew, only a gesture for the sake of company. Without changing her hard, brilliant smile, Esther whispered: "Wait! I'll get you later—"

He smiled back, his tortured, slashed face creasing painfully. All that could be changed by his being enormously pleasant to Rosie's young man. If he could slip Sammie a few dollars—more expense, he groaned—to take Rosie out, Esther would forgive everything.

He was too engaged in beaming and putting Sammie at ease to think of what would happen after he ate caviar canapes. Under other circumstances Greenberg would have been repulsed by Sammie's ultra-professional waxed mustache—an offensively small, pointed thing—and his commercial attitude toward poor Rosie; but Greenberg regarded him as a potential savior.

"You open an office yet, Doctor Katz?"

"Not yet. You know how things are. Anyhow, call me Sammie."

Greenberg recognized the gambit with satisfaction, since it seemed to please Esther so much. At one stroke Sammie had ingratiated himself and begun bargaining negotiations.

Without another word, Greenberg lifted his spoon to attack the soup. It would be easy to snare this eager doctor. A *doctor!* No wonder Esther and Rosie were so puffed with joy.

In the proper company way, he pushed his spoon away from him. The soup spilled onto the tablecloth.

"Not so hard, you dope," Esther hissed.

He drew the spoon toward him. The soup leaped off it like a live thing and splashed over him—turning, just before contact, to fall on the floor. He gulped and pushed the bowl away. This time the soup poured over the side of the plate and lay in a huge puddle on the table.

"I didn't want any soup anyhow," he said in a horrible attempt at levity. Lucky for him, he thought wildly, that Sammie was there to pacify Esther with his smooth college talk—not a bad fellow, Sammie, in spite of his mustache; he'd come in handy at times.

Greenberg lapsed into a paralysis of fear. He was thirsty after having eaten the caviar, which beats herring any time as a thirst raiser. But the knowledge that he could not touch water without having it recoil and perhaps spill, made his thirst a monumental craving. He attacked the problem cunningly.

The others were talking rapidly and rather hysterically. He waited until his courage was equal to his thirst; then he leaned over the table with a glass in his hand. "Sammie, do you mind—a little water, huh?"

Sammie poured from a pitcher while Esther watched for more of his tricks. It was to be expected, but still he was shocked when the water exploded out of the glass directly at Sammie's only suit.

"If you'll excuse me," Sammie said angrily, "I don't like to eat with lunatics."

And he left, though Esther cried and begged him to stay. Rosie was too stunned to move. But when the door closed, Greenberg raised his agonized eyes to watch his wife stalk murderously toward him.

Greenberg stood on the boardwalk outside his concession and glared blearily at the peaceful, blue, highly unpleasant ocean. He wondered what would happen if he started at the edge of the water and strode out. He could probably walk right to Europe on dry land.

It was early—much too early for business—and he was tired. Neither he nor Esther had slept; and it was practically certain that the neighbors hadn't either. But above all he was incredibly thirsty.

In a spirit of experimentation, he mixed a soda. Of course its high water content made it slop onto the floor. For breakfast he had surreptitiously tried fruit juice and coffee, without success.

With his tongue dry to the point of furriness, he sat weakly on a boardwalk bench in front of his concession. It was Friday morning, which meant that the day was clear with a promise of intense heat. Had it been Saturday, it naturally would have been raining.

"This year," he moaned, "I'll be wiped out. If I can't mix sodas, why should beer stay in a glass for me? I thought I could hire a boy for ten dollars a week to run the hot-dog griddle; I could make sodas, and Esther could draw beer; but twenty or maybe twenty-five a week I got to pay a sodaman. I won't even come out square—a fortune I'll lose!"

The situation really was desperate. Concessions depend on too many factors to be anything but capriciously profitable.

His throat was fiery and his soft brown eyes held a fierce glaze when the gas and electric were turned on, the beer pipes connected, the tank of carbon dioxide hitched to the pump, and the refrigerator started.

Gradually, the beach was filling with bathers. Greenberg writhed on his bench and envied them. They could swim and drink without having liquids draw away from them as if in horror. They were not thirsty—

And then he saw his first customers approach. His business experience was that morning customers buy only soft drinks. In a mad haste he put up the shutters and fled to the hotel.

"Esther!" he cried. "I got to tell you! I can't stand it—"

Threateningly, his wife held her broom like a baseball bat. "Go back to the concession, you crazy fool. Ain't you done enough already?"

He could not be hurt more than he had been. For once he did not cringe. "You got to help me, Esther."

"Why didn't you shave, you no-good bum? Is that any way—"

"That's what I got to tell you. Yesterday I got into an argument with a water gnome—"

"A what?" Esther looked at him suspiciously.

"A water gnome," he babbled in a rush of words. "A little man so high, with big ears that he swims with, and he makes it rain—"

"Herman!" she screamed. "Stop that nonsense. You're crazy!"

Greenberg pounded his forehead with his fist. "I *ain't* crazy. Look, Esther. Come with me into the kitchen."

She followed him readily enough, but her attitude made him feel more helpless and alone than ever. With her fists on her plump hips and her feet set wide, she cautiously watched him try to fill a glass of water.

"Don't you see?" he wailed. "It won't go in the glass. It spills over. It runs away from me."

She was puzzled. "What happened to you?"

Brokenly, Greenberg told of his encounter with the water ghome, leaving out no single degrading detail. "And now I can't touch water," he ended. "I can't drink it. I can't make sodas. On top of it all, I got such a thirst, it's killing me."

Esther's reaction was instantaneous. She threw her arms around him, drew his head down to her shoulder, and patted him comfortingly as if he were a child. "Herman, my poor Herman!" she breathed tenderly. "What did we ever do to deserve such a curse?"

"What shall I do, Esther?" he cried helplessly.

She held him at arm's length. "You got to go to a doctor," she said firmly. "How long can you go without drinking? Without water you'll die. Maybe sometimes I am a little hard on you, but you know I love you—"

"I know, mamma," he sighed. "But how can a doctor help me?"

"Am I a doctor that I should know? Go anyhow. What can you lose?"

He hesitated. "I need fifteen dollars for an electric razor," he said in a low, weak voice.

"So?" she replied. "If you got to, you got to. Go, darling. I'll take care of the concession."

Greenberg no longer felt deserted and alone. He walked almost confidently to a doctor's office. Manfully, he explained his symptoms. The doctor listened with professional sympathy, until Greenberg reached his description of the water gnome.

Then his eyes glittered and narrowed. "I know just the thing for you, Mr. Greenberg," he interrupted. "Sit there until I come back."

Greenberg sat quietly. He even permitted himself a surge of hope. But it seemed only a moment later that he was vaguely conscious of a siren screaming toward him; and then he was overwhelmed by the doctor and two internes who pounced on him and tried to squeeze him into a bag.

He resisted, of course. He was terrified enough to punch wildly. "What are you doing to me?" he shrieked. "Don't put that thing on me!"

"Easy now," the doctor soothed. "Everything will be all right."

It was on that humiliating scene that the policeman, required by law to accompany public ambulances, appeared. "What's up?" he asked.

"Don't stand there, you fathead," an interne shouted. "This man's crazy. Help us get him into this strait jacket."

But the policeman approached indecisively. "Take it easy, Mr. Greenberg. They ain't gonna hurt you while I'm here. What's it all about?"

"Mike!" Greenberg cried, and clung to his protector's sleeve. "They think I'm crazy—"

"Of course he's crazy," the doctor stated. "He came in here with a fantastic yarn about a water gnome putting a curse on him."

"What kind of a curse, Mr. Greenberg?" Mike asked cautiously.

"I got into an argument with the water ghome who makes it rain and takes care of the fish," Greenberg blurted. "I tore up his hat. Now he won't let water touch me. I can't drink, or anything—"

The doctor nodded. "There you are. Absolutely insane."

"Shut up." For a long moment Mike stared curiously at Greenberg. Then: "Did any of you scientists think of testing him? Here, Mr. Greenberg." He poured water into a paper cup and held it out.

Greenberg moved to take it. The water backed up against the cup's far lip; when he took it in his hand, the water shot out into the air.

"Crazy, is he?" Mike asked with heavy irony. "I guess you don't know there's things like gnomes and elves. Come with me, Mr. Greenberg."

They went out together and walked toward the boardwalk. Greenberg told Mike the entire story and explained how, besides being so uncomfortable to him personally, it would ruin him financially.

"Well, doctors can't help you," Mike said at length. "What do they know about the Little Folk? And I can't say I blame you for sassing the gnome. You ain't Irish or you'd have spoke with more respect to him. Anyhow, you're thirsty. Can't you drink *anything?*"

"Not a thing," Greenberg said mournfully.

They entered the concession. A single glance told Greenberg that business was very quiet, but even that could not lower his feelings more than they already were. Esther clutched him as soon as she saw them.

"Well?" she asked anxiously.

Greenberg shrugged in despair. "Nothing. He thought I was crazy."

Mike stared at the bar. Memory seemed to struggle behind his reflective eyes. "Sure," he said after a long pause. "Did you try beer, Mr. Greenberg? When I was a boy my old mother told me all about elves and gnomes and the rest of the Little Folk. She knew them, all right. They don't touch alcohol, you know. Try drawing a glass of beer—"

Greenberg trudged obediently behind the bar and held a glass under the spigot. Suddenly his despondent face brightened. Beer creamed into the glass—and stayed there! Mike and Esther grinned at each other as Greenberg threw back his head and furiously drank.

"Mike!" he crowed. "I'm saved. You got to drink with me!"

"Well—" Mike protested feebly.

By late afternoon, Esther had to close the concession and take her husband and Mike to the hotel.

The following day, being Saturday, brought a flood of rain. Greenberg nursed an imposing hang-over that was constantly aggravated by his having to drink beer in order to satisfy his recurring thirst. He thought of forbidden icebags and alkaline drinks in an agony of longing.

"I can't stand it!" he groaned. "Beer for breakfast—phooey!"

"It's better than nothing," Esther said fatalistically.

"So help me, I don't know if it is. But, darling, you ain't mad at me on account of Sammie, are you?"

She smiled gently, "Poo! Talk dowry and he'll come back quick."

"That's what I thought. But what am I going to do about my curse?"

Cheerfully, Mike furled an umbrella and strode in with a little old woman, whom he introduced as his mother. Greenberg enviously saw evidence of the effectiveness of icebags and alkaline drinks, for Mike had been just as high as he the day before.

"Mike told me about you and the gnome," the old lady said. "Now I know the Little Folk well, and I don't hold you to blame for insulting him, seeing you never met a gnome before. But I suppose you want to get rid of your curse. Are you repentant?"

Greenberg shuddered. "Beer for breakfast! Can you ask?"

"Well, just you go to this lake and give the gnome proof."

"What kind of proof?" Greenberg asked eagerly.

"Bring him sugar. The Little Folk love the stuff—"

Greenberg beamed. "Did you hear that, Esther? I'll get a barrel—"

"They love sugar, but they can't eat it," the old lady broke in. "It melts in water. You got to figure out a way so it won't. Then the little gentleman'll know you're repentant for real."

There was a sympathetic silence while his agitated mind attacked the problem from all angles. Then the old lady said in awe: "The minute I saw your place I knew Mike had told the truth. I never seen a sight like it in my life—rain coming down, like the flood, everywhere else; but all around this place, in a big circle, it's dry as a bone!"

While Greenberg scarcely heard her, Mike nodded and Esther seemed peculiarly interested in the phenomenon. When he admitted defeat and came out of his reflected stupor, he was alone in the concession, with only a vague memory of Esther's saying she would not be back for several hours.

"What am I going to do?" he muttered. "Sugar that won't melt—" He drew a glass of beer and drank it thoughtfully. "Particular they got to be yet. Ain't it good enough if I bring simple sirup—that's sweet."

He pottered about the place, looking for something to do. He could not polish the fountain on the bar, and the few frankfurters boiling on the griddle probably would go to waste. The floor had already been swept. So he sat uneasily and worried his problem.

"Monday, no matter what," he resolved, "I'll go to the lake. It don't pay to go tomorrow. I'll only catch a cold because it'll rain."

At last Esther returned, smiling in a strange way. She was extremely gentle, tender and thoughtful; and for that he was appreciative. But that night and all day Sunday he understood the reason for her happiness.

She had spread word that, while it rained in every other place all over town, their concession was miraculously dry. So, besides a headache that made his body throb in rhythm to its vast pulse, Greenberg had to work like six men satisfying the crowd who mobbed the place to see the miracle and enjoy the dry warmth.

How much they took in will never be known. Greenberg made it a practice not to discuss such personal matters. But it is quite definite that not even in 1929 had he done so well over a single week end.

Very early Monday morning he was dressing quietly, not to disturb his wife. Esther, however, raised herself on her elbow and looked at him doubtfully.

"Herman," she called softly, "do you really have to go?"

He turned, puzzled. "What do you mean—do I have to go?"

"Well—" She hesitated. Then: "Couldn't you wait until the end of the season, Herman, darling?"

He staggered back a step, his face working in horror. "What kind of an idea is that for my own wife to have?" he croaked. "Beer I have to drink instead of water. How can I stand it? Do you think I *like* beer? I can't wash myself. Already people don't like to stand near me; and how will they act at the end of the season? I go around looking like a bum because my beard is too tough for an electric razor, and I'm all the time drunk—the first Greenberg to be a drunkard. I want to be respected—"

"I know, Herman, darling," she sighed. "But I thought for the sake of our Rosie— Such a business we've never done like we did this week end. If it rains every Saturday and Sunday, but not on our concession, we'll make a *fortune!*"

"Esther!" Herman cried, shocked. "Doesn't my health mean anything?"

"Of course, darling. Only I thought maybe you could stand it for—"

He snatched his hat, tie, and jacket, and slammed the door. Outside, though, he stood indeterminedly. He could hear his wife crying, and he realized that, if he succeeded in getting the gnome to remove the curse, he would forfeit an opportunity to make a great deal of money.

He finished dressing more slowly. Esther was right, to a certain extent. If he could tolerate his waterless condition—

"No!" he gritted decisively. "Already my friends avoid me. It isn't right that a respectable man like me should always be drunk and not take a bath. So we'll make less money. Money isn't everything—"

And with great determination he went to the lake.

But that evening, before going home, Mike walked out of his way to stop in at the concession. He found Greenberg sitting on a chair, his head in his hands, and his body rocking slowly in anguish.

"What is it, Mr. Greenberg?" he asked gently.

Greenberg looked up. His eyes were dazed. "Oh, you, Mike," he said blankly. Then his gaze cleared, grew more intelligent, and he stood up and led Mike to the bar. Silently, they drank beer. "I went to the lake today," he said hollowly. "I walked all around it hollering like mad. The gnome didn't stick his head out of the water once."

"I know," Mike nodded sadly. "They're busy all the time."

Greenberg spread his hands imploringly. "So what can I do? I can't write him a letter or send him a telegram; he ain't got a door to knock on or a bell for me to ring. How do I get him to come up and talk?"

His shoulders sagged. "Here, Mike. Have a cigar. You been a real good friend, but I guess we're licked."

They stood in an awkward silence. Finally Mike blurted: "Real hot, today. A regular scorcher."

"Yeah. Esther says business was pretty good, if it keeps up."

Mike fumbled at the Cellophane wrapper. Greenberg said: "Anyhow, suppose I did talk to the gnome. What about the sugar?"

The silence dragged itself out, became tense and uncomfortable. Mike was distinctly embarrassed. His brusque nature was not adapted for comforting discouraged friends. With immense concentration he rolled the cigar between his fingers and listened for a rustle.

"Day like this's hell on cigars," he mumbled, for the sake of conversation. "Dries them like nobody's business. This one ain't, though."

"Yeah," Greenberg said abstractedly. "Cellophane keeps them—"

They looked suddenly at each other, their faces clean of expression.

"Holy smoke!" Mike yelled.

"Cellophane on sugar!" Greenberg choked out.

"Yeah," Mike whispered in awe. "I'll switch my day off with Joe, and I'll go to the lake with you tomorrow. I'll call for you early."

Greenberg pressed his hand, too strangled by emotion for speech. When Esther came to relieve him, he left her at the concession with only the inexperienced griddle boy to assist her, while he searched the village for cubes of sugar wrapped in Cellophane.

The sun had scarcely risen when Mike reached the hotel, but Greenberg had long been dressed and stood on the porch waiting impatiently. Mike was genuinely anxious for his friend. Greenberg staggered along toward the station, his eyes almost crossed with the pain of a terrific hang-over.

They stopped at a cafeteria for breakfast. Mike ordered orange juice, bacon and eggs, and coffee half-and-half. When he heard the order, Greenberg had to gag down a lump in his throat.

"What'll you have?" the counterman asked.

Greenberg flushed. "Beer," he said hoarsely.

"You kidding me?" Greenberg shook his head, unable to speak. "Want anything with it? Cereal, pie, toast—"

"Just beer." And he forced himself to swallow it. "So help me," he hissed at Mike, "another beer for breakfast will kill me!"

"I know how it is," Mike said around a mouthful of food.

On the train they attempted to make plans. But they were faced by a phenomenon that neither had encountered before, and so they got nowhere. They walked glumly to the lake, fully aware that they would have to employ the empirical method of discarding tactics that did not work.

"How about a boat?" Mike suggested.

"It won't stay in the water with me in it. And you can't row it."

"Well, what'll we do then?"

Greenberg bit his lip and stared at the beautiful blue lake. There the gnome lived, so near to them. "Go through the woods along the shore, and holler like hell. I'll go the opposite way. We'll pass each other and meet at the boathouse. If the gnome comes up, yell for me."

"O. K.," Mike said, not very confidently.

The lake was quite large and they walked slowly around it, pausing often to get the proper stance for particularly emphatic shouts. But two hours later, when they stood opposite each other with the full diameter of the lake between them, Greenberg heard Mike's hoarse voice: "Hey, gnome!"

"Hey, gnome!" Greenberg yelled. "Come on up!"

An hour later they crossed paths. They were tired, discouraged, and their throats burned; and only fishermen disturbed the lake's surface.

"The hell with this," Mike said. "It ain't doing any good. Let's go back to the boathouse."

"What'll we do?" Greenberg rasped. "I can't give up!"

They trudged back around the lake, shouting half-heartedly. At the boathouse, Greenberg had to admit that he was beaten. The boathouse owner marched threateningly toward him.

"Why don't you maniacs get away from here?" he barked. "What's the idea of hollering and scaring away the fish? The guys are sore—"

"We're not going to holler any more," Greenberg said. "It's no use."

When they bought beer and Mike, on an impulse, hired a boat, the owner cooled off with amazing rapidity, and went off to unpack bait.

"What did you get a boat for?" Greenberg asked. "I can't ride in it."

"You're not going to. You're gonna walk."

"Around the lake again?" Greenberg cried.

"Nope. Look, Mr. Greenberg. Maybe the gnome can't hear us through all that water. Gnomes ain't hardhearted. If he heard us and thought you were sorry, he'd take his curse off you in a jiffy."

"Maybe." Greenberg was not convinced. "So where do I come in?"

"The way I figure it, some way or other you push water away, but the water pushes you away just as hard. Anyhow, I hope so. If it does, you can walk on the lake." As he spoke, Mike had been lifting large stones and dumping them on the bottom of the boat. "Give me a hand with these."

Any activity, however useless, was better than none, Greenberg felt. He helped Mike fill the boat until just the gunwales were above water. Then Mike got in and shoved off.

"Come on," Mike said. "Try to walk on the water."

Greenberg hesitated. "Suppose I can't?"

"Nothing'll happen to you. You can't get wet; so you won't drown."

The logic of Mike's statement reassured Greenberg. He stepped out boldly. He experienced a peculiar sense of accomplishment when the water hastily retreated under his feet into pressure bowls, and an unseen, powerful force buoyed him upright across the lake's surface. Though his footing was not too secure, with care he was able to walk quite swiftly.

"Now what?" he asked, almost happily.

Mike had kept pace with him in the boat. He shipped his oars and passed Greenberg a rock. "We'll drop them all over the lake—make it damned noisy down there and upset the place. That'll get him up."

They were more hopeful now, and their comments, "Here's one that'll wake him," and "I'll hit him right on the noodle with this one," served to cheer them still further. And less than half the rocks had been dropped when Greenberg halted, a boulder in his hands. Something inside him wrapped itself tightly around his heart and his jaw dropped.

Mike followed his awed, joyful gaze. To himself, Mike had to admit that the gnome, propelling himself through the water with his ears, arms folded in tremendous dignity, was a funny sight.

"Must you drop rocks and disturb us at our work?" the gnome asked.

Greenberg gulped. "I'm sorry, Mr. Gnome," he said nervously. "I couldn't get you to come up by yelling."

The gnome looked at him. "Oh. You are the mortal who was disciplined. Why did you return?"

"To tell you that I'm sorry, and I won't insult you again."

"Have you proof of your sincerity?" the gnome asked quietly.

Greenberg fished furiously in his pocket and brought out a handful of sugar wrapped in Cellophane, which he tremblingly handed to the gnome.

"Ah, very clever, indeed," the little man said, unwrapping a cube and popping it eagerly into his mouth. "Long time since I've had some."

A moment later Greenberg spluttered and floundered under the surface. Even if Mike had not caught his jacket and helped him up, he could almost have enjoyed the sensation of being able to drown.

# CLOAK OF AESIR

*Astounding Science Fiction,*
March

## by Don A. Stuart
## (John W. Campbell, Jr., 1910–1971)

*"Don A. Stuart" was the name employed by the late John Campbell for a group of stories that helped change the texture of science fiction. Although Campbell was a legendary editor, his innovations as a writer have not received enough analysis (we badly need a first-rate critical biography of this complex and fascinating man)—indeed, future historians of the field may some day view the literary trends he established as equal in importance to his editorial skills. Primarily known as a writer of superior space opera like the Penton and Blake stories and THE MIGHTIEST MACHINE 1934 in the Stuart persona he changed to an emphasis on reflection and the responses of human beings to technology and the human condition. In this sense, he started the "Golden Age" all by himself.*

*"Cloak of Aesir" is an independent sequel to "Out of Night" 1937 and was the last story Campbell wrote under the Stuart byline. It is a memorable and moving contribution to the literature of science fiction.*

*(To science fiction fans who remember the 1930s, there has always been something sad about having had to choose between John Campbell, Writer and John Campbell, Editor. There was no way in which we could have given up the Editor and yet now and then we mourn the Writer and what we might have had. IA.)*

The Sarn Mother's tiny, almost-human face was lined with the fatigue of forty hours of continued strain. Now, she feared greatly, a new and greater tension was ahead. For the eight City Mothers, taking their places about the Conference Hall of the Sarn, were not going to be sympathetic to the Mother's story.

To them, the ancient Sarn Mother well knew, the humans of Earth were slaves. Slaves bred for work, of little mentality and no importance. Earth was the planet of the Sarn, the planet the Sarn had taken, some four thousand years before, from the race of small-bodied, small-minded weaklings called Man that had originally inhabited it.

And that idea was going to be extremely hard to change. Particularly, it would be hard for the Sarn Mother to change that idea, for she was somewhat—not of them. The Sarn Mother was the Immortal. She was, therefore, disliked.

These eight, these Mothers of Cities, were the matriarchic governors of Earth under the Sarn. Each had risen to over-lordship of a continent, or near-continental area, by competitive brilliance among all their people. They had won their places, merited them, they felt.

But the Sarn Mother? The ultimate ruler of all Earth, all Sarn and humans alike? She had not *inherited* her position exactly—she had simply been there forever. Her winning of it was forgotten in the mists of antiquity. The Sarn were a long-lived people—some lived a thousand years—but the Sarn Mother was immortal; she had lived in the mythical days of the Forgotten Planet, before the home world of the Sarn had disrupted in cosmic catastrophe, forcing the race to seek new worlds.

The Sarn Mother had won this world for them, but that— and all others who had fought mankind in that four-thou-sand-years-gone time—was forgotten. The Sarn Mother was simply a hang-over from an era that should have died. So felt the Mothers of Cities, ambitious Sarn who saw a place above them that—because of the Mother's cursed immortality—they could never hope to reach.

The Old Sarn Mother knew that, and knew, too, that only her own possession of secret science those millenniums of her life had given her, made her place safe. The City Mothers feared two things: that well-held secret science, and the jealousy of their sisters.

The old Sarn was tired with mental struggle, and she knew, as soundly as she knew the City Mothers hated her, that she was facing another struggle. The humans of Earth were rising in a slow, half-understood revolt. She and these eight City Mothers knew that.

But the City Mothers did not, and would not, admit that those humans were capable of revolt. For all their lives humans have been slaves, pets, a sort of domesticated animal. That they or the similarly domesticated cows might attempt to set up a civilization—

For the Sarn Mother alone had been alive the four thousand years that had passed since mankind's defense of Earth all but succeeded in defeating the invading Sarn. The City Mothers could not understand. Subconsciously they had no intention of understanding anything so unpleasant.

The Sarn Mother's pointed, elfin face smiled weary greeting. Her fluting, many-toned speech betrayed her fatigue as she spoke to them. "I call you together, daughters, because something of grave importance has arisen. You have heard, perhaps, of the judging of Grayth and Bartel?"

"Rumors," said the Mother of Targlan, the city perched high in the crystal clarity of the mighty Himalaya Mountains. "You reversed your judgment, I heard." Her voice was silky smooth—and bitter.

The Sarn Mother's small, pointed face did not change. The trouble, definitely, was beginning. "I told you at the last Council that the human stock was rebuilding, that the submerged intelligence and will that built, before our invasion of this planet, a high civilization, were mounting again. It is, believe, equal in power to that before the Conquest. And, under our rule, it has been purified in some respects. There is less violence, and more determination.

"It is somewhat hard for you to appreciate that, for you do not remember human beings as other than slaves.

"I recognize a certain growing restlessness at restraint. The majority of those humans do not yet know—understand—the reason for a vague restlessness that they feel. Their leaders do. They are restless of government and restraint, and I hoped to use that vagueness of feeling to destroy the tendency toward rebellion. I thought the rebellion might be turned against their own, proxy government. Therefore, I caused the humans to revolt against their government under us, instead of against the Sarn.

"Even I had underestimated them. Grayth and Bartel, the leaders of mankind, appeared before me accompanied by Drunnel, the rival leader. I will not detail their quarrel, save to say that Drunnel was my tool. I sentenced Grayth and Bartel.

"Then—Aesir, he called himself—appeared. He was a blackness—a three-dimensional shadow. He stood some four feet taller than I, nearly twelve feet tall, twice the height of humans. But he was shaped like a human in bulk, though the vague blackness made any feature impossible. He claimed that he was not made of any form of matter, but was the crystallization of the wills of all humans who have died in any age, while seeking freedom.

"Aesir spoke by telepathy. Mind to mind. We know the humans had been near that before the Conquest, and that our own minds are not so adapted to that as are the humans'. Aesir used that method.

"He stood before me, and made these statements that were clear to the minds of all humans and Sarn in the Hall of Judgment. His hand of blackness reached out and touched Drunnel, and the man fell to the floor and broke apart like a fragile vase. The corpse was frozen glass-hard in an instant of time.

"Therefore, I released Grayth and Bartel. But I turned on Aesir's blackness the forces of certain protective devices I have built. There is an atomic blast of one-sixteenth aperture. It is, at maximum, capable of disintegrating half a cubic mile of matter per minute. There was also a focused atomic flame of two-inch aperture, sufficient to fuse about twenty-two tons of steel per second.

"These were my first tests. At maximum aperture the blackness absorbed both without sound or static discharge, or any lightening of that three-dimensional shadow."

The Sarn Mother's mouth moved in a faint, ironic smile. "There are," she went on softly, "certain other weapons there. The Death of the Mother, which I employed once on a rebellious City Mother, some thirteen hundred years gone. Tathan Shoal, she was, of Bishop Waln." The Sarn Mother's slitted eyes lit amusedly on the present Mother of Bish-Waln, capital city of the continent of Africa.

"Tathan Shoal had the mistaken idea that she might gain

by attacking me. She came with many devices, including a screen capable of turning all the weapons she knew. It cost me the South Wall of the Hall of Judgment and an effective and efficient administrator to convince her. For she had been effective and efficient.

"Daughter of Targlan, it is best for the Race that we share knowledge. Tell your sister of Bish-Waln the remarkable progress your physicist has made with the field she knows as R-439-K."

The Mother of Targlan's face remained unchanged, save for a faint golden flush that spread over it, and the sudden angry fire of her eyes. Field R-439-K—her most treasured secret——

"It is a field," she said in a pleasant, friendly tone, "which causes the collapse of atoms within it, bringing about a spreading disruption that continues so long as the generator is activated. It is necessarily spherical in shape, destroying the generator very quickly, however. It would be excellent as a sort of bomb." She added that last as a sort of afterthought, a hazy, bitter dream in her voice.

The Sarn Mother smiled and nodded toward the Mother of Bish-Waln. That City Ruler's eyes were angry as had been her predecessor's as she responded to the unspoken command. But her voice betrayed no emotion.

"No, sister, it can be projected to some extent. The generator need not be destroyed, though the projector is, if you employ a field of ellipsoidal form."

The Mother of Uhrnol smiled, but her smile was only half amusement. "The projector can be saved, too. It is too bad I could not have known of your efforts. I could have saved you considerable work."

The three smiled at each other in seeming friendliness. Each felt slightly relieved; she stood alone neither in her chastisement nor in the loss of treasured secrets.

"The point of interest," the Sarn Mother pointed out softly, "is that none of you can stop that field. There is no protection. Some twenty-two centuries ago I discovered that interesting modification of the atomic-blast field, and within a century I had projected it. Ten centuries ago I had it tamed to the extent of a cylindrical tube of force of controllable dimensions. If Tathan Shoal had waited another five centuries before attacking me, she would not have cost me the South Wall. It still does not match perfectly the other three. But I cannot screen that force."

"Nor I," admitted the three City Mothers, in turn. There was a hint of bitter defeat in their tones, for each had hoped that field that could not be screened might make them safe in disposing of the old harridan, the Immortal Sarn Mother, who ruled them from a forgotten generation. She was a bitter, anachronistic hang-over from a forgotten time, from even the Forgotten Planet, and should have been forgotten with it.

"Aesir," said the Sarn Mother softly, "took the Death of the Mother into his blackness, and seemingly drew strength from it. At any rate, both the apparatus and the atomic generator which fed it were blown out from sudden overload.

"It might be wise to coöperate more closely than in the past. Once, remember, our race had a very bitter struggle with this race. What do you Mothers of Cities believe this Aesir to me?"

The Mother of Targlan stirred angrily. "There are clowns among the humans of my district who amuse their fellows by trickery. Humans have stiff legs, bending only in certain, few joints. That lack of flexibility gives them amusing powers. They can, for instance, advance the stiffness by the use of poles of light metal, representing longer, artificial bones. I have seen such clowns walk on legs that made them not twelve, but seventeen feet high."

"Yes," said the Sarn Mother sweetly, "the clowns of my North America are of a very inferior brand. They can appear but twelve feet tall. But——"

"Many," said the Mother of Bish-Waln, "of my humans have shown they can talk mind to mind among themselves. If it is new among your people here, it is——"

"Yes," said the Sarn Mother sweetly, "the humans of my North America are of an inferior brand, evidently. But——I am curious of these clowns and mind-talkers. Do they, perhaps, absorb atomic-blast beams for nourishment, and warm themselves at a focused flame? Do they so overload your atomic-collapse field generators as to burn them in molten rubbish?

"Or do they, perhaps, unlike yourselves, remember that the Sarn Mother has watched humans, and the minds and tricks of humans, for some eight times your not-inconsequential five hundred years?

"There were, in the Hall, humans, Sarn, and myself. By telepathy, Aesir spoke to us all, telling a myth of his origin among immaterial wills. He was, in his way, quite noisy, and quite conspicuous. Also, he was an excellent psychologist.

Had I been warned—had I known beforehand and had time to think—I would not have turned the blast, the focused flame, nor, certainly, the Death of the Mother against him.

"Now do any of you, who see so clearly through the trickery of my poor little, twelve-foot clown, and the trickery of my slow-developing telepathist—do any of you see through to the message Aesir meant for my intellect, and not my mind? A message he did not speak, but acted?" The Sarn Mother's elfin face looked down the Council table, and there was nothing of laughter in it.

The City Mothers moved uneasily under the lash of biting scorn. The Sarn Mother's voice dropped, softer still, till the tinklings of the atom flame above muffled her words.

"Mummery for fools, my daughters. I am interested that you are so attracted by the mummery as to forget the purpose, and so pleased with your cleverness that saw the human behind it.

"But I am—irritated that you underestimate, not merely of the mind of a human of deadly, blazingly brilliant intellect, but, even more, my own mind.

"Humans are a smaller people, better adapted to this somewhat heavier planet than we are. But we are no longer on the Forgotten World. The humans have learned to respect height; the ruling Race is tall.

"Is Aesir a fool, then, to make himself yet taller, and to fill out his slenderness with vague blackness?

"We have no hair on our skulls, as have humans, but the more useful *sterthan* which seems, to humans, practical telepathy, since we can talk among ourselves by what they know only through microwave radio sets.

"Is Aesir a fool, then, to use telepathy himself, talking truly mind to mind? Men know the limitations of microwave radio, that it ends at the horizon. But they do not know what vague limits telepathy may or may not have, and it is very wonderful, therefore.

"That mummery, my daughters, was intended only for humans, that mass of restless humans who do not know what they want. That was not meant for me—save that he wanted me to know what others heard.

"I am proud of my humans, daughters. But I am afraid, for you. You have not shown the intelligence that that man expected. That mind telepathy he used was not the message he meant for me. To me he said: 'Mother, a new balance must be reached. You are the ruler of Earth—but for me. I challenge you to try your weapons—which I know, as does everyone on Earth, you have in your throne—and see if you can destroy me.' And when I, not thinking, but reacting spontaneously to the evident menace of his blackness, did just this, he said more. He touched Drunnel, and Drunnel fell dead. 'I have an impregnable shield' his actions spoke, 'and it is more; a weapon. You cannot destroy me, Mother of the Sarn—but I can destroy you.

" 'Therefore, we seek a new balance. You could destroy all my people—but not destroy me. And I could destroy you, or any of your people.

" 'Release these two, Grayth and Bartel, and we will think again. This is not the time for hasty action.'

"Aesir, daughters, is no fool. He is no trickster—save for his own sound purposes—but a mind of astounding brilliance. He has discovered a principle, a weapon, unknown to us and of immense power.

"And, my daughters, I respect him. I released Grayth and Bartel, since they are, evidently, pawns in this game. Or, at least, they are two of the few humans on Earth I know are not—Aesir.

"And I have more liking"—the Sarn Mother's voice was bitter and ironic—"for one who expects my mind to see beyond mummery to a deep and important sincerity, than for those who explain trickery and point out the inferiority of my humans."

"You are reading words that are not written," said the Mother of Targlan flatly.

For an instant the eyes of the Sarn Mother burned with a white anger, a blazing intolerance of such sheer stupidity. Then it faded to a look of deep concern.

The Sarn Mother was unhuman, unhuman in the same way her elfin face was. It was very wrong, taken as a human face, with its pointed chin and tiny mouth, the slit-pupiled, golden eyes, and peaked hairline that was not hair. But there was the fundamental parallelism of two eyes, a mouth, a high, rounded forehead. Her body was grotesquely unhuman, but again there was a parallelism of articulated arms carried high on a strong torso and legs, though her arms were like four powerful snakes.

And—she was un-Sarn. The Mother was immortal, an unchanging intellect in a world that waxed and waned and changed about her. She had living memories of a world crushed in cosmic dust. She had memories of great Sarn who had dared and won a world, of a human civilization of magnitude near equal to this present Sarn world.

And the process that had made her immortal, had made her unable to have descendants. There was no direct link from her to this newer generation. Her only link was through a planet wiped from the face of time.

Four thousand years she had ruled this planet. Two thousand more she'd lived on the Forgotten World before the desperate colonization attempt had been conceived. These creatures—these Sarn—were ephemeral things about her, for all their five hundred years.

Sixty centuries are long, for any intellect. All things exhaust themselves in that long time, save one: the curiosity of the mind, the play and counterplay of intellect. The Mother was the perfect seeker after knowledge, for no other thoughts could ponderably intrude. Those others she had met long ago.

She was un-Sarn by her immortality, by her separation of six thousand years from all direct contact with her equals.

She was unhuman only by a different in body. And the body is wearied and forgotten in that time. Only the intellect, the mind, remains of interest, expanding and changing forever.

The intellect behind Aesir's cloak of blackness was the keenest, the finest, this planet had ever seen. And—that human appreciated that she, the Sarn Mother, was a keen intelligence.

The City Mothers did not.

The Sarn Mother turned her eyes slowly from the Mother of Targlan. "The words that spell the secret of that blackness are not written," she said mildly. (*These were the daughters of her race. These were the descendants of Sarn she had known and worked with and liked during six thousand years. These were—*)

"I must see more of that cloak, and investigate it more adequately." She sighed. "And you, my daughters, must not underestimate an enemy. And the humans are, I fear—or will be soon.

"They have been slaves for many generations—very short generations—and they have evolved. They evolve more swiftly than we, because of that short life span. And, remember this: at least one of them is sufficiently brilliant, of sufficient mental caliber, to develop a screen weapon superior to anything we know of. That alone makes him, potentially, extremely dangerous."

The City Mothers sat silent for long seconds. The thought was, as the Mother had known, extremely upsetting. Their matriarchic minds rebelled at the thought that there was a human—and a *male* human, at that—who was capable of developing something scientifically superior to anything in their possession.

"If," said the Mother of Targlan, "he has this remarkable weapon—proof against all ours, and deadly to us—I am extremely thankful that he has shown such kindliness toward our race." Her fluting voice was sugary. "He has not equipped any of his compatriots nor attacked us in any way."

The seven other City Mothers twitched slightly straighter in their chairs and looked with pleased smiles at the Sarn Mother's fine, small face.

The Mother smiled bitterly. "Undoubtedly that would be your own reaction were you possessed of such a weapon," she admitted. The Mother of Targlan stolidly continued to look into the Mother's half-angry, half-annoyed eyes.

"But you," the Mother explained, "have never done more than to say 'a thousand pounds of tungsten' when you had need of it. Or order fifty No. 27-R-29 oscillator tubes, when you hoped to make a satisfactory lie detector. Incidentally, daughter, I have an effective invisibility generator. And your lie detector will not operate. You'd do far better to use common sense and simplicity instead of outrageously expensive mummery that doesn't work. That spy you sent to—one of the other cities—last week had a very slipshod invisibility. I watched her a whole afternoon from here. She set off seven different alarms, and finally was caught in a delightful booby trap. Your sister believes in simplicity instead of gadgets."

The Mother of Targlan sat silent and stony. Her slitted eyes contracted slowly in flaming hatred. The old harridan was becoming cattish.

The old harridan was tired. She was wearied to death of the bickerings and annoyances of these City Mothers with too little to do to occupy their time. Furthermore, she hadn't slept in forty hours, and knew it. And the Mother of Targlan was being unbearably stupid.

The Mother of Bish-Waln was interested. So—that was the source of that spy. And the old Mother, for all her foolishness about these humans, had some sense. The secret of success is simplicity. Though that Targlan spy *had* had a fearful and wonderful array of apparatus strapped about her, it also had made her—even when dead—remarkably hard to see. She'd sounded like a collapse in a glass factory when she fell, though.

"To get back to my remarks," said the Sarn Mother abruptly, "you have never had to want something without getting it. Except," she added with a flash of tiny, pointed, green-white teeth, "understanding. If you want materials, they are brought.

"If a human wants materials, he steals them. And I will say this for you: you have all been remarkable organizers. The anti-theft measures you have developed are outstanding. But I should think that the fact that humans still succeed in thieving would convince you they are clever."

"So," snapped the Mother of Targlan, "are rats. But they aren't intelligent."

"Quite true," admitted the Mother. The Mother of Targlan was becoming annoyed, which vaguely pleased the old Sarn Mother, who was very annoyed. "But humans are both. It took me twelve years to find exactly how it was approximately thirty ounces of platinum disappeared each month, despite my electrostatic balance detectors. Now I make all workers clip their fingernails and hair. It was truly startling how much dust they could carry that way.

"To acquire materials, humans must steal them. And they must find it extremely difficult to gather such things as metallic caesium, gaseous fluorine, and rare gases like helium and neon. Unfortunately, I believe a considerable quantity of material is obtained from ingeniously acquired atom-flame lamps." The Mother nodded toward the softly rustling lamps overhead.

"So your workers secrete complete atom-flame lamps under their nails?" said the Mother of Targlan. "Your theft measures are indeed remarkable. The atom destructor of one atom lamp would power a dangerous weapon. They will stand a load of nearly ten thousand horsepower."

The Sarn Mother smiled. "How many atom-flame lamps have you lost through theft, daughter?"

"None. Not one!" snapped the Mother of Targlan.

"And what," asked the Mother kindly, "of lamps destroyed in burning human homes?"

"Perhaps ten a year."

"I'd say five a year, then, are acquired by humans. I've

proven two homes were burned to the ground to secure the atom lamps the occupants wanted."

"We," said the City Mother loftily, "require that the wreckage be produced."

"Excellent," sighed the Mother. "An excellent provision. Do you have a chemist analyze the molten waste? The humans generally find it very difficult to obtain scandium, and the analyses usually skimp badly on that. But the other elements you'll find. They smelt up a careful mixture of all the proper elements, with the exception of gallium. But they can always claim that boiled away."

The Mother of Targlan looked startled. The Sarn Mother's eyes twinkled slightly in satisfaction. She had discovered *that* trick only four days before, herself.

"As I said, the humans find it hard to get materials and appartus. But they are really ingenious, and I rather respect them for it. If you wish to assure yourselves of your cities," she added, looking about the table, "I'd advise you to acknowledge the power of your opponents.

"That is the reason this human, Aesir, has not done more. He has a weapon and a protection—for one. So long as he cannot obtain material, he cannot do more.

"But he will obtain materials." The Mother's annoyed air was dropped now. This, she knew, meant the safety of the Sarn race. "If he obtains sufficient materials before we learn the secret of that cloak, *the Sarn will not rule this planet.*"

The Mother of Bish-Waln looked at the Immortal steadily. Suddenly she spoke. "I have always considered the humans stupid. That they had the cleverness of other lower animals, in greater degree, I realized. But we, Mother, have no memories of their civilization before we came. How far advanced was it, actually?"

The Sarn Mother looked at the City Mother keenly for a moment. It was anomalous; this City Mother, less than one twentieth the Immortal's age, looked far older. Her face, pointed in the manner typical of her race, was graven with fine lines. There was a power and strength of purpose in its deeply tanned, leathery molding. Ruler of a tropical continent, her city centered in the warmth and cloudless air of the Sahara, she was one of the most active of the City Mothers.

The old Sarn Mother smiled slightly and nodded. "I can tell you very little now. But call in your archeologist. She is a brilliant and learned Sarn. Briefly, when we landed, the humans had had civilization for some fifteen thousand years. It was, by their calendar, 1977. They had recently developed atomic power of the first order, involving vapor turbines heated by atomic combustion, driving electromagnetic generators. They mined the world, their transportation systems were heavily interlinked and efficient.

"And—of our fifty-two ships, we lost thirty-nine during the Conquest. They were intelligent, efficient and deadly fighters. We captured and enslaved only the scum of the race; the best of humankind died fighting with a grim tenacity that appalled us. They were a fighting breed, slightly given to attack, but utterly and insanely given to defense.

"It is worth nothing in this case. If they once attack us, then we will, of course, attack, in reply. Whereupon their inherited defensiveness will come into play. If it does, I seriously assure you that, whether they have weapons or not, even if they fight with their bare hands, you will find the human race a perfectly deadly thing to tangle with. They have no conception of when to stop. It is good military tactics to stop, if any reasonably equitable settlement can be reached, after losing ten percent of your forces. The human race does not know that, and never will. They stop when, and only when, they are convinced they have won their point. They simply do not show good sense.

"But they are extremely deadly.

"That is true of the mass of humanity. They have leaders now, and Aesir is the principal leader. We can, and must, control them through him. He knows, instinctively, the attitude of his people, and will try, therefore, to prevent suicidal war.

"Wherefore, if we obtain the secret of his cloak of blackness, we can proceed."

"I will ask my archeologist, Mother," said the Mother of Bish-Waln.

"Whatever you may say of the dreadful, deadly, human race," said the Mother of Targlan ironically, "it would be interesting to know the mechanism of that shield. But—maybe he will not explain. And it would be extremely difficult to force him to, if what you say of it is true."

"We shall have to analyze it, of course," said the Mother wearily. There were many more hours of work and sleeplessness ahead. "Some hours ago I instructed my physicists to set up all the instruments they thought might be useful in the House of the Rocks."

The Mother of Targlan stared blankly; then, acidly, commented: "Of all places in the Sarn City here, I should say that that would show the absolute minimum of probability for an appearance of Aesir."

"And," continued the Mother, wearied of interruptions, "they will be ready for him in about an hour and a half. It is evident that Aesir will come to the aid of Grayth, if we capture him. To make assurance doubly sure—since Grayth is not, actually, absolutely necessary to them—we will take also Deya, Spokeswoman of Human Women. Grayth plans to marry her, and I am sure that Aesir will aid in releasing her."

The Mother of Bish-Waln frowned slightly. "Is it not bad policy, Mother, to arrest, and then release this man again? And—again at the insistence of Aesir."

"Therefore, the House of the Rocks. No human can approach. No human will know of the actual escape—save those humans already closely associated with Grayth, and, therefore, Aesir. Those humans already know what powers Aesir has, even better than we, and they will recognize this maneuver not as an arrest that failed, but as a test that did not fail. Our policy will be good, not bad, to those who know. The mass of humans simply will not know."

"They will not, I suppose," said the Mother of Drulon, at the far, stormy tip of South America, "notice that Grayth, their spokesman, is being taken in Sarn custody—and returns?"

"They will not," smiled the Mother. With an uncoiled finger, she pressed a tiny button.

At the far end of the long Council room, a silver door opened in the jet black of the wall. The heavy metal portal swung aside, and a guard snapped to attention in its opening, a giant Sarn standing over eight feet tall. Her powerful, supple arms were corded with the smooth-flowing muscles of a boa constrictor. Vaguely, her trappings indicated the rank of a Decalon—a commander of a Ten. Her cloak, though, with a deep, rich maroon, and in the center the gold, silver, and bright-purple metal threads wove a pattern that was the Mother's personal symbol.

And her face—to one who knew Sarn physiognomy—was not that of a mere Decalon. The slitted eyes were deepset and widely separated. Her mouth was firm, and the face, small and pointed to human experience, was square and powerful in a Sarn. The golden skin had been tanned to a leathery, weather-beaten brown, crossed by a myriad of fine lines of character. This was no mere commander over ten guards.

"Decalon," said the Mother softly, "bring the Cloaks of the Mother, and your command. There is an errand."

The Decalon turned sharply, noiselessly, closing the metal door.

"Once," explained the Mother, "Darath Toplar was Commander-in-chief of the Guard of the Sarn City. She is now a Decalon. That is because there are but ten in my personal guard.

"Now this is a time of emergency. I have revealed to each of you something of the things each thought a secret, and some of the things that I held secret. I am showing you the Cloaks of the Mother. That they existed, rumors have stated. They do. They have the properties the rumors suggest. Because it is necessary, they will be used."

The Decalon was back, behind her ten guards dressed in the same type of maroon uniform. Ten powerful, eight-foot Sarn warriors. On the face of each was stamped a keen, loyal intelligence. In the arms of the Decalon was a case of dark hardwood, inlaid with heavy, silvery metal straps. She put it down at the end of the great Council table, and the Mother's hand flicked out as her supple arm uncoiled to shoot a scrap of carefully cut metal the length of the polished table. The Decalon fitted it into a concealed lock with a motion of familiar dexterity.

The case, opened, revealed a space two by three by one-half foot. In it, racked neatly along one side, were twenty little battery cases, with coiled, flexible cables attached, and twenty headsets, bearing curiously complex goggles. The case was practically empty.

The Decalon reached in, and with practiced movements passed to her command the goggles and battery cases. Then she reached more carefully into the body of the case. The reaching hand vanished. Presently, queerly section by section, the Decalon was wiped out, till only a pair of feet remained, dwindling off into space. These vanished as some unseen boots were pulled over them.

In a moment, only the City Mothers and the Mother of the Sarn remained in the room—seemingly. The City Mothers stirred uneasily. The eyes of the Mother of Targlan were golden fires of anger and chagrin. These—these picked eleven of the Mother's personal guard and spy force—knew every secret of her laboratories.

And the old immortal harridan knew them, too. Her crackling laughter must have been spurred a thousand times by the futile attempts and doomed plans the Mother of Targlan had made and thought over. The Mother of Targlan felt a rising pressure of helpless anger well up, an anger that was suppressed by its very helplessness. Even the satisfaction that the Mother was old, a cackling hag, was denied. For—salt on her wounded pride—the Mother had done, seemingly centuries ago, what the Mother of Targlan struggled with vainly! The Mother was a far better scientist.

It was a very different Council room, this chamber where the Spokesmen of Man had met—an inner office of the elected representative of mankind, the Spokesman of Mankind. It was a warm room, mellowed by a thousand years of time; ancient woods, waxed and cared for for ten centuries and more, had taken on a fine, soft patina. Long-slanting fingers of afternoon sunlight did not glare on cold jet stone here; it was softened by the richness of the panels. Each was of a different wood; one from each of the continents, and one for each continental spokesman.

The great table in the center was worn in soft hummocks and swales by the arms of forty generations of Spokesmen, the thick rubberlike floor carven by their feet.

But as in the great Council room of the Hall of the Sarn in nearby Sarn City, here, too, atom-flame lamps rustled softly with dying atoms, whitening the light of the setting sun. Four men only were at this Council table, four who sat motioning, gesturing with a curious alertness, their faces intent. Yet—utterly silent.

Grayth, tall, lean, keen-faced Spokesman of Mankind, an elected representative who had won his honor by a keen understanding of the practical psychology of the men he represented before the Sarn Mother, political leader of mankind. Bartel, shorter, more solidly built Spokesman of North America, close friend of Grayth, who had stood beside him before the Sarn Mother, when—Aesir—had come.

And Carron, the gigantic commander of the legion of peace, the only semblance of an army allowed humans. A police force armed with tiny gas throwers capable of a single, stupefying shot, and rubber truncheons.

Also, one more. Darak, Grayth's subspokesman. He sat silent now, making occasional pothooks on the pad of paper, his round, uninteresting face bored and boring. Darak's office was appointive, given him at Grayth's order for the blank-

ly unimpressive face and uninteresting character of the man
made him few friends—as he had found by many years of
careful study of the subject. Few friends, and few who paid
him any attention whatever.

Darak had no need of the Cloak of the Mother; his own,
based not on laws of physics but of psychology, was nearly as
effective. People did not see Darak. He wasn't worth seeing.

Four humans at the ancient Council table, four men as
free as possible in this day of the Sarn, each wearing on his
cloak the symbol of his rank in human society. Each wearing
on a band round his forehead the medallion given every human at the age of eighteen. The band of Manhood or
Womanhood, the Sarn informed them. The mark of Mankind's submission to the Sarn.

Or was, till Ware made certain slight alterations, alterations that hollowed out the solid three-inch disk of silver to
contain a minute thing of spider-web coils and microscopic
crystal oscillators. The first of the telepaths that rendered this
soundless Council meaningful.

And rendered quite useless the listening devices that had
followed every Council of Mankind for a thousand years.
Grayth smiled upward to the swell of the atom-flame lamp.
In the mechanism of that device, in a dozen other places in
the room, the Sarn had long ago hidden radio transmitters.
For a millennium, every Council of Mankind had been
directly open to the strange radio-sense of the Mother and
her advisers. For the hairlike growth on the Sarn's skulls were
the sense organ of a type Man did not have, directly sensitive
to radio.

"Four men in here," Grayth thought to his companions,
"four men rustling papers. But the Sarn must be very curious
as to the silence."

Carron's broad, tanned face broke into a wide grin. "After
a thousand years, a bit of silence from this room is due. The
Mother knows well enough we aren't minding her business.
But I don't think she'll be anxious to investigate after—Aesir."

"The Sarn Mother," the thought whispered in their minds
from a more distant telepath, "is busy holding a conference
of her own. I've been trying for weeks to get the pattern of
Sarn thoughts. I get annoying flashes, but no more. The
Mother is tired, and the City Mothers are being stubborn, I
gather. But the thought patterns are just enough different
from human thought to make the telepaths ineffective at

more than about one hundred feet. And the most assiduous electrotechnician can't spend *all* his time tracing conduits in the Sarn Palace."

"I'd suggest you do absolutely nothing that an ordinary electrotechnician wouldn't do, Ware," Grayth hurriedly advised. "And for Aesir's sake, stay home when you're supposed to have off hours."

"Have you reached any conclusions? I've been sleeping, and woke only a few minutes ago." Ware's mental voice seemed to yawn. "I've been trying to think of some way to get more metal. Ye gods, if I could just get into one of the Sarn electrical plants for a day, I'd have a dozen things I need fixed up. The math was none too simple, but I've gotten it, I think." He chuckled. "Thanks, in fact, to a very wise old Sarn.

"Just below conscious level, a thought came to him, a bothersome equation. While a certain electrotechnician fussed with conduits fifty feet away, he fussed with the equation. The Sarn have some mathematical methods our ancestors never developed, and that I haven't had a chance to learn. Carron, if you ever feel urged to crack the skull of old Rath Largun, spare him for that."

"Can you use him again?" asked Carron amusedly.

"Oh, I have. He's old, and his mind wanders. Nearly a thousand years old, I think, which is exceptionally old for even a Sarn male. Since he is a male, he gets less credit among his people than he deserves, but he's the most brilliant mathematician the Sarn have. Because his mind wanders—he believes he thinks up the equations."

"Might they give him a clue later?" asked Grayth sharply.

"T . . . P . . ." said Ware easily. "What word am I spelling? When you have correctly answered that, the Sarn may get that clue."

"Good." Grayth nodded silently. "Ware, Carron has seven technicians in his legion of peace who will procure some of those things you need. They have volunteered."

"I have not said what I wanted, nor will I," Ware answered instantly. "Every technician caught stealing metal now will be destroyed by the Sarn instantly. No man is going to lose his life on something I wouldn't attempt myself. Further, we need two classes of men now more vitally than ever before: technicians and fighters. Humans haven't fought and are not fighters. Carron's legionnaires are the only trained, experienced fighters—with the will and emotion needed for fighting—that we have. And when they are also technicians, we can't spare them.

"Have you told Darak what's to be done, and given him the disks?" Ware changed the subject abruptly, with an air of "that's that." It was because Carron didn't know what metals Ware wanted; had he, he would have gotten them somehow, anyway.

Darak replied softly: "I have been told, and I have the disks. Twenty-five telepaths, each equipped with destroying apparatus reacting to one key thought. I know how the destroying mechanism is to be disconnected if successful delivery is made. Grayth has supplied me with sufficient official dispatches for both Durban City and Targlan. I am starting in twenty-two minutes."

"Then—good luck, Darak."

"Thank you. The wish is, perhaps, the luck of the gods?"

"Yes. The luck of Aesir—very appropriate." Ware chuckled. "You will lose contact with me, except when I use the large telepath here in the laboratory. You know the schedule hours for that?"

"Yes, thanks."

"We will be going, too, I think." Carron rose ponderously. His huge form dwarfed even the great Council table. And, since he spoke for the first time, his heavy voice seemed to explode in the room. "I'll see you to the Sarn City gates, Darak."

He glanced down at the subspokesman's busy fingers. They were chubby, soft-looking fingers, rather thick and clumsy. An ink bottle flickered and wavered in and out of existence under the flicking, incredibly deft fingers. Then it flickered, without seeming to move under his caressing, chubby hand, from a round, red ink bottle to a square black one. "Thank you, Carron. The dispatches, Grayth?" Darak's voice was rather high for a man, quite undistinguished. Darak was, next to Ware, the cleverest human on Earth in that era. But his mentality was as utterly different as was Grayth's. Grayth was a practical psychologist, the only living man capable of unifying and moving the masses of mankind. Ware was the scientist, the epitomization of centuries of the Sarn efforts to develop capable human technicians. And Darak?

Darak had the curiosity of the scientist in Ware, the psychological sense of Grayth, and the love of action that made giant Carron what he was.

Grayth tossed a mass of papers toward the subspokesman, a mass that bulged and crinkled. Darak leafed them swiftly into a brief case that he carried. "One thing I will have to remedy," he telepathed silently. "The metal gleams." Twenty-five silvery disks flickered momentarily among the rapidly leafed papers, and vanished as his thick fingers passed them. "All here," he said aloud. "Good-by. I should be back in about four days."

His feet made no noticeable noise on the floor—an accomplishment far more difficult than a soundless tread. An unnoticeable step involves exactly sufficient sound to satisfy the ear, without enough to attract it. A soundless tread is very startling, particularly in a rather stout, heavily built man.

He walked through the outer office, past a battery of secretaries and clerks working over statistics from all the human world, correlating and arranging them for Grayth and the human government. Two looked up as he passed, but neither saw him. They missed him as completely as they missed the passing of eleven eight-foot Sarn guards walking past in the opposite direction on the soundless toe pads nature had given them. For neither party wished to be seen, and each had its own unseen cloak wrapping it.

The door stood open a moment as giant Carron and Grayth spoke a few last words. Bartel stepped out, and then Carron, holding the door wide for his own exit, lingered a moment longer. Soundless feet carried the three Sarn, larger even than Carron's six feet six, through the door.

The door closed behind the commander of the legion of peace, and Grayth stood alone, silent. "Aesir—Aesir—Aesir—" his telepath was sending out.

"Yes?" snapped Ware.

"Three Sarn are standing in the room, invisible to me. Eight more are in the outer office. Both Carron and Bartel are trying to call you—they stood in the door delaying the entrance of the invisible three. All are invisible. Their thoughts I can detect, but not decipher."

"I know. I've learned to 'hear' their thoughts. It takes a little adjusting, due to the different patterns. I'm trying to get them now. Too distant. I don't like it."

"Grayth, Spokesman of Mankind." The Decalon spoke from the air in the curious accents of the Sarn, speaking the tongue common to humans and Sarn.

Grayth started, looked about him, shook his head violently, and reached for a call button with a look of unhappy doubt.

"Stop," snapped the Sarn. Grayth's hand halted in midair. "The Sarn Mother sent us for you. Stand up."

"Wh-where are you? Are you—"

Grayth stopped abruptly. A Sarn's powerful, muscle-corded arms gripped him suddenly, and simultaneously an intense blackness fell over him. A blackness more utterly complete than could have been produced by any substance thin enough and flexible enough to give the clothlike sensations that accompanied it. A very faint, rubbery rustling sound came to his ears, and simultaneously the jerking and pulling of the Sarn guard adjusting the cloak.

"We wear the Cloak of the Mother," the guard fluted sharply. "You will be quiet. You will make no sound, say no word. It is understood?"

"Yes," sighed Grayth. Then silently: "You've caught my impressions, Ware?"

"Yes." It whispered in his mind, the reassuring solidity of another human in close contact. The blackness, the utter blackness, baffled and brought a welling of panic. The huge corded arms of the Sarn, the secrecy of this invisible arrest, all brought a feeling of irrepressible panic.

Then Ware's calm mind obtruded powerfully, silently. "The blackness is not related to mine. It is caused, I suspect, by the complete refraction of light about your body. To be invisible, you must be rendered blind to visible light, since any organ capable of seeing must, by its nature, intercept light. Struggle slightly. Strike the face of one of the Guard."

Grayth shuddered. A guard was working swiftly at his feet. A tremor passed through him, and for a moment he fought off the powerful arms, surprising their grip by a sudden thrust and a gasp of panic. His arm flailed out gropingly. Then with a second gasp, half-sob, he quieted at the soft, tensely sharp command of the Decalon.

"Goggles," said Ware softly. "Transformers, probably, operating on ultravisible light, thus making vision possible with invisibility."

Tensely, in Grayth's mind came the impression of half a hundred other human minds attending this exchange, half a hundred humans throughout this central city, the Sarn City, capital alike of human and Sarn affairs.

"You must stop them," Grayth felt a mind whisper urgently. "Ware—you must release him. Secret capture—they hope to loose him where Aesir cannot find him to release him." Deya's mind, turbulent and fearful, now. Leader of human women, determined and ready to defy the age-long, mind-burdening hold of the Sarn, this sudden, half-magic descent of the invisible guards terrified her for the sake of the man she loved.

"Stay where you are, Ware," Grayth rapped out mentally. "They're moving me now—leading—no, carrying me out through my office. In thirty seconds, I'll be lost utterly; the darkness is totally blinding and bewildering." Grayth felt solid ground under his feet suddenly, then he was standing, and spinning in the four cable arms of the giant Sarn. The darkness spun madly about him for a moment, then he stood waveringly on his feet, without the faintest idea of position as powerful arms urged him forward. "Stay where you are. I don't know where I am, anyway, and I'm convinced this is intended as a trap to bring you where the Mother's prepared weapons can destroy you and all hope of the revolution. She wants me only as bait for you. Stay!"

Softly in Grayth's mind came Ware's easy chuckle. "If I knew where you were, my friend, I would come. I will know soon enough. In good time, the Mother will see that you—and hence I—know. She realizes you have telepathic communication with me. Never, to my knowledge, has she revealed these invisible cloaks—"

"There have been other unexplained disappearances; this is the first time a telepath has been available to carry word," Deya snapped out.

"No matter. In good time, for no force, no power, no weapon or ray, no bomb or any other thing can serve to disrupt the—Cloak of Aesir. No energy, however great, can break down that shield. That is not the Mother's hope, for this morning in the Hall of Judgment she tested that cloak to all her powers—and one or two, Grayth, no other Sarn of all Earth knows, save the Mother alone. It did not fail then, nor can it. She makes no further trial of it, but wants an analysis of its forces." Ware's easy jubilance rode through to Grayth, lessening the tension.

"She will not learn one iota of that, Grayth. No, she wants a demonstration, a demonstration on her own terms, at her own time, in her chosen place. By Aesir and all the gods of Earth, Grayth, we'll give her the demonstration she seeks. By every god from Mithra to Thor, we'll give her one, I'll chill her prized palace there on the Sarn Hill till her old bones ache. No Sarn yet ever had rheumatism, but, by Earth and man, we'll find out this night whether a Sarn's thousand bones can't breed a mighty case!"

"You'll stay where you are, you braggart fool," Grayth howled through his telepath. "You are the revolution, not I. Bartel's an abler man, if he does lack a bit in fine words and simple phrases. The Sarn Mother's lived five centuries to your year; she has studied space and time and all of energy with tools and instruments you never guessed, or will guess. You are a child, a prattling fool of a child, to her, Ware. Stay where you are! You may not know of any way to analyze or defeat that shield of yours, but what do you know of the Sarn's ten-thousand-year-old science?"

Ware's bubbling laughter echoed queerly in telepathy. "All Sarn science, Grayth, that has been published. The telepath, my friend, is not without its powers as an educator, tuned inward to catch, amplify and reflect each thought to a solid impression. And all human science, Grayth. Under my house—when I was trying to make a lab the Sarn wouldn't find—I found an ancient subway and a buried lab some striving humans had contrived in the last days before explosives and gas killed them. Books and periodicals, tons of them, heaped clumsily. A forgotten legacy."

Grayth groaned. The skin of his back seemed suddenly oppressed in the queer manner a telepath contrives when absolute rapport is established between two powerful minds. A heavy pack strapped on Ware's back. The screaming hiss of an atom-flame-lamp unit readjusted, rebuilt to carry a million times the load it had been designed for, a scream that vanished in inaudible shrillness. Sketchily, waveringly, the rock-walled, hidden laboratory of Ware's contriving stood out before Grayth's eyes, lighted against the utter blackness that shrouded him. Then that, too, became a blackness, a stranger, straining blackness and chill as Ware pressed a contact at his belt.

"Ware," pleaded Grayth, "I don't know where I am. If you don't promise now to stop this expedition at least until I give further intelligent information, I'll grind the Mother's medallion under my heel, and by the gods, you'll never know."

"I'll wait," sighed Ware.

"But—you'll go later, Ware—you'll go?" demanded Deya.

"I'll promise that, too, Deya." Ware's mind smiled to her.

"Grayth, I shall continue." Darak's thoughts, faint with distance, came in.

"Right," replied Grayth. "Bartel!"

"Yes."

"And Carron and Oburn, Tharnot, Barlmew, Todd—all of you, continue your duties, without any change or shift. Do not hint you know of my disappearance till the appropriate time. Todd, you take charge of that outer office; you did a good job, apparently, when you knew I was being carried by, invisible, ten feet from you. You are in charge there. Keep the girls out of my inner office, for any reason, until I can give some idea of what is to take place. Got it?"

"Right."

"Deya," said Ware, "has stopped sending. Further, she does not answer; she's blanked her mind."

"We've been walking—stopped now!" Grayth's mind raced. "Deya . . . Deya, answer me!"

There was a tense silence of mind; only the low, multitudinous mutter of a thousand human minds in normal thought about him.

"Oburn, where are you?" snapped Ware.

"At home."

"Stroll out in front; you live within three doors of Deya. Grayth, stumble in the dust—do you feel dust under your feet?"

"Yes." Grayth stumbled awkwardly against a giant Sarn guard, dragging his foot sharply across a dusty walk, unseen.

"Dust rose," said Oburn softly. "Deya, will you answer me?"

"Yes." Her telepath thoughts were half angry, half miserable. We're moving again, though, so—they spun me. I don't know which way."

"You will stop dragging your foot." A Sarn voice low and tense in Grayth's ear warned him.

"Ware, I . . . I don't like this." Grayth's thought was tense and very worried.

Deya's was bitter. "It was well enough when you were the one; now you are not so anxious that Ware stay back, I take it. Ware, you stay right where you are, because if that was wise for Grayth, the only one of us who can really move the men of his following, it is a hundred times wiser so far as I am concerned."

"I think," said Ware, annoyed, "that I had better start designing a telepath locating device. It should be relatively simple, and if this continues, we'll need one. I'll join you as soon as I know where you are. In the meantime, I have a little work to do preparing. Please stop ordering and counterordering. We need you both; the Mother wants to study this apparatus, and she won't stop taking people until she gets the chance. It won't do her any good whatever, so she'll get that chance."

"I fear you're right," Grayth agreed. "It should be getting dark now."

"It is. The moon rises at 1:45, so we have plenty of time. I think . . . I think it is going to be heavily overcast," predicted Ware suddenly. A chaos of thoughts raced suddenly through his mind, thoughts too lightly touched for others to follow.

Utter jet, and the sound of people moving, voices and low laughter. Hasty side steps to avoid unseen passers that brushed by, feet sounding softly on the dusty walks or grassy lanes. Then rough cobbles under their feet, rounded by the tread of more than a hundred generations of mankind, and behind them, the low murmur of the square fading away.

The rough cobbles gave way, suddenly, to the smooth, glassy pavement of the roads of the Sarn City. They had passed the low, ancient wall that marked the boundaries where men might walk unchallenged. Only low, sleepy cheeps of birds in nearby parklike gardens now, and the shrill notes of crickets and night insects tuning up.

The pace of the Sarn guards accelerated, their long legs, and the curious manner in which they retracted them with each step, making a pace swift for the humans to match. Grayth heard Deya's soft breathing accelerate as they moved at a near trot up the low rise that led to the Sarn Palace.

Then steps under his feet, strong Sarn arms guiding him upward, steadying stumbling feet. The echo of corridors answered to his tread, and for an instant he knew where he was; this was no unfamiliar walk to him now, and he was mentally readjusted. To the right, and a half-dozen turns, and he was beyond any area of the vast, sprawling Sarn Palace that he knew.

An arm detained him; he stood motionless in utter darkness, while, beyond, something hummed for an instant, then a soft shuffling of a sliding door, two steps forward, and the soft clang of the door's return. The sensation of a sudden drop in a swift elevator was nerve tearing in this darkness, this total unknowingness of place, time or intent of captors. Grayth stiffened, heard Deya's soft gasps as the floor seemed cut from beneath her. Then the steadiness of the floor returned, and only the soft humming of the gravity controls told of their movement downward. Time became confused, there was no clue to their speed, yet Grayth was certain that they dropped many thousands of feet. The air pressure mounted till swallowing had relieved it so many times he lost track of that crude barometric method. More than five thousand feet, though—

More than a mile! No human had ever guessed at the depths of the Sarn Palace. Only once had humans ever been permitted to see those depths, and then it was the upper caverns only, when Drunnel and his men had been given a few feeble weapons by the Mother's orders. Weapons to overcome Grayth and Ware.

"More than a mile—we're slowing, Ware. The air is thick; it must be nearly two miles down. The air itself seems denser and richer in my lungs. Unless we are brought upward again—"

"I'll come down to you," Ware's calm mind replied. "Can you receive there clearly?"

"Perfectly," Grayth acknowledged.

"Two facts I wanted; antigravity units of the cars do not disturb the reception. Two miles of solid rock do not disturb it. Thought waves are a level below all known radiations, a force unto themselves. The Cloak of Aesir stops all other things."

"We are walking down a corridor, wide, rock floored and walled, low ceilinged. There are columns," said Deya. "Ahead, I hear Sarn."

They halted, and the echoes of their feet died away slowly, the curious *zing-zing-zing* of sound reflected from rows of columns disappeared in unknown, unseeing distances.

"Mother of Sarn! Decalon Toplar reports with her Ten, and the two humans for whom she was sent," the Decalon's fluting voice called out.

"Remove the Cloak of the Mother, Decalon. Place all of the cloaks in this case, and with them the visors."

A giant Sarn tugged at Grayth, the curious rustle of the cloak rose about him, then abruptly he was blinded by a flood of intolerably brilliant light. Gradually his eyes adjusted themselves; it was no more than normal illumination from a score of giant atom-flame lamps set high above in the arched and groined stone of the ceiling. Black, glittering, granitic rock, studded with two huge plaques on opposite sides. A twenty-foot disk of gold mapping Earth, a twenty-foot golden disk mapping the Forgotten Planet. From a concealed atom-flame lamp in the lofty dome, two projectors shot stabbing rays against the golden disks. On Earth's, a ray of brilliant yellow-white; on the other, a ray of dim, chill blue.

The Mother sat on a chair of state, about her the eight Mothers of the Cities and a score of giant Sarn guards. From air, eleven more were emerging, as Deya emerged piecemeal, while goggled Sarn packed into the silver and hardwood case on the long table something unseen and tenderly treated. The Decalon stood by the case, tucking unseen folds carefully into its corners, taking goggles and batteries from the guards to place on tiny pins.

"It is the Given Law that no being, human or Sarn, shall twice be accused of a single thing," said Grayth. "Yesterday in the Hall of Judgment I was tried and acquitted. It is the Given Law that no being, human or Sarn, shall be brought for judging without an opportunity of defense, save he waive that right.

"Neither I nor this woman, Deya, has committed any offense against any being, human or Sarn. As is our right, we ask our accuser to appear and explain before us and the Mother the reason for this arrest."

The Mother's slitted eyes closed slowly and opened sleepily. Her powerful body remained as motionless as the stone of the Hall; the Mothers of the Cities neither moved nor seemed so much as to breathe.

The Mother spoke in the fluting tongue of the Sarn. "The Given Law is the Law of the Mother; by it I have promised to abide, save in time of emergency. This, Grayth, is such a time. You, this woman, and perhaps certain others have sought to plot against the Sarn and the Sarn Mother. That is the accusation; I am the accuser. What answer do you make?"

"If one be brought before the Mother, and faced with his accuser, he has then twenty-four hours to consider his reply. The accusation must have evidence enough to make it seem just in the Mother's eyes that an answer be made, and complete enough that the accused know why this thing is charged.

"The Mother is the accuser, but I may ask—by the Given Law—what reasoned facts bring forth this accusation?"

The Mother's eyes sparkled. Almost, a smile touched her tiny lips as she looked at Grayth's keen, gray eyes. The Sarn were proud that never in the millenniums of man's enslavement had cruelty been applied, nor intentional injustice. Where the Law of the Sarn could apply logically to humans, both races worked under the same law; where—as in the nature of two races such things must be—the laws could not apply identically, justice had been applied.

The Sarn were just; no human could say otherwise. The Sarn Mother's age covered six-score generations of mankind, and to some extent her immortality removed her alike from human and Sarn. Wherefore, it was easier for her, who had known man's greatness, to appreciate the keenness and strength that lay in Grayth's stubborn face. And, knowing mankind, to appreciate the steadfastness with which he would fight by every law or trick of law to win freedom back for Deya.

And—she appreciated the searching quickness with which Grayth had forced her once again on the defensive. Her case was true and solid—but made of ten thousand thousand little things, of things that had not happened as well as of things that had. Of subtle, reasoned psychology—and not half a dozen solid facts. Of those few, three were ruled out of this consideration, because they had been dealt with in that earlier trial, when Grayth was released.

She had no time to argue now with a mind that she knew was fully as keen as that of her own City Mothers. There were other, more important things afoot, as that gray-eyed man well knew. And he knew as well as she that her case was not a thing to be stated and in a dozen sentences. And also that it was a perfectly just, though unprovable, accusation.

"This is a time of emergency, Grayth," said the Mother softly. "I will give you the twenty-four hours you demand, however. And your companion, Deya.

"Decalon, let these two be taken to the fifteenth cell in the House of the Rocks."

The Decalon and her squad of ten moved forward. Grayth turned to Deya, a slight smile on his lips, as the Ten surrounded them. Back toward the great pillared corridor leading off into unseen distances, lighted by dwindling atom flames, the guards led them.

"The House of the Rocks. This, then, is the rumored prison of the Sarn. Ware . . . Ware—" Grayth called mentally.

"I am coming, Grayth. I will join you in an hour. You need not call continuously as I have made rapport with you and can follow your normal thoughts. The sky, as I suggested, is becoming overcast. It will be a very dark night."

"We could not leave unaided," sighed Deya.

"I do not believe it would be probable." Grayth laughed uneasily.

Grayth moved about the cell restlessly. The Decalon and her squadron were gone, down that tube that had brought them. The single huge old Sarn that served as warden, turnkey and guard had set the tumblers on the steel door, and left with soft, shuffling toe pads.

Grayth stopped in the center of the room, his head high and tense, furrows of concentration on his forehead. Deya, in her chair, sat motionless, her deep-blue eyes clouded in sudden thought. She rose slowly, a magnificent throwback to a race five thousand years forgotten, a viking's daughter, bearing a golden tan of the more southern sun of this region, but golden haired and blue eyed, tall and powerful.

Slowly her eyes cleared, and a slight frown of understanding met Grayth's eyes. "There are Sarn close by. At least a dozen. And if those Sarn are prisoners here, then all the Mother's laboratories have been stripped of talent," she said softly.

"Echoes," thought Grayth sharply. "Do not use voice."

Deya smiled. "They do, and yet no intelligible word is audible. The echoes do not carry words; they carry sounds, confusing, blended, intermingled sound. And concentration on telepaths might make impressions on instruments, where normal thought did not. Perhaps speech is better."

Grayth nodded. "There are a dozen Sarn, at least, all scientists. They are in the cell above, the cell below, the cells on each side. And the only clear things of their thoughts that I can make is—Aesir—and instruments."

"I've found that shaft," came Ware's thoughts. "I haven't traced every circuit of the palace for nothing, and as the palace electrotechnician, I've found many that were not on my charts. The sky is becoming heavily overcast. It will be very dark indeed. I will join you shortly."

The Mother pointed silently. Across the room, a section of rock had swung aside, and a broad signal board was revealed. A green light blinked irregularly, then went out. A blue bulb winked for a moment, and died in turn, as a yellow bulb glowed steadily. "By the shaft, then. The air is not open to him."

The Mothers of the Cities stirred restlessly. A second yellow light flashed. "If he goes below the sixth level—" suggested the Mother of Durban.

"The cage will remain down there, but probably he will not. He walked through a solid wall once; he may walk through solid rock." A third and fourth bulb flashed. The Mother watched quietly. The Mothers of Cities tensed as the fifth lighted. Abruptly it was out, and in sudden succession the blue and green bulbs winked.

"He knew," said the Mother, almost approvingly. "The car did not fall. Go."

A section of rock wall swung open. Silently the Mothers of Cities vanished behind it, and with them went the tall figures of the guards. The rock swung to. The Mother, alone on her tall throne, saw a darkening of the farther lights of the long corridor.

Aesir stood again before the Mother, a blackness, a thing that was not black, but was blackness incarnate. A thing some seven feet in height, vaguely manlike in form.

The Mother's thin lips smiled. "You have shrunk, Aesir. Have some of those billions of wills you mentioned left you, then?"

A voice stirred in her mind, a respecting, yet laughing voice. "Perhaps that may be it; a few wills more of cold metal than warm human flesh. But for the good of my race, two wills you hold captive must be freed. For this I have come again. And—perhaps that you and those who wait in five adjoining cells may know me somewhat better.

"I am the crystallization of a billion, and more than a billion wills, Mother of the Sarn."

"There are no humans here; the Sarn need no such tales." The Mother moved annoyedly.

"It is no tale; it, is pure fact. This blackness is their product, not as, perhaps, I might explain to humans, but still their product." The voice that stirred soundless in the Mother's mind smiled.

The Mother nodded slowly in comprehension. "Wills and knowledge. That may be. We seek a new balance, you and I."

"We seek a new balance, your race and mine," corrected that blackness. "You and I might reach a balance in this minute, if it were we two alone. The balance would be—that your plan went down to a depth that none, neither Sarn nor human, knows, while I remained."

"Yes," acknowledged the Mother. "I might be wiped out,

and you remain. But your race would go, and mine remain, save that you alone continued."

"There is no need to exchange these thoughts; each knows the other to that extent. Man has one great advantage over Sarn; that, as a race, man is more nearly developed to universal telepathy. A few of my people can already talk among themselves; I have learned the different pattern that is Sarn telepathy. I can speak with you as Grayth cannot."

"Though he appears aware of Sarn thoughts when near us," sighed the Mother, "I had not thought of that."

"We make an exchange now," Aesir's thoughts laughed. "You wanted observations of my . . . my body stuff. I will give you that, and in exchange—"

Aesir stepped forward, and swept from the long table the silver case that contained the cloaks of the Mother and the goggles. Simultaneously, the Mother's finger moved, and a carven bit of her high throne sank under it. From unseen projectors, a shrieking hell of flame screamed out, intolerable—blasting— The rocky floor of the great chamber screamed and puffed out in incandescent fury. The great table boomed dully in the corridors, a sudden, expanding blot of livid gas. The mad shrieking screamed and thundered down the corridors, the floor of the vast cavern slumped in annihilation that speared down through a hundred feet of rock in a single second of cosmic fury—

And died in silence. The Mother dropped three curled arms before her face, blinking tear-blurred eyes. Aesir stood, blackness against fiery incandescence of the cooling rocks, unsupported in the air. His form was altered, a clumsy thing with a strange, angular belly. An almost rectangular protuberance. But the thing was not rectangular; one corner was twisted and bitten away.

"I never knew," said Aesir softly, "but I am certain now; the world of the Sarn was not so heavy as Earth. You move slowly, Mother."

Silently the blackness glided down the corridor, dwindling from the Mother's sight. Furious golden eyes glittered after the hunched, disfigured mass. Slowly the glitter faded from her eyes, and a concentration of thought appeared, perhaps even a mischievous twinkle of approbation.

The Mother's finger touched another button, and instantly a score of tense-faced guards leaped through the door, clumsy seeming, funnel mouthed, hand weapons ready. They stopped at the door, staring at the fiery incandescence in the floor.

The Mothers of Cities crowded through their ranks, a slow, dawning smile of satisfaction on their thin lips as they looked into the glow. The Mother of Targlan took her seat slowly. "Then the revolution is ended," she said with soft satisfaction.

The Mother turned angry eyes on her. "Daughter," she asked bitterly, "do you think I mount here weapons of the power I have in the Hall of Judgment? I did not turn that weapon on him—but on the cloaks. No more than a corner of them did I get; he moved too swiftly. My thoughts have been disturbed in this emergency, and I have not rested in fifty hours, or I would never have left that case where he might reach it.

"Aesir must win on this exchange, for he *will* know what makes the Cloak of the Mother, while I *may* know what makes the Cloak of Aesir." The Mother looked calmly down the long corridor, where a figure of hunched blackness turned into a narrow cleft in the great wall of the rocky tunnel.

The old Sarn warder of the House of Rocks had been instructed. The Sarn Mother had no desire to lose Sarn lives—and she wanted Aesir in that grim citadel. The warder, as Aesir appeared, turned away and left the passages open to him. The invisible guards at the narrow cleft that led into the impregnable citadel remained inactive, wrapped in invisibility.

Up the stairways carved in the glinting rock the Blackness strode. Down the corridor to the gray steel door behind which Grayth's and Deya's minds acted as directive calls.

And—between ranks and files of recording instruments set in every wall, in every doorway he passed. Tiny atom flames finer than the slimmest wire reached out to touch and feel at the black texture of his cloak. Unseen force fields caressed delicately at the fringes of blackness. Bolometers and thermometers felt and sampled the chill that poured from the blackness. Frigid air, like chilled puddles, flowed from that blackness and trickled across the stone floor behind him. White of frost coated the corridor pavement as he, in his dead blackness, passed.

"Grayth—Deya—stand back from the door. The door will fade to a vague transparency. Step through it instantly." Through the impenetrable blackness, the subtle mystery of thought reached out to contact and explain to the imprisoned humans.

The formless blackness of Aesir's hand waved stubbily over the gray metal of the door. As though that hand were a wet

cloth, the door a chalked picture on slate, it vanished. Where
the hand had passed in quick circles, the grim metal roiled
and twisted—and vanished.

Deya's hand reached out uncertainly, touched the space
where the door had been to feel a vague opposition, as though
a thick and incredibly viscous gassy stuff remained. It was utterly without temperature sensation. She lunged through it
sharply, overcome by an instant's strangling suffocation, then
stood beside Aesir in the corridor. Grayth joined them
silently.

"The cloaks?" he asked.

"They are useless save for information. The Mother's rays
cut through the corner of the case, and cut strange patterns
in them, no doubt. You could not use them. We'll have to go
out as we are. Now come, and stay close behind me. We
must put walls behind us, and that won't be easy."

"Can we go into the rock—or would that be impossible?"
Deya asked.

Aesir's misshapen hand pointed. Behind them, the door of
the cell was · blackness similar to Aesir's own, a blackness
rapidly congealing about two bent shadows overlapping on
the surface. Two shadows were Deya and Grayth had
passed through. A deadly chill was radiating from the door, a
growing chill that sucked the light of the atom-flame lamps in
the ceiling, and ice from the air.

"You felt that momentary suffocation. You can't breathe
inside that steel, or inside rock. And that condition of inter-
penetrability is both temporary and frightfully treacherous.
We'll have to go."

Ware went ahead, and now, as he passed the hair-fine atom
flames that had probed for his cloak, a finger pointed and
shape cracklings of lightning snapped where the jet beam of
blackness struck the probing beams. Harmless to Aesir's
blackness, they were hairlines of death to unshielded humans.

The flames ahead on their course abruptly sputtered and
went out. The Sarn saw no reason to lose good instruments.

Down the stair, and out into the glare of the great atom
flames lighting the House of Rocks. "There are invisible
guards," said Aesir. "The Mother, I take it, warned them to
let me pass in unhindered. They may seek to stop you—"

It was against the Mother's orders. But those Sarn guards, in
their eight-foot power, in their contempt for humans, in the
pride they held that never had any being imprisoned in the

House of the Rocks escaped, raised unseen weapons toward Grayth and Deya.

A long, stretching finger of jet shot out from Aesir's stubby hand. Something cracked in the air, darting lightnings and a wild, many-toned shriek of agony chopped off abruptly. A Sarn figure black as Aesir's jet stumbled from nothingness and faded behind a swiftly formed white curtain of frost crystals. The black finger swept around, and the Sarn guards died in blue lightnings and blackness.

"Run," commanded Ware. The three started down the straight narrow cleft that led to the outer corridor. Aesir turned right, then right again, into a low-roofed tunnel. Another elevator bank, the cars undamaged. The heavy, locked metal door faded under his hand to disclose a black shaft leading down and up in emptiness to unseen depths and heights. Another door—and another—

Then a car was found, and the three hastened through. Behind them in the main corridor a heavy pounding of running feet and clanking accouterments sounded. The blunt, dull-glossed nose of a war-blast swerved clumsily round the corridor with half a dozen giant Sarn tugging at it. Degravitized, it floated free, but its tons of mass were clumsy and hard to manage there in narrow rock corridors. Shouting, musical commands twisted it into place, settled it, and it thudded to the floor as the degravitizer was cut. Two Sarn swung the trajectory controls, and a third held the lanyard ready.

Aesir reached for the controls of the elevator cab as the blast roared in throaty fury at dissolving, flaming walls. The rock walls to the left and right flared into deadly flame of dying atoms. And the view was lost as the translucency of the metal door snapped instantly into blackness, a blackness that licked up the furious energy greedily and pulled with freezing fingers at the heat of the two human bodies within.

"That button, Grayth. Quickly. I cannot touch it through this cloak," Ware snapped.

Grayth pushed the thing, one among a bank of hundreds. The floor of the cab pushed against them momentarily, then a sense of weightless falling gripped them as Ware's black finger pointed at something in the control mechanism. Blackness and frightful cold drained every trace of warmth from a resistor in the controls, and the full current drove through the degravitator control. The car shot madly upward.

"The Mother has many of these cars wired with power cut-offs. If this is one—as it probably is—and she learns in time which car we took, she may cut out our circuit. If so—we still have one chance, though I have never dared try it."

"Better cut that resistance back in," said Grayth quietly. "Listen to the howl of the air above."

The shriek was mounting. Far above in the closed tube, compressed by the upward plunge of the tube-fitting car, the air was howling through some vent. It was a vast organ pipe that changed its tune upward, upward—more and more swiftly as the tube length shortened and the pressure mounted—

"I can't." Ware's hidden head shook. "The air pressure must stop us. But not until we reach the top of the building and the automatic safeguards go into action. They'll cut the current in the car and apply brakes as we pass the topmost floor. If the Mother hasn't already—"

The shriek mounted. Abruptly the drive of the car vanished. Grayth, already firmly gripping the carved cage walls, flung a protecting arm about Deya and gripped more tightly. Aesir tumbled upward toward the roof of the cab, inverted himself somehow in midflight, and hung poised.

"Don't touch me," snapped Ware's thoughts in their minds. "It would be death—"

A new sibilant hiss cut through the roar of the air in the tube above, and Ware sighed in relief. "The Mother was too late. She cut the power—but not before we had come so high, and so fast that the automatic safeguards tripped. The emergency brakes have gone on."

The deceleration died, and Ware floated back to the floor. The car was stopped, was sinking slowly. It clicked again, and a ratchet locked somewhere beneath their feet. The door of the car opened with a rumble, and an outer door slipped aside. The three stepped out into a corridor, a corridor lighted by the atom-flame lamps of the Sarn, lamps carved in alabaster and golden amber stone. They were in the uppermost floor of the Palace of the Sarn.

Far below, the Sarn Mother looked thoughtfully at the little lighted column of signal lamps. The City Mothers followed her gaze, furious as they saw the double red bulbs of the safety guard signals go on. "I am curious," said the Sarn Mother softly. "He froze the resistor in the degravitizer circuit with his blackness, surely, to get any such mad climb rate. But I have a thought that Aesir does nothing that he does not know some remedy for, nor attempt anything that he does not have some second, saving escape. What would he have done had I been able to cut his power before he could reach the safety trips?"

The City Mothers were not curious. They waited impatiently as the Mother let seconds slip away without flinging a rank of guards about that upper floor.

The Mother made no move. She saw no gain in throwing her guards against the blackness, that, so far as she could see, had no weakness. She saw, rather, that her best policy was to wait the report of her scientists. Knowledge was the power she needed now. That, and the power she already had; control over all sources of the materials whose lack rendered Aesir harmless—so far as revolution went.

Aesir stood in the entranceway of the Hall of Judgment. Behind, through the ever-open doors, the Gardens of the Sarn were visible. Aesir—Ware—smiled. "I said it might be an overcast night," his thought whispered softly.

Grayth and Deya shivered. The gardens knelt before a wind that howled in maniac fury. In the reflected light that shone against the low-pressed sky, a wrack of storm boiled overhead. And it was cold. The wind that shrieked across the gardens was a breath of savage winter cutting through this summer night.

"I think," said Ware, "that it will rain."

As he spoke the sky burst into flame. Vast tongues of lightning ripped across the sky, stabbing down to Earth in a mighty network of electric fire. The air exploded with a blast of thunder that rattled the mighty fabric of the Sarn Palace to its bones. Instantly the floodgates opened. The clouds split up and tumbled down in liquid streams. The shouting wind lashed the water droplets before it in a horizontal spray that was half falling water, half water slashed from the ground that was suddenly a pond. The twinkling lights of the human city beyond the Sarn City walls were suddenly gone.

"Perhaps," said Ware pleasedly, "I used too much."

"You?" gasped Grayth. "*You* did this?"

"The Sarn hate cold, and they hate the wet more than any cat ever did. You'll find no Sarn loose in the gardens tonight. Our way should be clear to the gates."

Deya shuddered and looked at Aesir's blackness. "That wind is cold; that rain must be near sleet. And I am dressed for June—not a February night."

"I used too much power," Ware shrugged. "I never did this thing before. Put it down to inexperience."

"Experimental error," Grayth sighed. "Gods, man, you've washed the city away. Come, let's start before we have to swim."

"Not yet," said Ware. "I've something else to do. The Mother wanted to study this blackness of mine. Well, by all the gods there are, I'll give her all she wants. I'll make her think again before she summons Aesir for her pleasure!"

He turned about and faced into the great Hall of Judgment. It was magnificent beneath the dim light of a few big lamps. It was jet stone and chrome, gold and sparkling, inlaid crystal. Aesir's arm became a funnel of blackness that pointed in slow circles around the room. Where that arm passed, the sparkle of polished stone and shining metal or gem vanished. It became a dead blackness. The walls ceased to have the appearance of walls, but became empty spaces that stretched off to some eternity of night.

The glint and whisper of the atom flames died away; their strong light dulled to something somber and depressing.

And cold—cold welled out of the place in a tangible flood. The humans shivered violently and fled from the doorway that dripped, suddenly, with frozen mist. Puddled air, chilled near its freezing point, it seemed, flowed down the walls and out the door. A breeze sprang up, a throaty gurgle of air rushing into the room at the top of the great door to rush out at the bottom in a freezing, unseen torrent.

Grayth and Deya hurried aside, shivering in unbearable chill. The torrent of air poured out, across the vestibule to the entranceway of the palace. It flowed down the steps, and as they watched, the howling rain turned to snow and froze as sleet on the stone.

"Yes," said Ware in satisfaction, "the Sarn hate cold. It will be a month before that room is habitable again. Now come."

He walked through the flood, and down the steps toward the windlashed gardens. The wind howled by him, swirled around his cloak of blackness, and the figure was outlined in white that swirled and glinted in the faint light radiated from the building. Behind him, Grayth and Deya made their way, white figures against the blackness. In a moment they were lost behind driving, glistening curtains of rain.

They were soaked and freezing in an instant. In his arms Grayth felt Deya shivering violently. "Ware," he called abruptly. "Ware—go on; we will meet you. We can follow that blackness only by the snow that forms around you, and on a night like this, may I be cursed if I follow a walking snowstorm. I'm freezing now, and Deya, too."

"Frozen," the girl chattered.

"I can't cut off this shield," Ware answered. "The instruments aren't insulated well enough. If water touches them—there'll be neither Sarn nor human city to squabble over. Meet me at my house. You can find your way?"

"I think so," nodded Grayth, shivering.

"Strike for the road. It will glow tonight, as usual. And there will be no Sarn upon it, with this liquid blizzard howling."

"Good." Grayth and Deya set out half-running. Black wind and water thundered through the gardens. The sky exploded once more in blinding light, the waves of sound rocking the ground beneath their feet so that even half-frozen as they were, they felt its shaking.

In the rock of that wild night, no eyes saw Grayth and Deya reach their goal. Rain in solid, blinding sheets hid them as they slipped between wind-bowed trees to Ware's small stone cottage, into its unlighted doorway. Ware's hand found Grayth's, and led the shivering, dripping pair through the tiny room, abruptly brilliant in the explosion of another lightning flash. At the far wall, Ware fumbled at a stone that grated and moved. Silently he led them down to a yet smaller room lined with rough granite. The stone above them swung back, and a light sprang up. But again Ware was fumbling, and again he led them down, down to a musty cavernous place, walled with age-rusted steel, supported by rusted columns of steel hidden at the heart of thicker columns—stalagmites and stalactites formed about and buttressing the corroded metal.

"The old subway," Ware explained. "It goes for a quarter of a mile in that direction and nearly a mile in the other before cave-ins block it. All, you see, beneath the human city—and most at a depth of more than one hundred and twenty feet. My lab's over here." It was set up on the concrete platform of a forgotten station.

"But here—strip off those wet things and stand before these heaters." Ware turned to a crude control panel, and a network of iron bars grew warm, hot, then faintly red as a welcome heat poured out.

"Do we hide," asked Deya softly, "or frankly return?"

"If," said Ware sadly, "I knew how much longer this queer status of half-revealed half-concealed revolt was going to continue before I could get somewhere, we might be in a better position to know what to do."

"Which makes me wonder, Ware. Half-concealed half-revealed, I mean. The Mother's Cloaks have the goggles to make vision possible. I don't know what that blackness of yours is—beyond that it is infernally cold; I'm still congealed—but if no ray can pierce it, pray tell me how you see where you are going."

Ware looked up, laughing. "I don't. Yet I found my way across that swamp called the Garden of the Sarn more easily than you, tonight. The telepath is the answer—I see through others' eyes. The Mother told me where the cloaks were hidden." He nodded toward the truncated case. "Without her eyes—I'd never have seen to reach them."

"Perhaps," said Deya, "if we knew better what you have, and what you lack, we could help more efficiently."

"Perhaps," suggested Grayth grimly, "you can wash the blasted Sarn out of their city. Another such 'overcast night' and you may do it."

"The Sarn City's higher than we are." Ware smiled. "But our people do stand cold and wet better than theirs."

"But," said Deya, "it isn't practical—nor fast enough. What have you there? My slowly thawing bones give me a very personal interest in that cloak of yours."

Ware sighed gustily, "It's hard to explain. About ninety percent of it isn't in words, or explainable in words. It's a mathematical concept that has reality.

"Wherefore I will now give you a typical pre-Sarn analogy, because neither you nor Grayth can get pictures from mathematics. It's a language, you know—as much a language as the one we normally speak, or the Sarn language. Some terms you can translate, and some can't be. For instance $x^2 + y^2 = c^2$ is mathematics language for 'circle.' I will give you analogies which I guarantee are not sound, and neatly conceal the truth. But I can't do any better.

"Dirac, a physicist of the pre-Sarn days, explained the positron as a whole in a continuum of electrons in negative energy states. Space, he said, was completely filled with electrons possessed of negative energies. It was full to the brim, and overflowed into the electrons we can detect—ordinary matter electrons.

"Shortly before the Sarn came, men were developing hints that there might be more to that. There was. Electrons in positive energy states, when vibrated, gave off radiation—

light, heat, and so on. If you use energy concentrated enough, you can vibrate electrons in negative energy states. You might say they give off negative energy radiation. They produce photons of energy in negative energy states.

"As I said, it's an analogy that I can't honestly describe, but the effect is radiated negative energy. Radiant cold or radiant darkness or radiant lack-of-X-rays—whatever you want.

"Energy being conserved, of course, the result is that the source of that radiation, instead of consuming energy, gives it off. My pack does not radiate negative energy; it sets up a condition in the air about me that makes the air atoms radiate negative energy.

"The atomic flame the Mother turned on me satisfied, to some extent, the ravening demand for energy that negative energy setup caused. The force that makes the air atoms radiate in that way makes them unstable—sort of splits them into two parts, two half-formed atoms of matter. In that state, neither half is real, but each has a terrible demand for sufficient mass—in the form of energy—to raise it to reality. In that median state, matter is interpenetrable. We walk through steel doors and stone floors, for instance. It will hang on that unstable point of half-and-half momentarily, before re-forming to matter. It's as dependable as a rattlesnake or a 'tame' tiger. While we're interpenetrating, it may fall off that delicate balance and consume our mass-energy in re-forming. When Sarn guards send atomic flames after us, the unstable matter greedily drinks in the energy, and starts definitely toward reforming with the air of that energy. If left alone, one-half of the semiatoms absorbs the other half, and it's normal again. In the meantime, it's black. And cold—like the Mother's Hall of Judgment right now.

"When the Mother's beams were tearing at me, the energy was actively making extra atoms of air. It didn't make any difference what kind of beam she used—the energy was consumed. Her atomic flame had lots of power—and made a lot of air. Her curious atom-disruption beam didn't carry much energy, but the particular form of the beam was most deadly. The form passed through my shield quite unchanged, theoretically. But the energy had been removed from it.

"Naturally, the Mother's physicists are badly puzzled now by a completely unanimous report of 'nothing' on the part of their instruments. None of them, of course, read below absolute zero. That shield has a temperature of —55,000 Absolute—or thereabouts.

"I could wipe out the Sarn very readily. But"—Ware shrugged his shoulders—"they'd wipe out all humans while I was at it."

"What do you need?"

"An hour," Ware sighed. "One hour—in the Sarn workshops. A few pounds of molybdenum, some wire-drawing apparatus, a few ounces of scandium and special glass-blowing machinery. Then I'd have a duplicate of this toy of mine that would protect this whole city for fifty miles about."

"In other words," said Grayth, smiling slightly, "if you could drive the Sarn out, you could drive them away."

"Precisely," acknowledged Ware. "Which is comforting, if useless."

Deya rubbed her left arm with her right hand thoughtfully, and turned sideways to the heater. "How far," she asked, "will your present apparatus reach?"

"That, too, is helpful." Ware grinned. "Just about far enough to blanket completely the Sarn City. I could protect that against any attack. But not, by any means, the human city."

"That might help, though." Deya nodded. "I have something in mind. My dress is dry, if somewhat crumpled. Could you get us something to eat, Ware? My chill had left me hungry."

"What's your thought?" asked Ware eagerly, half annoyedly. The telepaths did not carry thoughts the wearer wished to conceal.

"I . . . I'd rather talk with Grayth first." Deya shook her head slowly. "I may be wrong."

Resignedly, Ware went up the crude stairway, up to the kitchen of his cottage one hundred and fifty feet above. Deya looked at Grayth as each in turn pulled off the telepath.

Deya pulled on her dress, smoothing the still slightly damp crinkles down. "How is Simons, Grayth?"

Grayth looked at her in slight puzzlement, his shirt half on. "Hopeless, as you know—but why do you ask now? He could not help us, anyway."

Deya's lips set in a slight, tight smile, her eyes bright and thoughtful. "I'm not so sure, Grayth. Not . . . so . . . sure. Ware has said that anything that he can run through an amplifier can be recorded, hasn't he? And if it can be recorded, it could be rebroadcast on a different wavelength, perhaps—"

Grayth started, went rigid. "By Aesir and all the gods of Earth! *Deya!* What fantastic idea have you now? That man is mad, horribly, loathsomely mad—"

"Negative energy," said Deya shortly, deft fingers arranging her hair. "If we could make the Sarn give up without fighting—in despair and hopelessness— And there are energies other than those purely physical ones that the Sarn are so thoroughly equipped to resist."

Grayth stood silent for a moment, his swift-working mind forgetting for the moment the task of driving his tired body. "You've talked with Dr. Wesson?" he asked intently.

Deya nodded slowly, "Yes—just this morning," then thought a moment before going on. "Or rather yesterday. It will be drawn in about three hours, if the storm has stopped. We should bring him here before then. You see what I have in mind?"

"Yes! I'll have Carron—"

Ware came down the steps, slowly, bearing two trays with bread and cheese and cold meat, some cups, cream and coffee. "If you will use those beakers for the water, the laboratory hot plates for a stove, Deya, I'd prefer your coffee to mine."

"Ware," asked Grayth tensely, "can you record a thought—a telepath thought?"

Ware stopped, brows suddenly furrowed. "Record it? Why? I've never tried—it's easier to think it again."

"Could it be done?"

"Hm-m-m . . . yes. I think so."

"How long to make the apparatus?" Grayth asked anxiously.

Ware hesitated. Shrugged. "A few hours. I can make that. Telepath apparatus, because of its very nature, has to be tiny. A few grains of the hard-to-get elements go a long way when the whole apparatus is less than a cubic millimeter in volume. But it takes time. A recorder and reproducer—say, two days, once I get the design. I think . . . yes, I know I can do it."

Grayth swept the telepath back to his head. Rapidly his thoughts drove out. "Carron—Carron—"

"Yes?" Sleepily Carron responded to the call.

"It's three hours to dawn. Carron—this must be done before the first people stir. Get Ohrman, the instrument maker, to Ware's at once. There are telepaths to be made. Get Dr. Wesson and tell him to call at Ware's. Then rouse one of the other men to receive and transmit my orders and get some sleep yourself.

"Now, Ware, draw out the plans for the parts you'll need for that apparatus, so Ohrman can start while you get some sleep. Oh . . . you can, I assume, make some translator arrangement that will twist human thought to Sarn telepath levels?"

"Eh? Human to Sarn levels—I don't know about that. I've been working on that problem on and off for weeks."

"Good—it'll be on, and not off, now. If you can do that, Ware, we win Earth again!"

The thing was incredibly tiny. It lay in Ware's palm, two small, inclosed reels connected by a bridge of bulging metal, the size, perhaps of a half peanut, between two slices of inch-thick steel rod. But the workmanship was wonderfully fine.

"This is only the reproducer," Ware sighed. His eyes were red and weary. "The recorder is there. You said that needn't be portable. And it records, as you wanted, in Sarn-type bands from the human thoughts, on a silver ribbon. The ribbon is endless, and repeats as long as this little spring is wound.

"Now, may I ask what you want of it? I've concentrated so on this that no question could enter my mind, I think. How is recorded thought to dislodge the Sarn? By repeating, 'Go away—go away.' Endlessly? Telepathic commands have no more force than words, you know."

"Not if they are resisted," Deya acknowledged. "But they can enter below conscious strength level. Do you want to see who—why—"

The stone above moved. Grayth and Deya and Ware looked up. Only the heavily sleeping, exhausted Ohrman remained unconscious of the intruder.

"Down, Simons," said Dr. Wesson's voice. There was a gentle urgency in it, a pitying yet firm tenderness. A pair of feet appeared, slowly, wearily, with an air of terrible, unending exhaustion—tired beyond all rest, misery and hopelessness subtly expressed in the dull, shambling descent of those heavy feet.

Loosely, miserably they came down the long flight, their mechanical, rhythmic drumming a muffled beat of defeat. The man came into view. His figure was lax, powerfully muscled arms and shoulders bent under a soul-deadening weight of overwhelming despair. Down—down—

"Down, Simons." The doctor's voice was weary with a queer despair caught somehow from that doom-weighted figure.

Ware turned slowly to look at Deya, at Grayth. "Who is he—Simons?"

They did not answer, and he turned back to look at the figure that stood unmoving now beneath the powerful lights of this buried laboratory. His face was pale and lined, powerful with the strength drained from it, set in a dead mask of uncaring despair. His eyes were black, black pits that looked without hope, or hope of hope, into the keen gray eyes of Aesir.

Ware felt something within him chill under the gaze of those eyes that no longer cared or hoped. The soul beyond them was not dead and longed for death. The lights of the bright room seemed cold and drear. Fatigue and hopelessness of the endless struggle against the overwhelming Sarn surged up in Ware, hopelessness and despair so deep he did not mind that the cause was lost before—

He tore his eyes away. "Deya—in the name of the gods, what—who—what is this thing!" he gasped.

"That is negative energy, Ware. That is the negative energy of the mind, the blackness of Aesir applied to all hope, all ambition. He is mad; he is a manic depressive. He has no hope, no thought of escape from that negative hell of despair that is beyond despair. He is mad, for no sane mind could conceive that awful blackness, the hopelessness that is a positive, devouring force that infests his being.

"If ever his mind should start to mend, he will become a suicidal maniac, driven to kill himself in any way he can, at any horrible expense. He cannot think of that escape now. That is struggle, that is in itself a hope—and he has none. To conceive of death as an escape is to hope, to believe that something better can be.

"That is beyond him now, for hope—struggle—effort to escape—all involve a will that mind has lost.

"He is mad, Ware, because no mind can hold the terrible despair his thoughts now know and remain sane.

"Record his thoughts. Record them there on that silver ribbon. Record that hopelessness that knows no resistance, no will to struggle. Record it, and broadcast that through the Sarn City!"

The Sarn Mother sat motionless at the high window of her tower, dull eyes looking out over the Gardens of the Sarn. Rich cloaks and heavy blankets wrapped her—useless things. The cold seeped through to her bones and drank her warmth. The great chamber, windowed on every side, was darkened by a heavy gloom, chilled by a cold that had grown slowly through the hours and the days she had sat here, almost unmoving. The bleak, cold stone of the walls was damp with a cold sweat of moisture. Great heaters in the walls ran at red heat and the dark air drank their warmth. Magnificent atomflame lamps rustled softly in the high ceiling; their faint, silken whisper mumbled meaningless in her ears, and their strong light had lost its sparkle. Some subtle change in the air made it seem gray and very cold.

The sun did not shine here. A cold, steady rain beat down on the gardens below, ran endlessly over the clear windowpanes, stirring under vague, listless winds. The sun did not shine here. Through the fog of slowly dripping rain, beyond the limits of her gardens, the sun shone. It was brilliant there, she knew, a bright, hot sun sparkling in the bright clean air. It was June out there. The year was dead here, dead in a creeping, growing chill that burdened the land. The creeping, growing chill of—

That hellish thing of blackness. Almost, she felt angered at it, squatting there, dejected, black, unutterably woeful in the center of her gardens. Or what had been her gardens. It was a ravaged place now, plowed and harrowed by howling beams of atomic death, a shrieking incandescent effort to move that crouched thing of blackness. It had meant only the destruction of one slight spot of beauty in a dreary, cold world.

But that meant little, for there was no beauty now, or ever would be again. Only the chill that stole the heat from the air, the walls, her tired old body and the subtle darkness that cut through the brilliance of the atom flames and left light without sparkle, colors that all tinged gray.

A finger stirred listlessly and pressed a control. No, it was over. Full heat. She had known that; what sense to try again what she had tried a thousand times before during these endless, sleepless days that changed only from one shade of gray to a deeper black.

Dull eyes looked at the sweating walls. Cold, stone walls. When had it ever been that she had ordered stone? Warm marbles of rose and green. Warm? The rose of dying day before night's chill. The green of endless arctic ice. It mocked her and drove its chill to her age-old body.

Age-old. Unending years that had wheeled and rolled while she waited, useless. Waited for the coming of her people, or when she might again seek in space. Useless years of fruitless attempts to learn that one, lost secret of speed bettering light's swift flight. Lost—lost with the ten trained Sarn that died those four thousand years gone in the blasting of this city once called New York. Too much else she'd had to do then to learn that secret.

Time she had now; four thousand wheeling years. But now she could not learn; it eluded her dulled mind, and the weakened minds of the decadent race.

As Aesir eluded her, and squatted miserable in the midst of misery his works had brought.

She stirred. The cold worked through. Hot food, hot drinks—they warmed a moment, then added dead, cold mass to the chill within her. A deadness that, she knew now, had been within her before this glooming chill had made her more aware. Her Sarn were weak; the soft product of an easy world, too sanely organized to require of them sharp, sharpening competition in endeavor.

And she was old. Immortality she had, and everlasting youth of tissue. But the mind grew old and dull, the courses of its thoughts narrowed and chilled with years and millenniums that passed. She was never to recall that exact age—but what matter? A stupid thing. What mattered that she thought of it or not; the years had passed, they'd graved their mark and narrowing on her. And on her race.

They had weakened. Humankind had strengthened, grown with the years that sapped the Sarn. Now, in her gardens, that hunched figure of dejection squatted, chilling all her city, defying the minds of all the Sarn. It had been a matter of time, inevitable as the fated motion of the planets. And the time had come. The humans were the stronger.

The door behind her opened slowly, but her brooding eyes remained fixed on the far wall till the intruder moved before her gaze. Barken Thil. Once, the Mother had thought her brilliant, hoped this physicist might find the forgotten secret of the speed drive. Now her eight-foot figure was shrunken, dimmed by the fog and gloom that curdled the air about them. "Yes?" The Mother spoke wearily.

"Nothing." The physicist shook her head. "It's useless, Mother of the Sarn. The blackness is there. No screen, no substance shuts it off. It registers no more than the cold we feel on our instruments; they tell us only what we know, that the air transmits less light, less heat. It is absorbed somehow, and yet does not warm thereby. A vacuum transmits energy as before—but we cannot live in vacua.

"Thard Nilo has gone mad. She sits on her stool and stares

at the wall, saying: 'The sun is warm . . . the sun is bright. The sun is warm . . . the sun is bright!' She will not move save when we lead her. She does not resist—but she does not act."

"The sun—is warm," the Mother said softly. "The sun—is bright. The sun—never shines here now. But the sun is bright and hot and the air is clean and dry in Bish-Waln."

The tired eyes looked up slowly toward the lax figure of the physicist. "I . . . I think I will visit. Bish-Waln. Where the sun is hot and bright and the air—

"I have never been there; never in all the time Earth became ours, four thousand years ago, have I left Sarn City. I have never seen Targlan of the ever-blue skies and the everwhite mountains. I have never seen Bish-Waln in the golden sands . . . the hot sands.

"I think that now, before humanity rises finally, I should like to see it. I think . . . yes, perhaps I will go."

Two hours later, she roused herself to give orders, vaguely, and hours later to enter her ship. The chill leaked out of metal and crystal as from the cold, green stone. She stared blankly through the rain-washed windows as the gloom-crowned gardens and the Sarn City dropped behind. One more ship rose slowly, listlessly behind her. Vaguely, she wondered that so few Sarn had been still there that these two ships could carry all.

For the first time in four thousand years she was leaving her city. For the first time in four thousand years no Sarn remained in Sarn City.

The clouds and gloom were suddenly below, a dull grayness that heaved and writhed like a living dome over Sarn City. June sunlight angled from the setting redness in the west across the human city stirring vaguely there below. A warmth she had not known in six unending days shot through her ancient body, and a blissfulness of sleep lapped her as the ship accelerated strongly, confidently, toward the sparkling waters beyond, toward Bish-Waln, bright and hot in the golden Sahara.

Her eyes closed, and she did not see through the dissolving clouds to the black figure that slowly rose erect, nor to the ordered division of the legion of peace that marched toward the blank, silent windows of the Sarn Palace. Behind them came a loose group of work-clad men to disperse among the dead, lightless shops of this, the city that had marked the landing of the Sarn.

# THE DAY IS DONE

*Astounding Science Fiction*, May

## by Lester del Rey (1915–     )

*Lester del Rey is important in the history of science fiction as an editor, critic, and writer. Best known for his stories "Helen O'Loy" (1938) and "Nerves" (1942), his 1962 novel THE ELEVENTH COMMANDMENT is one of the most interesting treatments of organized religion in sf.*

*"The Day Is Done" is a superb example of "prehistoric" science fiction, a category that is extremely difficult to write convincingly. That del Rey succeeds is obvious—what is not so obvious are the important things this story has to say about social relationships and the nature of evolutionary change in a revolutionary world.*

*(Lester is very fond of reminding me—at least once a month—that this story made me cry when I read it in the subway on the way to my classes at Columbia. Naturally, I always explain that I wept in agony over the excruciatingly bad writing, but it isn't true. Of all of Lester's stories this one is my favorite. IA)*

Hwoogh scratched the hair on his stomach and watched the sun climb up over the hill. He beat listlessly on his chest and yelled at it timidly, then grumbled and stopped. In his youth, he had roared and stumped around to help the god up, but now it wasn't worth the effort. Nothing was. He found a fine flake of sweaty salt under his hair, licked it off his fingers, and turned over to sleep again.

But sleep wouldn't come. On the other side of the hill there was a hue and cry, and somebody was beating a drum in a throbbing chant. The old Neanderthaler grunted and held his hands over his ears, but the Sun-Warmer's chant couldn't be silence. More ideas of the Talkers.

In his day, it had been a lovely world, full of hairy grumbling people; people a man could understand. There had been game on all sides, and the caves about had been filled with the smoke of cooking fires. He had played with the few young that were born—though each year fewer children had come into the tribe—and had grown to young manhood with the pride of achievement. But that was before the Talkers had made this valley one of their hunting grounds.

Old traditions, half told, half understood, spoke of the land in the days of old, when only his people roamed over the broad tundra. They had filled the caves and gone out in packs too large for any animal to withstand. And the animals swarmed into the land, driven south by the Fourth Glaciation. Then the great cold had come again, and times had been hard. Many of his people had died.

But many had lived, and with the coming of the warmer, drier climate again, they had begun to expand before the Talkers arrived. After that—Hwoogh stirred uneasily—for no good reason he could see, the Talkers took more and more of the land, and his people retreated and diminished before them. Hwoogh's father had made it understood that their little band in the valley were all that were left, and that this was the only place on the great flat earth where Talkers seldom came.

Hwoogh had been twenty when he first saw them, great long-legged men, swift of foot and eye, stalking along as if they owned the earth, with their incessant mouth noises. In the summer that year, they pitched their skin-and-wattle tents at the back of the hill, away from the caves, and made magic to their gods. There was magic on their weapons, and the beasts fell their prey. Hwoogh's people had settled back, watching fearfully, hating numbly, finally resorting to begging and stealing. Once a young buck had killed the child of a Talker, and been flayed and sent out to die for it. Thereafter, there had been a truce between Cro-Magnon and Neanderthaler.

Now the last of Hwoogh's people were gone, save only

himself, leaving no children. Seven years it had been since Hwoogh's brother had curled up in the cave and sent his breath forth on the long journey to his ancestors. He had always been dispirited and weak of will, but he had been the only friend left to Hwoogh.

. The old man tossed about and wished that Keyoda would return. Maybe she would bring food from the Talkers. There was no use hunting now, when the Talkers had already been up and killed all the easy game. Better that a man should sleep all the time, for sleep was the only satisfying thing left in the topsy-turvy world; even the drink the tall Cro-Magnons made from mashed roots left a headache the next day.

He twisted and turned in his bed of leaves at the edge of the cave, grunting surlily. A fly buzzed over his head provocatively, and he lunged at it. Surprise lighted his features as his fingers closed on the insect, and he swallowed it with a momentary flash of pleasure. It wasn't as good as the grub in the forest, but it made a tasty appetizer.

The sleep god had left, and no amount of lying still and snoring would lure him back. Hwoogh gave up and squatted down on his haunches. He had been meaning to make a new head for his crude spear for weeks, and he rummaged around in the cave for materials. But the idea grew farther away the closer he approached work, and he let his eyes roam idly over the little creek below him and the fleecy clouds in the sky. It was a warm spring, and the sun made idleness pleasant.

The sun god was growing stronger again, chasing the old fog and mist away. For years, he had worshiped the sun god as his, and now it seemed to grow strong again only for the Talkers. While the god was weak, Hwoogh's people had been mighty; now that its long sickness was over, the Cro-Magnons spread out over the country like the fleas on his belly.

Hwoogh could not understand it. Perhaps the god was mad at him, since gods are utterly unpredictable. He grunted, wishing again for his brother, who had understood such things better.

Keyoda crept around the boulder in front of the cave, interrupting his brooding. She brought scraps of food from the tent village and the half-chewed leg of a horse, which Hwoogh seized on and ripped at with his strong teeth. Evidently the Talkers had made a big kill the day before, for they were lavish with their gifts. He grunted at Keyoda, who sat under the cave entrance in the sun, rubbing her back.

Keyoda was as hideous as most of the Talkers were to Hwoogh, with her long dangling legs and short arms, and the ungainly straightness of her carriage. Hwoogh remembered the young girls of his own day with a sigh; they had been beautiful, short and squat, with forward-jutting necks and nice low foreheads. How the flat-faced Cro-Magnon women could get mates had been a puzzle to Hwoogh, but they seemed to succeed.

Keyoda had failed, however, and in her he felt justified in his judgment. There were times when he felt almost in sympathy with her, and in his own way he was fond of her. As a child, she had been injured, her back made useless for the work of a mate. Kicked around by the others of her tribe, she had gradually drifted away from them, and when she stumbled on Hwoogh, his hospitality had been welcome to her. The Talkers were nomads who followed the herds north in the summer, south in the winter, coming and going with the seasons, but Keyoda stayed with Hwoogh in his cave and did the few desultory tasks that were necessary. Even such a half-man as the Neanderthaler was preferable to the scornful pity of her own people, and Hwoogh was not unkind.

"Hwunkh?" asked Hwoogh. With his stomach partly filled, he felt more kindly toward the world.

"Oh, they come out and let me pick up their scraps—me, who was once a chief's daughter!—same as they always do." Her voice had been shrewish, but the weariness of failure and age had taken the edge from it. " 'Poor, poor Keyoda' thinks they, 'let her have what she wants, just so it don't mean nothin' we like.' Here." She handed him a roughly made spear, flaked on both sides of the point, but with only a rudimentary barb, unevenly made. "One of 'em give me this—it ain't the like of what they'd use, I guess, but it's good as you could make. One of the kids is practicing."

Hwoogh examined it; good, he admitted, very good, and the point was fixed nicely in the shaft. Even the boys, with their long limber thumbs that could twist any which way, made better weapons than he; yet once he had been famous among his small tribe for the nicety of his flint work.

Making a horse gesture, he got slowly to his feet. The shape of his jaw and the attachment of his tongue, together with a poorly developed left frontal lobe of his brain, made speech rudimentary, and he supplemented his glottals and labials with motions that Keyoda understood well enough. She shrugged and waved him out, gnawing on one of the bones.

Hwoogh wandered about without much spirit, conscious that he was growing old. And vaguely, he knew that age should not have fallen upon him for many snows; it was not the number of seasons, but something else, something that he could feel but not understand. He struck out for the hunting fields, hoping that he might find some game for himself that would require little effort to kill. The scornful gifts of the Talkers had become bitter in his mouth.

But the sun god climbed up to the top of the blue cave without Hwoogh's stumbling on anything. He swung about to return, and ran into a party of Cro-Magnons returning with the carcass of a reindeer strapped to a pole on their shoulders. They stopped to yell at him.

"No use, Hairy One!" they boasted, their voices light and gay. "We caught all the game this way. Turn back to your cave and sleep."

Hwoogh dropped his shoulders and veered away, his spear dragging limply on the ground. One of the party trotted over to him lightly. Sometimes Legoda, the tribal magic man and artist, seemed almost friendly, and this was one of the times.

"It was my kill, Hairy One," he said tolerantly. "Last night I drew strong reindeer magic, and the beast fell with my first throw. Come to my tent and I'll save a leg for you. Keyoda taught me a new song that she got from her father, and I would repay her."

Legs, ribs, bones! Hwoogh was tired of the outer meat. His body demanded the finer food of the entrails and liver. Already his skin was itching with a rash, and he felt that he must have the succulent inner parts to make him well; always, before, that had cured him. He grunted, between appreciation and annoyance, and turned off. Legoda pulled him back.

"Nay, stay, Hairy One. Sometimes you bring good fortune to me, as when I found the bright ocher for my drawing. There is meat enough in the camp for all. Why hunt today?" As Hwoogh still hesitated, he grew more insistent, not from kindness, but more from a wish to have his own way. "The wolves are running near today, and one is not enough against them. We carve the reindeer at the camp as soon as it comes from the poles. I'll give you first choice of the meat!"

Hwoogh grunted a surly acquiescence and waddled after the party. The dole of the Talkers has become gall to him, but liver was liver—if Legoda kept his bargain. They were chanting a rough marching song, trotting easily under the load of the reindeer, and he lumbered along behind, breathing hard at the pace they set.

As they neared the village of the nomads, its rough skin tents and burning fires threw out a pungent odor that irritated Hwoogh's nostrils. The smell of the long-limbed Cro-Magnons was bad enough without the dirty smell of a camp and the stink of their dung-fed fires. He preferred the accustomed moldy stench of his own musty cave.

Youths came swarming out at them, yelling with disgust at being left behind on this easy hunt. Catching sight of the Neanderthaler, they set up a howl of glee and charged at him, throwing sticks and rocks and jumping at him with play fury. Hwoogh shivered and crouched over, menacing them with his spear, and giving voice to throaty growls. Legoda laughed.

"In truth, O Hairy Chokanga, your voice should drive them from you. But see, they fear it not. Kuck, you two-legged pests! Out and away! Kuck, I say!" They leaped back at his voice and dropped behind, still yelling. Hwoogh eyed them warily, but so long as it suited the pleasure of Legoda, he was safe from their pranks.

Legoda was in a good mood, laughing and joking, tossing his quips at the women until his young wife came out and silenced it. She sprang at the reindeer with her flint knife, and the other women joined her.

"Heyo," called Legoda. "First choice goes to Chokanga, the Hairy One. By my word, it is his."

"Oh, fool!" There was scorn in her voice and in the look she gave Hwoogh. "Since when do we feed the beasts of the caves and the fish of the river? Art mad, Legoda. Let him hunt for himself."

Legoda tweaked her back with the point of his spear, grinning. "Aye, I knew thou'dst cry at that. But then, we owe his kind some pay—this was his hunting ground when we were but pups, straggling into this far land. What harm to give to an old man?" He swung to Hwoogh and gestured. "See, Chokanga, my word is good. Take what you want, but see that it is not more than your belly and that of Keyoda can hold this night."

Hwoogh darted in and came out with the liver and the fine sweet fat from the entrails. With a shrill cry of rage, Legoda's mate sprang for him, but the magic man pushed her back.

"Nay, he did right! Only a fool would choose the haunch when the heart of the meat was at hand. By the gods of my father, and I expected to eat of that myself! O Hairy One, you steal the meat from my mouth, and I like you for it. Go, before Heya gets free."

Tomorrow, Hwoogh knew, Legoda might set the brats on him for this day's act, but tomorrow was in another cave of the sun. He drew his legs under him and scuttled off to the left and around the hill, while the shrill yells of Heya and the lazy good humor of Legoda followed. A piece of liver dangled loose, and Hwoogh sucked on it as he went. Keyoda would be pleased, since she usually had to do the begging for both of them.

And a little of Hwoogh's self-respect returned. Hadn't he outsmarted Legoda and escaped with the choicest meat? And had Keyoda ever done as well when she went to the village of the Talkers? Ayeee, they had a thing yet to learn from the cunning brain of old Hwoogh!

Of course the Talkers were crazy; only fools would act as Legoda had done. But that was none of his business. He patted the liver and fat fondly and grinned with a slight return of good humor. Hwoogh was not one to look a gift horse in the mouth.

The fire had shrunk to a red bed of coals when he reached the cave, and Keyoda was curled up on his bed, snoring loudly, her face flushed. Hwoogh smelled her breath, and his suspicions were confirmed. Somehow, she had drunk of the devil brew of the Talkers, and her sleep was dulled with its stupor. He prodded her with his toe, and she sat up bleary-eyed.

"Oh, so you're back. Ayeee, and with liver and fat! But that never came from your spear throw; you been to the village and stole it. Oh, but you'll catch it!" She grabbed at the meat greedily and stirred up the fire, spitting the liver over it.

Hwoogh explained as best he could, and she got the drift of it. "So? Eh, that Legoda, what a prankster he is, and my own nephew, too." She tore the liver away, half raw, and they fell to eagerly, while she chuckled and cursed by turns. Hwoogh touched her nose and wrinkled his face up.

"Well, so what if I did?" Liquor had sharpened her tongue. "That no-good son of the chief come here, after me to be telling him stories. And to make my old tongue free, he brings me the root brew. Ah, what stories I'm telling—and some of 'em true, too!" She gestured toward a crude pot. "I reckon he steals it, but what's that to us? Help yourself, Hairy One. It ain't ever' day we're getting the brew."

Hwoogh remembered the headaches of former experiments, but he smelled it curiously and the lure of the magic water caught at him. It was the very essence of youth, the fire that brought life to his legs and memories to his mind. He held it up to his mouth, gasping as the beery liquid ran down his throat. Keyoda caught it before he could finish and drained the last quart.

"Ah, it strengthens my back and puts the blood a-running hot through me again." She swayed on her feet and sputtered out the fragments of an old skin-scraping song. "Now, there you go—can't you never learn not to drink it all to once? That way, it don't last as long, and you're out before you get to feeling good."

Hwoogh staggered as the brew took hold of him, and his knees bent even farther under him. The bed came up in his face, his head was full of bees buzzing merrily, and the cave spun around him. He roared at the cave, while Keyoda laughed.

"Heh! To hear you a-yelling, a body might think you was the only Chokanga left on earth. But you ain't—no, you ain't!"

"Hwunkh?" That struck home. To the best of Hwoogh's knowledge, there were no others of his kind left on earth. He grabbed at her and missed, but she fell and rolled against him, her breath against his face.

"So? Well, it's the truth. The kid up and told me. Legoda found three of 'em, just like you, he says, up the land to the east, three springs ago. You'll have to ask him—I dunno nothing about it." She rolled over against him, grunting half-formed words, and he tried to think of this new information. But the brew was too strong for his head, and he was soon snoring beside her.

Keyoda was gone to the village when he awoke, and the sun was a spear length high on the horizon. He rummaged around for a piece of the liver, but the flavor was not as good as it had been, and his stomach protested lustily at going to work again. He leaned back until his head got control of itself, then swung down to the creek to quench a thirst devil that had seized on him in the night.

But there was something he should do, something he half remembered from last night. Hadn't Keyoda said something about others of his people? Yes, three of them, and Legoda knew. Hwoogh hesitated, remembering that he had bested Legoda the day before; the young man might resent it today.

But he was filled with an overwhelming curiosity, and there was a strange yearning in his heart. Legoda must tell him.

Reluctantly, he went back to the cave and fished around in a hole that was a secret even from Keyoda. He drew out his treasures, fingering them reverently, and selecting the best. There were bright shells and colored pebbles, a roughly drilled necklace that had belonged to his father, a sign of completed manhood, bits of this and that with which he had intended to make himself ornaments. But the quest for knowledge was stronger than the pride of possession; he dumped them out into his fist and struck out for the village.

Keyoda was talking with the women, whining the stock formula that she had developed, and Hwoogh skirted around the camp, looking for the young artist. Finally he spotted the Talker out behind the camp, making odd motions with two sticks. He drew near cautiously, and Legoda heard him coming.

"Come near, Chokanga, and see my new magic." The young man's voice was filled with pride, and there was no threat to it. Hwoogh sighed with relief, but sidled up slowly. "Come nearer, don't fear me. Do you think I'm sorry of the gift I made? Nay, that was my own stupidity. See."

He held out the sticks and Hwoogh fingered them carefully. One was long and springy, tied end to end with a leather thong, and the other was a little spear with a tuft of feather on the blunt end. He grunted a question.

"A magic spear, Hairy One, that flies from the hand with wings, and kills beyond the reach of other spears."

Hwoogh snorted. The spear was too tiny to kill more than rodents, and the big stick had not even a point. But he watched as the young man placed the sharp stick to the tied one, and drew back on it. There was a sharp twang, and the little spear sailed out and away, burying its point in the soft bark of a tree more than two spear throws away. Hwoogh was impressed.

"Aye, Chokanga, a new magic that I learned in the south last year. There are many there who use it, and with it they can throw the point farther and better than a full-sized spear. One man may kill as much as three!"

Hwoogh grumbled: already they killed all the good game, and yet they must find new magic to increase their power. He held out his hand curiously, and Legoda gave him the long stick and another spear, showing him how it was held. Again there was a twang, and the leather thong struck at his wrist, but the weapon sailed off erratically, missing the tree by yards. Hwoogh handed it back glumly—such magic was not for his kind. His thumbs made the handling of it even more difficult.

Now, while the magic man was pleased with his superiority, was a good time to show the treasure. Hwoogh spread it out on the bare earth and gestured at Legoda, who looked down thoughtfully.

"Yes," the Talker conceded. "Some of it is good, and some would make nice trinkets for the women. What is it you want—more meat, or one of the new weapons? Your belly was filled yesterday; and with my beer, which was stolen, I think, though for that I blame you not. The boy has been punished already. And this weapon is not for you."

Hwoogh snorted, wriggled and fought for expression, while the young man stared. Little by little, his wants were made known, partly by the questions of the Cro-Magnon. Legoda laughed.

"So, there is a call of the kind in you, Old Man?" He pushed the treasure back to Hwoogh, except one gleaming bauble. "I would not cheat you, Chokanga, but this I take for the love I bear you, as a sign of our friendship." His grin was mocking as he stuck the valuable in a flap of his clout.

Hwoogh squatted down on his heels, and Legoda sat on a rock as he began. "There is but little to tell you, Hairy One. Three years ago I did run onto a family of your kind—a male and his mate, with one child. They ran from us, but we were near their cave, and they had to return. We harmed them not, and sometimes gave them food, letting them accompany us on the chase. But they were thin and scrawny, too lazy to hunt. When we returned next year, they were dead, and so far as I know, you are the last of your kind."

He scratched his head thoughtfully. "Your people die too easily, Chokanga; no sooner do we find them and try to help them than they cease hunting and become beggars. And then they lose interest in life, sicken and die. I think your gods must be killed off by our stronger ones."

Hwoogh grunted a half assent, and Legoda gathered up his bow and arrows, turning back toward camp. But there was a strange look on the Neanderthaler's face that did not escape the young man's eyes. Recognizing the misery in Hwoogh's expression, he laid a hand on the old man's shoulder and spoke more kindly.

"That is why I would see to your well-being, Hairy One. When you are gone, there will be no more, and my children will laugh at me and say I lie when I spin the tale of your race at the feast fire. Each time that I kill, you shall not lack for food."

He swung down the single street toward the tent of his family, and Hwoogh turned slowly back toward his cave. The assurance of food should have cheered him, but it only added to his gloom. Dully, he realized that Legoda treated him as a small child, or as one whom the sun god had touched with madness.

Hwoogh heard the cries and laughter of children as he rounded the hill, and for a minute he hesitated before going on. But the sense of property was well developed in him, and he leaped forward grimly. They had no business near his cave.

They were of all ages and sizes, shouting and chasing each other about in a crazy disorder. Having been forbidden to come on Hwoogh's side of the hill, and having broken the rule in a bunch, they were making the most of their revolt. Hwoogh's fire was scattered down the side of the hill into the creek, and they were busily sorting through the small store of his skins and weapons.

Hwoogh let out a savage yell and ran forward, his spear held out in jabbing position. Hearing him, they turned and jumped back from the cave entrance, clustering up into a tight group. "Go on away, Ugly Face," one yelled. "Go scare the wolves! Ugly Face. Ugly Face, waaaah!"

He dashed in among them, brandishing his spear, but they darted back on their nimble legs, slipping easily from in front of him. One of the older boys thrust out a leg and caught him, tripping him down on the rocky ground. Another dashed in madly and caught his spear away, hitting him roughly with it. From the time of the first primate, the innate cruelty of thoughtlessness had changed little in children.

Hwoogh let out a whooping bellow, scrambled up clumsily and was in among them. But they slipped nimbly out of his clutching hands. The little girls were dancing around gleefully, chanting, "Ugly Face ain't got no mother, Ugly Face ain't got no wife, waaaah on Ugly Face!" Frantically he caught at one of the boys, swung him about savagely, and tossed him on the ground, where the youth lay white and silent. Hwoogh felt a momentary glow of elation at his strength. Then somebody threw a rock.

The old Neanderthaler was tied down crudely when he swam back to consciousness, and three of the boys sat on his chest, beating the ground with their heels in time to a victory chant. There was a dull ache in his head, and bruises were swelling on his arms and chest where they had handled him roughly. He growled savagely, heaving up, and tumbled them off, but the cords were too strong for him. As surely as if grown men had done it, he was captured.

For years they had been his enemies, ever since they had found that Hwoogh-baiting was one of the pleasant occupations that might relieve the tedium of camp life. Now that the old feud was about finished, they went at the business of subduing him with method and ingenuity.

While the girls rubbed his face with soft mud from the creek, the boys ransacked the cave and tore at his clothes. The rough bag in which he had put his valuables came away in their hands, and they paused to distribute this new wealth. Hwoogh howled madly.

But a measure of sanity was returning to them, now that the first fury of the flight was over, and Kechaka, the chief's eldest son, stared at Hwoogh doubtfully. "If the elders hear of this," he muttered unhappily, "there will be trouble. They'd not like our bothering Ugly Face."

Another grinned. "Why tell them? He isn't a man, anyway, but an animal; see the hair on his body! Toss old Ugly Face in the river, clean up his cave, and hide these treasures. Who's to know?"

There were half-hearted protests, but the thought of the beating waiting for them added weight to the idea. Kechaka nodded finally and set them to straightening up the mess they had made. With broken branches, they eliminated the marks of their feet, leaving only the trail to the creek.

Hwoogh tossed and pitched in their arms as four of them picked him up; the bindings loosened somewhat, but not enough to free him. With some satisfaction, he noted that the boy he had caught was still retching and moaning, but that was no help to his present position. They waded relentlessly into the water, laid him on it belly down, and gave him a strong push that sent him gliding out through the rushing stream. Foaming and gasping, he fought the current, struggling against his bonds. His lungs ached for air, and the current buffeted him about; blackness was creeping up on his mind.

With a last desperate effort he tore loose the bonds and pushed up madly for the surface, gulping in air greedily. Water was unpleasant to him, but he could swim, and he struck out for the bank. The children were disappearing down the trail and were out of sight as he climbed from the water, bemoaning his lost fire that would have warmed him. He lumbered back to his cave and sank soddenly on the bed.

He, who had been a mighty warrior, bested by a snarling pack of Cro-Magnon brats! He clenched his fists savagely and growled, but there was nothing he could do. Nothing! The futility of his own effort struck down on him like a burning knife. Hwoogh was an old man, and the tears that ran from his eyes were the bitter, aching tears that only age can shed.

Keyoda returned late, cursing when she found the fire gone, but her voice softened as she spied him huddled in his bed, staring dully at the wall of the cave. Her old eyes spotted the few footprints the boys had missed, and she swore with a vigor that was almost youthful before she turned back to Hwoogh.

"Come, Hairy One, get out of that cold, wet fur!" Her hands were gentle on the straps, but Hwoogh shook her aside. "You'll be sick, lying there on them few leaves, all wet like that. Get off the fur, and I'll go back to the village for fire. Them kids! Wait'll I tell Legoda!"

Seeing there was nothing he would let her do for him, she turned away down the trail. Hwoogh sat up to change his furs, then lay back. What was the use? He grumbled a little when Keyoda returned with fire, but refused the delicacies she had wheedled at the village, and tumbled over into a fitful sleep.

The sun was long up when he awoke to find Legoda and Keyoda fussing over him. There was an unhappy feeling in his head, and he coughed. Legoda patted his back. "Rest, Hairy One. You have the sickness devil that burns the throat and runs at the nose, but that a man can overcome. Ayeee, how the boys were whipped! I, personally, attended to that, and this morning not one is less sore than you. Before they bother you again, the moon will eat up the sun."

Keyoda pushed a stew of boiled liver and kidneys at him, but he shoved it away. Though the ache in his head had gone down, a dull weight seemed to rest on his stomach, and he could not eat. It felt as though all the boys he had fought were sitting on his chest and choking him.

Legoda drew out a small painted drum and made heavy magic for his recovery, dancing before the old man and shaking the magic gourd that drove out all sickness devils. But this was a stronger devil. Finally the young man stopped and left for the village, while Keyoda perched on a stone to watch over the sick man. Hwoogh's mind was heavy and numb, and his heart was leaden in his breast. She fanned the flies away, covering his eyes with a bit of skin, singing him some song that the mothers lulled their children with.

He slept again, stirring about in a nightmare of Talker mockery, with a fever flushing his face. But when Legoda came back at night, the magic man swore he should be well in three days. "Let him sleep and feed him. The devil will leave him soon. See, there is scarce a mark where the stone hit."

Keyoda fed him, as best she could, forcing the food that she begged at the village down his throat. She lugged water from the creek as often as he cried for it, and bathed his head and chest when he slept. But the three days came and went, and still he was not well. The fever was little higher, and the cold little worse, than he had gone though many times before. But he did not throw it off as he should have done.

Legoda came again, bringing his magic and food, but they were of little help. As the day drew to a close, he shook his head and spoke low words to Keyoda. Hwoogh came out of a half stupor and listened dully.

"He tires of life, Keyoda, my father's sister." The young man shrugged. "See, he lies there not fighting. When a man will not try to live, he cannot."

"Ayyeah!" Her voice shrilled dolefully. "What man will not live if he can? Thou art foolish, Legoda."

"Nay. His people tire easily of life, O Keyoda. Why, I know not. But it takes little to make them die." Seeing that Hwoogh had heard, he drew closer to the Neanderthaler. "O Chokanga, put away your troubles and take another bite out of life. It can still be good, if you choose. I have taken your gift as a sign of friendship, and I would keep my word. Come to my fire, and hunt no more; I will tend you as I would my father."

Hwoogh grunted. Follow the camps, eat from Legoda's hunting, be paraded as a freak and a half-man! Legoda was kind, sudden and warm in his sympathy, but the others were scornful. And if Hwoogh should die, who was to mourn him? Keyoda would go back to her people, Legoda would forget him, and not one Chokanga would be there to show them the ritual for burial.

Hwoogh's old friends had come back to him in his dreams, visiting him and showing the hunting grounds of his youth. He had heard the grunts and grumblings of the girls of his race, and they were awaiting him. That world was still empty of the Talkers, where a man could do great things and make his own kills, without hearing the laughter of the Cro-Magnons. Hwoogh sighed softly. He was tired, too tired to care what happened.

The sun sank low, and the clouds were painted a harsh red. Keyoda was wailing somewhere, far off, and Legoda beat on his drum and muttered his magic. But life was empty, barren of pride.

The sun dropped from sight, and Hwoogh sighed again, sending his last breath out to join the ghosts of his people.

# THE ULTIMATE CATALYST

*Thrilling Wonder Stories*, June

## by John Taine (1902–1960)

*One of a number of professional scientists in this book, "John Taine" (Eric Temple Bell) was a famous mathematician at the California Institute of Technology and a former President of the Mathematics Association of America. However, most of his sf did not reflect his professional training (an exception is his novel THE TIME STREAM, 1946), and he employed a wide variety of themes in his fiction. Two of his most memorable works are THE IRON STAR (1930) and THE CRYSTAL HORDE (1952, magazine appearance, 1930).*

*"The Ultimate Catalyst" is about a subject that Taine knew well—the problems of the working scientist. It is unlikely, however, that any of his colleagues at Cal Tech (especially the chemists) ever faced a problem quite like this one.*

*(Whatever mark "John Taine" may make in the history of science fiction, and I am not as fond of his stories as some people are, there is no question but that his major work is "Men of Mathematics," a classic series of short biographies of great mathematicians. It is unlikely even to be surpassed in its field and if you want true pathos read his biography of Evariste Galois. IA)*

The Dictator shoved his plate aside with a petulant gesture. The plate, like the rest of the official banquet service, was solid gold with the Dictator's monogram, K. I.—Kadir Imperator, or Emperor Kadir—embosed in a design of machine guns round the edge. And, like every other plate on the long banquet table, Kadir's was piled high with a colorful assortment of raw fruits.

This was the dessert. The guests had just finished the main course, a huge plateful apiece of steamed vegetables. For an appetizer they had tried to enjoy an iced tumblerful of mixed fruit juices.

There had been nothing else at the feast but fruit juice, steamed vegetables, and raw fruit. Such a meal might have sustained a scholarly vegetarian, but for soldiers of a domineering race it was about as satisfying as a bucketful of cold water.

"Vegetables and fruit," Kadir complained. "Always vegetables and fruit. Why can't we get some red beef with blood in it for a change? I'm sick of vegetables. And I hate fruit. Blood and iron—that's what we need."

The guests stopped eating and eyed the Dictator apprehensively. They recognized the first symptoms of an imperial rage. Always when Kadir was about to explode and lose control of his evil temper, he had a preliminary attack of the blues, usually over some trifle.

They sat silently waiting for the storm to break, not daring to eat while their Leader abstained.

Presently a middle-aged man, halfway down the table on Kadir's right, calmly selected a banana, skinned it, and took a bite. Kadir watched the daring man in amazed silence. The last of the banana was about to disappear when the Dictator found his voice.

"Americano!" he bellowed like an outraged bull. "Mister Beetle!"

"*Doctor* Beetle, if you don't mind, Senhor Kadir," the offender corrected. "So long as every other white man in Amazonia insists on being addressed by his title, I insist on being addressed by mine. It's genuine, too. Don't forget that."

"Beetle!" The Dictator began roaring again.

But Beetle quietly cut him short. " 'Doctor' Beetle, please. I insist."

Purple in the face, Kadir subsided. He had forgotten what he intended to say. Beetle chose a juicy papaya for himself and a huge, greenish plum for his daughter, who sat on his left. Ignoring Kadir's impotent rage, Beetle addressed him as if there had been no unpleasantness. Of all the company, Beetle was the one man with nerve enough to face the Dictator as an equal.

"You say we need blood and iron," he began. "Do you mean that literally?" the scientist said slowly.

"How else should I mean it?" Kadir blustered, glowering at Beetle. "I always say what I mean. I am no theorist. I am a man of action, not words!"

"All right, all right," Beetle soothed him. "But I thought perhaps your 'blood and iron' was like old Bismarck's—blood and sabres. Since you mean just ordinary blood, like the blood in a raw beefsteak, and iron not hammered into sabres, I think Amazonia can supply all we need or want."

"But beef, red beef—" Kadir expostulated.

"I'm coming to that in a moment." Beetle turned to his daughter. "Consuelo, how did you like that greenbeefo?"

"That *what?*" Consuelo asked in genuine astonishment.

Although as her father's laboratory assistant she had learned to expect only the unexpected from him, each new creation of his filled her with childlike wonderment and joy. Every new biological creation her father made demanded a new scientific name. But, instead of manufacturing new scientific names out of Latin and Greek, as many reputable biologists do, Beetle used English, with an occasional lapse into Portuguese, the commonest language of Amazonia. He had even tried to have his daughter baptized Buglette, as the correct technical term of the immature female offspring of a Beetle. But his wife, a Portuguese lady of irreproachable family, had objected, and the infant was named Consuelo.

"I asked how you liked the greenbeefo," Beetle repeated. "That seedless green plum you just ate."

"Oh, so that's what you call it." Consuelo considered carefully, like a good scientist, before passing judgment on the delicacy. "Frankly, I didn't like it a little bit. It smelt like underdone pork. There was a distinct flavor of raw blood. And it all had a rather slithery wet taste, if you get what I mean."

"I get you exactly," Beetle exclaimed. "An excellent description." He turned to Kadir. "There! You see we've already done it."

"Done what?" Kadir asked suspiciously.

"Try a greenbeefo and see."

Somewhat doubtfully, Kadir selected one of the huge greenish plums from the golden platter beside him, and slowly ate it. Etiquette demanded that the guests follow their Leader's example.

While they were eating the greenbeefos, Beetle watched their faces. The women of the party seemed to find the juicy flesh of the plums unpalatable. Yet they kept on eating and several, after finishing one, reached for another.

The men ate greedily. Kadir himself disposed of the four greenbeefos on his platter and hungrily looked about for more. His neighbors on either side, after a grudging look at their own diminishing supplies, offered him two of theirs. Without a word of thanks, Kadir devoured the offerings.

As Beetle sat calmly watching their greed, he had difficulty in keeping his face impassive and not betraying his disgust. Yet these people were starving for flesh. Possibly they were to be pardoned for looking more like hungry animals than representatives of the conquering race at their first taste in two years of something that smelt like flesh and blood.

All their lives, until the disaster which had quarantined them in Amazonia, these people had been voracious eaters of flesh in all its forms from poultry to pork. Now they could get nothing of the sort.

The dense forests and jungles of Amazonia harbored only a multitude of insects, poisonous reptiles, gaudy birds, spotted cats, and occasional colonies of small monkeys. The cats and the monkeys eluded capture on a large scale, and after a few half-hearted attempts at trapping, Kadir's hardy followers had abandoned the forests to the snakes and the stinging insects.

The chocolate-colored waters of the great river skirting Amazonia on the north swarmed with fish, but they were inedible. Even the natives could not stomach the pulpy flesh of these bloated mud-suckers. It tasted like the water of the river, a foul soup of decomposed vegetation and rotting wood. Nothing remained for Kadir and his heroic followers to eat but the tropical fruits and vegetables.

Luckily for the invaders, the original white settlers from the United States had cleared enough of the jungle and forest to make intensive agriculture possible. When Kadir arrived, all of these settlers, with the exception of Beetle and his daughter, had fled. Beetle remained, partly on his own initiative, partly because Kadir insisted that he stay and "carry on" against the snakes. The others traded Kadir their gold mines in exchange for their lives.

The luscious greenbeefos had disappeared. Beetle suppressed a smile as he noted the flushed and happy faces of the guests. He remembered the parting words of the last of the mining engineers.

"So long, Beetle. You're a brave man and may be able to handle Kadir. If you do, we'll be back. Use your head, and make a monkey of this dictating brute. Remember, we're counting on you."

Beetle had promised to keep his friends in mind. "Give me three years. If you don't see me again by then, shed a tear and forget me."

*"Senhorina Beetle!"* It was Kadir roaring again. The surfeit of greenbeefos restored his old bluster.

"Yes?" Consuelo replied politely.

"I know now why your cheeks are always so red," Kadir shouted.

For a moment neither Consuelo nor her father got the drift of Kadir's accusation. They understood just as Kadir started to enlighten them.

"You and your traitorous father are eating while we starve."

Beetle kept his head. His conscience was clear, so far as the greenbeefos were concerned, and he could say truthfully that they were not the secret of Consuelo's rosy cheeks and his own robust health. He quickly forestalled his daughter's reply.

"The meat-fruit, as you call it, is not responsible for Consuelo's complexion. Hard work as my assistant keeps her fit. As for the greenbeefos, this is the first time anyone but myself has tasted one. You saw how my daughter reacted. Only a great actress could have feigned such inexperienced distaste. My daughter is a biological chemist, not an actress."

Kadir was still suspicious. "Then why did you not share these meatfruits with us before?"

"For a very simple reason. I created them by hybridization only a year ago, and the first crop of my fifty experimental plants ripened this week. As I picked the ripe fruit, I put it aside for this banquet. I thought it would be a welcome treat after two years of vegetables and fruit. And," Beetle continued, warming to his invention, "I imagined a taste of beef—

even if it is only green beef, 'greenbeefo'—would be a very suitable way of celebrating the second anniversary of the New Freedom in Amazonia."

The scientist's sarcasm anent the "new freedom" was lost upon Kadir, nor did Kadir remark the secret bitterness in Beetle's eyes. What an inferior human being a dictator was, the scientist thought! What stupidity, what brutality! So long as a single one remained—and Kadir was the last—the Earth could not be clean.

"Have you any more?" Kadir demanded.

"Sorry. That's all for the present. But I'll have tons in a month or less. You see," he explained, "I'm using hydroponics to increase production and hasten ripening."

Kadir looked puzzled but interested. Confessing that he was merely a simple soldier, ignorant of science, he deigned to ask for particulars. Beetle was only too glad to oblige.

"It all began a year ago. You remember asking me when you took over the country to stay and go on with my work at the antivenin laboratory? Well, I did. But what was I to do with all the snake venom we collected? There was no way of getting it out of the country now that the rest of the continent has quarantined us. We can't send anything down the river, our only way out to civilization—"

"Yes, yes," Kadir interrupted impatiently. "You need not remind anyone here that the mountains and the jungles are the strongest allies of our enemies. What has all this to do with the meat-fruit?"

"Everything. Not being able to export any venom, I went on with my research in biochemistry. I saw how you people were starving for flesh, and I decided to help you out. You had slaughtered and eaten all the horses at the antivenin laboratory within a month of your arrival. There was nothing left, for this is not a cattle country, and it never will be. There was nothing to do but try chemistry. I already had the greenhouses left by the engineers. They used to grow tomatoes and cucumbers before you came."

"So you made these meat-fruits chemically?"

Beetle repressed a smile at the Dictator's scientific innocence.

"Not exactly. But really it was almost as simple. There was nothing startlingly new about my idea. To see how simple it was, ask yourself what are the main differences between the higher forms of plant life and the lower forms of animal life.

"Both are living things. But the plants cannot move about

from place to place at will, whereas, the animals can. A plant is, literally, 'rooted to the spot.'

"There are apparent exceptions, of course, like water hyacinths, yeast spores, and others that are transported by water or the atmosphere, but they do not transport themselves as the living animal does. Animals have a 'dimension' of freedom that plants do not have."

"But the beef—"

"In a moment. I mentioned the difference between the freedoms of plants and animals because I anticipate that it will be of the utmost importance in the experiments I am now doing. However, this freedom was not, as you have guessed, responsible for the greenbeefos. It was another, less profound, difference between plants and animals that suggested the 'meat-fruits.' "

Kadir seemed to suspect Beetle of hidden and unflattering meanings, with all this talk of freedom in a country dedicated to the "New Freedom" of Kadir's dictatorship. But he could do nothing about it, so he merely nodded as if he understood.

"Plants and animals," Beetle continued, "both have a 'blood' of a sort. The most important constituents in the 'blood' of both differ principally in the metals combined chemically in each.

"The 'blood' of a plant contains chlorophyll. The blood of an animal contains haemoglobin. Chemically, chlorophyll and haemoglobin are strangely alike. The metal in chlorophyll is magnesium; in haemoglobin, it is iron.

"Well, it occurred to chemists that if the magnesium could be 'replaced' chemically by iron, the chlorophyll could be converted into haemoglobin! And similarly for the other way about: replace the iron in haemoglobin by magnesium, and get chlorophyll!

"Of course it is not all as simple or as complete as I have made it sound. Between haemoglobin and chlorophyll is a long chain of intermediate compounds. Many of them have been formed in the laboratory, and they are definite links in the chain from plant blood to animal blood."

"I see," Kadir exclaimed, his face aglow with enthusiasm at the prospect of unlimited beef from green vegetables. He leaned over the table to question Beetle.

"It is the blood that gives flesh its appetizing taste and nourishing strength. You have succeeded in changing the plant blood to animal blood?"

Beetle did not contradict him. In fact, he evaded the question.

"I expect," he confided, "to have tons of greenbeefos in a month, and thereafter a constant supply as great as you will need. Tray-culture—hydroponics—will enable us to grow hundreds of tons in a space no larger than this banquet hall."

The "banquet hall" was only a ramshackle dining room that had been used by the miners before Kadir arrived. Nevertheless, it could be called anything that suited the Dictator's ambition.

"Fortunately," Beetle continued, "the necessary chemicals for tray-culture are abundant in Amazonia. My native staff has been extracting them on a large scale for the past four months, and we will have ample for our needs."

"Why don't you grow the greenbeefos in the open ground?" one of Kadir's officers inquired a trifle suspiciously.

"Too inefficient. By feeding the plants only the chemicals they need directly, we can increase production several hundrodfold and cut down the time between successive crops to a few weeks. By properly spacing the propagation of the plants, we can have a constant supply. The seasons cut no figure."

They seemed satisfied, and discussion of the glorious future in store for Amazonia became general and animated. Presently Beetle and Consuelo asked the Dictator's permission to retire. They had work to do at the laboratory.

"Hydroponics?" Kadir enquired jovially. Beetle nodded, and they bowed themselves out of the banquet hall.

Consuelo withheld her attack until they were safe from possible eavesdroppers.

"Kadir is a lout," she began, "but that is no excuse for your filling him up with a lot of impossible rubbish."

"But it *isn't* impossible, and it *isn't* rubbish," Beetle protested. "You know as well as I do——"

"Of course I know about the work on chlorophyll and haemoglobin. But you didn't make those filthy green plums taste like raw pork by changing the chlorophyll of the plants into haemoglobin or anything like it. How did you do it, by the way?"

"Listen, Buglette. If I tell you, it will only make you sick. You ate one, you know."

"I would rather be sick than ignorant. Go on, you may as well tell me."

"Very well. It's a long story, but I'll cut it short. Amazonia is the last refuge of the last important dictator on earth. When Kadir's own people came to their senses a little over two years ago and kicked him out, he and his top men and their women came over here with their 'new freedom.' But the people of this continent didn't want Kadir's brand of freedom. Of course a few thousand crackpots in the larger cities welcomed him and his gang as their 'liberators,' but for once in history the mass of the people knew what they did not want. They combined forces and chased Kadir and his cronies up here.

"I never have been able to see why they did not exterminate Kadir and company as they would any other pests. But the presidents of the United Republics agreed that to do so would only be using dictatorial tactics, the very thing they had united to fight. So they let Kadir and his crew live— more or less—in strict quarantine. The temporary loss of a few rich gold mines was a small price to pay, they said, for world security against dictatorships.

"So here we are, prisoners in the last plague spot of civilization. And here is Kadir. He can dictate to his heart's content, but he can't start another war. He is as powerless as Napoleon was on his island.

"Well, when the last of our boys left, I promised to keep them in mind. And you heard my promise to help Kadir *out*. I am going to keep that promise, if it costs me my last snake."

They had reached the laboratory. Juan, the night-nurse for the reptiles, was going his rounds.

"Everything all right, Juan?" Beetle asked cordially.

He liked the phlegmatic Portuguese who always did his job with a minimum of talk. Consuelo, for her part, heartily disliked the man and distrusted him profoundly. She had long suspected him of being a stool-pigeon for Kadir.

"Yes, Dr. Beetle. Good night."

"Good night, Juan."

When Juan had departed, Consuelo returned to her attack.

"You haven't told me yet how you made these things taste like raw pork."

She strolled over to the tank by the north window where a luxuriant greenbeefo, like an overdeveloped tomato vine, grew rankly up its trellis to the ceiling. About half a dozen of the huge greenish "plums" still hung on the vine.

Consuelo plucked one and was thoughtfully sampling its quality.

"This one tastes all right," she said. "What did you do to the others?"

"Since you really want to know, I'll tell you. I took a hypodermic needle and shot them full of snake blood. My pet constrictor had enough juice in him to do the whole job without discomfort to himself or danger to his health."

Consuelo hurled her half-eaten fruit at her father's head, but missed. She stood wiping her lips with the back of her hand.

"So you can't change the chlorophyll in a growing plant into anything like haemoglobin? You almost had me believing you could."

"I never said I could. Nor can anybody else, so far as I know. But it made a good story to tell Kadir."

"But why?"

"If you care to analyze one of these greenbeefos in your spare time, you will find their magnesium content extraordinarily high. That is not accident, as you will discover if you analyze the chemicals in the tanks. I shall be satisfied if I can get Kadir and his friends to gorge themselves on greenbeefos when the new crop comes in. Now, did I sell Kadir the greenbeefo diet, or didn't I? You saw how they all fell for it. And they will keep on falling as long as the supply of snake blood holds out."

"There's certainly no scarcity of snakes in this charming country," Consuelo remarked. "I'm going to get the taste of one of them out of my mouth right now. Then you can tell me what you want me to do in this new culture of greenbeefos you've gone in for."

So father and daughter passed their days under the last dictatorship. Beetle announced that in another week the lush crop of greenbeefos would be ripe. Kadir proclaimed the following Thursday "Festal Thursday" as the feast day inaugurating "the reign of plenty" in Amazonia.

As a special favor, Beetle had requested Kadir to forbid any sightseeing or other interference with his work.

Kadir had readily agreed, and for three weeks Beetle had worked twenty hours a day, preparing the coming banquet with his own hands.

"You keep out of this," he had ordered Consuelo. "If there is any dirty work to be done, I'll do it myself. Your job is to keep the staff busy as usual, and see that nobody steals any of the fruit. I have given strict orders that nobody is to taste a greenbeefo till next Thursday, and Kadir has issued a proclamation to that effect. So if you catch anyone thieving, report to me at once."

The work of the native staff consisted in catching snakes. The workers could see but little sense in their job, as they knew that no venom was being exported. Moreover, the eccentric Doctor Beetle had urged them to bring in every reptile they found, harmless as well as poisonous, and he was constantly riding them to bestir themselves and collect more.

More extraordinary still, he insisted every morning that they carry away the preceding day's catch and dump it in the river. The discarded snakes, they noticed, seemed half dead. Even the naturally most vicious put up no fight when they were taken from the pens.

Between ten and eleven every morning Beetle absented himself from the laboratory, and forbade anyone to accompany him. When Consuelo asked him what he had in the small black satchel he carried with him on these mysterious trips, he replied briefly:

"A snake. I'm going to turn the poor brute loose."

And once, to prove his assertion, he opened the satchel and showed her the torpid snake.

"I must get some exercise, and I need to be alone," he explained, "or my nerves will snap. Please don't pester me."

She had not pestered him, although she doubted his explanation. Left alone for an hour, she methodically continued her daily inspection of the plants till her father returned, when she had her lunch and he resumed his private business.

On the Tuesday before Kadir's Festal Thursday, Consuelo did not see her father leave for his walk, as she was already busy with her inspection when he left. He had been gone about forty minutes when she discovered the first evidence of treachery.

The foliage of one vine had obviously been disturbed since the last inspection. Seeking the cause, Consuelo found that two of the ripening fruits had been carefully removed from their stems. Further search disclosed the theft of three dozen in all. Not more than two had been stolen from any plant.

Suspecting Juan, whom she had always distrusted, Consuelo hastened back to her father's laboratory to await his return and report. There she was met with an unpleasant surprise.

She opened the door to find Kadir seated at Beetle's desk, his face heavy with anger and suspicion.

"Where is your father?"

"I don't know."

"Come, come. I have made women talk before this when they were inclined to be obstinate. Where is he?"

"Again I tell you I don't know. He always takes his exercise at this time, and he goes alone. Besides," she flashed, "what business is it of yours where he is?"

"As to that," Kadir replied carelessly, "everything in Amazonia is my business."

"My father and I are not citizens—or subjects—of Amazonia."

"No. But your own country is several thousand miles away, Senhorina Beetle. In case of impertinent questions I can always report—with regrets, of course—that you both died by one of the accidents so common in Amazonia. Of snakebite, for instance."

"I see. But may I ask the reason for this sudden outburst?"

"So you have decided to talk? You will do as well as your father, perhaps better."

His eyes roved to one of the wire pens.

In it were half a dozen small red snakes.

"What do you need those for, now that you are no longer exporting venom?"

"Nothing much. Just pets, I suppose."

"Pets? Rather an unusual kind of pet, I should say." His face suddenly contorted in fear and rage. "Why is your father injecting snake blood into the unripe meat-fruit?" he shouted.

Consuelo kept her head. "Who told you that absurdity?"

"Answer me!" he bellowed.

"How can I? If your question is nonsense, how can anybody answer it?"

"So you refuse. I know a way to make you talk. Unlock that pen."

"I haven't the key. My father trusts nobody but himself with the keys to the pens."

"No? Well, this will do." He picked up a heavy ruler and lurched over to the pen. In a few moments he had sprung the lock.

"Now you answer my question or I force your arm into that pen. When your father returns I shall tell him that someone had broken the lock, and that you had evidently been trying to repair it when you got bitten. He will have to believe me. You will be capable of speech for just about three minutes after one of those red beauties strike. Once more, why did your father inject snake blood into the green meat-fruits?"

"And once more I repeat that you are asking nonsensical questions. Don't you dare—"

But he did dare. Ripping the sleeve of her smock from her arm, he gripped her bare wrist in his huge fist and began dragging her toward the pen. Her frantic resistance was no match for his brutal strength. Instinctively she resorted to the only defense left her. She let out a yell that must have carried half a mile.

Startled in spite of himself, Kadir paused, but only for an instant. She yelled again.

This time Kadir did not pause. Her hand was already in the pen when the door burst open. Punctual as usual, Beetle had returned exactly at eleven o'clock to resume his daily routine.

The black satchel dropped from his hand.

"What the hell—" A well-aimed laboratory stool finished the sentence. It caught the Dictator squarely in the chest. Consuelo fell with him, but quickly disengaged herself and stood panting.

"You crazy fool," Beetle spat at the prostrate man. "What do you think you are doing? Don't you know that those snakes are the deadliest of the whole lot?"

Kadir got to his feet without replying and sat down heavily on Beetle's desk. Beetle stood eying him in disgust.

"Come on, let's have it. What were you trying to do to my daughter?"

"Make her talk," Kadir muttered thickly. "She wouldn't—"

"Oh, she wouldn't talk. I get it, Consuelo! You keep out of this. I'll take care of our friend. Now, Kadir, just what did you want her to talk about?"

Still dazed, Kadir blurted out the truth.

"Why are you injecting snake blood into the unripe meat-fruit?"

Beetle eyed him curiously. With great deliberation he placed a chair in front of the Dictator and sat down.

"Let us get this straight. You ask why I am injecting snake blood into the greenbeefos. Who told you I was?"

"Juan. He brought three dozen of the unripe fruit to show me."

"To show you what?" Beetle asked in deadly calm. Had that fool Juan brains enough to look for the puncture-marks made by the hypodermic needle?

"To show me that you are poisoning the fruit."

"And did he show you?"

"How should I know? He was still alive when I came over here. I forced him to eat all three dozen."

"You had to use force?"

"Naturally. Juan said the snake blood would poison him."

"Which just shows how ignorant Juan is." Beetle sighed his relief. "Snake blood is about as poisonous as cow's milk."

"Why are you injecting—"

"You believed what that ignorant fool told you? He must have been drinking again and seeing things. I've warned him before. This time he goes. That is, if he hasn't come to his senses and gone already of his own free will."

"Gone? But where could he go from here?"

"Into the forest, or the jungle," Beetle answered indifferently. "He might even try to drape his worthless hide over a raft of rotten logs and float down the river. Anyhow, he will disappear after having made such a fool of himself. Take my word for it, we shan't see Juan again in a month of Sundays."

"On the contrary," Kadir retorted with a crafty smile, "I think we shall see him again in a very few minutes." He glanced at the clock. It showed ten minutes past eleven. "I have been here a little over half an hour. Juan promised to meet me here. He found it rather difficult to walk after his meal. When he comes, we can go into the question of those injections more fully."

For an instant Beetle looked startled, but quickly recovered his composure.

"I suppose as you say, Juan is slow because he has three dozen of those unripe greenbeefos under his belt. In fact I shouldn't wonder if he were feeling rather unwell at this very moment."

"So there is a poison in the fruits?" Kadir snapped.

"A poison? Rubbish! How would you or anyone feel if you had been forced to eat three dozen enormous green apples, to say nothing of unripe greenbeefos? I'll stake my reputation against yours that Juan is hiding in the forest and being very sick right now. And I'll bet anything you like that nobody ever sees him again. By the way, do you know which road he was to follow you by? The one through the clearing, or the cut-off through the forest?"

"I told him to take the cut-off, so as to get here quicker."

"Fine. Let's go and meet him—only we shan't. As for what I saw when I opened that door, I'll forget it if you will. I know Consuelo has already forgotten it. We are all quarantined here together in Amazonia, and there's no sense in harboring grudges. We've got to live together."

Relieved at being able to save his face, Kadir responded with a generous promise.

"If we fail to find Juan, I will admit that you are right, and that Juan has been drinking."

"Nothing could be fairer. Come on, let's go."

Their way to the Dictator's "palace"—formerly the residence of the superintendent of the gold mines—lay through the tropical forest.

The road was already beginning to choke up in the gloomier stretches with a rank web of trailing plants feeling their way to the trees on either side, to swarm up their trunks and ultimately choke the life out of them. Kadir's followers, soldiers all and new to the tropics, were letting nature take its course. Another two years of incompetence would see the painstaking labor of the American engineers smothered in rank jungle.

Frequently the three were compelled to abandon the road and follow more open trails through the forest till they again emerged on the road. Dazzling patches of yellow sunlight all but blinded them temporarily as they crossed the occasional barren spots that seem to blight all tropical forests like a leprosy. Coming out suddenly into one of these blinding patches, Kadir, who happened to be leading, let out a curdling oath and halted as if he had been shot.

"What's the matter?" Consuelo asked breathlessly, hurrying to overtake him. Blinded by the glare she could not see what had stopped the Dictator.

"I stepped on it." Kadir's voice was hoarse with disgust and fear.

"Stepped on what?" Beetle demanded. "I can't see in this infernal light. Was it a snake?"

"I don't know," Kadir began hoarsely. "It moved under my foot. Ugh! I see it now. Look."

They peered at the spot Kadir indicated, but could see nothing. Then, as their eyes became accustomed to the glare, they saw the thing that Kadir had stepped on.

A foul red fungus, as thick as a man's arm and over a yard long, lay directly in the Dictator's path.

"A bladder full of blood and soft flesh," Kadir muttered, shaking with fright and revulsion. "And I stepped on it."

"Rot!" Beetle exclaimed contemptuously, but there was a

bitter glint in his eyes. "Pull yourself together, man. That's nothing but a fungus. If there's a drop of blood in it, I'll eat the whole thing."

"But it moved," Kadir expostulated.

"Nonsense. You stepped on it, and naturally it gave beneath your weight. Come on. You will never find Juan at this rate."

But Kadir refused to budge. Fascinated by the disgusting object at his feet, the Dictator stood staring down at it with fear and loathing in every line of his face.

Then, as if to prove the truth of his assertion, the thing did move, slowly, like a wounded eel. But, unlike an eel, it did not move in the direction of its length. It began to roll slowly over.

Beetle squatted, the better to follow the strange motion. If it was not the first time he had seen such a freak of nature, he succeeded in giving a very good imitation of a scientist observing a novel and totally unexpected phenomenon. Consuelo joined her father in his researches. Kadir remained standing.

"Is it going to roll completely over?" Consuelo asked with evident interest.

"I think not," Beetle hazarded. "In fact, I'll bet three to one it only gets halfway over. There—I told you so. Look, Kadir, your fungus is rooted to the spot, just like any other plant."

In spite of himself, Kadir stooped down and looked. As the fungus reached the halfway mark in its attempted roll, it shuddered along its entire length and seemed to tug at the decayed vegetation. But shuddering and tugging got it nowhere. A thick band of fleshy rootlets, like coarse green hair, held it firmly to the ground. The sight of that futile struggle to move like a fully conscious thing was too much for Kadir's nerves.

"I am going to kill it," he muttered, leaping to his feet.

"How?" Beetle asked with a trace of contempt. "Fire is the only thing I know of to put a mess like that out of its misery—if it is in misery. For all I know, it may enjoy life. You can't kill it by smashing it or chopping it into mincemeat. Quite the contrary, in fact. Every piece of it will start a new fungus, and instead of one helpless blob rooted to the spot, you will have a whole colony. Better leave it alone, Kadir, to get what it can out of existence in its own way. Why must men like you always be killing something?"

"It is hideous and—"

"And you are afraid of it? How would you like someone to treat you as you propose treating this harmless fungus?"

"If I were like that," Kadir burst out," I should want somebody to put a torch to me."

"What if nobody knew that was what you wanted? Or if nobody cared? You have done some pretty foul things to a great many people in your time, I believe."

"But never anything like this!"

"Of course not. Nobody has ever done anything like this to anybody. So you didn't know how. What were you trying to do to my daughter an hour ago?"

"We agreed to forget all that," Consuelo reminded him sharply.

"Sorry. My mistake. I apologize, Kadir. As a matter of scientific interest, this fungus is not at all uncommon."

"I never saw one like it before," Consuelo objected.

"That is only because you don't go walking in the forest as I do," he reminded her. "Just to prove I'm right, I'll undertake to find a dozen rolling fungi within a hundred yards of here. What do you say?"

Before they could protest, he was hustling them out of the blinding glare into a black tunnel of the forest. Beetle seemed to know where he was going, for it was certain that his eyes were as dazed as theirs.

"Follow closely when you find your eyes," he called. "I'll go ahead. Look out for snakes. Ah, here's the first beauty! Blue and magenta, not red like Kadir's friend. Don't be prejudiced by its shape. Its color is all the beauty this poor thing has."

If anything, the shapeless mass of opalescent fungus blocking their path was more repulsive than the monstrosity that had stopped Kadir. This one was enormous, fully a yard in breadth and over five feet long. It lay sprawled over the rotting trunk of a fallen tree like a decomposing squid.

Yet, as Beetle insisted, its color was beautiful with an unnatural beauty. However, neither Consuelo nor Kadir could overcome their nausea at their living death. They fled precipitately back to the patch of sunlight. The fleshy magenta roots of the thing, straining impotently at the decaying wood which nourished them, were too suggestive of helpless suffering for endurance. Beetle followed at his leisure, chuckling to himself. His amusement drew a sharp reprimand from Consuelo.

"How can you be amused? That thing was in misery."

"Aren't we all?" he retored lightly, and for the first time in her life Consuelo doubted the goodness of her father's heart.

They found no trace of Juan. By the time they reached the Dictator's palace, Kadir was ready to agree to anything. He was a badly frightened man.

"You were right," he admitted to Beetle. "Juan was lying, and has cleared out. I apologize."

"No need to apologize," Beetle reassured him cordially. "I knew Juan was lying."

"Please honor me by staying to lunch," Kadir begged. "You cannot? Then I shall go and lie down."

They left him to recover his nerve, and walked back to the laboratory by the long road, not through the forest. They had gone over halfway before either spoke. When Beetle broke the long silence, he was more serious than Consuelo ever remembered his having been.

"Have you ever noticed," he began, "what arrant cowards all brutal men are?" She made no reply, and he continued, "Take Kadir, for instance. He and his gang have tortured and killed thousands. You saw how that harmless fungus upset him. Frightened half to death of nothing."

"Are you sure it was nothing?"

He gave her a strange look, and she walked rapidly ahead. "Wait," he called, slightly out of breath.

Breaking into a trot, he overtook her.

"I have something to say that I want you to remember. If anything should ever happen to me—I'm always handling those poisonous snakes—I want you to do at once what I tell you now. You can trust Felipe."

Felipe was the Portuguese foreman of the native workers.

"Go to him and tell him you are ready. He will understand. I prepared for this two years ago, when Kadir moved in. Before they left, the engineers built a navigable raft. Felipe knows where it is hidden. It is fully provisioned. A crew of six native river men is ready to put off at a moment's notice. They will be under Felipe's orders. The journey down the river will be long and dangerous, but with that crew you will make it. Anyhow, you will not be turned back by the quarantine officers when you do sight civilization. There is a flag with the provisions. Hoist it when you see any signs of civilization, and you will not be blown out of the water. That's all."

"Why are you telling me this now?"

"Because dictators never take their own medicine before they make someone else taste it for them."

"What do you mean?" she asked in sudden panic.

"Only that I suspect Kadir of planning to give me a dose of his peculiar brand of medicine the moment he is through with me. When he and his crew find out how to propagate the greenbeefos, I may be bitten by a snake. He was trying something like that on you, wasn't he?"

She gave him a long doubtful look. "Perhaps," she admitted. She was sure that there was more in his mind than he had told her.

They entered the laboratory and went about their business without another word. To recover lost time, Consuelo worked later than usual. Her task was the preparation of the liquid made up by Beetle's formula, in which the greenbeefos were grown.

She was just adding a minute trace of chloride of gold to the last batch when a timid rap on the door of the chemical laboratory startled her unreasonably. She had been worrying about her father.

"Come in," she called.

Felipe entered. The sight of his serious face gave her a sickening shock. What had happened? Felipe was carrying the familiar black satchel which Beetle always took with him on his solitary walks in the forest.

"What is it?" she stammered.

For answer Felipe opened his free hand and showed her a cheap watch. It was tarnished greenish blue with what looked like dried fungus.

"Juan's," he said. "When Juan did not report for work this afternoon, I went to look for him."

"And you found his watch? Where?"

"On the cut-off through the forest."

"Did you find anything else?"

"Nothing belonging to Juan."

"But you found something else?"

"Yes. I had never seen anything like them before."

He placed the satchel on the table and opened it.

"Look. Dozens like that one, all colors, in the forest. Doctor Beetle forgot to empty his bag when he went into the forest this morning."

She stared in speechless horror at the swollen monstrosity filling the satchel. The thing was like the one that Kadir had stepped on, except that it was not red but blue and magenta. The obvious explanation flashed through her mind, and she struggled to convince herself that it was true.

"You are mistaken," she said slowly. "Doctor Beetle threw the snake away as usual and brought this specimen back to study."

Felipe shook his head.

"No, Senhorina Beetle. As I always do when the Doctor comes back from his walk, I laid out everything ready for tomorrow. The snake was in the bag at twelve o'clock this morning. He came back at his regular time. I was busy then, and did not get to his laboratory till noon. The bag had been dropped by the door. I opened it, to see if everything was all right. The snake was still there. All its underside had turned to hard blue jelly. The back was still a snake's back, covered with scales. The head had turned green, but it was still a snake's head. I took the bag into my room and watched the snake till I went to look for Juan. The snake turned into this. I thought I should tell you."

"Thank you, Felipe. It is all right; just one of my father's scientific experiments. I understand. Goodnight, and thank you again for telling me. Please don't tell anyone else. Throw that thing away and put the bag in its usual place."

Left to herself, Consuelo tried not to credit her reason and the evidence of her senses. The inconsequential remarks her father had dropped in the past two years, added to the remark of today that dictators were never the first to take their own medicine, stole into her memory to cause her acute uneasiness.

What was the meaning of this new technique of his, the addition of a slight trace of chloride of gold to the solution? He had talked excitedly of some organic compound of gold being the catalyst he had sought for months to speed up the chemical change in the ripening fruit.

"What might have taken months the old way," he had exclaimed, "can now be done in hours. I've got it at last!"

What, exactly, had he got? He had not confided in her. All he asked of her was to see that the exact amount of chloride of gold which he prescribed was added to the solutions. Everything she remembered now fitted into its sinister place in one sombre pattern.

"This must be stopped," she thought.

It must be stopped, yes. But how?

The next day the banquet took place.

"Festal Thursday" slipped into the past, as the long shadows crept over the banquet tables—crude boards on trestles—spread in the open air. For one happy, gluttonous hour the bearers of the "New Freedom" to a benighted continent had stuffed themselves with a food that looked like green fruit but tasted like raw pork. Now they were replete and somewhat dazed.

A few were furtively mopping the perspiration from their foreheads, and all were beginning to show the sickly pallor of the gourmand who had overestimated his capacity for food. The eyes of some were beginning to wander strangely. These obviously unhappy guests appeared to be slightly drunk.

Kadir's speech eulogizing Beetle and his work was unexpectedly short. The Dictator's famous gift for oratory seemed to desert him, and he sat down somewhat suddenly, as if he were feeling unwell. Beetle rose to reply.

"Senhor Kadir! Guests and bearers to Amazonia of the New Freedom, I salute you! In the name of a freedom you have never known, I salute you, as the gladiators of ancient Rome saluted their tyrant before marching into the arena where they were to be butchered for his entertainment."

Their eyes stared up at him, only half-seeing. What was he saying? It all sounded like the beginning of a dream.

"With my own hands I prepared your feast, and my hands alone spread the banquet tables with the meat-fruits you have eaten. Only one human being here has eaten the fruit as nature made it, and not as I remade it. My daughter has not eaten what you have eaten. The cold, wet taste of the snake blood which you have mistaken for the flavor of swine-flesh, and which you have enjoyed, would have nauseated her. So I gave her uncontaminated fruit for her share of our feast."

Kadir and Consuelo were on their feet together, Kadir cursing incoherently, Consuelo speechless with fear. What insane thing had her father done? Had he too eaten of— But he must have, else Kadir would not have touched the fruit!

Beetle's voice rose above the Dictator's, shouting him down.

"Yes, you were right when you accused me of injecting snake blood into the fruit. Juan did not lie to you. But the snake blood is not what is making you begin to feel like a vegetable. I injected the blood into the fruit only to delude all you fools into mistaking it for flesh. I anticipated months of feeding before I could make of you what *should* be made of you.

"A month ago I was relying on the slow processes of nature to destroy you with my help. Light alone, that regulates the chemistry of the growing plant and to a lesser degree the chemistry of animals, would have done what must be done to rid Amazonia and the world of the threat of your New Freedom, and to make you expiate your brutal past.

"But light would have taken months to bring about the necessary *replacement of the iron in your blood by magnesium*. It would have been a slow transformation—almost, I might say, a lingering death. By feeding you greenbeefo I could keep your bodies full at all times with magnesium in chemically available form to *replace every atom of iron in your blood!*

"Under the slow action of photosynthesis—the chemical transformations induced by exposure to light—you would have suffered a lingering illness. You would not have died. No! You would have lived, but not as animals. Perhaps not even as degenerated vegetables, but as some new form of life between plant and the animal. You might even have retained your memories.

"But I have spared you this—so far as I can prophesy. You will live, but you will not remember—much. Instead of walking forward like human beings, you will roll. That will be your memory.

"Three weeks ago I discovered the organic catalyst to hasten the replacement of the iron in your blood by magnesium and thus to change your animal blood to plant blood, chlorophyll. The catalyst is merely a chemical compound which accelerates chemical reactions without itself being changed.

"By injecting a minute trace of chloride of gold into the fruits, I—and the living plant—produced the necessary catalyst. I have not yet had time to analyze it and determine its exact composition. Nor do I expect to have time. For I have, perforce, taken the same medicine that I prescribed for you!

"Not so much, but enough. I shall remain a thinking animal a little longer than the rest of you. That is the only unfair advantage I have taken. Before the sun sets we shall all have ceased to be human beings, or even animals."

Consuelo was tugging frantically at his arm, but he brushed her aside. He spoke to her in hurried jerks as if racing against time.

"I did not lie to you when I told you I could *not* change

the chlorophyll in a living plant into haemoglobin. Nobody has done that. But did I ever say I could not change *the haemoglobin in a living animal into chlorophyll?* If I have not done that, I have done something very close to it. Look at Kadir, and see for yourself. Let go my arm—I must finish."

Wrenching himself free, he began shouting against time.

"Kadir! I salute you. Raise your right hand and return the salute."

Kadir's right hand was resting on the bare boards of the table. If he understood what Beetle said, he refused to salute. But possibly understanding was already beyond him. The blood seemed to have ebbed from the blue flesh, and the coarse hairs on the back of the hand had lengthened perceptibly even while Beetle was demanding a salute.

"Rooted to the spot, Kadir! You are taking root already. And so are the rest of you. Try to stand up like human beings! Kadir! Do you hear me? Remember that blue fungus we saw in the forest? I have good reason for believing that was your friend Juan. In less than an hour you and I and all these fools will be exactly like him, except that some of us will be blue, others green, and still others red—like the thing you stepped on.

"It rolled. Remember, Kadir? That red abomination was one of my pet fungus snakes—shot full of salts of magnesium and the catalyst I extracted from the fruits. A triumph of science. I am the greatest biochemist that ever lived! But I shan't roll farther than the rest of you. We shall all roll together—or try to. 'Merrily we roll along, roll along'—I can see already you are going to be a blue and magenta mess like your friend Juan."

Beetle laughed harshly and bared his right arm. "I'm going to be red, like the thing you stepped on, Kadir. But I've stepped on the lot of you!"

He collapsed across the table and lay still. No sane human being could have stayed to witness the end. Half mad herself, Consuelo ran from the place of living death.

"Felipe, Felipe! Boards, wood—bring dry boards, quick, quick! Tear down the buildings and pile them up over the tables. Get all the men, get them all!"

Four hours later she was racing down the river through the night with Felipe and his crew. Only once did she glance back. The flames which she herself had kindled flapped against the black sky.

# THE GNARLY MAN    *Unknown,* June

# by L. Sprague de Camp (1907–    )

*Sprague de Camp is without doubt the most dis-
tinguished looking member of the science fiction
community. The body of work he has produced
since the late thirties is equally distinguished, and
covers a wide variety of forms and themes—science
fiction, fantasy, heroic fantasy, the popularization
of science, research into myths and legends, and
scholarship. He has written the so-far definitive biography of H. P. Lovecraft, and his LITERARY
SWORDSMEN AND SORCERERS is a trail-blaz-
ing study of heroic fantasy authors. His SCIENCE-
FICTION HANDBOOK (1953, revised 1975) remained the best single guide to writing sf for many
years.*

*It is very tempting to use the word "classic" to
describe the stories in this book. This one deserves
the term.*

*(I first met Sprague just about the time this story
appeared and in the forty years that has passed he
seems to have scarcely aged. He can still pass for
half his age—at least in my dazzled and envious
eyes—and so can his wife, the beautiful Catherine.
IA.)*

Dr. Matilda Saddler first saw the gnarly man on the evening
of June 14, 1946, at Coney Island.

The spring meeting of the Eastern Section of the American
Anthropological Association had broken up, and Dr. Saddler

141

had had dinner with two of her professional colleagues, Blue
of Columbia and Jeffcott of Yale. She mentioned that she
had never visited Coney, and meant to go there that evening.
She urged Blue and Jeffcott to come along, but they begged
off.

Watching Dr. Saddler's retreating back, Blue of Columbia
cackled: "The Wild Woman from Wichita. Wonder if she's
hunting another husband?" He was a thin man with a small
gray beard and a who-the-hell-are-you-sir expression.

"How many has she had?" asked Jeffcott of Yale.

"Two to date. Don't know why anthropologists lead the
most disorderly private lives of any scientists. Must be that
they study the customs and morals of all these different
peoples, and ask themselves, 'If the Eskimos can do it, why
can't we?' I'm old enough to be safe, thank God."

"I'm not afraid of her," said Jeffcott. He was in his early
forties and looked like a farmer uneasy in store clothes. "I'm
so very thoroughly married."

"Yeah? Ought to have been at Stanford a few years ago,
when she was there. Wasn't safe to walk across the campus,
with Tuthill chasing all the females and Saddler all the
males."

Dr. Saddler had to fight her way off the subway train, as
the adolescents who infest the platform of the B. M. T.'s
Stillwell Avenue station are probably the worst-mannered
people on earth, possibly excepting the Dobu Islanders, of the
western Pacific. She didn't much mind. She was a tall, strongly built woman in her late thirties, who had been kept in trim
by the outdoor rigors of her profession. Besides, some of
the inane remarks in Swift's paper on acculturation among
the Arapaho Indians had gotten her fighting blood up.

Walking down Surf Avenue toward Brighton Beach, she
looked at the concessions without trying them, preferring to
watch the human types that did and the other human types
that took their money. She did try a shooting gallery, but
found knocking tin owls off their perch with a .22 too easy
to be much fun. Long-range work with an army rifle was her
idea of shooting.

The concession next to the shooting gallery would have
been called a side show if there had been a main show for it
to be a side show to. The usual lurid banner proclaimed the
uniqueness of the two-headed calf, the bearded woman,
Arachne the spider girl, and other marvels. The pièce de
résistance was Ungo-Bungo, the ferocious ape-man, captured

in the Congo at a cost of twenty-seven lives. The picture showed an enormous Ungo-Bungo squeezing a hapless Negro in each hand, while others sought to throw a net over him.

Dr. Saddler knew perfectly well that the ferocious ape-man would turn out to be an ordinary Caucasian with false hair on his chest. But a streak of whimsicality impelled her to go in. Perhaps, she thought, she could have some fun with her colleagues about it.

The spieler went through his leather-lunged harangue. Dr. Saddler guessed from his expression that his feet hurt. The tattooed lady didn't interest her, as her decorations obviously had no cultural significance, as they have among the Polynesians. As for the ancient Mayan, Dr. Saddler thought it in questionable taste to exhibit a poor microcephalic idiot that way. Professor Yoki's legerdemain and fire eating weren't bad.

There was a curtain in front of Ungo-Bungo's cage. At the appropriate moment there were growls and the sound of a length of chain being slapped against a metal plate. The spieler wound up on a high note: "—ladies and gentlemen, the one and only UNGO-BUNGO!" The curtain dropped

The ape-man was squatting at the back of his cage. He dropped his chain, got up, and shuffled forward. He grasped two of the bars and shook them. They were appropriately loose and rattled alarmingly. Ungo-Bungo snarled at the patrons, showing his even, yellow teeth.

Dr. Saddler stared hard. This was something new in the ape-man line. Ungo-Bungo was about five feet three, but very massive, with enormous hunched shoulders. Above and below his blue swimming trunks thick, grizzled hair covered him from crown to ankle. His short, stout-muscled arms ended in big hands with thick, gnarled fingers. His neck projected slightly forward, so that from the front he seemed to have but little neck at all.

His face—well, thought Dr. Saddler, she knew all the living races of men, and all the types of freak brought about by glandular maladjustment, and none of them had a face like *that*. It was deeply lined. The forehead between the short scalp hair and the brows on the huge supraorbital ridges receded sharply. The nose, although wide, was not apelike; it was a shortened version of the thick, hooked Armenoid nose, so often miscalled Jewish. The face ended in a long upper lip and a retreating chin. And the yellowish skin apparently belonged to Ungo-Bungo.

The curtain was whisked up again.

Dr. Saddler went out with the others, but paid another dime, and soon was back inside. She paid no attention to the spieler, but got a good position in front of Ungo-Bungo's cage before the rest of the crowd arrived.

Ungo-Bungo repeated his performance with mechanical precision. Dr. Saddler noticed that he limped a little as he came forward to rattle the bars, and that the skin under his mat of hair bore several big whitish scars. The last joint of his left ring finger was missing. She noted certain things about the proportions of his shin and thigh, of his forearm and upper arm, and his big splay feet.

Dr. Saddler paid a third dime. An idea was knocking at her mind somewhere. If she let it in, either she was crazy or physical anthropology was haywire or—something. But she knew that if she did the sensible thing, which was to go home, the idea would plague her from now on.

After the third performance she spoke to the spieler. "I think your Mr. Ungo-Bungo used to be a friend of mine. Could you arrange for me to see him after he finishes?"

The spieler checked his sarcasm. His questioner was so obviously not a—not the sort of dame who asks to see guys after they finish.

"Oh, him," he said. "Calls himself Gaffney—Clarence Aloysius Gaffney. That the guy you want?"

"Why, yes."

"I guess you can." He looked at his watch. "He's got four more turns to do before we close. I'll have to ask the boss." He popped through a curtain and called, "Hey, Morrie!" Then he was back. "It's O. K. Morrie says you can wait in his office. Foist door to the right."

Morrie was stout, bald, and hospitable. "Sure, sure," he said, waving his cigar. "Glad to be of soivace, Miss Saddler. Chust a min while I talk to Gaffney's manager." He stuck his head out. "Hey, Pappas! Lady wants to talk to your ape-man later. I meant *lady*, O. K." He returned to orate on the difficulties besetting the freak business. "You take this Gaffney, now. He's the best damn ape-man in the business; all that hair rilly grows outa him. And the poor guy rilly has a face like that. But do people believe it? No! I hear 'em going out, saying about how the hair is pasted on, and the whole thing is a fake. It's mawtifying." He cocked his head, listening. "That rumble wasn't no rolly-coaster; it's gonna rain. Hope it's over by tomorrow. You wouldn't believe the way a rain can knock ya receipts off. If you drew a coive, it would be like this." He drew his finger horizontally through space, jerking it down sharply to indicate the effect of rain. "But as I said, people don't appreciate what you try to do for 'em. It's not just the money; I think of myself as an ottist. A creative ottist. A show like this got to have balance and propawtion, like any other ott—"

It must have been an hour later when a slow, deep voice at the door said: "Did somebody want to see me?"

The gnarly man was in the doorway. In street clothes, with the collar of his raincoat turned up and his hat brim pulled down, he looked more or less human, though the coat fitted his great, sloping shoulders badly. He had a thick, knobby walking stick with a leather loop near the top end. A small, dark man fidgeted behind him.

"Yeah," said Morrie, interrupting his lecture. "Clarence, this is Miss Saddler. Miss Saddler, this is Mr. Gaffney, one of our outstanding creative ottists."

"Pleased to meetcha," said the gnarly man. "This is my manager, Mr. Pappas."

Dr. Saddler explained, and said she'd like to talk to Mr. Gaffney if she might. She was tactful; you had to be to pry into the private affairs of Naga headhunters, for instance. The gnarly man said he'd be glad to have a cup of coffee with Miss Saddler; there was a place around the corner that they could reach without getting wet.

As they started out, Pappas followed, fidgeting more and more. The gnarly man said: "Oh, go home to bed, John. Don't worry about me." He grinned at Dr. Saddler. The effect would have been unnerving to anyone but an anthropologist. "Every time he sees me talking to anybody, he thinks it's some other manager trying to steal me." He spoke general American, with a suggestion of Irish brogue in the lowering of the vowels in words like "man" and "talk." "I made the lawyer who drew up our contract fix it so it can be ended on short notice."

Pappas departed, still looking suspicious. The rain had practically ceased. The gnarly man stepped along smartly despite his limp.

A woman passed with a fox terrier on a leash. The dog sniffed in the direction of the gnarly man, and then to all appearances went crazy, yelping and slavering. The gnarly man shifted his grip on the massive stick and said quietly, "Better hang onto him, ma'am." The woman departed hastily. "They just don't like me," commented Gaffney. "Dogs, that is."

They found a table and ordered their coffee. When the gnarly man took off his raincoat, Dr. Saddler became aware of a strong smell of cheap perfume. He got out a pipe with a big knobby bowl. It suited him, just as the walking stick did. Dr. Saddler noticed that the deep-sunk eyes under the beetling arches were light hazel.

"Well?" he said in his rumbling drawl.

She began her questions.

"My parents were Irish," he answered. "But I was born in South Boston . . . let's see . . . forty-six years ago. I can get you a copy of my birth certificate. Clarence Aloysius Gaffney, May 2, 1900." He seemed to get some secret amusement out of that statement.

"Were either of your parents of your somewhat unusual physical type?"

He paused before answering. He always did, it seemed. "Uh-huh. Both of 'em. Glands, I suppose."

"Were they both born in Ireland?"

"Yep. County Sligo." Again that mysterious twinkle.

She thought. "Mr. Gaffney, you wouldn't mind having some photographs and measurements made, would you? You could use the photographs in your business."

"Maybe." He took a sip. "Ouch! Gazooks, that's hot!"

"*What?*"

"I said the coffee's hot."

"I mean, before that."

The gnarly man looked a little embarrassed. "Oh, you mean the 'gazooks'? Well, I . . . uh . . . once knew a man who used to say that."

"Mr. Gaffney, I'm a scientist, and I'm not trying to get anything out of you for my own sake. You can be frank with me."

There was something remote and impersonal in his stare that gave her a slight spinal chill. "Meaning that I haven't been so far?"

"Yes. When I saw you I decided that there was something extraordinary in your background. I still think there is. Now, if you think I'm crazy, say so and we'll drop the subject. But I want to get to the bottom of this."

He took his time about answering. "That would depend." There was another pause. Then he said: "With your connections, do you know any really first-class surgeons?"

"But . . . yes, I know Dunbar."

"The guy who wears a purple gown when he operates? The guy who wrote a book on 'God, Man, and the Universe'?"

"Yes. He's a good man, in spite of his theatrical mannerisms. Why? What would you want of him?"

"Not what you're thinking. I'm satisfied with my . . . uh . . . unusual physical type. But I have some old injuries—broken bones that didn't knit properly—that I want fixed up. He'd have to be a good man, though. I have a couple of thousand dollars in the savings bank, but I know the sort of fees those guys charge. If you could make the necessary arrangements—"

"Why, yes, I'm sure I could. In fact, I could guarantee it. Then I *was* right? And you'll—" She hesitated.

"Come clean? Uh-huh. But remember, I can still prove I'm Clarence Aloysius if I have to."

"Who *are* you, then?"

Again there was a long pause. Then the gnarly man said: "Might as well tell you. As soon as you repeat any of it, you'll have put your professional reputation in my hands, remember.

"First off, I wasn't born in Massachusetts. I was born on the upper Rhine, near Mommenheim. And I was born, as nearly as I can figure out, about the year 50,000 B. C."

Matilda Saddler wondered whether she'd stumbled on the biggest thing in anthropology, or whether this bizarre personality was making Baron Munchausen look like a piker.

He seemed to guess her thoughts. "I can't prove that, of course. But so long as you arrange about that operation, I don't care whether you believe me or not."

"But . . . but . . . *how?*"

"I think the lightning did it. We were out trying to drive some bison into a pit. Well, this big thunderstorm came up, and the bison bolted in the wrong direction. So we gave up and tried to find shelter. And the next thing I knew I was lying on the ground with the rain running over me, and the rest of the clan standing around wailing about what had they done to get the storm god sore at them, so he made a bull's-eye on one of their best hunters. They'd never said *that* about me before. It's funny how you're never appreciated while you're alive.

"But I was alive, all right. My nerves were pretty well shot for a few weeks, but otherwise I was O. K., except for some burns on the soles of my feet. I don't know just what happened, except I was reading a couple of years ago that scientists had located the machinery that controls the replacement of tissue in the medulla oblongata. I think maybe the lightning did something to my medulla to speed it up. Anyway, I never got any older after that. Physically, that is. I was thirty-three at the time, more or less. We didn't keep track of ages. I look older now, because the lines in your face are bound to get sort of set after a few thousand years, and because our hair was always gray at the ends. But I can still tie an ordinary *Homo sapiens* in a knot if I want to."

"Then you're . . . you mean to say you're . . . you're trying to tell me you're—"

"A Neanderthal man? *Homo neanderthalensis?* That's right."

Matilda Saddler's hotel room was a bit crowded, with the gnarly man, the frosty Blue, the rustic Jeffcott, Dr. Saddler herself, and Harold McGannon, the historian. This McGannon was a small man, very neat and pink-skinned. He looked more like a New York Central director than a professor. Just now his expression was one of fascination. Dr. Saddler looked full of pride; Professor Jeffcott looked interested but puzzled; Dr. Blue looked bored—he hadn't wanted to come in the first place. The gnarly man, stretched out in the most comfortable chair and puffing his overgrown pipe, seemed to be enjoying himself.

McGannon was formulating a question. "Well, Mr.— Gaffney? I suppose that's your name as much as any."

"You might say so," said the gnarly man. "My original name meant something like Shining Hawk. But I've gone under hundreds of names since then. If you register in a hotel as 'Shining Hawk,' it's apt to attract attention. And I try to avoid that."

"Why?" asked McGannon.

The gnarly man looked at his audience as one might look at willfully stupid children. "I don't like trouble. The best way to keep out of trouble is not to attract attention. That's why I have to pull up stakes and move every ten or fifteen years. People might get curious as to why I never get any older."

"Pathological liar," murmured Blue. The words were barely audible, but the gnarly man heard them.

"You're entitled to your opinion, Dr. Blue," he said affably. "Dr. Saddler's doing me a favor, so in return I'm letting you all shoot questions at me. And I'm answering. I don't give a damn whether you believe me or not."

McGannon hastily threw in another question. "How is it that you have a birth certificate, as you say you have?"

"Oh, I knew a man named Clarence Gaffney once. He got killed by an automobile, and I took his name."

"Was there any reason for picking this Irish background?"

"Are you Irish, Dr. McGannon?"

"Not enough to matter."

"O. K. I didn't want to hurt any feelings. It's my best bet. There are real Irishmen with upper lips like mine."

Dr. Saddler broke in. "I meant to ask you, Clarence." She put a lot of warmth into his name. "There's an argument as to whether your people interbred with mine, when mine over-ran Europe at the end of the Mousterian. Some scientists have thought that some modern Europeans, especially along the west coast of Ireland, might have a little Neanderthal blood."

He grinned slightly. "Well—yes and no. There never was any back in the stone age, as far as I know. But these long-lipped Irish are my fault."

"How?"

"Believe it or not, but in the last fifty centuries there have been some women of your species that didn't find me too re-pulsive. Usually there was no offspring. But in the sixteenth century I went to Ireland to live. They were burning too many people for witchcraft in the rest of Europe to suit me at that time. And there was a woman. The result this time was a flock of hybrids—cute little devils, they were. So the Irishmen who look like me are my descendants."

"What did happen to your people?" asked McGannon. "Were they killed off?"

The gnarly man shrugged. "Some of them. We weren't at all warlike. But then the tall ones, as we called them, weren't either. Some of the tribes of the tall ones looked on us as le-gitimate prey, but most of them let us severely alone. I guess they were almost as scared of us as we were of them. Savages as primitive as that are really pretty peaceable people. You have to work so hard to keep fed, and there are so few of you, that there's no object in fighting wars. That comes later, when you get agriculture and livestock, so you have some-thing worth stealing.

"I remember that a hundred years after the tall ones had come, there were still Neanderthalers living in my part of the

country. But they died out. I think it was that they lost their
ambition. The tall ones were pretty crude, but they were so
far ahead of us that our things and our customs seemed silly.
Finally we just sat around and lived on the scraps we could
beg from the tall ones' camps. You might say we died of an
inferiority complex."

"What happened to you?" aksed McGannon.

"Oh, I was a god among my own people by then, and
naturally I represented them in their dealings with the tall
ones. I got to know the tall ones pretty well, and they were
willing to put up with me after all my own clan were dead.
Then in a couple of hundred years they'd forgotten all about
my people, and took me for a hunchback or something. I got
to be pretty good at flint working, so I could earn my keep.
When metal came in, I went into that, and finally into black-
smithing. If you'd put all the horseshoes I've made in a pile,
they'd—well, you'd have a damn big pile of horseshoes, anyway."

"Did you . . . ah . . . limp at that time?" asked McGannon.

"Uh-huh. I busted my leg back in the Neolithic. Fell out of
a tree, and had to set it myself, because there wasn't anybody
around. Why?"

"Vulcan," said McGannon softly.

"Vulcan?" repeated the gnarly man. "Wasn't he a Greek
god or something?"

"Yes. He was the lame blacksmith of the gods."

"You mean you think that maybe somebody got the idea
from me? That's an interesting theory. Little late to check up
on it, though."

Blue leaned forward and said crisply: "Mr. Gaffney, no
real Neanderthal man could talk so fluently and entertain-
ingly as you do. That's shown by the poor development of
the frontal lobes of the brain and the attachments of the
tongue muscles."

The gnarly man shrugged again. "You can believe what
you like. My own clan considered me pretty smart, and then
you're bound to learn something in fifty thousand years."

Dr. Saddler beamed. "Tell them about your teeth,
Clarence."

The gnarly man grinned. "They're false, of course. My
own lasted a long time, but they still wore out somewhere
back in the Paleolithic. I grew a third set, and they wore out,
too. So I had to invent soup."

"You *what?*" It was the usually taciturn Jeffcott.

"I had to invent soup, to keep alive. You know, the bark-dish-and-hot-stones method. My gums got pretty tough after a while, but they still weren't much good for chewing hard stuff. So after a few thousand years I got pretty sick of soup and mushy foods generally. And when metal came in I began experimenting with false teeth. Bone teeth in copper plates. You might say I invented them, too. I tried often to sell them, but they never really caught on until around 1750 A. D. I was living in Paris then, and I built up quite a little business before I moved on." He pulled the handkerchief out of his breast pocket to wipe his forehead; Blue made a face as the wave of perfume reached him.

"Well, Mr. Shining Hawk," snapped Blue with a trace of sarcasm, "how do you like our machine age?"

The gnarly man ignored the tone of the question. "It's not bad. Lots of interesting things happen. The main trouble is the shirts."

"Shirts?"

"Uh-huh. Just try to buy a shirt with a twenty neck and a twenty-nine sleeve. I have to order 'em special. It's almost as bad with hats and shoes. I wear an eight and one half hat and a thirteen shoe." He looked at his watch. "I've got to get back to Coney to work."

McGannon jumped up. "Where can I get in touch with you again, Mr. Gaffney? There's lots of things I'd like to ask you."

The gnarly man told him. "I'm free mornings. My working hours are two to midnight on weekdays, with a couple of hours off for dinner. Union rules, you know."

"You mean there's a union for you show people?"

"Sure. Only they call it a guild. They think they're artists, you know. Artists don't have unions; they have guilds. But it amounts to the same thing."

Blue and Jeffcott saw the gnarly man and the historian walking slowly toward the subway together. Blue said: "Poor old Mac! Always thought he had sense. Looks like he's swallowed this Gaffney's ravings, hook, line, and sinker."

"I'm not so sure," said Jeffcott, frowning. "There's something funny about the business."

"What?" barked Blue. "Don't tell me that *you* believe this story of being alive fifty thousand years? A caveman who uses perfume! Good God!"

"N-no," said Jeffcott. "Not the fifty thousand part. But I don't think it's a simple case of paranoia or plain lying, either. And the perfume's quite logical, if he were telling the truth."

"Huh?"

"Body odor. Saddler told us how dogs hate him. He'd have a smell different from ours. We're so used to ours that we don't even know we have one, unless somebody goes without a bath for a month. But we might notice his if he didn't disguise it."

Blue snorted. "You'll be believing him yourself in a minute. It's an obvious glandular case, and he's made up this story to fit. All that talk about not caring whether we believe him or not is just bluff. Come on, let's get some lunch. Say, see the way Saddler looked at him every time she said 'Clarence'? Like a hungry wolf. Wonder what she thinks she's going to do with him?"

Jeffcott thought. "I can guess. And if he *is* telling the truth, I think there's something in Deuteronomy against it."

The great surgeon made a point of looking like a great surgeon, to pince-nez and Vandyke. He waved the X-ray negatives at the gnarly man, pointing out this and that.

"We'd better take the leg first," he said. "Suppose we do that next Thursday. When you've recovered from that we can tackle the shoulder. It'll all take time, you know."

The gnarly man agreed, and shuffled out of the little private hospital to where McGannon awaited him in his car. The gnarly man described the tentative schedule of operations, and mentioned that he had made arrangements to quit his job. "Those two are the main thing," he said. "I'd like to try professional wrestling again some day, and I can't unless I get this shoulder fixed so I can raise my left arm over my head."

"What happened to it?" asked McGannon.

The gnarly man closed his eyes, thinking. "Let me see. I get things mixed up sometimes. People do when they're only fifty years old, so you can imagine what it's like for me.

"In 42 B. C. I was living with the Bituriges in Gaul. You remember that Cæsar shut up Werkinghetorich—Vercingetorix to you—in Alesia, and the confederacy raised an army of relief under Coswollon."

"Coswollon?"

The gnarly man laughed shortly. "I meant Warcaswollon.

Caswollon was a Briton, wasn't he? I'm always getting those two mixed up.

"Anyhow, I got drafted. That's all you can call it; I didn't want to go. It wasn't exactly *my* war. But they wanted me because I could pull twice as heavy a bow as anybody else.

"When the final attack on Cæsar's ring fortifications came, they sent me forward with some other archers to provide a covering fire for their infantry. At least, that was the plan. Actually, I never saw such a hopeless muddle in my life. And before I even got within bowshot, I fell into one of the Romans' covered pits. I didn't land on the point of the stake, but I fetched up against the side of it and busted my shoulder. There wasn't any help, because the Gauls were too busy running away from Cæsar's German cavalry to bother about wounded men."

The author of "God, Man, and the Universe" gazed after his departing patient. He spoke to his head assistant: "What do you think of him?"

"I think it's so," said the assistant. "I looked over those X rays pretty closely. That skeleton never belonged to a human being. And it has more healed fractures than you'd think possible."

"Hm-m-m," said Dunbar. "That's right, he wouldn't be human, would he? Hm-m-m. You know, if anything happened to him—"

The assistant grinned understandingly. "Of course, there's the S. P. C. A."

"We needn't worry about *them*. Hm-m-m." He thought, you've been slipping; nothing big in the papers for a year. But if you published a complete anatomical description of a Neanderthal man—or if you found out why his medulla functions the way it does—Hm-m-m. Of course, it would have to be managed properly—

"Let's have lunch at the Natural History Museum," said McGannon. "Some of the people there ought to know you."

"O. K.," drawled the gnarly man. "Only I've still got to get back to Coney afterward. This is my last day. Tomorrow, Pappas and I are going up to see our lawyer about ending our contract. Guy named Robinette. It's a dirty trick on poor old John, but I warned him at the start that this might happen."

"I suppose we can come up to interview you while you're

. . . ah . . . convalescing? Fine. Have you ever been to the museum, by the way?"

"Sure," said the gnarly man. "I get around."

"What did you . . . ah . . . think of their stuff in the Hall of the Age of Man?"

"Pretty good. There's a little mistake in one of those big wall paintings. The second horn on the woolly rhinoceros ought to slant forward more. I thought of writing them a letter. But you know how it is. They'd say: 'Were you there?' and I'd say, 'Uh-huh,' and they'd say, 'Another nut.' "

"How about the pictures and busts of Paleolithic men?"

"Pretty good. But they have some funny ideas. They always show us with skins wrapped around our middles. In summer we didn't wear skins, and in winter we hung them around our shoulders, where they'd do some good.

"And then they show those tall ones that you call Cro-Magnon men clean-shaven. As I remember, they all had whiskers. What would they shave with?"

"I think," said McGannon, "that they leave the beards off the busts to . . . ah . . . show the shape of the chins. With the beards they'd all look too much alike."

"Is that the reason? They might say so on the labels." The gnarly man rubbed his own chin, such as it was. "I wish beards would come back into style. I look much more human with a beard. I got along fine in the sixteenth century when everybody had whiskers.

"That's one of the ways I remember when things happened, by the haircuts and whiskers that people had. I remember when a wagon I was driving in Milan lost a wheel and spilled flour bags from hell to breakfast. That must have been in the sixteenth century, before I went to Ireland, because I remember that most of the men in the crowd that collected had beards. Now—wait a minute—maybe that was the fourteenth. There were a lot of beards then, too."

"Why, why didn't you keep a diary?" asked McGannon with a groan of exasperation.

The gnarly man shrugged characteristically. "And pack around six trunks full of paper every time I moved? No, thanks."

"I . . . ah . . . don't suppose you could give me the real story of Richard III and the princes in the tower?"

"Why should I? I was just a poor blacksmith, or farmer, or something most of the time. I didn't go around with the big shots. I gave up all my ideas of ambition a long time before that. I had to, being so different from other people. As far as I can remember, the only real king I ever got a good look at was Charlemagne, when he made a speech in Paris one day. He was just a big, tall man with Santa Claus whiskers and a squeaky voice."

Next morning McGannon and the gnarly man had a session with Svedberg at the museum. Then McGannon drove Gaffney around to the lawyer's office, on the third floor of a seedy office building in the West Fifties. James Robinette looked something like a movie actor and something like a chipmunk. He looked at his watch and said to McGannon: "This won't take long. If you'd like to stick around, I'd be glad to have lunch with you." The fact was that he was feeling just a trifle queasy about being left with this damn queer client, this circus freak or whatever he was, with his barrel body and his funny slow drawl.

When the business had been completed, and the gnarly man had gone off with his manager to wind up his affairs at Coney, Robinette said: "Whew! I thought he was a half-wit, from his looks. But there was nothing half-witted about the way he went over those clauses. You'd have thought the damn contract was for building a subway system. What is he, anyhow?"

McGannon told him what he knew.

The lawyer's eyebrows went up. "Do you *believe* his yarn? Oh, I'll take tomato juice and filet of sole with tartar sauce—only without the tartar sauce—on the lunch, please."

"The same for me. Answering your question, Robinette, I do. So does Saddler. So does Svedberg up at the museum. They're both topnotchers in their respective fields. Saddler and I have interviewed him, and Svedberg's examined him physically. But it's just opinion. Fred Blue still swears it's a hoax or . . . ah . . . some sort of dementia. Neither of us can prove anything."

"Why not?"

"Well . . . ah . . . how are you going to prove that he was, or was not, alive a hundred years ago? Take one case: Clarence says he ran a sawmill in Fairbanks, Alaska, in 1906 and '07, under the name of Michael Shawn. How are you going to find out whether there was a sawmill operator in Fairbanks at that time? And if you did stumble on a record of a Michael Shawn, how would you know whether he and Clarence were the same? There's not a chance in a thousand

that there'd be a photograph or a detailed description that
you could check with. And you'd have an awful time trying
to find anybody who remembered him at this late date.

"Then, Svedberg poked around Clarence's face, yesterday,
and said that no *Homo sapiens* ever had a pair of zygomatic
arches like that. But when I told Blue that, he offered to produce photographs of a human skull that did. I know what'll
happen. Blue will say that the arches are practically the same,
and Svedberg will say that they're obviously different. So
there we'll be."

Robinette mused, "He does seem damned intelligent for an
ape-man."

"He's not an ape-man, really. The Neanderthal race was a
separate branch of the human stock: they were more primitive in some ways and more advanced in others than we are.
Clarence may be slow, but he usually grinds out the right answer. I imagine that he was . . . ah . . . brilliant, for one of
his kind, to begin with. And he's had the benefit of so much
experience. He knows an incredible lot. He knows us; he sees
through us and our motives."

The little pink man puckered up his forehead. "I do hope
nothing happens to him. He's carrying around a lot of
priceless information in that big head of his. Simply priceless.
Not much about war and politics; he kept clear of those as a
matter of self-preservation. But little things, about how
people lived and how they thought thousands of years ago.
He gets his periods mixed up sometimes, but he gets them
straightened out if you give him time.

"I'll have to get hold of Pell, the linguist. Clarence knows
dozens of ancient languages, such as Gothic and Gaulish. I
was able to check him on one of them, like vulgar Latin; that
was one of the things that convinced me. And there are ar-
cheologists and psychologists—

"If only something doesn't happen to scare him off. We'd
never find him. I don't know. Between a man-crazy female
scientist and a publicity-mad surgeon—I wonder how it'll
work out—"

The gnarly man innocently entered the waiting room of
Dunbar's hospital. He, as usual, spotted the most comfortable
chair and settled luxuriously into it.

Dunbar stood before him. His keen eyes gleamed with anticipation behind their pince-nez. "There'll be a wait of about
half an hour, Mr. Gaffney," he said. "We're all tied up now,

you know. I'll send Mahler in; he'll see that you have anything you want." Dunbar's eyes ran lovingly over the gnarly man's stumpy frame. What fascinating secrets mightn't he discover once he got inside it?

Mahler appeared, a healthy-looking youngster. Was there anything Mr. Gaffney would like? The gnarly man paused as usual to let his massive mental machinery grind. A vagrant impulse moved him to ask to see the instruments that were to be used on him.

Mahler had his orders, but this seemed a harmless enough request. He went and returned with a tray full of gleaming steel. "You see," he said, "these are called scalpels."

Presently the gnarly man asked: "What's this?" He picked up a peculiar-looking instrument.

"Oh, that's the boss's own invention. For getting at the mid-brain."

"Mid-brain? What's that doing here?"

"Why, that's for getting at your— That must be there by mistake—"

Little lines tightened around the queer hazel eyes. "Yeah?" He remembered the look Dunbar had given him, and Dunbar's general reputation. "Say, could I use your phone a minute?"

"Why . . . I suppose . . . what do you want to phone for?"

"I want to call my lawyer. Any objections?"

"No, of course not. But there isn't any phone here."

"What do you call that?" The gnarly man got up and walked toward the instrument in plain sight on a table. But Mahler was there before him, standing in front of it.

"This one doesn't work. It's being fixed."

"Can't I try it?"

"No, not till it's fixed. It doesn't work, I tell you."

The gnarly man studied the young physician for a few seconds. "O. K., then I'll find one that does." He started for the door.

"Hey, you can't go out now!" cried Mahler.

"Can't I? Just watch me!"

"Hey!" It was a full-throated yell. Like magic more men in white coats appeared.

Behind them was the great surgeon. "Be reasonable, Mr. Gaffney," he said. "There's no reason why you should go out now, you know. We'll be ready for you in a little while."

"Any reason why I shouldn't?" The gnarly man's big face

swung on his thick neck, and his hazel eyes swiveled. All the exits were blocked. "I'm going."

"Grab him!" said Dunbar.

The white coats moved. The gnarly man got his hands on the back of a chair. The chair whirled, and became a dissolving blur as the men closed on him. Pieces of chair flew about the room, to fall with the dry, sharp *ping* of short lengths of wood. When the gnarly man stopped swinging, having only a short piece of the chair back left in each fist, one assistant was out cold. Another leaned whitely against the wall and nursed a broken arm.

"Go on!" shouted Dunbar when he could make himself heard. The white wave closed over the gnarly man, then broke. The gnarly man was on his feet, and held young Mahler by the ankles. He spread his feet and swung the shrieking Mahler like a club, clearing the way to the door. He turned, whirled Mahler around his head like a hammer thrower, and let the now mercifully unconscious body fly. His assailants went down in a yammering tangle.

One was still up. Under Dunbar's urging he sprang after the gnarly man. The latter had gotten his stick out of the umbrella stand in the vestibule. The knobby upper end went *whoosh* past the assistant's nose. The assistant jumped back and fell over one of the casualties. The front door slammed, and there was a deep roar of "Taxi!"

"Come on!" shrieked Dunbar. "Get the ambulance out!"

James Robinette was sitting in his office, thinking the thoughts that lawyers do in moments of relaxation, when there was a pounding of large feet in the corridor, a startled protest from Miss Spevak in the outer office, and the strange client of the day before was at Robinette's desk, breathing hard.

"I'm Gaffney," he growled between gasps. "Remember me? I think they followed me down here. They'll be up any minute. I want your help."

"They? Who's they?" Robinette winced at the impact of that damn perfume.

The gnarly man launched into his misfortunes, He was going well when there were more protests from Miss Spevak, and Dr. Dunbar and four assistants burst into the office.

"He's ours," said Dunbar, his glasses agleam.

"He's an ape-man," said the assistant with the black eye.

"He's a dangerous lunatic," said the assistant with the cut lip.

"We've come to take him away," said the assistant with the torn coat.

The gnarly man spread his feet and gripped his stick like a baseball bat by the small end.

Robinette opened a desk drawer and got out a large pistol. "One move toward him and I'll use this. The use of extreme violence is justified to prevent commission of a felony, to wit: kidnaping."

The five men backed up a little. Dunbar said: "This isn't kidnaping. You can only kidnap a person, you know. He isn't a human being, and I can prove it."

The assistant with the black eye snickered. "If he wants protection, he better see a game warden instead of a lawyer."

"Maybe that's what *you* think," said Robinette. "You aren't a lawyer. According to the law, he's human. Even corporations, idiots, and unborn children are legally persons, and he's a damn sight more human they they are."

"Then he's a dangerous lunatic," said Dunbar.

"Yeah? Where's your commitment order? The only persons who can apply for one are: (a) close relatives and (b) public officials charged with the maintenance of order. You're neither."

Dunbar continued stubbornly: "He ran amuck in my hospital and nearly killed a couple of my men, you know. I guess that gives us some rights."

"Sure," said Robinette. "You can step down to the nearest station and swear out a warrant." He turned to the gnarly man. "Shall we throw the book at 'em, Gaffney?"

"I'm all right," said that individual, his speech returning to its normal slowness. "I just want to make sure these guys don't pester me any more."

"O. K. Now listen, Dunbar. One hostile move out of you and we'll have a warrant out for you for false arrest, assault and battery, attempted kidnaping, criminal conspiracy, and disorderly conduct. *And* we'll slap on a civil suit for damages for sundry torts, to wit: assault, deprivation of civil rights, placing in jeopardy of life and limb, menace, and a few more I may think of later."

"You'll never make that stick," snarled Dunbar. "We have all the witnesses."

"Yeah? And wouldn't the great Evan Dunbar look sweet defending such actions? Some of the ladies who gush over your books might suspect that maybe you weren't such a damn knight in shining armor. We can make a prize monkey of you, and you know it."

"You're destroying the possibility of a great scientific discovery, you know, Robinette."

"To hell with that. My duty is to protect my client. Now beat it, all of you, before I call a cop." His left hand moved suggestively to the telephone.

Dunbar grasped at a last straw. "Hm-m-m. Have you got a permit for that gun?"

"Damn right. Want to see it?"

Dunbar sighed. "Never mind. You *would* have." His greatest opportunity for fame was slipping out of his fingers. He drooped toward the door.

The gnarly man spoke up. "If you don't mind, Dr. Dunbar, I left my hat at your place. I wish you'd send it to Mr. Robinette here. I have a hard time getting hats to fit me."

Dunbar looked at him silently and left with his cohorts.

The gnarly man was giving the lawyer further details when the telephone rang. Robinette answered: "Yes. . . . Saddler? Yes, he's here. . . . Your Dr. Dunbar was going to murder him so he could dissect him. . . . O. K." He turned to the gnarly man. "Your friend Dr. Saddler is looking for you. She's on her way up here."

"Zounds!" said Gaffney. "I'm going."

"Don't you want to see her? She was phoning from around the corner. If you go out now you'll run into her. How did she knew where to call?"

"I gave her your number. I suppose she called the hospital and my boardinghouse, and tried you as a last resort. This door goes into the hall, doesn't it? Well, when she comes in the regular door I'm going out this one. And I don't want you saying where I've gone. It's nice to have known you, Mr. Robinette."

"Why? What's the matter? You're not going to run out now, are you? Dunbar's harmless, and you've got friends. I'm your friend."

"You're durn tootin' I'm going to run out. There's too much trouble. I've kept alive all these centuries by staying away from trouble. I let down my guard with Dr. Saddler, and went to the surgeon she recommended. First he plots to take me apart to see what makes me tick. If that brain instrument hadn't made me suspicious, I'd have been on my way to the alcohol jars by now. Then there's a fight, and it's just pure luck I didn't kill a couple of those internes, or whatever they are, and get sent up for manslaughter. Now Matilda's after me with a more-than-friendly interest. I know what it means when a woman looks at you that way and calls you 'dear.' I wouldn't mind if she weren't a prominent person of the kind that's always in some sort of garboil. That would mean more trouble, sooner or later. You don't suppose I *like* trouble, do you?"

"But look here, Gaffney, you're getting steamed up over a lot of damn—"

"*Ssst!*" The gnarly man took his stick and tiptoed over to the private entrance. As Dr. Saddler's clear voice sounded in the outer office, he sneaked out. He was closing the door behind him when the scientist entered the inner office.

Matilda Saddler was a quick thinker. Robinette hardly had time to open his mouth when she flung herself at and through the private door with a cry of "Clarence!"

Robinette heard the clatter of feet on the stairs. Neither the pursued nor the pursuer had waited for the creaky elevator. Looking out the window, he saw Gaffney leap into a taxi. Matilda Saddler sprinted after the cab, calling: "Clarence! Come back!" But the traffic was light and the chase correspondingly hopeless.

They did hear from the gnarly man once more. Three months later Robinette got a letter whose envelope contained, to his vast astonishment, ten ten-dollar bills. The single sheet was typed, even to the signature.

DEAR MR. ROBINETTE:

I do not know what your regular fees are, but I hope that the inclosed will cover your services to me of last June.

Since leaving New York I have had several jobs. I pushed a hack—as we say—in Chicago, and I tried out as pitcher on a bush league baseball team. Once I made my living by knocking over rabbits and things with stones, and I can still throw fairly well. Nor am I bad at swinging a club, such as a baseball bat. But my lameness makes me too slow for a baseball career, and it will be some time before I try any remedial operations again.

I now have a job whose nature I cannot disclose because I do not wish to be traced. You need pay no attention to the postmark; I am not living in Kansas City, but had a friend post this letter there.

Ambition would be foolish for one in my peculiar position. I am satisfied with a job that furnishes me with the essentials, and allows me to go to an occasional movie, and a few friends with whom I can drink beer and talk.

I was sorry to leave New York without saying good-by to Dr. Harold McGannon, who treated me very nicely. I wish you would explain to him why I had to leave as I did. You can get in touch with him through Columbia University.

If Dunbar sent you my hat as I requested, pleased mail it to me: General Delivery, Kansas City, Mo. My friend will pick it up. There is not a hat store in this town where I live that can fit me. With best wishes, I remain,

Yours sincerely,
SHINING HAWK
Alias CLARENCE ALOYSIUS GAFFNEY

# BLACK DESTROYER

*Astounding Science Fiction,* July

## by A. E. van Vogt (1912– )

*"Black Destroyer" was the Canadian born van Vogt's first published story, and it propelled him to the top of the science fiction world. His was to be an important and contentious career, characterized by controversy, a long hiatus from sf (with the loss of what many felt were his potentially most creative years), and the production of many works of lasting interest.*

*There had been hundreds of stories about "space monsters" and BEMS before "Black Destroyer," the vast majority relying on the appearance of the creatures to frighten and amaze the reader. However, here it is not tentacles that provide the chills and frights, but Coeurl's insatiable* hunger. *Van Vogt would return to the theme of the menacing alien numerous times, and this story forms part of his popular "novel"* THE VOYAGE OF THE SPACE BEAGLE (1950).

*(The July, 1939,* Astounding *is sometimes taken as the opening of the two decades of science fiction's "Golden Age" when John Campbell, at the height of his powers, was undisputed Emperor of Science Fiction. Why this issue? Very largely because of* Black Destroyer *which had the wallop of a pile driver to those reading it then for the first time. I know, because I remember. IA)*

On and on Coeurl prowled! The black, moonless, almost starless night yielded reluctantly before a grim reddish dawn that crept up from his left. A vague, dull light, it was, that gave no sense of approaching warmth, no comfort, nothing but a cold, diffuse lightness, slowly revealing a nightmare landscape.

Black, jagged rock and black, unliving plain took form around him, as a pale-red sun peered at last above the grotesque horizon. It was then Coeurl recognized suddenly that he was on familiar ground.

He stopped short. Tenseness flamed along his nerves. His muscles pressed with sudden, unrelenting strength against his bones. His great forelegs—twice as long as his hindlegs— twitched with a shuddering movement that arched every razor-sharp claw. The thick tentacles that sprouted from his shoulders ceased their weaving undulation, and grew taut with anxious alertness.

Utterly appalled, he twisted his great cat head from side to side, while the little hairlike tendrils that formed each ear vibrated frantically, testing every vagrant breeze, every throb in the ether.

But there was no response, no swift tingling along his intricate nervous system, not the faintest suggestion anywhere of the presence of the all-necessary id. Hopelessly, Coeurl crouched, an enormous catlike figure silhouetted against the dim reddish skyline, like a distorted etching of a black tiger resting on a black rock in a shadow world.

He had known this day would come. Through all the centuries of restless search, this day had loomed ever nearer, blacker, more frightening—this inevitable hour when he must return to the point where he began his systematic hunt in a world almost depleted of id-creatures.

The truth struck in waves like an endless, rhythmic ache at the seat of his ego. When he had started, there had been a few id-creatures in every hundred square miles, to be mercilessly rooted out. Only too well Coeurl knew in this ultimate hour that he had missed none. There were no id-creatures left to eat. In all the hundreds of thousands of square miles that he had made his own by right of ruthless conquest—until no neighboring coeurl dared to question his sovereignty—there was no id to feed the otherwise immortal engine that was his body.

Square foot by square foot he had gone over it. And now—he recognized the knoll of rock just ahead, and the black rock bridge that formed a queer, curling tunnel to his right. It was in that tunnel he had lain for days, waiting for the simple-minded, snakelike id-creature to come forth from its hole in the rock to bask in the sun—his first kill after he had realized the absolute necessity of organized extermination.

He licked his lips in brief gloating memory of the moment his slavering jaws tore the victim into precious toothsome bits. But the dark fear of an idless universe swept the sweet remembrance from his consciousness, leaving only certainty of death.

He snarled audibly, a defiant, devilish sound that quavered on the air, echoed and re-echoed among the rocks, and shuddered back along his nerves—instinctive and hellish expression of his will to live.

And then—abruptly—it came.

He saw it emerge out of the distance on a long downward slant, a tiny glowing spot that grew enormously into a metal ball. The great shining globe hissed by above Coeurl, slowing visibly in quick deceleration. It sped over a black line of hills to the right, hovered almost motionless for a second, then sank down out of sight.

Coeurl exploded from his startled immobility. With tiger speed, he flowed down among the rocks. His round, black eyes burned with the horrible desire that was an agony within him. His ear tendrils vibrated a message of id in such tremendous quantities that his body felt sick with the pangs of his abnormal hunger.

The little red sun was a crimson ball in the purple-black heavens when he crept up from behind a mass of rock and gazed from its shadows at the crumbling, gigantic ruins of the city that sprawled below him. The silvery globe, in spite of its great size, looked strangely inconspicuous against that vast, fairylike reach of ruins. Yet about it was a leashed aliveness, a dynamic quiescence that, after a moment, made it stand out, dominating the foreground. A massive, rock-crushing thing of metal, it rested on a cradle made by its own weight in the harsh, resisting plain which began abruptly at the outskirts of the dead metropolis.

Coeurl gazed at the strange, two-legged creatures who stood in little groups near the brilliantly lighted opening that yawned at the base of the ship. His throat thickened with the immediacy of his need; and his brain grew dark with the first wild impulse to burst forth in furious charge and smash these flimsy, helpless-looking creatures whose bodies emitted the id-vibrations.

Mists of memory stopped that mad rush when it was still only electricity surging through his muscles. Memory that brought fear in an acid stream of weakness, pouring along his nerves, poisoning the reservoirs of his strength. He had time to see that the creatures wore things over their real bodies, shimmering transparent material that glittered in strange, burning flashes in the rays of the sun.

Other memories came suddenly. Of dim days when the city that spread below was the living, breathing heart of an age of glory that dissolved in a single century before flaming guns whose wielders knew only that for the survivors there would be an ever-narrowing supply of id.

It was the remembrance of those guns that held him there, cringing in a wave of terror that blurred his reason. He saw himself smashed by balls of metal and burned by searing flame.

Came cunning—understanding of the presence of these creatures. This, Coeurl reasoned for the first time, was a scientific expedition from another star. In the older days, the coeurls had thought of space travel, but disaster came too swiftly for it ever to be more than a thought.

Scientist meant investigation, not destruction. Scientists in their way were fools. Bold with his knowledge, he emerged into the open. He saw the creatures become aware of him. They turned and stared. One, the smallest of the group, detached a shining metal rod from a sheath, and held it casually in one hand. Coeurl loped on, shaken to his core by the action; but it was too late to turn back.

Commander Hal Morton heard little Gregory Kent, the chemist, laugh with the embarrassed half gurgle with which he invariably announced inner uncertainty. He saw Kent fingering the spindly metalite weapon.

Kent said: "I'll take no chances with anything as big as that."

Commander Morton allowed his own deep chuckle to echo along the communicators. "That," he grunted finally, "is one of the reasons why you're on this expedition, Kent—because you never leave anything to chance."

His chuckle trailed off into silence. Instinctively, as he watched the monster approach them across that black rock plain, he moved forward until he stood a little in advance of the others, his huge form bulking the transparent metalite suit. The comments of the men pattered through the radio communicator into his ears:

"I'd hate to meet that baby on a dark night in an alley."

"Don't be silly. This is obviously an intelligent creature. Probably a member of the ruling race."

"It looks like nothing else than a big cat, if you forget those tentacles sticking out from its shoulders, and making allowances for those monster forelegs."

"Its physical development," said a voice, which Morton recognized as that of Siedel, the psychologist, "presupposes an animal-like adaptation to surroundings, not an intellectual one. On the other hand, its coming to us like this is not the act of an animal but of a creature possessing a mental awareness of our possible identity. You will notice that its movements are stiff, denoting caution, which suggests fear and consciousness of our weapons. I'd like to get a good look at the end of its tentacles. If they taper into handlike appendages that can really grip objects, then the conclusion would be inescapable that it is a descendant of the inhabitants of this city. It would be a great help if we could establish communication with it, even though appearances indicate that it has degenerated into a historyless primitive."

Coeurl stopped when he was still ten feet from the foremost creature. The sense of id was so overwhelming that his brain drifted to the ultimate verge of chaos. He felt as if his limbs were bathed in molten liquid; his very vision was not quite clear, as the sheer sensuality of his desire thundered through his being.

The men—all except the little one with the shining metal rod in his fingers—came closer. Coeurl saw that they were frankly and curiously examining him. Their lips were moving, and their voices beat in a monotonous, meaningless rhythm on his ear tendrils. At the same time he had the sense of waves of a much higher frequency—his own communication level—only it was a machinelike clicking that jarred his brain. With a distinct effort to appear friendly, he broadcast his name from his ear tendrils. at the same time pointing at himself with one curving tentacle.

Gourlay, chief of communications, drawled: "I got a sort of static in my radio when he wiggled those hairs, Morton. Do you think—"

"Looks very much like it," the leader answered the unfinished question. "That means a job for you, Gourlay. If it speaks by means of radio waves, it might not be altogether impossible that you can create some sort of television picture of its vibrations, or teach him the Morse code."

"Ah," said Siedel. "I was right. The tentacles each develop into seven strong fingers. Provided the nervous system is complicated enough, those fingers could, with training, operate any machine."

Morton said: "I think we'd better go in and have some lunch. Afterward, we've got to get busy. The material men can set up their machines and start gathering data on the planet's metal possibilities, and so on. The others can do a little careful exploring. I'd like some notes on architecture and on scientific development of this race, and particularly what happened to wreck the civilization. On earth civilization after civilization crumbled, but always a new one sprang up in its dust. Why didn't that happen here? Any questions?"

"Yes. What about pussy? Look, he wants to come in with us."

Commander Morton frowned, an action that emphasized the deep-space pallor of his face. "I wish there was some way we could take it in with us, without forcibly capturing it. Kent, what do you think?"

"I think we should first decide whether it's an it or a him, and call it one or the other. I'm in favor of him. As for taking him in with us—" The little chemist shook his head decisively. "Impossible. This atmosphere is twenty-eight percent chlorine. Our oxygen would be pure dynamite to his lungs."

The commander chuckled. "He doesn't believe that, apparently." He watched the catlike monster follow the first two men through the great door. The men kept an anxious distance from him, then glanced at Morton questioningly. Morton waved his hand. "O.K. Open the second lock and let him get a whiff of the oxygen. That'll cure him."

A moment later, he cursed his amazement. "By Heaven, he doesn't even notice the difference! That means he hasn't any lungs, or else the chlorine is not what his lungs use. Let him in! You bet he can go in! Smith, here's a treasure house for a biologist—harmless enough if we're careful. We can always handle him. But what a metabolism!"

Smith, a tall, thin, bony chap with a long, mournful face, said in an oddly forceful voice: "In all our travels, we've found only two higher forms of life. Those dependent on chlorine, and those who need oxygen—the two elements that support combustion. I'm prepared to stake my reputation that no complicated organism could ever adapt itself to both gases in a natural way. At first thought I should say here is an extremely advanced form of life. This race long ago discovered truths of biology that we are just beginning to suspect. Morton, we mustn't let this creature get away if we can help it."

"If his anxiety to get inside is any criterion," Commander Morton laughed, "then our difficulty will be to get rid of him."

He moved into the lock with Coeurl and the two men. The automatic machinery hummed; and in a few minutes they were standing at the bottom of a series of elevators that led up to the living quarters.

"Does that go up?" One of the men flicked a thumb in the direction of the monster.

"Better send him up alone, if he'll go in."

Coeurl offered no objection, until he heard the door slam behind him; and the closed cage shot upward. He whirled with a savage snarl, his reason swirling into chaos. With one leap, he pounced at the door. The metal bent under his plunge, and the desperate pain maddened him. Now, he was all trapped animal. He smashed at the metal with his paws, bending it like so much tin. He tore great bars loose with his thick tentacles. The machinery screeched; there were horrible jerks as the limitless power pulled the cage along in spite of projecting pieces of metal that scraped the outside walls. And then the cage stopped, and he snatched off the rest of the door and hurtled into the corridor.

He waited there until Morton and the men came up with drawn weapons. "We're fools," Morton said. "We should have shown him how it works. He thought we'd double-crossed him."

He motioned to the monster, and saw the savage glow fade from the coal-black eyes as he opened and closed the door with elaborate gestures to show the operation.

Coeurl ended the lesson by trotting into the large room to his right. He lay down on the rugged floor, and fought down the electric tautness of his nerves and muscles. A very fury of

rage against himself for his fright consumed him. It seemed
to his burning brain that he had lost the advantage of appearing a mild and harmless creature. His strength must have
startled and dismayed them.

It meant greater danger in the task which he now knew he
must accomplish: To kill everything in the ship, and take the
machine back to their world in search of unlimited id.

With unwinking eyes, Coeurl lay and watched the two men
clearing away the loose rubble from the metal doorway of the
huge old building. His whole body ached with the hunger of
his cells for id. The craving tore through his palpitant
muscles, and throbbed like a living thing in his brain. His every nerve quivered to be off after the men who had wandered
into the city. One of them, he knew, had gone—alone.

The dragging minutes fled; and still he restrained himself,
still he lay there watching, aware that the men knew he
watched. They floated a metal machine from the ship to the
rock mass that blocked the great half-open door, under the
direction of a third man. No flicker of their fingers escaped
his fierce stare, and slowly, as the simplicity of the machinery
became apparent to him, contempt grew upon him.

He knew what to expect finally, when the flame flared in
incandescent violence and ate ravenously at the hard rock
beneath. But in spite of his preknowledge, he deliberately
jumped and snarled as if in fear, as that white heat burst
forth. His ear tendrils caught the laughter of the men, their
curious pleasure at his simulated dismay.

The door was released, and Morton came over and went
inside with the third man. The latter shook his head.

"It's a shambles. You can catch the drift of the stuff. Obviously, they used atomic energy, but . . . but it's in wheel
form. That's a peculiar development. In our science, atomic
energy brought in the nonwheel machine. It's possible that
here they've progressed—*further* to a new type of wheel
mechanics. I hope their libraries are better preserved than
this, or we'll never know. What could have happened to a
civilization to make it vanish like this?"

A third voice broke through the communicators: "This is
Siedel. I heard your question, Pennons. Psychologically and
sociologically speaking, the only reason why a territory becomes uninhabited is lack of food."

"But they're so advanced scientifically, why didn't they develop space flying and go elsewhere for their food?"

"Ask Gunlie Lester," interjected Morton. "I heard him expounding some theory even before we landed."

The astronomer answered the first call. "I've still got to verify all my facts, but this desolate world is the only planet revolving around that miserable red sun. There's nothing else. No moon, not even a planetoid. And the nearest star system is *nine hundred light-years* away.

"So tremendous would have been the problem of the ruling race of this world, that in one jump they would not only have had to solve interplanetary but interstellar space traveling. When you consider how slow our own development was—first the moon, then Venus—each success leading to the next, and after centuries to the nearest stars; and last of all to the anti-accelerators that permitted galactic travel. Considering all this, I maintain it would be impossible for any race to create such machines without practical experience. And, with the nearest star so far away, they had no incentive for the space adventuring that makes for experience."

Coeurl was trotting briskly over to another group. But now, in the driving appetite that consumed him, and in the frenzy of his high scorn, he paid no attention to what they were doing. Memories of past knowledge, jarred into activity by what he had seen, flowed into his consciousness in an ever developing and more vivid stream.

From group to group he sped, a nervous dynamo—jumpy, sick with his awful hunger. A little car rolled up, stopping in front of him, and a formidable camera whirred as it took a picture of him. Over on a mound of rock, a gigantic telescope was rearing up toward the sky. Nearby, a disintergrating machine drilled its searing fire into an ever-deepening hole, down and down, straight down.

Coeurl's mind became a blur of things he watched with half attention. And ever more imminent grew the moment when he knew he could no longer carry on the torture of acting. His brain strained with an irresistible impatience; his body burned with the fury of his eagerness to be off after the man who had gone alone into the city.

He could stand it no longer. A green foam misted his mouth, maddening him, he saw that, for the bare moment, nobody was looking.

Like a shot from a gun, he was off. He floated along in great, gliding leaps, a shadow among the shadows of the rocks. In a minute, the harsh terrain hid the spaceship and the two-legged beings.

Coeurl forgot the ship, forgot everything but his purpose, as if his brain had been wiped clear by a magic, memory-erasing brush. He circled widely, then raced into the city, along deserted streets, taking short cuts with the ease of familiarity, through gaping holes in time-weakened walls, through long corridors of moldering buildings. He slowed to a crouching lope as his ear tendrils caught the id vibrations.

Suddenly, he stopped and peered from a scatter of fallen rock. The man was standing at what must once have been a window, sending the glaring rays of his flashlight into the gloomy interior. The flashlight clicked off. The man, a heavy-set, powerful fellow, walked off with quick, alert steps. Coeurl didn't like that alertness. It presaged trouble; it meant lightning reaction to danger.

Coeurl waited till the human being had vanished around a corner, then he padded into the open. He was running now, tremendously faster than a man could walk, because his plan was clear in his brain. Like a wraith, he slipped down the next street, past a long block of buildings. He turned the first corner at top speed; and then, with dragging belly, crept into the hall-darkness between the building and a huge chunk of débris. The street ahead was barred by a solid line of loose rubble that made it like a valley, ending in a narrow, bottle-like neck. The neck had its outlet just below Coeurl.

His ear tendrils caught the log-frequency waves of whistling. The sound throbbed through his being; and suddenly terror caught with icy fingers at his brain. The man would have a gun. Suppose he leveled one burst of atomic energy—*one burst*—before his own muscles would whip out in murder fury.

A little shower of rocks streamed past. And then the man was beneath him. Coeurl reached out and struck a single crushing blow at the shimmering transparent headpiece of the spacesuit. There was a tearing sound of metal and a gushing of blood. The man doubled up as if part of him had been telescoped. For a moment, his bones and legs and muscles combined miraculously to keep him standing. Then he crumpled with a metallic clank of his space armor.

Fear completely evaporated, Coeurl leaped out of hiding. With ravenous speed, he smashed the metal and the body within it to bits. Great chunks of metal, torn piecemeal from the suit, sprayed the ground. Bones cracked. Flesh crunched.

It was simple to tune in on the virbrations of the id, and to create the violent chemical disorganization that freed it from the crushed bone. The id was, Coeurl discovered, mostly in the bone.

He felt revived, almost reborn. Here was more food than he had had in the whole past year.

Three minutes, and it was over, and Coeurl was off like a thing fleeing dire danger. Cautiously, he approached the glistening globe from the opposite side to that by which he had left. The men were all busy at their tasks. Gliding noiselessly, Coeurl slipped unnoticed up to a group of men.

Morton stared down at the horror of tattered flesh, metal and blood on the rock at his feet, and felt a tightening in his throat that prevented speech. He heard Kent say:

"He *would* go alone, damn him!" The little chemist's voice held a sob imprisoned; and Morton remembered that Kent and Jarvey had chummed together for years in the way only two men can.

"The worst part of it is," shuddered one of the men, "it looks like a senseless murder. His body is spread out like little lumps of flattened jelly, but it seems to be all there. I'd almost wager that if we weighed everything here, there'd still be one hundred and seventy-five pounds by earth gravity. That'd be about one hundred and seventy pounds here."

Smith broke in, his mournful face lined with gloom: "The killer attacked Jarvey, and then discovered his flesh was alien—uneatable. Just like our big cat. Wouldn't eat anything we set before him—" His words died out in sudden, queer silence. Then he said slowly: "Say, what about that creature? He's big enough and strong enough to have done this with his own little paws."

Morton frowned. "It's a thought. After all, he's the only living thing we've seen. We can't just execute him on suspicion, of course—"

"Besides," said one of the men, "he was never out of my sight."

Before Morton could speak, Siedel, the psychologist, snapped, "Positive about that?"

The man hesitated. "Maybe he was for a few minutes. He was wandering around so much, looking at everything."

"Exactly," said Siedel with satisfaction. He turned to Morton. "You see, commander, I, too, had the impression that he was always around; and yet, thinking back over it, I find gaps. There were moments—probably long minutes—when he was completely out of sight."

Morton's face was dark with thought, as Kent broke in fiercely: "I say, take no chances. Kill the brute on suspicion before he does any more damage."

Morton said slowly: "Korita, you've been wandering around with Cranessy and Van Horne. Do you think pussy is a descendant of the ruling class of this planet?"

The tall Japanese archeologist stared at the sky as if collecting his mind. "Commander Morton," he said finally, respectfully, "there is a mystery here. Take a look, all of you, at that majestic skyline. Notice the almost Gothic outline of the architecture. In spite of the magalopolis which they created, these people were close to the soil. The buildings are not simply ornamented. They are ornamental in themselves. Here is the equivalent of the Doric column, the Egyptian pyramid, the Gothic cathedral, growing out of the ground, earnest, big with destiny. If this lonely, desolate world can be regarded as a mother earth, then the land had a warm, a spiritual place in the hearts of the race.

"The effect is emphasized by the winding streets. Their machines prove they were mathematicians, but they were artists first; and so they did not create the geometrically designed cities of the ultra-sophisticated world metropolis. There is a genuine artistic abandon, a deep joyous emotion written in the curving and unmathematical arrangements of houses, buildings and avenues; a sense of intensity, of divine belief in an inner certainty. This is not a decadent, hoary-with-age civilization, but a young and vigorous culture, confident, strong with purpose.

"There it ended. Abruptly, as if at this point culture had its Battle of Tours, and began to collapse like the ancient Mohammedan civilization. Or as if in one leap it spanned the centuries and entered the period of contending states. In the Chinese civilization that period occupied 480–230 B.C., at the end of which the State of Tsin saw the beginning of the Chinese Empire. This phase Egypt experienced between 1780–1580 B.C., of which the last century was the 'Hyksos'—unmentionable—time. The classical experienced it from Chæronea—338—and, at the pitch of horror, from the Gracchi—133—to Actium—31 B.C. The West European Americans were devastated by it in the nineteenth and twentieth centuries, and modern historians agree that, nominally, we entered the same phase fifty years ago; though, of course, we have solved the problem.

"You may ask, commander, what has all this to do with

your question? My answer is: there is no record of a culture entering abruptly into the period of contending states. It is always a slow development; and the first step is a merciless questioning of all that was once held sacred. Inner certainties cease to exist, are dissolved before the ruthless probings of scientific and analytic minds. The skeptic becomes the highest type of being.

"I say that this culture ended abruptly in its most flourishing age. The sociological effects of such a catastrophe would be a sudden vanishing of morals, a reversion to almost bestial criminality, unleavened by any sense of ideal, a callous indifference to death. If this . . . this pussy is a descendant of such a race, then he will be a cunning creature, a thief in the night, a cold-blooded murderer, who would cut his own brother's throat for gain."

"That's enough!" It was Kent's clipped voice. "Commander, I'm willing to act the rôle of executioner."

Smith interrupted sharply: "Listen, Morton, you're not going to kill that cat yet, even if he is guilty. He's a biological treasure house."

Kent and Smith were glaring angrily at each other. Morton frowned at them thoughtfully, then said: "Korita, I'm inclined to accept your theory as a working basis. But one question: Pussy comes from a period earlier than our own? That is, we are entering the highly civilized era of our culture, while he became suddenly historyless in the most vigorous period of his. *But* is it possible that his culture is a later one on this planet than ours is in the galactic-wide system we have civilized?"

"Exactly. His may be the middle of the tenth civilization of his world; while ours is the end of the eighth sprung from earth, each of the ten, of course, having been builded on the the ruins of the one before it."

"In that case, pussy would not know anything about the skepticism that made it possible for us to find him out so positively as a criminal and murderer?"

"No; it would be literally magic to him."

Morton was smiling grimly. "Then I think you'll get your wish, Smith. We'll let pussy live; and if there are any fatalities, now that we know him, it will be due to rank carelessness. There's just the chance, of course, that we're wrong. Like Siedel, I also have the impression that he was always around. But now—we can't leave poor Jarvey here like this. We'll put him in a coffin and bury him."

"No, we won't!" Kent barked. He flushed. "I beg your pardon, commander. I didn't mean it that way. I maintain pussy wanted something from that body. It looks to be all there, but something must be missing. I'm going to find out what, and pin this murder on him so that you'll have to believe it beyond the shadow of a doubt."

It was late night when Morton looked up from the book and saw Kent emerge through the door that led from the laboratories below.

Kent carried a large, flat bowl in his hands; his tired eyes flashed across at Morton, and he said in a weary, yet harsh, voice: "Now watch!"

He started toward Coeurl, who lay sprawled on the great rug, pretending to be asleep.

Morton stopped him. "Wait a minute, Kent. Any other time, I wouldn't question your actions, but you look ill; you're overwrought. What have you got there?"

Kent turned, and Morton saw that his first impression had been but a flashing glimpse of the truth. There were dark pouches under the little chemist's gray eyes—eyes that gazed feverishly from sunken cheeks in an ascetic face.

"I've found the missing element," Kent said. "It's phosphorus. There wasn't so much as a square millimeter of phosphorus left in Jarvey's bones. Every bit of it had been drained out—by what superchemistry I don't know. There are ways of getting phosphorus out of the human body. For instance, a quick way was what happened to the workman who helped build this ship. Remember, he fell into fifteen tons of molten metalite—at least, so his relatives claimed—but the company wouldn't pay compensation until the metalite, on analysis, was found to contain a high percentage of phosphorus—"

"What about the bowl of food?" somebody interrupted. Men were putting away magazines and books, looking up with interest.

"It's got organic phosphorus in it. He'll get the scent, or whatever it is that he uses instead of scent—"

"I think he gets vibrations of things," Gourlay interjected lazily. "Sometimes, when he wiggles those tendrils, I get a distinct static on the radio. And then, again, there's no reaction, just as if he's moved higher or lower on the wave scale. He seems to control the vibrations at will."

Kent waited with obvious impatience until Gourlay's last

word, then abruptly went on: "All right, then, when he gets the vibration of the phosphorus and reacts to it like an animal, then—well, we can decide what we've proved by his reaction. Can I go ahead, Morton?"

"There are three things wrong with your plan," Morton said. "In the first place, you seem to assume that he is only animal; you seem to have forgotten he may not be hungry after Jarvey; you seem to think that he will not be suspicious. But set the bowl down. His reaction may tell us something."

Coeurl stared with unblinking black eyes as the man set the bowl before him. His ear tendrils instantly caught the id-vibrations from the contents of the bowl—and he gave it not even a second glance.

He recognized this two-legged being as the one who had held the weapon that morning. Danger! With a snarl, he floated to his feet. He caught the bowl with the fingerlike appendages at the end of one looping tentacle, and emptied its contents into the face of Kent, who shrank back with a yell.

Explosively, Coeurl flung the bowl aside and snapped a hawser-thick tentacle around the cursing man's waist. He didn't bother with the gun that hung from Kent's belt. It was only a vibration gun, he sensed—atomic powered, but not an atomic disintegrator. He tossed the kicking Kent onto the nearest couch—and realized with a hiss of dismay that he should have disarmed the man.

Not that the gun was dangerous—but, as the man furiously wiped the gruel from his face with one hand, he reached with the other for his weapon. Coeurl crouched back as the gun was raised slowly and a white beam of flame was discharged at his massive head.

His ear tendrils hummed as they canceled the efforts of the vibration gun. His round, black eyes narrowed as he caught the movement of men reaching for their metalite guns. Morton's voice lashed across the silence.

"Stop!"

Kent clicked off his weapon; and Coeurl crouched down, quivering with fury at this man who had forced him to reveal something of his power.

"Kent," said Morton coldly, "you're not the type to lose your head. You deliberately tried to kill pussy, knowing that the majority of us are in favor of keeping him alive. You know what our rule is: If anyone objects to my decisions, he must say so *at the time*. If the majority object, my decisions are overruled. In this case, no one but you objected, and, therefore, your action in taking the law into your own hands is most reprehensible, and automatically debars you from voting for a year."

Kent stared grimly at the circle of faces. "Korita was right when he said ours was a highly civilized age. It's decadent." Passion flamed harshly in his voice. "My God, isn't there a man here who can see the horror of the situation? Jarvey dead only a few hours, and this creature, whom we all know to be guilty, lying there unchained, planning his next murder; and the victim is right here in this room. What kind of men are we—fools, cynics, ghouls—or is it that our civilization is so steeped in reason that we can contemplate a murderer sympathetically?"

He fixed brooding eyes on Coeurl. "You were right, Morton, that's no animal. That's a devil from the deepest hell of this forgotten planet, whirling its solitary way around a dying sun."

"Don't go melodramatic on us," Morton said. "Your analysis is all wrong, so far as I am concerned. We're not ghouls or cynics; we're simply scientists, and pussy here is going to be studied. Now that we suspect him, we doubt his ability to trap any of us. One against a hundred hasn't a chance." He glanced around. "Do I speak for all of us?"

"Not for me, commander!" It was Smith who spoke, and, as Morton stared in amazement, he continued: "In the excitement and momentary confusion, no one seems to have noticed that when Kent fired his vibration gun, the beam hit this creature squarely on his cat head—and didn't hurt him."

Morton's amazed glance went from Smith to Coeurl, and back to Smith again. "Are you certain it hit him? As you say, it all happened so swiftly—when pussy wasn't hurt I simply assumed that Kent had missed him."

"He hit him in the face," Smith said positively. "A vibration gun, of course, can't even kill a man right away—but it can injure him. There's no sign of injury on pussy, though, not even a singed hair."

"Perhaps his skin is a good insulation against heat of any kind."

"Perhaps. But in view of our uncertainty, I think we should lock him up in the cage."

While Morton frowned darkly in thought, Kent spoke up. "Now you're talking sense, Smith."

Morton asked: "Then you would be satisfied, Kent, if we put him in the cage?"

Kent considered, finally: "Yes. If four inches of microsteel can't hold him, we'd better give him the ship."

Coeurl followed the men as they went out into the corridor. He trotted docilely along as Morton unmistakably motioned him through a door he had not hitherto seen. He found himself in a square, solid metal room. The door clanged metallically behind him; he felt the flow of power as the electric lock clicked home.

His lips parted in a grimace of hate, as he realized the trap, but he gave no other outward reaction. It occurred to him that he had progressed a long way from the sunk-into-primitiveness creature who, a few hours before, had gone incoherent with fear in an elevator cage. Now, a thousand memories of his powers were reawakened in his brain; ten thousand cunnings were, after ages of disuse, once again part of his very being.

He sat quite still for a moment on the short, heavy haunches into which his body tapered, his ear tendrils examining his surroundings. Finally, he lay down, his eyes glowing with contemptuous fire. The fools! The poor fools!

It was about an hour later when he heard the man—Smith—fumbling overhead. Vibrations poured upon him, and for just an instant he was startled. He leaped to his feet in pure terror—and then realized that the vibrations *were* vibrations, not atomic explosions. Somebody was taking pictures of the inside of his body.

He crouched down again, but his ear tendrils vibrated, and he thought contemptuously: the silly fool would be surprised when he tried to develop those pictures.

After a while the man went away, and for a long time there were noises of men doing things far away. That, too, died away slowly.

Coeurl lay waiting, as he felt the silence creep over the ship. In the long ago, before the dawn of immortality, the coeurls, too, had slept at night; and the memory of it had been revived the day before when he saw some of the men dozing. At last, the vibration of two pairs of feet, pacing, pacing endlessly, was the only human-made frequency that throbbed on his ear tendrils.

Tensely, he listened to the two watchmen. The first one walked slowly past the cage door. Then about thirty feet behind him came the second. Coeurl sensed the alertness of these men; knew that he could never surprise either while they walked separately. It meant—he must be doubly careful!

Fifteen minutes, and they came again. The moment they were past, he switched his senses from their vibrations to a vastly higher range. The pulsating violence of the atomic engines stammered its soft story to his brain. The electric dynamos hummed their muffled song of pure power. He felt the whisper of that flow through the wires in the walls of his cage, and through the electric lock of his door. He forced his quivering body into straining immobility, his senses seeking, searching to tune in on that sibilant tempest of energy. Suddenly, his ear tendrils vibrated in harmony—he caught the surging change into shrillness of that rippling force wave.

There was a sharp click of metal on metal. With a gentle touch of one tentacle, Coeurl pushed open the door, and glided out into the dully gleaming corridor. For just a moment, he felt contempt, a glow of superiority, as he thought of the stupid creatures who dared to match their wit against a coeurl. And in that moment, he suddenly thought of other coeurls. A queer, exultant sense of race pounded through his being; the driving hate of centuries of ruthless competition yielded reluctantly before pride of kinship with the future rulers of all space.

Suddenly, he felt weighed down by his limitations, his need for other coeurls, his aloneness—one against a hundred, with the stake all eternity; the starry universe itself beckoned his rapacious, vaulting ambition. If he failed, there would never be a second chance—no time to revive long-rotted machinery, and attempt to solve the secret of space travel.

He padded along on tensed paws—through the salon—into the next corridor—and came to the first bedroom door. It stood half open. One swift flow of synchronized muscles, one swiftly lashing tentacle that caught the unresisting throat of the sleeping man, crushing it; and the lifeless head rolled crazily, the body twitched once.

Seven bedrooms; seven dead men. It was the seventh taste of murder that brought a sudden return of lust, a pure, unbounded desire to kill, return of a millennium-old habit of destroying everything containing the precious id.

As the twelfth man slipped convulsively into death, Coeurl emerged abruptly from the sensuous joy of the kill to the sound of footsteps.

They were not near—that was what brought wave after wave of fright swirling into the chaos that suddenly became his brain.

The watchmen were coming slowly along the corridor

toward the door of the cage where he had been imprisoned. In a moment, the first man would see the open door—and sound the alarm.

Coeurl caught at the vanishing remnants of his reason. With frantic speed, careless now of accidental sounds, he raced—along the corridor with its bedroom doors—through the salon. He emerged into the next corridor, cringing in awful anticipation of the atomic flame he expected would stab into his face.

The two men were together, standing side by side. For one single instant, Coeurl could scarcely believe his tremendous good luck. Like a fool the second had come running when he saw the other stop before the open door. They looked up, paralyzed, before the nightmare of claws and tentacles, the ferocious cat head and hate-filled eyes.

The first man went for his gun, but the second, physically frozen before the doom he saw, uttered a shriek, a shrill cry of horror that floated along the corridors—and ended in a curious gurgle, as Coeurl flung the two corpses with one irresistible motion the full length of the corridor. He didn't want the dead bodies found near the cage. That was his one hope.

Shaking in every nerve and muscle, conscious of the terrible error he had made, unable to think coherently, he plunged into the cage. The door clicked softly shut behind him. Power flowed once more through the electric lock.

He crouched tensely, simulating sleep, as he heard the rush of many feet, caught the vibration of excited voices. He knew when somebody actuated the cage audioscope and looked in. A few moments now, and the other bodies would be discovered.

"Siedel gone!" Morton said numbly. "What are we going to do without Siedel? And Breckenridge! And Coulter and—Horrible!"

He covered his face with his hands, but only for an instant. He looked up grimly, his heavy chin outthrust as he stared into the stern faces that surrounded him. "If anybody's got so much as a germ of an idea, bring it out."

"Space madness!"

"I've thought of that. But there hasn't been a case of a man going mad for fifty years. Dr. Eggert will test everybody, of course, and right now he's looking at the bodies with that possibility in mind."

As he finished, he saw the doctor coming through the door. Men crowded aside to make way for him.

"I heard you, commander," Dr. Eggert said, "and I think I can say right now that the space-madness theory is out. The throats of these men have been squeezed to a jelly. No human being could have exerted such enormous strength without using a machine."

Morton saw that the doctor's eyes kept looking down the corridor, and he shook his head and groaned:

"It's no use suspecting pussy, doctor. He's in his cage, pacing up and down. Obviously heard the racket and—Man alive! You can't suspect him. That cage was built to hold literally *anything*—four inches of micro-steel—and there's not a scratch on the door. Kent, even you won't say, 'Kill him on suspicion,' because there can't be any suspicion, unless there's a new science here. Beyond anything we can imagine—"

"On the contrary," said Smith flatly, "we have all the evidence we need. I used the telefluor on him—you know the arrangement we have on top of the cage—and tried to take some pictures. They just blurred. Pussy jumped when the telefluor was turned on, as if he felt the vibrations.

"You all know what Gourlay said before? This beast can apparently receive and send vibrations of any lengths. The way he dominated the power of Kent's gun is final proof of his special ability to interfere with energy."

"What in the name of all the hells have. you got here?" One of the men groaned. "Why, if he can control that power, and send it out in any vibrations, there's nothing to stop him killing all of us."

"Which proves," snapped Morton, "that he isn't invincible, or he would have done it long ago."

Very deliberately, he walked over to the mechanism that controlled the prison cage.

"You're not going to open the door!" Ken gasped, reaching for his gun.

"No, but if I pull this switch, electricity will flow through the floor, and electrocute whatever's inside. We've never had to use this before, so you had probably forgotten about it."

He jerked the switch hard over. Blue fire flashed from the metal, and a bank of fuses above his head exploded with a single bang.

Morton frowned. "That's funny. Those fuses shouldn't have blown! Well, we can't even look in, now. That wrecked the audios, too."

Smith said: "If he could interfere with the electric lock, enough to open the door, then he probably probed every possible danger and was ready to interfere when you threw that switch."

"At least, it proves he's vulnerable to our energies!" Morton smiled grimly. "Because he rendered them harmless. The important thing is, we've got him behind four inches of the toughest of metal. At the worst we can open the door and ray him to death. But first, I think we'll try to use the telefluor power cable—"

A commotion from inside the cage interrupted his words. A heavy body crushed against a wall, followed by a dull thump.

"He knows what we were trying to do!" Smith grunted to Morton. "And I'll bet it's a very sick pussy in there. What a fool he was to go back into the cage and does he realize it!"

The tension was relaxing; men were smiling nervously, and there was even a ripple of humorless laughter at the picture Smith drew of the monster's discomfiture.

"What I'd like to know," said Pennons, the engineer, "is, why did the telefluor meter dial jump and waver at full power when pussy made that noise? It's right under my nose here, and the dial jumped like a house afire!"

There was silence both without and within the cage, then Morton said: "It may mean he's coming out. Back, everybody, and keep your guns ready. Pussy was a fool to think he could conquer a hundred men, but he's by far the most formidable creature in the galactic system. He may come out of that door, rather than die like a rat in a trap. And he's just tough enough to take some of us with him—if we're not careful."

The men backed slowly in a solid body; and somebody said: "That's funny. I thought I heard the elevator."

"Elevator!" Morton echoed. "Are you sure, man?"

"Just for a moment I was!" The man, a member of the crew, hesitated. "We were all shuffling our feet—"

"Take somebody with you, and go look. Bring whoever dared to run off back here—"

There was a jar, a horrible jerk, as the whole gigantic body of the ship careened under them. Morton was flung to the floor with a violence that stunned him. He fought back to consciousness, aware of the other men lying all around him. He shouted: "Who the devil started those engines!"

The agonizing acceleration continued; his feet dragged with awful exertion, as he fumbled with the nearest audioscope, and punched the engine-room number. The picture that flooded onto the screen brought a deep bellow to his lips:

"It's pussy! He's in the engine room—and we're heading straight out into space."

The screen went black even as he spoke, and he could see no more.

It was Morton who first staggered across the salon floor to the supply room where the spacesuits were kept. After fumbling almost blindly into his own suit, he cut the effects of the body-torturing acceleration, and brought suits to the semi-conscious men on the floor. In a few moments, other men were assisting him; and then it was only a matter of minutes before everybody was clad in metalite, with antiacceleration motors running at half power.

It was Morton then who, after first looking into the cage, opened the door and stood, silent as the others crowded about him, to stare at the gaping hole in the real wall. The hole was a frightful thing of jagged edges and horribly bent metal, and it opened upon another corridor.

"I'll swear," whispered Pennons, "that it's impossible. The ten-ton hammer in the machine shops couldn't more than dent four inches of micro with one blow—and we only heard one. It would take at least a minute for an atomic disintegrator to do the job. Morton, this is a super-being."

Morton saw that Smith was examining the break in the wall. The biologist looked up. "If only Breckenridge weren't dead! We need a metallurgist to explain this. Look!"

He touched the broken edge of the metal. A piece crumbled in his finger and slithered away in a fine shower of dust to the floor. Morton noticed for the first time that there was a little pile of metallic débris and dust.

"You've hit it." Morton nodded. "No miracle of strength here. The monster merely used his special powers to interfere with the electronic tensions holding the metal together. That would account, too, for the drain on the telefluor power cable that Pennons noticed. The thing used the power with his body as a transforming medium, smashed through the wall, ran down the corridor to the elevator shaft, and so down to the engine room."

"In the meantime, commander," Kent said quietly, "we are faced with a super-being in control of the ship, completely dominating the engine room, and its almost unlimited power, and in possession of the best part of the machine shops."

Morton felt the silence, while the men pondered the chemist's words. Their anxiety was a tangible thing that lay heavily upon their faces; in every expression was the growing realization that here was the ultimate situation in their lives; their **very** existence was at stake, and perhaps much more. Morton voiced the thought in everybody's mind:

"Suppose he wins. He's utterly ruthless, and he probably sees galactic power within his grasp."

"Kent is wrong," barked the chief navigator. "The thing doesn't dominate the engine room. We've still got the control room, and that gives us, *first* control of all the machines. You fellows may not know the mechanical set-up we have; but though he can eventually disconnect us, we can cut off all the switches in the engine room *now*. Commander, why didn't you just shut off the power instead of putting us into spacesuits? At the very least you could have adjusted the ship to the acceleration."

"For two reasons," Morton answered. "Individually, we're safer within the force fields of our spacesuits. And we can't afford to give up our advantages in panicky moves."

"Advantages. What other advantages have we got?"

"We know things about him," Morton replied. "And right now, we're going to make a test. Pennons, detail five men to each of the four approaches to the engine room. Take atomic disintegrators to blast through the big doors. They're all shut, I noticed. He's locked himself in.

"Selenski, you go up to the control room and shut off everything except the drive engines. Gear them to the master switch, and shut them off all at once. One thing though— leave the acceleration on full blast. No anti-acceleration must be applied to the ship. Understand?"

"Aye, sir!" The pilot saluted.

"And report to me through the communicators if any of the machines start to run again." He faced the men. "I'm going to lead the main approach. Kent, you take No. 2; Smith, No. 3, and Pennons, No. 4. We're going to find out right now if we're dealing with unlimited science, or a creature limited like the rest of us. I'll bet on the last possibility."

Morton had an empty sense of walking endlessly, as he moved, a giant of a man in his transparent space armor, along the glistening metal tube that was the main corridor of the engine-room floor. Reason told him the creature had already shown feet of clay, yet the feeling that here was an invincible being persisted.

He spoke into the communicator: "It's no use trying to sneak up on him. He can probably hear a pin drop. So just wheel up your units. He hasn't been in that engine room long enough to do anything."

"As I've said, this is largely a test attack. In the first place, we could never forgive ourselves if we didn't try to conquer him now, before he's had time to prepare against us. But, aside from the possibility that we can destroy him immediately, I have a theory.

"The idea goes something like this: Those doors are built to withstand accidental atomic explosions, and it will take fifteen minutes for the atomic disintegrators to smash them. During that period the monster will have no power. True, the drive will be on, but that's straight atomic explosion. My theory is, he can't touch stuff like that; and in a few minutes you'll see what I mean—I hope."

His voice was suddenly crisp: "Ready, Selenski?"

"Aye, ready."

"Then cut the master switch."

The corridor—the whole ship, Morton knew—was abruptly plunged into darkness. Morton clicked on the dazzling light of his spacesuit; the other men did the same, their faces pale and drawn.

"Blast!" Morton barked into his communicator.

The mobile units throbbed; and then pure atomic flame ravened out and poured upon the hard metal of the door. The first molten droplet rolled reluctantly, not down, but up the door. The second was more normal. It followed a shaky downward course. The third rolled sideways—for this was pure force, not subject to gravitation. Other drops followed until a dozen streams trickled sedately yet unevenly in every direction—streams of hellish, sparkling fire, bright as fairy gems, alive with the coruscating fury of atoms suddenly tortured, and running blindly, crazy with pain.

The minutes ate at time like a slow acid. At last Morton asked huskily:

"Selenski?"

"Nothing yet, commander."

Morton half whispered: "But he must be doing something. He can't be just waiting in there like a cornered rat. Selenski?"

"Nothing, commander."

Seven minutes, eight minutes, then twelve.

"Commander!" It was Selenski's voice, taut. "He's got the electric dynamo running."

Morton drew a deep breath, and heard one of his men say:

"That's funny. We can't get any deeper. Boss, take a look at this."

Morton looked. The little scintillating streams had frozen rigid. The ferocity of the disintegrators vented in vain against metal grown suddenly invulnerable.

Morton sighed. "Our test is over. Leave two men guarding every corridor. The others come up to the control room."

He seated himself a few minutes later before the massive control keyboard. "So far as I'm concerned the test was a success. We know that of all the machines in the engine room, the most important to the monster was the electric dynamo. He must have worked in a frenzy of terror while we were at the doors."

"Of course, it's easy to see what he did," Pennons said. "Once he had the power he increased the electronic tensions of the door to their ultimate."

"The main thing is this," Smith chimed in. "He works with vibrations only so far as his special powers are concerned, and the energy must come from outside himself. Atomic energy in its pure form, not being vibration, he can't handle any differently than we can."

Kent said glumly: "The main point in my opinion is that he stopped us cold. What's the good of knowing that his control over vibrations did it? If we can't break through those doors with our atomic disintegrators, we're finished."

Morton shook his head. "Not finished—but we'll have to do some planning. First, though, I'll start these engines. It'll be harder for him to get control of them when they're running."

He pulled the master switch back into place with a jerk. There was a hum, as scores of machines leaped into violent life in the engine room a hundred feet below. The noises sank to a steady vibration of throbbing power.

Three hours later, Morton paced up and down before the men gathered in the salon. His dark hair was uncombed; the space pallor of his strong face emphasized rather than detracted from the outthrust aggressiveness of his jaw. When he spoke, his deep voice was crisp to the point of sharpness:

"To make sure that our plans are fully co-ordinated, I'm going to ask each expert in turn to outline his part in the overpowering of this creature. Pennons first!"

Pennons stood up briskly. He was not a big man, Morton thought, yet he looked big, perhaps because of his air of authority. This man knew engines, and the history of engines. Morton had heard him trace a machine through its evolution from a simple toy to the highly complicated modern instrument. He had studied machine development on a hundred planets; and there was literally nothing fundamental that he didn't know about mechanics. It was almost weird to hear Pennons, who could have spoken for a thousand hours and still only have touched upon his subject, say with absurd brevity:

"We've set up a relay in the control room to start and stop every engine rhythmically. The trip lever will work a hundred times a second, and the effect will be to create vibrations of every description. There is just a possibility that one or more of the machines will burst, on the principle of soldiers crossing a bridge in step—you've heard that old story, no doubt—but in my opinion there is no real danger of a break of that tough metal. The main purpose is simply to interfere with the interference of the creature, and smash through the doors."

"Gourlay next!" barked Morton.

Gourlay climbed lazily to his feet. He looked sleepy, as if he was somewhat bored by the whole proceedings, yet Morton knew he loved people to think him lazy, a good-for-nothing slouch, who spent his days in slumber and his nights catching forty winks. His title was chief communication engineer, but his knowledge extended to every vibration field; and he was probably, with the possible exception of Kent, the fastest thinker on the ship. His voice drawled out, and—Morton noted—the very deliberate assurance of it had a soothing effect on the men—anxious faces relaxed, bodies leaned back more restfully:

"Once inside," Gourlay said, "we've rigged up vibration screens of pure force that should stop nearly everything he's got on the ball. They work on the principle of reflection, so that everything he sends will be reflected back to him. In addition, we've got plenty of spare electric energy that we'll just feed him from mobile copper cups. There must be a limit to his capacity for handling power with those insulated nerves of his."

"Selenski!" called Morton.

The chief pilot was already standing, as he had anticipated Morton's call. And that, Morton reflected, was the man. His

nerves had that rocklike steadiness which is the first require-
ment of the master controller of a great ship's movements;
yet that very steadiness seemed to rest on dynamite ready to
explode at its owner's volition. He was not a man of great
learning, but he "reacted" to stimuli so fast that he always
seemed to be anticipating.

"The impression I've received of the plan is that it must be
cumulative. Just when the creature thinks that he can't stand
any more, another thing happens to add to his trouble and
confusion. When the uproar's at its height, I'm supposed to
cut in the anti-accelerators. The commander thinks with Gunlie Lester that these creatures will know nothing about anti-
acceleration. It's a development, pure and simple, of the
science of interstellar flight, and couldn't have been developed in any other way. We think when the creature feels
the first effects of the anti-acceleration—you all remember
the caved-in feeling you had the first month—it won't know
what to think or do."

"Korita next."

"I can only offer you encouragement," said the archeologist, "on the basis of my theory that the monster has all the
characteristics of a criminal of the early ages of any civilization, complicated by an apparent reversion to primitiveness.
The suggestion has been made by Smith that his knowledge
of science is puzzling, and could only mean that we are
dealing with an actual inhabitant, not a descendant of the inhabitants of the dead city we visited. This would ascribe a
virtual immortality to our enemy, a possibility which is borne
out by his ability to breathe both oxygen and chlorine—or
neither—but even that makes no difference. He comes from a
certain age in his civilization; and he has sunk so low that his
ideas are mostly memories of that age.

"In spite of all the powers of his body, he lost his head in
the elevator the first morning, until he remembered. He
placed himself in such a position that he was forced to reveal
his special powers against vibrations. He bungled the mass
murders a few hours ago. In fact, his whole record is one of
the low cunning of the primitive, egotistical mind which has
little or no conception of the vast organization with which it
is confronted.

"He is like the ancient German soldier who felt superior to
the elderly Roman scholar, yet the latter was part of a mighty
civilization of which the Germans of that day stood in awe.

"You may suggest that the sack of Rome by the Germans

in later years defeats my argument; however, modern historians agree that the 'sack' was an historical accident, and not history in the true sense of the word. The movement of the 'Sea-peoples' which set in against the Egyptian civilization from 1400 B.C. succeeded only as regards the Cretan island-realm—their mighty expeditions against the Libyan and Phœnician coasts, with the accompaniment of Viking fleets, failed as those of the Huns failed against the Chinese Empire. Rome would have been abandoned in any event. Ancient, glorious Samarra was desolate by the tenth century; Pataliputra, Asoka's great capital, was an immense and completely uninhabited waste of houses when the Chinese traveler Hsinan-tang visited it about A.D. 635.

"We have, then, a primitive, and that primitive is now far out in space, completely outside of his natural habitat. I say, let's go in and win."

One of the men grumbled, as Korita finished: "You can talk about the sack of Rome being an accident, and about this fellow being a primitive, but the facts are facts. It looks to me as if Rome is about to fall again; and it won't be no primitive that did it, either. This guy's got plenty of what it takes."

Morton smiled grimly at the man, a member of the crew. "We'll see about that—right now!"

In the blazing brilliance of the gigantic machine shop, Coeurl slaved. The forty-foot, cigar-shaped spaceship was nearly finished. With a grunt of effort, he completed the laborious installation of the drive engines, and paused to survey his craft.

Its interior, visible through the one aperture in the outer wall, was pitifully small. There was literally room for nothing but the engines—and a narrow space for himself.

He plunged frantically back to work as he heard the approach of the men, and the sudden change in the tempest-like thunder of the engines—a rhythmical off-and-on hum, shriller in tone, sharper, more nerve-racking than the deep-throated, steady throb that had preceded it. Suddenly, there were the atomic disintegrators again at the massive outer doors.

He fought them off, but never wavered from his task. Every mighty muscle of his powerful body strained as he carried great loads of tools, machines and instruments, and dumped them into the bottom of his makeshift ship. There was no time to fit anything into place, no time for anything—no time—no time.

The thought pounded at his reason. He felt strangely weary for the first time in his long and vigorous existence. With a last, tortured heave, he jerked the gigantic sheet of metal into the gaping aperture of the ship—and stood there for a terrible minute, balancing it precariously.

He knew the doors were going down. Half a dozen disintegrators concentrating on one point were irresistibly, though slowly, eating away the remaining inches. With a gasp, he released his mind from the doors and concentrated every ounce of his mind on the yard-thick outer wall, toward which the blunt nose of his ship was pointing.

His body cringed from the surging power that flowed from the electric dynamo through his ear tendrils into that resisting wall. The whole inside of him felt on fire, and he knew that he was dangerously close to carrying his ultimate load.

And still he stood there, shuddering with the awful pain, holding the unfastened metal plate with hard-clenched tentacles. His massive head pointed as in dread fascination at that bitterly hard wall.

He heard one of the engine-room doors crash inward. Men shouted; disintegrators rolled forward, their raging power unchecked. Coeurl heard the floor of the engine room hiss in protest, as those beams of atomic energy tore everything in their path to bits. The machines rolled closer; cautious footsteps sounded behind them. In a minute they would be at the flimsy doors separating the engine room from the machine shop.

Suddenly, Coeurl was satisfied. With a snarl of hate, a vindictive glow of feral eyes, he ducked into his little craft, and pulled the metal plate down into place as if it were a hatchway.

His ear tendrils hummed, as he softened the edges of the surrounding metal. In an instant, the plate was more than welded—it was part of his ship, a seamless, rivetless part of a whole that was solid opaque metal except for two transparent areas, one in the front, one in the rear.

His tentacle embraced the power drive with almost sensuous tenderness. There was a forward surge of his fragile machine, straight at the great outer wall of the machine shops. The nose of the forty-foot craft touched—and the wall dissolved in a glittering shower of dust.

Coeurl felt the barest retarding movement; and then he

kicked the nose of the machine out into the cold of space, twisted it about, and headed back in the direction from which the big ship had been coming all these hours.

Men in space armor stood in the jagged hole that yawned in the lower reaches of the gigantic globe. The men and the great ship grew smaller. Then the men were gone; and there was only the ship with its blaze of a thousand blurring portholes. The ball shrank incredibly, too small now for individual portholes to be visible.

Almost straight ahead, Coeurl saw a tiny, dim, reddish ball—his own sun, he realized. He headed toward it at full speed. There were caves where he would hide and with other coeurls build secretly a spaceship in which they could reach other planets safely—now that he knew how.

His body ached from the agony of acceleration, yet he dared not let up for a single instant. He glanced back, half in terror. The globe was still there, a tiny dot of light in the immense blackness of space. Suddenly it twinkled and was gone.

For a brief moment, he had the empty, frightened impression that just before it disappeared, it moved. But he could see nothing. He could not escape the belief that they had shut off all their lights, and were sneaking up on him in the darkness. Worried and uncertain, he looked through the forward transparent plate.

A tremor of dismay shot through him. The dim red sun toward which he was heading was not growing larger. *It was becoming smaller* by the instant, and it grew visibly tinier during the next five minutes, became a pale-red dot in the sky—and vanished like the ship.

Fear came then, a blinding surge of it, that swept through his being and left him chilled with the sense of the unknown. For minutes, he stared frantically into the space ahead, searching for some landmark. But only the remote stars glimmered there, unwinking points against a velvet background of unfathomable distance.

Wait! One of the points was growing larger. With every muscle and nerve tense, Coeurl watched the point becoming a dot, a round ball of light—red light. Bigger, bigger, it grew. Suddenly, the red light shimmered and turned white—and there, before him, was the great globe of the spaceship, lights glaring from every porthole, the very ship which a few minutes before he had watched vanish behind him.

Something happened to Coeurl in that moment. His brain was spinning like a flywheel, faster, faster, more incoherently.

Suddenly, the wheel flew apart into a million aching fragments. His eyes almost started from their sockets as, like a maddened animal, he raged in his small quarters.

His tentacles clutched at precious instruments and flung them insensately; his paws smashed in fury at the very walls of his ship. Finally, in a brief flash of sanity, he knew that he couldn't face the inevitable fire of atomic disintegrators.

It was a simple thing to create the violent disorganization that freed every drop of id from his vital organs.

They found him lying dead in a little pool of phosphorus.

"Poor pussy," said Morton. "I wonder what he thought when he saw us appear ahead of him, after his own sun disappeared. Knowing nothing of anti-accelerators, he couldn't know that we could stop short in space, whereas it would take him more than three hours to decelerate; and in the meantime he'd be drawing farther and farther away from where he wanted to go. He couldn't know that by stopping, we flashed past him at millions of miles a second. Of course, he didn't have a chance once he left our ship. The whole world must have seemed topsy-turvy."

"Never mind the sympathy," he heard Kent say behind him. "We've got a job to kill every cat in that miserable world."

Korita murmured softly: "That should be simple. They are but primitives; and we have merely to sit down, and they will come to us, cunningly expecting to delude us."

Smith snapped: "You fellows make me sick! Pussy was the toughest nut we ever had to crack. He had everything he needed to defeat us—"

Morton smiled as Korita interrupted blandly: "Exactly, my dear Smith, except that he reacted according to the biological impulses of his type. His defeat was already foreshadowed when we unerringly analyzed him as a criminal from a certain era of his civilization.

"It was history, honorable Mr. Smith, our knowledge of history that defeated him," said the Japanese archeologist, reverting to the ancient politeness of his race.

# GREATER THAN GODS

*Astounding Science Fiction*, July

## by C. L. Moore (1911–      )

*One of the pioneer women science fiction writers,*
*Catherine (the C. L. is dramatic evidence of the*
*then status of women in the field) Moore wrote in*
*collaboration with Henry Kuttner after their mar-*
*riage in 1940. Previously, she was best known for*
*her female fantasy character "Jirel of Jory" who*
*appeared in a series of stories in* Weird Tales, *and*
*the "Northwest Smith" stories in the sf magazines*
*of the thirties. Both series were outstanding, and*
*very popular.*

*"Greater Than Gods" is a non-series story about*
*an alternate future. It is also about choosing, one of*
*the most difficult of all human activities.*

*(Science fiction in the Self-conscious Seventies is*
*as much a female activity, both in the reading and*
*writing, as it is a male activity, but it wasn't always*
*thus. Right through the Golden Age, it was almost*
*entirely masculine. But even in the depth of the*
*male-chauvinist Thirties there were women who*
*dared, successfully, to compete. C. L. Moore was*
*perhaps the best of these, but Leslie F. Stone and*
*A. R. Long were two others. Notice the use of ini-*
*tials and epicene given names to hide the fatal fem-*
*inism of the writers. IA)*

The desk was glass-clear steel, the mirror above it a window
that opened upon distance and sight and sound whenever the

televisor buzzer rang. The two crystal cubes on the desk were three-dimensional photographs of a sort undreamed of before the Twenty-third Century dawned. But between them on the desk lay a letter whose message was older than the history of writing itself.

*"My darling—"* it began in a man's strongly slanting handwriting. But there Bill Cory had laid down his pen and run despairing fingers through his hair, looking from one crystalcubed photograph to the other and swearing a little under his breath. It was fine stuff, he told himself savagely, when a man couldn't even make up his mind which of two girls he wanted to marry. Biology House of Science City, that trusted so faithfully the keenness and clarity of Dr. William Cory's decisions, would have shuddered to see him now.

For the hundredth time that afternoon he looked from one girl's face to the other, smiling at him from the crystal cubes, and chewed his lip unhappily. On his left, in the translucent block that had captured an immortal moment when dark Marta Mayhew smiled, the three-dimensional picture looked out at him with a flash of violet eyes. Dr. Marta Mayhew of Chemistry House, ivory whiteness and satin blackness. Not at all the sort of picture the mind conjures up of a leading chemist in Science City which houses the greatest scientists in the world.

Bill Cory wrinkled his forehead and looked at the other girl. Sallie Carlisle dimpled at him out of the crystal, as real as life itself to the last flying tendril of fair curls that seemed to float on a breeze frozen eternally into glass. Bill reached out to turn the cube a little, bringing the delicate line of her profile into view, and it was as if time stood still in the crystalline deeps and pretty Sallie in the breathing flesh paused for an eternal moment with her profile turned away.

After a long moment Bill Cory sighed and picked up his pen. After the *"darling"* of the letter he wrote firmly, *"Sallie."*

"Dr. Cory," hesitated a voice at the door. Bill looked up, frowning. Miss Brown blinked at him nervously behind her glasses. "Dr. Ashley's—"

"Don't announce me, Brownie," interrupted a languid voice behind her. " I want to catch him loafing. Ah, Bill, writing love letters? May I come in?"

"Could I stop you?" Bill's grin erased the frown from his forehead. The tall and tousled young man in the doorway was Charles Ashley, head of Telepathy House, and though their acquaintance had long been on terms of good-natured insult, behind it lay Bill's deep recognition of a quality of genius in Ashley that few men ever attain. No one could have risen to the leadership of Telepathy House whose mind did not encompass many more levels of infinite understanding than the ordinary mind even recognizes.

"I've worked myself into a stupor," announced the head of Telepathy House, yawning. "Come on up to the Gardens for a swim, huh?"

"Can't." Bill laid down his pen. "I've got to see the pups—"

"Damn the pups! You think Science City quivers every time those little mutts yap! Let Miss Brown look after 'em. She knows more than you do about genetics, anyhow. Some day the Council's going to find it out and you'll go back to working for a living."

"Shut up," requested Bill with a grin. "How are the pups, Miss Brown?"

"Perfectly normal, doctor. I just gave them their three o'clock feeding and they're asleep now."

"Do they seem happy?" inquired Ashley solicitously.

"That's right, scoff," sighed Bill. "Those pups and I will go ringing down the corridors of time, you mark my words."

Ashley nodded, half seriously. He knew it might well be true. The pups were the living proof of Bill's success in prenatal sex determination—six litters of squirming maleness with no female among them. They represented the fruit of long, painstaking experiments in the X-ray bombardment of chromosomes to separate and identify the genes carrying the factors of sex determination, of countless failures and immeasurable patience. If the pups grew into normal dogs— well, it would be one long, sure stride nearer the day when, through Bill's own handiwork, the world would be perfectly balanced between male and female in exact proportion to the changing need.

Miss Brown vanished with a shy, self-effacing smile. As the door closed behind her, Ashley, who had been regarding the two photograph cubes on Bill's desk with a lifted eyebrow, arranged his long length on the couch against the wall and was heard to murmur: "Eenie-meenie-minie-mo. Which is it going to be, Will-yum?"

They were on terms too intimate for Bill to misunderstand, or pretend to.

"I don't know," he admitted miserably, glancing down in some hesitation at the letter beginning, *"My darling Sallie—"*

Ashley yawned again and fumbled for a cigarette. "You know," he murmured comfortably, "it's interesting to speculate on your possible futures. With Marta or Sallie, I mean. Maybe some day somebody will find a way to look ahead down the branching paths of the future and deliberately select the turning points that will carry him toward the goal he chooses. Now if you could know beforehand where life with Sallie would lead, or life with Marta, you might alter the whole course of human history. That is, if you're half as important as you think you are."

"Huh-uh," grunted Bill. "If you predicate a fixed future, then it's fixed already, isn't it? And you'd have no real choice."

Ashley scratched a match deliberately and set his cigarette aglow before he said: "I think of the future as an infinite reservoir of an infinite number of futures, each of them fixed, yet malleable as clay. Do you see what I mean? At every point along our way we confront crossroads at which we make choices among the many possible things we may do the next moment. Each crossroad leads to a different future, all of them possible, all of them fixed, waiting for our choice to give them reality. Perhaps there's a—call it a Plane of Probability—where all these possible results of our possible choices exist simultaneously. Blueprints of things to come. When the physical time of matter catches up with, and fills in, any one particular plan, it becomes fixed in the present.

"But before time has caught up with it, while our choice at the crossroads is still unmade, an infinite number of possible futures must exist as it were in suspension, waiting for us in some unimaginable, dimensionless infinity. Can you imagine what it would be like to open a window upon that Probability Plane, look out into the infinities of the future, trace the consequences of future actions *before* we make them? We could mold the destiny of mankind! We could do what the gods must do, Bill! We'd be greater than gods! We could look into the Cosmic Mind—the very brain that planned us—and of our own will choose among those plans!"

"Wake up, Ash," said Bill softly.

"You think I'm dreaming? It's not a new idea, really. The old philosopher, Berkeley, had a glimpse of it when he taught his theories of subjective idealism, that we're aware of the cosmos only through a greater awareness all around us, an infinite mind—

"Listen, Bill. If you vision these . . . these blueprints of possible futures, you've got to picture countless generations, finite as ourselves, existing simultaneously and completely in all the circumstances of their entire lives—yet all of them still unborn, still even uncertain of birth if the course of the present is diverted from their particular path. To themselves, they must seem as real as we to each other.

"Somewhere on the Plane of Probability, Bill, there may be two diverging lines of your descendants, unborn generations whose very existence hinges on your choice here at the crossroads. Projections of yourself, really, their lives and deaths trembling in the balance. Think well before you choose!"

Bill grinned. "Suppose you go back to the Slum and dope out a way for me to look into the Cosmic Plan," he suggested.

Ashley shook his head.

"Wish I could. Boy, would you eat that word 'Slum' then! Telepathy House wouldn't be the orphan child around the City any longer if I could really open a window onto the Probability Plane. I wouldn't bother with you and your pint-sized problems. I'd look ahead into the future of the City. It's the heart of the world, now. Some day it may rule the world. And we're biased, you know. We can't help being. With all the sciences housed here under one city-wide roof, wielding powers that kings never dreamed of— No, it may go to our heads. We may overbalance into . . . into . . . well, I'd like to look ahead and prevent it. And if this be treason—" He shrugged and got up. "Sure you won't join me?"

"Go on—get out. I'm a busy man."

"So I see." Ashley twitched an eyebrow at the two crystal cubes. "Maybe it's good you can't look ahead. The responsibility of choosing might be heavier than you could bear. After all, we aren't gods and it must be dangerous to usurp a god's prerogative. Well, see you later."

Bill leaned in the doorway watching the lounging figure down the hall toward the landing platform where crystal cars waited to go flashing along the great tubes which artery Science City. Beyond, at the platform's edge, the great central plaza of the City dropped away in a breath-taking void a hundred stories deep. He stood looking out blind-eyed, wondering if Sallie or Marta would walk this hall in years to come.

Life would be more truly companionship with Marta, perhaps. But did a family need two scientists! A man wanted relaxation at home, and who could make life gayer than pretty Sallie with her genius for entertainment, her bubbling laughter? Yes, let it be Sallie. If there were indeed a Probability Plane where other possible futures hung suspended, halfway between waking and oblivion, let them wink out into nothingness.

He shut the door with a little slam to wake himself out of the dream, greeting the crystal-shrined girl on his desk with a smile. She was so real—the breeze blowing those curls was a breeze in motion. The lashes should flutter against the soft fullness of her lids—

Bill squeezed his eyes shut and shook his head to clear it. There was something wrong—the crystal was clouding—

A ringing in his ears grew louder in company with that curious blurring of vision. From infinitely far away, yet strangely in his own ears, a tiny voice came crying. A child's voice calling, "Daddy. . . . daddy!" A girl's voice, coming nearer, "Father—" A woman's voice saying over and over in a smooth, sweet monotone, "Dr. Cory. . . . Dr. William Cory—"

Upon the darkness behind his closed lids a streaked and shifting light moved blurrily. He thought he saw towers in the sun, forests, robed people walking leisurely—and it all seemed to rush away from his closed eyes so bewilderingly— he lifted his lids to stare at—

To stare at the cube where Sallie smiled. Only this was not Sallie. He gaped with the blankness of a man confronting impossibilities. It was not wholly Sallie now, but there was a look of Sallie upon the lovely, sun-touched features in the cube. All of her sweetness and softness, but with it—something more. Something familiar. What upon this living, lovely face, with its level brown eyes and courageous mouth, reminded Bill of—himself?

His hands began to shake a little. He thrust them into his pockets and sat down without once taking his eyes from the living stare in the cube. There was amazement in that other stare, too, and a half-incredulous delight that brightened as he gazed.

Then the sweet curved lips moved—lips with the softness of Sallie's closing on the firm, strong line of Bill's. They said

distinctly, in a sound that might have come from the cube itself or from somewhere deep within his own brain: "Dr.
Cory . . . Dr. Cory, do you hear me?"

"I hear you," he heard himself saying hoarsely, like a man
talking in a dream. "But—"

The face that was Sallie's and his blended blazed into joyful recognition, dimples denting the smooth cheeks with delicious mirth. "Oh, thank Heaven it *is* you! I've reached
through at last. I've tried so hard, so long—"

"But who . . . what—" Bill choked a little on his own
amazement and fell silent, marveling at the strange warm tenderness that was flooding up in him as he watched this familiar face he had never seen before. A tenderness more melting
and protective and passionately selfless than he had ever
imagined a man could feel. Dizzy with complete bewilderment, too confused to wonder if he dreamed, he tried again.
"Who are you? What are you doing here? How did—"

"But I'm not there—not really." The sweet face smiled
again, and Bill's heart swelled until his throat almost closed
with a warmth of pride and tenderness he was too dizzy to
analyze now. "I'm here—here at home in Eden, talking to
you across the millennium! Look—"

Somehow, until then he had not seen beyond her. Sallie's
face had smiled out of a mist of tulle, beyond which the cube
had been crystal-clear. But behind the face which was no
longer wholly Sallie's, a green hillside filled the cube. And,
very strangely, it had no look of smallness. Though the cube's
dimensions confined it, here was no miniature scene he gazed
upon. He looked through the cube as through a window, out
into a forest glade where upon a bank of green myrtle at the
foot of a white garden wall a little group of tanned men and
women reclined in a circle with closed eyes, lying almost like
corpses on the dark, glossy leaves. But there was no relaxation in them. Tensity more of the spirit than the body knit
the group into a whole, focused somehow upon the woman in
the circle's center—this fair-haired woman who leaned forward with her elbows on her knees, chin in hand, staring
brown-eyed and tensely into space—into Bill Cory's eyes.
Dimly he realized that his perception had expanded as he
stared. Awareness now of a whole countryside beyond her,
just over the garden wall, made this cube that had housed
Sallie's careless smile a window indeed, opening upon distance in space and time far outside his imagining.

He knew he was dreaming. He was sure of it, though the memory of what Ashley had been saying hovered uneasily in the back of his mind, too elusive now to be brought consciously into view. But in this impossible dream he clenched his hands hard in his pockets, taking a firm hold upon reality.

"Just who are you, and what do you want? And how did you—"

She chose to answer the last question first, breaking into it as if she could read his thoughts as she knelt staring on the myrtle leaves.

"I speak to you along an unbroken cord between us—father. Thousands of times removed, but—father. A cord that runs back through the lives that have parted us, yet which unite us. With the help of these people around me, their full mental strength supplementing mine, we've established contact at last, after so many failures, so much groping in mysteries which even I understand only partly, though my family for generations has been trained in the secrets of heredity and telepathy."

"But why—"

"Isn't the fact of achievement an end in itself? Success in establishing a two-way contact with the past, in talking to one's own ancestors—do I need more reason for attempting that than the pure joy of achieving it? You wonder why you were chosen. Is that it? Because you are the last man in a direct line of males to be born into my family before the blessed accident that saved the world from itself.

"Don't look so bewildered!" Laughter bubbled from the cube—or was it a sound in his own brain? "You aren't dreaming! Is it so incredible that along the unbroken cord of memories which links your mind to mine the current might run backward against the time flow?"

"But who are you? Your face—it's like—"

"My face is the face of the daughter that Sallie Cory bore you, thousands of years ago. That resemblance is a miracle and a mystery beyond all understanding—the mystery of heredity which is a stranger thing than the fact of our communication. We have wondered among ourselves if immortality itself—but no, I'll have mercy on you!"

This bewilderingly beloved face that had darkened with mystical brooding, flashed suddenly alive again with swift laughter, and hearing it, catching a lift of the brows that was his and a quirk of the soft lips that was Sallie's own, Bill made no effort to stem the tide of warm affection rising higher and higher in him. It was himself looking out of this cube through Sallie's brown eyes—himself exultant in achievement for the simple sake of achieving. She had called him father. Was this a father's love, selfless, unfathomable, for a lovely and beloved daughter?

"Don't wonder any more," laughed the voice in his ears. "Look—here's the past that lies between us. I want you to understand what parts your world from mine."

Softly the myrtle glade and the lovely smiling face that blended Sallie and Bill melted into the depths of a cloud forming inside the three dimensions of the cube. For a moment—nothing. Then motion was lifting behind the mist, shouldering the veils aside. Three-dimensional space seemed to open up all around him—

He saw a wedding procession coming down a church aisle toward him, Sallie smiling mistily through a cloud of silver tulle. And he knew at the sight of her that though it was only chance which had chosen her instead of dark Marta Mayhew, he could come to love Sallie Carlisle Cory with an intensity almost frightening.

He saw time go by with a swiftness like thought itself, events telescoping together with no sense of confusion, moving like memories through his mind, clear, yet condensed into split seconds. He was watching his own future, seeing a life that revolved around Sallie as the center of existence. He saw her flashing in and out of his laboratory as he worked, and whenever she entered, the whole room seemed to light up; whenever she left, he could scarcely work for the longing to follow.

He saw their first quarrel. Sallie, spinning in a shimmer of bright glass-silk as soft as gossamer, dimpled at the self which in this waking dream was more vividly Bill Cory than the Bill who watched. "See, darling, aren't I heavenly?" And he heard himself answering, "Edible, darling! But isn't that stuff expensive?"

Sallie's laughter was light. "Only fifteen hundred credits. That's dirt-cheap for a Skiparelle model."

He gasped. "Why Sallie, that's more than we're allowed for living expenses! I can't—"

"Oh, daddy'll pay for it if you're going to be stingy. I only wanted—"

"I'll buy my wife's clothes." Bill was grim. "But I can't afford Paris fashions, darling."

Sallie's pretty underlip pouted alarmingly. Tears sparkled

in the soft brown eyes she lifted to his, and his heart melted almost painfully in one hopeless rush.

"Don't cry, sweetheart! You can keep it, just this once. But we'll have to make it up next month. Never again, Sallie, understand?"

Her nod was bright and oblivious as a child's.

But they didn't make it up. Sallie loved partying, and Bill loved Sallie, and nowadays there was much more hilarity than work going on behind the door in Biology House marked "Dr. William Vincent Cory." The television's panels were tuned to orchestras playing strong rhythm now, not to lectures and laboratory demonstrations as of old.

No man can do two jobs well. The work on sex determination began to strike snags in the path that had seemed almost clear to success, and Bill had so little time any more to smooth them out. Always Sallie was in the back of his mind, sweet, smiling, adorable.

Sallie wanted the baby to be born in her father's home. It was a lovely place, white-walled on low green hills above the Pacific. Sallie loved it. Even when little Sue was big enough to travel she hated to think of leaving. And the climate was so wonderful for the baby there—

Anyhow, by then the Council had begun to frown over Bill Cory's work. After all, perhaps he wasn't really cut out to be a scientist—Sallie's happiness was more important than any man's job, and Sallie could never be really happy in Science City.

The second baby was a girl, too. There were a lot of girls being born nowadays. The telenews broadcasters joked about it. A good sign, they said. When a preponderance of boys was born, it had always meant war. Girls should bring peace and plenty for the new generation.

Peace and plenty—that was what mattered most to Bill and Sallie Cory now. That and their two exquisite daughters and their home on the green Pacific hills. Young Susan was growing up into a girlhood so enchanting that Bill suffused with pride and tenderness every time he thought of her. She had Sallie's beauty and blondeness, but there was a resolution in her that had been Bill's once, long ago. He liked to think of her, in daydreams, carrying on the work that he would never finish now.

Time ran on, years telescoping pleasantly into uneventful years. Presently the Cory girls were growing up . . . were married . . . were mothers. The grandchildren were girls, too. When Gandfather Cory joined his wife in the little graveyard on the sea-turned hill beyond the house, the Cory name died with him, though there was in his daughter's level eyes and in her daughter's look of serene resolution something more intrinsically Bill Cory than his name. The name might die, but something of the man who had borne it lived on in his descendants.

Girls continued to outnumber boys in the birth records as the generations passed. It was happening all over the world, for no reason that anyone could understand. It didn't matter much, really. Women in public offices were proving very efficient; certainly they governed more peacefully than men. The first woman president won her office on a platform that promised no war so long as a woman dwelt in the White House.

Of course, some things suffered under the matriarchy. Women as a sex are not scientists, not inventors, not mechanics or engineers or architects. There were men enough to keep these essentially masculine arts alive—that is, as much of them as the new world needed. There were many changes. Science City, for instance. Important, of course, but not to the extent of draining the country dry to maintain it. Life went on very nicely without too much machinery.

The tendency was away from centralized living in these new days. Cities spread out instead of up. Skyscrapers were hopelessly old-fashioned. Now parklands and gardens stretched between low-roofed houses where the children played all day. And war was a barbarous memory from those nightmare years when men still ruled the world.

Old Dr. Phillips, head of the dwindling and outmoded Science City, provoked President Wiliston into a really inspiring fury when he criticized the modern tendency toward a non-mechanized rural civilization. It happened on the tele-news, so that half the world heard it.

"But Madam President," he said, "don't you realize where we're heading? The world's going backward! It's no longer worth-while for our best minds to attempt bettering living conditions. We're throwing genius away! Do you realize that your cabinet yesterday flatly rejected the brilliant work of one of our most promising young men?"

"I do!" Alice Wiliston's voice rang with sudden violence over half the world. "That 'brilliant work,' as you call it, was a device that might have led to war! Do you think we want that? Remember the promise that the first woman president made the world, Dr. Phillips! So long as we sit in the White House there will be no need for war!"

And Elizabeth of England nodded in London; Julianna VII smiled into her Amsterdam telenews screen. While women ruled, war was outlawed. Peace and ease, and plenty would dominate civilization, leisure for cultivation of the arts, humankind coming into its own at last, after so many ages of pain and blood and heartbreak.

Years telescoped into centuries of peace and plenty in a garden world. Science had turned its genius to the stabilization of the climate so that nowhere was shelter necessary from cold or storms; food was freely abundant for all. The Garden that Adam and Eve forfeited in the world's beginning had returned again to their remotest descendants, and the whole earth was Eden.

And in this world that no longer demanded the slightest physical effort, mankind was turning to the cultivation of the mind. In these white, low-roofed houses set among garden parks, men and women increasingly adventured into the realms beyond the flesh, exploring the mysteries of the mind.

Bill Cory, leaning forward in his chair, had lost all identity with himself. He was simply a consciousness watching time unfold before him. The gravestone that bore his name on the California hillside had long since sunk into the sod, but if there is immortality at all, Bill Cory watched himself move forward through the centuries, down the long, expanding line of his descendants. Now and again, startlingly, his own face looked briefly at him from some faraway child of his remote grandchildren. His face, and Sallie's.

He saw pretty Sue come and go like reflections in a mirror. Not always Sue unmistakably and completely—sometimes only her brown eyes lighted the face of a many-times-great-granddaughter; sometimes the lift of her smile or the tilt of her pretty nose alone was familiar to him in a strange face. But sometimes Sue herself, perfect to the last detail, moved through the remote future. And every time he saw those familiar features, his heart contracted with an ache of tenderness for the daughter he yet might never have.

It was for these beloved Susans that he was becoming uneasy as he watched time go by in this lazy paradise world. People were slowing mentally and physically. What need any more for haste or trouble? Why worry because certain unimportant knowledge was being lost as time went on? The weather machines, the food machines were eternal; what else really mattered? Let the birth rate decline, let the dwindling race of the inventive and the ambitious fade like the anachronism it was. The body had taken mankind as far as it could; the mind was the vehicle for the future. In the vast reaches of infinity were fields aplenty for the adventurous spirit. Or one could simply drowse the days away—

Clouds thickened softly across the dreamy vistas of Eden. Bill Cory leaned back in his chair and rubbed his eyes with both hands. The hands were shaking, and he stared at them a little stupidly, still half lost in the wonder of what he had seen, in the strange welter of emotions that still warred in him—the memory of Sallie and his strong love for her, the memory of Sue's sweetness, the memory of pride in them both. And in the queer feeling that it had been himself in those many daughters of his through the ages, striving so hard for world peace to the ultimate end that mankind might achieve—*ruin*.

For it was wrong—it was bad. The whole world. The race of man was too splendid, too capable of working miracles, to end on a myrtle bank dreaming about abstractions. He had just seen a decadent, indolent, civilization going down the last incline into oblivion as a result—yes, as a direct result—of his own action. He'd seen himself sinking into a fat, idle old age, without honor of achievement.

Suddenly and desperately he hoped that Ashley had been right—that this was not the inevitable and changeless future. If he tore up the letter lying on his desk now, if he never married Sallie, would not his work be finished successfully some day, and the catastrophe of unbalanced births avoided? Or could a man change his ordained future?

Almost fearfully he reached for the letter lying beside that clouded cube in which the years had mirrored themselves. Would he be able to take the letter up and rip it across—like this? The sound of tearing paper reassured him. So far, at least, he was still a free agent.

And knowing that, suddenly he was sorry. Not to marry Sallie, with her bubbling laugh. Never to see young Sue growing into beauty and courage and sweetness. Old age without achievement, had he said to himself a moment ago? Sue herself was achievement enough for any man. Sue and those other Susans down the long line of his descendants, incarnating again and again all that was finest in him, eternal as life itself through millenniums.

He did not want to meet again the brown eyes of this latest Susan who had come to him in the depths of the cube. While he looked, his reason was lost in his love for her, and not even against reason could he believe the world which had produced her to be anything but perfect, simply because this beloved daughter moved and breathed in it.

But the letter was torn. He would never marry Sallie if he could help himself. The cost was too high, even for such a reward as Sue. And an almost tremulous awe broke over him in a sudden tide as he realized what he was doing. This was what Ashley had dreamed of—opening a window into the Plane of Probability and learning enough to force the Cosmic Mind out of its course. Changing the shape of his own future and that of all mankind. Greater than gods—but he was no god. And Ashley had warned him that it might be dangerous to usurp a god's prerogative. Suddenly he was afraid.

He looked away from that cube which held his future, and across from it on his desk the violet eyes of Marta Mayhew caught his, fixed in their changeless smile. She was a girl, he thought, he remembered from half a lifetime ago, so much had happened since he glanced last into her face. Dark and lovely she was, her eyes meeting his almost as if there were vision behind their deep, long stare. Almost as if—

Light flared out in one white, blinding sheet that blotted out the cube and the violet-eyed face and the room around him. Involuntarily Bill clapped his hands to his eyes, seeing behind the darkness of his lids a dazzle of blurring colors. It had happened too quickly for wonder—he was not even thinking as he opened his eyes and looked into the cube where Marta's gaze had met him a moment before.

And then a great tide of awe and wonder came washing up into his consciousness, and he knew that Ashley had been right. There was an alternative future. There comes a point beyond which bewilderment and shock no longer affect the human brain, and Bill was outside wondering now, or groping for logical explanations. He only knew that he stood here staring into the cube from which Marta's eyes had smiled at him so short an instant ago—

They were still Marta's eyes, deep-colored in a boy face almost Bill's own, feature for feature, under a cap of blue steel. Somehow that other future had come to him, too. He was aware of a sudden urgent wonder *why* they had come so nearly together, though neither could be conscious of the other— But things were moving in the depths of the cube.

Behind the boy's face, three-dimensional perspective had started vividly back from the crystal surfaces, as if the cube were a wide window flung suddenly open upon a new world. In that world, a place of glass and shining chromium, faces crowded as if indeed at an open window, peering into his room. Steel-helmed faces with staring eyes. And foremost among them, leaning almost through the opened window into his own past, the steel-capped boy whose features were Bill's looked eagerly out, the sound of quickened breath through his lips a soft, clear sound in the room. They were Bill's lips, Bill's features—but Marta's gentle courage had somehow grown masculine in the lines of the boy's face, and her eyes met Bill's in his.

In the instant before those parted lips spoke, Bill knew him, and his throat closed on an unuttered cry of recognition—recognition of this face he had never seen before, yet could not mistake. The deep welling of love and pride in his heart would have told him the boy's identity, he thought, had he not known at sight who he was—would be—might one day be—

He heard his own voice saying doubtfully, "Son—?"

But if the boy heard he must not have understood. He was handicapped by no such emotion as stirred Bill. His clipped, metallic voice spoke as clearly as if indeed through an opened window: "Greetings from the United World, William Vincent Cory! Greetings from the Fifteenth Leader in the Fifth New Century, A.G."

Behind the disciplined, stern-featured young face others crowded, men with steel-hard features under steel caps. As the boy's voice paused, a dozen right arms slanted high, a dozen open palms turned forward in a salute that was old when Caesar took it in ancient Rome. A dozen voices rolled out in clipped accents, "Greetings, William Vincent Cory!"

Bill's bewildered stammer was incoherent, and the boy's face relaxed a little into a smile. He said: "We must explain, of course. For generations our scientists have been groping in the past, Dr. Cory. This is our first successful two-way contact, and for its demonstration to our Council, connection with you was selected as the most appropriate and fitting contact possible. Because your name is holy among us; we know all there is to know of your life and work, but we have wished to look upon your face and speak to you of our grati-

tude for molding mankind into the patterns of the United
World.

"As a matter of record, I have been instructed to ask first
at what point we have intersected the past. What date is it in
your calendar?"

"Why, it's July 7, 2240," Bill heard his own voice stammer
a little as he answered, and he was conscious of a broad and
rather foolish grin overspreading his face. He couldn't help it.
This was his boy—the child who wouldn't be born for years
yet, who might, really, never be born. Yet he knew him, and
he couldn't help smiling with pride, and warm, delighted
amusement. So stern-faced, so conscious of his own responsibility! Marta's son and his—only of course it couldn't be, exactly. This scene he looked into must be far ahead in time—

"Twenty-two forty!" exclaimed the boy who was not his
son. "Why, the Great Work isn't even finished yet then!
We're earlier than we knew!"

"Who are you, son?" Bill couldn't keep the question back
any longer.

"I'm John Williams Cory IV, sir," said the boy proudly.
"Your direct descendant through the Williams line, and—
first in the Candidates Class." He said it proudly, a look of
almost worshiping awe lighting his resolute young face. "That
means, of course, that I shall be the Sixteenth Leader when
the great Dunn retires, and the sixth Cory—the sixth, sir!—to
be called to that highest of all human stations, the Leadership!" The violet eyes so incongruous in that disciplined
young face blazed with almost fanatic exaltation.

Behind him, a heavy-faced man moved forward, lifting the
Roman salute, smiling wintrily beneath his steel helmet.

"I am Dunn, sir," he said in a voice as heavy as his features. "We've let Candidate Cory contact you because of the
relationship, but it's my turn now to extend greetings from the
System you made possible. I want to show it to you, but first
let me thank you for founding the greatest family the United
World has ever known. No other name has appeared more
than twice on the great rôle of Leaders, but we have had five
Corys—and the finest of them all is yet to come!"

Bill saw a wave of clear red mount his boy's proud, exalted
face, and his own heart quickened with love and pride. For
this was his son, by whatever name he went here. The
memory of his lovely daughter had been drowned out momentarily in the deep uprushing of pride in this tall, blue-eyed
boy with his disciplined face and his look of leashed eager-

ness. There was drive and strength and power of will in that
young face now.

He scarcely heard Dunn's heavy voice from the room beyond the cube, so eagerly was he scanning the face of his son
he yet might never have, learning almost hungrily the already
familiar features, at once hard and eager and exultant. That
mouth was his, tight and straight, and the cheeks that creased
with deep hollows when he smiled, but the violet eyes were
his mother's eyes, and the gentle inflexibility of Marta's courage at once strengthened and softened the features that were
Bill's own. The best of them both was here, shining now with
something more than either had ever known—an almost fanatic devotion to some stern purpose as exalting as worship,
as inflexible as duty—

"Your own future, sir," Dunn was saying. "But our past,
of course. Would you like to see it, Dr. Cory, so that you
may understand just how directly we owe to you all that our
world is today?"

"Yes—v-very much." Bill grinned at his own stammer,
suddenly light-hearted and incredulous. All this was a dream.
He knew that, of course. Why, the very coincidences in it
proved that. Or—were they coincidences? Desperately he
tried to clarify the thought taking form in his own mind, a
terrifyingly vast thought, terrifyingly without explanation.
And yet it must be a dream— If it were real, then there was
more than chance here. It could be no accident that these
two children of his, groping blindly in the dark for contact
with him, had succeeded at so nearly the same moment.
There would be reason behind it, reason too vast for comprehension. He parted his lips to speak, but Dunn was already
speaking.

"Look then, William Vincent Cory! Watch your own
greatness unfolding in the years that lie ahead."

Hazily the scene in the cube blurred. The beloved, blue-
eyed face of the boy he might never have, faded as a dream
fads—a dream fading in a dream, he thought dimly—

This time it was Marta coming down the church aisle
toward him, looking like a violet-eyed madonna coifed and
veiled in white lace. He knew that he did not love her, now.
His heart was still sore with the memory of Sallie. But love
would come; with a woman like this it could not but come.
There was tenderness and humor and passion on that raptly
lifted face, and a strength that would call out the strength in
him, not a weakness such as dimpled in Sallie's face to evoke

an underlying weakness in himself. For weakness was in him. He knew it. It would depend upon the woman who shared his life which quality overcame the other.

Life would be good with Marta. He saw it unfolding before him in a long succession of days, work and play and companionship that brought out the best in both. And the memory of the strange vision in which he thought he loved Sallie faded. This was the woman he loved. Her courage and humor, her violet eyes bright with pride of him—

Life went by—clear, condensed, swift. He saw his own work moving steadily toward success, Marta's eager encouragement tiding him over the low ebbs when difficulties threatened. She was so full of pride in her brilliant young husband that her enthusiasm almost ran away with her. It was she who insisted upon making the discovery public.

"I want to flaunt you before the world!" she urged. "Let's report to the Council now, darling. Aw, please, Bill!"

"We're not ready yet," he protested feebly. "Let's wait—"

"What for? Look." She shook a record sheet under his nose. "A hundred per cent success in the last dozen experiments! What more do you want? It's time to make an official report—anounce what you're doing to the world! You've been all the way from fruit flies to monkeys. You'll have to make a report to the Council anyhow before you can take the next step. And remember, darling, when you come to that, I'm first in line as a candidate."

He seized her shoulders in a heavy grip, frowning down into the eagerness of her lifted face. "There'll be no guinea pigs in this family! When Junior Cory comes into the world he—or she—will do it without benefit of X-rays. Understand?"

"But darling, I thought the whole idea was to give parents their choice of boys or girls in the family."

"The thing's not perfected yet to the point where I'd want to risk my own wife. And anyhow . . . anyhow, I've got a funny notion I'd rather just take what comes. Don't know why, exactly, but—"

"Bill, I do believe you're superstitious! Well, we'll fight that out later. But right now, you're going to make a full report of your success to the Council, and I'm going to be the proudest wife in the City. And that's final!"

So the report was made public. It created a tremendous furor; the world clamored for the magical stuff that would put the molding of the future into their hands. Bill Cory blushed and grinned for a delighted public in the telenews screens, promising the great gift soon, and Marta glowed with vicarious pride.

By the time he had made his first experiment with a human subject, the puppies which were the result of his first successful mammalian experiment were beginning to worry him a little. Miss Brown was the first to notice it. She came in from the kennels one day with a frown behind her steel-rimmed spectacles.

"Dr. Cory, has someone been training those dogs?"

"Training them?" Bill looked up, puzzled. "Of course not. Why?"

"Well, they've got the makings of the finest trained dogs on Earth. Either the whole lot of them is exceptionally intelligent or . . . or . . . something. They just fall over each other obeying every command you can make clear to them."

Bill straightened from his microscope. "Um-m-m . . . funny. Usually one or two dogs in a litter are more intelligent and obedient than the rest. But to have every one in six litters a canine genius is something pretty queer. What do you make of it?"

"I wouldn't call it genius, exactly. As I say, I'm not sure if it's unusual intelligence or . . . well, maybe a strong strain of obedience, or lack of initiative, or . . . it's too soon to say. But they're not normal dogs, Dr. Cory."

It was too soon to say. Tests simply showed the pups to be extraordinarily amenable to training, but what quality in them made this so was difficult to determine. Bill was not sure just what it implied, but an uneasiness in him woke and would not be quieted.

The first "X-ray" babies began to be born. Without exception they were fine, strong, healthy infants, and without exception of the predetermined sex. The Council was delighted; the parents were delighted; everyone was delighted except Bill. The memory of those oddly obedient pups haunted him—

Within three years the Cory System was available to the public. The experimental babies had made such an excellent showing that, in the end, Bill gave in to the insistent world, though something in the recesses of his mind urged delay. Yet he couldn't explain it. The babies were all healthy, normal, intelligent children. Unusually amenable to authority, yes, but that was an asset, not a liability.

Presently all over the world the first crops of Cory System babies began to appear, and gradually Bill's misgivings faded. By then Bill Junior had arrived to take his mind off other people's children, but even now he was obscurely glad that little Bill was a boy on his own initiative, not because his parents had forced masculinity upon him. There was no rhyme or reason to Bill's queer obsession that his own child should not be a product of the X-ray system, but he had been firm about it.

And in later years he had reason to be glad. Bill Jr. grew up fast. He had Marta's violet eyes and his father's darkly blond hair, and a laughing resolution all his own. He was going to be an architect, and neither his mother's shocked protest at this treason to the family profession, nor Bill's not wholly concealed disappointment could swerve him. But he was a good lad. Between school terms he and his father had entirely marvelous vacations together, and for Bill the world revolved about this beloved, talented, headstrong youngster whose presence upon Earth seemed reason enough for Bill's whole existence.

He was glad, even, that the boy *was* stubborn. For there could be no question now about a weakness in the children of the Cory System births. In all ways but one they were quite normal, it was true, but initiative seemed to have been left out of them. It was as if the act of predetermining their sex had robbed them of all ability to make any decisions of their own. Excellent followers they were—but no leaders sprang up among them.

And it was dangerous to fill with unquestioning followers of the strongest man a world in which General George Hamilton controlled the United States. He was in his fourth term as president as the first great group of Cory System children came to maturity. Fiercely and sincerely he believed in the subjugation of the many to the State, and this new generation found in him an almost divinely inspired leader.

General George dreamed of a United World in which all races lived in blind obedience and willing sacrifice for the common good. And he was a man to make his dreams come true. Of course, he admitted, there would be opposition at first. There might be bloody wars, but in his magnificent dreams he believed sincerely that no price could be too high, that the end justified any means necessary to achieve it. And it seemed like the coöperation of Heaven itself to find almost an entire generation coming into adulthood ready to accept his leadership implicitly.

He understood why. It was no secret now what effect the Cory System had upon the children it produced. They would follow the strongest leader with blind faith. But upon this one generation of followers General George knew he could build a future that would live after him in the magnificent fulfillment of his most magnificent dreams. For a war lord needs a nation of soldiers, a great crop of boy babies to grow into armies, and surprisingly few saw the real motive behind General George's constant cry for boys, boys, boys—huge families of them. Fathers of many sons were feted and rewarded. Everybody knew there was the certainty of war behind this constant appeal for families of sons, but comparatively few realized that since the best way to be sure of boys was the use of the Cory System, the whole new generation would be blind followers of the strongest leader, just as their fathers were. Perhaps the Cory System might have died of its own great weakness, its one flaw, had not General George so purposefully demanded sons of his followers.

General George died before the first great war was over. His last words, gasped in the bursting tumult of a bomb raid over Washington were, "Carry on—unite the world!" And his vice-president and second in command, Phillip Spaulding, was ready to snatch up the falling torch and light the world to union.

Half the United States lay in smoking ruins before the Great War ended. But General George had builded well upon that most enduring of all foundations—the faith of men. "Be fruitful and multiply," was a command his followers had obeyed implicitly, and Spaulding had mighty resources of human brawn and human obedience to draw upon.

The great general had died gladly for his dream, and he had not died in vain. Half the world was united under his starry banners within a decade after his death; the United World of his vision came into being less than fifty years later.

With peace and blind faith and prosperity, Science City indeed came into its own. And because a taste of power had made the Leaders hungry, the eyes of the City turned upward toward starry space. During the command of the Fourth Leader after the immortal General George, the first successful space voyage was achieved. The first living man stood knee-deep in the dead pumice dust of the moon and a mighty forward stride for mankind was recorded.

It was only a step. Mars came next, three generations later. After a brief and bloody war, its decadent inhabitants surrendered and the Seventh Leader began to have giddily intoxicating dreams of a United Solar System—

Time telescoped by. Generation melted into generation in changing tides over a world population that seemed unaltering in its by now age-old uniforms of George Blue. And in a sense they were unaltering. Mankind was fixed in a mold—a good enough mold for the military life of the U. W.—the United World. The Cory System had long ago become compulsory, and men and women were produced exactly in the ratio that the Leaders decreed. But it was significant that the Leader class came into the world in the old haphazard fashion of the days before the legendary Dr. Cory's discovery.

The name of Cory was a proud one. It had long been a tradition in that famous family that the founder's great System should not be used among themselves. They were high among the Leader class. Several of the Leaders had borne the surname of Cory, though the office of course was not hereditary, but passed after rigid training and strict examination to the most eligible of the Candidates Class when an old Leader passed his prime.

And among the mighty Corys, family resemblance was strong. Generations saw the inevitable dilution of the original strain, but stubbornly through the years the Cory features came and went. Sometimes only the darkly blond hair of the first great Bill, sometimes the violet eyes which his pretty Marta had bequeathed her son, sometimes the very face of young Bill Jr. himself, that had roused an ache of pride and love in his father's heart whenever he saw those beloved features.

The Cory eyes looked now upon two worlds, triumphantly regimented to the last tiny detail. Mankind was proving his supremacy over himself—over his weaknesses and his sentimental, selfish desires for personal happiness as opposed to the great common good. Few succumbed to such shameful yearnings, but when they did, every man was a spy against his neighbor, as stern as the Leader himself in crushing these threats to the U. W.'s strength. It should be the individual's holiest and most mystically passionate dream to sacrifice his happiness for the Leader and the U. W., and the Leader and the United World lived for the sole purpose of seeing that he did.

Marvelous was the progress of mankind. The elements had long since been conquered; the atom had yielded up its incalculable power in the harness of the machines, space itself was a highway for the vehicles of the U. W.

Under the blue-black skies of Mars, mankind's checkerboard cities patterned the hot red soil; under the soft gray clouds of Venus, those roofed and checkered cities spread from a common center through jungles steaming in more than tropic heat. Many-mooned Jupiter was drawing the covetous eyes of the Leaders in their sky-high cities of glass and steel.

And moving through these patterned cities upon three worlds, the followers of the Leader went about their ways, resolute, unfaltering, their faces set in one pattern of determination.

It was not a happy pattern. There was little laughter here; the only emotion upon the serious faces, aside from the shadow of that same exaltation that blazed in the Leader's eyes, was a subtle furtiveness, a sidelong quality that by intuition seemed to distrust its neighbors. Bill recognized it. Every man's duty was to sacrifice for the Cause not only his personal desires and happiness, but his personal honor as well; he must keep relentlessly alert for traitorous weakness in his friends, his associates, his own family.

Mistily the panorama of the centuries began to melt into itself, to fade, while behind it a blue-eyed face, helmed in blue steel, took form to smile straight into Bill's eyes. A tense, expectant smile, supremely confident.

Bill sat back and breathed deeply, avoiding for a moment the proudly smiling face of his son. "I'm—there!" he was thinking. "That was me being born again and again, working with all my heart to crush out human happiness— But there was Sue, too, generations of her—yes, and of me—working just as sincerely toward an opposite goal, a world without war. Either way they've got me. If I don't finish my work, the world unbalances toward matriarchy; if I do, mankind turns into a machine. It's bad. Either way it's bad—"

"The doctor is almost overwhelmed at the realization of his own greatness," Dunn's voice murmured from the window into the future. Bill recognized it for a sort of apology, and sat up with an effort to meet the pride-bright eyes of the boy who one day might be his son. There was nothing but happy expectancy of praise on the boy's face, but Dunn must have read a little doubt in Bill's, for he said heavily, as if to overwhelm that doubt:

"We build toward one common end, all of us—we have no thought for any smaller purpose than the conquest of the Solar System for the mighty race of man! And this great purpose is yours no less than ours, Dr. Cory."

"Manpower is what counts, you know, sir." Young Billy's voice took up the tale as Dunn's died. "We've got tremendous reserves, and we're piling up still more. Lots of room yet on Mars to fill up, and Venus is almost untouched yet. And after that, we'll breed men and women adapted to Jupiter's gravity, perhaps . . . oh, there'll be no end to our power, sir! We'll go on and on— Who knows? There may come a day when we're a United Universe!"

For an instant, hearing the young voice shake with eagerness, Bill doubted his own doubtfulness. The mighty race of man! And he was part of it, living in this far-off future no less than he lived now in the flesh, in the burning ardor of this iron-faced boy. For a moment he forgot to be amazed and incredulous that he stood in the Twenty-third Century and looked as if through a window into the Thirtieth, talking with the unborn descendant of his yet unconceived son. For this moment it was all accomplished reality, a very magnificent and blood-stirring present achieved directly through his own efforts.

*"Father . . . father!"* The voice was sweet and high in the core of his brain. And memory came back in an overwhelming rush that for an instant drowned out everything but a father's awareness of special love for a favorite daughter.

"Yes, Susan . . . yes, dear." He murmured it aloud, swinging around toward the cube that housed his other future. Sue leaned forward upon her knees among the myrtle leaves, her brown eyes wide and a little frightened upon his. There was a crease between her winged brows that dented Bill's own forehead as he faced her. For a moment it was almost as if each of them looked into a mirror which reflected the features of the other, identical in nearly every detail. Then Sallie's smile dimpled the cheeks of her far-descended daughter, and Sue laughed a small, uneasy laugh.

"What is it, father? Is something wrong?"

He opened his lips to speak—but what could he say? What could he possibly say to her, who did not even dream that her own time was anything but inevitable? How could he explain to a living, warmly breathing woman that she did not exist, might never exist?

He stared at her unhappily, groping for words he could not find. But before he spoke—

"Dr. Cory, sir— Is anything wrong?" He turned back to Billy with a harried crease between his brows and then stared wildly from one face to the other. How could they help hearing one another? But obviously Billy, from his window into the present, saw simply the cube that held Sallie's immortal smile, while Sue, from hers, looked upon Marta's changeless face. It seemed to Bill that the boy and the girl had spoken in voices almost identical, using words nearly the same, though neither was aware of the other. How could they be? They could not even exist simultaneously in the same world. He might have one of these beloved children or the other; not both. Equally beloved children, between whom he must choose—and how could he choose?

"Father—" said Sue on a rising inflection of alarm. "There *is* something wrong. I . . . feel it in your mind— Oh, what is it, father?"

Bill sat speechless, staring from one face to the other of these mutually exclusive children. Here they stood, with their worlds behind them, looking anxiously at him with the same little crease between the brows of each. And he could not even speak to either without convincing the other he was a madman talking to empty air. He wanted insanely to laugh. It was a deadlock beyond all solution. Yet he must answer them—he must make his choice—

As he sat there groping in vain for words, a curious awareness began to take shape in his mind. How strange it was that these two should have been the ones to reach him, out of all the generations behind each that had been searching the past. And why had they established contact at so nearly the same time, when they had all his life span to grope through, hunting him for such different reasons, in such different ways? There was more than accident here, if all this were not a dream—

Billy and Sue—so similar despite the wide divergence of their words, a wider divergence than the mind can well grasp, for how can one measure the distance between mutually incompatible things? Billy who was all of Bill Cory that was strong and resolute and proud; Sue, who incarnated his gentler qualities, the tenderness, the deep desire for peace. They were such poles apart—why, *they were the poles!* The positive and negative qualities that, together, made up all that was best in Bill Cory. Even their worlds were like two halves of a whole; one all that was strong and ruthless, the other the epitome of gentle, abstract idealism. And both were bad, as all extremes must be.

And if he could understand the purpose behind the fact that these two poles of human destiny had reached back in their own pasts to find him at the same moment—if he could understand why the two halves of his soul, split into positive and negative entities, stood here clothed almost in his own flesh to torture him with indecision, perhaps—

He could not choose between them, for there was no choice, but there was a deeper question here than the simple question of conduct. He groped for it blindly, wondering if the answer to everything might not lie in the answer to that question. For there was purpose here vaster than anything man has words for—something loomed behind it to shadowy heights that made his mind reel a little as he tried to understand.

He said inadequately to both his staring children: "But why . . . how did you . . . at this very moment out of all time—"

To Billy it was mere gibberish, but Sue must have understood the question in his mind, for after a moment, in a puzzled murmur, she said:

"I—don't know, exactly. There *is* something here beyond the simple fact of success. I . . . I feel it— I can sense something behind my own actions that . . . that frightens me. Something guiding and controlling my own mind—Oh, father, father, I'm afraid!"

Every protective instinct in him leaped ahead of reason in Bill's instant, "Don't be frightened, honey! I won't let anything happen to you!"

"*Dr. Cory!*" Young Billy's voice cracked a little in horror at what must have sounded to him like raving madness. Behind him, staring faces went tense with bewilderment. Above their rising murmurs Sue wailed, "Father!" in a frightened echo to Billy's, "Dr. Cory, are you ill, sir?"

"Oh, wait a minute, both of you!" said Bill wildly. And then in a stammer, to stop Billy's almost hysterical questions, "Your . . . your sister— Oh, Sue, honey, I hear you! I'll take care of you! Wait a minute!"

In the depths of the cube the boy's face seemed to freeze, the eyes that were Marta's going blank beneath the steel cap, Bill's very mouth moving stiffly with the stiffness of his lips.

"But you never had a daughter—"

"No, but I might have, if—I mean, if I'd married Sallie of course you'd never even— Oh, God!" Bill gave it up and pressed both hands over his eyes to shut out the sight of the boy's amazed incredulity, knowing he's said too much, yet too numbed and confused now for diplomacy. The only clear idea in his head was that he must somehow be fair to both of them, the boy and the girl. Each must understand why he—

"Is the doctor ill, Candidate Cory?" Dunn's voice was heavy from the cube.

Bill heard the boy's voice stammering: "No—that is, I don't—" And then, faltering, more softly: "Leader, was the great doctor ever—mad?"

"Good God, boy!"

"But—speak to him, Leader!"

Bill looked up haggardly as Dunn's voice rolled out with the sternness of a general addressing armies. "Pull yourself together, sir! You never had a daughter! Don't you remember?"

Bill laughed wildly. "Remember? I've never had a son yet! I'm not married—not even engaged! How can I remember what hasn't happened?"

"But you *will* marry Marta Mayhew! You did marry her! You founded the great line of Corys and gave the world your—"

"Father . . . father! What's wrong?" Sue's sweet wail was in his ears. He glanced toward her window momentarily, seeing the terror in the soft brown eyes that stared at him, but he could only murmur: "Hush, darling—wait, please!" before he faced the Leader and said with a strong effort at calmness, "None of all that has happened—yet."

"But it will—it must—it *did!*"

"Even if I never married Marta, never had a son?"

Dunn's dark face convulsed with a grimace of exasperated anger.

"But good Lord, man, look here!" He seized Billy's blue-uniformed shoulders with both hands, thrusting him forward. "You did have a son! This is his descendant, the living likeness of young Cory Junior! This world . . . I myself . . . all of us . . . we're the result of that marriage of yours! And you never had a daughter! Are you trying to tell us we don't exist? Is this a . . . a dream I'm showing you?" And he shook the boy's broad young shoulders between his hands. "You're looking at us, hearing us, talking to us! Can't you see that you must have married Marta Mayhew?"

"Father, I want you! Come back!" Sue's wail was insistent.

Bill groaned. "Wait a minute, Dunn." And then, turning, "Yes, honey, what is it?"

On her knees among the myrtle leaves Sue leaned forward among the sun-flecked shadows of her cool green glade, crying: "Father, you won't . . . you can't believe them? I heard . . . through your ears I heard them, and I can understand a little through your mind linked with mine. I can understand what you're thinking . . . but it can't be true! You're telling yourself that we're still on the Probability Plane . . . but that's just a theory! That's nothing but a speculation about the future! How could I be anything but real? Why, it's silly! Look at me! Listen to me! Here I am! Oh, don't let me go on thinking that maybe . . . maybe you're right, after all. But it *was* Sallie Carlisle you married, wasn't it, father? Please say it was!"

Bill gulped. "Wait, honey. Let me explain to them first." He knew he shouldn't have started the whole incredible argument. You can't convince a living human that he doesn't exist. They'd only think him mad. Well—Sue might understand. Her training in metaphysics and telepathy might make it possible. But Billy—

He turned with a deep breath and a mental squaring of shoulders, determined to try, anyhow. For he must be fair. He began: "Dunn, did you ever hear of the Plane of Probability?"

At the man's incredulous stare he knew a dizzy moment of wonder whether he, too, lived in an illusion as vivid as theirs, and in that instant the foundations of time itself rocked beneath his feet. But he had no time now for speculation. Young Billy must understand, no matter how mad Dunn believed him, and Sue must know why he did what he must do—though he didn't understand himself, yet, what that would be. His head was ringing with bewilderment.

"The . . . the Plane of Probability?" In Dunn's eyes upon his he saw a momentary conviction flare that, reality or not, and history be damned, this man was mad. And then, doubtfully, the Leader went on, "Hm-m-m . . . yes, somewhere I *have* heard— Oh, I remember. Some clap-trap jargon the old

Telepathy House fakers used to use before we cleared them
out of Science City. But what's that nonsense got to—"

"It's not nonsense." Bill closed his eyes in a sudden, almost
intolerable longing for peace, for time to think what he must
do. But no, the thing must be settled now, without time for
thinking. And perhaps that was the best way, after all. A
man's brain would crack if he paused to think out this
madness. Only he must say something to young Billy— And
what could he say? How could he face either of these beloved
children and, to their uncomprehending, pleading faces, refuse them life? If he could only break the connection that
riveted them all into a sort of triple time balance— But he
couldn't. He must make it clear to Billy—

"It's not nonsense," he heard his own voice repeating
wildly. "The future—you and your world—is a probability
only. I'm a free agent. If I never marry Marta, never perfect
the sex-determination idea, the probable future shifts to . . .
to another pattern. *And that as bad as yours, or worse!*" he
finished to himself.

"Is he mad?" Billy's voice was a whisper in the screen.

The Leader said as if to himself, in an awed and stumbling
voice, "I don't . . . I can't . . . the thing's preposterous! And
yet he *is* unmarried, the Great Work's still unfinished. Suppose he never— But we're real! We're flesh and blood, aren't
we?" He stamped a booted foot on the floor as if to test the
foundations of his world. "We're descended in an unbroken
line from this . . . this madman. Lord in heaven, are we all
mad?"

"Father! Come back!" Sue's voice shrilled in Bill's ears. He
turned desperately, glad of an excuse to escape the haunted
stares from that other window even though he must face hers.
She had risen to her feet among the myrtle leaves. The glade
was cool and still about her in this lazy, sunlit world of her
own future. She was crying desperately, "Don't listen, father!
I can feel the confusion in your mind. I know what they're
saying! But they aren't real, father—they can't be! You never
had a son, don't you remember? All this you're saying is just
. . . just talk, isn't it? That silly stuff about the Probability
Plane—it's nothing but speculation! Oh, say it is, father!
We've got such a lovely world, we love living so . . . I want
to live, father! I *am* real! We've fought so hard, for so many
centuries, for peace and happiness and our beautiful garden
world. Don't let it snuff out into nothingness! But"—she
laughed uncertainly—"how could you, when it's all around

us, and has been for thousands of years? I . . . oh, father!" Her voice broke on a little quivering gulp that made Bill's heart quiver with it, and he ached intolerably with the rising of her tears. She was his to protect and cherish, forever. How could he—

"Dr. Cory—do you hear me? Oh, please listen!" Young Billy's familiar voice reached out to him from that other future. He glanced toward him once, and then put his hands to his ears and whirled from them both, the two voices mingling in an insane chaos of pleading.

Sue on her myrtle bank in a future immeasurably far ahead, child of a decadent world slipping easily down the slope of oblivion.

Billy's world might be as glorious as he believed, but the price was too high to pay for it. Bill remembered the set, unsmiling faces he had seen in the streets of that world. These were men his own work had robbed of the initiative that was their birthright. Happiness was their birthright, too, and the power to make the decisions that determined their own futures.

No, not even for such achievements as theirs must mankind be robbed of the inalienable right to choose for himself. If it lay in Bill Cory's power to outlaw a system which destroyed men's freedom and honor and joy, even for such an end as mankind's immortal progress, he had no choice to make. The price was too high. Confusedly he remembered something out of the dim past: "What shall it profit a man if he gain the whole world and lose his own soul. . .?"

But—the alternative. Bill groaned. Happiness, peace, freedom, honor—yes, Sue's world had all that Billy's lacked. And to what end? Indolence and decadence and extinction for the great race that Billy's civilization would spread gloriously among the stars.

"But I'm thinking of *choice*," groaned Bill to himself. "And, I haven't got any choice! If I marry Sallie and don't finish my work—one future follows. If I marry Marta and do finish it, the other comes. And both are bad—but what can I do? Man or mankind; which has the stronger claim? Happiness and extinction—or unhappiness and splendid immortality; which is better?"

"Cory—Dr. Cory!" It was Dunn's voice, heavy enough to break through the daze of bewilderment that shrouded Bill's brain. He turned. The Leader's iron-hard face under the steel helmet was settling into lines of fixed resolution. Bill saw that he had reached some decision, and knew a sudden, dazed admiration for the man. After all, he had not been chosen Leader for nothing.

"You're a fool to tell us all this, Cory. Mad, or a fool, or both. Don't you know what it means? Don't think we established this connection unprepared for trouble! The same force that carries the sight and sound of us from our age to yours can carry destruction, too! Nowhere in our past is there a record that William Cory was killed by a blast of atom-gun fire as he sat at his desk—but, by God, sir, if you can change that past, so can we!"

"It would mean wiping yourself out, you know," Bill reminded him as steadily as he could, searching the angry eyes of this man who must never have faced resolute opposition before, and wondering if the man had yet accepted a truth that must seem insanely impossible to him. He wanted overwhelmingly to laugh, and yet somewhere inside him a chilly conviction was growing that it might be possible for the children of his unborn son, in a future that would never exist, to blast him out of being. He said: "You and your whole world would vanish if I died."

"But not unavenged!" The Leader said it savagely, and then hesitated. "But what am I saying? You've driven me almost as mad as you! Look, man, try to be sensible! Can you imagine yourself dissolving into nothingness that never existed? Neither can I!"

"But if you could kill me, then how could your world ever have been born?"

"To hell with all that!" exploded Dunn. "I'm no metaphysician! I'm a fighting man! I'll take the chance!"

"Please, Dr. Cory—" Billy pressed forward against the very surface of the cube, as if he could thrust himself back into his own past and lay urgent hands upon this man so like him, staring white-faced and stubborn into the future. Perhaps it was more than the desire for peace that spoke in his shaken voice. If Bill Cory, looking into that young face so like his own, had felt affection and recognition for it, then must not the boy know a feeling akin to it as he saw himself in Cory's features? Perhaps it was that subtle, strange identification between the two that made the boy's voice tremble a little as if with the first weakening of belief. When he spoke he seemed to be acknowledging the possibility of doubt, almost without realizing it. He said in that shaken, ardent voice:

"Please, try to understand! It's not death we're afraid of. All of us would die now, willingly, if our deaths could further the common good. What we can't endure to face is the death of our civilization, this marvelous thing that makes mankind immortal. Think of that, sir! This is the only right thing possible for you to do! Would we feel so strongly if we weren't *sure?* Can you condemn your own race to eternity on one small planet, when you could give them the universe to expand in and every good thing science can offer?"

"Father . . . father!" It was Sue again, frantic and far away.

But before Bill could turn to her, Dunn's voice broke in heavily over both the others. "Wait—I've made up my mind!" Billy fell back a little, turning to his Leader with a blaze of sudden hope. Bill stared. "As I see it," went on Dunn, "the whole preposterous question hinges on the marriage you make. Naturally I can't concede even to myself that you could possibly marry anyone but the woman you *did* marry—but if you honestly feel that there's any question in your mind about it, I'll settle it for you."

He turned to nod toward a corner of the room in which he stood that was outside Bill's range, and in a moment the blue-uniformed, staring crowd about him parted and a low, rakish barrel of blue-gleaming steel glided noiselessly forward toward that surface of the cube which was a window into the past-future that parted Bill and themselves. Bill had never seen anything like it before, but he recognized its lethal quality. It crouched streamlined down upon its base as if for a lunge, and its mouth facing him was a dark doorway for death itself. Dunn bent behind it and laid his hand upon a half-visible lever in its base.

"Now," he said heavily. "William Cory, there seems to be a question in your mind as to whether we could reach you with our weapons. Let me assure you that the force-beam which connects us can carry more than sight and sound into your world! I hope I shan't have to demonstrate that. I hope you'll be sensible enough to turn to that televisor screen in the wall behind you and call Marta Mayhew."

"M—Marta?" Bill heard the quiver in his voice. "Why—"

"You will call her, and in our sight and hearing you are going to ask her to marry you. That much choice is yours, marriage or death. Do you hear me?"

Bill wanted insanely to laugh. Shotgun wedding from a mythical future—"You can't threaten me with that popgun forever," he said with a quaver of mirth he could not control. "How do you know I'll marry her once you're away?"

"You'll keep your word," said Dunn serenely. "Don't forget, Cory, we know you much better than you know yourself. We know your future far more completely than you saw it. We know how your character will develop with age. Yes, you're an honorable man. Once you've asked her to marry you, and heard her say yes—and she will—you won't try to back out. No, the promise given and received between you constitutes a marriage as surely as if we'd seen the ceremony performed. You see, we trust your honor, William Cory."

"But—" Bill got no further than that, for explosively in his brain a sweet, high voice was sobbing:

"Father, father, what are you doing? What's happened? Why don't you speak to me?"

In the tension Bill had nearly forgotten Sue, but the sound of that familiar voice tore at him with sudden, almost intolerable poignancy. Sue—the promise to protect her had risen to his lips involuntarily at the very mention of danger. It was answer to an urgency rooted race-deep, the instinct to protect the helpless and the loved. For a moment he forgot the gun trained on him from the other window; he forgot Billy and the world behind him. He was conscious only of his daughter crying in terror for help—for help from him and for protection against him at once, in a dizzy confusion that made his head swim.

"Sue—" he began uncertainly.

"Cory, we're waiting!" Dunn's voice had an ominous undernote.

But there was a solution. He never knew just when he first became aware of it. A long while ago, perhaps, subconsciously, the promise of it had begun to take shape in his mind. He did not know when he first realized that—but he thought he knew whence it came. There was a sureness and a vastness about it that did not originate in himself. It was the Cosmic Mind indeed in which his own small soul was floundering, and out of that unthinkably limitless Plan, along with the problem came at last the solution. (*There must be balance . . . the force that swings the worlds in their orbits can permit of no question without an answer—*)

There was no confusion here; there had never been. This was not chance. Purpose was behind it, and sudden confidence came flooding into him from outside. He turned with resolution so calm upon his face that Billy sighed and smiled, and Dunn's tense face relaxed.

"Thank God, sir," breathed Billy, "I knew you'd come to your senses. Believe me, sir, you won't be sorry."

"Wait," said Bill to them both, and laid his hand on the button beneath his desk that rang a bell in his laboratory. "Wait and see."

In three worlds and times, three people very nearly identical in more than the flesh alone—perhaps three facets of the same personality, who can say?—stood silent and tense and waiting. It seemed like a very long time before the door opened and Miss Brown came into the room, hesitating on the threshold with her calm, pleasant face questioning.

"You want me, Dr. Cory?"

Bill did not answer for a moment. He was pouring his whole soul into this last long stare that said good-by to the young son he would never know. For understanding from some vast and nameless source was flooding his mind now, and he knew what was coming and why it would be so. He looked across the desk and gazed his last upon Sue's familiar face so like his own, the fruit of a love he would never share with pretty Sallie. And then, drawing a deep breath, he gulped and said distinctly:

"Miss Brown, will you marry me?"

Dunn had given him the key—a promise given and received between this woman and himself would be irrevocable, would swing the path of the future into a channel that led to no world that either Billy or Sue could know.

Bill got his first glimmer of hope for that future from the way the quiet woman in the doorway accepted his question. She did not stare or giggle or stammer. After one long, deep look into his eyes—he saw for the first time that hers were gray and cool behind the lenses—she answered calmly.

"Thank you, Dr. Cory. I shall be very happy to marry you."

And then—it came. In the very core of his brain, heartbreak and despair exploded in a long, wailing scream of faith betrayed as pretty Sue, his beloved, his darling, winked out into the oblivion from which she would never now emerge. The lazy green Eden was gone forever; the sweet fair girl on her knees among the myrtle leaves had never been—would never be.

Upon that other window surface, in one last flash of unbearable clearness, young Billy's incredulous features stared at him. Behind that beloved, betrayed face he saw the face of the Leader twisting with fury. In the last flashing instant while the vanishing, never-to-exist future still lingered in the cube, Bill saw an explosion of white-hot violence glare blindingly from the gun mouth, a heat and violence that seared the very brain. Would it have reached him—could it have harmed him? He never knew, for it lasted scarcely a heartbeat before eternity closed over the vanishing world in a soundless, fathomless, all-swallowing tide.

Where that world had stretched so vividly a moment ago, now Marta's violet gaze looked out into the room through crystal. Across the desk Sallie's lovely, careless smile glowed changelessly. They had been gateways to the future—but the gates were closed. There would never be such futures now; there never had been. In the Cosmic Mind, the great Plan of Things, two half-formed ideas went out like blown candle flames.

And Bill turned to the gray-eyed woman in the doorway with a long, deep, shaken sigh. In his own mind as he faced her, thoughts too vast for formulation moved cloudily.

"I know now something no man was ever sure of before—our oneness with the Plan. There are many, many futures. I couldn't face the knowledge of another, but I think—yes, I believe, ours will be the best. She won't let me neglect the work we're doing, but neither will she force me to give it to the world unperfected. Maybe, between us, we can work out that kink that robs the embryo of determination, and then—who knows?

"Who knows why all this had to happen? There was Purpose behind it—all of it—but I'll never understand just why. I only know that the futures are infinite—and that I haven't lost Billy or Sue. I couldn't have done what I did without being sure of that. I couldn't lose them, because they're me—the best of me, going on forever. Perhaps I'll never die, really—not the real me—until these incarnations of the best that's in me, whatever form and face and name they wear, work out mankind's ultimate destiny in some future I'll never see. There was reason behind all this. Maybe, after all, I'll understand—some day."

He said nothing aloud, but he held out his hand to the woman in the door and smiled down confidently into her cool, gray eyes.

# TRENDS    *Astounding Science Fiction*, July

# by Isaac Asimov (1920–    )

*"Trends" was not my first published story, but
my third. The first two, however, did not appear in
Astounding and so I rarely count them. This was
the very first story I sold to John Campbell, and I
became the youngest member of the "stable" of
writers he had already gathered around himself.*

*Though others still younger came his way later, I
don't think that ever in his career did he have an
acolyte less worldly and more naive than I was. I
believe that amused him and that it pleased him to
have so excellent an opportunity to do a bit of
molding. At any rate, I have always thought that of
all his writers I was his favorite and that he spent
more time and effort on me than on anyone else. I
believe it still shows.*

*I have always been proud that my first Astound-
ing story appeared in the first issue of the Golden
Age, but I know very well that there was no connection. In fact, in the blaze of Van Vogt's lead
story* Black Destroyer, *I doubt that anyone noticed
the twinkle of my own presence. IA*

John Harman was sitting at his desk, brooding, when I entered the office that day. It had become a common sight, by
then, to see him staring out at the Hudson, head in hand, a
scowl contorting his face—all too common. It seemed unfair
for the little bantam to be eating his heart out like that day
after day, when by rights he should have been receiving the
praise and adulation of the world.

229

I flopped down into a chair. "Did you see the editorial in today's *Clarion*, boss?"

He turned weary, bloodshot eyes toward me. "No, I haven't. What do they say? Are they calling the vengeance of God down upon me again?" His voice dripping with bitter sarcasm.

"They're going a little farther *now*, boss," I answered. "Listen to this:

" 'Tomorrow is the day of John Harman's attempt at profaning the heavens. Tomorrow, in defiance of world opinion and world conscience, this man will defy God.

" 'It is not given to man to go wheresoever ambition and desire lead him. There are things forever denied him, and aspiring to the stars is one of these. Like Eve, John Harman wishes to eat of the forbidden fruit, and like Eve he will suffer due punishment therefor.

" 'But it is not enough, this mere talk. If we allow him thus to brook the vengeance of God, the trespass is mankind's and not Harman's alone. In allowing him to carry out his evil designs, we make ourselves accessory to the crime, and Divine vengeance will fall on all alike.

" 'It is, therefore, essential that immediate steps be taken to prevent Harman from taking off in his so-called rocketship tomorrow. The government in refusing to take such steps may force violent action. If it will make no move to confiscate the rocketship, or to imprison Harman, our enraged citizenry may have to take matters into their own hands—' "

Harman sprang from his seat in a rage and, snatching the paper from my hands, threw it into the corner furiously. "It's an open call to a lynching," he raved. "Look at this!"

He cast five or six envelopes in my direction. One glance sufficed to tell what they were.

"More death threats?" I asked.

"Yes, exactly that. I've had to arrange for another increase in the police patrol outside the building and for a motorcycle police escort when I cross the river to the testing ground tomorrow."

He marched up and down the room with agitated stride. "I don't know what to do, Clifford. I've worked on the *Prometheus* almost ten years. I've slaved, spent a fortune of money, given up all that makes life worth while—and for what? So that a bunch of fool revivalists can whip up public sentiment against me until my very life isn't safe."

"You're in advance of the times, boss," I shrugged my shoulders in a resigned gesture which made him whirl upon me in a fury.

"What do you mean 'in advance of the times'? This is 1973. The world has been ready for space travel for half a century now. Fifty years ago, people were talking, dreaming of the day when man could free himself of Earth and plumb the depths of space. For fifty years, science has inched toward this goal, and now . . . now I finally have it, and behold! you say the world is not ready for me."

"The '20s and '30s were years of anarchy, decadence, and misrule, if you remember your history," I reminded him gently. "You cannot accept them as criteria."

"I know, I know. You're going to tell me of the First War of 1914, and the Second of 1940. It's an old story to me; my father fought in the Second and my grandfather in the First. Nevertheless, those were the days when science *flourished*. Men were not afraid then; somehow they dreamed and dared. There was no such thing as conversation when it came to matters mechanical and scientific. No theory was too radical to advance, no discovery too revolutionary to publish. Today, dry rot has seized the world when a great vision, such as space travel, is hailed as 'defiance of God.' "

His head sank slowly down, and he turned away to hide his trembling lips and the tears in his eyes. Then he suddenly straightened again, eyes blazing: "But I'll show them. I'm going through with it, in spite of Hell, Heaven and Earth. I've put too much into it to quit now."

"Take it easy, boss," I advised. "This isn't going to do you any good tomorrow, when you get into that ship. Your chances of coming out alive aren't too good now, so what will they be if you start out worn to pieces with excitement and worry?"

"You're right. Let's not think of it any more. Where's Shelton?"

"Over at the Institute arranging for the special photographic plates to be sent us."

"He's been gone a long time, hasn't he?"

"Not especially; but listen, boss, there's something wrong with him. I don't like him."

"Poppycock! He's been with me two years, and I have no complaints."

"All right." I spread my hands in resignation. "If you won't listen to me, you won't. Just the same I caught him reading one of those infernal pamphlets Otis Eldredge puts out. You know the kind: 'Beware, O mankind, for judgment draws near. Punishment for your sins is at hand. Repent and be saved.' And all the rest of the time-honored junk."

Harman snorted in disgust. "Cheap tub-thumping rivivalist! I suppose the world will never outgrow his type—not while sufficient morons exist. Still you can't condemn Shelton just because he reads it. I've read them myself on occasion."

"He *says* he picked it up on the sidewalk and read it in 'idle curiosity,' but I'm pretty sure I saw him take it out of his wallet. Besides, he goes to church every Sunday."

"Is *that* a crime? Everyone does, nowadays!"

"Yes, but not to the Twentieth Century Evangelical Society. That's Eldredge's."

That jolted Harman. Evidently, it was the first he had heard of it. "Say, that *is* something, isn't it? We'll have to keep an eye on him, then."

But after that, things started to happen, and we forgot all about Shelton—until it was too late.

There was nothing much left to do that last day before the test, and I wandered into the next room, where I went over Harman's final report to the Institute. It was my job to correct any errors or mistakes that crept in, but I'm afraid I wasn't very thorough. To tell the truth, I couldn't concentrate. Every few minutes, I'd fall into a brown study.

It seemed queer, all this fuss over space travel. When Harman had first announced the approaching perfection of the *Prometheus,* some six months before, scientific circles had been jubilant. Of course, they were cautious in their statements and qualified everything they said, but there was real enthusiasm.

However, the masses didn't take it that way. It seems strange, perhaps, to you of the twenty-first century, but perhaps we should have expected it in those days of '73. People weren't very progressive then. For years there had been a swing toward religion, and when the churches came out unanimously against Harman's rocket—well, there you were.

At first, the opposition confined itself *to* the churches and we thought it might play itself out. But it didn't. The papers got hold of it, and literally spread the gospel. Poor Harman became an anathema to the world in a remarkably short time, and then his troubles began.

He received death threats, and warnings of divine vengeance every day. He couldn't walk the streets in safety. Dozens of sects, to none of which he belonged—he was one of the very rare free-thinkers of the day, which was another count against him—excommunicated him and placed him under special interdict. And, worst of all, Otis Eldredge and his Evangelical Society began stirring up the populace.

Eldridge was a queer character—one of those geniuses, in their way, that arise every so often. Gifted with a golden tongue and a sulphurous vocabulary, he could fairly hypnotize a crowd. Twenty thousand people were so much putty in his hands, could he only bring them within earshot. And for four months, he thundered against Harman; for four months, a pouring stream of denunciation rolled forth in oratorical frenzy. And for four months, the temper of the world rose.

But Harman was not to be daunted. In his tiny, five-foot-two body, he had enough spirit for five six-footers. The more the wolves howled, the firmer he held his ground. With almost divine—his enemies said, diabolical—obstinacy, he refused to yield an inch. Yet his outward firmness was to me, who knew him, but an imperfect concealment of the great sorrow and bitter disappointment within.

The ring of the doorbell interrupted my thoughts at that point and brought me to my feet in surprise. Visitors were very few those days.

I looked out the window and saw a tall, portly figure talking with Police Sergeant Cassidy. I recognized him at once as Howard Winstead, head of the Institute. Harman was hurrying out to greet him, and after a short exchange of phrases, the two entered the office. I followed them in, being rather curious as to what could have brought Winstead, who was more politician than scientist, here.

Winstead didn't seem very comfortable, at first; not his usual suave self. He avoided Harman's eyes in an embarrassed manner and mumbled a few conventionalities concerning the weather. Then he came to the point with direct, undiplomatic bluntness.

"John," he said, "how about postponing the trial for a time?"

"You really mean abandoning it altogether, don't you? Well, I won't, and that's final."

Winstead lifted his hand. "Wait now, John, don't get excited. Let me state my case. I know the Institute agreed to give you a free hand, and I know that you paid at least half the expenses out of your own pocket, but—you can't go through with it."

"Oh, can't I, though?" Harman snorted derisively.

"Now listen, John, you know your science, but you don't know your human nature and I do. This is not the world of the 'Mad Decades,' whether you realize it or not. There have been profound changes since 1940." He swung into what was evidently a carefully prepared speech.

"After the First World War, you know, the world as a whole swung away from religion and toward freedom from convention. People were disgusted and disillusioned, cynical and sophisticated. Eldredge calls them 'wicked and sinful.' In spite of that, science flourished—some say it always fares best in such an unconventional period. From *its* standpoint it was a 'Golden Age.'

"However, you know the political and economic history of the period. It was a time of political chaos and international anarchy; a suicidal, brainless, insane period—and it culminated in the Second World War. And just as the First War led to a period of sophistication, so the Second initiated a return to religion.

"People were disgusted with the 'Mad Decades.' They had had enough of it, and feared, beyond all else, a return to it. To remove that possibility, they put the ways of those decades behind them. Their motives, you see, were understandable and laudable. All the freedom, all the sophistication, all the lack of convention were gone—swept away clean. We are living now in a second Victorian age; and naturally so, because human history goes by swings of the pendulum and this is the swing toward religion and convention.

"One thing only is left over since those days of half a century ago. That one thing is respect of humanity for science. We have prohibition; smoking for women is outlawed; cosmetics are forbidden; low dresses and short skirts are unheard of; divorce is frowned upon. But science has not been confined—*as yet*.

"It behooves science, then, to be circumspect, to refrain from arousing the people. It will be very easy to make them believe—and Otis Eldredge has come perilously close to doing it in some of his speeches—that it was science that brought about the horrors of the Second World War. Science outstripped culture, they will say, technology outstripped sociology, and it was that unbalance that came so near to destroying the world. Somehow, I am inclined to believe they are not so far wrong, at that.

"But do you know what would happen, if it ever *did* come to that? Scientific research may be forbidden or, if they don't go that far, it will certainly be so strictly regulated as to stifle in its own decay. It will be a calamity from which humanity would not recover for a millennium.

"And it is your trial flight that may precipitate all this. You are arousing the public to a stage where it will be difficult to calm them. I warn you, John. The consequences will be on your head."

There was absolute silence for a moment and then Harman forced a smile. "Come, Howard, you're letting yourself be frightened by shadows on the wall. Are you trying to tell me that it is your serious belief that the world as a whole is ready to plunge into a second Dark Ages? After all, the intelligent men are on the side of science, aren't they?"

"If they are, there aren't many of them left from what I see." Winstead drew a pipe from his pocket and filled it slowly with tobacco as he continued: "Eldridge formed a League of the Righteous two months ago—they call it the L. R.—and it has grown unbelievably. *Twenty million is its membership in the United States alone.* Eldredge boasts that after the next election Congress will be his; and there seems to be more truth than bluff in that. Already there has been strenuous lobbying in favor of a bill outlawing rocket experiments, and laws of that type have been enacted in Poland, Portugal, and Rumania. Yes, John, we are perilously close to open persecution of science." He was smoking now in rapid, nervous puffs.

"But if I succeed, Howard, if I succeed! What then?"

"Bah! You know the chances for that. Your own estimate gives you only one chance in ten of coming out alive."

"What does that signify? The next experimenter will learn by my mistakes, and the odds will improve. That's the scientific method."

"The mob doesn't know anything about the scientific method; and they don't want to know. Well, what do you say? Will you call it off?"

Harman sprang to his feet, his chair tumbling over with a crash. "Do you know what you ask? Do you want me to give up my life's work, my dream, just like that? Do you think I'm going to sit back and wait for your *dear* public to become benevolent? Do you think they'll change in *my* lifetime?

"Here's my answer: I have an inalienable right to pursue knowledge. Science has an inalienable right to progress and develop without interference. The world, in interfering with me, is wrong; I am right. And it shall go hard, but I *will not* abandon my rights."

Winstead shook his head sorrowfully. "You're wrong, John, when you speak of 'inalienable' rights. What you call a 'right' is merely a *privilege, generally agreed upon.* What society accepts, is right; what it does not, is wrong."

"Would your friend, Eldredge, agree to such a definition of his 'righteousness'?" questioned Harmon bitterly.

"No, he would not, but that's irrelevant. Take the case of those African tribes who used to be cannibals. They were brought up as cannibals, have the long tradition of cannibalism, and their society accepts the practice. To *them*, cannibalism is *right*, and why shouldn't it be? So you see how relative the whole notion is, and how inane your conception of 'inalienable' rights to perform experiments is."

"You know, Howard, you missed your calling when you didn't become a lawyer." Harman was really growing angry. "You've been bringing out every moth-eaten argument you can think of. For God's sake, man, are you trying to pretend that it is a crime to refuse to run with the crowd? Do you stand for absolute uniformity, ordinariness, orthodoxy, commonplaceness? Science would die far sooner under the program you outline than under governmental prohibition."

Harman stood up and pointed an accusing finger at the other. "You're betraying science and the tradition of those glorious rebels: Galileo, Darwin, Einstein and their kind. My rocket leaves tomorrow on schedule in spite of you and every other stuffed shirt in the United States. That's that, and I refuse to listen to you any longer. So you can just get out."

The head of the Institute, red in the face, turned to me. "You're my witness, young man, that I warned this obstinate nitwit, this . . . this hare-brained fanatic." He spluttered a bit, and then strode out, the picture of fiery indignation.

Harman turned to me when he had gone: "Well, what do *you* think? I suppose you agree with him."

There was only one possible answer and I made it:

"You're not paying me to do anything else but follow orders, boss. I'm sticking with you."

Just then Shelton came in and Harman packed us both off to go over the calculations of the orbit of flight for the umpteenth time, while he himself went off to bed.

The next day, July 15th, dawned in matchless splendor, and Harman, Shelton, and myself were in an almost gay mood as we crossed the Hudson to where the *Prometheus*—surrounded by an adequate police guard—lay in gleaming grandeur.

Around it, roped off at an apparently safe distance, rolled a crowd of gigantic proportions. Most of them were hostile, raucously so. In fact, for one fleeting moment, as our motorcycle police escort parted the crowds for us, the shouts and imprecations that reached our ears almost convinced me that we should have listened to Winstead.

But Harman paid no attention to them at all, after one supercilious sneer at a shout of: "There goes John Harman, son of Belial." Calmly, he directed us about our task of inspection. I tested the foot-thick outer walls and the air locks for leaks, then made sure the air purifier worked. Shelton checked up on the repellent screen and the fuel tanks. Finally, Harman tried on the clumsy spacesuit, found it suitable, and announced himself ready.

The crowd stirred. Upon a hastily erected platform of wooden planks piled in confusion by some in the mob, there rose up a striking figure. Tall and lean; with thin, ascetic countenance; deep-set, burning eyes, peering and half closed; a thick, white mane crowning all—it was Otis Eldredge. The crowd recognized him at once and many cheered. Enthusiasm waxed and soon the entire turbulent mass of people shouted themselves hoarse over him.

He raised a hand for silence, turned to Harman, who regarded him with surprise and distaste, and pointed a long, bony finger at him:

"John Harman, son of the devil, spawn of Satan, you are here for an evil purpose. You are about to set out upon a blasphemous attempt to pierce the veil beyond which man is forbidden to go. You are tasting of the forbidden fruit of Eden and beware that you taste not of the fruits of sin."

The crowd cheered him to the echo and he continued: "The finger of God is upon you, John Harman. He shall not allow His works to be defiled. You die today, John Harman."

His voice rose in intensity and his last words were uttered in truly prophetlike fervor.

Harman turned away in disdain. In a loud, clear voice, he addressed the police sergeant: "Is there any way, officer, of removing these spectators? The trial flight may be attended by some destruction because of the rocket blasts, and they're crowding too close."

The policeman answered in a crisp, unfriendly tone: "If you're afraid of being mobbed, say so, Mr. Harman. You don't have to worry, though, we'll hold them back. And as for danger—from *that* contraption—" He sniffed loudly in the direction of the *Prometheus,* evoking a torrent of jeers and yells.

Harman said nothing further, but climbed into the ship in silence. And when he did so, a queer sort of stillness fell over the mob; a palpable tension. There was no attempt at rushing the ship, an attempt I had thought inevitable. On the contrary, Otis Eldredge himself shouted to everyone to move back.

"Leave the sinner to his sins," he shouted. " 'Vengeance is mine,' saith the Lord."

As the moment approached, Shelton nudged me. "Let's get out of here," he whispered in a strained voice. "Those rocket blasts are poison." Saying this, he broke into a run, beckoning anxiously for me to follow.

We had not yet reached the fringes of the crowd when there was a terrific roar behind me. A wave of heated air swept over me. There was the frightening hiss of some speeding object past my ear, and I was thrown violently to the ground. For a few minutes I lay dazed, my ears ringing and my head reeling.

When I staggered drunkenly to my feet again, it was to view a dreadful sight. Evidently, the entire fuel supply of the *Prometheus* had exploded at once, and where it had lain a moment ago there was now only a yawning hole. The ground was strewn with wreckage. The cries of the hurt were heart-rending and the mangled bodies—but I won't try to describe those.

A weak groan at my feet attracted my attention. One look, and I gasped in horror, for it was Shelton, the back of his head a bloody mass.

"I did it." His voice was hoarse and triumphant but withal so low that I could scarcely hear it. "I did it. I broke open the liquid-oxygen compartments and when the spark went through the acetyline mixture the whole cursed thing exploded." He gasped a bit and tried to move but failed. "A piece of wreckage must have hit me, but I don't care. I'll die knowing that—"

His voice was nothing more than a rasping rattle, and on his face was the ecstatic look of a martyr. He died then, and I could not find it in my heart to condemn him.

It was then I first thought of Harman. Ambulances from Manhattan and from Jersey City were on the scene, and one had sped to a wooden patch some five hundred yards distant where, caught in the treetops, lay a splintered fragment of the *Prometheus'* forward compartment. I limped there as fast as I could, but they had dragged out Harman and clanged away long before I could reach them.

After that, I didn't stay. The disorganized crowd had no thought but for the dead and wounded *now*, but when they recovered, and bent their thoughts to revenge, my life would not be worth a straw. I followed the dictates of the better part of valor and quietly disappeared.

The next week was a hectic one for me. During that time, I lay in hiding at the home of a friend, for it would have been more than my life was worth to allow myself to be seen and recognized. Harman, himself, lay in a Jersey City hospital, with nothing more than superficial cuts and bruises— thanks to the backward force of the explosion and the saving clump of trees which cushioned the fall of the *Prometheus*. It was on him that the brunt of the world's wrath fell.

New York, and the rest of the world also, just about went crazy. Every last paper in the city came out with gigantic headlines, "28 Killed, 73 Wounded—the Price of Sin," printed in blood-red letters. The editorials howled for Harman's life, demanding he be arrested and tried for first-degree murder.

The dreaded cry of "Lynch him!" was raised throughout the five boroughs, and milling thousands crossed the river and converged on Jersey City. At their head was Otis Eldredge, both legs in splints, addressing the crowd from an open automobile as they marched. It was a veritable army.

Mayor Carson of Jersey City called out every available policeman and phoned frantically to Trenton for the State militia. New York clamped down on every bridge and tunnel leaving the city—but not till after many thousands had left.

There were pitched battles on the Jersey coast that sixteenth of July. The vastly outnumbered police clubbed indiscriminately but were gradually pushed back and back. Mounties rode down upon the mob relentlessly but were swallowed up and pulled down by sheer force of numbers. Not until tear gas was used, did the crowd halt—and even then they did not retreat.

The next day, martial law was declared, and the State militia entered Jersey City. That was the end for the lynchers. Eldredge was called to confer with the mayor, and after the conference ordered his followers to disperse.

In a statement to the newspapers, Mayor Carson said: "John Harman must needs suffer for his crime, but it is essential that he do so legally. Justice must take its course, and the State of New Jersey will take all necessary measures."

By the end of the week, normality of a sort had returned and Harman slipped out of the public spotlight. Two more weeks and there was scarcely a word about him in the newspapers, excepting such casual references to him in the discussion of the new Zittman antirocketry bill that had just passed both houses of Congress by unanimous votes.

Yet he remained in the hospital still. No legal action had been taken against him, but it began to appear that a sort of indefinite imprisonment "for his own protection" might be his eventual fate. Therefore, I bestirred myself to action.

Temple Hospital is situated in a lonely and outlying district of Jersey City, and on a dark, moonless night I experienced no difficulty at all in invading the grounds unobserved. With a facility that surprised me, I sneaked in through a basement window, slugged a sleepy interne into insensibility and proceeded to Room 15E, which was listed in the books as Harman's.

"Who's there?" Harman's surprised shout was music in my ears.

"Sh! Quiet! It's I, Cliff McKenny."

"You! What are you doing here?"

"Trying to get you out. If I don't, you're liable to stay here the rest of your life. Come on, let's go."

I was hustling him into his clothes while we were speaking, and in no time at all we were sneaking down the corridor. We were out safely and into my waiting car before Harman collected his scattered wits sufficiently to begin asking questions.

"What's happened since that day?" was the first question.

"I don't remember a thing after starting the rocket blasts until I woke up in the hospital."

"Didn't they tell you anything?"

"Not a damn thing," he swore. "I asked until I was hoarse."

So I told him the whole story from the explosion on. His eyes were wide with shocked surprise when I told of the dead and wounded, and filled with wild rage when he heard of Shelton's treachery. The story of the riots and attempted lynching evoked a muffled curse fom between set lips.

"Of course, the papers howled 'murder,' " I concluded, "but they couldn't pin *that* on you. They tried manslaughter, but there were too many eye-witnesses that had heard your request for the removal of the crowd and the police sergeant's absolute refusal to do so. That, of course, absolved you from all blame. The police sergeant himself died in the explosion, and they couldn't make him the goat.

"Still, with Eldredge yelling for your hide, you're never safe. It would be best to leave while able."

Harman nodded his head in agreement. "Eldredge survived the explosion, did he?"

"Yes, worse luck. He broke both legs, but it takes more than that to shut his mouth."

Another week had passed before I reached our future haven—my uncle's farm in Minnesota. There, in a lonely and out-of-the-way rural community, we stayed while the hullabaloo over Harman's disappearance gradually died down and the perfunctory search for us faded away. The search, by the way, was short indeed, for the authorities seemed more relieved than concerned over the disappearance.

Peace and quiet did wonders with Harman. In six months he seemed a new man—quite ready to consider a second attempt at space travel. Not all the misfortunes in the world could stop him, it seemed, once he had his heart set on something.

"My mistake the first time," he told me one winter's day, "lay in announcing the experiment. I should have taken the temper of the people into account, as Winstead said. This time, however"—he rubbed his hands and gazed thoughtfully into the distance—"I'll steal a march on them. The experiment will be performed in secrecy—absolute secrecy."

I laughed grimly. "It would have to be. Do you know that

all future experiments in rocketry, even entirely theoretical research, is a crime punishable by death?"

"Are you afraid, then?"

"Of course not, boss. I'm merely stating a fact. And here's another plain fact. We two can't build a ship all by ourselves, you know."

"I've thought of that and figured a way out, Cliff. What's more, I can take care of the money angle, too. You'll have to do some traveling, though.

"First, you'll have to go to Chicago and look up the firm of Roberts & Scranton and withdraw everything that's left of my father's inheritance, which," he added in a rueful aside, "is more than half gone on the first ship. Then, locate as many of the old crowd as you can: Harry Jenkins, Joe O'Brien, Neil Stanton—all of them. And get back as quickly as you can. I am tired of delay."

Two days later, I left for Chicago. Obtaining my uncle's consent to the entire business was a simple affair. "Might as well be strung up for a herd of sheep as for a lamb," he grunted, "so go ahead. I'm in enough of a mess now and can afford a bit more, I guess."

It took quite a bit of traveling and even more smooth talk and persuasion before I managed to get four men to come: the three mentioned by Harman and one other, a Saul Simonoff. With that skeleton force and with the half million still left Harman out of the reputed millions left him by his father, we began work.

The building of the *New Prometheus* is a story in itself—a long story of five years of discouragement and insecurity. Little by little, buying girders in Chicago, beryl-steel plates in New York, a vanadium cell in San Francisco, miscellaneous items in scattered corners of the nation, we constructed the sister ship to the ill-fated *Prometheus*.

The difficulties in the way were all but unsuperable. To prevent drawing suspicion down upon us, we had to spread our purchases over periods of time, and to see to it, as well, that the orders were made out to various places. For this we required the co-operation of various friends, who, to be sure, did not know at the time for exactly what purpose the purchases were being used.

We had to synthesize our own fuel, ten tons of it, and that was perhaps the hardest job of all; certainly it took the most time. And finally, as Harman's money dwindled, we came up against our biggest problem—the necessity of economizing.

From the beginning we had known that we could never make the *New Prometheus* as large or as elaborate as the first ship had been, but it soon developed that we would have to reduce its equipment to a point perilously close to the danger line. The repulsive screen was barely satisfactory and all attempts at radio communication were perforce abandoned.

And as we labored through the years, there in the backwoods of northern Minnesota, the world moved on, and Winstead's prophecies proved to have hit amazingly near the mark.

The events of those five years—from 1973 to 1978—are well known to the schoolboys of today, the period being the climax of what we now call the "Neo-Victorian Age." The happenings of those years seem well-nigh unbelievable as we look back upon them now.

The outlawing of all research on space travel came in the very beginning, but was a bare start compared to the anti-scientific measures taken in the ensuing years. The next congressional elections, those of 1974, resulted in a Congress in which Eldredge controlled the House and held the balance of power in the Senate.

Hence, no time was lost. At the first session of the ninety-third Congress, the famous Stonely-Carter bill was passed. It established the Federal Scientific Research Investigatory Bureau—the FSRIB—which was given full power to pass on the legality of all research in the country. Every laboratory, industrial or scholastic, was required to file information, in advance, on all projected research before this new bureau, which could, and did, ban absolutely all such as it disapproved of.

The inevitable appeal to the supreme court came on November 9, 1974, in the case of Westly vs. Simmons, in which Joseph Westly of Stanford upheld his right to continue his investigations on atomic power on the grounds that the Stonely-Carter act was unconstitutional.

How we five, isolated amid the snowdrifts of the Middle West, followed that case! We had all the Minneapolis and St. Paul papers sent to us—always reaching us two days late—and devoured every word of print concerning it. For the two months of suspense work ceased entirely on the *New Prometheus*.

It was rumored at first that the court would declare the act unconstitutional, and monster parades were held in every large town against this eventuality. The League of the Righteous brought its powerful influence to bear—and even the supreme court submitted. It was five to four for constitutionality. *Science strangled by the vote of one man.*

And it was strangled beyond a doubt. The members of the bureau were Eldredge men, heart and soul, and nothing that would not have immediate industrial use was passed.

"Science has gone too far," said Eldredge in a famous speech at about that time. "We must halt it indefinitely, and allow the world to catch up. Only through that and trust in God may we hope to achieve universal and permanent prosperity."

But this was one of Eldredge's last statements. He had never fully recovered from the broken legs he received that fateful day in July of '73, and his strenuous life since then strained his constitution past the breaking point. On February 2, 1976, he passed away amid a burst of mourning unequaled since Lincoln's assassination.

His death had no immediate effect on the course of events. The rules of the FSRIB grew, in fact, in stringency as the years passed. So starved and choked did science become, that once more colleges found themselves forced to reinstate philosophy and the classics as the chief studies—and at that the student body fell to the lowest point since the beginning of the twentieth century.

These conditions prevailed more or less throughout the civilized world, reaching even lower depths in England, and perhaps least depressing in Germany, which was the last to fall under the "Neo-Victorian" influence.

The nadir of science came in the spring of 1978, a bare month before the completion of the *New Prometheus,* with the passing of the "Easter Edict"—it was issued the day before Easter. By it, *all* independent research or experimentation was absolutely forbidden. The FSRIB thereafter reserved the right to allow only such research as it *specifically requested.*

John Harman and I stood before the gleaming metal of the *New Prometheus* that Easter Sunday; I in the deepest gloom, and he in an almost jovial mood.

"Well, Clifford, my boy," said he, "the last ton of fuel, a few polishing touches, and I am ready for my second attempt. This time there will be no Sheltons among us." He hummed a hymn. That was all the radio played those days, and even we rebels sang them from sheer frequency of repetition.

I grunted sourly: "It's no use, boss. Ten to one, you end up somewhere in space, and even if you come back, you'll most likely be hung by the neck. We can't win." My head shook dolefully from side to side.

"Bah! This state of affairs can't last, Cliff."

"I think it will. Winstead was right that time. The pendulum swings, and since 1945 it's been swinging against us. We're ahead of the times—or behind them."

"Don't speak of that fool Winstead. You're making the same mistake he did. Trends are things of centuries and millenniums, not years or decades. For five hundred years we have been moving toward science. You can't reverse that in thirty years."

"Then what are we doing?" I asked sarcastically.

"We're going through a momentary reaction following a period of too-rapid advance in the Mad Decades. Just such a reaction took place in the Romantic Age—the first Victorian Period—following the too-rapid advance of the eighteenth-century Age of Reason."

"Do you really think so?" I was shaken by his evident self-assurance.

"Of course. This period has a perfect analogy in the spasmodic 'revivals' that used to hit the small towns in America's Bible Belt a century or so ago. For a week, perhaps, everyone would get religion and virtue would reign triumphant. Then, one by one, they would backslide and the Devil would resume his sway.

"In fact, there are symptoms of backsliding even now. The L. R. has indulged in one squabble after another since Eldredge's death. There have been half a dozen schisms already. The very extremities to which those in power are going are helping us, for the country is rapidly tiring of it."

And that ended the argument—I in total defeat, as usual.

A month later, the *New Prometheus* was complete. It was nowhere near as glittering and as beautiful as the original, and bore many a trace of makeshift workmanship, but we were proud of it—proud and triumphant.

"I'm going to try again, men"—Harman's voice was husky, and his little frame vibrant with happiness—"and I may not make it, but for that I don't care." His eyes shone in anticipation. "I'll be shooting through the void at last, and the dream of mankind will come true. Out around the Moon and back; the first to see the other side. It's worth the chance."

"You won't have fuel enough to land on the Moon, boss, which is a pity," I said.

"That doesn't matter. There'll be other flights after this, better prepared and better equipped."

At that a pessimistic whisper ran through the little group surrounding him, to which he paid no attention.

"Good-by," he said. "I'll be seeing you." And with a cheerful grin he climbed into the ship.

Fifteen minutes later, the five of us sat about the living-room table, frowning, lost in thought, eyes gazing out the building at the spot where a burned section of soil marked the spot where a few minutes earlier the *New Prometheus* had lain.

Simonoff voiced the thought that was in the mind of each one of us: "Maybe it would be better for him *not* to come back. He won't be treated very well if he does, I think." And we all nodded in gloomy assent.

How foolish that prediction seems to me now from the hindsight of three decades.

The rest of the story is really not mine, for I did not see Harman again until a month after his eventful trip ended in a safe landing.

It was almost thirty-six hours after the take-off that a screaming projectile shot its way over Washington and buried itself in the mud just across the Potomac.

Investigators were at the scene of the landing within fifteen minutes, and in another fifteen minutes the police were there, for it was found that the projectile was a *rocketship*. They stared in involuntary awe at the tired, disheveled man who staggered out in near-collapse.

There was utter silence while he shook his fist at the gawking spectators and shouted: "Go ahead, hang me, fools. But I've reached the Moon, and you can't hang *that*. Get the FSRIB. Maybe they'll declare the flight illegal and, therefore, nonexistent." He laughed weakly and suddenly collapsed.

Someone shouted: "Take him to a hospital. He's sick." In stiff unconsciousness Harman was bundled into a police car and carried away, while the police formed a guard about the rocketship.

Government officials arrived and investigated the ship, read the log, inspected the drawings and photographs he had taken of the Moon, and finally departed in silence. The crowd grew and the word spread that a man had reached the Moon.

Curiously enough, there was little resentment of the fact. Men were impressed and awed; the crowd whispered and cast inquisitive glances at the dim crescent of Luna, scarcely seen in the bright sunlight. Over all, an uneasy pall of silence, the silence of indecision, lay.

Then, at the hospital, Harman revealed his identity, and the fickle world went wild. Even Harman himself was stunned in surprise at the rapid change in the world's temper. It seemed almost incredible, and yet it was true. Secret discontent, combined with a heroic tale of man against overwhelming odds—the sort of tale that had stirred man's soul since the beginning of time—served to sweep everyone into an ever-swelling current of anti-Victorianism. And Eldredge was dead—no other could replace him.

I saw Harman at the hospital shortly after that. He was propped up and still half buried with papers, telegrams and letters. He grinned at me and nodded. "Well, Cliff," he whispered, "the pendulum swung back again."

# THE BLUE GIRAFFE

*Astounding Science Fiction*, August

## by L. Sprague de Camp

*Sprague possesses a sharp wit and a fine sense of
humor, never better expressed than in this delightful tale.*

*(The craft of the short story, by the way, is by
no means identical with that of the novel. Many an
excellent short-story writer writes novels with difficulty, if at all, and vice versa. Sprague, however,
could do either with equal skill and, as a matter of
fact, I think his novels are even more effective than
his short stories. How I wish it were possible to include* Divide and Rule *or* Lest Darkness Fall *or*
The Roaring Trumpet, *but alas, we must stick to
reasonably short stories. IA)*

Athelstan Cuff was, to put it very mildly, astonished that his
son should be crying. It wasn't that he had exaggerated ideas
about Peter's stoicism, but the fact was that Peter never cried.
He was, for a twelve-year-old boy, self-possessed to the point
of grimness. And now he was undeniably sniffling. It must be
something jolly well awful.

Cuff pushed aside the pile of manuscript he had been reading. He was the editor of *Biological Review;* a stoutish Englishman with prematurely white hair, prominent blue eyes,
and a complexion that could have been used for painting box
cars. He looked a little like a lobster who had been boiled
once and was determined not to repeat the experience.

"What's wrong, old man?" he asked.

Peter wiped his eyes and looked at his father calculatingly.
Cuff sometimes wished that Peter wasn't so damned rational.

248

A spot of boyish unreasonableness would be welcome at times.

"Come on, old fella, out with it. What's the good of having a father if you can't tell him things?"

Peter finally got it out. "Some of the guys——" He stopped to blow his nose. Cuff winced slightly at the "guys." His one regret about coming to America was the language his son picked up. As he didn't believe in pestering Peter all the time, he had to suffer in silence.

"Some of the guys say you aren't really my father."

It had come, thought Cuff, as it was bound to sooner or later. He shouldn't have put off telling the boy for so long.

"What do you mean, old man?" he stalled.

"They say," *sniff*, "I'm just a 'dopted boy."

Cuff forced out, "So what?" The despised Americanism seemed to be the only thing that covered the situation.

"What do you mean, 'so what'?"

"I mean just that. What of it? It doesn't make a particle of difference to your mother or me, I assure you. So why should it to you?"

Peter thought. "Could you send me away some time, on account of I was only 'dopted?"

"Oh, so that's what's worrying you? The answer is no. Legally you're just as much our son as if . . . as anyone is anybody's son. But whatever gave you the idea we'd ever send you away? I'd like to see that chap who could get you away from us."

"Oh, I just wondered."

"Well, you can stop wondering. We don't want to, and we couldn't if we did. It's perfectly all right, I tell you. Lots of people start out as adopted children, and it doesn't make any difference to anybody. You wouldn't get upset if somebody tried to make fun of you because you had two eyes and a nose, would you?"

Peter had recovered his composure. "How did it happen?"

"It's quite a story. I'll tell you, if you like."

Peter only nodded.

"I've told you," said Athelstan Cuff, "about how before I came to America I worked for some years in South Africa. I've told you about how I used to work with elephants and lions and things, and about how I transplanted some white rhino from Swaziland to the Kruger Park. But I've never told you about the blue giraffe——"

In the 1940's the various South African governments were considering the problem of a park that would be not merely a game preserve available to tourists, but a completely wild area in which no people other than scientists and wardens would be allowed. They finally agreed on the Okvango River Delta in Ngamiland, as the only area that was sufficiently large and at the same time thinly populated.

The reasons for its sparse population were simple enough: nobody likes to settle down in a place when he is likely to find his house and farm under three feet of water some fine morning. And it is irritating to set out to fish in a well-known lake only to find that the lake has turned into a grassy plain, around the edges of which the mopane trees are already springing up.

So the Batawana, in whose reserve the Delta lay, were mostly willing to leave this capricious stretch of swamp and jumble to the elephant and the lion. The few Batawana who did live in and around the Delta were bought out and moved. The Crown Office of the Bechuanaland Protectorate got around its own rules against alienation of tribal lands by taking a perpetual lease on the Delta and surrounding territory from the Batawana, and named the whole area Jan Smuts Park.

When Athelstan Cuff got off the train at Francistown in September of 1976, a pelting spring rain was making the platform smoke. A tall black in khaki loomed out of the grayness, and said: "You are Mr. Cuff, from Cape Town? I'm George Mtengeni, the warden at Smuts. Mr. Opdyck wrote me you were coming. The Park's car is out this way."

Cuff followed. He'd heard of George Mtengeni. The man wasn't a Chwana at all, but a Zulu from near Durban. When the Park had been set up, the Batawana had thought that the warden ought to be  a Tawana. But the Makoba, feeling chesty about their independence from their former masters, the Batawana, had insisted on his being one of their nation. Finally the Crown Office in disgust had hired an outsider. Mtengeni had the dark skin and narrow nose found in so many of the Kaffir Bantu. Cuff guessed that he probably had a low opinion of the Chwana people in general and the Batawana in particular.

They got into the car. Mtengeni said: "I hope you don't mind coming way out here like this. It's too bad that you couldn't come before the rains started; the pans they are all full by now."

"So?" said Cuff. "What's the Mababe this year?" He referred to the depression known variously as Mababe Lake, Swamp, or Pan, depending on whether at a given time it contained much, little, or no water.

"The Mababe, it is a lake, a fine lake full of drowned trees and hippo. I think the Okavango is shifting north again. That means Lake Ngami it will dry up again."

"So it will. But look here, what's all this business about a blue giraffe? Your letter was dashed uninformative."

Mtengeni showed his white teeth. "It appeared on the edge of the Mopane Forest seventeen months ago. That was just the beginning. There have been other things since. If I'd told you more, you would have written the Crown Office saying that their warden was having a nervous breakdown. Me, I'm sorry to drag you into this, but the Crown Office keeps saying they can't spare a man to investigate."

"Oh, quite all right, quite," answered Cuff. "I was glad to get away from Cape Town anyway. And we haven't had a mystery since old Hickey disappeared."

"Since who disappeared? You know me, I can't keep up with things out in the wilds."

"Oh, that was many years ago. Before your time, or mine for that matter. Hickey was a scientist who set out into the Kalahari with a truck and a Xosa assistant, and disappeared. Men flew all over the Kalahari looking for him, but never found a trace, and the sand had blown over his tire tracks. Jolly odd, it was."

The rain poured down steadily as they wallowed along the dirt road. Ahead, beyond the gray curtain, lay the vast plains of northern Bechuanaland with their great pans. And beyond the plains were, allegedly, a blue giraffe, and other things.

The spidery steelwork of the tower hummed as they climbed. At the top, Mtengeni said: "You can look over that way . . . west . . . to the other side of the forest. That's about twenty miles."

Cuff screwed up his eyes at the eyepieces. "Jolly good 'scope you've got here. But it's too hazy beyond the forest to see anything."

"It always is, unless we have a high wind. That's the edge of the swamps."

"Dashed if I see how you can patrol such a big area all by yourself."

"Oh, these Bechuana they don't give much trouble. They are honest. Even I have to admit that they have some good qualities. Anyway, you can't get far into the Delta without getting lost in the swamps. There are ways, but then, I only know them. I'll show them to you, but please don't tell these Bechuana about them. Look, Mr. Cuff, there's our blue giraffe."

Cuff started. Mtengeni was evidently the kind of man who would announce an earthquake as casually as the morning mail.

Several hundred yards from the tower half a dozen giraffes were moving slowly through the brush, feeding on the tops of the scrubby trees. Cuff swung the telescope on them. In the middle of the herd was the blue one. Cuff blinked and looked again. There was no doubt about it; the animal was as brilliant a blue as if somebody had gone over it with paint. Athelstan Cuff suspected that that was what somebody *had* done. He said as much to Mtengeni.

The warden shrugged. "That, it would be a peculiar kind of amusement. Not to say risky. Do you see anything funny about the others?"

Cuff looked again. "Yes . . . by Jove, one of 'em's got a beard like a goat; only it must be six feet long, at least, now look here, George, what's all this leading up to?"

"I don't know myself. Tomorrow, if you like, I'll show you one of those ways into the Delta. But that, it's quite a walk, so we'd better take supplies for two or three days."

As they drove toward the Tamalakane, they passed four Batawana, sad-looking reddish-brown men in a mixture of native and European clothes. Mtengeni slowed the car and looked at them suspiciously as they passed, but there was no evidence that they had been poaching.

He said: "Ever since their Makoba slaves were freed, they've been going on a . . . decline, I suppose you would call it. They are too dignified to work."

They got out at the river. "We can't drive across the ford this time of year," explained the warden, locking the car. "But there's a rapid a little way down, where we can wade."

They walked down the trail, adjusting their packs. There wasn't much to see. The view was shut off by the tall soft-bodied swamp plants. The only sound was the hum of insects.

The air was hot and steamy already, though the sun had been up only half an hour. The flies drew blood when they bit, but the men were used to that. They simply slapped and waited for the next bite.

Ahead there was a deep gurgling noise, like a foghorn with water in its works. Cuff said: "How are your hippo doing this year?"

"Pretty good. There are some in particular that I want you to see. Ah, here we are."

They had come in sight of a stretch of calm water. In the foreground a hippopotamus repeated its foghorn bellow. Cuff saw others, of which only the eyes, ears, and nostrils were visible. One of them was moving; Cuff could make out the little V-shaped wakes pointing back from its nearly submerged head. It reached the shallows and lumbered out, dripping noisily.

Cuff blinked. "Must be something wrong with my eyes."

"No," said Mtengeni. "That hippo she is one of those I wanted you to see."

The hippopotamus was green with pink spots.

She spied the men, grunted suspiciously, and slid back into the water.

"I still don't believe it," said Cuff. "Dash it, man, that's impossible."

"You will see many more things," said Mtengeni. "Shall we go on?"

They found the rapid and struggled across; then walked along what might, by some stretch of the imagination, be called a trail. There was little sound other than their sucking footfalls, the hum of insects, and the occasional screech of a bird or the crashing of a buck through the reeds.

They walked for some hours. Then Mtengeni said: "Be careful. There is a rhino near."

Cuff wondered how the devil the Zulu knew, but he was careful. Presently they came on a clear space in which the rhinoceros was browsing.

The animal couldn't see them at that distance, and there was no wind to carry their smell. It must have heard them, though, for it left off its feeding and snorted, once, like a locomotive. It had two heads.

It trotted toward them sniffing.

The men got out their rifles. "My God!" said Athelstan Cuff. "Hope we don't have to shoot him. My God!"

"I don't think so," said the warden. "That's Tweedle. I know him. If he gets too close, give him one at the base of the horn and he . . . he will run."

"Tweedle?"

"Yes. The right head is Tweedledum and the left is Tweedledee," said Mtengeni solemnly. "The whole rhino I call Tweedle."

The rhinoceros kept coming. Mtengeni said: "Watch this." He waved his hat and shouted: "Go away! *Footsack!*"

Tweedle stopped and snorted again. Then he began to circle like a waltzing mouse. Round and round he spun.

"We might as well go on," said Mtengeni. "He will keep that up for hours. You see Tweedledum is fierce, but Tweedledee, he is peaceful, even cowardly. So when I yell at Tweedle, Tweedledum wants to charge us, but Tweedledee he wants to run away. So the right legs go forward and the left legs go back, and Tweedle, he goes in circles. It takes him some time to agree on a policy."

"*Whew!*" said Athelstan Cuff. "I say, have you got any more things like this in your zoo?"

"Oh, yes, lots. That's what I hope you'll do something about."

Do something about this! Cuff wondered whether this was touching evidence of the native's faith in the white omni-science, or whether Mtengeni had gotten him there for the cynical amusement of watching him run in useless circles. Mtengeni himself gave no sign of what he was thinking.

Cuff said: "I can't understand, George, why somebody hasn't looked into this before."

Mtengeni shrugged. "Me, I've tried to get somebody to, but the government won't send anybody, and the scientific expeditions, there haven't been any of them for years. I don't know why."

"I can guess," said Cuff. "In the old days people even in the so-called civilized countries expected travel to be a jolly rugged proposition, so they didn't mind putting up with a few extra hardships on trek. But now that you can ride or fly almost anywhere on soft cushions, people won't put themselves out to get to a really uncomfortable and out-of-the-way place like Ngamiland."

Over the swampy smell came another, of carrion. Mtengeni pointed to the carcass of a waterbuck fawn, which the scavengers had apparently not discovered yet.

"That's why I want you to stop this whatever-it-is," he said. There was real concern in his voice.

"What do you mean, George?"

"Do you see its legs?"

Cuff looked. The forelegs were only half as long as the hind ones.

"That buck," said the Zulu. "It naturally couldn't live long. All over the Park, freaks like this they are being born. Most of them don't live. In ten years more, maybe twenty, all my animals will have died out because of this. Then my job, where is it?"

They stopped at sunset. Cuff was glad to. It had been some time since he'd done fifteen miles in one day, and he dreaded the morrow's stiffness. He looked at his map and tried to figure out where he was. But the cartographers had never seriously tried to keep track of the changes in the Okavango's multifarious branches, and had simply plastered the whole Delta with little blue dashes with tufts of blue lines sticking up from them, meaning simply "swamp." In all directions the country was a monotonous alternation of land and water. The two elements were inextricably mixed.

The Zulu was looking for a dry spot free of snakes. Cuff heard him suddenly shout *"Footsack!"* and throw a clod at a log. The log opened a pair of jaws, hissed angrily, and slid into the water.

"We'll have to have a good fire," said Mtengeni, hunting for dry wood. "We don't want a croc or hippo wandering into our tent by mistake."

After supper they set the automatic bug sprayer going, inflated their mattresses, and tried to sleep. A lion roared somewhere in the west. That sound no African, native or Africander, likes to hear when he is on foot at night. But the men were not worried; lions avoided the swampy areas. The mosquitoes presented a more immediate problem.

Many hours later, Athelstan Cuff heard Mtengeni getting up.

The warden said: "I just remembered a high spot half a mile from here, where there's plenty of firewood. Me, I'm going out to get some."

Cuff listened to Mtengeni's retreating steps in the soft ground; then to his own breathing. Then he listened to something else. It sounded like a human yell.

He got up and pulled on his boots quickly. He fumbled around for the flashlight, but Mtengeni had taken it with him.

The yell came again.

Cuff found his rifle and cartridge belt in the dark and went out. There was enough starlight to walk by if you were careful. The fire was nearly out. The yells seemed to come from a direction opposite to that in which Mtengeni had gone. They were high-pitched, like a woman's screams.

He walked in their direction, stumbling over irregularities in the ground and now and then stepping up to his calves in unexpected water. The yells were plainer now. They weren't in English. Something was also snorting.

He found the place. There was a small tree, in the branches of which somebody was perched. Below the tree a noisy bulk moved around. Cuff caught the outline of a sweeping horn, and knew he had to deal with a buffalo.

He hated to shoot. For a Park official to kill one of his charges simply wasn't done. Besides, he couldn't see to aim for a vital spot, and he didn't care to try to dodge a wounded buffalo in the dark. They could move with race-horse speed through the heaviest growth.

On the other hand, he couldn't leave even a poor fool of a native woman treed. The buffalo, if it was really angry, would wait for days until its victim weakened and fell. Or it would butt the tree until the victim was shaken out. Or it would rear up and try to hook the victim out with its horns.

Athelstan Cuff shot the buffalo. The buffalo staggered about a bit and collapsed.

The victim climbed down swiftly, pouring out a flood of thanks in Xosa. It was very bad Xosa, even worse than the Englishman's. Cuff wondered what she was doing here, nearly a thousand miles from where the Maxosa lived. He assumed that she was a native, though it was too dark to see. He asked her if she spoke English, but she didn't seem to understand the question, so he made shift with the Bantu dialect.

"*Uveli phi na?*" he asked sternly. "Where do you come from? Don't you know that nobody is allowed in the Park without special permission?"

"*Izwe kamafene wabantu,*" she replied.

"What? Never heard of the place. Land of the baboon people, indeed! What are you?"

"*Ingwamza.*"

"You're a white stork? Are you trying to be funny?"

"I didn't say I was a white stork. Ingwamza's my name."

"I don't care about your name. I want to know what you *are*."

"*Umfene umfazi.*"

Cuff controlled his exasperation. "All right, all right, you're a baboon woman. I don't care what clan you belong to. What's your tribe? Batawana, Bamangwato, Bangwaketse, Barolong, Herero, or what? Don't try to tell me you're a Xosa; no Xosa ever used an accent like that."

"*Amafene abantu.*"

"What the devil are the baboon people?"

"People who live in the Park."

Cuff resisted the impulse to pull out two handfuls of hair by the roots. "But I tell you nobody lives in the Park! It isn't allowed! Come now, where do you really come from and what's your native language and why are you trying to talk Xosa?"

"I told you, I live in the Park. And I speak Xosa because all we *amafene abantu* speak it. That's the language Mqhavi taught us."

"Who is Mqhavi?"

"The man who taught us to speak Xosa."

Cuff gave up. "Come along, you're going to see the warden. Perhaps he can make some sense out of your gabble. And you'd better have a good reason for trespassing, my good woman, or it'll go hard with you. Especially as it resulted in the killing of a good buffalo." He started off toward the camp, making sure that Ingwamza followed him closely.

The first thing he discovered was that he couldn't see the light of any fire to guide him back. Either he'd come farther than he thought, or the fire had died altogether while Mtengeni was getting wood. He kept on for a quarter of an hour in what he thought was the right direction. Then he stopped. He had, he realized, not the vaguest idea of where he was.

He turned. "*Sibaphi na?*" he snapped. "Where are we?"

"In the Park."

Cuff began to wonder whether he'd ever succeed in delivering this native woman to Mtengeni before he strangled her with his bare hands. "I know we're in the Park," he snarled. "But *where* in the Park?"

"I don't know exactly. Somewhere near my people's land."

"That doesn't do me any good. Look: I left the warden's

camp when I heard you yell. I want to get back to it. Now how do I do it?"

"Where is the warden's camp?"

"I don't know, stupid. If I did I'd go there."

"If you don't know where it is, how do you expect me to guide you thither? I don't know either."

Cuff made strangled noises in his throat. Inwardly he had to admit that she had him there, which only made him madder. Finally he said: "Never mind, suppose you take me to your people. Maybe they have somebody with some sense."

"Very well," said the native woman, and she set off at a rapid pace, Cuff stumbling after her vague outline. He began to wonder if maybe she wasn't right about living in the Park. She seemed to know where she was going.

"Wait," he said. He ought to write a note to Mtengeni, explaining what he was up to, and stick it on a tree for the warden to find. But there was no pencil or paper in his pockets. He didn't even have a match safe or a cigarette lighter. He'd taken all those things out of his pockets when he'd lain down.

They went on a way, Cuff pondering on how to get in touch with Mtengeni. He didn't want himself and the warden to spend a week chasing each other around the Delta. Perhaps it would be better to stay where they were and build a fire—but again, he had no matches, and didn't see much prospect of making a fire by rubbing sticks in this damned damp country.

Ingwamza said: "Stop. There are buffalo ahead."

Cuff listened and heard faintly the sound of snapping grass stems as the animals fed.

She continued: "We'll have to wait until it gets light. Then maybe they'll go away. If they don't, we can circle around them, but I couldn't find the way around in the dark."

They found the highest point they could and settled down to wait. Something with legs had crawled inside Cuff's shirt. He mashed it with a slap.

He strained his eyes into the dark. It was impossible to tell how far away the buffalo were. Overhead a nightjar brought its wings together with a single startling clap. Cuff told his nerves to behave themselves. He wished he had a smoke.

The sky began to lighten. Gradually Cuff was able to make out the black bulks moving among the reeds. They were at least two hundred yards away. He'd have preferred that they were at twice the distance, but it was better than stumbling right on them.

It became lighter and lighter. Cuff never took his eyes off the buffalo. There was something queer about the nearest one. It had six legs.

Cuff turned to Ingwamza and started to whisper: "What kind of buffalo do you call—" Then he gave a yell of pure horror and jumped back. His rifle went off, tearing a hole in his boot.

He had just gotten his first good look at the native woman in the rapidly waxing dawn. Ingwamza's head was that of an overgrown chacma baboon.

The buffalo stampeded through the feathery papyrus. Cuff and Ingwamza stood looking at each other. Then Cuff looked at his right foot. Blood was running out of the jagged hole in the leather.

"What's the matter? Why did you shoot yourself?" asked Ingwamza.

Cuff couldn't think of an answer to that one. He sat down and took off his boot. The foot felt numb, but there seemed to be no harm done aside from a piece of skin the size of a sixpence gouged out of the margin. Still, you never knew what sort of horrible infection might result from a trifling wound in these swamps. He tied his foot up with his handkerchief and put his boot back on.

"Just an accident," he said. "Keep going, Ingwamza."

Ingwamza went, Cuff limping behind. The sun would rise any minute now. It was light enough to make out colors. Cuff saw that Ingwamza, in describing herself as a baboon-woman, had been quite literal, despite the size, general proportions, and posture of a human being. Her body, but for the greenish-yellow hair and the short tail, might have passed for that of a human being, if you weren't too particular. But the astonishing head with its long bluish muzzle gave her the appearance of an Egyptian animal-headed god. Cuff wondered vaguely if the *'fene abantu* were a race of man-monkey hybrids. That was impossible, of course. But he'd seen so many impossible things in the last couple of days.

She looked back at him. "We shall arrive in an hour or two. I'm sleepy." She yawned. Cuff repressed a shudder at the sight of four canine teeth big enough for a leopard. Ingwamza could tear the throat out of a man with those fangs as easily as biting the end off a banana. And he'd been using his most hectoring colonial-administrator tone on her in the dark!

He made a resolve never to speak harshly to anybody he couldn't see.

Ingwamza pointed to a carroty baobab against the sky. "*Izew kamagene wabantu.*" They had to wade a little stream to get there. A six-foot monitor lizard walked across their path, saw them, and disappeared with a scuttle.

The *'fene abantu* lived in a village much like that of any Bantu people, but the circular thatched huts were smaller and cruder. Baboon people ran out to peer at Cuff and to feel his clothes. He gripped his rifle tightly. They didn't act hostile, but it gave you a dashed funny feeling. The males were larger than the females, with even longer muzzles and bigger tusks.

In the center of the village sat a big *umfene umntu* scratching himself in front of the biggest hut. Ingwamza said, "That is my father, the chief. His name is Indlovu." To the baboon-man she told of her rescue.

The chief was the only *umfene umntu* that Cuff had seen who wore anything. What he wore was a necktie. The necktie had been a gaudy thing once.

The chief got up and made a speech, the gist of which was that Cuff had done a great thing, and that Cuff would be their guest until his wound healed. Cuff had a chance to observe the difficulties that the *'fene abantu* had with the Xosa tongue. The clicks were blurred, and they stumbled badly over the lipsmack. With those mouths, he could see how they might.

But he was only mildly interested. His foot was hurting like the very devil. He was glad when they led him into a hut so he could take off his boot. The hut was practically unfurnished. Cuff asked the *'fene abantu* if he might have some of the straw used for thatching. They seemed puzzled by his request, but complied, and he made himself a bed of sorts. He hated sleeping on the ground, especially on ground infested with arthropodal life. He hated vermin, and knew he was in for an intimate acquaintance with them.

He had nothing to bandage his foot with, except the one handkerchief, which was now thoroughly blood-soaked. He'd have to wash and dry it before it would be fit to use again. And where in the Okavango Delta could he find water fit to wash the handkerchief in? Of course he could boil the water. In what? He was relieved and amazed when his questions brought forth the fact that there was a large iron pot in the village, obtained from God knew where.

The wound had clotted satisfactorily, and he dislodged the handkerchief with infinite care from the scab. While his water was boiling, the chief, Indlovu, came in and talked to him. The pain in his foot had subsided for the moment, and he was able to realize what an extraordinary thing he had come across, and to give Indlovu his full attention. He plied Indlovu with questions.

The chief explained what he knew about himself and his people. It seemed that he was the first of the race; all the others were his descendants. Not only Ingwamza but all the other *amafene abafazi* were his daughters. Ingwamza was merely the last. He was old now. He was hazy about dates, but Cuff got the impression that these beings had a shorter life span than human beings, and matured much more quickly. If they were in fact baboons, that was natural enough.

Indlovu didn't remember having had any parents. The earliest he remembered was being led around by Mqhavi. Stanley H. Mqhavi had been a black man, and worked for the machine man, who had been a pink man like Cuff. He had had a machine up on the edge of the Chobe Swamp. His name had been Heeky.

Of course, Hickey! thought Cuff. Now he was getting somewhere. Hickey had disappeared by simply running his truck up to Ngamiland without bothering to tell anybody where he was going. That had been before the Park had been established; before Cuff had come out from England. Mqhair must have been his Xosa assistant. His thoughts raced ahead of Indlovu's words.

Indlovu went on to tell about how Heeky had died, and how Mqhavi, not knowing how to run the machine, had taken him, Indlovu, and his now numerous progeny in an attempt to find his way back to civilization. He had gotten lost in the Delta. Then he had cut his foot somehow, and gotten sick, very sick. Cuff had come out from England. Mqhavi must have Mqhavi, had gotten well he had been very weak. So he had settled down with Indlovu and his family. They already walked upright and spoke Xosa, which Mqhavi had taught them. Cuff got the idea that the early family relationships among the *'fene abantu* had of necessity involved close inbreeding. Mqhavi had taught them all he knew, and then died, after warning them not to go within a mile of the machine, which, as far as they knew, was still up at the Chobe Swamp.

Cuff thought, that blasted machine is an electronic tube of some sort, built to throw short waves of the length to affect animal genes. Probably Indlovu represented one of Hickey's early experiments. Then Hickey had died, and—left the thing going. He didn't know how it got power; some solar system, perhaps.

Suppose Hickey had died while the thing was turned on. Mqhavi might have dragged his body out and left the door open. He might have been afraid to try to turn it off, or he might not have thought of it. So every animal that passed that doorway got a dose of the rays, and begat monstrous off-spring. These super-baboons were one example; whether an accidental or a controlled mutation, might never be known.

For every useful mutation there were bound to be scores of useless or harmful ones. Mtengeni had been right: it had to be stopped while there was still normal stock left in the Park. He wondered again how to get in touch with the warden. He'd be damned if anything short of the threat of death would get him to walk on that foot, for a few days anyhow.

Ingwamza entered with a wooden dish full of a mess of some sort. Athelstan Cuff decided resignedly that he was expected to eat it. He couldn't tell by looking whether it was animal or vegetable in nature. After the first mouthful he was sure it was neither. Nothing in the animal and vegetable worlds could taste as awful as that. It was too bad Mqhavi hadn't been a Bamangwato; he'd have really known how to cook, and could have taught these monkeys. Still, he had to eat something to support life. He fell to with the wooden spoon they gave him, suppressing an occasional gag and watching the smaller solid particles closely. Sure enough, he had to smack two of them with the spoon to keep them from crawling out.

"How it is?" asked Ingwamza. Indlovu had gone out.

"Fine," lied Cuff. He was chasing a slimy piece of what he suspected was waterbuck tripe around the dish.

"I am glad. We'll feed you a lot of that. Do you like scorpions?"

"You mean to *eat?*"

"Of course. What else are they good for?"

He gulped. "No."

"I won't give you any then. You see I'm glad to know what my future husband likes."

"What?" He thought he had misunderstood her.

"I said, I am glad to know what you like, so I can please you after you are my husband."

Athelstan Cuff said nothing for sixty seconds. His naturally prominent eyes bulged even more as her words sank in. Finally he spoke.

"*Gluk*," he said.

"What's that?"

"*Gug. Gah.* My God. Let me out of here!" His voice jumped two octaves, and he tried to get up. Ingwamza caught his shoulders and pushed him gently, but firmly, back on his pallet. He struggled, but without visibly exerting herself the *'fene umfazi* held him as in a vise.

"You can't go," she said. "If you try to walk on that foot you will get sick."

His ruddy face was turning purple! "Let me up! Let me up, I say! I can't stand this!"

"Will you promise not to try to go out if I do? Father would be furious if I let you do anything unwise."

He promised, getting a grip on himself again. He already felt a bit foolish about his panic. He was in a nasty jam, certainly, but an official of His Majesty didn't act like a frightened schoolgirl at every crisis.

"What," he asked, "is this all about?"

"Father is so grateful to you for saving my life that he intends to bestow me on you in marriage, without even asking a bride price."

"But . . . but . . . I'm married already," he lied.

"What of it? I'm not afraid of your other wives. If they got fresh, I'd tear them in pieces like this." She bared her teeth and went through the motions of tearing several Mistresses Cuff in pieces. Athelstan Cuff shut his eyes at the horrid sight.

"Among my people," he said, "you're allowed only one wife."

"That's too bad," said Ingwamza. "That means that you couldn't go back to your people after you married me, doesn't it?"

Cuff sighed. These *'fene abantu* combined the mental outlook of uneducated Maxosa with physical equipment that would make a lion think twice before attacking one. He'd probably have to shoot his way out. He looked around the hut craftily. His rifle wasn't in sight. He didn't dare ask about it for fear of arousing suspicion.

"Is your father set on this plan?" he asked.

"Oh, yes, very. Father is a good *umntu*, but he gets set on ideas like this and nothing will make him change them. And he has a terrible temper. If you cross him when he has his heart set on something, he will tear you in pieces. *Small pieces.*" She seemed to relish the phrase.

"How do *you* feel about it, Ingwamza?"

"Oh, I do everything father says. He knows more than any of us."

"Yes, but I mean you personally. Forget about your father for the moment."

She didn't quite catch on for a moment, but after further explanation she said: "I wouldn't mind. It would be a great thing for my people if one of us was married to a man."

Cuff silently thought that that went double for him.

Indlovu came in with two other *amafene abantu*. "Run along, Ingwamza," he said. The three baboon-men squatted around Athelstan Cuff and began questioning him about men and the world outside the Delta.

When Cuff stumbled over a phrase, one of the questioners, a scarred fellow named Sondlo, asked why he had difficulty. Cuff explained that Xosa wasn't his native language.

"Men do speak other languages?" asked Indlovu. "I remember now, the great Mqhavi once told me something to that effect. But he never taught me any other languages. Perhaps he and Heeky spoke one of these other languages, but I was too young when Heeky died to remember."

Cuff explained something about linguistics. He was immediately pressed to "say something in English." Then they wanted to learn English, right then, that afternoon.

Cuff finished his evening meal and looked without enthusiasm at his pallet. No artificial light, so these people rose and set with the sun. He stretched out. The straw rustled. He jumped up, bringing his injured foot down hard. He yelped, swore, and felt the bandage. Yes, he'd started it bleeding again. Oh, to hell with it. He attacked the straw, chasing out a mouse, six cockroaches, and uncounted smaller bugs. Then he stretched out again. Looking up, he felt his scalp prickle. A ten-inch centipede was methodically hunting its prey over the underside of the roof. If it missed its footing when it was right over him—He unbuttoned his shirt and pulled it up over his face. Then the mosquitoes attacked his midriff. His foot throbbed.

A step brought him up; it was Ingwamza.

"What is it now?" he asked.

*"Ndiya kuhlaha apha,"* she answered.

"Oh no, you're not going to stay here. We're not . . . well, anyway, it simply isn't done among my people."

"But Esselten, somebody must watch you in case you get sick. My father—"

"No, I'm sorry, but that's final. If you're going to marry me you'll have to learn how to behave among men. And we're beginning right now."

To his surprise and relief, she went without further objection, albeit sulkily. He'd never have dared to try to put her out by force.

When she had gone, he crawled over to the door of the hut. The sun had just set, and the moon would follow it in a couple of hours. Most of the *'fene abantu* had retired. But a couple of them squatted outside their huts, in sight of his place, watchfully.

Heigh ho, he thought, they aren't taking any chances. Perhaps the old boy *is* grateful and all that rot. But I think my fiancée let the cat out when she said that about the desirability of hitching one of the tribe to a human being. Of course the poor things don't know that it wouldn't have any legal standing at all. But that fact wouldn't save me from a jolly unpleasant experience in the meantime. Suppose I haven't escaped by the time of the ceremony. Would I go through with it? *Br-r-r!* Of course not. I'm an Englishman and an officer of the Crown. But if it meant my life . . . I don't know. I'm dashed if I do. Perhaps I can talk them out of it . . . being careful not to get them angry in the process—

He was tied to the straw, and enormous centipedes were dropping off the ceiling onto his face. Then he was running through the swamp, with Ingwamza and her irate pa after him. His feet stuck in the mud so he couldn't move, and there was a light in his face. Mtengeni—good old George!—was riding a two headed rhino. But instead of rescuing him, the warden said: "Mr. Cuff, you must do something about these Bechuana. Them, they are catching all my animals and painting them red with green stripes." Then he woke up.

It took him a second to realize that the light was from the

setting moon, not the rising sun, and that he therefore had
been asleep less than two hours. It took him another second
to realize what had wakened him. The straw of the hut wall
had been wedged apart, and through the gap a *'fene umntu*
was crawling. While Cuff was still wondering why one of his
hosts, or captors, should use this peculiar method of getting
in, the baboon-man stood up. He looked enormous in the
faint light.

"What is it?" asked Cuff.

"If you make a noise," said the stranger, "I will kill you."

"What? What's the idea? Why should you want to kill
me?"

"You have stolen my Ingwamza."

"But . . . but—" Cuff was at a loss. Here the gal's old
man would tear him in pieces—*small* pieces—if he didn't
marry her, and a rival or something would kill him if he did.
"Let's talk it over first," he said, in what he hoped was a normal voice. "Who are you, by the way?"

"My name is Cukata. I was to have married Ingwamza
next month. And then you came."

"What . . . what—"

"I won't kill you. Not if you make no noise. I will just fix
you so you won't marry Ingwamza." He moved toward the
pile of straw.

Cuff didn't waste time inquiring into the horrid details.
"Wait a minute," he said, cold sweat bedewing not merely his
brow, but his whole torso. "My dear fellow, this marriage
wasn't my idea. It was Indlovu's, entirely. I don't want to
steal your girl. They just informed me that I was going to
marry her, without asking me about it at all. I don't *want* to
marry her. In fact there's nothing I want to do less."

The *'fene umntu* stood still for a moment, thinking. Then
he said softly: "You wouldn't marry my Ingwamza if you
had the chance? You think she is ugly?"

"Well—"

"By u-Qamata, that's an insult! Nobody shall think such
thoughts of my Ingwamza! Now I will kill you for sure!"

"Wait, wait!" Cuff's voice, normally a pleasant low .bari-
tone, became a squeak. "That isn't it at all! She's beautiful,
intelligent, industrious, all that a *'ntu* could want. But I can
never marry her." Inspiration! Cuff went on rapidly. Never
had he spoken Xosa so fluently. "You know that if lion mates
with leopard, there are no offspring." Cuff wasn't sure that
was so, but he took a chance. "It is that way with my people

and yours. We are too different. There would be no issue to our marriage. And Indlovu would not have grandchildren by us to gladden his old age."

Cukata, after some thought, saw, or thought he did. "But," he said, "how can I prevent this marriage without killing you?"

"You could help me escape."

"So. Now that's an idea. Where do you want to go?"

"Do you know where the Hickey machine is?"

"Yes, though I have never been close to it. That is forbidden. About fifteen miles north of here, on the edge of the Chobe Swamp, is a rock. By the rock are three baobab trees, close together. Between the trees and the swamp are two houses. The machine is in one of those houses."

He was silent again. "You can't travel fast with that wounded foot. They would overtake you. Perhaps Indlovu would tear you in pieces, or perhaps he would bring you back. If he brought you back, we should fail. If he tore you in pieces, I should be sorry, for I like you, even if you are a feeble little *isi-pham-pham*." Cuff wished that the simian brain would get around to the point. "I have it. In ten minutes I shall whistle. You will then crawl out through this hole in the wall, making no noise. You understand?"

When Athelstan Cuff crawled out, he found Cukata in the alley between two rows of huts. There was a strong reptilian stench in the air. Behind the baboon-man was something large and black. It walked with a swaying motion. It brushed against Cuff, and he almost cried out at the touch of cold, leathery hide.

"This is the largest," said Cukata. "We hope some day to have a whole herd of them. They are fine for traveling across the swamps, because they can swim as well as run. And they grow much faster than the ordinary crocodile."

The thing was a crocodile but such a crocodile! Though not much over fifteen feet in length, it had long, powerful legs that raised its body a good four feet off the ground, giving it a dinosaurian look. It rubbed against Cuff, and the thought occurred to him that it had taken an astonishing mutation indeed to give a brainless and voracious reptile an affection for human beings.

Cukata handed Cuff a knobkerry, and explained: "Whistle, loudly, when you want him to come. To start him, hit him on the tail with this. To stop him, hit him on the nose. To make him go to the left, hit him on the right side of the neck, not too hard. To make him go to the right, hit him—"

"On the left side of the neck, but not too hard," finished Cuff. "What does he eat?"

"Anything that is meat. But you needn't feed him for two or three days; he has been fed recently."

"Don't you use a saddle?"

"Saddle? What's that?"

"Never mind." Cuff climbed aboard, wincing as he settled onto the sharp dorsal ridges of the animal's hide.

"Wait," said Cukata. "The moon will be completely gone in a moment. Remember, I shall say that I know nothing about your escape, but that you go out and stole him yourself. His name Soga."

There were the baobab trees, and there were the houses. There were also a dozen elephants, facing the rider and his bizarre mount and spreading their immense ears. Athelstan Cuff was getting so blasé about freaks that he hardly noticed that two of the elephants had two trunks apiece; that another of them was colored a fair imitation of a Scotch tartan; that another of them had short legs like a hippopotamus, so that it looked like something out of a dachshund breeder's nightmare.

The elephants, for their part, seemed undecided whether to run or to attack, and finally compromised by doing nothing. Cuff realized when he was already past them that he had done a wickedly reckless thing in going so close to them unarmed except for the useless kerry. But somehow he couldn't get excited about mere elephants. His whole life for the past forty-eight hours had had a dreamlike quality. Maybe he was dreaming. Or maybe he had a charmed life. Or something. Though there was nothing dreamlike about the throb in his foot, or the acute soreness in his gluteus maximus.

Soga, being a crocodile, bowed his whole body at every stride. First the head and tail went to the right and the body to the left; then the process was reversed. Which was most unpleasant for his rider.

Cuff was willing to swear that he'd ridden at least fifty miles instead of the fifteen Cukata had mentioned. Actually he had done about thirty, not having been able to follow a straight line and having to steer by stars and, when it rose, the sun. A fair portion of the thirty had been hugging Soga's barrel while the croc's great tail drove them through the water like a racing shell. No hippo or other crocs had bothered them; evidently they knew when they were well off.

Athelstan Cuff slid—almost fell—off, and hobbled up to the entrance of one of the houses. His practiced eye took in the roof cistern, the solar boiler, the steam-electric plant, the batteries, and finally the tube inside. He went in. Yes, by Jove, the tube was in operation after all these years. Hickey must have had something jolly unusual. Cuff found the main switch easily enough and pulled it. All that happened was that the little orange glow in the tube died.

The house was so silent it made Cuff uncomfortable, except for the faint hum of the solar power plant. As he moved about, using the kerry for a crutch, he stirred up the dust which lay six inches deep on the floor. Maybe there were notebooks or something which ought to be collected. There had been, he soon discovered, but the termites had eaten every scrap of paper, and even the imitation-leather covers, leaving only the metal binding rings and their frames. It was the same with the books.

Something white caught his eye. It was paper. lying on a little metal-legged stand that the termites evidently hadn't thought well enough of to climb. He limped toward it eagerly. But it was only a newspaper, *Umlindi we Nyanga*— "The Monthly Watchman"—published in East London. Evidently, Stanley H. Mqhavi had subscribed to it. It crumbled at Cuff's touch.

Oh, well, he thought, can't expect much. We'll run along, and some of the bio-physicist chappies can come in and gather up the scientific apparatus.

He went out, called Soga, and started east. He figured that he could strike the old wagon road somewhere north of the Mababe, and get down to Mtengeni's main station that way.

Were those human voices? Cuff shifted uneasily on his Indian fakir's seat. He had gone about four miles after leaving Hickey's scientific station.

They were voices, but not human ones. They belonged to a dozen *'fene abantu*, who came loping through the grass with old Indlovu at their head.

Cuff reached back and thumped Soga's tail. If he could get the croc going all out, he might be able to run away from his late hosts. Soga wasn't as fast as a horse, but he could trot right along. Cuff was relieved to see that they hadn't brought his rifle along. They were armed with kerries and spears, like any of the more savage *abantu*. Perhaps the fear of injuring their pet would make them hesitate to throw things at him. At least he hoped so.

A familiar voice caught up with him in a piercing yell of "Soga!" The croc slackened his pace and tried to turn his head. Cuff whacked him unmercifully. Indlovu's yell came again, followed by a whistle. The croc was now definitely off his stride. Cuff's efforts to keep him headed away from his proper masters resulted in his zigzagging erratically. The contrary directions confused and irritated him. He opened his jaws and hissed. The baboon-men were gaining rapidly.

So, thought Cuff, this is the end. I hate like hell to go out before I've had a chance to write my report. But mustn't show it. Not an Englishman and an officer of the Crown. Wonder what poor Mtengeni'll think.

Something went *whick* past him; a fraction of a second later, the crash of an elephant rifle reached him. A big puff of dust ballooned up in front of the baboon-men. They skittered away from it as if the dust and not the bullet that made it were something deadly. George Mtengeni appeared from behind the nearest patch of thorn scrub, and yelled, "Hold still there, or me, I'll blow your heads off." If the *'fene abantu* couldn't understand his English, they got his tone.

Cuff thought vaguely, good old George, he could shoot their ears off at that distance, but he has more sense then to kill any of them before he finds out. Cuff slid off Soga and almost fell in a heap.

The warden came up. "What . . . what in the heavens has been happening to you, Mr. Cuff? What are these?" He indicated the baboon-men.

"Joke," giggled Cuff. "Good joke on you, George. Been living in your dashed Park for years, and you never knew— Wait, I've got to explain something to these chaps. I say, Indlovu . . . hell, he doesn't know English. Got to use Xosa. You know Xosa, don't you George?" He giggled again.

"Why, me, I . . . I can follow it. It's much like Zulu. But my God, what happened to the seat of your pants?"

Cuff pointed a wavering finger at Soga's sawtoothed back. "Good old Soga. Should have had a saddle. Dashed outrage, not providing a saddle for His Majesty's representative."

"But you look as if you'd been skinned! Me, I've got to get you to a hospital . . . and what about your foot?"

"T'hell with the foot. 'Nother joke, Can't stand up, can't sit down. Jolly, what? Have to sleep on my stomach. But, Indlovu! I'm sorry I had to run away. I couldn't marry Ingwamza. Really. Because . . . because—" Athelstan Cuff swayed and collapsed in a small, ragged pile.

Peter Cuff's eyes were round. He asked the inevitable small-boy question: "What happened then?"

Athelstan Cuff was stuffing his pipe. "Oh, about what you'd expect. Indlovu was jolly vexed, I can tell you, but he didn't dare do anything with George standing there with the gun. He calmed down later after he understood what I had been driving at, and we became good friends. When he died, Cukata was elected chief in his place. I still get Christmas cards from him."

"Christmas cards from a baboon?"

"Certainly. If I get one next Christmas, I'll show it to you. It's the same card every year. He's an economical fella, and he bought a hundred cards of the same pattern because he could get them at a discount."

"Were you all right?"

"Yes, after a month in the hospital. I still don't know why I didn't get sixteen kinds of blood poisoning. Fool's luck, I suppose."

"But what's that got to do with me being a 'dopted boy?"

"Peter!" Cuff gave the clicks represented in the Bantu languages by *x* and in English by *tsk*. "Isn't it obvious? That tube of Hickey's was on when I approached his house. So I got a full dose of the radiations. Their effect was to produce violent mutations in the germ-plasm. You know what that is, don't you? Well, I never dared have any children of my own after that, for fear they'd turn out to be some sort of monster. That didn't occur to me until afterward. It fair bowled me over, I can tell you, when I did think of it. I went to pieces, rather, and lost my job in South Africa. But now that I have you and your mother, I realize that it wasn't so important after all."

"Father—" Peter hesitated.

"Go on, old man."

"If you'd thought of the rays before you went to the house, would you have been brave enough to go ahead anyway?"

Cuff lit his pipe and looked off at nothing. "I've often wondered about that myself. I'm dashed if I know. I wonder . . . just what would have happened—"

# THE MISGUIDED HALO

*Unknown*, August

## by Henry Kuttner (1915–1958)

*The late Henry Kuttner accomplished much in his too-short life, but some of his accomplishments were unappreciated because most observers of science fiction felt "his" best work was that done in collaboration with his wife, the gifted C. L. Moore, under the name "Lewis Padgett." Although it was really impossible to separate out who did what in these collaborative efforts, it seemed to many that Moore was more responsible for their success than Kuttner. This is always a problem in collaborations, and it was a shame because Kuttner, although he turned out a number of stories for the pulps that even he was not proud of, was a very talented writer, especially of "science-fantasy."*

*His particular specialty was a most effective use of irony, a device as demanding and difficult for a writer as any in literature. "The Misguided Halo" is an excellent example.*

*(I met Henry Kuttner only once, in the mid-1940s, at a party which nearly drowned in the combined noise of Bob Heinlein, Sprague de Camp and myself. He sat through it all quietly, holding hands with his wife, and listening with patent amusement. He must have said something, but I don't remember what that might have been. IA.)*

The youngest angel could scarcely be blamed for the error. They had given him a brand-new, shining halo and pointed down to the particular planet they meant. He had followed directions implicitly, feeling quite proud of the responsibility. This was the first time the youngest angel had ever been commissioned to bestow sainthood on a human.

So he swooped down to the earth, located Asia, and came to rest at the mouth of a cavern that gaped halfway up a Himalayan peak. He entered the cave, his heart beating wildly with excitement, preparing to materalize and give the holy lama his richly earned reward. For ten years the ascetic Tibetan Kai Yung had sat motionless, thinking holy thoughts. For ten more years he had dwelt on top of a pillar, acquiring additional merit. And for the last decade he had lived in this cave, a hermit, forsaking fleshly things.

The youngest angel crossed the threshold and stopped with a gasp of amazement. Obviously he was in the wrong place. An overpowering odor of fragrant *sake* assailed his nostrils, and he stared aghast at the wizened, drunken little man who squatted happily beside a fire, roasting a bit of goat flesh. A den of iniquity!

Naturally, the youngest angel, knowing little of the ways of the world, could not understand what had led to the lama's fall from grace. The great pot of *sake* that some misguidedly pious one had left at the cave mouth was an offering, and the lama had tasted, and tasted again. And by this time he was clearly not a suitable candidate for sainthood.

The youngest angel hesitated. The directions had been explicit. But surely this tippling reprobate could not be intended to wear a halo. The lama hiccuped loudly and reached for another cup of *sake* and thereby decided the angel, who unfurled his wings and departed with an air of outraged dignity.

Now, in a Midwestern State of North America there is a town called Tibbett. Who can blame the angel if he alighted there, and, after a brief search, discovered a man apparently ripe for sainthood, whose name, as stated on the door of his small suburban home, was K. Young?

"I may have got it wrong," the youngest angel thought. "They said it was Kai Yung. But this is Tibbett, all right. He must be the man. Looks holy enough, anyway.

"Well," said the youngest angel, "here goes. Now, where's that halo?"

Mr. Young sat on the edge of his bed, with head lowered, brooding. A depressing spectacle. At length he arose and donned various garments. This done, and shaved and washed and combed, he descended the stairway to breakfast.

Jill Young, his wife, sat examining the paper and sipping

orange juice. She was a small, scarcely middle-aged, and quite pretty woman who had long ago given up trying to understand life. It was, she decided, much too complicated. Strange things were continually happening. Much better to remain a bystander and simply let them happen. As a result of this attitude, she kept her charming face unwrinkled and added numerous gray hairs to her husband's head.

More will be said presently of Mr. Young's head. It had, of course, been transfigured during the night. But as yet he was unaware of this, and Jill drank orange juice and placidly approved a silly-looking hat in an advertisement.

"Hello, Filthy," said Young. "Morning."

He was not addressing his wife. A small and raffish Scotty had made its appearance, capering hysterically about its master's feet, and going into a fit of sheer madness when the man pulled its hairy ears. The raffish Scotty flung its head sidewise upon the carpet and skated about the room on its muzzle, uttering strangled squeaks of delight. Growing tired of this at last, the Scotty, whose name was Filthy McNasty, began thumping its head on the floor with the apparent intention of dashing out its brains, if any.

Young ignored the familiar sight. He sat down, unfolded his napkin, and examined his food. With a slight grunt of appreciation he began to eat.

He became aware that his wife was eying him with an odd and distrait expression. Hastily he dabbed at his lips with the napkin. But Jill still stared.

Young scrutinized his shirt front. It was, if not immaculate, at least free from stray shreds of bacon or egg. He looked at his wife, and realized that she was staring at a point slightly above his head. He looked up.

Jill started slightly. She whispered, "Kenneth, what *is* that?"

Young smoothed his hair. "Er ... what, dear?"

"That thing on your head."

The man ran exploring fingers across his scalp. "My head? How do you mean?"

"It's shining," Jill explained. "What on earth have you been doing to yourself?"

Mr. Young felt slightly irritated. "I have been doing nothing to myself. A man grows bald eventually."

Jill frowned and drank orange juice. Her fascinated gaze crept up again. Finally she said, "Kenneth, I wish you'd—"

"What?"

She pointed to a mirror on the wall.

With a disgusted grunt Young arose and faced the image in the glass. At first he saw nothing unusual. It was the same face he had been seeing in mirrors for years. Not an extraordinary face—not one at which a man could point with pride and say: "Look. *My face.*" But, on the other hand, certainly not a countenance which would cause consternation. All in all, an ordinary, clean, well-shaved, and rosy face. Long association with it had given Mr. Young a feeling of tolerance, if not of actual admiration.

But topped by a halo it acquired a certain eerieness.

The halo hung unsuspended about five inches from the scalp. It measured perhaps seven inches in diameter, and seemed like a glowing, luminous ring of white light. It was impalpable, and Young passed his hand through it several times in a dazed manner.

"It's a . . . halo," he said at last, and turned to stare at Jill.

The Scotty, Filthy McNasty, noticed the luminous adornment for the first time. He was greatly interested. He did not, of course, know what it was, but there was always a chance that it might be edible. He was not a very bright dog.

Filthy sat up and whined. He was ignored. Barking loudly, he sprang forward and attempted to climb up his master's body in a mad attempt to reach and rend the halo. Since it had made no hostile move, it was evidently fair prey.

Young defended himself, clutched the Scotty by the nape of its neck, and carried the yelping dog into another room, where he left it. Then he returned and once more looked at Jill.

At length she observed, "Angels wear halos."

"Do I look like an angel?" Young asked. "It's a . . . a scientific manifestation. Like . . . like that girl whose bed kept bouncing around. You read about that."

Jill had. "She did it with her muscles."

"Well, I'm not," Young said definitely. "How could I? It's scientific. Lots of things shine by themselves."

"Oh, yes. Toadstools."

The man winced and rubbed his head. "Thank you, my dear. I suppose you know you're being no help at all."

"Angels have halos," Jill said with a sort of dreadful insistence.

Young was at the mirror again. "Darling, would you mind

keeping your trap shut for a while? I'm scared as hell, and you're far from encouraging."

Jill burst into tears, left the room, and was presently heard talking in a low voice to Filthy.

Young finished his coffee, but it was tasteless. He was not as frightened as he had indicated. The manifestation was strange, weird, but in no way terrible. Horns, perhaps, would have caused horror and consternation. But a halo— Mr. Young read the Sunday newspaper supplements, and had learned that everything odd could be attributed to the bizarre workings of science. Somewhere he had heard that all mythology had a basis in scientific fact. This comforted him, until he was ready to leave for the office.

He donned a derby. Unfortunately the halo was too large. The hat seemed to have two brims, the upper one whitely luminous.

"Damn!" said Young in a heartfelt manner. He searched the closet and tried on one hat after another. None would hide the halo. Certainly he could not enter a crowded bus in such a state.

A large furry object in a corner caught his gaze. He dragged it out and eyed the thing with loathing. It was a deformed, gigantic woolly headpiece, resembling a shako, which had once formed a part of a masquerade costume. The suit itself had long since vanished, but the hat remained to the comfort of Filthy, who sometimes slept on it.

Yet it would hide the halo. Gingerly Young drew the monstrosity on his head and crept toward the mirror. One glance was enough. Mouthing a brief prayer, he opened the door and fled.

Choosing between two evils is often difficult. More than once during that nightmare ride downtown Young decided he had made the wrong choice. Yet, somehow, he could not bring himself to tear off the hat and stamp it underfoot, though he was longing to do so. Huddled in a corner of the bus, he steadily contemplated his fingernails and wished he was dead. He heard titters and muffled laughter, and was conscious of probing glances riveted on his shrinking head.

A small child tore open the scar tissue on Young's heart and scrabbled about in the open wound with rosy, ruthless fingers.

"Mamma," said the small child piercingly, "look at the funny man."

"Yes, honey," came a woman's voice. "Be quiet."

"What's that on his head?" the brat demanded.

There was a significant pause. Finally the woman said, "Well, I don't really know," in a baffled manner.

"What's he got it on for?"

No answer.

"Mamma!"

"Yes, honey."

"Is he crazy?"

"Be quiet," said the woman, dodging the issue.

"But what *is* it?"

Young could stand it no longer. He arose and made his way with dignity through the bus, his glazed eyes seeing nothing. Standing on the outer platform, he kept his face averted from the fascinated gaze of the conductor.

As the vehicle slowed down Young felt a hand laid on his arm. He turned. The small child's mother was standing there, frowning.

"Well?" Young inquired snappishly.

"It's Billy," the woman said. "I try to keep nothing from him. Would you mind telling me just what that is on your head?"

"It's Rasputin's beard," Young grated. "He willed it to me." The man leaped from the bus and, ignoring a half-heard question from the still-puzzled woman, tried to lose himself in the crowd.

This was difficult. Many were intrigued by the remarkable hat. But, luckily, Young was only a few blocks from his office, and at last, breathing hoarsely, he stepped into the elevator, glared murderously at the operator, and said, "Ninth floor."

"Excuse me, Mr. Young," the boy said mildly. "There's something on your head."

"I know," Young replied. "I put it there."

This seemed to settle the question. But after the passenger had left the elevator, the boy grinned widely. When he saw the janitor a few minutes later he said:

"You know Mr. Young? The guy—"

"I know him. So what?"

"Drunk as a lord."

"Him? You're screwy."

"Tighter'n a drum," declared the youth, "swelp me Gawd."

Meanwhile, the sainted Mr. Young made his way to the office of Dr. French, a physician whom he knew slightly, and who was conveniently located in the same building. He had not long to wait. The nurse, after one startled glance at the re-markable hat, vanished, and almost immediately reappeared to usher the patient into the inner sanctum.

Dr. French, a large, bland man with a waxed, yellow mustache, greeted Young almost effusively.

"Come in, come in. How are you today? Nothing wrong, I hope. Let me take your hat."

"Wait," Young said, fending off the physician. "First let me explain. There's something on my head."

"Cut, bruise or fracture?" the literal-minded doctor inquired. "I'll fix you up in a jiffy."

"I'm not *sick*," said Young. "At least, I hope not. I've got a ... um ... a halo."

"Ha, ha," Dr. French applauded. "A halo, eh? Surely you're not that good."

"Oh, the hell with it!" Young snapped, and snatched off his hat. The doctor retreated a step. Then, interested, he approached and tried to finger the halo. He failed.

"I'll be— This is odd," he said at last. "Does look rather like one, doesn't it?"

"What is it? That's what I want to know."

French hesitated. He plucked at his mustache. "Well, it's rather out of my line. A physicist might— No. Perhaps Mayo's. Does it come off?"

"Of course not. You can't even touch the thing."

"Ah. I see. Well, I should like some specialists' opinions. In the meantime, let me see—" There was orderly tumult. Young's heart, temperature, blood, saliva and epidermis were tested and approved.

At length French said: "You're fit as a fiddle. Come in tomorrow, at ten. I'll have some other specialists here then."

"You ... uh ... you can't get rid of this?"

"I'd rather not try just yet. It's obviously some form of radioactivity. A radium treatment may be necessary—"

Young left the man mumbling about alpha and gamma rays. Discouraged, he donned his strange hat and went down the hall to his own office.

The Atlas Advertising Agency was the most conservative of all advertising agencies. Two brothers with white whiskers had started the firm in 1820, and the company still seemed to wear dignified mental whiskers. Changes were frowned upon by the board of directors, who, in 1938, were finally convinced that radio had come to stay, and had accepted contracts for advertising broadcasts.

Once a junior vice president had been discharged for wearing a red necktie.

Young slunk into his office. It was vacant. He slid into his chair behind the desk, removed his hat, and gazed at it with loathing. The headpiece seemed to have grown even more horrid than it had appeared at first. It was shedding, and, moreover, gave off a faint but unmistakable aroma of unbathed Scotties.

After investigating the halo, and realizing that it was still firmly fixed in its place, Young turned to his work. But the Norns were casting baleful glances in his direction, for presently the door opened and Edwin G. Kipp, president of Atlas, entered. Young barely had time to duck his head beneath the desk and hide the halo.

Kipp was a small, dapper, and dignified man who wore pince-nez and Vandyke with the air of a reserved fish. His blood had long since been metamorphosed into ammonia. He moved, if not in beauty, at least in an almost visible aura of grim conservatism.

"Good morning, Mr. Young," he said. "Er . . . is that you?"

"Yes," said the invisible Young. "Good morning. I'm tying my shoelace."

To this Kipp made no reply save for an almost inaudible cough. Time passed. The desk was silent.

"Er . . . Mr. Young?"

"I'm . . . still here," said the wretched Young. "It's knotted. The shoelace, I mean. Did you want me?"

"Yes."

Kipp waited with gradually increasing impatience. There were no signs of a forthcoming emergence. The president considered the advisability of his advancing to the desk and peering under it. But the mental picture of a conversation conducted in so grotesque a manner was harrowing. He simply gave up and told Young what he wanted.

"Mr. Devlin has just telephoned," Kipp observed. "He will arrive shortly. He wishes to . . . er . . . to be shown the town, as he put it."

The invisible Young nodded. Devlin was one of their best clients. Or, rather, he had been until last year, when he suddenly began to do business with another firm, to the discomfiture of Kipp and the board of directors.

The president went on. "He told me he is hesitating about his new contract. He had planned to give it to World, but I had some correspondence with him on the matter, and suggested that a personal discussion might be of value. So he is visiting our city and wishes to go . . . er . . . sightseeing."

Kipp grew confidential. "I may say that Mr. Devlin told me rather definitely that he prefers a less conservative firm. 'Stodgy,' his term was. He will dine with me tonight, and I shall endeavor to convince him that our service will be of value. Yet"—Kipp coughed again—"yet diplomacy is, of course, important. I should appreciate your entertaining Mr. Devlin today."

The desk had remained silent during this oration. Now it said convulsively: "I'm sick. I can't—"

"You are ill? Shall I summon a physician?"

Young hastily refused the offer, but remained in hiding. "No, I . . . but I mean—"

"You are behaving most strangely," Kipp said with commendable restraint. "There is something you should know, Mr. Young. I had not intended to tell you as yet, but . . . at any rate, the board has taken notice of you. There was a discussion at the last meeting. We have planned to offer you a vice presidency in the firm."

The desk was stricken dumb.

"You have upheld our standards for fifteen years," said Kipp. "There has been no hint of scandal attached to your name. I congratulate you, Mr. Young."

The president stepped forward, extending his hand. An arm emerged from beneath the desk, shook Kipp's, and quickly vanished.

Nothing further happened. Young tenaciously remained in his sanctuary. Kipp realized that, short of dragging the man out bodily, he could not hope to view an entire Kenneth Young for the present. With an admonitory cough he withdrew.

The miserable Young emerged, wincing as his cramped muscles relaxed. A pretty kettle of fish. How could he entertain Devlin while he wore a halo? And it was vitally necessary that Devlin be entertained, else the elusive vice presidency would be immediately withdrawn. Young knew only too well that employees of Atlas Advertising Agency trod a perilous pathway.

His reverie was interrupted by the sudden appearance of an angel atop the bookcase.

It was not a high bookcase, and the supernatural visitor sat there calmly enough, heels dangling and wings furled. A scanty robe of white samite made up the angel's wardrobe—that and a shining halo, at sight of which Young felt a wave of nausea sweep him.

"This," he said with rigid restraint, "is the end. A halo may be due to mass hypnotism. But when I start seeing angels—"

"Don't be afraid," said the other. "I'm real enough."

Young's eyes were wild. "How do I know? I'm obviously talking to empty air. It's schizo-something. Go away."

The angel wriggled his toes and looked embarrassed. "I can't, just yet. The fact is, I made a bad mistake. You may have noticed that you've a slight halo—"

Young gave a short, bitter laugh. "Oh, yes. I've *noticed* it."

Before the angel could reply the door opened. Kipp looked in, saw that Young was engaged, and murmured, "Excuse me," as he withdrew.

The angel scratched his golden curls. "Well, your halo was intended for somebody else—a Tibetan lama, in fact. But through a certain chain of circumstances I was led to believe that you were the candidate for sainthood. So—" The visitor made a comprehensive gesture.

Young was baffled. "I don't quite—"

"The lama . . . well, sinned. No sinner may wear a halo. And, as I say, I gave it to you through error."

"Then you can take it away again?" Amazed delight suffused Young's face. But the angel raised a benevolent hand.

"Fear not. I have checked with the recording angel. You have led a blameless life. As a reward, you will be permitted to keep the halo of sainthood."

The horrified man sprang to his feet, making feeble swimming motions with his arms. "But . . . but . . . but—"

"Peace and blessings be upon you," said the angel, and vanished.

Young fell back into his chair and massaged his aching brow. Simultaneously the door opened and Kipp stood on the threshold. Luckily Young's hands temporarily hid the halo.

"Mr. Devlin is here," the president said. "Er . . . who was that on the bookcase?"

Young was too crushed to lie plausibly. He muttered, "An angel."

Kipp nodded in satisfaction. "Yes, of course. . . . *What?* You say an angel . . . an angel? Oh, my gosh!" The man turned quite white and hastily took his departure.

Young contemplated his hat. The thing still lay on the desk, wincing slightly under the baleful stare directed at it.

To go through life wearing a halo was only less endurable than the thought of continually wearing the loathsome hat. Young brought his fist down viciously on the desk.

"I won't stand it! I . . . I don't have to—" He stopped abruptly. A dazed look grew in his eyes.

"I'll be . . . that's right! I don't *have* to stand it. If that lama got out of it . . . of course. 'No sinner may wear a halo.' " Young's round face twisted into a mask of sheer evil. "I'll be a sinner, then! I'll break all the Commandments—"

He pondered. At the moment he couldn't remember what they were. "Thou shalt not covet thy neighbor's wife." That was one.

Young thought of his neighbor's wife—a certain Mrs. Clay, a behemothic damsel of some fifty summers, with a face like a desiccated pudding. That was one Commandment he had no intention of breaking.

But probably one good, healthy sin would bring back the angel in a hurry to remove the halo. What crimes would result in the least inconvenience? Young furrowed his brow.

Nothing occurred to him. He decided to go for a walk. No doubt some sinful opportunity would present itself.

He forced himself to don the shako and had reached the elevator when a hoarse voice was heard hallooing after him. Racing along the hall was a fat man.

Young knew instinctively that this was Mr. Devlin.

The adjective "fat," as applied to Devlin, was a considerable understatement. The man bulged. His feet, strangled in biliously yellow shoes, burst out at the ankles like blossoming flowers. They merged into calves that seemed to gather momentum as they spread and mounted, flung themselves up with mad abandon, and revealed themselves in their complete, unrestrained glory at Devlin's middle. The man resembled, in silhouette, a pineapple with elephantiasis. A great mass of flesh poured out of his collar, forming a pale, sagging lump in which Young discerned some vague resemblance to a face.

Such was Devlin, and he charged along the hall, as mammoths thunder by, with earth-shaking tramplings of his crashing hoofs.

"You're Young!" he wheezed. "Almost missed me, eh? I was waiting in the office—" Devlin paused, his fascinated gaze upon the hat. Then, with an effort at politeness, he laughed falsely and glanced away. "Well, I'm all ready and r'aring to go."

Young felt himself impaled painfully on the horns of a dilemma. Failure to entertain Devlin would mean the loss of that vice presidency. But the halo weighed like a flatiron on Young's throbbing head. One thought was foremost in his mind: he *had* to get rid of the blessed thing.

Once he had done that, he would trust to luck and diplomacy. Obviously, to take out his guest now would be fatal, insanity. The hat alone would be fatal.

"Sorry," Young grunted. "Got an important engagement. I'll be back for you as soon as I can."

Wheezing laughter, Devlin attached himself firmly to the other's arm. "No, you don't. You're showing me the town! Right now!" An unmistakable alcoholic odor was wafted to Young's nostrils. He thought quickly.

"All right," he said at last. "Come along. There's a bar downstairs. We'll have a drink, eh?"

"Now you're talking," said the jovial Devlin, almost incapacitating Young with a comradely slap on the back. "Here's the elevator."

They crowded into the cage. Young shut his eyes and suffered as interested stares were directed upon the hat. He fell into a state of coma, arousing only at the ground floor, where Devlin dragged him out and into the adjacent bar.

Now Young's plan was this: he would pour drink after drink down his companion's capacious gullet, and await his chance to slip away unobserved. It was a shrewd scheme, but it had one flaw—Devlin refused to drink alone.

"One for you and one for me," he said. "That's fair. Have another."

Young could not refuse, under the circumstances. The worst of it was that Devlin's liquor seemed to seep into every cell of his huge body, leaving him, finally, in the same state of glowing happiness which had been his originally. But poor Young was, to put it as charitably as possible, tight.

He sat quietly in a booth, glaring across at Devlin. Each time the waiter arrived, Young knew that the man's eyes were riveted upon the hat. And each round made the thought of that more irritating.

Also, Young worried about his halo. He brooded over sins. Arson, burglary, sabotage, and murder passed in quick review through his befuddled mind. Once he attempted to snatch the waiter's change, but the man was too alert. He laughed pleasantly and placed a fresh glass before Young.

The latter eyed it with distaste. Suddenly coming to a decision, he arose and wavered toward the door. Devlin overtook him on the sidewalk.

"What's the matter? Let's have another—"

"I have work to do," said Young with painful distinctness. He snatched a walking cane from a passing pedestrian and made threatening gestures with it until the remonstrating victim fled hurriedly. Hefting the stick in his hand, he brooded blackly.

"But why work?" Devlin inquired largely. "Show me the town."

"I have important matters to attend to." Young scrutinized a small child who had halted by the curb and was returning the stare with interest. The tot looked remarkably like the brat who had been so insulting on the bus.

"What's important?" Devlin demanded. "Important matters, eh? Such as what?"

"Beating small children," said Young, and rushed upon the startled child, brandishing his cane. The youngster uttered a shrill scream and fled. Young pursued for a few feet and then became entangled with a lamp-post. The lamp-post was impolite and dictatorial. It refused to allow Young to pass. The man remonstrated and, finally, argued, but to no avail.

The child had long since disappeared. Administering a brusque and snappy rebuke to the lamp-post, Young turned away.

"What in Pete's name are you trying to do?" Devlin inquired. "That cop's looking at us. Come along." He took the other's arm and led him along the crowded sidewalk.

"What am I trying to do?" Young sneered. "It's obvious, isn't it? I wish to sin."

"Er . . . sin?"

"Sin."

"Why?"

Young tapped his hat meaningly, but Devlin put an altogether wrong interpretation on the gesture. "You're nuts?"

"Oh, shut up," Young snapped in a sudden burst of rage, and thrust his cane between the legs of a passing bank president whom he knew slightly. The unfortunate man fell heavily to the cement, but arose without injury save to his dignity.

"I beg your pardon!" he barked.

Young was going through a strange series of gestures. He had fled to a show-window mirror and was doing fantastic things to his hat, apparently trying to lift it in order to catch a glimpse of the top of his head—a sight, it seemed, to be shielded jealously from profane eyes. At length he cursed loudly, turned, gave the bank president a contemptuous stare, and hurried away, trailing the puzzled Devlin like a captive balloon.

Young was muttering thickly to himself.

"Got to sin—really sin. Something big. Burn down an orphan asylum. Kill m' mother-in-law. Kill . . . anybody!" He looked quickly at Devlin, and the latter shrank back in sudden fear. But finally Young gave a disgusted grunt.

"Nrgh. Too much blubber. Couldn't use a gun or a knife. Have to blast—Look!" Young said, clutching Devlin's arm. "Stealing's a sin, isn't it?"

"Sure is," the diplomatic Devlin agreed. "But you're not—"

Young shook his head. "No. Too crowded here. No use going to jail. Come on!"

He plunged forward. Devlin followed. And Young fulfilled his promise to show his guest the town, though afterward neither of them could remember exactly what had happened. Presently Devlin paused in a liquor store for refueling, and emerged with bottles protruding here and there from his clothing.

Hours merged into an alcoholic haze. Life began to assume an air of foggy unreality to the unfortunate Devlin. He sank presently into a coma, dimly conscious of various events which marched with celerity through the afternoon and long into the night. Finally he roused himself sufficiently to realize that he was standing with Young confronting a wooden Indian which stood quietly outside a cigar store. It was, perhaps, the last of the wooden Indians. The outworn relic of a bygone day, it seemed to stare with faded glass eyes at the bundle of wooden cigars it held in an extended hand.

Young was no longer wearing a hat. And Devlin suddenly noticed something decidedly peculiar about his companion.

He said softly, "You've got a halo."

Young started slightly. "Yes," he replied, "I've got a halo. This Indian—" He paused.

Devlin eyed the image with disfavor. To his somewhat fuzzy brain the wooden Indian appeared even more horrid than the surprising halo. He shuddered and hastily averted his gaze.

"Stealing's a sin," Young said under his breath, and then, with an elated cry, stooped to lift the Indian. He fell immediately under its weight, emitting a string of smoking oaths as he attempted to dislodge the incubus.

"Heavy," he said, rising at last. "Give me a hand."

Devlin had long since given up any hope of finding sanity in this madman's actions. Young was obviously determined to sin, and the fact that he possessed a halo was somewhat disquieting, even to the drunken Devlin. As a result, the two men proceeded down the street, bearing with them the rigid body of a wooden Indian.

The proprietor of the cigar shop came out and looked after them, rubbing his hands. His eyes followed the departing statue with unmitigated joy.

"For ten years I've tried to get rid of that thing," he whispered gleefully. "And now ... aha!"

He re-entered the store and lit a Corona to celebrate his emancipation.

Meanwhile, Young and Devlin found a taxi stand. One cab stood there; the driver sat puffing a cigarette and listening to his radio. Young hailed the man.

"Cab, sir?" The driver sprang to life, bounced out of the car, and flung open the door. Then he remained frozen in a half-crouching position, his eyes revolving wildly in their sockets.

He had never believed in ghosts. He was, in fact, somewhat of a cynic. But in the face of a bulbous ghoul and a decadent angel bearing the stiff corpse of an Indian, he felt with a sudden, blinding shock of realization that beyond life lies a black abyss teeming with horror unimaginable. Whining shrilly, the terrified man leaped back into his cab, got the thing into motion, and vanished as smoke before the gale.

Young and Devlin looked at one another ruefully.

"What now?" the latter asked.

"Well," said Young, "I don't live far from here. Only ten blocks or so. Come on!"

It was very late, and few pedestrians were abroad. These few, for the sake of their sanity, were quite willing to ignore the wanderers and go their separate ways. So eventually Young, Devlin, and the wooden Indian arrived at their destination.

The door of Young's home was locked, and he could not locate the key. He was curiously averse to arousing Jill. But, for some strange reason, he felt it vitally necessary that the wooden Indian be concealed. The cellar was the logical place. He dragged his two companions to a basement window, smashed it as quietly as possible, and slid the image through the gap.

"Do you really live here?" asked Devlin, who had his doubts.

"Hush!" Young said warningly. "Come on!"

He followed the wooden Indian, landing with a crash in a heap of coal. Devlin joined him after much wheezing and grunting. It was not dark. The halo provided about as much illumination as a twenty-five-watt globe.

Young left Devlin to nurse his bruises and began searching for the wooden Indian. It had unaccountably vanished. But he found it at last cowering beneath a washtub, dragged the object out, and set it up in a corner. Then he stepped back and faced it, swaying a little.

"That's a sin, all right," he chuckled. "Theft. It isn't the amount that matters. It's the principle of the thing. A wooden Indian is just as important as a million dollars, eh, Devlin?"

"I'd like to chop that Indian into fragments," said Devlin with passion. "You made me carry it for three miles." He paused, listening. "What in heaven's name is that?"

A small tumult was approaching. Filthy, having been instructed often in his duties as a watchdog, now faced opportunity. Noises were proceeding from the cellar. Burglars, no doubt. The raffish Scotty cascaded down the stairs in a babel of frightful threats and oaths. Loudly declaring his intention of eviscerating the intruders, he flung himself upon Young, who made hasty clucking sounds intended to soothe the Scotty's aroused passions.

Filthy had other ideas. He spun like a dervish, yelling bloody murder. Young wavered, made a vain snatch at the air, and fell prostrate to the ground. He remained face down, while Filthy, seeing the halo, rushed at it and trampled upon his master's head.

The wretched Young felt the ghosts of a dozen and more drinks rising to confront him. He clutched at the dog, missed, and gripped instead the feet of the wooden Indian. The image swayed perilously. Filthy cocked up an apprehensive eye and fled down the length of his master's body, pausing halfway as he remembered his duty. With a muffled curse he sank his teeth into the nearest portion of Young and attempted to yank off the miserable man's pants.

Meanwhile, Young remained face down, clutching the feet of the wooden Indian in a despairing grip.

There was a resounding clap of thunder. White light blazed through the cellar. The angel appeared.

Devlin's legs gave way. He sat down in a plump heap, shut his eyes, and began chattering quietly to himself. Filthy swore at the intruder, made an unsuccessful attempt to attain a firm grasp on one of the gently fanning wings, and went back to think it over, arguing throatily. The wing had an unsatisfying lack of substantiality.

The angel stood over Young with golden fires glowing in his eyes, and a benign look of pleasure molding his noble features. "This," he said quietly, "shall be taken as a symbol of your first successful good deed since your enhaloment." A wingtip brushed the dark and grimy visage of the Indian. Forthwith, there was no Indian. "You have lightened the heart of a fellow man—little, to be sure, but some, and at a cost of much labor on your part.

"For a day you have struggled with this sort to redeem him, but for this no success has rewarded you, albeit the morrow's pains will afflict you.

"Go forth, K. Young, rewarded and protected from all sin alike by your halo." The youngest angel faded quietly, for which alone Young was grateful. His head was beginning to ache and he'd feared a possible thunderous vanishment.

Filthy laughed nastily, and renewed his attack on the halo. Young found the unpleasant act of standing upright necessary. While it made the walls and tubs spin round like all the hosts of heaven, it made impossible Filthy's dervish dance on his face.

Some time later he awoke, cold sober and regretful of the fact. He lay between cool sheets, watching morning sunlight lance through the windows, his eyes, and feeling it splinter in jagged bits in his brain. His stomach was making spasmodic attempts to leap up and squeeze itself out through his burning throat.

Simultaneous with awakening came realization of three things: the pains of the morrow had indeed afflicted him; the halo mirrored still in the glass above the dressing table—and the parting words of the angel.

He groaned a heartfelt triple groan. The headache would pass, but the halo, he knew, would not. Only by sinning could one become unworthy of it, and—shining protector!—it made him unlike other men. His deeds must all be good, his works a help to men. He could not sin!

# HEAVY PLANET

*Astounding Science Fiction*, August

# by Milton A. Rothman (1919–     )

*The pen name originally appearing on this was
"Lee Gregory." Lee Gregory was really Milton
Rothman, long-time Philadelphia sf fan and working
scientist (Ph.D., Physics, University of Pennsylvania, 1952). "Heavy Planet" was probably the
finest "hard" science fiction story of 1939—published when the author was all of twenty.*

*(Milt threatens to be something that is common
in Hollywood but rare in science fiction, the
founder of a dynasty. It is rare for a science fiction
writer to have offspring who turn to science fiction—perhaps the force of the dreadful example
makes it unlikely. Young Tony Rothman, who is as
bright as his father (and taller) is now beginning to
make it in the field. I.A.)*

Ennis was completing his patrol of Sector EM, Division 426
of the Eastern Ocean. The weather had been unusually fine,
the liquid-thick air roaring along in a continuous blast that
propelled his craft with a rush as if it were flying, and lifting
short, choppy waves that rose and fell with a startling suddenness. A short savage squall whirled about, pounding down
on the ocean like a million hammers, flinging the little boat
ahead madly.

Ennis tore at the controls, granite-hard muscles standing
out in bas-relief over his short, immensely thick body, skin
gleaming scalelike in the slashing spray. The heat from the
sun that hung like a huge red lantern on the horizon was a
tangible intensity, making an inferno of the gale.

289

The little craft, that Ennis maneuvered by sheer brawn, took a leap into the air and seemed to float for many seconds before burying its keel again in the sea. It often floated for long distances, the air was so dense. The boundary between air and water was sometimes scarcely defined at all—one merged into the other imperceptibly. The pressure did strange things.

Like a dust mote sparkling in a beam, a tiny speck of light above caught Ennis' eye. A glider, he thought, but he was puzzled. Why so far out here on the ocean? They were nasty things to handle in the violent wind.

The dust mote caught the light again. It was lower, tumbling down with a precipitancy that meant trouble. An upward blast caught it, checked its fall. Then it floated down gently for a space until struck by another howling wind that seemed to distort its very outlines.

Ennis turned the prow of his boat to meet the path of the falling vessel. Curious, he thought; where were its wings? Were they retracted, or broken off? It ballooned closer, and it wasn't a glider. Far larger than any glider ever made, it was of a ridiculous shape that would not stand up for an instant. And with the sharp splash the body made as it struck the water—a splash that fell in almost the same instant it rose—a thought seemed to leap up in his mind. A thought that was more important than anything else on that planet; or was to him, at least. For if it was what he thought it was—and it had to be that—it was what Shadden had been desperately seeking for many years. What a stroke of inconceivable luck, falling from the sky before his very eyes!

The silvery shape rode the ragged waters lightly. Ennis' craft came up with a rush; he skillfully checked its speed and the two came together with a slight jar. The metal of the strange vessel dented as if it were made of rubber. Ennis stared. He put out an arm and felt the curved surface of the strange ship. His finger prodded right through the metal. What manner of people were they who made vessels of such weak materials?

He moored his little boat to the side of the larger one and climbed to an opening. The wall sagged under him. He knew he must be careful; it was frightfully weak. It would not hold together very long; he must work fast if it were to be saved. The atmospheric pressure would have flattened it out long ago, had it not been for the jagged rent above which had allowed the pressure to be equalized.

He reached the opening and lowered himself carefully into the interior of the vessel. The rent was too small; he enlarged it by taking the two edges in his hands and pulling them apart. As he went down he looked askance at the insignificant plates and beams that were like tissue paper on his world. Inside was wreckage. Nothing was left in its original shape. Crushed, mutilated machinery, shattered vacuum tubes, sagging members, all ruined by the gravity and the pressure.

There was a pulpy mess on the floor that he did not examine closely. It was like red jelly, thin and stalky, pulped under a gravity a hundred times stronger and an atmosphere ten thousand times heavier than that it had been made for.

He was in a room with many knobs and dials on the walls, apparently a control room. A table in the center with a chart on it, the chart of a solar system. It had nine planets; his had but five.

Then he knew he was right. If they came from another system, what he wanted must be there. It could be nothing else.

He found a staircase, descended. Large machinery bulked there. There was no light, but he did not notice that. He could see well enough by infra red, and the amount of energy necessary to sustain his compact gianthood kept him constantly radiating.

Then he went through a door that was of a comfortable massiveness, even for his planet—and there it was. He recognized it at once. It was big, squat, strong. The metal was soft, but it was thick enough even to stand solidly under the enormous pull of this world. He had never seen anything quite like it. It was full of coils, magnets, and devices of shapes unknown to him. But Shadden would know. Shadden, and who knows how many other scientists before him, had tried to make something which would do what this could do, but they had all failed. And without the things this machine could perform, the race of men on Heavyplanet was doomed to stay down on the surface of the planet, chained there immovably by the crushing gravity.

It was atomic energy. That he had known as soon as he knew that the body was not a glider. For nothing else but atomic energy and the fierce winds was capable of lifting a body from the surface of Heavyplanet. Chemicals were impotent. There is no such thing as an explosion where the atmosphere pressed inward with more force than an explosion could press outward. Only atomic, of all the theoretically possible sources of energy, could supply the work necessary to lift a vessel away from the planet. Every other source of energy was simply too weak.

Yes, Shadden, all the scientists must see this. And quickly, because the forces of sea and storm would quickly tear the ship to shreds, and, even more vital, because the scientists of Bantin and Marak might obtain the secret if there was delay. And that would mean ruin—the loss of its age-old supremacy—for his nation. Bantin and Marak were war nations; did they obtain the secret they would use it against all the other worlds that abounded in the Universe.

The Universe was big. That was why Ennis was so sure there was atomic energy on this ship. For, even though it might have originated on a planet that was so tiny that *chemical energy*—although that was hard to visualize—would be sufficient to lift it out of the pull of gravity, to travel the distance that stretched between the stars only one thing would suffice.

He went back through the ship, trying to see what had happened.

There were pulps lying behind long tubes that pointed out through clever ports in the outer wall. He recognized them as weapons, worth looking into.

There must have been a battle. He visualized the scene. The forces that came from atomic energy must have warped even space in the vicinity. The ship pierced, the occupants killed, the controls wrecked, the vessel darting off at titanic speed, blindly into nothing. Finally it had come near enough to Heavyplanet to be enmeshed in its huge web of gravity.

*Weeaao-o-ow!* It was the wailing roar of his alarm siren, which brought him spinning around and dashing for his boat. Beyond, among the waves that leaped and fell so suddenly, he saw a long, low craft making way toward the derelict spaceship. He glimpsed a flash of color on the rounded, gray superstructure, and knew it for a battleship of Marak. Luck was going strong both ways; first good, now bad. He could easily have eluded the battleship in his own small craft, but he couldn't leave the derelict. Once lost to the enemy he could never regain it, and it was too valuable to lose.

The wind howled and buffeted about his head, and he strained his muscles to keep from being blasted away as he crouched there, half on his own boat and half on the derelict. The sun had set and the evening winds were beginning to blow. The hulk scudded before them, its prow denting from the resistance of the water it pushed aside.

He thought furiously fast. With a quick motion he flipped the switch of the radiophone and called Shadden. He waited with fierce impatience until the voice of Shadden was in his ear. At last he heard it, then: "Shadden! This is Ennis. Get your glider, Shadden, fly to a45j on my route! Quickly! It's come, Shadden! But I have no time. Come!"

He flipped the switch off, and pounded the valve out of the bottom of his craft, clutching at the side of the derelict. With a rush the ocean came up and flooded his little boat and in an instant it was gone, on its way down to the bottom. That would save him from being detected for a short time.

Back into the darkness of the spaceship. He didn't think he had been noticed climbing through the opening. Where could he hide? Should he hide? He couldn't defeat the entire battleship singlehanded, without weapons. There were no weapons that could be carried anyway. A beam of concentrated actinic light that ate away the eyes and the nervous system had to be powered by the entire output of a battleship's generators. Weapons for striking and cutting had never been developed on a world where flesh was tougher than metal. Ennis was skilled in personal combat, but how could he overcome all that would enter the derelict?

Down again, into the dark chamber where the huge atomic generator towered over his head. This time he looked for something he had missed before. He crawled around it, peering into its recesses. And then, some feet above, he saw the opening, and pulled himself up to it, carefully, not to destroy the precious thing with his mass. The opening was shielded with a heavy, darkly transparent substance through which seeped a dim glow from within. He was satisfied then. Somehow, matter was still being disintegrated in there, and energy could be drawn off if he knew how.

There were leads—wires of all sizes, and busbars, and thick, heavy tubes that bent under their own weight. Some must lead in and some must lead out; it was not good to tamper with them. He chose another track. Upstairs again, and to the places where he had seen the weapons.

They were all mounted on heavy, rigid swivels. He carefully detached the tubes from the bases. The first time he tried it he was not quite careful enough, and part of the projector itself was ripped away, but next time he knew what he was doing and it came away nicely. It was a large thing, nearly as thick as his arm and twice as long. Heavy leads trailed from its lower end and a lever projected from behind. He hoped it was in working condition. He dared not try it; all he could do was to trace the leads back and make sure they were intact.

He ran out of time. There came a thud from the side, and then smaller thuds, as the boarding party incautiously leaped over. Once there was a heavy sound, as someone went all the way through the side of the ship.

"Idiots!" Ennis muttered, and moved forward with his weapon toward the stairway. Noises came from overhead, and then a loud crash buckled the plates of the ceiling. Ennis leaped out of the way, but the entire section came down, with two men on it. The floor sagged, but held for the moment. Ennis, caught beneath the downcoming mass, beat his way free. He came up with a girder in his hand, which he bent over the head of one of the Maraks. The man shook himself and struck out for Ennis, who took the blow rolling and countered with a buffet that left a black splotch on a skin that was like armor plate and sent the man through the opposite wall. The other was upon Ennis, who whirled with the quickness of one who maneuvers habitually under a pressure of ten thousand atmospheres, and shook the Marak from him, leaving him unconscious with a twist in a sensitive spot.

The first opponent returned, and the two grappled, searching for nerve centers to beat upon. Ennis twisted frantically, conscious of the real danger that the frail vessel might break to pieces beneath his feet. The railing of a staircase gave behind the two, and they hurtled down it, crashing through the steps to the floor below. Their weight and momentum carried them through. Ennis released his grip on the Marak, stopped his fall by grasping one of the girders that was part of the ship's framework. The other continued his devastating way down, demolishing the inner shell, and then the outer shell gave way with a grinding crash that ominously became a burbling rush of liquid.

Ennis looked down into the space where the Marak had fallen, hissed with a sudden intake of breath, then dove down himself. He met rising water, gushing in through a rent in the keel. He braced himself against a girder which sagged under his hand and moved onward against the rushing water. It geysered through the hole in a heavy stream that pushed him back and started to fill the bottom level of the ship. Against that terrific pressure he strained forward slowly, beating against the resisting waves, and then, with a mighty flounder, was at the opening. Its edges had been folded back upon themselves by the inrushing water, and they gaped inward like a jagged maw. He grasped them in a huge hand and exerted force. They strained for a moment and began to straighten. Irresistibly he pushed and stretched them into their former position, and then took the broken ends in his hands and squeezed. The metal grew soft under his grip and began to flow. The edges of the plate welded under that mighty pressure. He moved down the crack and soon it was watertight. He flexed his hands as he rose. They ached; even his strength was beginning to be taxed.

Noises from above; pounding feet. Men were coming down to investigate the commotion. He stood for a moment in thought, then turned to a blank wall, battered his way through it, and shoved the plates and girders back into position. Down to the other end of the craft, and up a staircase there. The corridor above was deserted, and he stole along it, hunting for the place he had left the weapon he had prepared. There was a commotion ahead as the Maraks found the unconscious man.

Two men came pounding up the passageway, giving him barely enough time to slip into a doorway to the side. The room he found himself in was a sleeping chamber. There were two red pulps there, and nothing that could help him, so he stayed in there only long enough to make sure that he would not be seen emerging into the hall. He crept down it again, with as little noise as possible. The racket ahead helped him; it sounded as though they were tearing the ship apart. Again he cursed their idiocy. Couldn't they see how valuable this was?

They were in the control room, ripping apart the machinery with the curiosity of children, wondering at the strange weakness of the paperlike metal, not realizing that, on the world where it was fabricated, it was sufficiently strong for any strain the builders could put upon it.

The strange weapon Ennis had prepared was on the floor of the passage, and just outside the control room. He looked anxiously at the trailing cables. Had they been stepped on and broken? Was the instrument in working condition? He had to get it and be away; no time to experiment to see if it would work.

A noise from behind, and Ennis again slunk into a doorway as a large Marak with a colored belt around his waist strode jarringly through the corridor into the control room. Sharp orders were barked, and the men ceased their havoc with the machinery of the room. All but a few left and scattered through the ship. Ennis' face twisted into a scowl. This made things more difficult. He couldn't overcome them all single-handed, and he couldn't use the weapon inside the ship if it was what he thought it was from the size of the cables.

A Marak was standing immediately outside the room in which Ennis lurked. No exit that way. He looked around the room; there were no other doors. A porthole in the outer wall was a tiny disk of transparency. He looked at it, felt it with his hands, and suddenly pushed his hands right through it. As quietly as he could, he worked at the edges of the circle until the hole was large enough for him to squeeze through. The jagged edges did not bother him. They felt soft, like a ragged pat of butter.

The Marak vessel was moored to the other side of the spaceship. On this side the wind howled blankly, and the sawtooth waves stretched on and on to a horizon that was many miles distant. He cautiously made his way around the glistening rotundity of the derelict, past the prow, straining silently against the vicious backward sweep of the water that tore at every inch of his body. The darker hump of the battleship loomed up as he rounded the curve, and he swam across the tiny space to grasp a row of projections that curved up over the surface of the craft. He climbed up them, muscles that were hard as carborundum straining to hold against all the forces of gravity and wind that fought him down. Near the top of the curve was a rounded, streamlined projection. He felt around its base and found a lever there, which he moved. The metal hump slid back, revealing a rugged swivel mounting with a stubby cylindrical projector atop it.

He swung the mounting around and let loose a short, sudden blast of white fire along the naked deck of the battleship. Deep voices yelled within and men sprang out, to fall back with abrupt screams clogged in their throats as Ennis caught them in the intolerable blast from the projector. Men, shielded by five thousand miles of atmosphere from actinic light, used to receiving only red and infra red, were painfully vulnerable to this frightful concentration of ultraviolet.

Noise and shouts burst from the derelict spaceship alongside, sweeping away eerily in the thundering wind that seemed to pound down upon them with new vigor in that moment. Heads appeared from the openings in the craft.

Ennis suddenly stood up to his full height, bracing himself against the wind, so dense it made him buoyant. With a deep bellow he bridged the space to the derelict. Then, as a squad of Maraks made their difficult, slippery way across the flank of the battleship toward him, and as the band that had boarded the spaceship crowded out on its battered deck to see what the noise was about, he dropped down into a crouch behind his ultraviolet projector, and whirled it around, pulling the firing lever.

That was what he wanted. Make a lot of noise and disturbance, get them all on deck, and then blow them to pieces. The ravening blast spat from the nozzle of the weapon, and the men on the battleship dropped flat on the deck. He found he could not depress the projector enough to reach them. He spun it to point at the spaceship. The incandescence reached out, and then seemed to waver and die. The current was shut off at the switchboard.

Ennis rose from behind the projector, and then hurtled from the flank of the battleship as he was struck by two Maraks leaping on him from behind the hump of the vessel. The three struck the water and sank, Ennis struggling violently. He was on the last lap, and he gave all his strength to the spurt. The water swirled around them in little choppy waves that fell more quickly than the eye could follow. Heavier blows than those from an Earthly trip hammer were scoring Ennis' face and head. He was in a bad position to strike back, and suddenly he became limp and sank below the surface. The pressure of the water around him was enormous, and it increased very rapidly as he went lower and lower. He saw the shadowy bulk of the spaceship above him. His lungs were fighting for air, but he shook off his pretended stupor and swam doggedly through the water beneath the derelict. He went on and on. It seemed as though the distance were endless following the metal curve. It was so big from beneath, and trying to swim the width without air made it bigger.

Clear, finally, his lungs drew in the saving breaths. No time to rest, though. He must make use of his advantage while it was his; it wouldn't last long. He swam along the side of the ship looking for an opening. There was none within reach from the water, so he made one, digging his stubby fingers into the metal, climbing up until it was safe to tear a rent in the thick outer and inner walls of the ship.

He found himself in one of the machine rooms of the second level. He went out into the corridor and up the stairway which was half-wrecked, and found himself in the main passage near the control room. He darted down it, into the room. There was nobody there, although the noises from above indicated that the Maraks were again descending. There was his weapon on the floor, where he had left it. He was glad that they had not gotten around to pulling that instrument apart. There would be one thing saved for intelligent examination.

The clatter from the descending crowd turned into a clamor of anger as they discovered him in the passageway. They stopped there for a moment, puzzled. He had been in the ocean, and had somehow magically reappeared within the derelict. It gave him time to pick up the weapon.

Ennis debated rapidly and decided to risk the unknown. How powerful the weapon was he did not know, but with atomic energy it would be powerful. He disliked using it inside the spaceship; he wanted to have enough left to float on the water until Shadden arrived; but they were beginning to advance on him, and he had to start something.

He pulled a lever. The cylinder in his arms jerked back with great force; a bolt of fierce, blinding energy tore out of it and passed with the quickness of light down the length of the corridor.

When he could see again there was no corridor. Everything that had been in the way of the projector was gone, simply disappeared.

Unmindful of the heat from the object in his hands, he turned and directed it at the battleship that was plainly outlined through the space that had been once the walls of the derelict. Before the men on the deck could move, he pulled the lever again.

And the winds were silenced for a moment. The natural elements were still in fear at the incredible forces that came from the destruction of atoms. Then with an agonized scream the hurricane struck again, tore through the spot where there had been a battleship.

Far off in the sky Ennis detected motion. It was Shadden, speeding in a glider.

Now would come the work that was important. Shadden would take the big machine apart and see how it ran. That was what history would remember.

# LIFE-LINE

*Astounding Science Fiction*, August

# by Robert A. Heinlein (1907–    )

*More than any other single individual next to John Campbell himself, Robert A. Heinlein changed modern science fiction. Born in Butler, Missouri, he was in his early thirties when he began his sf career, which saw him become the greatest luminary of the Golden Age.*

*His "Future History" series (collected as THE PAST THROUGH TOMORROW, 1967) is one of the seminal works in the canon of science fiction. Although his political and social views have generated much controversy in the last twenty years, his emphasis on order, individualism, and discipline aroused little comment early in his career, with America in a struggle against an illegal, disorderly, and undisciplined fascism.*

*"Life-Line" was the first in the series and the first published science fiction of one of modern sf's founding fathers. It made him a star at once.*

*(Bob Heinlein gave me my very first alcoholic drink. It was a Cuba Libre. I sniffed at it suspiciously, but he assured me it was a Coca-Cola and I wouldn't dream of doubting the man who in a matter of months was suddenly the universally acknowledged "best writer" of science fiction. I drank it as though it was indeed a Coca-Cola and was promptly assailed by the most unpleasant symptoms. Although I had been my usually quiet self till then, I now crept into a corner to recover. Bob shouted, "No wonder he doesn't drink. It sobers him up!"—I still don't drink. IA)*

The chairman rapped loudly for order. Gradually the catcalls and boos died away as several self-appointed sergeant-at-arms persuaded a few hot-headed individuals to sit down. The speaker on the rostrum by the chairman seemed unaware of the disturbance. His bland, faintly insolent face was impassive. The chairman turned to the speaker and addressed him in a voice in which anger and annoyance were barely restrained.

"Dr. Pinero"—the "Doctor" was faintly stressed—"I must apologize to you for the unseemly outburst during your remarks. I am surprised that my colleagues should so far forget the dignity proper to men of science as to interrupt a speaker, no matter"—he paused and set his mouth—"no matter how great the provocation." Pinero smiled in his face, a smile that was in some way an open insult. The chairman visibly controlled his temper and continued: "I am anxious that the program be concluded decently and in order. I want you to finish your remarks. Nevertheless, I must ask you to refrain from affronting our intelligence with ideas that any educated man knows to be fallacious. Please confine yourself to your discovery—if you have made one."

Pinero spread his fat, white hands, palms down. "How can I possibly put a new idea into your heads, if I do not first remove your delusions?"

The audience stirred and muttered. Someone shouted from the rear of the hall: "Throw the charlatan out! We've had enough."

The chairman pounded his gavel.

"Gentlemen! Please!"

Then to Pinero, "Must I remind you that you are not a member of this body, and that we did not invite you?"

Pinero's eyebrows lifted. "So? I seem to remember an invitation on the letterhead of the Academy."

The chairman chewed his lower lip before replying. "True. I wrote that invitation myself. But it was at the request of one of the trustees—a fine, public-spirited gentleman, but not a scientist, not a member of the Academy."

Pinero smiled his irritating smile. "So? I should have guessed. Old Bidwell, not so, of Amalgamated Life Insurance? And he wanted his trained seals to expose me as a fraud, yes? For if I can tell a man the day of his own death, no one will buy his pretty policies. But how can you expose me, if you will not listen to me first? Even supposing you had the wit to understand me? Bah! He has sent jackals to tear down a lion." He deliberately turned his back on them.

The muttering of the crowd swelled and took on a vicious tone. The chairman cried vainly for order. There arose a figure in the front row.

"Mr. Chairman!"

The chairman grasped the opening and shouted: "Gentlemen! Dr. van Rhein Smitt has the floor." The commotion died away.

The doctor cleared his throat, smoothed the forelock of his beautiful white hair, and thrust one hand into a side pocket of his smartly tailored trousers. He assumed his women's-club manner.

"Mr. Chairman, fellow members of the Academy of Science, let us have tolerance. Even a murderer has the right to say his say before the State exacts its tribute. Shall we do less? Even though one may be intellectually certain of the verdict? I grant Dr. Pinero every consideration that should be given by this august body to any unaffiliated colleague, even though"—he bowed slightly in Pinero's direction—"we may not be familiar with the university which bestowed his degree. If what he has to say is false, it cannot harm us. If what he has to say is true, we should know it." His mellow, cultivated voice rolled on, soothing and calming. "If the eminent doctor's manner appears a trifle inurbane of our tastes, we must bear in mind that the doctor may be from a place, or a stratum, not so meticulous in these matters. Now our good friend and benefactor has asked us to hear this person and carefully assess the merit of his claims. Let us do so with dignity and decorum."

He sat down to a rumble of applause, comfortably aware that he had enhanced his reputation as an intellectual leader. Tomorrow the papers would again mention the good sense and persuasive personality of "America's Handsomest University President." Who knows; maybe now old Bidwell would come through with that swimming-pool donation.

When the applause had ceased, the chairman turned to where the center of the disturbance sat, hands folded over his little round belly, face serene.

"Will you continue, Dr. Pinero?"

"Why should I?"

The chairman shrugged his shoulders. "You came for that purpose."

Pinero arose. "So true. So very true. But was I wise to come? Is there anyone here who has an open mind, who can stare a bare fact in the face without blushing? I think not. Even that so-beautiful gentleman who asked you to hear me out has already judged me and condemned me. He seeks order, not truth. Suppose truth defies order, will he accept it? Will you? I think not. Still, if I do not speak, you will win your point by default. The little man in the street will think that you little men have exposed me, Pinero, as a hoaxer, a pretender.

"I will repeat my discovery. In simple language, I have invented a technique to tell how long a man will live. I can give you advance billing of the Angel of Death. I can tell you when the Black Camel will kneel at your door. In five minutes' time, with my apparatus, I can tell any of you how many grains of sand are still left in your hour-glass." He paused and folded his arms across his chest. For a moment no one spoke. The audience grew restless.

Finally the chairman intervened, "You aren't finished, Dr. Pinero?"

"What more is there to say?"

"You haven't told us how your discovery works."

Pinero's eyebrows shot up. "You suggest that I should turn over the fruits of my work for children to play with? This is dangerous knowledge, my friend. I keep it for the man who understands it, myself." He tapped his chest.

"How are we to know that you have anything back of your wild claims?"

"So simple. You send a committee to watch me demonstrate. If it works, fine. You admit it and tell the world so. If it does not work, I am discredited, and will apologize. Even I, Pinero, will apologize."

A slender, stoop-shouldered man stood up in the back of the hall. The chair recognized him and he spoke.

"Mr. Chairman, how can the eminent doctor seriously propose such a course? Does he expect us to wait around for twenty or thirty years for someone to die and prove his claims?"

Pinero ignored the chair and answered directly.

"*Pfui!* Such nonsense! Are you so ignorant of statistics that you do not know that in any large group there is at least one who will die in the immediate future? I make you a proposition. Let me test each one of you in this room, and I will name the man who will die within the fortnight, yes, and the day and hour of his death." He glanced fiercely around the room. "Do you accept?"

Another figure got to his feet, a portly man who spoke in measured syllables. "I, for one, cannot countenance such an experiment. As a medical man, I have noted with sorrow the plain marks of serious heart trouble in many of our elder colleagues. If Dr. Pinero knows those symptoms, as he may, and were he to select as his victim one of their number, the man so selected would be likely to die on schedule, whether the distinguished speaker's mechanical egg timer works or not."

Another speaker backed him up at once. "Dr. Shepard is right. Why should we waste time on voodoo tricks? It is my belief that this person who calls himself *Dr*. Pinero wants to use this body to give his statements authority. If we participate in this farce, we play into his hands. I don't know what his racket is, but you can bet that he has figured out some way to use us for advertising his schemes. I move, Mr. Chairman, that we proceed with our regular business."

The motion carried by acclamation, but Pinero did not sit down. Amidst cries of "Order! Order!" he shook his untidy head at them, and had his say.

"Barbarians! Imbeciles! Stupid dolts! Your kind have blocked the recognition of every great discovery since time began. Such ignorant canaille are enough to start Galileo spinning in his grave. That fat fool down there twiddling his elk's tooth calls himself a medical man. Witch doctor would be a better term! That little bald-headed runt over there— You! You style yourself a philosopher, and prate about life and time in your neat categories. What do you know of either one? How can you ever learn when you won't examine the truth when you have a chance? Bah!" He spat upon the stage. "You call this an Academy of Science. I call it an undertakers' convention, interested only in embalming the ideas of your red-blooded predecessors."

He paused for breath and was grasped on each side by two members of the platform committee and rushed out the wings. Several reporters arose hastily from the press table and followed him. The chairman declared the meeting adjourned.

The newspapermen caught up with Pinero as he was going out by the stage door. He walked with a light, springy step, and whistled a little tune. There was no trace of the belligerence he had shown a moment before. They crowded about him. "How about an interview, doc?" "What d'yuh think of modern education?" "You certainly told 'em. What are your views on life after death?" "Take off your hat, doc, and look at the birdie."

He grinned at them all. "One at a time, boys, and not so fast. I used to be a newspaperman myself. How about coming up to my place?"

A few minutes later they were trying to find places to sit down in Pinero's messy bed-living room, and lighting his cigars. Pinero looked around and beamed. "What'll it be, boys? Scotch or Bourbon?" When that was taken care of he got down to business. "Now, boys, what do you want to know?"

"Lay it on the line, doc. Have you got something, or haven't you?"

"Most assuredly I have something, my young friend."

"Then tell us how it works. That guff you handed the profs won't get you anywhere now."

"Please, my dear fellow. It is my invention. I expect to make some money with it. Would you have me give it away to the first person who asks for it?"

"See here, doc, you've got to give us something if you expect to get a break in the morning papers. What do you use? A crystal ball?"

"No, not quite. Would you like to see my apparatus?"

"Sure. Now we're getting somewhere."

He ushered them into an adjoining room, and waved his hand. "There it is, boys." The mass of equipment that met their eyes vaguely resembled a medico's office X-ray gear. Beyond the obvious fact that it used electrical power, and that some of the dials were calibrated in familiar terms, a casual inspection gave no clue to its actual use.

"What's the principle, doc?"

Pinero pursed his lips and considered. "No doubt you are all familiar with the truism that life is electrical in nature. Well, that truism isn't worth a damn, but it will help to give you an idea of the principle. You have also been told that time is a fourth dimension. Maybe you believe it, perhaps not. It has been said so many times that it has ceased to have any meaning. It is simply a cliché that windbags use to impress fools. But I want you to try to visualize it now, and try to feel it emotionally."

He stepped up to one of the reporters. "Suppose we take you as an example. Your name is Rogers, is it not? Very well, Rogers, you are a space-time event having duration four ways. You are not quite six feet tall, you are about twenty inches wide and perhaps ten inches thick. In time, there stretches behind you more of this space-time event, reaching to, perhaps, 1905, of which we see a cross section here at right angles to the time axis, and as thick as the present. At the far end is a baby, smelling of sour milk and drooling its breakfast on its bib. At the other end lies, perhaps, an old man some place in the 1980s. Imagine this space-time event, which we call Rogers, as a long pink worm, continuous through the years. It stretches past us here in 1939, and the cross section we see appears as a single, discreet body. But that is illusion. There is physical continuity to this pink worm, enduring through the years. As a matter of fact, there is physical continuity in this concept to the entire race, for these pink worms branch off from other pink worms. In this fashion the race is like a vine whose branches intertwine and send out shoots. Only by taking a cross section of the vine would we fall into the error of believing that the shootlets were discreet individuals."

He paused and looked around at their faces. One of them, a dour, hard-bitten chap, put in a word.

"That's all very pretty, Pinero, if true, but where does that get you?"

Pinero favored him with an unresentful smile. "Patience, my friend. I asked you to think of life as electrical. Now think of our long, pink worm as a conductor of electricity. You have heard, perhaps, of the fact that electrical engineers can, by certain measurements, predict the exact location of a break in a transatlantic cable without ever leaving the shore. I do the same with our pink worms. By applying my instruments to the cross section here in this room I can tell where the break occurs; that is to say, where death takes place. Or, if you like, I can reverse the connections and tell you the date of your birth. But that is uninteresting; you already know it."

The dour individual sneered. "I've caught you, doc. If what you say about the race being like a vine fo pink worms is true, you can't tell birthdays, because the connection with the race is continuous at birth. Your electrical conductor reaches on back through the mother into a man's remotest ancestors."

Pinero beamed. "True, and clever, my friend. But you have pushed the analogy too far. It is not done in the precise manner in which one measures the length of an electrical conductor. In some ways it is more like measuring the length of a long corridor by bouncing an echo off the far end. At birth there is a sort of twist in the corridor, and, by proper calibration, I can detect the echo from that twist."

"Let's see you prove it."

"Certainly, my dear friend. Will you be a subject?"

One of the others spoke up. "He's called your bluff, Luke. Put up or shut up."

"I'm game. What do I do?"

"First write the date of your birth on a sheet of paper, and hand it to one of your colleagues."

Luke complied. "Now what?"

"Remove your outer clothing and step upon these scales. Now tell me, were you ever very much thinner, or very much fatter, than you are now? No? What did you weigh at birth? Ten pounds? A fine bouncing baby boy. They don't come so big any more."

"What is all this flubdubbery?"

"I am trying to approximate the average cross section of our long pink conductor, my dear Luke. Now will you seat yourself here? Then place this electrode in your mouth. No, it will not hurt you; the voltage is quite low, less than one micro-volt, but I must have a good connection." The doctor left him and went behind his apparatus, where he lowered a hood over his head before touching his controls. Some of the exposed dials came to life and a low humming came from the machine. It stopped and the doctor popped out of his little hide-away.

"I get sometime in February, 1902. Who has the piece of paper with the date?"

It was produced and unfolded. The custodian read, "February 22, 1902."

The stillness that followed was broken by a voice from the edge of the little group. "Doc, can I have another drink?"

The tension relaxed, and several spoke at once: "Try it on me, doc." "Me first, doc; I'm an orphan and really want to know." "How about it, doc? Give us all a little loose play."

He smilingly complied, ducking in and out of the hood like a gopher from its hole. When they all had twin slips of paper to prove the doctor's skill, Luke broke a long silence.

"How about showing how you predict death, Pinero?"

"If you wish. Who will try it?"

No one answered. Several of them nudged Luke forward. "Go ahead, smart guy. You asked for it." He allowed himself to be seated in the chair. Pinero changed some of the switches, then entered the hood. When the humming ceased he came out, rubbing his hands briskly together.

"Well, that's all there is to see, boys. Got enough for a story?"

"Hey, what about the prediction? When does Luke get his 'thirty'?"

Luke faced him. "Yes, how about it?"

Pinero looked pained. "Gentlemen, I am surprised at you. I give that information for a fee. Besides, it is a professional confidence. I never tell anyone but the client who consults me."

"I don't mind. Go ahead and tell them."

"I am very sorry, I really must refuse. I only agreed to show you how; not to give the results."

Luke ground the butt of his cigarette into the floor. "It's a hoax, boys. He probably looked up the age of every reporter in town just to be ready to pull this. It won't wash, Pinero."

Pinero gazed at him sadly. "Are you married, my friend?"

"No."

"Do you have anyone dependent on you? Any close relatives?"

"No. Why? Do you want to adopt me?"

Pinero shook his head. "I am very sorry for you, my dear Luke. You will die before tomorrow."

### DEATH PUNCHES TIME CLOCK

. . . within twenty minutes of Pinero's strange prediction, Timons was struck by a falling sign while walking down Broadway toward the offices of the *Daily Herald* where he was employed.

Dr. Pinero declined to comment but confirmed the story that he had predicted Timons' death by means of his so-called chrono-vitameter. Chief of Police Roy.

Legal Notice

To whom it may concern, greetings, I, John Cabot Winthrop III, of the firm of Winthrop, Winthrop, Ditmars and Winthrop, Attorneys-at-law, do affirm that Hugo Pinero of this city did hand to me ten thousand dollars in lawful money of the United States, and did instruct me to place it in escrow with a chartered bank of my selection with escrow instructions as follows:

The entire bond shall be forfeit, and shall forthwith be paid to the first client of Hugo Pinero and/or Sands of Time, Inc. who shall exceed his life tenure as predicted by Hugo Pinero by one per centum, or to the estate of the first client who shall fail of such predicted tenure in a like amount, whichever occurs first in point of time.

Subscribed and sworn,
John Cabot Winthrop III.

Subscribed and sworn to before
me this 2nd day of April, 1939.
Albert M. Swanson
Notary Public in and for this
county and State. My commission
expires June 17, 1939.

"Good evening, Mr. and Mrs. Radio Audience, let's go to press! Flash! Hugo Pinero, the Miracle Man from Nowhere, has made his thousandth death prediction without anyone claiming the reward he offered to the first person who catches him failing to call the turn. With thirteen of his clients already dead, it is mathematically certain that he has a private line to the main office of the Old Man with the Scythe. That is one piece of news I don't want to know about before it happens. Your coast-to-coast correspondent will *not* be a client of Prophet Pinero—"

The judge's watery baritone cut through the stale air of the courtroom. "Please, Mr. Weems, let us return to our subject. This court granted your prayer for a temporary restraining order, and now you ask that it be made permanent. In rebuttal, Dr. Pinero claims that you have presented no cause and asks that the injunction be lifted, and that I order your client to cease from attempts to interfere with what Pinero describes as a simple, lawful business. As you are not addressing a jury, please omit the rhetoric and tell me in plain language why I should not grant his prayer."

Mr. Weems jerked his chin nervously, making his flabby gray dewlap drag across his high stiff collar, and resumed:

"May it please the honorable court, I represent the public—"

"Just a moment. I thought you were appearing for Amalgamated Life Insurance."

"I am, your honor, in a formal sense. In a wider sense I represent several other of the major assurance, fiduciary and financial institutions, their stockholders and policy holders, who constitute a majority of the citizenry. In addition we feel that we protect the interests of the entire population, unorganized, inarticulate and otherwise unprotected."

"I thought that I represented the public," observed the judge dryly. "I am afraid I must regard you as appearing for your client of record. But continue. What is your thesis?"

The elderly barrister attempted to swallow his Adam's apple, then began again: "Your honor, we contend that there are two separate reasons why this injunction should be made permanent, and, further, that each reason is sufficient alone.

"In the first place, this person is engaged in the practice of soothsaying, an occupation proscribed both in common law and statute. He is a common fortuneteller, a vagabond charlatan who preys on the gullibility of the public. He is cleverer than the ordinary gypsy palm reader, astrologer or table tipper, and to the same extent more dangerous. He makes false claims of modern scientific methods to give a spurious dignity to the thaumaturgy. We have here in court leading representatives of the Academy of Science to give expert witness as to the absurdity of his claims.

"In the second place, even if this person's claims were true—granting for the sake of argument such an absurdity"—Mr. Weems permitted himself a thin-lipped smile—"we contend that his activities are contrary to the public interest in general, and unlawfully injurious to the interests of my client in particular. We are prepared to produce numerous exhibits with the legal custodians to prove that this person did publish, or cause to have published, utterances urging the public to dispense with the priceless boon of life insurance to the great detriment of their welfare and to the financial damage of my client."

Pinero arose in his place. "Your honor, may I say a few words?"

"What is it?"

"I believe I can simplify the situation if permitted to make a brief analysis."

"Your honor," put in Weems, "this is most irregular."

"Patience, Mr. Weems. Your interests will be protected. It seems to me that we need more light and less noise in this matter. If Dr. Pinero can shorten the proceedings by speaking at this time, I am inclined to let him. Proceed, Dr. Pinero."

"Thank you, your honor. Taking the last of Mr. Weems' points first, I am prepared to stipulate that I published the utterances he speaks of—"

"One moment, doctor. You have chosen to act as your own attorney. Are you sure you are competent to protect your own interests?"

"I am prepared to chance it, your honor. Our friends here can easily prove what I stipulate."

"Very well. You may proceed."

"I will stipulate that many persons have canceled life-insurance policies as a result thereof, but I challenge them to show that anyone so doing has suffered any loss or damage therefrom. It is true that the Amalgamated has lost business through my activities, but that is the natural result of my discovery, which has made their policies as obsolete as the bow and arrow. If an injunction is granted on that ground, I shall set up a coal-oil-lamp factory, and then ask for an injunction against the Edison and General Electric companies to forbid them to manufacture incandescent bulbs.

"I will stipulate that I am engaged in the business of making predictions of death, but I deny that I am practicing magic, black, white or rainbow-colored. If to make predictions by methods of scientific accuracy is illegal, then the actuaries of the Amalgamated have been guilty for years, in that they predict the exact percentage that will die each year in any given large group. I predict death retail; the Amalgamated predicts it wholesale. If their actions are legal, how can mine be illegal?

"I admit that it makes a difference whether I can do what I claim, or not; and I will stipulate that the so-called expert witnesses from the Academy of Science will testify that I cannot. But they know nothing of my method and cannot give truly expert testimony on it—"

"Just a moment, doctor. Mr. Weems, is it true that your expert witnesses are not conversant with Dr. Pinero's theory and methods?"

Mr. Weems looked worried. He drummed on the table top, then answered, "Will the court grant me a few moments' indulgence?"

"Certainly."

Mr. Weems held a hurried whispered consultation with his cohorts, then faced the bench. "We have a procedure to suggest, your honor. If Dr. Pinero will take the stand and explain the theory and practice of his alleged method, then these distinguished scientists will be able to advise the court as to the validity of his claims."

The judge looked inquiringly at Pinero, who responded: "I will not willingly agree to that. Whether my process is true or false, it would be dangerous to let it fall into the hands of fools and quacks"—he waved his hand at the group of professors seated in the front row, paused and smiled maliciously—"as these gentlemen know quite well. Furthermore, it is not necessary to know the process in order to prove that it will work. Is it necessary to understand the complex miracle of biological reproduction in order to observe that a hen lays eggs? Is it necessary for me to re-educate this entire body of self-appointed custodians of wisdom—cure them of their ingrown superstitions—in order to prove that my predictions are correct?

"There are but two ways of forming an opinion in science. One is the scientific method; the other, the scholastic. One can judge from experiment, or one can blindly accept authority. To the scientific mind, experimental proof is all-important, and theory is merely a convenience in description, to be junked when it no longer fits. To the academic mind, authority is everything, and facts are junked when they do not fit theory laid down by authority.

"It is this point of view—academic minds clinging like oysters to disproved theories—that has blocked every advance of knowledge in history. I am prepared to prove my method by experiment, and, like Galileo in another court, I insist, 'It still moves!'

"Once before I offered such proof to this same body of self-styled experts, and they rejected it. I renew my offer; let me measure the life length of the members of the Academy of Science. Let them appoint a committee to judge the results. I will seal my findings in two sets of envelopes; on the outside of each envelope in one set will appear the name of a member; on the inside, the date of his death. In the other envelopes I will place names; on the outside I will place dates. Let the committee place the envelopes in a vault, then meet from time to time to open the appropriate envelopes. In such a large body of men some deaths may be expected, if Amalgamated actuaries can be trusted, every week or two. In such a fashion they will accumulate data very rapidly to prove that Pinero is a liar, or no."

He stopped, and thrust out his chest until it almost caught up with his little round belly. He glared at the sweating savants. "Well?"

The judge raised his eyebrows, and caught Mr. Weems' eye. "Do you accept?"

"Your honor, I think the proposal highly improper—"

The judge cut him short. "I warn you that I shall rule against you if you do not accept, or propose an equally reasonable method of arriving at the truth."

Weems opened his mouth, changed his mind, looked up and down the faces of the learned witnesses, and faced the bench. "We accept, your honor."

"Very well. Arrange the details between you. The temporary injunction is lifted and Dr. Pinero must not be molested in the pursuit of his business. Decision on the petition for permanent injunction is reserved without prejudice pending the accumulation of evidence. Before we leave this matter I wish to comment on the theory implied by you, Mr. Weems, when you claimed damage to your client. There has grown up in the minds of certain groups in this country the notion that because a man or corporation has made a profit out of the public for a number of years, the government and the courts are charged with the duty of guaranteeing such profit in the future, even in the face of changing circumstances and contrary to public interest. This strange doctrine is not supported by statute nor common law. Neither individuals nor corporations have any right to come into court and ask that the clock of history be stopped, or turned back."

Bidwell grunted in annoyance. "Weems, if you can't think up anything better than that, Amalgamated is going to need a new chief attorney. It's been ten weeks since you lost the injunction, and that little wart is coining money hand over fist. Meantime, every insurance firm in the country's going broke. Hoskins, what's our loss ratio?"

"It's hard to say, Mr. Bidwell. It gets worse every day. We've paid off thirteen big policies this week; all of them taken out since Pinero started operations."

A spare little man spoke up. "I say, Bidwell, we aren't accepting any new applicants for United, until we have time to check and be sure that they have not consulted Pinero. Can't we afford to wait until the scientists show him up?"

Bidwell snorted. "You blasted optimist! They won't show

him up. Aldrich, can't you face a fact? The fat little pest has something; how, I don't know. This is a fight to the finish. If we wait, we're licked." He threw his cigar into a cuspidor, and bit savagely into a fresh one. "Clear out of here, all of you! I'll handle this my own way. You, too, Aldrich. United may wait, but Amalgamated won't."

Weems cleared his throat apprehensively. "Mr. Bidwell, I trust you will consult me before embarking on any major change in policy?"

Bidwell grunted. They filed out. When they were all gone and the door closed, Bidwell snapped the switch of the inter-office announcer. "O.K.; send him in."

The outer door opened. A slight, dapper figure stood for a moment at the threshold. His small, dark eyes glanced quickly about the room before he entered, then he moved up to Bidwell with a quick, soft tread. He spoke to Bidwell in a flat, emotionless voice. His face remained impassive except for the live, animal eyes. "You wanted to talk to me?"

"Yes."

"What's the proposition?"

"Sit down, and we'll talk."

Pinero met the young couple at the door of his inner office.

"Come in, my dears, come in. Sit down. Make yourselves at home. Now tell me, what do you want of Pinero? Surely such young people are not anxious about the final roll call?"

The boy's pleasant young face showed slight confusion. "Well, you see, Dr. Pinero, I'm Ed Hartley and this is my wife, Betty. We're going to have . . . that is, Betty is expecting a baby and, well—"

Pinero smiled benignly. "I understand. You want to know how long you will live in order to make the best possible provision for the youngster. Quite wise. Do you both want readings, or just yourself?"

The girl answered, "Both of us, we think."

Pinero beamed at her. "Quite so. I agree. Your reading presents certain technical difficulties at this time, but I can give you some information now. Now come into my laboratory, my dears, and we'll commence."

He rang for their case histories, then showed them into his workshop. "Mrs. Hartley first, please. If you will go behind that screen and remove your shoes and your outer clothing, please."

He turned away and made some minor adjustments of his

apparatus. Ed nodded to his wife, who slipped behind the screen and reappeared almost at once, dressed in a slip. Pinero glanced up.

"This way, my dear. First we must weigh you. There. Now take your place on the stand. This electrode in your mouth. No, Ed, you mustn't touch her while she is in the circuit. It won't take a minute. Remain quiet."

He dove under the machine's hood and the dials sprang into life. Very shortly he came out, with a perturbed look on his face. "Ed, did you touch her?"

"No, doctor." Pinero ducked back again and remained a little longer. When he came out this time, he told the girl to get down and dress. He turned to her husband.

"Ed, make yourself ready."

"What's Betty's reading, doctor?"

"There is a little difficulty. I want to test you first."

When he came out from taking the youth's reading, his face was more troubled than ever. Ed inquired as to his trouble. Pinero shrugged his shoulders and brought a smile to his lips.

"Nothing to concern you, my boy. A little mechanical misadjustment, I think. But I shan't be able to give you two your readings today. I shall need to overhaul my machine. Can you come back tomorrow?"

"Why, I think so. Say, I'm sorry about your machine. I hope it isn't serious."

"It isn't, I'm sure. Will you come back into my office and visit for a bit?"

"Thank you, doctor. You are very kind."

"But, Ed, I've got to meet Ellen."

Pinero turned the full force of his personality on her. "Won't you grant me a few moments, my dear young lady? I am old, and like the sparkle of young folks' company. I get very little of it. Please." He nudged them gently into his office and seated them. Then he ordered lemonade and cookies sent in, offered them cigarettes and lit a cigar.

Forty minutes later Ed listened entranced, while Betty was quite evidently acutely nervous and anxious to leave, as the doctor spun out a story concerning his adventures as a young man in Tierra del Fuego. When the doctor stopped to relight his cigar, she stood up.

"Doctor, we really must leave. Couldn't we hear the rest tomorrow?"

"Tomorrow? There will not be time tomorrow."

"But you haven't time today, either. Your secretary has rung five times."

"Couldn't you spare me just a few more minutes?"

"I really can't today, doctor. I have an appointment. There is someone waiting for me."

"There is no way to induce you?"

"I'm afraid not. Come, Ed."

After they had gone, the doctor stepped to the window and stared out over the city. Presently, he picked out two tiny figures as they left the office building. He watched them hurry to the corner, wait for the lights to change, then start across the street. When they were part way across, there came the scream of a siren. The two little figures hesitated, started back, stopped and turned. Then the car was upon them. As the car slammed to a stop, they showed up from beneath it, no longer two figures, but simply a limp, unorganized heap of clothing.

Presently the doctor turned away from the window. Then he picked up his phone and spoke to his secretary.

"Cancel my appointments for the rest of the day. . . . No. . . . No one. . . . I don't care; cancel them."

Then he sat down in his chair. His cigar went out. Long after dark he held it, still unlighted.

Pinero sat down at his dining table and contemplated the gourmet's luncheon spread before him. He had ordered this meal with particular care, and had come home a little early in order to enjoy it fully.

Somewhat later he let a few drops of fiori d'Alpini roll around his tongue and trickle down his throat. The heavy, fragrant sirup warmed his mouth and reminded him of the little mountain flowers for which it was named. He sighed. It had been a good meal, an exquisite meal and had justified the exotic liqueur.

His musing was interrupted by a disturbance at the front door. The voice of his elderly maidservant was raised in remonstrance. A heavy male voice interrupted her. The commotion moved down the hall and the dining-room door was pushed open.

"Mia Madonna! Non si puo entrare! The master is eating!"

"Never mind, Angela. I have time to see these gentlemen. You may go."

Pinero faced the surly-faced spokesman of the intruders. "You have business with me; yes?"

"You bet we have. Decent people have had enough of your damned nonsense."

"And so?"

The caller did not answer at once. A smaller, dapper individual moved out from behind him and faced Pinero.

"We might as well begin." The chairman of the committee placed a key in the lock box and opened it. "Wonzoll, will you help me pick out today's envelopes?" He was interrupted by a touch on his arm.

"Dr. Baird, you are wanted on the telephone."

"Very well. Bring the instrument here."

When it was fetched he placed the receiver to his ear. "Hello. . . . Yes; speaking. . . . What? . . . No, we have heard nothing. . . . Destroyed the machine, you say. . . . Dead! How? . . . No! No statement. None at all. . . . Call me later."

He slammed the instrument down and pushed it from him.

"What's up?"

"Who's dead now?"

Baird held up one hand. "Quiet, gentlemen, please! Pinero was murdered a few moments ago at his home."

"Murdered!"

"That isn't all. About the same time vandals broke into his office and smashed his apparatus."

No one spoke at first. The committee members glanced around at each other. No one seemed anxious to be the first to comment.

Finally one spoke up. "Get it out."

"Get what out?"

"Pinero's envelope. It's in there, too. I've seen it."

Baird located it, and slowly tore it open. He unfolded the single sheet of paper and scanned it.

"Well? Out with it!"

"One thirteen p.m. . . . today."

They took this in silence.

Their dynamic calm was broken by a member across the table from Baird reaching for the lock box. Baird interposed a hand.

"What do you want?"

"My prediction. It's in there—we're all in there."

"Yes, yes."

"We're all in there."

"Let's have them."

Baird placed both hands over the box. He held the eye of
the man opposite him, but did not speak. He licked his lips.
The corner of his mouth twitched. His hands shook. Still he
did not speak. The man opposite relaxed back into his chair.
"You're right, of course," he said.

"Bring me that wastebasket." Baird's voice was low and
strained, but steady.

He accepted it and dumped the litter on the rug. He placed
the tin basket on the table before him. He tore half a dozen
envelopes across, set a match to them, and dropped them in
the basket. Then he started tearing a double handful at a
time, and fed the fire steadily. The smoke made him cough,
and tears ran out of his smarting eyes. Someone got up and
opened a window. When Baird was through, he pushed the
basket away from him, looked down and spoke.

"I'm afraid I've ruined this table top."

# ETHER BREATHER

*Astounding Science Fiction*, September

## by Theodore Sturgeon (1918–    )

*Until the early seventies, Theodore Sturgeon (Edward H. Waldo) was the most heavily reprinted writer in the science fiction universe. This was a richly deserved honor, for he had produced a long line of outstanding, well-crafted stories featuring memorable characters. Working within the fantasy and science fiction genres, he excelled at both, and influenced an entire generation of writers, including Ray Bradbury.*

*Here is his first published story—one that exhibits all of the talent he would develop and nurture in succeeding years.*

*(Good Heavens! I've known Ted Sturgeon for forty years and never knew till now that that wasn't his real name. Are you sure, Marty? Anyway, an editor said to me once, "If you had to publish a collection of stories by Theodore Sturgeon, what would you call it?" I thought for a while and said, "Caviar!" The editor said triumphantly to someone else who was in the office, "See!!!" and that was indeed the name of the collection. IA)*

*Yes, Isaac, I'm sure. He legally changed his name to Sturgeon when his mother remarried.*

It was "The Seashell." It *would* have to be "The Seashell." I wrote it first as a short story, and it was turned down. Then I made a novelette out of it, and then a novel. Then a short

short. Then a three-line gag. And it still wouldn't sell. It got to be a fetish with me, rewriting that "Seashell." After a while editors got so used to it that they turned it down on sight. I had enough rejection slips from that number alone to paper every room in the house of tomorrow. So when it sold—well, it was like the death of a friend. It hit me. I hated to see it go.

It was a play by that time, but I hadn't changed it much. Still the same pastel, froo-froo old "Seashell" story, about two children who grew up and met each other only three times as the years went on, and a little seashell that changed hands each time they met. The plot, if any, doesn't matter. The dialogue was—well, pastel. Naïve. Unsophisticated. Very pretty, and practically salesproof. But it just happened to ring the bell with an earnest young reader for Associated Television, Inc., who was looking for something about that length that could be dubbed "artistic"; something that would not require too much cerebration on the part of an audience, so that said audience could relax and appreciate the new polychrome technique of television transmission. You know; pastel.

As I leaned back in my old relic of an armchair that night, and watched the streamlined version of my slow-moving brainchild, I had to admire the way they put it over. In spots it was almost good, that "Seashell." Well suited for the occasion, too. It was a full-hour program given free to a perfume house by Associated, to try out the new color transmission as an advertising medium. I liked the first two acts, if I do say so as shouldn't. It was at the half-hour mark that I got my first kick on the chin. It was a two-minute skit for the advertising plug.

A tall and elegant couple were seen standing on marble steps in an elaborate theater lobby. Says she to he:

"And how do you like the play, Mr. Robinson?"

Says he to she: "It stinks."

Just like that. Like any radio-television listener, I was used to paying little, if any, attention to a plug. That certainly snapped me up in my chair. After all, it was my play, even if it was "The Seashell." They couldn't do that to me.

But the girl smiling archly out of my television set didn't seem to mind. She said sweetly, "I think so, too."

He was looking slushily down into her eyes. He said: "That goes for you, too, my dear. What *is* that perfume you are using?"

"Berbelot's *Doux Rêves*. What do you think of it?"

He said, "You heard what I said about the play."

I didn't wait for the rest of the plug, the station identification, and act three. I headed for my visiphono and dialed Associated. I was burning up. When their pert-faced switchboard girl flashed on my screen I snapped: "Get me Griff. Snap it up!"

"Mr. Griff's line is busy, Mr. Hamilton," she sang to me. "Will you hold the wire, or shall I call you back?"

"None of that, Dorothe," I roared. Dorothe and I had gone to high school together; as a matter of fact I had got her the job with Griff, who was Associated's head script man. "I don't care who's talking to Griff. Cut him off and put me through. He can't do that to me. I'll sue, that's what I'll do. I'll break the company. I'll—"

"Take it easy, Ted," she said. "What's the matter with everyone all of a sudden, anyway? If you must know, the man gabbing with Griff now is old Berbelot himself. Seems he wants to sue Associated, too. What's up?"

By this time I was practically incoherent. "Berbelot, hey? I'll sue him, too. The rat! The dirty—What are you laughing at?"

"He wants to sue you!" she giggled. "And I'll bet Griff will, too, to shut Berbelot up. You know, this might turn out to be really funny!" Before I could swallow that she switched me over to Griff.

As he answered he was wiping his heavy jowls with a handkerchief. "Well?" he asked in a shaken voice.

"What are you, a wise guy?" I bellowed. "What kind of a stunt is that you pulled on the commercial plug on my play? Whose idea was that, anyway? Berbelot's? What the—"

"Now, Hamilton," Griff said easily, "don't excite yourself this way." I could see his hands trembling—evidently old Berbelot had laid it on thick. "Nothing untoward has occurred. You must be mistaken. I assure you—"

"You pompous old sociophagus," I growled, wasting a swell two-dollar word on him, "don't call me a liar. I've been listening to that program and I know what I heard. I'm going to sue you. And Berbelot. And if you try to pass the buck onto the actors in that plug skit, I'll sue them, too. And if you make any more cracks about me being mistaken, I'm going to come up there and feed you your teeth. Then I'll sue you personally as well as Associated."

I dialed out and went back to my television set, fuming. The program was going on as if nothing had happened. As I cooled—and I cool slowly—I began to see that the last half of "The Seashell" was even better than the first. You know, it's poison for a writer to fall in love with his own stuff; but, by golly, sometimes you turn out a piece that really has something. You try to be critical, and you can't be. The Ponta Delgada sequence in "The Seashell" was like that.

The girl was on a cruise and the boy was on a training ship. They met in the Azores Islands. Very touching. The last time they saw each other was before they were in their teens, but in the meantime they had had their dreams. Get the idea of the thing? Very pastel. And they did do it nicely. The shots of Ponta Delgada and the scenery of the Azores were swell. Came the moment, after four minutes of ickey dialogue, when he gazed at her, the light of true, mature love dawning on his young face.

She said shyly, "Well—"

Now, his lines, as written—and I should know!—went:

"Rosalind . . . it *is* you, then, isn't it? Oh, I'm afraid"—he grasps her shoulders—"afraid that it can't be real. So many times I've seen someone who might be you, and it has never been . . . Rosalind, Rosalind, guardian angel, reason for living, beloved . . . beloved—" Clinch.

Now, as I say, it went off as written, up to and including the clinch. But then came the payoff. He took his lips from hers, buried his face in her hair and said clearly: "I hate your————guts." And that "————" was the most perfectly enunciated present participle of a four-letter verb I have ever heard.

Just what happened after that I couldn't tell you. I went haywire, I guess. I scattered two hundred and twenty dollars' worth of television set over all three rooms of my apartment. Next thing I knew I was in a 'press tube, hurtling toward the three-hundred-story skyscraper that housed Associated Television. Never have I seen one of those 'press cars, forced by compressed air through tubes under the city, move so slowly, but it might have been my imagination. If I had anything to do with it, there was going to be one dead script boss up there.

And who should I run into on the 229th floor but old Berbelot himself. The perfume king had blood in his eye. Through the haze of anger that surrounded me, I began to realize that things were about to be very tough on Griff. And I was quite ready to help out all I could.

Berbelot saw me at the same instant, and seemed to read my thought. "Come on," he said briefly, and together we ran the gantlet of secretaries and assistants and burst into Griff's office.

Griff rose to his feet and tried to look dignified, with little success. I leaped over his glass desk and pulled the wings of his stylish open-necked collar together until he began squeaking.

Berbelot seemed to be enjoying it. "Don't kill him, Hamilton," he said after a bit. "I want to."

I let the script man go. He sank down to the floor, gasping. He was like a scared kid, in more ways than one. It was funny.

We let him get his breath. He climbed to his feet, sat down at his desk, and reached out toward a battery of push buttons. Berbelot snatched up a Dow-metal paper knife and hacked viciously at the chubby hand. It retreated.

"Might I ask," said Griff heavily, "the reason for this unprovoked rowdiness?"

Berbelot cocked an eye at me. "Might he?"

"He might tell us what this monkey business is all about," I said.

Griff cleared his throat painfully. "I told both you . . . er . . . gentlemen over the phone that, as far as I know, there was nothing amiss in our interpretation of your play, Mr. Hamilton, nor in the commercial section of the broadcast, Mr. Berbelot. After your protests over the wire, I made it a point to see the second half of the broadcast myself. Nothing was wrong. And as this is the first commercial color broadcast, it has been recorded. If you are not satisfied with my statements, you are welcome to see the recording yourselves, immediately."

What else could we want? It occurred to both of us that Griff was really up a tree; that he was telling the truth as far as he knew it, and that he thought we were both screwy. I began to think so myself.

Berbelot said, "Griff, didn't you hear that dialogue near the end, when those two kids were by that sea wall?"

Griff nodded.

"Think back now," Berbelot went on. "What did the boy say to the girl when he put his muzzle into her hair?"

" 'I love you,' " said Griff self-consciously, and blushed. "He said it twice."

Berbelot and I looked at each other. "Let's see that recording," I said.

Well, we did, in Griff's luxurious private projection room. I hope I never have to live through an hour like that again. If it weren't for the fact that Berbelot was seeing the same thing I saw, and feeling the same way about it, I'd have reported to an alienist. Because that program came off Griff's projector positively shimmering with innocuousness. My script was A-1; Berbelot's plugs were right. On that plug that had started everything, where the man and the girl were gabbing in the theater lobby, the dialogue went like this:

"And how do you like the play, Mr. Robinson?"

"Utterly charming . . . and that goes for you, too, my dear. What *is* that perfume you are using?"

"Berbelot's *Doux Rêves*. What do you think of it?"

"You heard what I said about the play."

Well, there you are. And by the recording, Griff had been right about the repetitious three little words in the Azores sequence. I was floored.

After it was over, Berbelot said to Griff: "I think I can speak for Mr. Hamilton when I say that if this is an actual recording, we owe you an apology; also when I say that we do not accept your evidence until we have compiled our own. I recorded that program as it came over my set, as I have recorded all my advertising. We will see you tomorrow, and we will bring that sound film. Coming, Hamilton?"

I nodded and we left, leaving Griff to chew his lip.

I'd like to skip briefly over the last chapter of that evening's nightmare. Berbelot picked up a camera expert on the way, and we had the films developed within an hour after we arrived at the fantastic "house that perfume built." And if I was crazy, so was Berbelot; and if he was, then so was the camera. So help me, that blasted program came out on Berbelot's screen exactly as it had on my set and his. If anyone ever took a long-distance cussing out, it was Griff that night. We figured, of course, that he had planted a phony recording on us, so that we wouldn't sue. He'd do the same thing in court, too. I told Berbelot so. He shook his head.

"No, Hamilton, we can't take it to court. Associated gave me that broadcast, the first color commercial, on condition that I sign away their responsibility for 'incomplete, or inadequate, or otherwise unsatisfactory performance.' They didn't quite trust that new apparatus, you know."

"Well, I'll sue for both of us, then," I said.

"Did they buy all rights?" he asked.

"Yes . . . damn! They got me, too! They have a legal right to do anything they want." I threw my cigarette into the electric fire, and snapped on Berbelot's big television set, tuning it to Associated's XZB.

Nothing happened.

"Hey! Your set's on the bum!" I said. Berbelot got up and began fiddling with the dial. I was wrong. There was nothing the matter with the set. It was Associated. All of their stations were off the air—all four of them. We looked at each other.

"Get XZW," said Berbelot. "It's an Associated affiliate, under cover. Maybe we can—"

XZW blared out at us as I spun the dial. A dance program, the new five-beat stuff. Suddenly the announcer stuck his face into the transmitter.

"A bulletin from Iconoscope News Service," he said conversationally. "FCC has clamped down on Associated Television and its stations. They are off the air. The reasons were not given, but it is surmised that it has to do with a little strong language used on the world premiere of Associated's new color transmission. That is all."

"I expected that," smiled Berbelot. "Wonder how Griff'll alibi himself out of that? If he tries to use that recording of his, I'll most cheerfully turn mine over to the government, and we'll have him for perjury."

"Sorta tough on Associated, isn't it?" I said.

"Not particularly. You know these big corporations. Associated gets millions out of their four networks, but those millions are just a drop in the bucket compared with the other pies they've got their fingers in. That color technique, for instance. Now that they can't use it for a while, how many other outfits will miss the chance of bidding for the method and equipment? They lose some advertising contracts, and they save by not operating. They won't even feel it. I'll bet you'll see color transmission within forty-eight hours over a rival network."

He was right. Two days later Cineradio had a color broadcast scheduled, and all hell broke loose. What they'd done to the Berbelot hour and my "Seashell" was really tame.

The program was sponsored by one of the antigravity industries— I forget which. They'd hired Raouls Stavisk, the composer, to play one of the ancient Gallic operas he'd exhumed. It was a piece called "Carmen" and had been practically forgotten for two centuries. News of it had created quite a stir among music lovers, although, personally, I don't go for it. It's too barbaric for me. Too hard to listen to, when you've been hearing five-beat all your life. And those old-timers had never heard of a quarter tone.

Anyway, it was a big affair, televised right from the huge Citizens' Auditorium. It was more than half full—there were about 130,000 people there. Practically all of the select high-brow music fans from that section of the city. Yes, 130,000 pairs of eyes saw that show in the flesh, and countless millions saw it on their own sets; remember that.

Those that saw it at the Auditorium got their money's worth, from what I hear. They saw the complete opera; saw it go off as scheduled. The coloratura, Maria Jeff, was in perfect voice, and Stavisk's orchestra rendered the ancient tones perfectly. So what?

So, those that saw it at home saw the first half of the program the same as broadcast—of course. But—and get this— they saw Maria Jeff, on a close-up, in the middle of an aria, throw back her head, stop singing, and shout raucously: "The hell with this! Whip it up, boys!"

They heard the orchestra break out of that old two-four music—"Habañera," I think they called it—and slide into a wicked old-time five-beat song about "alco-pill Alice," the girl who didn't believe in eugenics. They saw her step lightly about the stage, shedding her costume—not that I blame her for that; it was supposed to be authentic, and must have been warm. But there was a certain something about the way she did it.

I've never seen or heard of anything like it. First, I thought that it was part of the opera, because from what I learned in school I gather that the ancient people used to go in for things like that. I wouldn't know. But I knew it wasn't opera when old Stavisk himself jumped up on the stage and started dancing with the prima donna. The televisors flashed around to the audience, and there they were, every one of them, dancing in the aisles. And I mean dancing. Wow!

Well, you can imagine the trouble that that caused. Cineradio, Inc., was flabbergasted when they were shut down by FCC like Associated. So were 130,000 people who had seen the opera and thought it was good. Every last one of them denied dancing in the aisles. No one had seen Stavisk jump on the stage. It just didn't make sense.

Cineradio, of course, had a recording. So, it turned out, did FCC. Each recording proved the point of its respective

group. That of Cineradio, taken by a sound camera right
there in the auditorium, showed a musical program. FCC's,
photographed right off a government standard receiver,
showed the riot that I and millions of others had seen over
the air. It was too much for me. I went out to see Berbelot.
The old boy had a lot of sense, and he'd seen the beginning
of this crazy business.

He looked pleased when I saw his face on his house televisor. "Hamilton!" he exclaimed. "Come on in! I've been phoning all over the five downtown boroughs for you!" He pressed
a button and the foyer door behind me closed. I was whisked
up into his rooms. That combination foyer and elevator of his
is a nice gadget.

"I guess I don't have to ask you why you came," he said as
we shook hands. "Cineradio certainly pulled a boner, hey?"

"Yes and no," I said. "I'm beginning to think that Griff
was right when he said that, as far as he knew, the program
was on the up and up. But if he was right, what's it all
about? How can a program reach the transmitters in perfect
shape, and come out of every receiver in the nation like a
practical joker's idea of paradise?"

"It can't," said Berbelot. He stroked his chin thoughtfully.
"But it did. Three times."

"Three? When—"

"Just now, before you got in. The secretary of state was
making a speech over XZM, Consolidated Atomic, you know.
XZM grabbed the color equipment from Cineradio as soon as
they were blacked out by FCC. Well, the honorable secretary
droned on as usual for just twelve and a half minutes. Suddenly he stopped, grinned into the transmitter, and said, 'Say,
have you heard the one about the traveling farmer and the
salesman's daughter?' "

"I have," I said. "My gosh, don't tell me he spieled it?"

"Right," said Berbelot. "In detail, over the unsullied airwaves. I called up right away, but couldn't get through.
XZM's trunk lines were jammed. A very worried-looking
switchboard girl hooked up I don't know how many lines together and announced into them: 'If you people are calling
up about the secretary's speech, there is nothing wrong with
it.Now please get off the lines!' "

"Well," I said, "let's see what we've got. First, the broadcasts leave the studios as scheduled and as written. Shall we
accept that?"

"Yes," said Berbelot. "Then, since so far no black-and-white broadcasts have been affected, we'll consider that this strange behavior is limited to the polychrome technique."

"How about the recordings at the studios? They were in polychrome, and they weren't affected."

Berbelot pressed a button, and an automatic serving table rolled out of its niche and stopped in front of each of us. We helped ourselves to smokes and drinks, and the table returned to its place.

"Cineradio's wasn't a television recording, Hamilton. It was a sound camera. As for Associated's . . . I've got it! Griff's recording was transmitted to his recording machines by wire, from the studios! It didn't go out on the air at all!"

"You're right. Then we can assume that the only programs affected are those in polychrome, actually aired. Fine, but where does that get us?"

"Nowhere," admitted Berbelot. "But maybe we can find out. Come with me."

We stepped into an elevator and dropped three floors. "I don't know if you've heard that I'm a television bug," said my host. "Here's my lab. I flatter myself that a more complete one does not exist anywhere."

I wouldn't doubt it. I never in my life saw a layout like that. It was part museum and part workshop. It had in it a copy of a genuine relic of each and every phase of television down through the years, right from the old original scanning-disk sets down to the latest three-dimensional atomic jobs. Over in the corner was an extraordinarily complicated mass of apparatus which I recognized as a polychrome transmitter.

"Nice job, isn't it?" said Berbelot. "It was developed in here, you know, by one of the lads who won the Berbelot scholarship." I hadn't known. I began to have real respect for this astonishing man.

"Just how does it work?" I asked him.

"Hamilton," he said testily, "we have work to do. I would be talking all night if I told you. But the general idea is that the vibrations sent out by this transmitter are all out of phase with each other. Tinting in the receiver is achieved by certain blendings of these out-of-phase vibrations as they leave this rig. The effect is a sort of irregular vibration—a vibration in the electromagnetic waves themselves, resulting in a totally new type of wave which is still receivable in a standard set."

"I see," I lied. "Well, what do you plan to do?"

"I'm going to broadcast from here to my country place up north. It's eight hundred miles away from here, which ought to be sufficient. My signals will be received there and automatically returned to us by wire." He indicated a receiver standing close by. "If there is any difference between what we send and what we get, we can possibly find out just what the trouble is."

"How about FCC?" I asked. "Suppose—it sounds funny to say it—but just suppose that we get the kind of strong talk that came over the air during my 'Seashell' number?"

Berbelot snorted. "That's taken care of. The broadcast will be directional. No receiver can get it but mine."

What a man! He thought of everything. "O.K.," I said. "Let's go."

Berbelot threw a couple of master switches and we sat down in front of the receiver. Lights blazed on, and through a bank of push buttons at his elbow, Berbelot maneuvered the transmitting cells to a point above and behind the receiver, so that we could see and be seen without turning our heads. At a nod from Berbelot I leaned forward and switched on the receiver.

Berbelot glanced at his watch. "If things work out right, it will be between ten and thirty minutes before we get any interference." His voice sounded a little metallic. I realized that it was coming from the receiver as he spoke.

The images cleared on the view-screen as the set warmed up. It gave me an odd sensation. I saw Berbelot and myself sitting side by side—just as if we were sitting in front of a mirror, except that the images were not reversed. I thumbed my nose at myself, and my image returned the compliment.

Berbelot said: "Go easy, boy. If we get the same kind of interference the others got, your image will make something out of that." He chuckled.

"Damn right," said the receiver.

Berbelot and I stared at each other, and back at the screen. Berbelot's face was the same, but mine had a vicious sneer on it. Berbelot calmly checked with his watch. "Eight forty-six," he said. "Less time each broadcast. Pretty soon the interference will start with the broadcast, if this keeps up."

"Not unless you start broadcasting on a regular schedule," said Berbelot's image.

It had apparently dissociated itself completely from Berbelot himself. I was floored.

Berbelot sat beside me, his face frozen. "You see?" he whispered to me. "It takes a minute to catch up with itself. Till it does, it is my image."

"What does it all mean?" I gasped.

"Search me," said the perfume king.

We sat and watched. And so help me, so did our images. They were watching *us!*

Berbelot tried a direct question. "Who are you?" he asked.

"Who do we look like?" said my image; and both laughed uproariously.

Berbelot's image nudged mine. "We've got 'em on the run, hey, pal?" it chortled.

"Stop your nonsense!" said Berbelot sharply. Surprisingly, the merriment died.

"Aw," said my image plaintively. "We don't mean anything by it. Don't get sore. Let's all have fun. *I'm* having fun."

"Why, they're like kids!" I said.

"I think you're right," said Berbelot.

"Look," he said to the images, which sat there expectantly, pouting. "Before we have any fun, I want you to tell me who you are, and how you are coming through the receiver, and how you messed up the three broadcasts before this."

"Did we do wrong?" asked my image innocently. The other one giggled.

"High-spirited sons o' guns, aren't they?" said Berbelot.

"Well, are you going to answer my questions, or *do I turn the transmitter off?*" he asked the images.

They chorused frantically: "We'll tell! We'll tell! Please don't turn it off!"

"What on earth made you think of that?" I whispered to Berbelot.

"A stab in the dark," he returned. "Evidently they like coming through like this and can't do it any other way but on the polychrome wave."

"What do you want to know?" asked Berbelot's image, its lip quivering.

"Who are you?"

"Us? We're . . . I don't know. You don't have a name for us, so how can I tell you?"

"Where are you?"

"Oh, everywhere. We get around."

Berbelot moved his hand impatiently toward the switch.

The images squealed: "Don't! Oh, please don't! This is fun!"

"Fun, is it?" I growled. "Come on, give us the story, or we'll black you out!"

My image said pleadingly: "Please believe us. It's the truth. We're everywhere."

"What do you look like?" I asked. "Show yourselves as you are!"

"We can't," said the other image, "because we don't 'look' like anything. We just . . . are, that's all."

"We don't reflect light," supplemented my image.

Berbelot and I exchanged a puzzled glance. Berbelot said, "Either somebody is taking us for a ride or we've stumbled on something utterly new and unheard-of."

"You certainly have," said Berbelot's image earnestly. "We've known about you for a long time—as you count time—"

"Yes," the other continued. "We knew about you some two hundred of your years ago. We had felt your vibrations for a long time before that, but we never knew just who you were until then."

"Two hundred years—" mused Berbelot. "That was about the time of the first atomic-powered television sets."

"That's right!" said my image eagerly. "It touched our brain currents and we could see and hear. We never could get through to you until recently, though, when you sent us that stupid thing about a seashell."

"None of that, now," I said angrily, while Berbelot chuckled.

"How many of you are there?" he asked them.

"One, and many. We are finite and infinite. We have no size or shape as you know it. We just . . . are."

We just swallowed that without comment. It was a bit big.

"How did you change the programs? How are you changing this one?" Berbelot asked.

"These broadcasts pass directly through our brain currents. Our thoughts change them as they pass. It was impossible before; we were aware, but we could not be heard. This new wave has let us be heard. Its convolutions are in phase with our being."

"How did you happen to pick that particular way of breaking through?" I asked. "I mean all that wisecracking business."

For the first time one of the images—Berbelot's—looked abashed. "We wanted to be liked. We wanted to come through to you and find you laughing. We knew how. Two hundred years of listening to every single broadcast, public and private, has taught us your language and your emotions and your ways of thought. Did we really do wrong?"

"Looks as if we have walked into a cosmic sense of humor," remarked Berbelot to me.

To his image: "Yes, in a way, you did. You lost three huge companies their broadcasting licenses. You embarrassed exceedingly a man named Griff and a secretary of state. You"—he chuckled—"made my friend here very, very angry. That wasn't quite the right thing to do, now, was it?"

"No," said my image. It actually blushed. "We won't do it any more. We were wrong. We are sorry."

"Aw, skip it," I said. I was embarrassed myself. "Everybody makes mistakes."

"That *is* good of you," said my image on the television screen. "We'd like to do something for you. And you, too, Mr.—"

"Berbelot," said Berbelot. Imagine introducing yourself to a television set!

"You can't do anything for us," I said, "except to stop messing up color televising."

"You really want us to stop, then?" My image turned to Berbelot's. "We have done wrong. We have hurt their feelings and made them angry."

To us: "We will not bother you again. Good-by!"

"Wait a minute!" I yelped, but I was too late. The viewscreen showed the same two figures, but they had lost their peculiar life. They were Berbelot and me. Period.

"Now look what you've done," snapped Berbelot.

He began droning into the transmitter: "Calling interrupter on polychrome wave! Can you hear me? Can you hear me? Calling—"

He broke off and looked at me disgustedly. "You dope," he said quietly, and I felt like going off into a corner and bursting into tears.

Well, that's all. The FCC trials reached a "person or persons unknown" verdict, and color broadcasting became a universal reality. The world has never learned, until now, the real story of that screwy business. Berbelot spent every night for three months trying to contact that ether-intelligence, without success. Can you beat it? It waited two hundred years for a chance to come through to us and then got its feelings hurt and withdrew!

My fault, of course. That admission doesn't help any. I wish I could do something—

# PILGRIMAGE *Amazing Stories*, October

## by Nelson Bond (1908–      )

*Another writer best known for his series charac-
ters (Lancelot Biggs, Meg the Priestess, Pat Pending),
Nelson Bond was a steady, competent professional
who occasionally attained brilliance. His best work
can be found (if you can find the book) in NO
TIME LIKE THE FUTURE, 1954.*

*"Meg the Priestess" was a significant series which
consisted of only three stories (all in different magazines) that appeared from 1939–1941. It was one
of the first series to feature a female protaganist,
and this story began her adventures.*

*(I met Nelson Bond, only once, to my knowl-
edge, and that was at the first world science
fiction convention of 1939. He did me a great service some time later, though. I was unable to forget
I was a fan and I argued with readers over my stories in the letter columns of the magazines—until
Nelson dropped me a short note saying, "You're a
writer, now, Isaac. Let the readers have their opinions."—And I followed his advice. IA)*

In her twelfth summer, the illness came upon Meg and she
was afraid. Afraid, yet turbulent with a strange feeling of exaltation unlike anything she had ever before known. She was
a woman now. And she knew, suddenly and completely, that
which was expected of her from this day on. Knew—and
dreaded.

She went immediately to the *hoam* of the Mother. For
such was the Law. But as she moved down the walk-avenue,

she stared, with eyes newly curious, at the Men she passed. At their pale, pitifully hairless bodies. At their soft, futile hands and weak mouths. One lolling on the doorstep of 'Ana's *hoam*, returned her gaze brazenly; made a small, enticing gesture. Meg shuddered, and curled her lips in a refusal-face.

Only yesterday she had been a child. Now, suddenly, she was a woman. And for the first time, Meg saw her people as they really were.

The warriors of the Clan. She looked with distaste upon the tense angularity of their bodies. The corded legs, the grim, set jaws. The cold eyes. The brawny arms, scarred to the elbow with ill-healed cicatrices. The tiny, thwarted breasts, flat and hard beneath leather harness-plates. Fighters they were, and nothing else.

This was not what she wanted.

She saw, too, the mothers. The full-lipped, flabby breasted bearers of children, whose skins were soft and white as those of the Men. Whose eyes were humid; washed barren of all expression by desires too oft aroused, too often sated. Their bodies bulged at hip and thigh, swayed when they walked like ripe grain billowing in a lush and fertile field. They lived only that the tribe might live, might continue to exist. They reproduced.

This was not what she wanted.

Then there were the workers. Their bodies retained a vestige of womankind's inherent grace and nobility. But if their waists were thin, their hands were blunt-fingered and thick. Their shoulders were bent with the weight of labor, coarsened from adze and hod. Their faces were grim from the eternal struggle with an unyielding earth. And the earth, of which they had made themselves a part, had in return made itself a part of them. The workers' skin was browned with soil, their bodies stank of dirk and grime and unwashed perspiration.

No, none of these was what she wanted. None of these was what she would *have*, of that she was positively determined.

So great was Meg's concentration that she entered into the *hoam* of the Mother without crying out, as was required. Thus it was that she discovered the Mother making great magic to the gods.

In her right hand, the Mother held a stick. With it she scratched upon a smooth, bleached, calfskin scroll. From time to time she let the stick drink from a pool of midnight cupped in a dish before her. When she moved it again on the hide, it left its spoor; a spidery trail of black.

For a long moment Meg stood and watched, wondering. Then dread overcame her; fear-thoughts shook her body. She thought suddenly of the gods. Of austere Jarg, their leader; of lean Ibrim and taciturn Taamuz. Of far-seeing Tedhi, she whose laughter echoes in the roaring summer thunders. What wrath would they visit upon one who had spied into their secrets?

She covered her eyes and dropped to her knees. But there were footsteps before her, and the Mother's hands upon her shoulders. And there was but gentle chiding in the voice of the Mother as she said, "My child, know you not the Law? That all must cry out before entering the Mother's *hoam?*"

Meg's fear-thoughts went away. The Mother was good. It was she who fed and clothed the Clan; warmed them in dark winter and found them meat when meat was scarce. If she, who was the gods' spokesman on earth, saw no evil in Meg's unintentional prying—

Meg dared look again at the magic stick. There was a question in her eyes. The Mother answered that question.

"It is 'writing,' Meg. Speech without words."

Speech-without-words? Meg crept to the table; bent a curious ear over the spider-marks. But she heard no sound. Then the Mother was beside her again saying, "No, my child. It does not speak to the ears, but to the eyes. Listen, and I will make it speak through my mouth."

She read aloud.

"Report of the month of June, 3478 A.D. There has been no change in the number of the Jinnia Clan. We are still five score and seven, with nineteen Men, twelve cattle, thirty horses. But there is reason to believe that 'Ana and Sahlee will soon add to our number.

"Last week Darthee, Lina and Alis journeyed into the Clina territory in search of game. They met there several of the Durm Clan and exchanged gifts of salt and bacca. Pledges of friendship were given. On the return trip, Darthee was linberred by one of the Wild Ones, but was rescued by her companions before the strain could be crossed. The Wild One was destroyed.

"We have in our village a visitor from the Delwurs of the east, who says that in her territory the Wild Ones have almost disappeared. Illness she says, has depleted their Men—and she begs that I lend her one or two for a few months. I am thinking of letting her have Jak and Ralf, both of whom are proven studs—"

The Mother stopped. "That is as far as I had gone, my child, when you entered."

Meg's eyes were wide with wonder. It was quite true that Darthee, Lina and Alis had recently returned from a trip to China. And that there was now a visitor in camp. But how could the speech-without-words know these things, *tell* these things? She said, "But, Mother—will not the speech-without-words forget?"

"No, Meg. *We* forget. The books remember always."

"Books, Mother?"

"These are books." The Mother moved to the sleeping part of her *hoam;* selected one of a tumbled pile of calfskin scrolls. "Here are the records of our Clan from ages past— since the time of the Ancient Ones. Not all are here. Some have been lost. Others were ruined by flood or destroyed by fire.

"But it is the Mother's duty to keep these records. That is why the Mother must know the art of making the speech-without-words. It is hard work, my little one. And a labor without end—"

Meg's eyes were shining. The trouble that had been cold within her before was vanished now. In its place had come a great thought. A thought *so* great, *so* daring, that Meg had to open her lips twice before the words came.

"Is it—" she asked breathlessly, "Is it very hard to become a—Mother?"

The Mother smiled gently. "A very great task, Meg. But you should not think of such things. It is not yet time for you to decide—" She paused, looking at Meg strangely. "Or—is it, my child?"

Meg flushed, and her eyes dropped.

"It is, Mother."

"Then be not afraid, my daughter. You know the Law. At this important hour it is yours to decide what station in life will be yours. What is your wish, Meg? Would you be a warrior, a worker, or a breeding mother?"

Meg looked at the Clan leader boldly.

"I would be," she said, "a Mother!" Then, swiftly, "But not a breeding mother. I mean a *Clan* Mother—like you, O Mother!"

The Mother stared. Then the harsh lines melted from her face and she said, thoughtfully, "Thrice before has that request been made of me, Meg. Each time I have refused. It was Beth who asked first, oh, many years ago. She became a warrior, and died gallantly lifting the siege of Loovil. . . .

"Then Haizl. And the last time it was Hein. When I refused, she became the other type of mother.

"But I was younger then. Now I am old. And it is right that there should be someone to take my place when I am gone—" She stared at the girl intently.

"It is not easy, my daughter. There is much work to be done. Work, not of the body but of the mind. There are problems to be solved, many vows to be taken, a hard pilgrimage to be made—"

"All these," swore Meg, "would I gladly do, O Mother! If you will but let me—" Her voice broke suddenly. "But I cannot become anything else. I would not be a warrior, harsh and bitter. Nor a worker, black with dirt. And the breeders— I would as soon mate with one of the Wild Ones as with one of the Men! The thought of their soft hands—"

She shuddered. And the Clan Mother nodded, understanding. "Very well, Meg. Tomorrow you will move into this *hoam*. You will live with me and study to become the Jinnia Clan's next Mother. . . ."

So began Meg's training. Nor was the Mother wrong in saying that the task was not an easy one. Many were the times when Meg wept bitterly, striving to learn that which a Mother must know. There was the speech-without-words, which Meg learned to call "writing." It looked like a simple magic when the Mother did it. But that slender stick, which moved so fluidly beneath the Mother's aged fingers slipped and skidded and made ugly blotches of midnight on the hide whenever Meg tried to make spider-marks.

Meg learned that these wavering lines were not meaningless. Each line was made of "sentences," each sentence of "words," and each word was composed of "letters." And each letter made a sound, just as each combination of letters made a word-sound.

These were strange and confusing. A single letter, out of place, changed the whole meaning of the word ofttimes. Sometimes it altered the meaning of the whole sentence. But Meg's determination was great. There came, finally, the day when the Mother allowed her to write the monthly report in the Clan history. Meg was thirteen, then. But already she was older in wisdom than the others of her Clan.

It was then that the Mother began to teach her yet another

magic. It was the magic of "numbers." Where there had been twenty-six "letters," there were only ten numbers. But theirs was a most peculiar magic. Put together, ofttimes they formed other and greater numbers. Yet the same numbers taken away from each other formed still a third group. The names of these magics, Meg never did quite learn. They were strange, magical, meaningless terms. "Multiplication" and "subtraction." But she learned how to do them.

Her task was made the harder, for it was about this time that the Evil Ones sent a little pain-imp to torment her. He stole in through her ear one night while she was sleeping. And for many months he lurked in her head, above her eyes. Every time she would sit down to study the magic of the numbers, he would begin dancing up and down, trying to stop her. But Meg persisted. And finally the pain-imp either died or was removed. And Meg knew the numbers. . . .

There were rites and rituals to be learned. There was the Sacred Song which had to be learned by heart. This song had no tune, but was accompanied by the beating of the tribal drums. Its words were strange and terrible; echoing the majesty of the gods in its cryptic phrasing.

"O, Sakan! you see by Tedhi on his early Light—"

This was a great song. A powerful magic. It was the only tribal song Meg learned which dared name one of the gods. And it had to be sung reverently, lest far-seeing Tedhi be displeased and show her monstrous teeth and destroy the invoker with her mirthful thunders.

Meg learned, too, the tribal song of the Jinnia Clan. She had known it from infancy, but its words had been obscure. Now she learned enough to probe into its meaning. She did not know the meanings of some of the forgotten words, but for the most part it made sense when the tribe gathered on festive nights to sing, "Caamé back to over Jinnia—"

And Meg grew in age and stature and wisdom. In her sixteenth summer, her legs were long and firm and straight as a warrior's spear. Her body was supple; bronzed by sunlight save where her doeskin breech-cloth kept the skin white. Unbound, her hair would have trailed the earth, but she wore it piled upon her head, fastened by a netting woven by the old mothers, too ancient to bear.

The vanity-god had died long ages since, and Meg had no way of knowing she was beautiful. But sometimes, looking at her reflection in the pool as she bathed, she approved the soft curves of her slim young body, and was more than ever glad and proud that she had become a neophyte to the Mother. She liked her body to be this way. Why, she did not know. But she was glad that she had not turned lean and hard, as had those of her age who had become warriors. Or coarse, as had become the workers. Or soft and flabby, as were the breeding-mothers. Her skin was golden-brown, and pure gold where the sunlight burnished the fine down on her arms and legs, between her high, firm breasts.

And finally there came the day when the Mother let Meg conduct the rites at the Feast of the Blossoms. This was in July, and Meg had then entered upon her seventeenth year. It was a great occasion, and a great test. But Meg did not fail. She conducted the elaborate rite from beginning to end without a single mistake.

That night, in the quiet of their *hoam*, the Mother made a final magic. She drew from her collection of aged trophies a curl of parchment. This she blessed. Then she handed it to Meg.

"You are ready now, O my daughter," she said. "In the morning you will leave."

"Leave, Mother?" said Meg.

"For the final test. This that I give you is a map. A shower-of-places. You will see, here at this joining of mountain and river, our village in the heart of the Jinnia territory. Far off, westward and to the north, as here is shown, is the Place of the Gods. It is there you must go on pilgrimage before you return to take your place as Mother."

Now, at this last moment, Meg felt misgivings.

"But you, Mother?" she asked. "If I become Mother, what will become of you?"

"The rest will be welcome, daughter. It is good to know that the work will be carried on—" The aged Mother pondered. "There is much, yet, that you do not know, Meg. It is forbidden that I should tell you all until you have been to the Place of the Gods. There will you see, and understand—"

"The—the books?" faltered Meg.

"Upon your return you may read the books. Even as I read them when I returned. And all will be made clear to you. Even that final secret which the clan must not know—"

"I do not understand, Mother."

"You will, my daughter—later. And now, to sleep. For at dawn tomorrow begins your pilgrimage. . . ."

Off in the hills, a wild dog howled his melancholy farewell to the dying moon. His thin song clove the stirring silence of the trees, the incessant movement of the forest. Meg wakened at that cry; wakened and saw that already the red edge of dawn tinged the eastern sky.

She uncurled from the broad treecrotch in which she had spent the night. Her horse was already awake, and with restless movements was nibbling the sparse grass beneath the giant oak. Meg loosed his tether, then went to the spring she had found the night before.

There she drank, and in the little rill that trickled from the spring, bathed herself as best she could. Her ablutions finished, she set about making breakfast. There was not much food in her saddlebags. A side of rabbit, carefully saved from last night's dinner. Two biscuits, slightly dry now. A precious handful of salt. She ate sparingly, resolved to build camp early tonight in order to set a few game traps and bake another batch of biscuit.

She cleared a space, scratching a wide circle of earth bare of all leaves and twigs, then walking around it widdershins thrice to chase away the firedemon. Then she scratched the firestone against a piece of the black metal from the town of the Ancient Ones—a gift of the Mother—and kindled her little fire.

Two weeks had passed since Meg had left the Jinnia territory. She had come from the rugged mountainlands of her home territory, through the river valleys of the Hyan Clan. On the flat plains of the Yana section, she had made an error. Her map had shown the route clearly, but she had come upon a road built by the Ancient Ones. A road of white creet, still in fair repair. And because it was easier to travel on this highway than to thread a way through the jungle, she had let herself drift southward.

It was not until she reached the timeworn village of Slooie that friendly Zuries had pointed out her mistake. Then she had to turn northward and westward again, going up the Big River to the territory of the Demoys.

Now, her map showed, she was in Braska territory. Two more weeks—perhaps less than that—should bring her to her goal. To the sacred Place of the Gods.

Meg started and roused from her speculations as a twig snapped in the forest behind her. In one swift motion she had wheeled, drawn her sword, and was facing the spot from which the sound had come. But the green bushes did not tremble; no further crackling came from the underbrush. Her fears allayed, she turned to the important business of roasting her side of rabbit.

It was always needful to be on the alert. Meg had learned that lesson early; even before her second day's journey had led her out of Jinnia territory. For, as the Mother had warned, there were still many Wild Ones roaming through the land. Searching for food, for the precious firemetal from the ruined villages of the Ancient Ones—most of all for mates. The Wild Ones were dying out, slowly, because of their lack of mates. There were few females left among them. Most of the Wild Ones were male. But there was little in their shaggy bodies, their thick, brutish faces, their hard, gnarled muscles, to remind one of the Men.

A Wild One had attacked Meg in her second night's camp. Fortunately she had not yet been asleep when he made his foray—else her pilgrimage would have ended abruptly. Not that he would have killed her. The Wild Ones did not kill the women they captured. They took them to their dens. And— Meg had heard tales. A priestess could not cross her strain with a Wild One and still become a Mother.

So Meg had fought fiercely, and had been victorious. The Wild One's bones lay now in the Jinnia hills, picked bare by the vultures. But since that escape, Meg had slept nightly in trees, her sword clenched in her hand. . . .

The food was cooked now. Meg removed it from the spit, blew upon it, and began to eat. She had many things on her mind. The end of her pilgrimage was nigh. The hour when she would enter into the Place of the Gods, and learn the last and most carefully guarded secret.

That is why her senses failed her. That is why she did not even know the Wild One lurked near until, with a roar of throaty satisfaction, he had leaped from the shrubbery, seized her, and pinioned her struggling arms to her sides with tight grip.

It was a bitter fight, but a silent one. For all her slimness, Meg's body was sturdy. She fought pantherlike; using every weapon with which the gods had endowed her. Her fists, legs, teeth.

But the Wild One's strength was as great as his ardor was strong. He crushed Meg to him bruisingly; the stink of his sweat burning her nostrils. His arms bruised her breasts; choked the breath from her straining lungs. One furry arm tensed about her throat, cutting off the precious air.

Meg writhed, broke free momentarily, buried her strong

teeth in his arm. A howl of hurt and rage broke from the Wild One's lips. Meg tugged at her sword. But again the Wild One threw himself upon her; this time with great fists flailing. Meg saw a hammerlike hand smashing down on her, felt the shocking concussion of the Wild One's strength. A lightning flashed. The ground leaped up to meet her. Then all was silent. . . .

She woke, groaning weakly. Her head was splitting, and the bones of her body arched. She started to struggle to her feet; had risen halfway before she discovered with a burst of hope that she *could* move! She was not bound! Then the Wild One—

She glanced about her swiftly. She was still lying in the little glade where she had been attacked. The sun's full orb had crept over the horizon now, threading a lacework of light through the tiny glen. Her fire smouldered still. And beside it crouched a—a—

Meg could not decide what it was. It looked like a Man, but that of course was impossible. Its body was smooth and almost as hairless as her own. Bronzed by the sun. But it was not the pale, soft body of a man. It was muscular, hard, firm; taller and stronger than a warrior.

Flight was Meg's first thought. But her curiosity was even stronger than her fear. This was a mystery. And her sword was beside her. Whoever, or whatever, this Thing might be, it did not seem to wish her harm. She spoke to it.

"Who are you?" asked Meg. "And where is the Wild One?"

The stranger looked up, and a happy look spread over his even features. He pointed briefly to the shrubbery. Meg followed the gesture; saw lying there the dead body of the Wild One. Her puzzled gaze returned to the Man-thing.

"You killed him? Then you are not one of the Wild Ones? But I do not understand. You are not a man—"

"You," said the man-thing in a voice deeper than Meg had ever heard from a human throat, "talk too much. Sit down and eat, Woman!"

He tossed Meg a piece of her own rabbit-meat. Self unaware that she did so, Meg took it and began eating. She stared at the stranger as he finished his own repast, wiped his hands on his clout and moved toward her. Meg dropped her half-eaten breakfast, rose hastily and groped for her sword.

"Touch me not, Hairless One!" she cried warningly. "I am a priestess of the Jinnia Clan. It is not for such as you to—"

The stranger brushed by her without even deigning to hear her words. He reached the spot where her horse had been tethered; shook a section of broken rein ruefully.

"You women!" he spat. "Bah! You do not know how to train a horse. See—he ran away!"

Meg thought anger-thoughts. Her face burned with the sun, though the sun's rays were dim in the glade. She cried, "Man-thing, know you no better than to talk thus to a Woman and a master? By Jarg, I should have you whipped—"

"You talk too much!" repeated the Man-thing wearily. Once more he squatted on his hunkers; studied her thoughtfully. "But you interest me. Who are you? What are you doing so far from the Jinnia territory? Where are you going?"

"A priestess," said Meg coldly, "does not answer the questions of a Man-thing—"

"I'm not a Man-*thing*," said the stranger pettishly, "I am a Man. A Man of the Kirki tribe which lives many miles south of here. I am Daiv, known as He-who-would-learn. So tell me, Woman."

His candor confused Meg. Despite herself, she found the words leaving her lips. "I—I am Meg. I am making pilgrimage to the Place of the Gods. It is my final task ere I become Mother of my clan."

The Man's eyes appraised her with embarrassing frankness. "So?" he said. "Mother of a Clan? Meg, would you not rather stay with me and become mother of your own clan?"

Meg gasped. Men were the mates of Women—yes! But never had any Man the audacity to *suggest* such a thing. Matings were arranged by the Mother, with the agreement of the Woman. And surely this Man must know that priestesses did not mate.

"Man!" she cried, "Know you not the Law? I am soon to become a Clan Mother. Guard your words, or the wrath of the Gods—"

The Man, Daiv, made happy-sounds again. "It was I who saved you from the Wild One," he chuckled. "Not the Gods. In my land, Golden One, we think it does no harm to ask. But if you are unwilling—" he shrugged. "I will leave you now."

Without further adieu, he rose and started to leave. Meg's face reddened. She cried out angrily, "Man!"

He turned, "Yes?"

"I have no horse. How am I to get to the Place of the Gods?"

"Afoot, Golden One. Or are you Women too weak to make such a journey?"

He laughed again—and was gone.

For a long moment Meg stared after him, watching the green fronds close behind his disappearing form, feeling the stark desolation of utter aloneness close in upon her and envelop her. Then she did a thing she herself could not understand. She put down her foot upon the ground, hard, in an angry-movement.

The sun was high, and growing warmer. The journey to the Place of the Gods was longer, now that she had no mount. But the pilgrimage was a sacred obligation. Meg scraped dirt over the smoldering embers of her fire. She tossed her saddle-bags across her shoulder and faced westward. And she pressed on. . . .

The way was long; the day hot and tedious. Before the sun rode overhead, Meg was sticky with sweat and dust. Her feet were sore, and her limbs ached with the unaccustomed exercise of walking. By afternoon, every step was an agony. And while the sun was still too-strong-to-be-looked-at, she found a small spring of fresh water and decided to make camp there for the night.

She set out two seines for small game; took the flour and salt from her saddle-bags and set about making a batch of biscuit. As the rocks heated, she went to the stream and put her feet in it, letting the water-god lick the fever from her tender soles.

From where she sat, she could not see the fire. She had been there perhaps a half an hour when a strange, unfamiliar smell wrinkled her nostrils. It was at once a sweet-and-bitter smell; a pungent odor like strong herbs, but one that set the water to running in her mouth.

She went back to her camp hastily—and found there the Man, Daiv, once again crouching over her stone fireplace. He was watching a pot on the stones. From time to time he stirred the pot with a long stick. Drawing closer, Meg saw a brown water in the pot. It was this which made the aromatic smell. She would have called out to the Man, but he saw her first. And,

"Hello, Golden One!" he said.

Meg said stonily, "What are you doing here?"

The Man shrugged.

"I am Daiv. He-who-would-learn. I got to thinking about this Place of the Gods, and decided I too, would come and see it." He sniffed the brown, bubbling liquid; seemed satisfied. He poured some of it out into an earthen bowl and handed it to Meg. "You want some?"

Meg moved toward him cautiously. This might be a ruse of the Man from the Kirki tribe. Perhaps this strange, aromatic liquid was a drug. The Mother of the Clan had the secret of such drinks. There was one which caused the head to pucker, the mouth to dry and the feet to reel. . . .

"What is it?" she demanded suspiciously.

"Cawfi, of course." Daiv looked surprised. "Don't you know? But, no—I suppose the bean-tree would not grow in your northern climate. It grows near my land. In Sippe and Weezian territories. Drink it!"

Meg tasted the stuff. It was like its smell; strong and bitter, but strangely pleasing. Its heat coursed through her, taking the tired-pain from her body as the water of the spring had taken the burn from her feet.

"It's good, Man," she said.

"Daiv," said the Man. "My name is Daiv, Golden One."

Meg made a stern-look with her brows.

"It is not fitting," she said, "that a priestess should call a Man by his name."

Daiv seemed to be given to making happy-sounds. He made one again.

"You have done lots of things today that are not fitting for a priestess, Golden One. You are not in Jinnia now. Things are different here. And as for me—" He shrugged. "My people do things differently, too. We are one of the chosen tribes, you know. We come from the land of the Escape."

"The Escape?" asked Meg.

"Yes." As he talked, Daiv busied himself. He had taken meat from his pouch, and was wrapping this now in clay. He tossed the caked lumps into the embers of the crude oven. He had also some taters, which Meg had not tasted for many weeks. He took the skins off these, cut them into slices with his hunting-knife and browned the pieces on a piece of hot, flat rock. "The Escape of the Ancient Ones, you know."

"I—I'm not sure I understand," said Meg.

"Neither do I—quite. It happened many years ago. Before my father's father's father's people. There are books in the tribe Master's *hoam* which tell. I have seen some of them. . . .

"Once things were different, you know. In the days of the Ancient Ones, Men and Women were equal throughout the world. In fact, the Men were the Masters. But the Men were warlike and fierce—"

"Like the Wild Ones, you mean?"

"Yes. But they did not make war with clubs and spears, like the Wild Ones. They made war with great catapults that threw fire and flame and exploding death. With little bows that shot steel arrowheads. With gases that destroy, and waters that burn the skin.

"On earth and sea they made these battles, and even in the air. For in those days, the Ancient Ones had wings, like birds. They soared high, making great thunders. And when they warred, they dropped huge eggs of fire which killed others."

Meg cried sharply, "Oh—"

"Don't you believe me?"

"The taters, Daiv! They're burning!"

"Oh!" Daiv made a happy-face and carefully turned the scorching tater slices. Then he continued.

"It is told that there came a final greatest war of all. It was a conflict not only between the Clans, but between the forces of the entire earth. It started in the year which is known as nineteen and sixty—whatever *that* means—"

"I know!" said Meg.

Daiv looked at her with sudden respect. "You do? Then the Master of my tribe must meet you and—"

"It is impossible," said Meg. "Go on!"

"Very well. For many years this war lasted. But neither side could gain a victory. In those days it was the Men who fought, while the Women remained *hoam* to keep the Men's houses. But the Men died by thousands. And there came a day when the Women grew tired of it.

"They got together . . . all of them who lived in the civilized places. And they decided to rid themselves of the brutal Men. They stopped sending supplies and fire-eggs to the battling Men across the sea. They built walled forts, and hid themselves in them.

"The war ended when the Men found they had no more to fight with. They came back to their *hoams,* seeking their Women. But the Women would not receive them. There was bitter warfare once again—between the sexes. But the Women held their walled cities. And so—"

"Yes?" said Meg.

"The Men," said Daiv somberly, "became the Wild Ones of the forest. Mateless, save for the few Women they could linber.* Their numbers died off. The Clans grew. Only in a few places—like Kirki, my land—did humanity not become a matriarchy."

He looked at Meg. "You believe?"

Meg shook her head. Suddenly she felt very sorry for this stranger, Daiv. She knew, now, why he had not harmed her. Why, when she had been powerless before him, he had not forced her to become his mate. He was mad. Totally and completely mad. She said, gently, "Shall we eat, Daiv?"

Mad or not, there was great pleasure in having some company on the long, weary, remaining marches of her pilgrimage. Thus it was that Meg made no effort to discourage Daiv in his desire to accompany her. He was harmless, and he was pleasant company—for a Man. And his talk, wild as it was at times, served to pass boring hours.

They crossed the Braska territory and entered at last into the 'Kota country. It was here the Place of the Gods was—only at the far western end, near Yomin. And the slow days passed, turning into weeks. Not many miles did they cover in those first few days, while Meg's feet were tender and her limbs full of jumping little pain-imps. But when hard walking had destroyed the pain-imps, they traveled faster. And the time was drawing near. . . .

"You started, once, to tell me about the Escape, Daiv," said Meg one evening. "But you did not finish. What is the legend of the Escape?"

Daiv sprawled languidly before the fire. His eyes were dreamy.

"It happened in the Zoni territory," he said, "Not far from the lands of my own tribe. In those days was there a Mangod named Renn, who foresaw the death of the Ancient Ones. He built a gigantic sky-bird of metal, and into its bowels climbed two score Men and Women.

"They flew away, off there—" Daiv pointed to a shining white dot in the sky above. "To the evening star. But it is said that one day they will return. That is why our tribe tries to preserve the customs of the Ancient Ones. Why even misguided tribes like yours preserve the records—"

Meg's face reddened.

"Enough!" she cried. "I have listened to many of your tales without making comment, Daiv. But now I command you to tell me no more such tales as this. This is—this is blas--phemy!"

*Linber—to kidnap (derived from Lindbergh?)—Ed.

"Blasphemy?"

"It is not bad enough that your deranged mind should tell of days when *Men* ruled the earth? Now you speak of a *Man*-god!"

Daiv looked worried. He said, "But, Golden One, I thought you understood that all the gods were Men—"

"Daiv!" Without knowing why she did so, Meg suddenly swung to face him; covered his lips with her hands. She sought the darkness fearfully; made a swift gesture and a swifter prayer. "Do not tempt the wrath of the Gods! I am a priestess, and I know. All the Gods are—*must* be—Women!"

"But why?"

"Why—why, because they are!" said Meg. "It could not be otherwise. All Women know the gods are great, good and strong. How, then, could they be men? Jarg, and Ibram, and Taamuz. The mighty Tedhi—"

Daiv's eyes narrowed in wonderthought.

"I do not know their names," he mused. "They are not gods of our tribe. And yet—Ibrim . . . Tedhi. . . ."

There was vast pity in Meg's voice.

"We have been comrades for a long journey, Daiv," she pleaded. "Never before, since the world began, have a Man and a Woman met as you and I. Often you have said mad, impossible things. But I have forgiven you because—well, because you are, after all, only a Man.

"But tomorrow, or the day after that, we should come to the Place of the Gods. Then will my pilgrimage be ended, and I will learn that which is the ultimate secret. Then I shall have to return to my Clan, to become the Mother. And so let us not spoil our last hours of comradeship with vain argument."

Daiv sighed.

"The elder ones are gone, and their legends tell so little. It may be you are right, Golden One. But I have a feeling that it is my tribal lore that does not err. Meg—I asked this once before. Now I ask again. Will you become my mate?"

"It is impossible, Daiv. Priestesses and Mothers do not mate. And soon I will take you back with me to Jinnia, if you wish. And I will see to it that you are taken care of, always, as a Man should be taken care of."

Daiv shook his head.

"I cannot, Meg. Our ways are not the same. There is a custom in our tribe . . . a mating custom which you do not know. Let me show you—"

He leaned over swiftly. Meg felt the mighty strength of his bronzed arms closing about her, drawing her close. And he was touching his mouth to hers; closely, brutally, terrifyingly.

She struggled and tried to cry out, but his mouth bruised hers. Angerthoughts swept through her like a flame. But it was not anger—it was something else—that gave life to that flame. Suddenly her veins were running with liquid fire. Her heart beat upon rising, panting breasts like something captive that would be free. Her fists beat upon his shoulders vainly ... but there was little strength in her blows.

Then he released her, and she fell back, exhausted. Her eyes glowed with anger and her voice was husky in her throat. She tried to speak, and could not. And in that moment, a vast and terrible weakness trembled through Meg. She knew, fearfully, that if Daiv sought to mate with her, not all the priestessdom of the gods could save her. There was a body-hunger throbbing within her that hated his Manness ... but cried for it!

But Daiv, too, stepped back. And his voice was low as he said, "Meg?"

She wiped her mouth with the back of her hand. Her voice was vibrant.

"What magic is that, Daiv? What custom is that? I hate it. I hate *you!* I—"

"It is the touching-of-mouths, Golden One. It is the right of the Man with his mate. It is my plea that you enter not the Place of the Gods, but return with me, now, to Kirki, there to become my mate."

For a moment, indecision swayed Meg. But then, slowly, "No! I must go to the Place of the Gods," she said.

And thus it was. For the next day Meg marked on the shower-of-places the last time that indicated the path of her pilgrimage. And at eventide, when the sun threw long, ruddy rays upon the rounded hills of black, she and Daiv entered into the gateway which she had been told led to the Place of the Gods.

It was here they lingered for a moment. There were many words each would have said to the other. But both knew that this was the end.

"I know no Law, Daiv," said Meg, "which forbids a Man from entering the Place of the Gods. So you may do so if you wish. But it is not fitting that we should enter together. Therefore I ask you to wait here while I enter alone.

"I will learn the secret there. And learning, I will go out by another path, and return to Jinnia."

"You will go—alone?"

"Yes, Daiv."

"But if you should—" he persisted.

"If by some strangeness I should change my mind," said Meg, "I will return to you—here. But it is unlikely. Therefore do not wait."

"I will wait, Golden One," said Daiv soberly, "until all hope is dead."

Meg turned away, then hesitated and turned back. A great sorrow was within her. She did not know why. But she knew of one magic that could hear her heart for the time.

"Daiv—" she whispered.

"Yes, Golden One?"

"No one will ever know. And before I leave you forever—could we once more do the—the touching-of-mouths?"

So it was that alone and with the recollection of a moment of stirring glory in her heart, Meg strode proudly at last into the Place of the Gods.

It was a wild and desolate place. Barren hills of sand rose about here, and of vegetation there was none save sparse weeds and scrubby stumps that flowered miserly in the bleak, chill air.

The ground was harsh and salt beneath her feet, and no birds sang an evening carillon in that drab wilderness. Afar, a wild dog pierced the sky with its lonely call. The great hills echoed that cry dismally.

Above the other hills towered a greater one. To this, with unerring footsteps, Meg took her way. She knew not what to expect. It might be that here a band of singing virgins would appear to her, guiding her to a secret altar before which she would kneel and learn the last mystery.

It might be that the gods themselves reigned here, and that she would fall in awe before the sweeping skirts of austere Jarg, to hear from the gods' own lips the secret she had come so far to learn.

Whatever it was that would be revealed to her, Meg was ready. Others had found this place, and had survived. She did not fear death. But—death-in-life? Coming to the Place of the Gods with a blasphemy in her heart? With the memory of a Man's mouth upon hers—

For a moment, Meg was afraid. She had betrayed her priestessdom. Her body was inviolate, but would not the gods search her soul and know that her heart had forgotten the Law; had mated with a Man?

But if death must be her lot—so be it. She pressed on.

So Meg turned through a winding path, down between two tortuous clefts of rock, and came at last unto the Place of the Gods. Nor could she have chosen a better moment for the ultimate reaching of this place. The sun's roundness had now touched the western horizon.

There was still light. And Meg's eyes, wondering, sought that light. Sought—and saw! And then, with awe in her heart, Meg fell to her knees.

She had glimpsed that-which-was-not-to-be-seen! The Gods themselves, standing in omnipotent majesty, upon the crest of the towering rock.

For tremulous moments Meg knelt there, whispering the ritual prayers of appeasement. At any moment she expected to hear the thunderous voice of Tedhi, or to feel upon her shoulder the judicial hand of Jarg. But there came no sound but the frenzied beating of her own heart, of the soft stirring of dull grasses, of the wind touching the grim rocks.

And she lifted her head and looked once more. . . .

It was they! A race recollection, deeper and more sure than her own haulting memory told her at once that she had not erred. This was, indeed, the Place of the Gods. And these were the Gods she faced—stern, implacable, everlasting. Carven in eternal rock by the hands of those long ago.

Here they were; the Great Four. Jarg and Taamuz, with ringletted curls framing their stern, judicial faces. Sad Ibrim, lean of cheek and hollow of eye. And far-seeing Tedhi, whose eyes were concealed behind the giant telescopes. Whose lips, even now, were peeled back as though to loose a peal of his thunderous laughter.

And the Secret?

But even as the question leaped to her mind, it had its answer. Suddenly Meg knew that there was no visitation to be made upon her here. There would be no circle of singing virgins, no communication from those great stone lips. For the Secret which the Mother had hinted . . . the Secret which the Clanswomen must not know . . . was a secret Daiv had confided to her during those long marches of the pilgrimage.

The Gods—were Men!

Oh, not men like Jak or Ralf, whose pale bodies were but the instruments through which the breeding mothers' bodies were fertilized! Nor male creatures like the Wild Ones.

But—Men like Daiv! Lean and hard of jaw, strong of muscle, sturdy of body.

Even the curls could not conceal the inherent masculinity of Jarg and Taamuz. And Tedhi's lip was covered with Manhair, clearcut and bristling above his happy-mouth. And Ibrim's cheeks were haired, even as Daiv's had been from time to time before he made his tribal cut-magic with a keen knife.

The gods, the rulers, the Masters of the Ancient Ones *had* been Men. It had been as Daiv said—that many ages ago the Women had rebelled. And now they pursued their cold and loveless courses, save where—in a few places like the land of Kirki—the old way still maintained.

It was a great knowledge, and a bitter one. Now Meg understood why the Mother's lot was so unhappy. Because only the Mother knew how artificial this new life was. How soon the Wild Ones would die out, and the captive Men along with them. When that day came, there would be no more young. No more Men *or* Women. No more civilization. . . .

The Gods knew this. That is why they stood here in the grey hills of 'Kota, sad, forlorn, forgotten. The dying gods of a dying race. That because of an ill-conceived vengeance humankind was slowly destroying itself.

There was no hope. Knowing, now, this Secret, Meg must return to her Clan with lips sealed. There, like the Mother before her, she must watch with haunted eyes the slow dwindling of their tiny number . . . see the weak and futile remnants of Man die off. Until at last—

Hope was not dead! The Mother had been wrong. For the Mother had not been so fortunate in her pilgrimage as had Meg. She had never learned that there were still places in the world where Man had preserved himself in the image of the Ancient Ones. In the image of the Gods.

But she, Meg, knew! And knowing, she was presented with the greatest choice a Woman could know.

Forward into the valley, lay the path through which she could return to her Clan. There she would become Mother, and would guide and guard her people through a lifetime. She would be all-wise, all-powerful, all-important. But she would be a virgin unto death; sterile with the sanctity of tradition.

This she might do. But there was yet another way. And Meg threw her arms high, crying out that the Gods might hear and decide her problem.

The Gods spoke not. Their solemn features, weighted with

the gravity of time, moved not nor spoke to her. But as she searched their faces piteously for an answer to her vast despair, there came to Meg a memory. It was a passage from the Prayer of Ibrim. And as her lips framed those remembered words, it seemed that the dying rays of the sun centered on Ibrim's weary face, and those great stone eyes were alive for a moment with understanding . . . and approval.

" . . . shall not perish from the earth, but have everlasting Life. . . ."

Then Meg, the priestess, decided. With a sharp cry that broke from her heart, she turned and ran. Not toward the valley, but back . . . back . . . back . . . on feet that were suddenly stumbling and eager. Back through the towering shadow of Mt. Rushmore, through a desolate grotto that led to a gateway wherein awaited the Man who had taught her the touching-of-mouths.

# RUST     *Astounding Science Fiction*, October

# by Joseph E. Kelleam (1913–     )

*Joseph E. Kelleam had a handful of stories in the sf magazines in the late thirties and early forties, then disappeared for almost fifteen years, resurfacing in the mid-fifties with a novel and later with a few more stories and three more novels. In addition to the present selection, a noteworthy story is "The Eagles Gather," Astounding, 1942. His later work did not fulfill the promise of these two.*

*"Rust" vividly captures the mood of that portion of modern science fiction characterized by alienation and despair. World War II had not started when Kelleam wrote this story, but all the signs of a coming holocaust were there, and we think he was trying to warn us.*

*(We were a small group as the Thirties waned, and we huddled together for comfort, caught as we were in the least regarded branch of that unregarded world of the pulp magazine. And yet even so it was possible to pass in the night. Kelleam's path and mine never crossed. IA)*

The sun, rising over the hills, cast long shadows across the patches of snow and bathed the crumbling ruins in the pale light. Had men been there they could have reckoned the month to be August. But men had gone, long since, and the sun had waned; and now, in this late period of the earth's age, the short spring was awakening.

Within the broken city, in a mighty-columned hall that still supported a part of a roof, life of a sort was stirring. Three grotesque creatures were moving, their limbs creaking dolefully.

X-120 faced the new day and the new spring with a feeling of exhilaration that nearly drove the age-old loneliness and emptiness from the corroded metal of what might be called his brain. The sun was the source of his energy, even as it had been the source of the fleshy life before him; and with the sun's reappearance he felt new strength coursing through the wires and coils and gears of his complex body.

He and his companions were highly developed robots, the last ever to be made by the Earthmen. X-120 consisted of a globe of metal, eight feet in diameter, mounted upon four many-jointed legs. At the top of this globe was a protuberance like a kaiser's helmet which caught and stored his power from the rays of the sun.

From the "face" of the globe two ghostly quartz eyes bulged. The globe was divided by a heavy band of metal at its middle, and from this band, at each side, extended a long arm ending in a powerful claw. This claw was like the pincers of a lobster and had been built to shear through metal. Four long cables, which served as auxiliary arms, were drawn up like springs against the body.

X-120 stepped from the shadows of the broken hall into the ruined street. The sun's rays striking against his tarnished sides sent new strength coursing through his body. He had forgotten how many springs he had seen. Many generations of twisted oaks that grew among the ruins had sprung up and fallen since X-120 and his companions had been made. Countless hundreds of springs had flitted across the dying earth since the laughter and dreams and follies of men had ceased to disturb those crumbling walls.

"The sunlight is warm," called X-120. "Come out, G-3a and L-1716. I feel young again."

His companions lumbered into the sunlight. G-3a had lost one leg, and moved slowly and with difficulty. The steel of his body was nearly covered with red rust, and the copper and aluminum alloys that completed his make-up were pitted with deep stains of greenish black. L-1716 was not so badly tarnished, but he had lost one arm; and the four auxiliary cables were broken and dangled from his sides like trailing wires. Of the three X-120 was the best preserved. He still had the use of all his limbs, and here and there on his body shone the gleam of untarnished metal. His masters had made him well.

The crippled G-3a looked about him and whined like an old, old man. "It will surely rain," he shivered. "I cannot stand another rain.

"Nonsense," said L-1716, his broken arms, scraping along the ground as he moved, "there is not a cloud in the sky. Already I feel better."

G-3a looked about him in fear. "And are we all?" he questioned. "Last winter there were twelve."

X-120 had been thinking of the other nine, all that had been left of the countless horde that men had once fashioned. "The nine were to winter in the jade tower," he explained. "We will go there. Perhaps they do not think it is time to venture out."

"I cannot leave my work," grated G-3a. "There is so little time left. I have almost reached the goal." His whirring voice was raised to a pitch of triumph. "Soon I shall make living robots, even as men made us."

"The old story," sighed L-1716. "How long have we been working to make robots who will take our places? And what have we made? Usually nothing but lifeless blobs of steel. Sometimes we have fashioned mad things that had to be destroyed. But never in all the years have we made a single robot that resembled ourselves."

X-120 stood in the broken street, and the sunlight made a shimmering over his rust-dappled sides.

"That is where we have failed," he mused as he looked at his clawlike arms. "We have tried to make robots like ourselves. Men did not make us for life; they fashioned us for death." He waved his huge lobster claw in the air. "What was this made for? Was it made for the shaping of other robots? Was it made to fashion anything? Blades like that were made for slaughter—nothing else."

"Even so," whined the crippled robot, "I have nearly succeeded. With help I can win."

"And have we ever refused to help?" snapped L-1716. "You are getting old, G-3a. All winter you have worked in that little dark room, never allowing us to enter."

There was a metallic cackle in G-3a's voice. "But I have nearly won. They said I wouldn't, but I have nearly won. I need help. One more operation. If it succeeds, the robots may yet rebuild the world."

Reluctantly X-120 followed the two back into the shadowy

ruins. It was dark in there; but their round, glassy eyes had been made for both day and night.

"See," squeaked old G-3a, as he pointed to a metal skeleton upon the floor. "I have remade a robot from parts that I took from the scrap heap. It is perfect, all but the brain. Still, I believe this will work." He motioned to a gleaming object upon a littered table. It was a huge copper sphere with two black squares of a tarlike substance set into it. At the pole opposite from these squares was a protuberance no larger than a man's fist.

"This," said G-3a thoughtfully, "is the only perfect brain that I could find. You see, I am not trying to create something; I am merely rebuilding. Those"—he nodded to the black squares—"are the sensory organs. The visions from the eyes are flashed upon these as though they were screens. Beyond those eyes is the response mechanism, thousands and thousands of photo-electric cells. Men made it so that it would react mechanically to certain images. Movement, the simple avoidance of objects, the urge to kill, these are directed by the copper sphere.

"Beyond this"—he gestured to the bulge at the back of the brain—"is the thought mechanism. It is what made us different from other machines."

"It is very small," mocked X-120.

"So it is," replied G-3a. "I have heard that it was the reverse with the brains of men. But enough! See, this must fit into the body—so. The black squares rest behind the eyes. That wire brings energy to the brain, and those coils are connected to the power unit which operates the arms and legs. That wire goes to the balancing mechanism—" He droned on and on, explaining each part carefully. "And now," he finished, "someone must connect it. I cannot."

L-1716 stared at his one rusty claw with confusion. Then both he and G-3a were looking at X-120.

"I can only try," offered the robot. "But remember what I said. We were not fashioned to make anything; only to kill."

Clumsily he lifted the copper sphere and its cluster of wires from the table. He worked slowly and carefully. One by one the huge claws crimped the tiny wires together. The job was nearly finished. Then the great pincers, hovering so carefully above the last wire, came into contact with another. There was a flash as the power short-circuited. X-120 reeled back. The copper sphere melted and ran before their eyes.

X-120 huddled against the far wall. "It is as I said," he moaned; "we can build nothing. We were not made to work at anything. We were only made for one purpose, to kill." He looked at his bulky claws, and shook them as though he might cast them away.

"Do not take on so," pacified old G-3a. "Perhaps it is just as well. We are things of steel, and the world seems to be made for creatures of flesh and blood—little, puny things that even I can crush. Still, that thing there"—he pointed to the metal skeleton which now held the molten copper like a crucible—"was my last hope. I have nothing else to offer."

"Both of you have tried," agreed L-1716. "No one could blame either of you. Sometimes of nights when I look into the stars, it seems that I see our doom written there; and I can hear the worlds laughing at us. We have conquered the earth, but what of it? We are going now, following the men who fashioned us."

"Perhaps it is better," nodded X-120. "I think it is the fault of our brains. You said that men made us to react mechanically to certain stimuli. And though they gave us a thought mechanism, it has no control over our reactions. I never wanted to kill. Yet, I have killed many men-things. And sometimes, even as I killed, I would be thinking of other things. I would not even know what had happened until after the deed was done."

G-3a had not been listening. Instead, he had been looking dolefully at the metal ruin upon the floor. "There was one in the jade tower," he said abruptly, "who thought he had nearly learned how to make a brain. He was to work all winter on it. Perhaps he has succeeded."

"We will go there," shrilled L-1716 laconically.

But even as they left the time-worn hall G-3a looked back ruefully at the smoking wreckage upon the floor.

X-120 slowed his steps to match the feeble gait of G-3a. Within sight of the tower he saw that they need go no farther. At some time during the winter the old walls had buckled. The nine were buried beneath tons and tons of masonry.

Slowly the three came back to their broken hall. "I will not stay out any longer," grumbled G-3a. "I am very old. I am very tired." He crept back into the shadows.

L-1716 stood looking after him. "I am afraid that he is nearly done," he spoke sorrowfully. "The rust must be within him now. He saved me once, long ago, when we destroyed this city."

"Do you still think of that?" asked X-120. "Sometimes it troubles me. Men were our masters."

"And they made us as we are," growled L-1716. "It was not our doing. We have talked of it before, you know. We were machines, made to kill—"

"But we were made to kill the little men in the yellow uniforms."

"Yes, I know. They made us on a psychological principle: stimulus, response. We had only to see a man in a yellow uniform and our next act was to kill. Then, after the Great War was over, or even before it was over, the stimulus and response had overpowered us all. It was only a short step from killing men in yellow uniforms to killing all men."

"I know," said X-120 wearily. "When there were more of us I heard it explained often. But sometimes it troubles me."

"It is all done now. Ages ago it was done. You are different, X-120. I have felt for long that there is something different about you. You were one of the last that they made. Still, you were here when we took this city. You fought well, killing many."

X-120 sighed. "There were small men-things then. They seemed so soft and harmless. Did we do right?"

"Nonsense. We could not help it. We were made so. Men learned to make more than they could control. Why, if I saw a man today, crippled as I am, I would kill him without thinking."

"L-1716," whispered X-120, "do you think there are any men left in the world?"

"I don't think so. Remember, the Great War was general, not local. We were carried to all parts of the earth, even to the smallest islands. The robots' rebellion came everywhere at almost the same time. There were some of us who were equipped with radios. Those died first, long ago, but they talked with nearly every part of the world." Suddenly he wearied of speech. "But why worry now. It is spring. Men made us for killing men. That was their crime. Can we help it if they made us too well?"

"Yes," agreed X-120, "it is spring. We will forget. Let us go toward the river. It was always peaceful and beautiful there."

L-1716 was puzzled. "What peace and beauty?" he asked.

"They are but words that men taught us. I have never known them. But perhaps you have. You were always different."

"I do not know what peace and beauty are, but when I think of them I am reminded of the river and of—" X-120 stopped suddenly, careful that he might not give away a secret he had kept so long.

"Very well," agreed L-1716, "we will go to the river. I know a meadow there where the sun always seemed warmer."

The two machines, each over twelve feet high, lumbered down the almost obliterated street. As they pushed their way over the débris and undergrowth that had settled about the ruins, they came upon many rusted skeletons of things that had once been like themselves. And toward the outskirts of the city they crossed over an immense scrap heap where thousands of the shattered and rusted bodies lay.

"We used to bring them here after—" said L-1716. "But the last centuries we have left them where they have fallen. I have been envying those who wintered in the jade tower." His metallic voice hinted of sadness.

They came at last to an open space in the trees. Farther they went and stood at the edge of a bluff overlooking a gorge and a swirling river below. Several bridges had once been there but only traces remained.

"I think I will go down to the river's edge," offered X-120.

"Go ahead. I will stay here. The way is too steep for me."

So X-120 clambered down a half-obliterated roadway alone. He stood at last by the rushing waters. Here, he thought, was something that changed the least. Here was the only hint of permanence in all the world. But even it changed. Soon the melting snow would be gone and the waters would dwindle to a mere trickle. He turned about and looked at the steep side of the gorge. Except for the single place where the old roadbed crept down, the sides rose sheer, their crests framed against the blue sky. These cliffs, too, were lasting.

Even in spring the cliffs and river seemed lonely and desolate. Men had not bothered to teach X-120 much of religion or philosophy. Yet somewhere in the combination of cells in his brain was a thought which kept telling him that he and his kind were suffering for their sins and for the sins of men before them.

And perhaps the thought was true. Certainly, men had

never conquered their age-old stupidity, though science had bowed before them. Countless wars had taken more from men than science had given them. X-120 and his kind were the culmination of this primal killer instinct.

In the haste of a war-pressed emergency man had not taken the time to refine his last creation, or to calculate its result. And with that misstep man had played his last card on the worn gaming table of earth. That built-in urge to kill men in yellow uniforms had changed, ever so slightly, to an urge to kill—men.

Now there were only X-120, his two crippled comrades, the heaps of rusted steel, and the leaning, crumbling towers.

He followed the river for several miles until the steep sides lessened. Then he clambered out, and wandered through groves of gnarled trees. He did not wish to go back to L-1716, not just yet. The maimed robot was always sad. The rust was eating into him, too. Soon he would be like G-3a. Soon the two of them would be gone. Then he would be the last. An icy surge of fear stole over him. He did not want to be left alone.

He lumbered onward. A few birds were stirring. Suddenly, almost at his feet, a rabbit darted from the bushes. X-120's long jointed arms swung swiftly. The tiny animal lay crushed upon the ground. Instinctively he stamped upon it, leaving only a bloody trace upon the new grass.

Then remorse and shame stole over him. He went on silently. Somehow the luster of the day had faded for him. He did not want to kill. Always he was ashamed, after the deed was done. And the age-old question went once more through the steel meshes of his mind: Why had he been made to kill?

He went on and on, and out of long habit he went furtively. Soon he came to an ivy-covered wall. Beyond this were the ruins of a great stone house. He stopped at what had once been a garden. Near a broken fountain he found what he had been seeking, a little marble statue of a child, weathered and discolored. Here, unknown to his companions, he had been coming for years upon countless years. There was something about this little sculpturing that had fascinated him. And he had been half ashamed of his fascination.

He could not have explained his feelings, but there was something about the statue that made him think of all the things that men had possessed. It reminded him of all the qualities that were so far beyond his kind. He stood looking at the statue for long. It possessed an ethereal quality that still defied time. It made him think of the river and of the overhanging cliffs. Some long-dead artist almost came to life before his quartz eyes.

He retreated to a nearby brook and came back with a huge ball of clay. This in spite of the century-old admonitions that all robots should avoid the damp. For many years he had been trying to duplicate the little statue. Now, once more, he set about his appointed task. But his shearlike claws had been made for only one thing, death. He worked clumsily. Toward sundown he abandoned the shapeless mass that he had fashioned and returned to the ruins.

Near the shattered hall he met L-1716. At the entrance they called to G-3a, telling him of the day's adventures. But no answer came. Together they went in. G-3a was sprawled upon the floor. The rust had conquered.

The elusive spring had changed into even a more furtive summer. The two robots were coming back to their hall on an afternoon which had been beautiful and quiet. L-1716 moved more slowly now. His broken cables trailed behind him, making a rustling sound in the dried leaves that had fallen.

Two of the cables had become entangled. Unnoticed, they caught in the branches of a fallen tree. Suddenly L-1716 was whirled about. He sagged to his knees. X-120 removed the cables from the tree. But L-1716 did not get up. "A wrench," he said brokenly; "something is wrong."

A thin tendril of smoke curled up from his side. Slowly he crumpled. From within him came a whirring sound that ended in a sharp snap. Tiny flames burst through his metal sides. L-1716 fell forward.

And X-120 stood over him and begged, "Please, old friend, don't leave me now." It was the first time that the onlooking hills had seen any emotion in centuries.

A few flakes of snow were falling through the air. The sky looked gray and low. A pair of crows were going home, their raucous cries troubling an otherwise dead world.

X-120 moved slowly. All that day he had felt strange. He found himself straying from the trail. He could only move now by going in a series of arcs. Something was wrong within him. He should be back in the hall, he knew, and not out in this dangerous moisture. But he was troubled, and all day he had wandered, while the snowflakes had fallen intermittently about him.

On he went through the gray, chill day. On and on until he came to crumbling wall, covered with withered ivy. Over this he went into a ruined garden, and paused at a broken fountain, before an old and blackened statue.

Long he stood, looking down at the carving of a little child, a statue that men had made so long before. Then his metal arm swung through the air. The marble shivered into a hundred fragments.

Slowly he turned about and retraced his steps. The cold sun was sinking, leaving a faint amethyst stain in the west. He must get back to the hall. Mustn't stay out in the wet, he thought.

But something was wrong. He caught himself straying from the path, floundering in circles. The light was paling, although his eyes had been fashioned for both day and night.

Where was he? He realized with a start that he was lying on the ground. He must get back to the hall. He struggled, but no movement came. Then, slowly, the light faded and flickered out.

And the snow fell, slowly and silently, until only a white mound showed where X-120 had been.

# THE FOUR-SIDED TRIANGLE
*Amazing Stories*, November

# by William F. Temple (1914–     )

*William F. Temple was a former roommate of Arthur C. Clarke as well as former editor of the Journal of the British Interplanetary Society. In addition to this story, he is best known for his novel SHOOT AT THE MOON (1966) and the novelette "The Two Shadows"* (Startling Stories, 1951).*

*"The Four-Sided Triangle" is about love and the duplication (not cloning) of life. The story was later expanded into an interesting novel (1949) and an underrated film (1953).*

*(In the Thirties, science fiction, to the American magazine-reading public at least, was a completely American phenomenon. We knew vaguely that the greatest science fiction writers, Jules Verne, H. G. Wells were not American, but that didn't count. When we held the first Science Fiction Convention, attended by Americans only, there was no hesitation in giving it the adjective "World." And yet even in those days there were important British writers: Eric Frank Russell, for instance. William F. Temple was another.)*

Three people peered through a quartz window.

The girl was squashed uncomfortably between the two men, but at the moment neither she nor they cared. The object they were watching was too interesting.

The girl was Joan Leeton. Her hair was an indeterminate brown, and owed its curls to tongs, not to nature. Her eyes were certainly brown, and bright with unquenchable good humour. In repose her face was undistinguished, though far from plain; when she smiled, it was beautiful.

Her greatest attraction (and it was part of her attraction that she did not realise it) lay in her character. She was soothingly sympathetic without becoming mushy, she was very level-headed (a rare thing in a woman) and completely unselfish. She refused to lose her temper over anything, or take offence, or enlarge upon the truth in her favour, and yet she was tolerant of such lapses in others. She possessed a brain that was unusually able in its dealing with science, and yet her tastes and pleasures were simple.

William Fredericks (called 'Will') had much in common with Joan, but his sympathy was a little more disinterested, his humour less spontaneous, and he had certain prejudices. His tastes were reserved for what he considered the more worthy things. But he was calm and good-tempered, and his steadiness of purpose was reassuring. He was black-haired, with an expression of quiet content.

William Josephs (called 'Bill') was different. He was completely unstable. Fiery of hair, he was alternately fiery and depressed of spirit. Impulsive, generous, highly emotional about art and music, he was given to periods of gaiety and moods of black melancholia. He reached, at his best, heights of mental brilliance far beyond the other two, but long bouts of lethargy prevented him from making the best of them.

Nevertheless, his sense of humour was keen, and he was often amused at his own absurdly over-sensitive character; but he could not change it.

Both these men were deeply in love with Joan, and both tried hard to conceal it. If Joan had any preference, she concealed it just as ably, although they were aware that she was fond of both of them.

The quartz window, through which the three were looking, was set in a tall metal container, and just a few feet away was another container, identical even to the thickness of the window-glass.

Overhead was a complex assemblage of apparatus: bulbous, silvered tubes, small electric motors that hummed in various unexpected places, makeshift screens of zinc, roughly soldered, coils upon coils of wire, and a network of slung cables that made the place look like a creeper-tangled tropical jungle. A large dynamo churned out a steady roar in the corner, and a pair of wide sparkgaps crackled continuously, filling the laboratory with a weird, jumping blue light as the day waned outside the windows and the dusk crept in.

An intruder in the laboratory might have looked through the window of the other container and seen, standing on a steel frame in a cubical chamber, an oil painting of 'Madame Croignette' by Boucher, delicately illuminated by concealed lights. He would not have known it, but the painting was standing in a vacuum.

If he had squeezed behind the trio at the other container and gazed through their window he would have seen an apparently identical sight: an oil painting of 'Madame Croignette' by Boucher, standing on a steel frame in a vacuum, delicately illuminated by concealed lights.

From which he would probably not gather much.

The catch was that the painting at which the three were gazing so intently was not quite the same as the one in the first container—not yet. There were minute differences in colour and proportion.

But gradually these differences were righting themselves, for the whole of the second canvas was being built up atom by atom, molecule by molecule, into an exactly identical twin of the one which had felt the brush of Francis Boucher.

The marvellously intricate apparatus, using an adaption of a newly-discovered magnetic principle, consumed only a moderate amount of power in arranging the lines of sympathetic fields of force which brought every proton into position and every electron into its respective balancing orbit. It was a machine which could divert the flow of great forces without the ability to tap their energy.

'Any minute now!' breathed Will.

Bill rubbed his breath off the glass impatiently.

'Don't do that!' he said, and promptly fogged the glass over again. Not ungently, he attempted to rub a clear patch with Joan's own pretty nose. She exploded into laughter, fogging the glass hopelessly, and in the temporary confusion of this they missed seeing the event they had been waiting days for—the completion of the duplicate painting to the ultimate atom.

The spark-gaps died with a final snap, a lamp sprang into being on the indicator panel, and the dynamo began to run whirringly down to a stop.

They cleaned out the window, and there stood 'Madame Croignette' looking rather blankly out at them with wide brown eyes that exactly matched the sepia from Boucher's palette, and both beauty spots and every hair of her powdered wig in place to a millionth of a millimetre.

Will turned a valve, and there was the hiss of air rushing into the chamber. He opened the window, and lifted the painting out gingerly, as if he half-expected it to crumble in his hands.

'Perfect—a beauty!' he murmured. He looked up at Joan with shining eyes. Bill caught that look, and unaccountably checked the impulsive whoop of joy he was on the point of letting loose. He coughed instead, and leaned over Joan's shoulder to inspect 'Madame Croignette' more closely.

'The gamble's come off,' went on Will. 'We've sunk every cent into this, but it won't be long before we have enough money to do anything we want to do—anything.'

'Anything—except to get Bill out of bed on Sunday mornings,' smiled Joan, and they laughed.

'No sensible millionaire would get out of bed any morning,' said Bill.

The steel and glass factory of Art Replicas, Limited, shone like a diamond up in the green hills of Surrey. In a financial sense, it had actually sprung from a diamond—the sale of a replica of the Koh-i-noor. That had been the one and only product of Precious Stones, Limited, an earlier company which was closed down by the government when they saw that it would destroy the world's diamond market.

A sister company, Radium Products, was going strong up in the north because its scientific necessity was recognised. But the heart of the three company directors lay in Art Replicas, and there they spent their time.

Famous works of art from all over the world passed through the factory's portals, and gave birth to innumerable replicas of themselves for distribution and sale at quite reasonable prices.

Families of only moderate means found it pleasing to have a Constable or Turner in the dining room and a Rodin statuette in the hall. And this widely-flung ownership of *objets d'art,* which were to all intents and purposes the genuine articles, strengthened interest in art enormously. When people had lived with these things for a little while, they began to perceive the beauty in them—for real beauty is not always obvious at a glance—and to become greedy for more knowledge of them and the men who originally conceived and shaped them.

So the three directors—Will, Bill, and Joan—put all their energy into satisfying the demands of the world for art, and conscious of their part in furthering civilisation, were deeply content.

For a time.

Then Bill, the impatient and easily-bored, broke out one day in the middle of a Directors' Meeting.

'Oh to hell with the Ming estimates!' he cried, sweeping a pile of orders from the table.

Joan and Will, recognising the symptoms, exchanged wry glances of amusement.

'Look here,' went on Bill, 'I don't know what you two think, but I'm fed up! We've become nothing but dull business people now. It isn't our sort of life. Repetition, repetition, repetition! I'm going crazy! We're *research* workers, not darned piece-workers. For heaven's sake, let's start out in some new line!'

This little storm relieved him, and almost immediately he smiled too.

'But, really, aren't we?' he appealed.

'Yes,' responded Joan and Will in duet.

'Well, what about it?'

Will coughed, and prepared himself.

'Joan and I were talking about that this morning, as a matter of fact,' he said. 'We were going to suggest that we sell the factory, and retire to our old laboratory and re-equip it.'

Bill picked up the ink-pot and emptied it solemnly over the Ming estimates. The ink made a shining lake in the centre of the antique and valuable table.

'At last we're sane again,' he said. 'Now you know the line of investigation I want to open up. I'm perfectly convinced that the reason for our failure to create a living duplicate of any living creature was because the quotiety we assumed for the $xy$ action—'

'Just a moment, Bill,' interrupted Will. 'Before we get on with that work, I—I mean, one of the reasons Joan and me wanted to retire was because—well—'

'What he's trying to say,' said Joan quietly, 'is that we plan to get married and settle down for a bit before we resume research work.'

Bill stared at them. He was aware that his cheeks were slowly reddening. He felt numb.

'Well!' he said. 'Well!' (He could think of nothing else. This was unbelievable! He must postpone consideration of it until he was alone, else his utter mortification would show.)

He put out his hand automatically, and they both clasped it.

'You know I wish you every possible happiness,' he said, rather huskily. His mind seemed empty. He tried to form some comment, but somehow he could not compose one sentence that made sense.

'I think we'll get on all right,' said Will, smiling at Joan. She smiled back at him, and unknowingly cut Bill to the heart.

With an effort, Bill pulled himself together and rang for wine to celebrate. He ordered some of the modern reconstruction of an exceedingly rare '94.

The night was moonless and cloudless, and the myriads of glittering pale blue points of the Milky Way sprawled across the sky as if someone had cast a handful of brilliants upon a black velvet cloth. But they twinkled steadily, for strong air currents were in motion in the upper atmosphere.

The Surrey lane was dark and silent. The only signs of life were the occasional distant glares of automobile headlights passing on the main highway nearly a mile away, and the red dot of a burning cigarette in a gap between the hedgerows.

The cigarette was Bill's. He sat there on a gate staring up at the array in the heavens and wondering what to do with his life.

He felt completely at sea, purposeless, and unutterably depressed. He had thought the word 'heartache' just a vague descriptive term. Now he knew what it meant. It was a solid physical feeling, an ache that tore him inside, unceasingly. He yearned to see Joan, to be with Joan, with his whole being. This longing would not let him rest. He could have cried out for a respite.

He tried to argue himself to a more rational viewpoint.

'I am a man of science,' he told himself. 'Why should I allow old Mother Nature to torture and badger me like this? I can see through all the tricks of that old twister. These feelings are purely chemical reactions, the secretions of the glands mixing with the blood-stream. My mind is surely strong enough to conquer that? Else I have a third-rate brain, not the scientific instrument I've prided myself on.'

He stared up at the stars glittering in their seeming calm

stability, age-old and unchanging. But were they? They may look just the same when all mankind and its loves and hates had departed from this planet, and left it frozen and dark. But he knew that even as he watched, they were changing position at a frightful speed, receding from him at thousands of miles a second.

'Nature is a twister, full of illusions,' he repeated. . . .

There started a train of thought, a merciful anaesthetic in which he lost himself for some minutes.

Somewhere down in the deeps of his subconscious an idea which had, unknown to him, been evolving itself for weeks, was stirred, and emerged suddenly into the light. He started, dropped his cigarette, and left it on the ground.

He sat there stiffly on the gate and considered the idea.

It was wild—incredibly wild. But if he worked hard and long at it, there was a chance that it might come off. It would provide a reason for living, anyway, so long as there was any hope at all of success.

He jumped down from the gate and started walking quickly and excitedly along the lane back to the factory. His mind was already turning over possibilities, planning eagerly. In the promise of this new adventure, the heart-ache was temporarily submerged.

Six months passed.

Bill had retired to the old laboratory, and spent much of that time enlarging and re-equipping it. He added a rabbit pen, and turned an adjacent patch of ground into a burial-ground to dispose of those who died under his knife. This cemetery was like no cemetery in the world, for it was also full of dead things that had never died—because they had never lived.

His research got nowhere. He could build up, atom by atom, the exact physical counterpart of any living animal, but all such duplicates remained obstinately inanimate. They assumed an extraordinary life-like appearance, but it was frozen life. They were no more alive than waxwork images, even though they were as soft and pliable as the original animals in sleep.

Bill thought he had hit upon the trouble in a certain equation, but re-checking confirmed that the equation had been right in the first place. There was no flaw in either theory or practice as far as he could see.

Yet somehow he could not duplicate the force of life in action. Must he apply that force himself? How?

He applied various degrees of electrical impulses to the nerve centers of the rabbits, tried rapid alternations of temperatures, miniature 'iron lungs', vigorous massage—both external and internal—intra-venous and spinal injections of everything from adrenalin to even more powerful stimulants which his agile mind concocted. And still the artificial rabbits remained limp bundles of fur.

Joan and Will returned from their honeymoon and settled down in a roomy, comfortable old house a few miles away. They sometimes dropped in to see how the research was going. Bill always seemed bright and cheerful enough when they came, and joked about his setbacks.

'I think I'll scour the world for the hottest thing in female bunnies and teach her to do a hula-hula on the lab. bench,' he said. 'That ought to make some of these stiffs sit up!'

Joan said she was seriously thinking of starting an eating-house specialising in rabbit pie, if Bill could keep up the supply of dead rabbits. He replied that he'd already buried enough to feed an army.

Their conversation was generally pitched in this bantering key, save when they really got down to technicalities. But when they had gone, Bill would sit and brood, thinking constantly of Joan. And he could concentrate on nothing else for the rest of that day.

Finally, more or less by accident, he found the press-button which awoke life in the rabbits. He was experimenting with a blood solution he had prepared, thinking that it might remain more constant than the natural rabbit's blood, which became thin and useless too quickly. He had constructed a little pump to force the natural blood from a rabbit's veins and fill them instead with his artificial solution.

The pump had not been going for more than a few seconds before the rabbit stirred weakly and opened its eyes. It twitched its nose, and lay quite still for a moment, save for one foot which continued to quiver.

Then suddenly it roused up and made a prodigious bound from the bench. The thin rubber tubes which tethered it by the neck parted in midair, and it fell awkwardly with a heavy thump on the floor. The blood continued to run from one of the broken tubes, but the pump which forced it out was the rabbit's own heart—beating at last.

The animal seemed to have used all its energy in that one powerful jump, and lay still on the floor and quietly expired.

Bill stood regarding it, his fingers still on the wheel of the pump.

Then, when he realised what it meant, he recaptured some of his old exuberance, and danced around the laboratory carrying a carboy of acid as though it were a Grecian urn.

Further experiments convinced him that he had set foot within the portals of Nature's most carefully guarded citadel. Admittedly he could not himself create anything original or unique in Life. But he could create a living image of any living creature under the sun.

A hot summer afternoon, a cool green lawn shaded by elms and on it two white-clad figures, Joan and Will, putting through their miniature nine-hole course. A bright-striped awning by the hedge, and below it, two comfortable canvas chairs and a little Moorish table with soft drinks. An ivy-covered wall of an old red-brick mansion showing between the trees. The indefinable smell of new-cut grass in the air. The gentle but triumphant laughter of Joan as Will foozled his shot.

That was the atmosphere Bill entered at the end of his duty tramp along the lane from the laboratory—it was his first outdoor excursion for weeks—and he could not help comparing it with the sort of world he had been living in: the benches and bottles and sinks, the eye-tiring field of the microscope, the sheets of calculations under the glare of electric light in the dark hours of the night, the smell of blood and chemicals and rabbits.

And he realised completely that science wasn't the greatest thing in life. Personal happiness was. That was the goal of all men, whatever way they strove to reach it.

Joan caught sight of him standing on the edge of the lawn, and came hurrying across to greet him.

'Where have you been all this time?' she asked. 'We've been dying to hear how you've been getting on.'

'I've done it,' said Bill.

'Done it? Have you really?' Her voice mounted excitedly almost to a squeak. She grabbed him by the wrist and hauled him across to Will. 'He's done it!' she announced, and stood between them, watching both their faces eagerly.

Will took the news with his usual calmness, and smilingly gripped Bill's hand.

'Congratulations, old lad,' he said. 'Come and have a drink and tell us all about it.'

They squatted on the grass and helped themselves from the table. Will could see that Bill had been overworking himself badly. His face was drawn and tired, his eyelids red, and he was in the grip of a nervous tension which for the time held him dumb and uncertain of himself.

Joan noticed this, too, and checked the questions she was going to bombard upon him. Instead, she quietly withdrew to the house to prepare a pot of the China tea which she knew always soothed Bill's migraine.

When she had gone, Bill, with an effort, shook some of the stupor from him, and looked across at Will. His gaze dropped, and he began to pluck idly at the grass.

'Will,' he began, presently, 'I'—He cleared his throat nervously, and started again in a none too steady voice. 'Listen, Will, I have something a bit difficult to say, and I'm not so good at expressing myself. In the first place, I have always been crazily in love with Joan.'

Will sat, and looked at him curiously. But he let Bill go on.

'I never said anything because—well, because I was afraid I wouldn't make a success of marriage. Too unstable to settle down quietly with a decent girl like Joan. But I found I couldn't go on without her, and was going to propose—when you beat me to it. I've felt pretty miserable since, though this work has taken something of the edge off.'

Will regarded the other's pale face—and wondered.

'This work held out a real hope to me. And now I've accomplished the major part of it. I can make a living copy of any living thing. Now—do you see *why* I threw myself into this research? *I want to create a living, breathing twin of Joan, and marry her!*'

Will started slightly. Bill got up and paced restlessly up and down.

'I know I'm asking a hell of a lot. This affair reaches deeper than a scientific curiosity. No feeling man can contemplate such a proposal without misgivings, for his wife and for himself. But honestly, Will, I cannot see any possible harm arising from it. Though, admittedly, the only good thing would be to make a selfish man happy. For heaven's sake, let me know what you think.'

Will sat contemplating, while the distracted Bill continued to pace.

Presently, he said, 'You are sure no physical harm could come to Joan in the course of the experiment?'

'Certain—completely certain,' said Bill.

'Then I personally have no objection. Anything but objection. I had no idea you felt that way, Bill, and it would make me, as well as Joan, very unhappy to know you had to go on like that.'

He caught sight of his wife approaching with a laden tray.

'Naturally, the decision rests with her,' he said. 'If she'd rather not, there's no more to it.'

'No, of course not,' agreed Bill.

But they both knew what her answer would be.

'Stop the car for a minute, Will,' said Joan suddenly, and her husband stepped on the foot-brake.

The car halted in the lane on the brow of the hill. Through a gap in the hedge the two occupants had a view of Bill's laboratory as it lay below in the cradle of the valley.

Joan pointed down. In the field behind the 'cemetery' two figures were strolling. Even at this distance, Bill's flaming hair marked his identity. His companion was a woman in a white summer frock. And it was on her that Joan's attention was fixed.

'She's alive now!' she whispered, and her voice trembled slightly.

Will nodded. He noticed her apprehension, and gripped her hand encouragingly. She managed a wry smile.

'It's not every day one goes to pay a visit to oneself,' she said. 'It was unnerving enough last week to see her lying on the other couch in the lab., dressed in my red frock—which *I* was wearing—so pale, and—Oh, it was like seeing myself dead!'

'She's not dead now, and Bill's bought her some different clothes, so cheer up,' said Will. 'I know it's a most queer situation, but the only possible way to look at it is from the scientific viewpoint. It's a unique scientific event. And it's made Bill happy into the bargain.'

He ruminated a minute.

'Wish he'd given us a hint as to how he works his resuscitation process, though,' he went on. 'Still, I suppose he's right to keep it a secret. It's a discovery which could be appallingly abused. Think of dictators manufacturing loyal, stupid armies from one loyal, stupid soldier! Or industrialists manufacturing cheap labour! We should soon have a world of robots, all traces of individuality wiped out. No variety, nothing unique—life would not be worth living.'

'No,' replied Joan, mechanically, her thoughts still on that white-clad figure down there.

Will released the brake, and the car rolled down the hill toward the laboratory. The two in the field saw it coming, and walked back through the cemetery to meet it. They reached the road as the car drew up.

'Hello, there!' greeted Bill. 'You're late—we've had the kettle on the boil for half an hour. Doll and I were getting anxious.'

He advanced into the road, and the woman in the white frock lingered hesitantly behind him. Joan tightened her lips and braced herself to face this unusual ordeal. She got out of the car, and while Will and Bill were grasping hands, she walked to meet her now living twin.

Apparently Doll had decided to face it in the same way, and they met with oddly identical expressions of smiling surface ease, with an undercurrent of curiosity and doubt. They both saw and understood each other's expression simultaneously, and burst out laughing. That helped a lot.

'It's not so bad, after all,' said Doll, and Joan checked herself from making the same instinctive remark.

'No, not nearly,' she agreed.

And it wasn't. For although Doll looked familiar to her, she could not seem to identify her with herself to any unusual extent. It was not that her apparel and hair-style were different, but that somehow her face, figure and voice seemed like those of another person.

She did not realise that hitherto she had only seen parts of herself in certain mirrors from certain angles, and the complete effect was something she had simply never witnessed. Nor that she had not heard her own voice outside her own head, so to speak—never from a distance of some feet.

Nevertheless, throughout the meal she felt vaguely uneasy, though she tried to hide it, and kept up a fire of witty remarks. And her other self, too, smiled at her across the table and talked easily.

They compared themselves in detail, and found they were completely identical in every way, even to the tiny mole on their left forearm. Their tastes, too, agreed. They took the same amount of sugar in their tea, and liked and disliked the same foodstuffs.

'I've got my eye on that pink iced cake,' laughed Doll. 'Have you?'

Joan admitted it. So they shared it.

'You'll never have any trouble over buying each other birthday or Christmas presents,' commented Will. 'How nice to know exactly what the other wants!'

Bill had a permanent grin on his face, and beamed all over the table all the time. For once he did not have a great deal to say. He seemed too happy for words, and kept losing the thread of the conversation to gaze upon Doll fondly.

'We're going to be married tomorrow!' he announced unexpectedly, and they protested their surprise at the lack of warning. But they promised to be there.

There followed an evening of various sorts of games, and the similar thought-processes of Joan and Doll led to much amusement, expecially in the guessing games. And twice they played checkers and twice they drew.

It was a merry evening, and Bill was merriest of all. Yet when they came to say goodnight, Joan felt the return of the old uneasiness. As they left in the car, Joan caught a glimpse of Doll's face as she stood beside Bill at the gate. And she divined that under that air of gaiety, Doll suffered the same uneasiness as she.

Doll and Bill were married in a distant registry office next day, using a fictitious name and birthplace for Doll to avoid any publicity—after all, no one would question her identity.

Winter came and went.

Doll and Bill seemed to have settled down quite happily, and the quartet remained as close friends as ever. Both Doll and Joan were smitten with the urge to take up flying as a hobby, and joined the local flying club. They each bought a single-seater, and went for long flights, cruising side by side.

Almost in self-protection from this neglect (they had no interest in flying) Bill and Will began to work again together, delving further into the mysteries of the atom. This time they were searching for the yet-to-be-discovered secret of tapping the potential energy which the atom held.

And almost at once they stumbled onto a new lead.

Formerly they had been able to divert atomic energy without being able to transform it into useful power. It was as if they had constructed a number of artificial dams at various points in a turbulent river, which altered the course of the river without tapping any of its force—though that is a poor and misleading analogy.

But now they had conceived, and were building, an amazingly complex machine which, in the same unsatisfactory analogy, could be likened to a turbine-generator, tapping some of the power of that turbulent river.

The 'river' however, was very turbulent indeed, and needed skill and courage to harness. And there was a danger of the harness suddenly slipping.

Presently, the others became aware that Doll's health was gradually failing. She tried hard to keep up her usual air of brightness and cheerfulness, but she could not sleep, and became restless and nervous.

And Joan, who was her almost constant companion, suddenly realised what was worrying that mind which was so similar to hers. The realisation was a genuine shock, which left her trembling, but she faced it.

'I think it would be a good thing for Doll and Bill to come and live here for a while, until Doll's better,' she said rather diffidently to Will one day.

'Yes, okay, if you think you can persuade them,' replied Will. He looked a little puzzled.

'We have far too many empty rooms here,' she said defensively. 'Anyway, I can help Doll if I'm with her more.'

Doll seemed quite eager to come, though a little dubious, but Bill thought it a great idea. They moved within the week.

At first, things did improve. Doll began to recover, and became more like her natural self. She was much less highly strung, and joined in the evening games with the other three with gusto. She studied Will's favourite game, backgammon, and began to enjoy beating him thoroughly and regularly.

And then Joan began to fail.

She became nerveless, melancholy, and even morose. It seemed as though through helping Doll back to health, she had been infected with the same complaint.

Will was worried, and insisted on her being examined by a doctor.

The doctor told Will in private: 'There's nothing physically wrong. She's nursing some secret worry, and she'll get worse until this worry is eased. Persuade her to tell you what it is—she refuses to tell me.'

She also refused to tell Will, despite his pleadings.

And now Doll, who knew what the secret was, began to

worry about Joan, and presently she relapsed into her previous nervous condition.

So it continued for a week, a miserable week for the two harassed and perplexed husbands, who did not know which way to turn. The following week, however, both women seemed to make an effort, and brightened up somewhat, and could even laugh at times.

The recovery continued, and Bill and Will deemed it safe to return to their daily work in the lab., completing the atom-harnessing machine.

One day Will happened to return to the house unexpectedly, and found the two women in each other's arms on a couch, crying their eyes out. He stood staring for a moment. They suddenly became aware of him, and parted, drying their eyes.

'What's up, Will? Why have you come back?' asked Joan, unsteadily, sniffing.

'Er—to get my slide-rule: I'd forgotten it,' he said. 'Bill wanted to trust his memory, but I think there's something wrong with his figures. I want to check up before we test the machine further. But—what's the matter with you two?'

'Oh, we're all right,' said Doll, strainedly and not very convincingly. She blew her nose, and endeavoured to pull herself together. But almost immediately she was overtaken by another burst of weeping, and Joan put her arms around her comfortingly.

'Look here,' said Will, in sudden and unusual exasperation, 'I've had about enough of this. You know what Bill and I are only too willing to deal with whatever you're worrying about. Yet the pair of you won't say a word—only cry and fret. How can we help if you won't tell us? Do you think we like to see you going on like this?'

'I'll tell you, Will,' said Joan quietly.

Doll emitted a muffled 'No!' but Joan ignored her, and went on: 'Don't you see that Bill has created another me in *every* detail? Every memory and every feeling? And because Doll thinks and feels exactly as I do, she's in love with you! She has been that way from the very beginning. All this time she's been trying to conquer it, to suppress it, and make Bill happy instead.'

Doll's shoulders shook with the intensity of her sobbing. Will laid his hands gently on them, consolingly. He could think of nothing whatever to say. He had not even dreamt of such a situation, obvious as it appeared now.

'Do you wonder the conflict got her down?' said Joan. 'Poor girl! I brought her here to be nearer to you, and that eased things for her.'

'But it didn't for you,' said Will, quietly, looking straight at her. 'I see now why you began to worry. Why didn't you tell me then, Joan?'

'How could I?'

He bit his lip, paced nervously over to the window, and stood with his back to the pair on the couch.

'What a position!' he thought. 'What can we do? Poor Bill!'

He wondered how he could break the sorry news to his best friend, and even as he wondered, the problem was solved for him.

From the window there was a view down the length of the wide, shallow valley, and a couple miles away the white concrete laboratory could just be seen nestling at the foot of one of the farther slopes. There were fields all around it, and a long row of great sturdy oak trees started from its northern corner.

From this height and distance the whole place looked like a table-top model. Will stared moodily at that little white box where Bill was, and tried to clarify his chaotic thoughts.

And suddenly, incredibly, before his eyes the distant white box spurted up in a dusty cloud of chalk-powder, and ere a particle of it had neared its topmost height, the whole of that part of the valley was split across by a curtain of searing, glaring flame. The whole string of oak trees, tough and amazingly deep-rooted though they were, floated up through the air like feathers of windblown thistledown before the blast of that mighty eruption.

The glaring flame vanished suddenly, like a light that had been turned out, and left a thick, brown, heaving fog in its place, a cloud of earth that had been pulverised. Will caught a glimpse of the torn oak trees falling back into this brown, rolling cloud, and then the blast wave, which had travelled up the valley, smote the house.

The window was instantly shattered and blown in, and he went flying backwards in a shower of glass fragments. He hit the floor awkwardly, and sprawled there, and only then did his laggard brain realise what had happened.

Bill's habitual impatience had at last been his undoing. He had refused to wait any longer for Will's return, and gone on with the test, trusting to his memory. And he had been wrong.

The harness had slipped.

A man sat on a hill with a wide and lovely view of the country, bright in summer sunshine, spread before him. The rich green squares of the fields, the white ribbons of the lanes, the yellow blocks of haystacks and grey spires of village churches, made up a pattern infinitely pleasing to the eye.

And the bees hummed drowsily, nearby sheep and cattle made the noises of their kind, and a neighbouring thicket fairly rang with the unending chorus of a hundred birds.

But all this might as well have been set on another planet, for the man could neither see nor hear the happy environment. He was in hell.

It was a fortnight now since Bill had gone. When that grief had begun to wear off, it was succeeded by the most perplexing problem that had ever beset a member of the human race.

Will had been left to live with two women who loved him equally violently. Neither could ever conquer or suppress that love, whatever they did. They knew that.

On the other hand, Will was a person who was only capable of loving one of the women. Monogamy is deep-rooted in most normal people, and particularly so with Will. He had looked forward to travelling through life with one constant companion, and only one—Joan.

But now there were two Joans, identical in appearance, feeling, thought. Nevertheless, they were two separate people. And between them he was a torn and anguished man, with his domestic life in shapeless ruins.

He could not ease his mental torture with work, for since Bill died so tragically, he could not settle down to anything in a laboratory.

It was no easier for Joan and Doll. Probably harder. To have one's own self as a rival—even a friendly, understanding rival—for a man's companionship and affection was almost unbearable.

This afternoon they had both gone to a flying club, to attempt to escape for a while the burden of worry, apparently. Though neither was in a fit condition to fly, for they were tottering on the brink of a nervous breakdown.

The club was near the hill where Will was sitting and striving to find some working solution to a unique human problem which seemed quite unsoluble. So it was no coincidence that presently a humming in the sky caused him to lift dull eyes to see both the familiar monoplanes circling and curving across the blue spaces between the creamy, cumulus clouds.

He lay back on the grass watching them. He wondered which plane was which, but there was no means of telling, for they were similar models. And anyway, that would not tell him which was Joan and which was Doll, for they quite often used each other's planes, to keep the 'feel' of both. He wondered what they were thinking up there. . . .

One of the planes straightened and flew away to the west, climbing as it went. Its rising drone became fainter. The other plane continued to bank and curve above.

Presently, Will closed his eyes and tried to doze in the warm sunlight. It was no use. In the darkness of his mind revolved the same old maddening images, doubts, and questions. It was as if he had become entangled in a nightmare from which he could not awake.

The engine of the plane overhead suddenly stopped. He opened his eyes, but could not locate it for a moment.

Then he saw it against the sun, and it was falling swiftly in a tailspin. It fell out of the direct glare of the sun, and he saw it in detail, revolving as it plunged so that the wings glinted like a flashing heliograph. He realised with a shock that it was but a few hundred feet from the ground.

He scrambled to his feet, in an awful agitation.

'Joan!' he cried, hoarsely. 'Joan!'

The machine continued its fall steadily and inevitably, spun down past his eye-level, and fell into the centre of one of the green squares of the fields below.

He started running down the hill even as it landed. As the sound of the crash reached him, he saw a rose of fire blossom like magic in that green square, and from it a wavering growth of black, oily smoke mounted into the heavens. The tears started from his eyes, and ran freely.

When he reached the scene, the inferno was past its worst, and as the flames died he saw that nothing was left, only black, shapeless, scattered things, unrecognisable as once human or once machine.

There was a squeal of brakes from the road. An ambulance had arrived from the flying club. Two men jumped out, burst through the hedge. It did not take them more than a few seconds to realise that there was no hope.

'Quick, Mr. Fredericks, jump in,' cried one of them, recognising Will. 'We must go straight to the other one.'

*The other one!*

Before he could question them, Will was hustled between

them into the driving cabin of the ambulance. The vehicle was quickly reversed, and sped off in the opposite direction.

'Did—did the other plane—' began Will, and the words stuck in his throat.

The driver, with his eye on the road which was scudding under their wheels at sixty miles an hour, nodded grimly.

'Didn't you see, sir? They both crashed at exactly the same time, in the same way—tailspin. A shocking accident—terrible. I can't think how to express my sympathy, sir. I only pray that this one won't turn out so bad.'

It was as if the ability to feel had left Will. His thoughts slowed up almost to a standstill. He sat there numbed. He dare not try to think.

But, sluggishly, his thoughts went on. Joan and Doll had crashed at exactly the same time in exactly the same way. That was above coincidence. They must have both been thinking along the same lines again, and that meant they had crashed *deliberately!*

He saw now the whole irony of it, and groaned.

Joan and Doll had each tried to solve the problem in their own way, and each had reached the same conclusion without being aware what the other was thinking. They saw that one of them would have to step out of the picture if Will was ever to be happy. They knew that that one would have to step completely out, for life could no longer be tolerated by her if she had to lose Will.

And, characteristically, they had each made up their minds to be the self-sacrificing one.

Doll felt that she was an intruder, wrecking the lives of a happily married pair. It was no fault of hers: she had not asked to be created full of love for a man she could never have.

But she felt that she was leading an unnecessary existence, and every moment of it was hurting the man she loved. So she decided to relinquish the gift of life.

Joan's reasoning was that she had been partly responsible for bringing Doll into this world, unasked, and with exactly similar feelings and longings as herself. Ever since she had expected, those feelings had been ungratified, cruelly crushed and thwarted. It wasn't fair. Doll had as much right to happiness as she. Joan had enjoyed her period of happiness with Will. Now let Doll enjoy hers.

So it was that two planes, a mile apart, went spinning into crashes that were meant to appear accidental—and did, except to one man, the one who most of all was intended never to know the truth.

The driver was speaking again.

'It was a ghastly dilemma for us at the club. We saw 'em come down on opposite sides and both catch fire. We have only one fire engine, one ambulance. Had to send the engine to one, and rush this ambulance to the other. The engine couldn't have done any good at this end, as it happens. Hope it was in time where we're going!'

Will's dulled mind seemed to take this in quite detachedly. Who had been killed in the crash he saw? Joan or Doll? Joan or Doll?

Then suddenly it burst upon him that it was only the original Joan that he loved. That was the person whom he had known so long, around whom his affection had centred. The hair he had caressed, the lips he had pressed, the gay brown eyes which had smiled into his. He had never touched Doll in that way.

Doll seemed but a shadow of all that. She may have had memories of those happenings, but she had never actually experienced them. They were only artificial memories. Yet they must have seemed real enough to her.

The ambulance arrived at the scene of the second crash.

The plane had flattened out a few feet from the ground, and not landed so disastrously as the other. It lay crumpled athwart a burned and blackened hedge. The fire engine had quenched the flames within a few minutes. And the pilot had been dragged clear, unconscious, badly knocked about and burned.

They got her into the ambulance, and rushed her to a hospital.

Will had been sitting by the bedside for three hours before the girl in the bed had opened her eyes.

Blank, brown eyes they were, which looked at him, then at the hospital ward, without the faintest change of expression.

'Joan!' he whispered, clasping her free arm—the other was in a splint. There was no response of any sort. She lay back gazing unseeingly at the ceiling. He licked his dry lips. It couldn't be Joan after all.

'Doll!' he tried. 'Do you feel all right?'

Still no response.

'I know that expression,' said the doctor, who was standing by. 'She's lost her memory.'

'For good, do you think?' asked Will, perturbed.

The doctor pursed his lips indicating he didn't know.

'Good lord! Is there no way of finding out whether she is my wife or my sister-in-law?'

'If you don't know, no one does, Mr. Fredericks,' replied the doctor. 'We can't tell which plane who was in. We can't tell anything from her clothes, for they were burned in the crash, and destroyed before we realized their importance. We've often remarked their uncanny resemblance. Certainly you can tell them apart.'

'I can't!' answered Will, in anguish. 'There is no way.'

The next day, the patient had largely recovered her senses, and was able to sit up and talk. But a whole tract of her memory had been obliterated. She remembered nothing of her twin, and in fact nothing at all of the events after the duplication experiment.

Lying on the couch in the laboratory, preparing herself under the direction of Bill, was the last scene she remembered.

The hospital psychologist said that the shock of the crash had caused her to unconsciously repress a part of her life which she did not want to remember. She could not remember now if she wanted to. He said she might discover the truth from her eventually, but if he did, it would take months—maybe even years.

But naturally her memories of Will, and their marriage, were intact, and she loved him as strongly as ever.

Was she Joan or Doll?

Will spent a sleepless night, turning the matter over. Did it really matter? There was only one left now—why not assume she was Joan, and carry on? But he knew that as long as doubt and uncertainty existed, he would never be able to recover the old free life he had had with Joan.

It seemed that he would have to surrender her to the psychologist, and that would bring to light all sorts of details which neither he, Joan, nor Bill had ever wished to be revealed.

But the next day something turned up which changed the face of things.

While he was sitting at the bedside, conversing with the girl who might or might not be Joan, a nurse told him a man was waiting outside to see him. He went, and found a police officer standing there.

Ever since the catastrophe which had wrecked Bill's laboratory, the police had been looking around that locality, searching for any possible clues.

Buried in the ground they had found a safe, burst and broken. Inside were the charred remains of books, papers, and letters. They had examined them, without gleaning much, and now the officer wished to know if Will could gather anything from them.

Will took the bundle and went through it. There was a packet of purely personal letters, and some old tradesmen's accounts, paid and receipted. These with the officer's consent, were destroyed. But also there were the burnt remains of three of Bill's experimental notebooks.

They were written in Bill's system of shorthand, which Will understood. The first two were old, and of no particular interest. The last, however—unfortunately the most badly charred of the three—was an account of Bill's attempts to infuse life into his replicas of living creatures.

The last pages were about the experiment of creating another Joan, and the last recognisable entry read:

*'This clumsy business of pumping through pipes, in the manner of a blood transfusion, left a small scar at the base of Doll's neck, the only flaw in an otherwise perfect copy of Joan. I resented. . . .'*

The rest was burned away.

To the astonishment of the police inspector, Will turned without saying a word and hurried back into the ward.

'Let me examine your neck, dear, I want to see if you've been biting yourself,' he said, with a false lightness.

Wondering, the girl allowed herself to be examined.

There was not the slightest sign of a scar anywhere on her neck.

'You are Joan,' he said, and embraced her as satisfactorily as her injuries would permit.

'I am Joan,' she repeated, kissing and hugging him back.

And at last they knew again the blessedness of peace of mind.

For once, Fate, which had used them so hardly, showed mercy, and they never knew that in the packet of Bill's receipted accounts, which Will had destroyed, was one from a plastic surgeon, which began:

'To removing operation scar from neck, and two days' nursing and attention.'

# STAR BRIGHT

*Argosy*, November

# by Jack Williamson (1908–          )

*Jack Williamson has been witness to the development of modern science fiction as reader, writer, and scholar. He has produced a solid body of work spanning fifty years, and has had little trouble in keeping up with the competition. Still writing today, he will always be remembered for his "Legion of Space" and "Seetee" stories, although there is much more in his canon, most notably THE HU-MANOIDS (1949) and that wonderful fantasy, DARKER THAN YOU THINK (1940, in book form 1948). The best of his short fiction is available in THE BEST OF JACK WILLIAMSON, 1978.*

*Jack did not include this story in the latter collection, although he did select it for MY BEST SCIENCE FICTION STORY in 1949. He should have, because even though tastes change, this is a powerful story of hope, of desperation, and of a form of fulfillment.*

*(Once John Campbell took over* Astounding *and began to remold science fiction, many of the star writers of the previous decade fell by the way. There was the kind of slaughter we associate with the passing of the silents and the coming of the talkies. There were survivors, though, and one of the most remarkable of these was Jack Williamson whose* Legion of Space *had dazzled my teen-age years and who now went on to adapt himself, effortlessly, to Campbell's standards. IA)*

385

Mr. Jason Peabody got off the street car. Taking a great, relieved breath of the open air, he started walking up Bannister Hill. His worried eyes saw the first pale star come out of the dusk ahead.

It made him grope back wistfully into the mists of childhood, for the magic of words he once had known. He whispered the chant of power:

> *Star light, star bright,*
> *First star I've seen tonight,*
> *I wish I may, I wish I might,*
> *Have the wish I wish tonight.*

Mr. Peabody was a brown, bald little wisp of a man. Now defiantly erect, his thin shoulders still betrayed the stoop they had got from twenty years of bending over adding machines and ledgers. His usually meek face now had a hurt and desperate look.

"I wish—"

With his hopeful eyes on the star, Mr. Peabody hesitated. His harried mind went back to the painful domestic scene from which he had just escaped. A wry little smile came to his troubled face.

"I wish," he told the star, "that I could work miracles!"

The star faded to a pale malevolent red.

"You've got to work miracles," added Mr. Peabody, "to bring up a family on a bookkeeper's pay. A family, that is, like mine."

The star winked green with promise.

Mr. Peabody still owed thirteen thousand dollars on the little stucco house, two blocks off the Locust Avenue car line: the payments were as easy as rent, and in ten more years it would be his own. Ella met him at the door, this afternoon, with a moist kiss.

Ella was Mrs. Peabody. She was a statuesque blonde, an inch taller than himself, with a remarkable voice. Her clinging kiss made him uneasy. He knew instantly, from twenty-two years of experience, that it meant she wanted something.

"It's good to be home, dear." He tried to start a counter-campaign. "Things were tough at the office today." His tired sigh was real enough. "Old Berg has fired until we're all doing two men's work. I don't know who will be next."

"I'm sorry, darling." She kissed him moistly again, and her

voice was tenderly sympathetic. "Now get washed. I want to have dinner early, because tonight is Delphian League."

Her voice was too sweet. Mr. Peabody wondered what she wanted. It always took her a good while to work up to the point. When she arrived there, however, she was likely to be invincible. He made another feeble effort.

"I don't know what things are coming to." He made a weary shrug. "Berg is threatening to cut our pay. With the insurance, and the house payments, and the children, I don't see how we'd live."

Ella Peabody came back to him, and put her soft arm around him. She smelled faintly of the perfume she had used on the evening before, faintly of kitchen odors.

"We'll manage, dear," she said bravely.

She began to talk brightly of the small events of the day. Her duties in the kitchen caused no interruption. Her remarkable voice reached him clearly, even through the closed bathroom door.

With an exaggerated show of fatigue, Mr. Peabody settled himself into an easy chair. He found the morning paper—which he never had time to read in the morning—opened it, and then dropped it across his knees as if too tired to read. Feebly attempting another diversion, he asked:

"Where are the children?"

"William is out to see the man about his car."

Mr. Peabody forgot his fatigue.

"I told William he couldn't have a car," he said, with some heat. "I told him he's too young and irresponsible. If he insists on buying some pile of junk, he'll have to pay for it himself. Don't ask me how."

"And Beth," Mrs. Peabody's voice continued, "is down at the beauty shop." She came to the kitchen door. "But I have the most thrilling news for you, darling!"

The lilt in her voice told Mr. Peabody to expect the worst. The dreaded moment had come. Desperately he lifted the paper from his knees, became absorbed in it.

"Yes, dear," he said. "Here—I see the champ is going to take on this Australian palooka, if—"

"Darling, did you hear me?" Ella Peabody's penetrating voice could not be ignored. "At the Delphian League tonight, I'm going to read a paper on the Transcendental Renaissance. Isn't that a perfectly gorgeous opportunity?"

Mr. Peabody dropped the paper. He was puzzled. The

liquid sparkle in her voice was proof enough that her moment of victory was at hand. Yet her purpose was still unrevealed.

"Ella, dear," he inquired meekly, "what do you know about the Transcendental Renaissance?"

"Don't worry about that, darling. The young man at the library did the research and typed the paper for me, for only ten dollars. But it's so sweet of you to want to help me, and there's one thing that you can do."

Mr. Peabody squirmed uncomfortably in his chair. The trap was closing, and he could see no escape.

"I knew you'd understand, darling." Her voice had a little tender throb. "And you know I didn't have a decent rag to wear. Darling, I'm getting that blue jersey that was in the window of the Famous. It was marked sixty-nine eighty, but the manager let me have it for only forty-nine ninety-five."

"I'm awfully sorry, dear," Mr. Peabody said slowly. "But I'm afraid we simply can't manage it. I'm afraid you had better send it back."

Ella's blue eyes widened, and began to glitter.

"Darling!" Her throbbing voice broke. "Darling—you must understand. I can't read my paper in those disgraceful old rags. Besides, it has already been altered."

"But, dear—we just haven't got the money."

Mr. Peabody picked up his paper again, upside down. After twenty-two years, he knew what was to come. There would be tearful appeals to his love and his pride and his duty. There would be an agony of emotion, maintained until he surrendered.

And he couldn't surrender: that was the trouble. In twenty-two years, his affection had never swerved seriously from his wife and his children. He would have given her the money, gladly; but the bills had to be paid tomorrow.

He sighed with momentary relief when an unfamiliar motor horn honked outside the drive. William Peabody slouched, in ungraceful indolence, through the side door.

William was a lank, pimpled sallow-faced youth, with unkempt yellow hair and prominent buck teeth. Remarkably, in spite of the fact that he was continually demanding money for clothing, he always wore the same dingy leather jacket and the same baggy pants.

Efforts to send him to the university, to a television school, and to a barber college, had all collapsed for want of William's cooperation.

"Hi, Gov." He was filling a black college-man pipe. "Hi, Mom. Dinner up?"

"Don't call me Gov," requested Mr. Peabody, mildly. "William!" He had risen and walked to the window, and his voice was sharper. "Whose red roadster is that in the drive?"

William dropped himself into the easy chair which Mr. Peabody had just vacated.

"Oh, the car?" He exhaled blue smoke. "Why, didn't Mom tell you, Gov? I just picked it up."

Mr. Peabody's slight body stiffened.

"So you bought a car? Who's going to pay for it?"

William waved the pipe, carelessly.

"Only twenty a month," he drawled. "And it's a real buy, Gov. Only eighty thousand miles, and it's got a radio. Mom said you could manage it. It will be for my birthday, Gov."

"Your birthday is six months off."

Silver, soothing, Mrs. Peabody's voice floated from the kitchen:

"But you'll still be paying for it when his birthday comes, Jason. So I told Bill it would be all right. A boy is so left out these days, if he hasn't a car. Now, if you will just give me the suit money—"

Mr. Peabody began a sputtering reply. He stopped suddenly, when his daughter Beth came in the front door. Beth was the bright spot in his life. She was a tall slim girl, with soft sympathetic brown eyes. Her honey-colored hair was freshly set in exquisite waves.

Perhaps it was natural for father to favor daughter. But Mr. Peabody couldn't help contrasting her cheerful industry to William's idleness. She was taking a business course, so that she would be able to keep books for Dr. Rex Brant, after they were married.

"Hello, Dad." She came to him and put her smooth arms around him and gave him an affectionate little squeeze. "How do you like my new permanent? I got it because I have a date with Rex tonight. I didn't have enough money, so I said I would leave the other three dollars at Mrs. Larkin's before seven. Have you got three dollars, Dad?"

"Your hair looks pretty, dear."

Mr. Peabody patted his daughter's shoulder, and dug cheerfully into his pocket. He never minded giving money to Beth—when he had it. Often he regretted that he had not been able to do more for her.

"Thanks, Dad." Kissing his temple, she whispered, "You dear!"

Tapping out his black pipe, William looked at his mother.

"It just goes to show," he drawled. "If it was Sis that wanted a car—"

"I told you, son," Mr. Peabody declared positively, "I'm not going to pay for that automobile. We simply haven't the money."

William got languidly to his feet.

"I say, Gov. You wouldn't want to lose your fishing tackle."

Mr. Peabody's face stiffened with anxiety.

"My fishing tackle?"

In twenty-two years, Mr. Peabody had actually found the time and money to make no more than three fishing trips. He still considered himself, however, an ardent angler. Sometimes he had gone without his lunches, for weeks, to save for some rod or reel or special fly. He often spent an hour in the back yard, casting at a mark on the ground.

Trying to glare at William, he demanded hoarsely:

"What about my fishing tackle?"

"Now, Jason," interrupted the soothing voice of Mrs. Peabody, "don't get yourself all wrought up. You know you haven't used your old fishing tackle in the last ten years."

Stiffly erect, Mr. Peabody strode toward his taller son.

"William, what have you done with it?"

William was filling his pipe again.

"Keep your shirt on, Gov," he advised. "Mom said it would be all right. And I had to have the dough to make the first payment on the bus. Now don't bust an artery. I'll give you the pawn tickets."

"Bill!" Beth's voice was sharp with reproof. "You *didn't*—"

Mr. Peabody, himself, made a gasping incoherent sound. He started blindly toward the front door.

"Now, Jason!" Ella's voice was silver with a sweet and unendurable reason. "Control yourself, Jason. You haven't had your dinner—"

He slammed the door violently behind him.

This was not the first time in twenty-two years that Mr. Peabody had fled to the windy freedom of Bannister Hill. It was not even the first time he had spoken a wish to a star. While he had no serious faith in that superstition of his childhood, he still felt that it was a very pleasant idea.

An instant after the words were uttered, he saw the shooting star. A tiny point of light, drifting a little upward through the purple dusk. It was not white, like most falling stars, but palely green.

It recalled another old belief, akin to the first. If you saw a falling star, and if you could make a wish before the star went out, the wish would come true. Eagerly, he caught his breath.

"I wish," he repeated, "I could do miracles!"

He finished the words in time. The star was still shining. Suddenly, in fact, he noticed that its greenish radiance was growing brighter.

Far brighter! And exploding!

Abruptly, then, Mr. Peabody's vague and wistful satisfaction changed to stark panic. He realized that one fragment of the green meteor, like some celestial bullet, was coming straight at him! He made a frantic effort to duck, to shield his face with his hand—

Mr. Peabody woke, lying on his back on the grassy hill. He groaned and lifted his head. The waning moon had risen. Its slanting rays shimmered from the dew on the grass.

Mr. Peabody felt stiff and chilled. His clothing was wet with the dew. And something was wrong with his head. Deep at the base of his brain, there was a queer dull ache. It was not intense, but it had a slow, unpleasant pulsation.

His forehead felt oddly stiff and drawn. His fingers found a streak of dried blood, and then the ragged, painful edge of a small wound.

"Golly!"

With that little gasping cry, he clapped his hand to the back of his head. But there was no blood in his hair. That small leaden ache seemed close beneath his hand, but there was no other surface wound.

"Great golly!" whispered Mr. Peabody. "It has lodged in my brain!"

The evidence was clear enough. He had seen the meteor hurtling straight at him. There was a tiny hole in his forehead, where it must have entered. There was none where it could have emerged.

Why hadn't it already killed him? Perhaps because the heat of it had cauterized the wound. He remembered reading a believe-it-or-not about a man who had lived for years with a bullet in his brain.

A meteor lodged in his brain! The idea set him to shuddering. He and Ella had met their little ups and downs, but his life had been pretty uneventful. He could imagine being shot by a bandit or run over by a taxi. But this—

"Better go to Beth's Dr. Brant," he whispered.

He touched his bleeding forehead, and hoped the wound would heal safely. When he tried to rise, a faintness seized him. A sudden thirst parched his throat.

"Water!" he breathed.

As he sank giddily back on his elbow, that thirst set in his mind the image of a sparkling glass of water. It sat on a flat rock, glittering in the moonlight. It looked so substantial that he reached out and picked it up.

Without surprise, he drank. A few swallows relieved his thirst, and his mind cleared again. Then the sudden realization of the incredible set him to quivering with reasonless panic.

The glass dropped out of his fingers, and shattered on the rock. The fragments glittered mockingly under the moon. Mr. Peabody blinked at them.

"It was real!" he whispered. "I made it real—out of nothing. A miracle—I worked a miracle!"

The word was queerly comforting. Actually, he knew no more about what had happened than before he had found a word for it. Yet much of its disquieting unfamiliarity was dispelled.

He remembered a movie that the Englishman, H. G. Wells, had written. It dealt with a man who was able to perform the most surprising and sometimes appalling miracles. He had finished, Mr. Peabody recalled, by destroying the world.

"I want nothing like that," he whispered in some alarm, and then set out to test his gift. First he tried mentally to lift the small flat rock upon which the miraculous glass had stood.

"Up," he commanded sharply. "Up!"

The rock, however, refused to move. He tried to form a mental picture of it, rising. Suddenly, where he had tried to picture it, there was another and apparently identical rock.

The miraculous stone crashed instantly down upon its twin, and shattered. Flying fragments stung Mr. Peabody's face. He realized that his gift, whatever his nature, held potentialities of danger.

"Whatever I've got," he told himself, "it's different from what the man had in the movie. I can make things—small things, anyhow. But I can't move them." He sat up on the wet grass. "Can I—unmake them?"

He fixed his eyes upon the fragments of the broken glass.

"Go!" he ordered. "Go away—vanish!"

They shimmered unchanged in the moonlight.

"No," concluded Mr. Peabody, "I can't unmake things."

That was, in a way, too bad.

He made another mental note of caution. Large animals and dangerous creations of all kinds had better be avoided. He realized suddenly that he was shivering in his dew-soaked clothing. He slapped his stiff hands against his sides, and wished he had a cup of coffee.

"Well—why not?" He tried to steady his voice against a haunting apprehension. "Here—a cup of coffee!"

Nothing appeared.

"Come!" he shouted. "Coffee!"

Still there was nothing. And doubt returned to Mr. Peabody. Probably he had just been dazed by the meteor. But the hallucinations had looked so queerly real. That glass of water, glittering in the moonlight on the rock—

And there it was again!

Or another, just like it. He touched the glass uncertainly, sipped at the ice-cold water. It was as real as you please. Mr. Peabody shook his bald aching head, baffled.

"Water's easy," he muttered. "But how do you get coffee?"

He let his mind picture a heavy white cup, sitting in its saucer on the rock, steaming fragrantly. The image of it shimmered oddly, half-real.

He made a kind of groping effort. There was a strange brief roaring in his head, beyond that slow painful throb. And suddenly the cup was real.

With awed and trembling fingers, he lifted it. The scalding coffee tasted like the cheaper kind that Ella bought when she was having trouble with the budget. But it was coffee.

Now he knew how to get the cream and sugar. He simply pictured the little creamer and the three white cubes, and made that special grasping effort—and there they were. And he was weak with a momentary unfamiliar fatigue.

He made a spoon and stirred the coffee. He was learning about the gift. It made no difference what he said. He had only the power to *realize* the things he pictured in his mind. It required a peculiar kind of effort, and the act was accompanied by that mighty, far-off roaring in his ears.

The miraculous objects, moreover, had all the imperfections of his mental images. There was an irregular gap in the heavy saucer, behind the cup—where he had failed to complete his picture of it.

Mr. Peabody, however, did not linger long upon the mechanistic details of his gift. Perhaps Dr. Brant would be able to explain it: he was really a very clever young surgeon. Mr. Peabody turned to more immediate concerns.

He was shivering with cold. He decided against building a miraculous fire, and set out to make himself an overcoat. This turned out to be more difficult than he had anticipated. It was necessary to picture clearly the fibers of the wool, the details of buttons and buckle, the shape of every piece of material, the very thread in the seams.

In some way, moreover, the process of materializing was very trying. He was soon quivering with a strange fatigue. The dull little ache at the base of his brain throbbed faster. Again he sensed that roaring beyond, like some Niagara of supernal power.

At last, however, the garment was finished. Attempting to put it on, Mr. Peabody discovered that it was a very poor fit. The shoulders were grotesquely loose. What was worse, he had somehow got the sleeves sewed up at the cuffs.

Wearily, his bright dreams dashed a little, he drew it about his shoulders like a cloak. With a little care and practice, he was sure, he could do better. He ought to be able to make anything he wanted.

Feeling a tired contentment, Mr. Peabody started back down Bannister Hill. Now he could go home to a triumphant peace. His cold body anticipated the comforts of his house and his bed. He dwelt pleasantly upon the happiness of Ella and William and Beth, when they should learn about his gift.

He pushed the ungainly overcoat into a trash container, and swung aboard the car. Fumbling for change to pay the twenty-cent fare, he found one lone dime. A miraculous twin solved the problem. He relaxed on the seat with a sigh of quiet satisfaction.

His son, William, as it happened, was the first person to whom Mr. Peabody attempted to reveal his unusual gift. William was sprawled in the easiest chair, his sallow face decorated with scraps of court plaster. He woke with a start. His eyes rolled glassily. Seeing Mr. Peabody, he grinned with relief.

"Hi, Gov," he drawled. "Got over your tantrum, huh?"

Consciousness of the gift lent Mr. Peabody a new authority.

"Don't call me Gov." His voice was louder than usual. "I wasn't having a tantrum." He felt a sudden apprehension. "What has happened to you, William?"

William fumbled lazily for his pipe.

"Guy crocked me," he drawled. "Some fool in a new Buick. Claims I was on his side of the road. He called the cops, and had a wrecker tow off the bus.

"Guess you'll have a little damage suit on your hands, Gov. Unless you want to settle for cash. The wrecker man said the bill would be about nine hundred. . . . Got any tobacco, Gov?"

The old helpless fury boiled up in Mr. Peabody. He began to tremble, and his fists clenched. After a moment, however, the awareness of his new power allowed him to smile. Things were going to be different now.

"William," he said gravely, "I would like to see a little more respect in your manner in the future." He was building up to the dramatic revelation of his gift. "It was your car and your wreck. You can settle it as you like."

William gestured carelessly with his pipe.

"Wrong as usual, Gov. You see, they wouldn't sell *me* the car. I had to get Mom to sign the papers. So you can't slip out of it that easy, Gov. You're the one that's liable. Got any tobacco?"

A second wave of fury set Mr. Peabody to dancing up and down. Once more, however, consciousness of the gift came to his rescue. He decided upon a double miracle. That ought to put William in his place.

"There's your tobacco." He gestured toward the bare center of the library table. "Look!" He concentrated upon a mental image of the red tin container. "Presto!"

William's mild curiosity changed to a quickly concealed surprise. Lazily he reached for the tin box, drawling:

"Fair enough, Gov. But that magician at the Palace last year pulled the same trick a lot slicker and quicker—" He looked up from the open can, with a triumphant reproof. "Empty, Gov. I call that a pretty flat trick."

"I forgot." Mr. Peabody bit his lip. "You'll find half a can on my dresser."

As William ambled out of the room, he applied himself to a graver project. In his discomfiture and general excitement, he failed to consider a certain limitation upon acts of creation, miraculous or otherwise, existing through Federal law.

His flat pocketbook yielded what was left of the week's pay. He selected a crisp new ten-dollar bill, and concentrated on it. His first copy proved to be blank on the reverse. The second was blurred on both sides. After that, however, he seemed to get the knack of it.

By the time William came swaggering back, lighting up his pipe, there was a neat little stack of miraculous money on the table. Mr. Peabody leaned back in his chair, closing his eyes. That pulsing ache diminished again, and the roar of power receded.

"Here, William," he said in a voice of weary triumph. "You said you needed nine hundred to settle for your wreck."

He counted off the bills, while William stared at him, mouth open and buck teeth gleaming.

"Whatsis, Gov?" he gasped. A note of alarm entered his voice. "Where have you been tonight, Gov? Old Berg didn't leave the safe open?"

"If you want the money, take it," Mr. Peabody said sharply. "And watch your language, son."

William picked up the bills. He stared at them incredulously for a moment, and then stuffed them into his pocket and ran out of the house.

His mind hazy with fatigue, Mr. Peabody relaxed in the big chair. A deep satisfaction filled him. This was one use of the gift which hadn't gone wrong. There was enough of the miraculous money left so that he could give Ella the fifty dollars she wanted. And he could make more, without limit.

A fly came buzzing into the lamplight. Watching it settle upon a candy box on the table, and crawl across the picture of a cherry, Mr. Peabody was moved to another experiment. A mere instant of effort created another fly!

Only one thing was wrong with the miraculous insect. It looked, so far as he could see, exactly like the original. But, when he reached his hand toward it, it didn't move. It wasn't alive.

Why? Mr. Peabody was vaguely bewildered. Did he merely lack some special knack that was necessary for the creation of life? Or was that completely beyond his new power, mysteriously forbidden?

He applied himself to experiment. The problem was still unsolved, although the table was scattered with lifeless flies and the inert forms of a cockroach, a frog, and a sparrow, when he heard the front door.

Mrs. Peabody came in. She was wearing the new blue suit. The trim lines of it seemed to give a new youth to her ample figure, and Mr. Peabody thought that she looked almost beautiful.

She was still angry. She returned his greeting with a stiff little nod, and started regally past him toward the stair. Mr. Peabody followed her anxiously.

"That's your new suit, Ella? You look pretty in it."

With a queen's dignity, she turned. The lamplight shimmered on her blonde indignant head.

"Thank you, Jason." Her voice was cool. "I had no money to pay the boy. It was most embarrassing. He finally left it, when I promised to take the money to the store in the morning."

Mr. Peabody counted off ten of the miraculous bills.

"Here it is, dear," he said. "And fifty more."

Ella was staring, her jaw hanging.

Mr. Peabody smiled at her.

"From now on, dear," he promised her, "things are going to be different. Now I'll be able to give you everything that you've always deserved."

Puzzled alarm tensed Ella Peabody's face, and she came swiftly toward him.

"What's this you say, Jason?"

She saw the lifeless flies that he had made, and then started back with a little muffled cry from the cockroach, the frog, and the sparrow.

"What are these things?" Her voice was shrill. "What are you up to?"

A pang of fear struck into Mr. Peabody's heart. He perceived that it was going to be difficult for other people to understand his gift. The best plan was probably a candid demonstration of it.

"Watch, Ella. I'll show you."

He shuffled through the magazines on the end of the table. He had learned that it was difficult to materialize anything accurately from memory alone. He needed a model.

"Here." He had found an advertisement that showed a platinum bracelet set with diamonds. "Would you like this, my dear?"

Mrs. Peabody retreated from him, growing pale.

"Jason, are you crazy?" Her voice was quick and apprehensive. "You know you can't pay for the few things I simply must have. Now—this money—diamonds—I don't understand you!"

Mr. Peabody dropped the magazine on his knees. Trying to close his ears to Ella's penetrating voice, he began to concentrate on the jewel. This was more difficult than the paper money had been. His head rang with that throbbing pain. But he completed that peculiar final effort, and the thing was done.

"Well—do you like it, my dear?"

He held it toward her. The gleaming white platinum had a satisfying weight. The diamonds glittered with a genuine fire. But she made no move to take it.

Her bewildered face went paler. A hard accusing stare came into her eyes. Suddenly she advanced upon him, demanding:

"Jason, where did you get that bracelet?"

"I—I made it." His voice was thin and husky. "It's—miraculous."

Her determined expression made that statement sound very thin, even to Mr. Peabody.

"Miraculous lie!" She sniffed the air. "Jason, I believe you are drunk!" She advanced on him again. "Now I want to know the truth. What have you done? Have you been—stealing?"

She snatched the bracelet from his fingers, shook it threateningly in front of him.

"Now where did you get it?"

Looking uneasily about, Mr. Peabody saw the kitchen door opening slowly. William peered cautiously through. He was pale, and his trembling hand clutched a long bread knife.

"Mom!" His whisper was hoarse. "Mom, you had better watch out! The Gov is acting plenty weird. He was trying to pull some crummy magic stunts. And then he gave me a bale of queer."

His slightly bulging eyes caught the glitter of the dangling bracelet, and he started.

"Hot ice, huh?" His voice grew hard with an incredible moral indignation. "Gov, cantcher remember you got a decent respectable family? Hot jools, and pushing the queer! Gov, how could you?"

"Queer?" The word croaked faintly from Mr. Peabody's dry throat. "What do you mean—queer?"

"The innocence gag, huh?" William sniffed. "Well, let me

tell you, Gov. Queer is counterfeit. I thought that dough looked funny. So I took it down to a guy at the pool hall that used to shove it. A mess, he says. A blind man could spot it. It ain't worth a nickel on the dollar. It's a sure ticket, he says, for fifteen years!"

This was a turn of affairs for which Mr. Peabody had not prepared himself. An instant's reflection told him that, failing in his confusion to distinguish the token of value from the value itself, he had indeed been guilty.

*"Counterfeit—"*

He stared dazedly at the tense suspicious faces of his wife and son. A chill of ultimate frustration was creeping into him. He collected himself to fight it.

"I didn't—didn't think," he stammered. "We'll have to burn the money that I gave you, too, Ella."

He mopped at his wet forehead, and caught his breath.

"But look." His voice was louder. "I've still got the gift. I can make anything I want—out of nothing at all. I'll show you. I'll make—I'll make you a brick of gold."

His wife retreated, her face white and stiff with dread. William made an ominous flourish with the bread knife, and peered watchfully.

"All right, Gov. Strut your stuff."

There couldn't be any crime about making real gold. But the project proved more difficult than Mr. Peabody had expected. The first dim outlines of the brick began to waver, and he felt sick and dizzy.

The steady beat of pain filled all his head, stronger than it had ever been. The rush of unseen power became a mighty hurricane, blowing away his consciousness. Desperately, he clutched at the back of a chair.

The massive yellow ingot at last shimmered real, under the lamp. Mopping weakly at the sweat on his face, Mr. Peabody made a gesture of weary triumph and sat down.

"What's the matter, darling?" his wife said anxiously. "You look so tired and white. Are you ill?"

William's hands were already clutching at the yellow block. He lifted one end of it, with an effort, and let it fall. It made a dull solid thud.

"Gosh, Gov!" William whispered. "It *is* gold!" His eyes popped again, and narrowed grimly. "Better quit trying to string us, Gov. You cracked a safe tonight."

"But I made it." Mr. Peabody rose in anxious protest. "You saw me."

Ella caught his arm, steadied him.

"We know, Jason," she said soothingly. "But now you look so tired. You had better come up to bed. You'll feel better in the morning."

Digging into the gold brick with his pocket knife, William cried out excitedly:

"Hey, Mom! Lookit—"

With a finger on her lips and a significant nod, Mrs. Peabody silenced her son. She helped Mr. Peabody up the stairs, to the door of their bedroom, and then hurried back to William.

Mr. Peabody undressed wearily and put on his pajamas. With a tired little sigh, he snuggled down under the sheets and closed his eyes.

Naturally he had made little mistakes at first, but now everything was sure to be all right. With just a little more practice, he would be able to give his wife and children all the good things they deserved.

"Daddy?"

Mr. Peabody opened his eyes, and saw Beth standing beside the bed. Her brown eyes looked wide and strange, and her voice was anxious.

"Daddy, what dreadful thing has happened to you?"

Mr. Peabody reached from beneath the sheet, and took her hand. It felt tense and cold.

"A very wonderful thing, Bee, dear," he said. "Not dreadful at all. I simply have a miraculous gift. I can create things. I want to make something for you. What would you like, Bee? A pearl necklace, maybe?"

"Dad—darling!"

Her voice was choked with concern. She sat down on the side of the bed, and looked anxiously into his face. Her cold hand quivered in his.

"Dad, you aren't—insane?"

Mr. Peabody felt a tremor of ungovernable apprehension.

"Of course not, daughter. Why?"

"Mother and Bill have been telling me the most horrid things," she whispered, staring at him. "They said you were playing with dead flies and a cockroach, and saying you could work miracles, and giving them counterfeit money and stolen jewelry and a fake gold brick—"

"Fake?" He gulped. "No; it was real gold."

Beth shook her troubled head.

"Bill showed me," she whispered. "It looks like gold on the outside. But when you scratch it, it's only lead."

Mr. Peabody felt sick. He couldn't help tears of frustration from welling into his eyes.

"I tried," he sobbed. "I don't know why everything goes wrong." He caught a determined breath, and sat up in bed. "But I *can* make gold—real gold. I'll show you."

"Dad!" Her voice was low and dry and breathless. "Dad, you *are* going insane." Quivering hands covered her face. "Mother and Bill were right," she sobbed faintly. "But the police—oh, I can't stand it!"

"Police?" Mr. Peabody leaped out of bed. "What about the police?"

The girl moved slowly back, watching him with dark, frightened eyes.

"Mother and Bill phoned them, before I came in. They think you're insane, and mixed up in some horrid crimes besides. They're afraid of you."

Twisting his hands together, Mr. Peabody padded fearfully to the window. He had an instinctive dread of the law, and his wide reading of detective stories had given him a horror of the third degree.

"They mustn't catch me!" he whispered hoarsely. "They wouldn't believe, about my gift. Nobody does. They'd grill me about the counterfeit and the gold brick and the bracelet. Grill me!" He shuddered convulsively. "Bee, I've got to get away!"

"Dad, you mustn't." She caught his arm, protestingly. "They'll catch you, in the end. Running away will only make you seem guilty."

He pushed away her hand.

"I've got to get away, I tell you. I don't know where. If there were only someone who would understand—"

"Dad, listen!" Beth clapped her hands together, making a sound from which he started violently. "You must go to Rex. He can help you. Will you Dad?"

After a moment, Mr. Peabody nodded.

"He's a doctor. He might understand."

"I'll phone him to expect you. And you get dressed."

He was tying his shoes, when she ran back into the room. "Two policemen, downstairs," she whispered. "Rex said he would wait up for you. But now you can't get out—"

Her voice dropped with amazement, as a coil of rope appeared magically upon the carpet. Mr. Peabody hastily knotted one end of it to the bedstead, and tossed the other out the window.

"Goodby, Bee," he gasped. "Dr. Rex will let you know."

She hastily thumb-bolted the door, as an authoritative hammering began on the other side. Mrs. Peabody's remarkable voice came unimpeded through the panels:

"Jason! Open the door, this instant. Ja-a-a-son!"

Mr. Peabody was still several feet from the ground when the miraculous rope parted unexpectedly. He pulled himself out of a shattered trellis, glimpsed the black police sedan parked in front of the house, and started down the alley.

Trembling from the peril and exertion of his flight across the town, he found the door of Dr. Brant's modest two-room apartment unlocked. He let himself in quietly. The young doctor laid aside a book and stood up, smiling, to greet him.

"I'm glad to see you, Mr. Peabody. Won't you sit down and tell me about yourself?"

Breathless, Mr. Peabody leaned against the closed door. He thought that Brant was at once too warm and too watchful. It came to him that he must yet step very cautiously to keep out of a worse predicament than he had just escaped.

"Beth probably phoned you to expect a lunatic," he began. "But I'm not insane, doctor. Not yet. I have simply happened to acquire a unique gift. People won't believe that it exists. They misunderstand me, suspect me."

Depite his effort for a calm, convincing restraint, his voice shook with bitterness.

"Now my own family has set the police on me!"

"Yes, Mr. Peabody." Dr. Brant's voice was very soothing. "Now just sit down. Make yourself comfortable. And tell me all about it."

After snapping the latch on the door, Mr. Peabody permitted himself to sink wearily into Brant's easy chair. He met the probing eyes of the doctor.

"I didn't mean to do wrong." His voice was still protesting, ragged. "I'm not guilty of any deliberate crime. I was only trying to help the ones I loved."

"I know," the doctor soothed him.

A sharp alarm stiffened Mr. Peabody. He realized that Brant's soothing professional manner was intended to calm a dangerous madman. Words would avail him nothing.

"Beth must have told you what they think," he said desperately. "They won't believe it, but I can create. Let me show you."

Brant smiled at him, gently and without visible skepticism. "Very well. Go on."

"I shall make you a goldfish bowl."

He looked at a little stand, that was cluttered with the doctor's pipes and medical journals, and concentrated upon that peculiar, painful effort. The pain and the rushing passed, and the bowl was real. He looked inquiringly at Brant's suave face.

"Very good, Mr. Peabody. "Now can you put the fish in it?"

"No." Mr. Peabody pressed his hands against his dully aching head. "It seems that I can't make anything alive. That is one of the limitations that I have discovered."

"Eh?"

Brant's eyes widened a little. He walked slowly to the small glass bowl, touched it gingerly, and put a testing finger into the water it contained. His jaw slackened.

"Well." He repeated the word, with increasing emphasis. "Well, well, *well!*"

His staring gray eyes came back to Mr. Peabody. "You are being honest with me? You'll give your word there's no trickery? You materialized this object by mental effort alone?"

Mr. Peabody nodded.

It was Brant's turn to be excited. While Mr. Peabody sat quietly recovering his breath, the lean young doctor paced up and down the room. He lit his pipe and let it go out, and asked a barrage of tense-voiced questions.

Wearily, Mr. Peabody tried to answer the questions. He made new demonstrations of his gift, materializing a nail, a match, a cube of sugar, and a cuff link that was meant to be silver. Commenting upon the leaden color of the latter, he recalled his misadventures with the gold brick.

"A minor difficulty, I should think—always assuming that this is a fact."

Brant took off his rimless glasses, and polished them nervously. "Possibly due merely to lack of familiarity with atomic structure. . . . But—my word!"

He began walking the floor again.

All but dead with fatigue, Mr. Peabody was mutely grateful at last to be permitted to crawl into the doctor's bed. Despite that small dull throbbing in his brain, he slept soundly.

And up in the heavens a bright star winked, greenly.

Brant, if he slept at all, did so in the chair. The next morning, wrinkled, hollow-eyed, dark-chinned, he woke Mr. Peabody; refreshed his bewildered memory with a glimpse of a nail, a match, a cube of sugar, and a lead cuff link; and inquired frantically whether he still possessed the gift.

Mr. Peabody felt dull and heavy. The ache at the back of his head was worse, and he felt reluctant to attempt any miracles. He remained able, however, to provide himself with a cup of inexplicable coffee.

"Well!" exclaimed Brant. "Well, well, well! All through the night I kept doubting even my own senses. My word—it's incredible. But what an opportunity for medical science!"

"Eh?" Mr. Peabody started apprehensively. "What do you mean?"

"Don't alarm yourself," Brant said soothingly. "Of course we must keep your case a secret, at least until we have data enough to support an announcement. But, for your sake as well as for science, you must allow me to study your new power."

Nervously, he was polishing his glasses.

"You are my uncle," he declared abruptly. "Your name is Homer Brown. Your home is in Pottsville, upstate. You are staying with me for a few days, while you undergo an examination at the hospital."

"Hospital?"

Mr. Peabody began a feeble protest. Ever since Beth was born, he had felt a horror of hospitals. Even the odor, he insisted, was enough to make him ill.

In the midst of his objections, however, he found himself bundled into a taxi.

Brant whisked him into the huge gray building, past nurses and interns. There was an endless series of examinations; from remote alert politeness that surrounded him, he guessed that he was supposed to be insane. At last Brant called him into a tiny consultation room, and locked the door.

His manner was suddenly respectful—and oddly grave.

"Mr. Peabody, I must apologize for all my doubts," he said. "The X-ray proves the incredible. Here, you may see it for yourself."

He made Mr. Peabody sit before two mirrors, that each reflected a rather gruesome-looking skull. The two images emerged into one. At the base of the skull, beyond the staring eye sockets, Brant pointed out a little ragged black object.

"That's it."

"You mean the meteor?"

"It is a foreign body. Naturally, we can't determine its true nature, without recourse to brain surgery. But the X-ray shows the scars of its passage through brain tissue and frontal bone—miraculously healed. It is doubtless the object which struck you."

Mr. Peabody had staggered to his feet, gasping voicelessly.

"Brain surgery!" he whispered hoarsely. "You aren't—"

Very slowly, Brant shook his head.

"I wish we could," he said gravely. "But the operation is impossible. It would involve a section of the cerebrum itself. No surgeon I know would dare attempt it."

Gently, he took Mr. Peabody's arm. His voice fell.

"It would be unfair to conceal from you the fact that your case is extremely serious."

Mr. Peabody's knees were shaking.

"Doctor, what do you mean?"

Brant pointed solemnly at the X-ray films.

"That foreign body is radioactive," he said deliberately. "I noticed that the film tended to fog, and you sound like hail on the Geiger counter." The doctor's face was tense and white.

"You understand that it can't be removed," he said. "And the destructive effect of its radiations upon the brain tissue will inevitably be fatal, within a few weeks."

He shook his head, while Mr. Peabody stared uncomprehendingly.

Brant's smile was tight, bitter.

"Your life, it seems, is the price you must pay for your gift."

Mr. Peabody let Brant take him back to the little apartment. The throbbing in his head was an incessant reminder that the rays of the stone were destroying his brain. Despair numbed him, and he felt sick with pain.

"Now that I know I'm going to die," he told the doctor, "there is just one thing I've got to do. I must use the gift to make money enough so that my family will be cared for."

"You'll be able to do that, I'm sure," Brant agreed. Filling a pipe, he came to Mr. Peabody's chair. "I don't want to excite your hopes unduly," he said slowly. "But I want to suggest one possibility."

"Eh?" Mr. Peabody half rose. "You mean the stone might be removed?"

Brant was shaking his head.

"It can't be, by any ordinary surgical technique," he said.

"But I was just thinking: your extraordinary power healed the wound it made in traversing the brain. If you can acquire control over the creation and manipulation of living matter, we might safely attempt the operation—depending on your gift to heal the section."

"There's no use to it." Mr. Peabody sank wearily back into Brant's easy chair. "I've tried, and I can't make anything alive. The power was simply not granted me."

"Nonsense," Brant told him. "The difficulty, probably, is just that you don't know enough biology. A little instruction in bio-chemistry, anatomy, and psysiology ought to fix you up."

"I'll try," Mr. Peabody agreed. "But first my family must be provided for."

After the doctor had given him a lesson on the latest discoveries about atomic and molecular structures, he found himself able to create objects of the precious metals, with none of them turning out like the gold brick.

For two days he drove himself to exhaustion, making gold and platinum. He shaped the metal into watch cases, old-fashioned jewelry, dental work, and medals, so that it could be disposed of without arousing suspicion.

Brant took a handful of the trinkets to a dealer in old gold. He returned with five hundred dollars, and the assurance that the entire lot, gradually marketed, would net several thousand.

Mr. Peabody felt ill with the pain and fatigue of his creative efforts, and he was still distressed with a fear of the law. He learned from the newspapers that the police were watching his house, and he dared not even telephone his daughter Beth.

"They all think I'm insane; even Beth does," he told Brant. "Probably I'll never see any of them again. I want you to keep the money, and give it to them after I am gone."

"Nonsense," the young doctor said. "When you get a little more control over your gift, you will be able to fix everything up."

But even Brant had to admit that Mr. Peabody's increasing illness threatened to cut off the research before they had reached success.

Unkempt and hollow-eyed, muttering about "energy-conversion" and "entropy-reverse," and "telurgic psi capacity," Brant sat up night after night while Mr. Peabody slept, plowing through heavy tomes on relativity and atomic physics and parapsychology trying to discover a sane explanation of the gift.

"I believe that roaring you say you hear," he told Mr. Peabody, "is nothing less than a sense of the free radiant energy of cosmic space. The radioactive stone has somehow enabled your brain—perhaps by stimulation of the psychophysical faculty that is rudimentary in all of us—has enabled you to concentrate and convert that diffuse energy into material atoms."

Mr. Peabody shook his fevered, throbbing head.

"What good is your theory to me?" Despair moved him to a bitter recital of his case.

"I can work miracles, but what good has the power done me? It has driven me from my family. It has made me a fugitive from justice. It has turned me into a sort of guinea pig, for your experiments. It is nothing but a headache—a real one, I mean. And it's going to kill me, in the end."

"Not," Brant assured him, "if you can learn to create living matter."

Not very hopefully, for the pain and weakness that accompanied his miraculous efforts were increasing day by day. Mr. Peabody followed Brant's lectures in anatomy and physiology. He materialized blobs of protoplasm and simple cells and bits of tissue.

The doctor evidently had grandiose ideas of a miraculous human being. He set Mr. Peabody to studying and creating human limbs and organs. After a few days, the bathtub was filled with a strange lot of miraculous debris, swimming in a preservative solution.

Then Mr. Peabody rebelled.

"I'm getting too weak, doctor," he insisted faintly. "My power is somehow—going. Sometimes it seems that things are going to flicker out again, instead of getting real. I know I can't make anything as large as a human being."

"Well, make something small," Brant told him. "Remember, if you give up, you are giving up your life."

And presently, with a manual of marine biology on his knees, Mr. Peabody was forming small miraculous goldfish in the bowl he had made on the night of his arrival. They were gleaming, perfect—except that they always floated to the top of the water, dead.

Brant had gone out. Mr. Peabody was alone before the bowl, when Beth slipped silently into the apartment. She looked pale and distressed.

"Dad!" she cried anxiously. "How are you?" She came to him, and took his trembling hands. "Rex warned me on the phone not to come: he was afraid the police would follow me. But I don't think they saw me. And I had to come, Dad. I was so worried. But how are you?"

"I think I'll be all right," Mr. Peabody lied stoutly, and tried to conceal the tremor in his voice. "I'm glad to see you, dear. Tell me about your mother and Bill."

"They're all right. But Dad, you look so ill!"

"Here, I've something for you." Mr. Peabody took the five hundred dollars out of his wallet, and put it in her hands. "There will be more, after—later."

"But, Dad—"

"Don't worry, dear, it isn't counterfeit."

"It isn't that." Her voice was distressed. "Rex has tried to tell me about these miracles. I don't understand them, Dad; I don't know what to believe. But I do know we don't want the money you make with them. None of us."

Mr. Peabody tried to cover his hurt.

"But my dear," he asked, "how are you going to live?"

"I'm going to work, next week," she said. "I'm going to be a reception clerk for a dentist—until Rex has an office of his own. And Mom is going to take two boarders, in the spare room."

"But," said Mr. Peabody, "there is William."

"Bill already has a job," Beth informed him. "You know the fellow he ran into? Well, the man has a garage. He let Bill go to work for him. Bill gets fifty a week, and pays back thirty for the accident. Bill's doing all right."

The way she looked when she said it made it clear to Mr. Peabody that there had been a guiding spirit in his family's remarkable reformation—and that Beth had had a lot to do with it. Mr. Peabody smiled at her gratefully to show that he understood, but he said nothing.

She refused to watch him demonstrate his gift.

"No, Dad." She moved back almost in horror from the little bowl with the lifeless goldfish floating in it. "I don't like magic, and I don't believe in something for nothing. There is always a catch to it."

She came and took his hand again, earnestly.

"Dad," she begged softly, "why don't you give up this gift? Whatever it is. Why don't you explain to the police and your boss, and try to get your old job back?"

Mr. Peabody shook his head, with a wry little smile.

"I'm afraid it wouldn't be so easy, explaining," he said. "But I'm ready to give up the gift—whenever I can."

"I don't understand you, Dad." Her face was trembling. "Now I must go. I hope the police didn't see me. I'll come back, whenever I can."

She departed, and Mr. Peabody wearily returned to his miraculous goldfish.

Five minutes later the door was flung unceremoniously open. Mr. Peabody looked up, startled. And the gleaming ghost of a tiny fish, half-materialized, shimmered and vanished.

Mr. Peabody had expected to see Brant, returning. But four policemen, two in plain clothes, trooped into the room. They triumphantly informed him that he was under arrest, and began searching the apartment.

"Hey, Sergeant!" came an excited shout from the bathroom. "Looks like Doc Brant is in the ring, too. And it ain't only jewel-robbery and fraud and counterfeiting. It's murder—with mutilation!"

The startled officers converged watchfully upon Mr. Peabody, and handcuffs jingled. Mr. Peabody, however, was looking curiously elated for a man just arrested under charge of the gravest of crimes. The haunting shadow of pain cleared from his face, and he smiled happily.

"Hey, they're gone!" It was the patrolman in the bathroom. His horror-tinged excitement had changed to bewildered consternation. "I saw 'em, a minute ago. I swear it. But now there ain't nothing in the tub but water."

The sergeant stared suspiciously at Mr. Peabody, who looked bland but exhausted. Then he made a few stinging remarks to the bluecoat standing baffled in the doorway. Finally he swore with much feeling.

Mr. Peabody's hollow eyes had closed. The smile on his face softened into weary relaxation. The detective sergeant caught him, as he swayed and fell. He had gone to sleep.

He woke next morning in a hospital room. Dr. Brant was standing beside the bed. In answer to Mr. Peabody's first alarmed question, he grinned reassuringly.

"You are my patient," he explained. "You have been under my care for an unusual case of amnesia. Very convenient disorder, amnesia. And you are doing very well."

"The police?"

Brant gestured largely.

"You've nothing to fear. There's no evidence that you were

guilty of any criminal act. Naturally they wonder how you came into possession of the counterfeit; but certainly they can't prove you made it. I have already told them that, as a victim of amnesia, you will not be able to tell them anything."

Mr. Peabody sighed and stretched himself under the sheets, gratefully.

"Now, I've got a couple of questions," Brant said. "What was it that happened so fortunately to the debris in the bathtub? And to the stone in your head? For the X-ray shows that it is gone."

"I just undid them," Mr. Peabody said.

Brant caught his breath, and nodded very slowly.

"I see," he said at last. "I suppose the inevitable counterpart of creation must be annihilation. But how did you do it?"

"It came to me, just as the police broke in," Mr. Peabody said. "I was creating another one of those damned goldfish, and I was too tired to finish it. When I heard the door, I made a little effort to—well, somehow let it go, push it away."

He sighed again, happily.

"That's the way it happened. The goldfish flickered out of existence; it made an explosion in my head, like a bomb. That gave me the feel of unmaking. Annihilation, you call it. Much easier than creating, once you get the knack of it. I took care of the things in the bathroom, and the stone in my brain."

"I see." Brant took a restless turn across the room, and came back to ask a question. "Now that the stone is gone," he said, "I suppose your remarkable gift is—lost?"

It was several seconds before Mr. Peabody replied. Then he said softly:

"It was lost."

That statement, however, was a lie. Mr. Peabody had learned a certain lesson. The annihilation of the meteoric stone had ended his pain. But, as he had just assured himself by the creation and instant obliteration of a small goldfish under the sheets, his power was intact.

Still a bookkeeper, Mr. Peabody is still outwardly very much the same man as he was that desperate night when he walked upon Bannister Hill. Yet there is now a certain subtle difference in him.

A new confidence in his bearing has caused Mr. Berg to increase his responsibilities and his pay. The yet unsolved mysteries surrounding his attack of amnesia cause his family and his neighbors to regard him with a certain awe. William now only very rarely calls him "Gov."

Mr. Peabody remains very discreet in the practice of his gift. Sometimes, when he is quite alone, he ventures to provide himself with a miraculous cigarette. Once, in the middle of the night, a mosquito which had tormented him beyond endurance simply vanished.

And he has come, somehow, into the possession of a fishing outfit which is the envy of his friends—and which he now finds time to use.

Chiefly, however, his gift is reserved for performing inexplicable tricks for the delight of his two grandchildren, and the creation of tiny and miraculous toys.

All of which, he strictly enjoins them, must be kept secret from their parents, Beth and Dr. Brant.

# by Robert A. Heinlein

*Heinlein's second story (in this volume and his second published), "Misfit" contains all the elements that made him great—attention to detail, narrative flow, young protaganist, and interesting social extrapolation. The "Cosmic Construction Corps" owes an obvious debt to the depression-era CCC. There was to be a great deal more from where this came from—for evidence, see Volume II, 1940.*

*(No one ever dominated the science fiction field as Bob did in the first few years of his career. It was a one-man phenomenon that will probably never be repeated. The field has grown too large, its nature too varied, its writers too many for any one person to overshadow it. IA)*

> "... for the purpose of conserving and improving our interplanetary resources, and providing useful, healthful occupations for the youth of this planet."
> Excerpt from the enabling act, H.R. 7118, setting up the Cosmic Construction Corps.

"Attention to muster!" The parade ground voice of a First Sergeant of Space Marines cut through the fog and drizzle of a nasty New Jersey morning. "As your names are called, answer 'Here', step forward with your baggage, and embark. Atkins!"

"Here!"

"Austin!"

"Hyar!"

"Ayres!"

"Here!"

One by one they fell out of ranks, shouldered the hundred and thirty pounds of personal possessions allowed them, and trudged up the gangway. They were young—none more than twenty-two—in some cases luggage outweighed the owner.

"Kaplan!"

"Here!"

"Keith!"

"Heah!"

"Libby!"

"Here!" A thin gangling blonde had detached himself from the line, hastily wiped his nose, and grabbed his belongings. He slung a fat canvas bag over his shoulder, steadied it, and lifted a suitcase with his free hand. He started for the companionway in an unsteady dog trot. As he stepped on the gangway his suitcase swung against his knees. He staggered against a short wiry form dressed in the powder-blue of the Space Navy. Strong fingers grasped his arm and checked his fall.

"Steady, son. Easy does it." Another hand readjusted the canvas bag.

"Oh, excuse me, uh"—the embarrassed youngster automatically counted the four bands of silver braid below the shooting star—"Captain. I didn't—"

"Bear a hand and get aboard, son."

"Yes, sir."

The passage into the bowels of the transport was gloomy. When the lad's eyes adjusted he saw a gunner's mate wearing the brassard of a Master-at-Arms, who hooked a thumb towards an open air-tight door.

"In there. Find your locker and wait by it." Libby hurried to obey. Inside he found a jumble of baggage and men in a wide low-ceilinged compartment. A line of glow-tubes ran around the junction of bulkhead and ceiling and trisected the overhead; the soft roar of blowers made a background to the voices of his shipmates. He picked his way through heaped luggage, and located his locker, seven-ten, on the far wall outboard. He broke the seal on the combination lock, glanced at the combination, and opened it. The locker was very small, the middle of a tier of three. He considered what he should keep in it. A loudspeaker drowned out the surrounding voices and demanded his attention:

"Attention! Man all space details; first section. Raise ship in twelve minutes. Close air-tight doors. Stop blowers at minus two minutes. Special orders for passengers; place all gear on deck, and lie down on red signal light. Remain down until release is sounded. Masters-at-Arms check compliance."

The gunner's mate popped in, glanced around and immediately commenced supervising rearrangement of the baggage. Heavy items were lashed down. Locker doors were closed. By the time each boy had found a place on the deck and the Master-at-Arms had okayed the pad under his head, the glow-tubes turned red and the loudspeaker brayed out.

"All hands—Up Ship! Stand by for acceleration." The Master-at-Arms hastily reclined against two cruise bags, and watched the room. The blowers sighed to a stop. There followed two minutes of dead silence. Libby felt his heart commence to pound. The two minutes stretched interminably. Then the deck quivered and a roar like escaping high-pressure steam beat at his ear drums. He was suddenly very heavy and a weight lay across his chest and heart. An indefinite time later the glow-tubes flashed white, and the announcer bellowed:

"Secure all getting underway details; regular watch, first section." The blowers droned into life. The Master-at-Arms stood up, rubbed his buttocks and pounded his arms, then said:

"Okay, boys." He stepped over and undogged the airtight door to the passageway. Libby got up and blundered into a bulkhead, nearly falling. His legs and arms had gone to sleep, besides which he felt alarmingly light, as if he had sloughed off at least half of his inconsiderable mass.

For the next two hours he was too busy to think, or to be homesick. Suitcases, boxes, and bags had to be passed down into the lower hold and lashed against angular acceleration. He located and learned how to use a waterless water closet. He found his assigned bunk and learned that it was his only eight hours in twenty-four; two other boys had the use of it too. The three sections ate in three shifts, nine shifts in all—twenty-four youths and a master-at-arms at one long table which jam-filled a narrow compartment off the galley.

After lunch Libby restowed his locker. He was standing before it, gazing at a photograph which he intended to mount on the inside of the locker door, when a command filled the compartment:

"Attention!"

Standing inside the door was the Captain flanked by the Master-at-Arms. The Captain commenced to speak. "At rest, men. Sit down. McCoy, tell control to shift this compartment to smoke filter." The gunner's mate hurried to the communicator on the bulkhead and spoke into it in a low tone. Almost at once the hum of the blowers climbed a half-octave and stayed there. "Now light up if you like. I'm going to talk to you.

"You boys are headed out on the biggest thing so far in your lives. From now on you're men, with one of the hardest jobs ahead of you that men have ever tackled. What we have to do is part of a bigger scheme. You, and hundreds of thousands of others like you, are going out as pioneers to fix up the solar system so that human beings can make better use of it.

"Equally important, you are being given a chance to build yourselves into useful and happy citizens of the Federation. For one reason or another you weren't happily adjusted back on Earth. Some of you saw the jobs you were trained for abolished by new inventions. Some of you got into trouble from not knowing what to do with the modern leisure. In any case you were misfits. Maybe you were called bad boys and had a lot of black marks chalked up against you.

"But everyone of you starts even today. The only record you have in this ship is your name at the top of a blank sheet of paper. It's up to you what goes on that page.

"Now about your job—We didn't get one of the easy repair-and-recondition jobs on the Moon, with week-ends at Luna City, and all the comforts of home. Nor did we draw a high-gravity planet where a man can eat a full meal and expect to keep it down. Instead we've got to go out to Asteroid HS-5388 and turn it into Space Station E-M3. She has no atmosphere at all, and only about two percent Earth-surface gravity. We've got to play human fly on her for at least six months, no girls to date, no television, no recreation that you don't devise yourselves, and hard work every day. You'll get space sick, and so homesick you can taste it, and agoraphobia. If you aren't careful, you'll get ray-burnt. Your stomach will act up, and you'll wish to God you'd never enrolled.

"But if you behave yourself, and listen to the advice of the old spacemen, you'll come out of it strong and healthy, with a little credit stored up in the bank, and a lot of knowledge and experience that you wouldn't get in forty years on Earth. You'll be men, and you'll know it.

"One last word. It will be pretty uncomfortable to those that aren't used to it. Just give the other fellow a little consideration, and you'll get along all right. If you have any complaint and can't get satisfaction any other way, come see me. Otherwise, that's all. Any questions?"

One of the boys put up his hand. "Captain?" he enquired timidly.

"Speak up, lad, and give your name."

"Rogers, sir. Will we be able to get letters from home?"

"Yes, but not very often. Maybe every month or so. The chaplain will carry mail, and any inspection and supply ships."

The ship's loudspeaker blatted out, "All hands! Free flight in ten minutes. Stand by to lose weight." The Master-at-Arms supervised the rigging of grab-lines. All loose gear was made fast, and little cellulose bags were issued to each man. Hardly was this done when Libby felt himself get light on his feet—a sensation exactly like that experienced when an express elevator makes a quick stop on an upward trip, except that the sensation continued and became more intense. At first it was a pleasant novelty, then it rapidly became distressing. The blood pounded in his ears, and his feet were clammy and cold. His saliva secreted at an abnormal rate. He tried to swallow, choked, and coughed. Then his stomach shuddered and contracted with a violent, painful, convulsive reflex and he was suddenly, disastrously nauseated. After the first excruciating spasm, he heard McCoy's voice shouting.

"Hey! Use your sick-kits like I told you. Don't let that stuff get in the blowers." Dimly Libby realized that the admonishment included him. He fumbled for his cellulose bag just as a second temblor shook him, but he managed to fit the bag over his mouth before the eruption occurred. When it subsided, he became aware that he was floating near the overhead and facing the door. The chief Master-at-Arms slithered in the door and spoke to McCoy.

"How are you making out?"

"Well enough. Some of the boys missed their kits."

"Okay. Mop it up. You can use the starboard lock." He swam out.

McCoy touched Libby's arm. "Here, Pinkie, start catching them butterflies." He handed him a handful of cotton waste, then took another handful himself and neatly dabbed up a globule of the slimy filth that floated about the compartment. "Be sure your sick-kit is on tight. When you get sick, just stop and wait until it's over." Libby imitated him as best as he could. In a few minutes the room was free of the worst of the sickening debris. McCoy looked it over, and spoke:

"Now peel off them dirty duds, and change your kits.

Three or four of you bring everything alone to the starboard lock."

At the starboard spacelock, the kits were put in first, the inner door closed, and the outer opened. When the inner door was opened again the kits were gone—blown out into space by the escaping air. Pinkie addressed McCoy,

"Do we have to throw away our dirty clothes too?"

"Huh uh, we'll just give them a dose of vacuum. Take 'em into the lock and stop 'em to those hooks on the bulkheads. Tie 'em tight."

This time the lock was left closed for about five minutes. When the lock was opened the garments were bone dry—all the moisture boiled out by the vacuum of space. All that remained of the unpleasant rejecta was a sterile powdery residue. McCoy viewed them with approval. "They'll do. Take them back to the compartment. Then brush them— hard—in front of the exhaust blowers."

The next few days were an eternity of misery. Homesickness was forgotten in the all-engrossing wretchedness of spacesickness. The Captain granted fifteen minutes of mild acceleration for each of the nine meal periods, but the respite accentuated the agony. Libby would go to a meal, weak and ravenously hungry. The meal would stay down until free flight was resumed, then the sickness would hit him all over again.

On the fourth day he was seated against a bulkhead, enjoying the luxury of a few remaining minutes of weight while the last shift ate, when McCoy walked in and sat down beside him. The gunner's mate fitted a smoke filter over his face and lit a cigarette. He inhaled deeply and started to chat.

"How's it going, bud?"

"All right, I guess. This spacesickness—Say, McCoy, how do you ever get used to it?"

"You get over it in time. Your body acquires new reflexes, so they tell me. Once you learn to swallow without choking, you'll be all right. You even get so you like it. It's restful and relaxing. Four hours sleep is as good as ten."

Libby shook his head dolefully. "I don't think I'll ever get used to it."

"Yes, you will. You'd better anyway. This here asteroid won't have any surface gravity to speak of; the Chief Quartermaster says it won't run over two per cent Earth normal.

That ain't enough to cure spacesickness. And there won't be any way to accelerate for meals either."

Libby shivered and held his head between his hands.

Locating one asteroid among a couple of thousand is not as easy as finding Trafalgar Square in London—especially against the star-crowded backdrop of the galaxy. You take off from Terra with its orbital speed of about nineteen miles per second. You attempt to settle into a composite conoid curve that will not only intersect the orbit of the tiny fast-moving body, but also accomplish an exact rendezvous. Asteroid HS-5388, 'Eighty-eight,' lay about two and two-tenths astronomical units out from the sun, a little more than two hundred million miles; when the transport took off it lay beyond the sun better than three hundred million miles. Captain Doyle instructed the navigator to plot the basic ellipsoid to tack in free flight around the sun through an elapsed distance of some three hundred and forty million miles. The principle involved is the same as used by a hunter to wing a duck in flight by 'leading' the bird in flight. But suppose that you face directly into the sun as you shoot; suppose the bird cannot be seen from where you stand, and you have nothing to aim by but some old reports as to how it was flying when last seen?

On the ninth day of the passage Captain Doyle betook himself to the chart room and commenced punching keys on the ponderous integral calculator. Then he set his orderly to present his compliments to the navigator and to ask him to come to the chartroom. A few minutes later a tall heavyset form swam through the door, steadied himself with a grabline and greeted the captain.

"Good morning, Skipper."

"Hello, Blackie." The Old Man looked up from where he was strapped into the integrator's saddle. "I've been checking your corrections for the meal time accelerations."

"It's a nuisance to have a bunch of ground-lubbers on board, sir."

"Yes, it is, but we have to give those boys a chance to eat, or they couldn't work when we got there. Now I want to decelerate starting about ten o'clock, ship's time. What's our eight o'clock speed and co-ordinates?"

The Navigator slipped a notebook out of his tunic. "Three hundred fifty-eight miles per second; course is right ascension fifteen hours, eight minutes, twenty-seven seconds, declination minus seven degrees, three minutes; solar distance one hundred and ninety-two million four hundred eighty thousand miles. Our radial position is twelve degrees above course, and almost dead on course in R.A. Do you want Sol's co-ordinates?"

"No, not now." The captain bent over the calculator, frowned and chewed the tip of his tongue as he worked the controls. "I want you to kill the acceleration about one million miles inside Eighty-eight's orbit. I hate to waste the fuel, but the belt is full of junk and this damned rock is so small that we will probably have to run a search curve. Use twenty hours on deceleration and commence changing course to port after eight hours. Use normal asymptotic approach. You should have her in a circular trajectory abreast of Eighty-eight, and paralleling her orbit by six o'clock tomorrow morning. I shall want to be called at three."

"Aye aye, sir."

"Let me see your figures when you get 'em. I'll send up the order book later."

The transport accelerated on schedule. Shortly after three the Captain entered the control room and blinked his eyes at the darkness. The sun was still concealed by the hull of the transport and the midnight blackness was broken only by the dim blue glow of the instrument dials, and the crack of light from under the chart hood. The Navigator turned at the familiar tread.

"Good morning, Captain."

"Morning, Blackie. In sight yet?"

"Not yet. We've picked out half a dozen rocks, but none of them checked."

"Any of them close?"

"Not uncomfortably. We've overtaken a little sand from time to time."

"That can't hurt us—not on a stern chase like this. If pilots would only realize that the asteroids flow in fixed directions at computable speeds nobody would come to grief out here." He stopped to light a cigarette. "People talk about space being dangerous. Sure, it used to be; but I don't know of a case in the past twenty years that couldn't be charged up to some fool's recklessness."

"You're right, Skipper. By the way, there's coffee under the chart hood."

"Thanks; I had a cup down below." He walked over by the lookouts at stereoscopes and radar tanks and peered up at the star-flecked blackness. Three cigarettes later the lookout nearest him called out.

"Light ho!"

"Where away?"

His mate read the exterior dials of the stereoscope. "Plus point two, abaft one point three, slight drift astern." He shifted to radar and added, "Range seven nine oh four three."

"Does that check?"

"Could be, Captain. What is her disk?" came the Navigator's muffled voice from under the hood. The first lookout hurriedly twisted the knobs of his instrument, but the Captain nudged him aside.

"I'll do this, son." He fitted his face to the double eye guards and surveyed a little silvery sphere, a tiny moon. Carefully he brought two illuminated cross-hairs up until they were exactly tangent to the upper and lower limbs of the disc. "Mark!"

The reading was noted and passed to the Navigator, who shortly ducked out from under the hood.

"That's our baby, Captain."

"Good."

"Shall I make a visual triangulation?"

"Let the watch officer do that. You go down and get some sleep. I'll ease her over until we get close enough to use the optical range finder."

"Thanks, I will."

Within a few minutes the word had spread around the ship that Eighty-eight had been sighted. Libby crowded into the starboard troop deck with a throng of excited mess mates and attempted to make out their future home from the view port. McCoy poured cold water on their excitement.

"By the time that rock shows up big enough to tell anything about it with your naked eye we'll all be at our grounding stations. She's only about a hundred miles thick, yuh know."

And so it was. Many hours later the ship's announcer shouted:

"All hands! Man your grounding stations. Close all airtight doors. Stand by to cut blowers on signal."

McCoy forced them to lie down throughout the ensuing two hours. Short shocks of rocket blasts alternated with nauseating weightlessness. Then the blowers stopped and check valves clicked into their seats. The ship dropped free for a few moments—a final quick blast—five seconds of falling, and a short, light, grinding bump. A single bugle note came over the announcer, and the blowers took up their hum.

McCoy floated lightly to his feet and poised, swaying, on his toes. "All out, troops—this is the end of the line."

A short chunky lad, a little younger than most of them, awkwardly emulated him, and bounded toward the door, shouting as he went, "Come on, fellows! Let's go outside and explore!"

The Master-at-Arms squelched him. "Not so fast, kid. Aside from the fact that there is no air out there, go right ahead. You'll freeze to death, burn to death, and explode like a ripe tomato. Squad leader, detail six men to break out spacesuits. The rest of you stay here and stand by."

The working party returned shortly loaded down with a couple of dozen bulky packages. Libby let go the four he carried and watched them float gently to the deck. McCoy unzipped the envelope from one suit, and lectured them about it.

"This is a standard service type, general issue, Mark IV, Modification 2." He grasped the suit by the shoulders and shook it out so that it hung like a suit of long winter underwear with the helmet lolling helplessly between the shoulders of the garment. "It's self-sustaining for eight hours, having an oxygen supply for that period. It also has a nitrogen trim tank and a carbon-dioxide-water-vapor cartridge filter."

He droned on, repeating practically verbatim the description and instructions given in training regulations. McCoy knew these suits like his tongue knew the roof of his mouth; the knowledge had meant his life on more than one occasion.

"The suit is woven from glass fibre laminated with nonvolatile asbestocellutite. The resulting fabric is flexible, very durable; and will turn all rays normal to solar space outside the orbit of Mercury. It is worn over your regular clothing, but notice the wire-braced accordion pleats at the major joints. They are so designed as to keep the internal volume of the suit nearly constant when the arms or legs are bent. Otherwise the gas pressure inside would tend to keep the suit blown up in an erect position, and movement while wearing the suit would be very fatiguing.

"The helmet is moulded from a transparent silicone, leaded and polarized against too great ray penetration. It may be equipped with external visors of any needed type. Orders are to wear not less than a number-two amber on this body. In addition, a lead plate covers the cranium and extends on down the back of the suit, completely covering the spinal column.

"The suit is equipped with two-way telephony. If your radio quits, as these have a habit of doing, you can talk by putting your helmets in contact. Any questions?"

"How do you eat and drink during the eight hours?"

"You don't stay in 'em any eight hours. You can carry sugar balls in a gadget in the helmet, but you boys will always eat at the base. As for water, there's a nipple in the helmet near your mouth which you can reach by turning your head to the left. It's hooked to a built-in canteen. But don't drink any more water when you're wearing a suit than you have to. These suits ain't got any plumbing."

Suits were passed out to each lad, and McCoy illustrated how to don one. A suit was spread supine on the deck, the front zipper that stretched from neck to crotch was spread wide and one sat down inside this opening, whereupon the lower part was drawn on like long stockings. Then a wiggle into each sleeve and the heavy flexible gauntlets were smoothed and patted into place. Finally an awkward backward stretch of the neck with shoulders hunched enabled the helmet to be placed over the head.

Libby followed the motions of McCoy and stood up in his suit. He examined the zipper which controlled the suit's only opening. It was backed by two soft gaskets which would be pressed together by the zipper and sealed by internal air pressure. Inside the helmet a composition mouthpiece for exhalation led to the filter.

McCoy bustled around, inspecting them, tightening a belt here and there, instructing them in the use of the external controls. Satisfied, he reported to the conning room that his section had received basic instruction and was ready to disembark. Permission was received to take them out for thirty minutes acclimatization.

Six at a time, he escorted them through the air lock, and out on the surface of the planetoid. Libby blinked his eyes at the unaccustomed luster of sunshine on rock. Although the sun lay more than two hundred million miles away and bathed the little planet with radiation only one fifth as strong as that lavished on mother Earth, nevertheless the lack of atmosphere resulted in a glare that made him squint. He was glad to have the protection of his amber visor. Overhead the sun, shrunk to penny size, shone down from a dead black sky in which unwinking stars crowded each other and the very sun itself.

The voice of a mess mate sounded in Libby's earphones, "Jeepers! That horizon looks close. I'll bet it ain't more'n a mile away."

Libby looked out over the flat bare plain and subconsciously considered the matter. "It's less," he commented, "than a third of a mile away."

"What the hell do you know about it, Pinkie? And who asked you, anyhow?"

Libby answered defensively, "As a matter of fact, it's one thousand six hundred and seventy feet, figuring that my eyes are five feet three inches above ground level."

"Nuts. Pinkie, you are always trying to show off how much you think you know."

"Why, I am not," Libby protested. "If this body is a hundred miles thick and as round as it looks: why, naturally the horizon *has* to be just that far away."

"Says *who?*"

McCoy interrupted.

"Pipe down! Libby is a lot nearer right than you were."

"He is exactly right," put in a strange voice. "I had to look it up for the navigator before I left control."

"Is that so?"—McCoy's voice again—"If the Chief Quartermaster says you're right, Libby, you're right. How did you know?"

Libby flushed miserably. "I—I don't know. That's the only way it could be."

The gunner's mate and the quartermaster stared at him but dropped the subject.

By the end of the 'day' (ship's time, for Eighty-eight had a period of eight hours and thirteen minutes), work was well under way. The transport had grounded close by a low range of hills. The Captain selected a little bowl-shaped depression in the hills, some thousand feet long and half as broad, in which to establish a permanent camp. This was to be roofed over, sealed, and an atmosphere provided.

In the hill between the ship and the valley, quarters were to be excavated; dormitories, mess hall, officers' quarters, sick bay, recreation room, offices, store rooms, and so forth. A tunnel must be bored through the hill, connecting the sites of these rooms, and connecting with a ten foot airtight metal tube sealed to the ship's portside air-lock. Both the tube and tunnel were to be equipped with a continuous conveyor belt for passengers and freight.

Libby found himself assigned to the roofing detail. He helped a metalsmith struggle over the hill with a portable atomic heater, difficult to handle because of a mass of eight hundred pounds, but weighing here only sixteen pounds. The rest of the roofing detail were breaking out and preparing to move by hand the enormous translucent tent which was to be the 'sky' of the little valley.

The metalsmith located a landmark on the inner slope of the valley, set up his heater, and commenced cutting a deep horizontal groove or step in the rock. He kept it always at the same level by following a chalk mark drawn along the rock wall. Libby enquired how the job had been surveyed so quickly.

"Easy," he was answered, "two of the quartermasters went ahead with a transit, leveled it just fifty feet above the valley floor, and clamped a searchlight to it. Then one of 'em ran like hell around the rim, making chalk marks at the height at which the beam struck."

"Is this roof going to be just fifty feet high?"

"No, it will average maybe a hundred. It bellies up in the middle from the air pressure."

"Earth normal?"

"Half Earth normal."

Libby concentrated for an instant, then looked puzzled. "But look—This valley is a thousand feet long and better than five hundred wide. At half of fifteen pounds per square inch, and allowing for the arch of the roof, that's a load of one and an eighth billion pounds. What fabric can take that kind of a load?"

"Cobwebs."

"Cobwebs?"

"Yeah, cobwebs. Strongest stuff in the world, stronger than the best steel. Synthetic spider silk. This gauge we're using for the roof has a tensile strength of four thousand pounds a running inch."

Libby hesitated a second, then replied, "I see. With a rim about eighteen hundred thousand inches around, the maximum pull at the point of anchoring would be about six hundred and twenty-five pounds per inch. Plenty safe margin."

The metalsmith leaned on his tool and nodded. "Something like that. You're pretty quick at arithmetic, aren't you, bud?"

Libbly looked startled. "I just like to get things straight."

They worked rapidly around the slope, cutting a clean smooth groove to which the 'cobweb' would be anchored and sealed. The white-hot lava spewed out of the discharge vent and ran slowly down the hillside. A brown vapor boiled off the surface of the molten rock, arose a few feet and sublimed almost at once in the vacuum to white powder which settled to the ground. The metalsmith pointed to the powder.

"That stuff 'ud cause silicosis if we let it stay there, and breathed it later."

"What do you do about it?"

"Just clean it out with the blowers of the air conditioning plant."

Libby took this opening to ask another question. "Mister—?"

"Johnson's my name. No mister necessary."

"Well, Johnson, where do we get the air for this whole valley, not to mention the tunnels? I figure we must need twenty-five million cubic feet or more. Do we manufacture it?"

"Naw, that's too much trouble. We brought it in with us."

"On the transport?"

"Uh huh, at fifty atmospheres."

Libby considered this. "I see—that way it would go into a space eighty feet on a side."

"Matter of fact it's in three specially constructed holds— giant air bottles. This transport carried air to Ganymede. I was in her then—a recruit, but in the air gang even then."

In three weeks the permanent camp was ready for occupancy and the transport cleared of its cargo. The storerooms bulged with tools and supplies. Captain Doyle had moved his administrative offices underground, signed over his command to his first officer, and given him permission to proceed on 'duty assigned'—in this case; return to Terra with a skeleton crew.

Libby watched them take off from a vantage point on the hillside. An overpowering homesickness took possession of him. Would he ever go home? He honestly believed at the time that he would swap the rest of his life for thirty minutes each with his mother and with Betty.

He started down the hill toward the tunnel lock. At least

the transport carried letters to them, and with any luck the chaplain would be by soon with letters from Earth. But to-morrow and the days after that would be no fun. He had en-joyed being in the air gang, but tomorrow he went back to his squad. He did not relish that—the boys in his squad were all right, he guessed, but he just could not seem to fit in.

This company of the C.C.C. started on its bigger job; to pock-mark Eighty-eight with rocket tubes so that Captain Doyle could push this hundred-mile marble out of her orbit and herd her in to a new orbit between Earth and Mars, to be used as a space station—a refuge for ships in distress, a haven for life boats, a fueling stop, a naval outpost.

Libby was assigned to a heater in pit H-16. It was his business to carve out carefully calculated emplacements in which the blasting crew then set off the minute charges which accomplished the major part of the excavating. Two squads were assigned to H-16, under the general supervision of an elderly marine gunner. The gunner sat on the edge of the pit, handling the plans, and occasionally making calculations on a circular slide rule which hung from a lanyard around his neck.

Libby had just completed a tricky piece of cutting for a three-stage blast, and was waiting for the blasters, when his phones picked up the gunner's instructions concerning the size of the charge. He pressed his transmitter button.

"Mr. Larsen! You've made a mistake!"

"Who said that?"

"This is Libby. You've made a mistake in the charge. If you set off that charge, you'll blow this pit right out of the ground, and us with it."

Marine Gunner Larsen spun the dials on his slide rule be-fore replying, "You're all het up over nothing, son. That charge is correct."

"No, I'm not, sir," Libby persisted, "you've multiplied where you should have divided."

"Have you had any experience at this sort of work?"

"No, sir."

Larsen addressed his next remark to the blasters. "Set the charge."

They started to comply. Libby gulped, and wiped his lips with his tongue. He knew what he had to do, but he was afraid. Two clumsy stiff-legged jumps placed him beside the blasters. He pushed between them and tore the electrodes from the detonator. A shadow passed over him as he worked, and Larsen floated down beside him. A hand grasped his arm.

"You shouldn't have done that, son. That's direct disobedience of orders. I'll have to report you." He commenced reconnecting the firing circuit.

Libby's ears burned with embarrassment, but he answered back with the courage of timidity at bay. "I had to do it, sir. You're still wrong."

Larsen paused and ran his eyes over the dogged face. "Well,—it's a waste of time, but I don't like to make you stand by a charge you're afraid of. Let's go over the calculation together."

Captain Doyle sat at his ease in his quarters, his feet on his desk. He stared at a nearly empty glass tumbler.

"That's good beer, Blackie. Do you suppose we could brew some more when it's gone?"

"I don't know, Cap'n. Did we bring any yeast?"

"Find out, will you?" He turned to a massive man who occupied the third chair. "Well, Larsen, I'm glad it wasn't any worse than it was."

"What beats me, Captain, is how I could have made such a mistake. I worked it through twice. It it had been a nitro explosive, I'd have known off hand that I was wrong. If this kid hadn't had a hunch, I'd have set it off."

Captain Doyle clapped the old warrant officer on the shoulder. "Forget it, Larsen. You wouldn't have hurt anybody; that's why I require the pits to be evacuated even for small charges. These isotope explosives are tricky at best. Look what happened in pit A-9. Ten days' work shot with one charge, and the gunnery officer himself approved that one. But I want to see this boy. What did you say his name was?"

"Libby, A.J."

Doyle touched a button on his desk. A knock sounded at the door. A bellowed "Come in!" produced a stripling wearing the brassard of Corpsman Mate-of-the-Deck.

"Have Corpsman Libby report to me."

"Aye aye, sir."

Some few minutes later Libby was ushered into the Captain's cabin. He looked nervously around, and noted Larsen's presence, a fact that did not contribute to his peace of mind. He reported in a barely audible voice, "Corpsman Libby, sir."

The Captain looked him over. "Well, Libby, I hear that

you and Mr. Larsen had a difference of opinion this morning. Tell me about it."

"I—I didn't mean any harm, sir."

"Of course not. You're not in any trouble; you did us all a good turn this morning. Tell me, how did you know that the calculation was wrong? Had any mining experience?"

"No, sir. I just saw that he had worked it out wrong."

"But how?"

Libby shuffled uneasily. "Well, sir, it just seemed wrong— It didn't fit."

"Just a second, Captain. May I ask this young man a couple of questions?" It was Commander "Blackie" Rhodes who spoke.

"Certainly. Go ahead."

"Are you the lad they call 'Pinkie'?"

Libby blushed. "Yes, sir."

"I've heard some rumors about this boy." Rhodes pushed his big frame out of his chair, went over to a bookshelf, and removed a thich volume. He thumbed through it, then with open book before him, started to question Libby.

"What's the square root of ninety-five?"

"Nine and seven hundred forty-seven thousandths."

"What's the cube root?"

"Four and five hundred sixty-three thousandths."

"What's its logarithm?"

"Its what, sir?"

"Good Lord, can a boy get through school today without knowing?"

The boy's discomfort became more intense. "I didn't get much schooling, sir. My folks didn't accept the Covenant until Pappy died, and we had to."

"I see. A logarithm is a name for a power to which you raise a given number, called the base, to get the number whose logarithm it is. Is that clear?"

Libby thought hard. "I don't quite get it, sir."

"I'll try again. If you raise ten to the second power— square it—it gives one hundred. Therefore the logarithm of a hundred to the base ten is two. In the same fashion the logarithm of a thousand to the base ten is three. Now what is the logarithm of ninety-five?"

Libby puzzled for a moment. "I can't make it come out even. It's a fraction."

"That's okay."

"Then it's one and nine hundred seventy-eight thousandths —just about."

Rhodes turned to the Captain. "I guess that about proves it, sir."

Doyle nodded thoughtfully. "Yes, the lad seems to have intuitive knowledge of arithmetical relationships. But let's see what else he has."

"I am afraid we'll have to send him back to Earth to find out properly."

Libby caught the gist of this last remark. "Please, sir, you aren't going to send me home? Maw 'ud be awful vexed with me."

"No, no, nothing of the sort. When your time is up, I want you to be checked over in the psychometrical laboratories. In the meantime I wouldn't part with you for a quarter's pay. I'd give up smoking first. But let's see what you can do."

In the ensuing hour the Captain and the Navigator heard Libby: one, deduce the Pythagorean proposition; two, derive Newton's laws of motion and Kepler's laws of ballistics from a statement of the conditions in which they obtained; three, judge length, area, and volume by eye with no measurable error. He had jumped into the idea of relativity and non-rectilinear space-time continua, and was beginning to pour forth ideas faster than he could talk, when Doyle held up a hand.

"That's enough, son. You'll be getting a fever. You run along to bed, now, and come see me in the morning. I'm taking you off field work."

"Yes, sir."

"By the way, what is your full name?"

"Andrew Jackson Libby, sir."

"No, your folks wouldn't have signed the Covenant. Good night."

"Good night, sir."

After he had gone, the two older men discussed their discovery."

"How do you size it up, Captain?"

"Well, he's a genius, of course—one of those wild talents that will show up once in a blue moon. I'll turn him loose among my books and see how he shapes up. Shouldn't wonder if he were a page-at-a-glance reader, too."

"It beats me what we turn up among these boys—and not a one of 'em any account back on Earth."

Doyle nodded. "That was the trouble with these kids. They didn't feel needed."

Eighty-eight swung some millions of miles further around the sun. The pock-marks on her face grew deeper, and were lined with durite, that strange close-packed laboratory product which (usually) would confine even atomic disintegration. Then Eighty-eight received a series of gentle pats, always on the side headed along her course. In a few weeks' time the rocket blasts had their effect and Eighty-eight was plunging in an orbit toward the sun.

When she reached her station one and three-tenths the distance from the sun of Earth's orbit, she would have to be coaxed by another series of pats into a circular orbit. Thereafter she was to be known as E-M3, Earth-Mars Space Station Spot Three.

Hundreds of millions of miles away two other C.C.C. companies were inducing two other planetoids to quit their age-old grooves and slide between Earth and Mars to land in the same orbit as Eighty-eight. One was due to ride this orbit one hundred and twenty degrees ahead of Eighty-eight, the other one hundred and twenty degrees behind. When E-M1, E-M2, and E-M3 were all on station no hard-pushed traveler of the spaceways on the Earth-Mars passage would ever again find himself far from land—or rescue.

During the months that Eighty-eight fell free toward the sun, Captain Doyle reduced the working hours of his crew and turned them to the comparatively light labor of building a hotel and converting the little roofed-in valley into a garden spot. The rock was broken down into soil, fertilizers applied, and cultures of anaerobic bacteria planted. Then plants, conditioned by thirty-odd generations of low gravity at Luna City, were set out and tenderly cared for. Except for the low gravity, Eighty-eight began to feel like home.

But when Eighty-eight approached a tangent to the hypothetical future orbit of E-M3, the company went back to maneuvering routine, watch on and watch off, with the Captain living on black coffee and catching catnaps in the plotting room.

Libby was assigned to the ballistic calculator, three tons of thinking metal that dominated the plotting room. He loved the big machine. The Chief Fire Controlman let him help adjust it and care for it. Libby subconsciously thought of it as a person—his own kind of person.

On the last day of the approach, the shocks were more frequent. Libby sat in the right-hand saddle of the calculator and droned out the predictions for the next salvo, while gloating over the accuracy with which the machine tracked. Captain Doyle fussed around nervously, occasionally stopping to peer over the Navigator's shoulder. Of course the figures were right, but what if it didn't work? No one had ever moved so large a mass before. Suppose it plunged on and on—and on. Nonsense! It couldn't. Still he would be glad when they were past the critical speed.

A marine orderly touched his elbow. "Helio from the Flagship, sir."

"Read it."

"Flag to Eighty-eight; private message, Captain Doyle; am lying off to watch you bring her in.—Kearney."

Doyle smiled. Nice of the old geezer. Once they were on station, he would invite the Admiral to ground for dinner and show him the park.

Another salvo cut loose, heavier than any before. The room trembled violently. In a moment the reports of the surface observers commenced to trickle in. "Tube nine, clear!" "Tube ten, clear!"

But Libby's drone ceased.

Captain Doyle turned on him. "What's the matter, Libby? Asleep? Call the polar stations. I have to have a parallax."

"Captain—" The boy's voice was low and shaking.

"Speak up, man!"

"Captain—the machine isn't tracking."

"Spiers!" The grizzled head of the Chief Fire Controlman appeared from behind the calculator.

"I'm already on it, sir. Let you know in a moment."

He ducked back again. After a couple of long minutes he reappeared. "Gyros tumbled. It's a twelve hour calibration job, at least."

The Captain said nothing, but turned away, and walked to the far end of the room. The Navigator followed him with his eyes. He returned, glanced at the chronometer, and spoke to the Navigator.

"Well, Blackie, if I don't have that firing data in seven minutes, we're sunk. Any suggestions?"

Rhodes shook his head without speaking.

Libby timidly raised his voice. "Captain—"

Doyle jerked around. "Yes?"

"The firing data is tube thirteen, seven point six three; tube twelve, six point nine oh; tube fourteen, six point eight nine."

Doyle studied his face. "You sure about that, son?"

"It *has* to be that, Captain."

Doyle stood perfectly still. This time he did not look at Rhodes but started straight ahead. Then he took a long pull on his cigarette, glanced at the ash, and said in a steady voice,

"Apply the data. Fire on the bell."

Four hours later, Libby was still droning out firing data, his face grey, his eyes closed. Once he had fainted but when they revived him he was still muttering figures. From time to time the Captain and the Navigator relieved each other, but there was no relief for him.

The salvos grew closer together, but the shocks were lighter.

Following one faint salvo, Libby looked up, stared at the ceiling, and spoke.

"That's all, Captain."

"Call the polar stations!"

The reports came back promptly, "Parallax constant, sidereal-solar rate constant."

The Captain relaxed into a chair. "Well, Blackie, we did it—thanks to Libby!" Then he noticed a worried, thoughtful look spread over Libby's face. "What's the matter, man? Have we slipped up?"

"Captain, you know you said the other day that you wished you had Earth-normal gravity in the park?"

"Yes. What of it?"

"If that book on gravitation you lent me is straight dope, I think I know a way to accomplish it."

The Captain inspected him as if seeing him for the first time. "Libby, you have ceased to amaze me. Could you stop doing that sort of thing long enough to dine with the Admiral?"

"Gee, Captain, that would be swell!"

The audio circuit from Communications cut in.

"Helio from Flagship: 'Well done, Eighty-eight.' "

Doyle smiled around at them all. "That's pleasant confirmation."

The audio brayed again.

"Helio from Flagship: 'Cancel last signal, stand by for correction.' "

A look of surprise and worry sprang into Doyle's face—then the audio continued:

"Helio from Flagship: 'Well done, E-M3.' "

# ISAAC ASIMOV
## PRESENTS

# THE GOLDEN YEARS OF SCIENCE FICTION

*Volume 2*

# ACKNOWLEDGMENTS

# CONTENTS

# Introduction

In the world outside reality, it was another bad year. The war that had started in 1939 continued, and on April 9 Germany invaded Norway and Denmark. On May 10, under tremendous pressure, Neville Chamberlain took his umbrella and went home, dissolving the British government, which was replaced by one under the leadership of Winston S. Churchill. On the same day, Germany invaded Belgium and Holland. Within three days the Dutch army surrendered and Churchill, noting the despair now growing in many British hearts, responded with his famous "Blood, Tears, Toil and Sweat," speech. It had no effect on the fighting, as Belgium surrendered on the 28th, and the British Expeditionary Force was evacuated from the beaches of Dunkirk, barely escaping destruction at the hands of the advancing Germans.

On June 14, the Germans entered Paris and France formally capitulated on the 22nd. The Battle of Britain raged during the daylight hours through the month of August, reaching a peak the week of 11-18th, as the RAF fought to survive—and the Germans switched to city bombing on the night of the 23rd, initiating the Blitz on London. On September 3 the U.S. drew closer to the war as Roosevelt concluded a "Lend Lease" arrangement with the British that exchanged American destroyers for long-term leases on bases in Newfoundland and in the Caribbean.

On September 16, the Selective Training and Service Act went into effect in the United States, and the draft began. Few cards were burned.

On November 3 Franklin Delano Roosevelt defeated Wendell Wilkie and prepared to start his third term as President of the United States.

During 1940 Albert Einstein presented a paper in which he argued that there was no theory that could provide a logical basis for physics as it was presently formulated. Carl Jung

9

published *The Interpretation of Personality*. Tom Harmon of the University of Michigan won the Heisman Trophy. Darius Milhaud composed *Medea*. Ernest Hemingway made a big splash with *For Whom the Bell Tolls*, while Minnesota captured the national college football championship. Charlie Chaplin directed and starred in *The Great Dictator* (Hitler was not amused). There were 32,400,000 private cars in the United States. The record for the mile run was *still* the 4:06:4 set in 1937 by Sydney Wooderson.

Construction of the first cyclotron began at the University of California. George Santayana published *The Realm of Spirit*. Whistler painted "Miss Laura Ridly." Alice Marble was still the best woman tennis player and Joe Louis was still heavyweight champion of the world. Igor Stravinsky wrote his *Symphony in C*. Eugene O'Neill's masterpiece, *Long Day's Journey into Night* was written, but would have to wait sixteen years to see production. Lawson Little won the U.S. Open Golf Championship, while the great Jimmy Demaret took the Masters.

Alfred Hitchcock's *Rebecca* and *Gaslight* were two of the top films of the year. Under the direction of Howard Florey, a team of researchers developed penicillin. The most widely sung song of the year was the German Army's "Lili Marlene." James Stewart and Ginger Rogers won Academy Awards. Johnny Mize led the majors in home runs with 43 (Hank Greenberg had 41), while somebody named Debs Garms took the batting title with a .355 average. There were 264,000 divorces in the United States. Death took Leon Trotsky (of an ice-pick in the brain) and Neville Chamberlain (of disillusionment as well as cancer).

Mel Brooks was still Melvin Kaminsky.

But in the real world it was another very good year.

In the real world the second World Science Fiction Convention (the Chicon) was held in faraway Chicago. In the real world nineteen-year-old Fred Pohl became editor (at $10 a week) of two new science fiction magazines—*Astonishing Stories* and *Super Science Stories*, while *three* more magazines, *Captain Future, Science Fiction Quarterly* and *Comet Stories* also saw the light of day for the first time.

In the real world, more important people made their maiden voyages into reality: in February—Leigh Brackett with *Martian Quest*, and H. B. Fyfe with *Locked Out*; in March—James Blish with *Emergency Refueling*; in April—

C. M. Kornbluth and Richard Wilson with *Stepsons of Mars*; and in July—Frederik Pohl with the co-authored *Before the Universe*.

More wonderous things happened in the real world: "Typewriter in the Sky" by L. Ron Hubbard and "Darker Than You Think" by Jack Williamson were published in *Unknown. Astounding Science Fiction* had three great serials— *If This Goes On* by Robert A. Heinlein, *Final Blackout* by L. Ron Hubbard (what a great one he could have been), and the immmortal *Slan* by A. E. van Vogt.

Death took fantasy writers E. F. Benson and Talbot Mundy as well as Farnsworth Wright, the great editor of the immortal *Weird Tales*.

But the distant wings were beating as Angela Carter, Thomas Disch, Peter Haining, Alexei Panshin, and Norman Spinrad were born.

Let us travel back to that honored year of 1940 and enjoy the best stories that the real world bequeathed to us.


## EDITORIAL NOTE

The reader should note that three selections by Robert A. Heinlein are missing because arrangements for their use could not be made. We regret their absence and direct the reader to *The Past Through Tomorrow* (New York: Putnam, 1967, paperback edition by Berkley), which contains all three stories.

# REQUIEM*   *Astounding Science Fiction*
## January

## by Robert A. Heinlein (1907-      )

> 1940 was to be the year of Robert Heinlein, and this
> story is the first of three in this book. "Requiem" is
> one of his most memorable stories, written at a time
> when the moon was a mystery and a fascination to
> most people. The struggle of the heroic Harriman to
> reach his objective left its mark on all who read the
> story.
> Forget the faulty predictions and enjoy a tale that
> contains the elixir of science fiction—the sense of
> wonder.

(How much more exciting the thought of reaching the
moon was *before* we reached it. We had the moon all to ourselves then. Bob's fascination with the moon weaved itself
through many stories and reached a peak with the first adult
science fiction movie, "Destination: Moon," which Bob, of
course, wrote. I never forgave Bob, though, for introducing—or allowing the introduction of—a comic Brooklynite. It
was such a silly stereotype and Bob *knew* I was from Brooklyn and would resent it. At least they might have obtained an
actor who had lived in Brooklyn and spoke the language. The
actor they did get, whom I have never seen before or since,
must have been brought up in Montana for his Brooklyn accent was simply pitiful. I.A.)

* See note following end of Introduction.

# THE DWINDLING SPHERE

*Astounding Science Fiction*

March

## by Willard Hawkins

*This fine story was rescued from oblivion by Laurence M. Janifer, who reprinted it in* Master's Choice. *Although early science fiction had (and has) a reputation for accurate prediction and stories about "today's fiction, tomorrow's fact," there were some subjects that received relatively little attention. This was especially true of issues like resource consumption, with too many writers simply "inventing" new sources of energy or not dealing with the problem at all.*

*Here is one of the early few that considered the consequences of this particular human activity.*

(It's a lucky thing I have good old Marty around. I like to think I know every story that was published in the 1930s and 1940s but for some reason I missed this one completely and I don't know Willard Hawkins either then or now. Very upsetting, especially since this is one more story that discusses fission before Hiroshima. Of course, fission of elements less complex than iron involves an *input* of energy, but what the heck. No one's perfect. The important thing in the story is a certain element of satire.)

I.A.

*EXTRACTS FROM THE DIARY OF*

*FRANK BAXTER, B.S., M.Sc.*

*June 23, 1945.* I thought today I was on the track of something, but the results, while remarkable in their way, were disapppointing. The only thing of importance I can be

13

said to have demonstrated is that, with my new technique of neutron bombardment, it is unnecessary to confine experiments to the heavier elements. This broadens the field of investigation enormously. Substituted a lump of common coal for uranium in today's experiment, and it was reduced to a small cinder. Probably oxidized, owing to a defect in the apparatus or in my procedure.

However, it seems remarkable that, despite the almost instantaneous nature of the combustion, there was no explosion. Nor, as far as I could detect, was any heat generated. In fact, I unthinkingly picked up the cinder—a small, smooth buttonlike object—and it was scarcely warm.

*June 24, 1945.* Repeated yesterday's experiment carefully checking each step, with results practically identical to yesterday's. Can it be that I am on the verge of success? But that is absurd. If—as might be assumed from the evidence—my neutron bombardment started a self-perpetuating reaction which continued until every atom in the mass had been subjected to fission, enormous energy would have been generated. In fact, I would no longer be here, all in one piece, to tell about it. Even the combustion of my lump of coal at such a practically instantaneous rate would be equivalent to exploding so much dynamite.

It is very puzzling, for the fact remains that the lump has been reduced to a fraction of its original weight and size. There is, after all, only one possible answer: the greater part of its mass must have been converted into energy. The question, then, is what became of the energy?

*June 28, 1945.* Have been continuing my experiments, checking and rechecking. I have evidently hit upon some new principle in the conversion of matter into energy. Here are some of the results thus far:

Tried the same experiment with a chuck of rock—identical result. Tried it with a lump of earth, a piece of wood, a brass doorknob. Only difference in results was the size and consistency of the resulting cinder. Have weighed the substance each time, then the residue after neutron bombardment. The original substance seems to be reduced to approximately one twentieth of its original mass, although this varies somewhat according to the strength of the magnetic field and various adjustments in the apparatus. These factors also seem to affect the composition of the cinder.

The essence of the problem, however, has thus far baffled me. Why is it that I cannot detect the force generated? What is its nature? Unless I can solve this problem, the whole discovery is pointless.

I have written to my old college roommate, Bernard Ogilvie, asking him to come and check my results. He is a capable engineer and I have faith in his honesty and common sense—even though he appears to have been lured away from scientific pursuits by commercialism.

*July 15, 1945.* Ogilvie has been here now for three days. He is greatly excited, but I am sorry that I sent for him. He has given me no help at all on my real problem—in fact, he seems more interested in the by-products than in the experiment itself. I had hoped he would help me to solve the mystery of what becomes of the energy generated by my process. Instead, he appears to be fascinated by those little chunks of residue—the cinders.

When I showed that it was possible, by certain adjustments in the apparatus, to control their texture and substance, he was beside himself with excitement. The result is that I have spent all my time since his arrival in making these cinders. We have produced them in consistency ranging all the way from hard little buttons to a mushy substance resembling cheese.

Analysis shows them to be composed of various elements, chiefly carbon and silica. Ogilvie appears to think there has been an actual transmutation of elements into this final result. I question it. The material is simply a form of ash—a residue.

We have enlarged the apparatus and installed a hopper, into which we shovel rock, debris—in fact, anything that comes handy, including garbage and other waste. If my experiment after all proves a failure, I shall at least have the ironic satisfaction of having produced an ideal incinerator. Ogilvie declares there is a fortune in that alone.

*July 20, 1945.* Bernard Ogilvie has gone. Now I can get down to actual work again. He took with him a quantity of samples and plans for the equipment. Before he left, he revealed what is on his mind. He thinks my process may revolutionize the plastics industry. What a waste of time to have called him in! A fine mind spoiled by commercialism. With an epochal discovery in sight, all he can think of is that here is an opportunity to convert raw material which costs practically nothing into commercial gadgets. He thinks the stuff can be molded and shaped—perhaps through a matrix principle incorporated right in the apparatus.

Partly, I must confess, to get rid of him, I signed the agreement he drew up. It authorizes him to patent the process in my name, and gives me a major interest in all subsidiary devices and patents that may be developed by his engineers. He himself is to have what he calls the promotion rights, but there is some sort of a clause whereby the control reverts wholly to me or to my heirs at his death. Ogilvie says it will mean millions to both of us.

He undoubtedly is carried away by his imagination. What could I do with such an absurd sum of money? However, a few thousand dollars might come in handy for improved equipment. I must find a means of capturing and controlling that energy.

## EXTRACTS FROM THE DIARY OF QUENTIN BAXTER, PRESIDENT OF PLASTOSCENE PRODUCTS, INC.

*August 3, 2065.* I have made a discovery today which moved me profoundly—so profoundly that I have opened this journal so that my own thoughts and reactions may be likewise recorded for posterity. Diary-keeping has heretofore appeared to me as a rather foolish vanity—it now appears in an altogether different light.

The discovery which so altered my viewpoint was of a diary kept by my great-grandfather, Frank Baxter, the actual inventor of plastoscene.

I have often wondered what sort of a man this ancestor of mine could have been. History tells us almost nothing about him. I feel that I know him as intimately as I know my closest associates. And what a different picture this diary gives from the prevailing concept!

Most of us have no doubt thought of the discoverer of the plastoscene principle as a man who saw the need for a simple method of catering to humanity's needs—one which would supplant the many laborious makeshifts of his day—and painstakingly set out to evolve it.

Actually, the discovery appears to have been an accident. Frank Baxter took no interest in its development—regarded it as of little account. Think of it! An invention more revolutionary than the discovery of fire, yet its inventor failed entirely to grasp its importance! To the end of his days it was to him merely a by-product. He died considering himself a failure, because he was unable to attain the goal he sought—the creation of atomic power.

In a sense, much of the credit apparently belongs to his friend Bernard Ogilvie, who grasped the possibilities inherent in the new principle. Here again, what a different picture the diary gives from that found in our schoolbooks! The historians would have us regard Frank Baxter as a sort of master mind, Bernard Ogilvie as his humble disciple and Man Friday.

Actually, Ogilvie was a shrewd promoter who saw the possibilities of the discovery and exploited them—not especially to benefit humanity, but for personal gain. We must give him credit, however, for a scrupulous honesty which was amazing for his time. It would have been easy for him to take advantage of the impractical, dreamy scientist. Instead, he arranged that the inventor of the process should reap its rewards, and it is wholly owing to his insistence that control reverted to our family, where it has remained for more than a century.

All honor to these two exceptional men!

Neither, it is true, probably envisioned the great changes that would be wrought by the discovery. My ancestor remained to the end of his days dreamy and aloof, concerned solely with his futile efforts to trap the energy which he was sure he had released. The wealth which rolled up for him through Plastoscene Products, Inc.—apparently the largest individual fortune of his time—was to him a vague abstraction. I find a few references to it in his diary, but they are written in a spirit of annoyance. He goes so far as to mention once—apparently exasperated because the responsibilities of his position called him away from his experiments for a few hours—that he would like to convert the millions into hard currency and pour them into a conversion hopper, where at least they might be turned into something useful.

It is strange, by the way, that the problem he posed has never been demonstrably solved. Scientists still are divided in their allegiance to two major theories—one, that the force generated by this conversion of elements escapes into the fourth dimension; the other that it is generated in the form of radiations akin to cosmic rays, which are dissipated with a

velocity approaching the infinite. These rays do not affect ordinary matter, according to the theory, because they do not
impinge upon it, but instead pass through it, as light passes
through a transparent substance.

*August 5, 2065.* I have read and reread my grandfather's
diary, and confess that I more and more find in him a
kindred spirit. His way of life seems to me infinitely more ap-
pealing than that which inheritance has imposed upon me.
The responsibilities resting on my shoulders, as reigning head
of the Baxter dynasty, become exceedingly onerous at times. I
even find myself wondering whether plastoscene has, after all,
proved such an unmixed blessing for mankind.

Perhaps the greatest benefits may lie in the future. Certainly each stage in its development has been marked by
economic readjustments—some of them well-night world-
shattering. I have often been glad that I did not live through
those earlier days of stress, when industry after industry was
wiped out by the remorseless juggernaut of technological
progress. When, for example, hundreds of thousands were
thrown out of employment in the metal-mining and -refining
and allied industries. It was inevitable that plastoscene substi-
tutes, produced at a fraction of the cost from common dirt of
the fields, should wipe out this industry—but the step could
have been taken, it seems to me, without subjecting the dis-
possessed workers and employers to such hardship, thereby
precipitating what amounted to a civil war. When we pause
to think of it, almost every article in common use today
represents one or more of those industries which was similarly wiped out, and on which vast numbers of people depended for their livelihood.

We have, at length, achieved a form of stable society—but
I, for one, am not wholly satisfied with it. What do we have?
A small owning class—a cluster of corporations grouped
around the supercorporation, Plastoscene Products, Inc., of
which I am—heaven help me!—the hereditary ruler. Next, a
situation-holding class, ranging from scientists, executives and
technicians down to the mechanical workers. Here again—because there are so few situations open, compared with the
vast reservoir of potential producers—the situation holders
have developed what amounts to a system of hereditary succession. I am told that it is almost impossible for one whose
father was not a situation holder even to obtain the training

necessary to qualify him for any of the jealously guarded positions.

Outside of this group is that great, surging mass, the major part of human society. These millions, I grant, are fed and clothed and housed and provided with a standard of living which their ancestors would have regarded as luxurious. Nevertheless, their lot is pitiful. They have no incentives; their status is that of a subject class. Particularly do I find distasteful the law which makes it a crime for any member of this enforced leisure group to be caught engaging in useful labor. The appalling number of convictions in our courts for this crime shows that there is in mankind an instinct to perform useful service, which cannot be eradicated merely by passing laws.

The situation is unhealthy as well from another standpoint. To me it seems a normal thing that society should progress. Yet we cannot close our eyes to the fact that the most highly skilled scientific minds the world has ever known have failed to produce a worthwhile advance in technology for over a quarter of a century. Has science become sterile? No. In fact, every schoolboy knows the answer.

Our scientists do not dare to announce their discoveries. I am supposed to shut my eyes to what I know—that every vital discovery along the lines of technology has been suppressed. The plain, blunt truth is that we dare not introduce any technical advance which would eliminate more situation holders. A major discovery—one that reduced an entire class of situation holders to enforced leisure—would precipitate another revolution.

Is human society, as a result of its greatest discovery, doomed to sterility?

*October 17, 2089.* It has been nearly a quarter of a century since I first read the diary of my great-grandfather, Frank Baxter. I felt an impulse to get it out to show to my son, and before I realized it I had reread the volume in its entirety. It stirred me even more than it did back in my younger days. I must preserve its crumbling pages in facsimile, on permanent plastoscene parchment, so that later descendants—finding our two journals wrapped together— will thrill as I have thrilled to that early record of achievement.

The reading has crystallized thoughts long dormant in my mind. I am nearing the end of the trail. Soon I will turn over the presidency of Plastoscene Products, Inc. to my son—if he desires it. Perhaps he will have other ideas. He is now a full-fledged Pl. T.D. Doctor of Plastoscene Technology. It may be that power and position will mean as little to him as they have come to mean to me. I shall send for him tomorrow.

*October 18, 2089.* I have had my discussion with Philip, but I fear I bungled matters. He talked quite freely of his experiments. It seems that he has been working along the line of approach started by Levinson some years ago. As we know, the plastoscene principle in use involves the making of very complex adjustments. That is to say, if we wish to manufacture some new type of object—say a special gyroscope bearing—the engineer in charge first sets the machine to produce material of a certain specific hardness and temper, then he adjusts the controls which govern size and shape, and finally, having roughly achieved the desired result, he refines the product with micrometer adjustments—but largely through the trial-and-error method—until the quality, dimensions and so on meet the tests of his precision instruments. If the object involved is complex—involving two or more compounds, for example—the adjustments are correspondingly more difficult. We have not succeeded in producing palatable foodstuffs, though our engineers have turned out some messes which are claimed to have nourishing qualities. I suspect that the engineers have purposely made them nauseating to the taste.

True, once the necessary adjustments have been made, they are recorded on microfilm. Thereafter, it is only necessary to feed this film into the control box, where the electric eye automatically makes all the adjustments for which the skill of the technician was initially required. Levinson, however, proposed to reproduce natural objects in plastoscene by photographic means.

It is this process which Philip appparently has perfected. His method involves a three-dimensional "scanning" device which records the texture, shape and the exact molecular structure of the object to be reproduced. The record is made on microfilm, which then needs only to be passed through the control box to re-create the object as many times as may be required.

"Think of the saving of effort!" Philip remarked enthusiastically. "Not only can objects of the greatest intricacy be reproduced without necessity of assembling, but even natural foods can be created in all their flavor and nourishing quality. I have eaten synthetic radishes—I have even tasted synthetic chicken—that could not be told from the original which formed its matrix."

"You mean," I demanded in some alarm, "that you can reproduce life?"

His face clouded. "No. That is a quality that seems to elude the scanner. But I can reproduce the animal, identical with its live prototype down to the last nerve tip and hair, except that it is inert—lifeless. The radishes I spoke of will not grow in soil—they cannot reproduce themselves—but chemically and in cell structure they image the originals."

"Philip," I declared, "this is an amazing achievement! It removes the last limitation upon the adaptability of plastoscene. It means that we can produce not merely machine parts but completely assembled machines. It means that foodstuffs can be—"

I stopped, brought to myself by his sudden change in expression.

"True, Father," he observed coldly, "except that it happens to be a pipe dream. I did not expect that you would be taken in by my fairy talc. I have an engagement and must go."

He hurried from the room before I could get my wits about me.

*October 23, 2089.* Philip has been avoiding me, but I managed at last to corner him.

I began this time by mentioning that it would soon be necessary for me to turn over the burden of Plastoscene Products, Inc. to him as my logical successor.

He hesitated, then blurted, "Father, I know this is going to hurt you, but I don't want to carry on the succession. I prefer to remain just a cog in the engineering department."

"Responsibility," I reminded him, "is something that cannot be honorably evaded."

"Why should it be my responsibility?" he demanded vehemently. "I didn't ask to be your son."

"Nor," I countered, "did I ask to be my father's son, nor the great-grandson of a certain inventor who died in the twentieth century. Philip, I want you to do one thing for me. Take this little book, read it, then bring it back and tell me what you think of it." I handed him Frank Baxter's diary.

*October 24, 2089.* Philip brought back the diary today. He admitted that he had sat up all night reading it.

"But I'm afraid the effect isn't what you expected," he told me frankly. "Instead of instilling the idea that we Baxters have a divine mission to carry on the dynasty, it makes me feel that our responsibility is rather to undo the damage already caused by our meddling. That old fellow back there—Frank Baxter—didn't intend to produce this hideous stuff."

"Hideous stuff?" I demanded.

"Don't be shocked, Father," he said, a trifle apologetically. "I can't help feeling rather deeply about this. Perhaps you think we're better off than people in your great-grandfather's time. I doubt it. They had work to do. There may have been employment problems, but it wasn't the enforced idleness of our day. Look at Frank Baxter—he could work and invent things with the assurance that he was doing something to advance mankind. He wasn't compelled to cover up his discoveries for fear they'd cause further—"

He stopped suddenly, as if realizing that he had said more than he intended.

"My boy," I told him, speaking slowly, "I know just how you feel—and knowing it gives me more satisfaction than you can realize."

He stared at me, bewildered. "You mean—you don't want me to take on the succession?"

I unfolded my plan.

*FROM THE DIARY OF RAN RAXLER, TENTH-RANKING HONOR STUDENT, NORTH-CENTRAL FINALS, CLASS OF 2653*

*December 28, 2653.* I have had two thrills today—an exciting discovery right on the heels of winning my diploma in the finals. Being one of the high twenty practically assures me of a chance to serve in the production pits this year.

But the discovery—I must record that first of all. It consists of a couple of old diaries. I found them in a chestful of family heirlooms which I rescued as they were about to be tossed into the waste tube. In another minute, they would have been on their way to the community plastoscene converter.

There has been a legend in our family that we are descended from the original discoverer of plastoscene, and this find surely tends to prove it. Even the name is significant. Frank Baxter. Given names as well as surnames are passed down through the generations. My grandfather before me was Ran Raxler. The dropping of a letter here, the corruption of another there, could easily have resulted in the modification of Frank Baxter to Ran Raxler.

What a thrill it will be to present to the world the authentic diary of the man who discovered the plastoscene principle! Not the impossible legendary figure, but the actual, flesh-and-blood man. And what a shock it will be to many! For it appears that Frank Baxter stumbled upon this discovery quite by accident, and regarded it to the end of his days as an unimportant by-product of his experiments.

And this later Baxter—Quentin—who wrote the companion diary and sealed the two together. What a martyr to progress he proved himself—he and his son, Philip. The diary throws an altogether different light on their motives than has been recorded in history. Instead of being selfish oligarchs who were overthrown by a mass uprising, this diary reveals that they themselves engineered the revolution.

The final entry in Quentin Baxter's diary consists of these words: "I unfolded my plan." The context—when taken with the undisputed facts of history—makes it clear what the plan must have been. As I reconstruct it, the Baxters, father and son, determined to abolish the control of plastoscene by a closed corporation of hereditary owners, and to make it the property of the whole people.

The son had perfected the scanning principle which gives plastoscene its present unlimited range. His impulse was to withhold it—in fact, it had become a point of honor among technicians to bury such discoveries, after showing them to a few trusted associates. Incomprehensible? Perhaps so at first, but not when we understand the upheavals such discoveries might cause in the form of society then existing. To make this clear, I should, perhaps, point to the record of history, which proves that up to the time of plastoscene, foodstuffs had been largely produced by growing them in the soil. This was accomplished through a highly technical process, which I cannot explain, but I am told that the University of Antarctica maintains an experimental laboratory in which the method is actually demonstrated to advanced classes. Moreover, we know what these foods were like through the microfilm matrices which still reproduce some of them for us.

The right to produce such foods for humanity's needs was jealously guarded by the great agricultural aristocracy. And, of course, this entire situation-holding class, together with many others, would be abolished by Philip's invention.

We know what happened. Despite the laws prohibiting the operation of plastoscene converters except by licensed technicians and situation holders, contraband machines suddenly began to appear everywhere among the people. Since these machines were equipped with the new scanning principle, it is obvious, in view of the diary, that they must have been deliberately distributed at strategic points by the Baxters.

At first, the contraband machines were confiscated and destroyed—but since they were, of course, capable of reproducing themselves through the matrix library of microfilm which was standard equipment, the effort to keep pace with their spread through the masses was hopeless. The ruling hierarchies appealed to the law, and to the Baxters, whose hereditary control of the plastoscene monopoly had been supposedly a safeguard against its falling into the hands of the people as a whole. The Baxters, father and son, then played their trump card. They issued a proclamation deeding the plastoscene principle in perpetuity to all the people. History implies that they were forced to do this—but fails to explain how or why. There was a great deal of confusion and bloodshed during this period; no wonder that historians jumped at conclusions—even assuming that the Baxters were assassinated by revolutionists, along with others of the small owning group who made a last stand, trying to preserve their monopolies. In light of Quentin Baxter's diary, there is far better ground for believing that they were executed by members of their own class, who regarded them as traitors.

We should be thankful indeed that those ancient days of war and bloodshed are over. Surely such conditions can never reappear on Earth. What possible reason can there be for people to rise up against each other? Just as we can supply all our needs with plastoscene, so can our neighbors on every continent supply theirs.

*March 30, 2654.* I have completed my service in the production pits, and thrilling weeks they have been. To have a part in the great process which keeps millions of people alive, even for a brief four weeks' period, makes one feel that life has not been lived in vain.

One could hardly realize, without such experience, what enormous quantities of raw material are required for the sustenance and needs of the human race. How fortunate I am to have been one of the few to earn this privilege of what the ancients called "work."

The problem must have been more difficult in the early days. Where we now distribute raw-material concentrates in the form of plastoscene-B, our forefathers had to transport the actual rock as dredged from the gravel pits. Even though the process of distribution was mechanical and largely automatic, still it was cumbersome, since material for conversion is required in a ratio of about twenty to one as compared with the finished product.

Today, of course, we have the intermediate process, by which soil and rock are converted at the pits into blocks of plastoscene-B. This represents, in a sense, the conversion process in an arrested stage. The raw material emerges in these blocks reduced to a tenth of its original weight and an even smaller volume than it will occupy in the finished product—since the mass has been increased by close packing of molecules.

A supply of concentrate sufficient to last the ordinary family for a year can now easily be stored in the standard-sized converter, and even the huge community converters have a capacity sufficient to provide for all the building, paving of roadways, recarpeting of recreation grounds, and like purposes, that are likely to be required in three months' time. I understand that experimental stations in South America are successfully introducing liquid concentrate, which can be piped directly to the consumers from the vast production pits.

I was amused on my last day by a question asked by a ten-year-old boy, the son of one of the supervisors. We stood on a rampart overlooking one of the vast production pits, several hundred feet deep and miles across—the whole space filled with a bewildering network of towers, girders, cranes, spires and cables, across and through which flashed transports of every variety. Far below us, the center of all this activity, could be discerned the huge conversion plant, in which the rock is reduced to plastoscene-B.

The little boy looked with awe at the scene, then turned his face upward, demanding, "What are we going to do when this hole gets so big that it takes up the whole world?"

We laughed, but I could sympathize with the question. Man is such a puny creature that it is difficult for him to realize what an infinitesimal thing on the Earth's surface is a cavity which to him appears enormous. The relationship, I

should say, is about the same as a pinprick to a ball which a
child can toss in the air.

*FROM THE INTRODUCTION TO OUR EIGHTY
YEARS' WAR, SIGNED BY GLUX GLUXTON, CHIEF
HISTORIAN, THE NAPHALI INSTITUTE OF SCIENCE
(DATED AS OF THE SIXTH DAY, SIXTH LUNAR
MONTH, YEAR 10,487)*

The Eighty Years' War is over. It has been concluded by a
treaty of eternal amity signed at Latex on the morning of the
twenty-ninth day of the fifth month.

By the terms of the treaty, all peoples of the world agree
to subject themselves to the control by the World Court. The
Court, advised through surveys continuously conducted by
the International Institute of Science, will have absolute authority over the conversion of basic substance into plastoscene, to the end that further disputes between regions and
continents shall be impossible.

To my distinguished associates and to myself was allotted
the task of compiling a history of the causes behind this prolonged upheaval and of its course. How well we have
succeeded posterity must judge. In a situation so complex,
how, indeed, may one declare with assurance which were the
essential causes? Though known as *the* Eighty Years' War, a
more accurate expression would be "the Eighty Years *of*
War," for the period has been one marked by a constant succession of wars—of outbreaks originating spontaneously and
from divers causes in various parts of the world.

Chief among the basic causes, of course, were the disputes
between adjoining districts over the right to extend their conversion pits beyond certain boundaries. Nor can we overlook
the serious situation precipitated when it was realized that the
Antarctican sea-water conversion plants were sucking up such
great quantities that the level of the oceans was actually
being lowered—much as the Great Lakes once found on the
North American continent were drained of their water centuries ago. Disputes, alliances and counteralliances, regions
arrayed against each other, and finally engines of war raining
fearful destruction. What an unprecedented bath of blood the
world has endured!

The whole aim, from this time forth, will be to strip off the
earth's surface evenly, so that it shall become smooth and
even, not rough and unsightly and covered with abandoned

pits as now viewed from above. To prevent a too rapid lowering of sea level, it is provided that Antarctica and some other sections which have but a limited amount of land surface shall be supplied with concentrate from the more favored regions.

Under such a treaty, signed with fervent good will by the representatives of a war-weary world population, is it far-fetched to assert that permanent peace has been assured? Your historian holds that it is not.

## FROM THE REPORT OF RAGNAR DUGH, DELEGATE TO THE WORLD PEACE CONFERENCE, TO THE 117th DISTRICT (CIRCUIT 1092, REV. 148)

Honored confrères: It gives me pleasure to present, on behalf of the district which has honored me as its representative, concurrence in the conditions for peace as proposed in the majority report.

As I view your faces in the televisor, I see in them the same sense of deep elation that I feel in the thought that this exhausting era of bloodshed and carnage has run its course, and that war is to be rendered impossible from this time forth. Is this too strong a statement? I read in your eyes that it is not, for we are at last abolishing the cause of war—namely, the overcrowding of the earth's surface.

The proposed restrictions may seem drastic, but the human race will accustom itself to them. And let us remember that they would be even more drastic if the wars themselves had not resulted in depopulating the world to a great extent. I am glad that it has not been found necessary to impose a ten-year moratorium on all childbearing. As matters stand, by limiting childbirth to a proportion of one child per circuit of the sun for each three deaths within any given district, scientists agree that the population of the earth will be reduced at a sufficient rate to relieve the tension.

The minority report, which favors providing more room for the population by constructing various levels or concentric shells, which would gird the world's surface and to which addditional levels would be added as needed, I utterly condemn. It is impractical chiefly for the reason that the conversion of so much material into these various dwelling surfaces would cause a serious shrinkage in the earth's mass.

Let us cast our votes in favor of the majority proposition, thus insuring a long life for the human race and for the sphere on which we dwell, and removing the last cause of war between peoples of the earth.

## FROM THE MEMOIRS OF XLAR XVII, PRINCEP OF PLES

*Cycle 188, 400-43.* What an abomination is this younger generation! I am glad the new rules limit offspring to not more than one in a district per cycle. My nephew, Ryk LVX, has been saturating himself with folklore at the Museum of Antiquity, and had the audacity to assure me that there are records which suggest the existence of mankind before plastoscope. Why will people befog their minds with the supernatural?

"There is a theory," he brazenly declared, "that at one time the world was partly composed of food, which burst up through its crust ready for the eating. It is claimed that even the carpet we now spread over the earth's surface had its correspondence in a substance which appeared there spontaneously."

"In that case," I retorted sarcastically, "what became of this—this exudation of the rocks?"

Of course, he had an answer ready: "Plastoscene was discovered and offered mankind an easier method of supplying its needs, with the result that the surface of the earth, containing the growth principle, was stripped away. I do not say that this is a fact," he hastened to add, "but merely that it may have some basis."

Here is what I told my nephew. I sincerely tried to be patient and to appeal to his common sense. "The basis in fact is this: It is true that the earth's surface has been many times stripped during the long existence of the human race. There is only one reasonable theory of life on this planet. Originally man—or rather his evolutionary predecessor—possessed within himself a digestive apparatus much wider in scope than at present. He consumed the rock, converted it into food, and thence into the elements necessary to feed his tissues, all within his own body. Eventually, as he developed intelligence, man learned how to produce plastoscene by mechanical means. He consumed this product as food, as well as using it for the myriad other purposes of his daily life. As a result, the organs within his own body no longer were needed to produce plastoscene directly from the rock. They gradually atrophied and disappeared, leaving only their vestiges in the present digestive tract."

This silenced the young man for a time, but I have no doubt he will return later with some other fantastic delusion. On one occasion it was the legend that, instead of being twin planets, our earth and Luna were at one time of differing sizes, and that Luna revolved around the earth as some of the distant moons revolve around their primaries. This theory has been thoroughly discredited. It is true that there is a reduction of the earth's mass every time we scrape its surface to produce according to our needs; but it is incredible that the earth could ever have been several times the size of its companion planet, as these imaginative theorists would have us believe. They forget, no doubt, that the volume and mass of a large sphere is greater, in proportion to its area and consequent human population, than that of a smaller sphere. Our planet even now would supply man for an incomprehensible time, yet it represents but a tiny fraction of such a mass as these theorists would have us believe in. They forget that diminution would proceed at an ever-mounting rate as the size decreased; that such a huge sphere as they proposed would have lasted forever.

It is impossible. As impossible as to imagine that a time will come when there will be no more Earth for man's conversion—

# THE AUTOMATIC PISTOL

*Weird Tales*
May

## by Fritz Leiber (1910-        )

*Fritz Leiber has been getting away with murder
for many years in the sense that he is a major
science fiction writer who writes mainly fantasy. He
has won six Hugo and two Nebula Awards for stories and novels like "Gonna Roll the Bones"
(1967) and The Big Time (1958), but it is his
"Gray Mouser" stories that have the most devoted
following. Two of his early novels are classics:
Conjure Wife (Unknown, 1943) and Gather,
Darkness, originally a three-part serial in Astounding in 1943. Few writers have maintained such a
high standard over so long a period.*

*"The Automatic Pistol" is one of his best short
stories, despite the fact that it was passed over in
The Best of Fritz Leiber in 1974.*

(The thing about Fritz that is entirely unfair—and I've
complained about this in print before—is that he is tall, distinguished and good-looking. He looks like a Shakespearian
actor and, in fact, his father *was* one, and a good one. Why
is this unfair? Because writers are supposed to be eccentric
and peculiar, darn it. I get away with murder because of that
notion. I can be sloppy or do childish things and everyone
smiles and says, forgivingly, "Oh, well, you know what
writers are like." Then they see Fritz and suddenly I find myself held to an impossibly high standard. Oh, well. I.A.)

Inky never let anyone but himself handle his automatic pistol, or even touch it. It was blue-black and hefty and when

30

you just pressed the trigger once, eight .45 caliber slugs came out of it almost on top of each other.

Inky was something of a mechanic, as far as his automatic went. He would break it down and put it together again, and every once in a while carefully rub a file across the inside trigger catch.

Glasses once told him, "You will make that gun into such a hair-trigger that it will go off in your pocket and blast off all your toes. You will only have to think about it and it will start shooting."

Inky smiled at that, I remember, and didn't bother to say anything. He was a little wiry man with a pale face, from which he couldn't ever shave off the blue-black of his beard, no matter how close he shaved. His hair was black too. When he talked, there was a foreign sound to his voice. He got together with Anton Larsen just after prohibition came, in the days when sea-skiffs with converted automobile motors used to play tag with revenue cutters in New York Bay and off the Jersey coast, both omitting to use lights in order to make the game more difficult. Larsen and Kozacs used to get their booze off a steamer and run it in near the Twin Lights in New Jersey.

It was there that Glasses and I started to work for them. Glasses, who looked like a cross between a college professor and an automobile salesman, came from I don't know where in New York City, and I was a local small-town policeman until I determined to lead a more honest life. We used to ride the stuff back toward Newark in a truck.

Inky always rode in with us; Larsen only occasionally. Neither of them used to talk much; Larsen, because he didn't see any sense in talking unless to give a guy orders or make a proposition; and Inky, well, I guess because he wasn't any too happy talking American. And there wasn't a ride Inky took with us but he didn't slip out his automatic and sort of pet it and mutter at it under his breath. Once when we were restfully chugging down the highway Glasses asked him, polite but inquiring:

"Just what is it makes you so fond of that gun? After all, there must be thousands identically like it."

"You think so?" says Inky, giving us a quick stare from his little, glinty black eyes and making a speech for once. "Let me tell you, Glasses" (he made the word sound like 'Hlasses'), "nothing is alike in this world. People, guns, bottles of Scotch—nothing. Everything in the world is different. Every man has different fingerprints; and, of all guns made in the same factory as this one, there is not one like mine. I could pick mine out from a hundred. Yes, even if I hadn't filed the trigger catch, I could do that."

We didn't contradict him. It sounded pretty reasonable. He sure loved that gun, all right. He slept with it under his pillow. I don't think it ever got more than three feet away from him as long as he lived. There is something crazy in a man feeling that way about a gun.

Once when Larsen was riding in with us, he remarked sarcastically in his heavy voice, "That is a pretty little gun, Inky, but I am getting very tired of hearing you talk to it so much, especially when no one can understand what you are saying. Doesn't it ever talk back to you?"

Inky didn't smile at this. "My gun only knows eight words," he said, "and they are practically all alike. They are eight lead slugs."

This was such a good crack that we laughed.

"Let's have a look at it," said Larsen, reaching out his hand.

But Inky put it back in his pocket and didn't take it out for the rest of the trip.

After that Larsen was always kidding Inky about the gun, and trying to get his goat. He was a persistent guy with a very peculiar sense of humor, and he kept it up for a long time after it had stopped being funny. Finally he took to acting as if he wanted to buy it, making Inky crazy offers of one or two hundred dollars.

"Two hundred and seventy-five dollars, Inky," he said one evening as we were rattling past Keansburg with a load of cognac and Irish whisky. "That's my last offer, and you better take it."

Inky shook his head and made a funny grimace that was almost like a snarl. Then, to my great surprise (I almost ran the truck off the pavement) Larsen lost his temper.

"Hand over that damn gun!" he bellowed, grabbing Inky's shoulders and shaking him. I was almost knocked off the seat. Somebody would have been hurt, or worse, if a motorcycle cop hadn't stopped us just at that moment to ask for his hush-money. By the time he was gone, Larsen and Inky were both cooled down below the danger point, and there was no more fighting. We got our load safely into the warehouse, nobody saying a word.

Afterward, when Glasses and I were having a cup of coffee

at a little open-all-night restaurant, I said, "Those two guys are crazy, and I don't like it a bit. Why the devil do they have to act that way, now that the business is going so swell? I haven't got the brains Larsen has, but you won't ever find me fighting about a gun as if I was a kid."

Glasses only smiled as he poured a precise half-spoonful of sugar into his cup.

"And Inky's as bad as *he* is," I went on. "I tell you, Glasses, it ain't natural or normal for a man to feel that way about a piece of metal. I can understand him being fond of it and feeling lost without it. I feel the same way about my lucky half-dollar. It's the way he pets it and makes love to it that gets on my nerves. And now Larsen's acting the same way."

Glasses shrugged. "We're all getting a little jittery, although we won't admit it," he said. "Too many bootleggers being shot up by hijackers. And so we start getting on each other's nerves and fighting about trifles—such as automatic pistols."

"There may be something there."

Glasses winked at me. "Why, certainly, No Nose; that's something else again. I even have another explanation of tonight's events."

"What?"

He leaned over and whispered in a mock-mysterious way, "Maybe there's something queer about the gun itself."

I told him in impolite language to go chase himself.

From that night, however, things were changed. Larsen and Inky Kozacs never spoke to each other any more except in the line of business. And there was no more talk, kidding or serious, about the gun. Inky only brought it out when Larsen wasn't along.

Well, the years kept passing and the bootlegging business stayed good except that the hijackers became more numerous and Inky got a couple of chances to show us what a nice noise his automatic made. Then, too, we got into a row with another gang in our line under an Irishman named Luke Dugan, and had to watch our step very carefully and change our routes about every other trip.

Still, business was good. I continued to support almost all my relatives, and Glasses put away a few dollars every month for what he called his Persian Cat Fund, Larsen, I believe, spent about everything he got on women and all that goes with them. He was the kind of guy who would take all the pleasures of life without cracking a smile, but who lived for them just the same.

As for Inky Kozacs, we never knew what happened to the money he made. We never heard of him spending much, so we finally figured he must be saving it—probably in bills in a safety deposit box, if I know his kind. Maybe he was planning to go back to the Old Country, wherever that was, and be somebody. At any rate he never told us. By the time Congress took our profession away from us, he must have had a whale of a lot of dough. We hadn't had a big racket, but we'd been very careful.

Finally the night came when we ran our last load. We'd have had to quit the business pretty soon anyway, because the big syndicates were demanding more protection money each week. There was no chance left for a small independent operator, even if he was as clever as Larsen. So Glasses and I took a couple of months off for vacation before thinking what to do next for his Persian cats and my shiftless relatives. For the time being we stuck together.

Then one morning I read in the paper that Inky Kozacs had been taken for a ride. He'd been found shot dead on a dump heap near Elizabeth, New Jersey.

"I guess Luke Dugan finally got him," said Glasses.

"A nasty break," I said, "especially figuring all that money he hadn't gotten any fun out of. I am glad that you and I, Glasses, aren't important enough for Dugan to bother about."

"Yeah. Say, No Nose, does it say if they found Inky's gun on him?"

I said it told that the dead man was unarmed and that no weapon was found on the scene.

Glasses remarked that it was queer to think of Inky's gun being in anyone else's pocket. I agreed, and we spent some time wondering whether Inky had had a chance to defend himself.

About two hours later Larsen called and told us to meet him at the hideout. He said Luke Dugan was gunning for him too.

The hideout is a three-room frame bungalow with a big corrugated iron garage next to it. The garage was for the truck, and sometimes we would store a load of booze there when we heard that the police were going to make some arrests for the sake of variety. It is near Keansburg, and is about a mile and a half from the cement highway and about a quarter of a mile from the bay and the little inlet in which we used to hide our boat. Stiff, knife-edged sea-grass, taller than a man, comes up near to the house on the bay side, which is north, and on the west too. Under the sea-grass the ground is marshy, though in hot weather and when the tides aren't high, it gets dry and caked; here and there creeks of tidewater go through it. Even a little breeze will make the blades of sea-grass scrape each other with a funny dry sound.

To the east are some fields, and beyond them, Keansburg. Keansburg is a very cheap summer resort town and many of the houses are built up on poles because of the tides and storms. It has a little lagoon for the boats of the fishermen who go out after crabs.

To the south of the hideout is the dirt road leading to the cement highway. The nearest house is about half a mile away.

It was late in the afternoon when Glasses and I got there. We brought groceries for a couple of days, figuring Larsen might want to stay. Then, along about sunset, we heard Larsen's coupé turning in, and I went out to put it in the big, empty garage and carry in his suitcase. When I got back Larsen was talking to Glasses. He was a big man and his shoulders were broad both ways, like a wrestler's. His head was almost bald and what was left of his hair was a dirty yellow. His eyes were little and his face wasn't given much to expression. And there wasn't any expression to it when he said, "Yeah, Inky got it."

"Luke Dugan's crazy gunmen sure hold a grudge," I observed.

Larsen nodded his head and scowled.

"Inky got it," he repeated, taking up his suitcase and starting for the bedroom. "And I'm planning to stay here for a few days, just in case they're after me too. I want you and Glasses to stay here with me."

Glasses gave me a funny wink and began throwing a meal together. I turned on the lights and pulled down the blinds, taking a worried glance down the road, which was empty. This waiting around in a lonely house for a bunch of gunmen to catch up with you didn't appeal to me. Nor to Glasses either, I guessed. It seemed to me that it would have been a lot more sensible for Larsen to put a couple of thousand miles between him and New York. But, knowing Larsen, I had sense enough not to make any comments.

After canned corned-beef hash and beans and beer, we sat around the table drinking coffee.

Larsen took an automatic out of his pocket and began fooling with it, and right away I saw it was Inky's. For about five minutes nobody said a word. The silence was so thick you could have cut it in chunks and sold it for ice cubes. Glasses played with his coffee, pouring in the cream one drop at a time. I wadded a piece of bread into little pellets and kicked myself for feeling so uneasy and sick at the stomach.

Finally Larsen looked up at us and said, "Too bad Inky didn't have this with him when he was taken for a ride. He gave it to me just before he planned sailing for the old country. He didn't want it with him any more, now that the racket's all over."

"I'm glad the guy that killed him hasn't got it now," said Glasses quickly. He talked nervously and at random, as if he didn't want the silence to settle down again. "It's a funny thing, Inky giving up his gun—but I can understand his feeling; he mentally associated the gun with our racket; when the one was over he didn't care about the other."

Larsen grunted, which meant for Glasses to shut up.

"What's going to happen to Inky's dough?" I asked.

Larsen shrugged his shoulders and went on fooling with the automatic, throwing a shell into the chamber, cocking it, and so forth. It reminded me so much of the way Inky used to handle it that I got fidgety and began to imagine I heard Luke Dugan's gunmen creeping up through the sea-grass. Finally I got up and started to walk around.

It was then that the accident happened. Larsen, after cocking the gun, was bringing up his thumb to let the hammer down easy, when it slipped out of his hand. As it hit the floor it went off with a flash and a bang, sending the slug gouging the floor too near my foot for comfort.

As soon as I realized I wasn't hit, I yelled without thinking, "I always told Inky he was putting too much of a hair-trigger on his gun! The crazy fool!"

"Inky is too far away to hear you," remarked Glasses.

Larsen sat with his pig eyes staring down at the gun where it lay between his feet. Then he gave a funny little snort, picked it up and put it on the table.

"That gun ought to be thrown away. It's too dangerous to handle. It's bad luck," I said to Larsen—and then wished I hadn't, for he gave me the benefit of a dirty look and some fancy Swedish swearing.

"Shut up, No Nose," he finished, "and don't tell me what I

can do and what I can't. I can take care of you, and I can take care of Inky's gun. Right now I'm going to bed."

He shut the bedroom door behind him, leaving it up to me and Glasses to guess that we were supposed to take our blankets and sleep on the floor.

But we didn't want to go to sleep right away, if only because we were still thinking about Luke Dugan. So we got out a deck of cards and started a game of stud poker, speaking very low. Stud poker is like the ordinary kind, except that four of the five cards are dealt face up and one at a time.

You bet each time a card is dealt, and so considerable money is apt to change hands, even when you're playing with a ten-cent limit, like we were. It's a pretty good game for taking money away from suckers, and Glasses and I used to play it by the hour when we had nothing better to do. But since we were both equally dumb or equally wise (whichever way you look at it) neither one of us won consistently.

It was very quiet, except for Larsen's snoring and the rustling of the sea-grass and the occasional chink of a dime.

After about an hour, Glasses happened to look down at Inky's automatic lying on the other side of the table, and something about the way his body twisted around sudden made me look too. Right away I felt something was wrong, but I couldn't tell what; it gave me a funny feeling in the back of the neck. Then Glasses put out two thin fingers and turned the gun halfway around, and I realized what had been wrong—or what I thought had been wrong. When Larsen had put the gun down, I thought it had been pointing at the outside door; but when Glasses and I looked at it, it was pointing more in the direction of the bedroom door. When you have the fidgets your memory gets tricky.

A half-hour later we noticed the gun pointed toward the bedroom door again. This time Glasses spun it around quick, and I got the fidgets for fair. Glasses gave a low whistle and got up, and tried putting the gun on different parts of the table and jiggling the table to see if the gun would move.

"I see what happened now," he whispered finally. "When the gun is lying on its side, it sort of balances on its safety catch.

"Now this table has got a wobble to it, and when we are playing cards the wobble is persistent enough to edge the gun slowly around in a circle."

"I don't care about that," I whispered back. "I don't want to be shot in my sleep just because the table has a persistent wobble. I think the rumble of a train two miles away would be enough to set off that crazy hair-trigger. Give me it."

Glasses handed it over and, taking care always to point it at the floor, I unloaded it, put it back on the table, and put the bullets in my coat pocket. Then we tried to go on with our card game.

"My red bullet bets ten cents," I said. (A "bullet" means an ace, and I called mine a red bullet because it was the ace of hearts.)

"My king raises you ten cents," responded Glasses.

But it was no use. Between Inky's automatic and Luke Dugan I couldn't concentrate on my cards.

"Do you remember, Glasses," I said, "the evening you said that there was maybe something queer about Inky's gun?"

"I do a lot of talking, No Nose, and not much of it is worth remembering. We'd better stick to our cards. My pair of sevens bets a nickel."

I followed his advice, but didn't have much luck, and lost five or six dollars. By two o'clock we were both pretty tired and not feeling quite so jittery; so we got the blankets and wrapped up in them and tried to grab a little sleep. I listened to the sea-grass and the tooting of a locomotive about two miles away, and worried some over the possible activities of Luke Dugan, but finally dropped off.

It must have been about sunrise that the clicking noise woke me up. There was a faint, greenish light coming in through the shades. I lay still, not knowing exactly what I was listening for, but so on edge that it didn't occur to me how prickly hot I was from sleeping without sheets, or how itchy my face and hands were from mosquito bites. Then I heard it again, and it sounded like nothing but the sharp click the hammer of a gun makes when it snaps down on an empty chamber. Twice I heard it. It seemed to be coming from the inside of the room. I slid out of my blankets and rustled Glasses awake.

"It's that damned automatic of Inky's," I whispered shakily. "It's trying to shoot itself."

When a person wakes up sudden and before he should, he's apt to feel just like I did and say crazy things without thinking. Glasses looked at me for a moment, and then he rubbed his eyes and smiled. I could hardly see the smile in the dim light, but I could feel it in his voice when he said, "No Nose, you are getting positively psychic."

"I tell you I'd swear to it," I insisted. "It was the click of the hammer of a gun."

Glasses yawned. "Next you will be telling me that the gun was Inky's familiar."

"Familiar what?" I asked him, scratching my head and beginning to get mad and feel foolish. There are times when Glasses' college professor stuff gets me down.

"No Nose," he continued, "have you ever heard of witches?"

I was walking around to the windows and glancing out from behind the blinds to make sure there was no one around. I didn't see anyone. For that matter, I didn't really expect to.

"What d'you mean?" I said. "Sure I have. Why, I knew a guy, a Pennsylvania Dutchman, and he told me about witches putting what he called hexes on people. He said his uncle had a hex put on him, and he died afterward. He was a traveling salesman—the Dutchman that told me all that, I mean."

Glasses nodded his head, and then went on, "Well, No Nose, the devil gives each witch a pet black cat or dog or maybe a toad to follow them around and instruct them and protect them and revenge injuries. Those little creatures were called familiars—stooges sent out by the Big Boy in hell to watch over his chosen, you might say. The witches used to talk to them in a language no one else could understand. Now this is what I'm getting at. Times change and styles change—and the style in familiars along with them. Inky's gun is black, isn't it? And he used to mutter at it in a language we couldn't understand, didn't he? And—"

"You're crazy," I told him, not wanting to be kidded and made a fool of.

"Why, No Nose," he said, giving me a very innocent look, "you were telling me yourself just now that you thought the gun had a life of its own, that it could cock itself and shoot itself without any human assistance. Weren't you?"

"You're crazy," I repeated, feeling like an awful fool and wishing I hadn't waked Glasses up. "See, the gun's here where I left it on the table, and the bullets are still in my pocket."

"Luckily," he said in a stagy voice he tried to make a sound like an undertaker's. "Well, now that you've called me early, I shall wander off and avail us of our neighbor's newspaper. Meanwhile, you may run my bath."

I waited until I was sure he was gone, because I didn't

want him to make a fool of me again. Then I went over and examined the gun. First I looked for the trademark or the name of the maker. I found a place which had been filed down, where it may have once been, but that was all. Before this I would have sworn I could have told the make after a quick inspection, but now I couldn't. Not that *in general* it didn't look like an ordinary automatic; it was the details—the grip, the trigger guard, the safety catch—that were different and *unfamiliar*. I figured it was some foreign make I'd never happened to see before.

After I'd been handling it for about two minutes I began to notice something queer about the feel of the metal. As far as I could see it was just ordinary blued steel, but somehow it was too smooth and slick and made me want to keep stroking the barrel back and forth. I can't explain it any better; the metal just didn't seem *right* to me. Finally I realized that the gun was getting on my nerves and making me imagine things; so I put it down on the mantel.

When Glasses got back, the sun was up and he wasn't smiling any more. He shoved a newspaper on my lap and pointed. It was open to page five. I read:

ANTON LARSEN SOUGHT
IN KOZACS KILLING

*Police Believe Ex-Bootlegger
Slain by Pal*

I looked up to see Larsen standing in the bedroom door. He was in his pajama trousers and looked yellow and seedy, his eyelids puffed and his pig eyes staring at us.

"Good morning, boss," said Glasses slowly. "We just noticed in the paper that they are trying to do you a dirty trick. They're claiming you, not Dugan, had Inky shot."

Larsen grunted, came over and took the paper, looked at it quickly, grunted again, and went to the sink to splash some cold water on his face.

"So," he said, turning to us. "So. All the better that we are here at the hideout."

That day was the longest and most nervous I've ever gone through. Somehow Larsen didn't seem to be completely waked up. If he'd have been a stranger I'd have diagnosed it as a laudanum jag. He just sat around in his pajama trousers, so that by noon he still looked as if he'd only that minute rolled out of bed. The worst thing was that he wouldn't talk or tell us anything about his plans. Of course he never did much talking, but this time there was a difference. His funny pig eyes began to give me the jim-jams; no matter how still he sat they were always moving—like a guy in a laudanum nightmare who's about to run amok.

Finally it started to get on Glasses' nerves, which surprised me, for Glasses usually knows how to take things quietly. He began by making little suggestions—that we should get a later paper, that we should call up a certain lawyer in New York, that I should get my cousin Jake to mosey around to the police station at Keansburg and see if anything was up, and so on. Each time Larsen shut him up quick.

Once I thought he was going to take a crack at Glasses. And Glasses, like a fool, kept on pestering. I could see a blow-up coming, plain as the No Nose in front of my face. I couldn't figure what was making him do it. I guess when the college professor type gets the jim-jams they get them worse than a dummy like me. They've got trained brains which they can't stop from pecking away at ideas, and that's a disadvantage sometimes.

As for me, I tried to keep hold of my nerves. I kept saying to myself, "Larsen is O.K. He's just a little on edge. We all are. Why, I've known him ten years. He's O.K." I only half realized I was saying those things because I was beginning to believe that Larsen *wasn't* O.K.

The blow-up came at about two o'clock. Larsen's eyes opened wide, as if he'd just remembered something, and he jumped up so quick that I started to look around for Luke Dugan's firing-squad—or the police. But it wasn't either of those. Larsen had spotted the automatic on the mantel. Right away, as he began fingering it, he noticed it was unloaded.

"Who monkeyed with this?" he asked in a very nasty, thick voice. "And why?"

Glasses couldn't keep quiet.

"I thought you might hurt yourself with it," he said.

Larsen walked over to him and slapped him on the side of the face, knocking him down. I took firm hold of the chair I had been sitting on, ready to use it like a club—and waited. Glasses twisted on the floor for a moment, until he got control of the pain. Then he looked up, tears beginning to drip out of his left eye—the side he had been hit on. He had sense enough not to say anything, or to smile. Some fools might have smiled in such a situation, thinking it showed courage. It would have showed courage, I admit, but not good sense.

After about twenty seconds Larsen decided not to kick him in the face.

"Well, are you going to keep your mouth shut?" he asked.

Glasses nodded. I let go my grip on the chair.

"Where's the load?" asked Larsen.

I took the bullets out of my pocket and put them on the table, moving deliberately.

Larsen reloaded the gun. It made me sick to see his big hands sliding along the blue-black metal, because I remembered the *feel* of it.

"Nobody touches this but me, see?" he said.

And with that he walked into the bedroom and closed the door.

All I could think was, "Glasses was right when he said Larsen was crazy on the subject of Inky's automatic. And it's just the same as it was with Inky. He has to have the gun close to him. That's what was bothering him all morning, only he didn't know."

Then I kneeled down by Glasses, who was still lying on the floor, propped up on his elbows looking at the bedroom door. The mark of Larsen's hand was brick-red on the side of his face, with a little trickle of blood on the cheekbone, where the skin was broken.

I whispered, very low, just what I thought of Larsen. "Let's beat it first chance and get the police on him," I finished. "Or else maybe jump him when he comes out."

Glasses shook his head a little. He kept staring at the door, his left eye blinking spasmodically. Then he shivered, and gave a funny grunt deep down in his throat.

"I can't believe it," he said. "It's horrible!"

"He killed Inky," I whispered in his ear. "I'm almost sure of it. And he was within an inch of killing you."

"I don't mean that," said Glasses.

"What do you mean then?"

Glasses shook his head, as if he were trying to change the subject of his thoughts.

"Something I saw," he said, "or, rather, something I realized."

"The . . . the gun?" I questioned. My lips were dry and it was hard for me to say the word.

He gave me a funny look and got up.

"We'd better both be sensible from now on," he said, and

then added in a whisper, "We can't do anything now. He's on guard and we're unarmed. Maybe we'll get a chance tonight."

After a long while Larsen called to me to heat some water so he could shave. I brought it to him, and by the time I was frying hash he came out and sat down at the table. He was all washed and shaved and the straggling patches of hair around his bald head were brushed smooth. He was dressed and had his hat on. But in spite of everything he still had that yellow, seedy, laudanum-jag look. We ate our hash and beans and drank our beer, no one talking. It was dark now, and a tiny wind was making the blades of sea-grass scrape together and whine.

Finally Larsen got up and walked around the table once and said, "Let's have a game of stud poker."

While I was clearing off the dishes he brought out his suitcase and planked it down on the side table. Then he took Inky's automatic out of his pocket and looked at it a second. A fleeting expression passed across his stolid face—an expression in which it seemed to me indecision and puzzlement and maybe even fear were mingled. Then he laid the automatic in the suitcase, and shut it and strapped it tight.

"We're leaving after the game," he said.

I wasn't quite sure whether to feel relieved or not.

We played with a ten-cent limit, and right from the start Larsen began to win. It was a queer game, what with me feeling so jittery, and Glasses sitting there with the left side of his face all swollen, squinting through the right lens of his spectacles because the left lens had been cracked when Larsen hit him, and Larsen all dressed up as if he were waiting for a train. The shades were all down and the hanging light bulb, which was shaded with a foolscap of newspaper, threw a bright circle of light on the table but left the rest of the room shadowy. And afterward we were going to leave, he'd said. For where?

It was after Larsen had won about five dollars from each of us that I began hearing the noise. At first I couldn't be sure, because it was very low and because of the dry whining of the sea-grass, but right from the first it bothered me.

Larsen turned up a king and raked in another pot.

"You can't lose tonight," observed Glasses, smiling—and winced because the smile hurt his cheek.

Larsen scowled. He didn't seem pleased at his luck, or at Glasses' remark. His pig eyes were moving in the same way that had given us the jim-jams earlier in the day. And I kept thinking, "Maybe he killed Inky Kozacs. Glasses and me are just small fry to him. Maybe he's trying to figure out whether to kill us too. Or maybe he's got a use for us, and he's wondering how much to tell us. If he starts anything I'll shove the table over on him; that is, if I get the chance." He was beginning to look like a stranger to me, although I'd known him for ten years and he'd been my boss and paid me good money.

Then I heard the noise again, a little plainer this time. It was very peculiar and hard to describe—something like the noise a rat would make if it were tied up in a lot of blankets and trying to work its way out. I looked up and saw that Glasses' face was pale. It made the bruise on his left cheek stand out plainer.

"My black bullet bets ten cents," said Larsen, pushing a dime into the pot.

"I'm with you," I answered, shoving in two nickels. My voice sounded so dry and choked it startled me.

Glasses put in his money and dealt another card to each of us.

Then *I* felt my face going pale, for it seemed to me that the noise was coming from Larsen's suitcase, and I remembered that he had put Inky's automatic into the suitcase with its muzzle pointing *away* from us.

The noise was louder now. Glasses couldn't bear to sit still without saying anything. He pushed back his chair and started to whisper, "I think I hear—"

Then he saw the crazy, murderous look that came into Larsen's eyes, and he had sense enough to finish lamely, "I think I hear the eleven o'clock train."

"Sit still," said Larsen, "very still. It's only ten forty-five. You don't hear anything. My ace bets another ten cents."

"I'll raise you," I croaked.

I didn't know what I was saying. I wanted to jump up. I wanted to throw Larsen's suitcase out the door. I wanted to run out myself. Yet I sat tight. We all sat tight. We didn't dare make a move, for if we had, it would have shown that we believed the impossible was happening. And if a man does that he's crazy. I kept rubbing my tongue against my dry lips.

I stared at the cards, trying to shut out everything else. The hand was all dealt now. I had a jack and some little ones, and I knew my face-down card was a jack. That made a pair of jacks. Glasses had a king showing. Larsen's ace of clubs was the highest card on the board.

And still the sound kept coming. Something twisting, straining, scuffling. A muffled sound.

"And I raise *you* ten cents," said Glasses loudly. I got the idea he did it just to make a noise, not because he thought his cards were especially good.

I turned to Larsen, trying to pretend I was interested in whether he would raise or stop betting. His eyes had stopped moving and were staring straight ahead at the suitcase. His mouth was twisted in a funny, set way. After a while his lips began to move. His voice was so low I could barely catch the words.

"Ten cents more. *I killed Inky, you know.* What does your jack say, No Nose?"

"It raises you," I said automatically.

His reply came in the same almost inaudible voice. "You haven't a chance of winning, No Nose. *But, you see, he didn't bring the money with him, like he said he would. However, I found out where he keeps it hidden in his room. I can't pull the job myself; the cops would recognize me. But you two ought to be able to do it for me. That's why we're going to New York tonight. I raise you ten cents more.* What do you say?"

"I'll see you," I heard myself saying.

The noise stopped, not gradually but all of a sudden. Right away I wanted ten times worse to jump up and do something. But I was frozen to my seat.

Larsen turned up the ace of diamonds. Again I barely heard his words.

"Two aces. *Inky's little gun didn't protect him, you know. He didn't have a chance to use it.* Clubs and diamonds. A pair of bullets. I win."

Then it happened.

I don't need to tell you much about what we did afterward. We buried the body in the sea-grass. We cleaned everything up and drove the coupé a couple of miles inland before abandoning it. We carried the gun away with us and took it apart and hammered it out of shape and threw it into the bay, part by part. We never found out anything more about Inky's money, or tried to. The police never bothered us. We counted ourselves lucky that we had enough sense left to get away safely, after what happened.

For, with smoke and flame squirting through the little round holes and the whole suitcase jerking and shaking with the recoils, eight slugs drummed out and almost cut Anton Larsen in two.

# HINDSIGHT    *Astounding Science Fiction*
                                    May

## by Jack Williamson (1908-      )

*1978 marked the fiftieth anniversary of Jack Williamson as a published science fiction writer, and he is still going strong as the current "Dean" of sf authors. From his first story, "The Metal Man,"* in the December 1928 issue of Amazing Stories, *he has produced a steady stream of first-rate science fiction and fantasy. His long list of serials in the sf pulps of the thirties earned him his reputation, but he steadily improved his work, both in content and in style.*

*It is often charged (and with considerable validity) that Golden Age sf lacked character development. This powerful story of betrayal and realization, written at a time of intense nationalism in the United States, offers proof that there were some notable exceptions.*

(Jack Williamson is one of the most lovable people in the entire lovable band of science fiction writers. He is quiet and gentle and yet doesn't in the least mind being surrounded by such loudmouths as Randall Garrett, Lester del Rey, Harlan Ellison and myself. In fact, Jack was the very first professional writer to accept me. When my very first published story appeared—"Marooned Off Vesta" in the March 1939 *Amazing*—I at once received a postcard from Jack which read, "Welcome to the ranks." I valued that tremendously. It was my union card, even more than the story was, and I've never forgotten it. Jack has, for I've asked him if he remembered and he looked blank—but I haven't. I.A.)

Something was wrong with the cigar.

But Brek Veronar didn't throw it away. Earth-grown tobacco was precious, here on Ceres. He took another bite off the end, and pressed the lighter cone again. This time, imperfectly, the cigar drew—with an acrid, puzzling odor of scorching paper.

Brek Veronar—born William Webster, Earthman—was sitting in his well-furnished office, adjoining the arsenal laboratory. Beyond the perdurite windows, magnified in the crystalline clarity of the asteroid's synthetic atmosphere, loomed a row of the immense squat turret forts that guarded the Astrophon base—their mighty twenty-four-inch rifles, coupled to the Veronar autosight, covered with their theoretical range everything within Jupiter's orbit. A squadron of the fleet lay on the field beyond, seven tremendous dead-black cigar shapes. Far off, above the rugged red palisades of a second plateau, stood the many-colored domes and towers of Astrophon itself, the Astrarch's capital.

A tall, gaunt man, Brek Veronar wore the bright, close-fitting silks of the Astrarchy. Dyed to conceal the increasing streaks of gray, his hair was perfumed and curled. In abrupt contrast to the force of his gray, wide-set eyes, his face was white and smooth from cosmetic treatments. Only the cigar could have betrayed him as a native of Earth, and Brek Veronar never smoked except here in his own locked laboratory.

He didn't like to be called the Renegade.

Curiously, that whiff of burning paper swept his mind away from the intricate drawing of a new rocket-torpedo gyropilot pinned to a board on the desk before him, and back across twenty years of time. It returned him to the university campus, on the low yellow hills beside the ancient Martian city of Toran—to the fateful day when Bill Webster had renounced allegiance to his native Earth, for the Astrarch.

Tony Grimm and Elora Ronee had both objected. Tony was the freckled, irresponsible redhead who had come out from Earth with him six years before, on the other of the two annual engineering scholarships. Elora Ronee was the lovely dark-eyed Martian girl—daughter of the professor of geodesics, and a proud descendant of the first colonists—whom they both loved.

He walked with them, that dry, bright afternoon, out from the yellow adobe buildings, across the rolling, stony, ocher-colored desert. Tony's sunburned, blue-eyed face was grave for once, as he protested.

"You can't do it, Bill. No Earthman could."

"No use talking," said Bill Webster, shortly. "The Astrarch wants a military engineer. His agents offered me twenty thousand eagles a year, with raises and bonuses—ten times what any research scientist could hope to get, back on Earth."

The tanned, vivid face of Elora Ronee looked hurt. "Bill—what about your own research?" the slender girl cried. "Your new reaction tube! You promised you were going to break the Astrarch's monopoly on space transport. Have you forgotten?"

"The tube was just a dream," Bill Webster told her, "but probably it's the reason he offered the contract to me, and not Tony. Such jobs don't go begging."

Tony caught his arm. "You can't turn against your own world, Bill," he insisted. "You can't give up everything that means anything to an Earthman. Just remember what the Astrarch is—a superpirate."

Bill Webster's toe kicked up a puff of yellow dust. "I know history," he said. "I know that the Astrarchy had its beginnings from the space pirates who established their bases in the asteroids, and gradually turned to commerce instead of raiding."

His voice was injured and defiant. "But, so far as I'm concerned, the Astrarchy is just as respectable as such planet nations as Earth and Mars and the Jovian Federation. And it's a good deal more wealthy and powerful than any of them."

Tense-faced, the Martian girl shook her dark head. "Don't blind yourself, Bill," she begged urgently. "Can't you see that the Astrarch really is no different from any of the old pirates? His fleets still seize any independent vessel, or make the owners ransom it with his space-patrol tax."

She caught an indignant breath. "Everywhere—even here on Mars—the agents and residents and traders of the Astrarchy have brought graft and corruption and oppression. The Astrarch is using his wealth and his space power to undermine the government of every independent planet. He's planning to conquer the system!"

Her brown eyes flashed. "You won't aid him, Bill. You—couldn't!"

Bill Webster looked into the tanned, intent loveliness of her face—he wanted suddenly to kiss the smudge of yellow dust on her impudent little nose. He had loved Elora Ronee, had once hoped to take her back to Earth. Perhaps he still loved her. But now it was clear that she had always wanted Tony Grimm.

Half angrily, he kicked an iron-reddened pebble. "If things had been different, Elora, it might have been—" With an abrupt little shrug, he looked back at Tony. "Anyhow," he said flatly, "I'm leaving for Astrophon tonight."

That evening, after they had helped him pack, he made a bonfire of his old books and papers. They burned palely in the thin air of Mars, with a cloud of acrid smoke.

That sharp odor was the line that had drawn Brek Veronar back across the years, when his nostrils stung to the scorched-paper scent. The cigar came from a box that had just arrived from Earth—made to his special order.

He could afford such luxuries. Sometimes, in fact, he almost regretted the high place he had earned in the Astrarch's favor. The space officers, and even his own jealous subordinates in the arsenal laboratory, could never forget that he was an Earthman—the Renegade.

The cigar's odor puzzled him.

Deliberately, he crushed out the smoldering tip, peeled off the brown wrapper leaves. He found a tightly rolled paper cylinder. Slipping off the rubber bands, he opened it. A glimpse of the writing set his heart to thudding.

It was the hand of Elora Ronee!

Brek Veronar knew that fine graceful script. For once Bill Webster had received a little note that she had written him, when they were still in school. He read it eagerly:

DEAR BILL: This is the only way we can hope to get word to you, past the Astrarch's spies. Your old name, Bill, may seem strange to you. But both Tony and I—want you to remember that you are an Earthman.

You can't know the oppression that Earth now is suffering, under the Astrarch's heel. But independence is almost gone. Weakened and corrupted, the government yields everywhere. Every Earthman's life is burdened with taxes and unjust penalties and the unfair competition of the Astrarch traders.

The Earth, Bill, has not completely yielded. We are going to strike for liberty. Many years of our lives—Tony's and mine—have gone into the plan. And the toil and the sacrifices of millions of our fellow Earthmen. We have at least a chance to recover our lost freedom.

But we need you, Bill—desperately.

For your own world's sake, come back. Ask for a vacation trip to Mars. The Astrarch will not deny you that. On April 8th, a ship will be waiting for you in the desert outside Toran—where we walked the day you left.

Whatever your decision, Bill, we trust you to destroy this letter and keep its contents secret. But we believe that you will come back. For Earth's sake, and for your old friends,                                   TONY AND ELORA

Brek Veronar sat for a long time at his desk, staring at the charred, wrinkled sheet. His eyes blurred a little, and he saw the tanned vital face of the Martian girl, her brown eyes imploring. At last he sighed and reached slowly for the lighter cone. He held the letter until the flame had consumed it.

Next day four space officers came to the laboratory. They were insolent in the gaudy gold and crimson of the Astrarch, and the voice of the captain was suave with a triumphant hate:

"Earthman, you are under technical arrest, by the Astrarch's order. You will accompany us at once to his quarters aboard the *Warrior Queen*."

Brek Veronar knew that he was deeply disliked, but very seldom had the feeling been so openly shown. Alarmed, he locked his office and went with the four.

Flagship of the Astrarch's space fleets, the *Warrior Queen* lay on her cradle, at the side of the great field beyond the low gray forts. A thousand feet and a quarter of a million tons of fighting metal, with sixty-four twenty-inch rifles mounted in eight bulging spherical turrets, she was the most powerful engine of destruction the system had ever seen.

Brek Veronar's concern was almost forgotten in a silent pride, as a swift electric car carried them across the field. It was his autosight—otherwise the Veronar achronic field detector geodesic achron-integration self-calculating range finder—that directed the fire of those mighty guns. It was the very fighting brain of the ship—of all the Astrarch's fleet.

No wonder these men were jealous.

"Come, Renegade!" The bleak-faced captain's tone was ominous. "The Astrarch is waiting."

Bright-uniformed guards let them into the Astrarch's compact but luxurious suite, just aft the console room and forward of the autosight installation, deep in the ship's armored bowels. The Astrarch turned from a chart projector, and crisply ordered the two officers to wait outside.

"Well, Veronar?"

A short, heavy, compact man, the dictator of the Astrarchy was vibrant with a ruthless energy. His hair was waved and perfumed, his face a rouged and powdered mask, his silk-swathed figure loaded with jewels. But nothing could hide the power of his hawklike nose and his burning black eyes.

The Astrarch had never yielded to the constant pressure of jealousy against Brek Veronar. The feeling between them had grown almost to friendship. But now the Earthman sensed, from the cold inquiry of those first words, and the probing flash of the ruler's eyes, that his position was gravely dangerous.

Apprehension strained his voice. "I'm under arrest?"

The Astrarch smiled, gripped his hand. "My men are over-zealous, Veronar." The voice was warm, yet Brek Veronar could not escape the sense of something sharply critical, deadly. "I merely wish to talk with you, and the impending movements of the fleet allowed little time."

Behind that smiling mask, the Astrarch studied him. "Veronar, you have served me loyally. I am leaving Astrophon for a cruise with the fleet, and I feel that you, also, have earned a holiday. Do you want a vacation from your duties here—let us say, to Mars?"

Beneath those thrusting eyes, Brek Veronar flinched. "Thank you, Gorro," he gulped—he was among the few privileged to call the Astrarch by name. "Later, perhaps. But the torpedo guide isn't finished. And I've several ideas for improving the autosight. I'd much prefer to stay in the laboratory."

For an instant, the short man's smile seemed genuine. "The Astrarchy is indebted to you for the autosight. The increased accuracy of fire had in effect quadrupled our fleets." His eyes were sharp again, doubtful. "Are further improvements possible?"

Brek Veronar caught his breath. His knees felt a little weak. He knew that he was talking for his life. He swallowed, and his words came at first unsteadily.

"Geodesic analysis and integration is a completely new

science," he said desperately. "It would be foolish to limit the possibilities. With a sufficiently delicate pick-up, the achronic detector fields ought to be able to trace the world lines of any object almost indefinitely. Into the future—"

He paused for emphasis. "Or into the past!"

An eager interest flashed in the Astrarch's eyes. Brek felt confidence returning. His breathless voice grew smoother.

"Remember, the principle is totally new. The achronic field can be made a thousand times more sensitive than any telescope—I believe, a million times! And the achronic beam eliminates the time lag of all electromagnetic methods of observation. Timeless, paradoxically it facilitates the exploration of time."

"Exploration?" questioned the dictator. "Aren't you speaking rather wildly, Veronar?"

"Any range finder, in a sense, explores time," Brek assured him urgently. "It analyzes the past to predict the future—so that a shell fired from a moving ship and deflected by the gravitational fields of space may move thousands of miles to meet another moving ship, minutes in the future.

"Instruments depending on visual observation and electromagnetic transmission of data were not very successful. One hit in a thousand used to be good gunnery. But the autosight has solved the problem—now you reprimand gunners for failing to score two hits in a hundred."

Brek caught his breath. "Even the newest autosight is just a rough beginning. Good enough, for a range finder. But the detector fields can be made infinitely more sensitive, the geodesic integration infinitely more certain.

"It ought to be possible to unravel the past for years, instead of minutes. It ought to be possible to foretell the position of a ship for weeks ahead—to anticipate every maneuver, and even watch the captain eating his breakfast!"

The Earthman was breathless again, his eyes almost feverish. "From geodesic analysis," he whispered, "there is one more daring step—control. You are aware of the modern view that there is no absolute fact, but only probability. I can prove it! And probability can be manipulated through pressure of the achronic field.

"It is possible, even, I tell you—"

Brek's rushing voice faltered. He saw that doubt had drowned the flash of interest in the Astrarch's eyes. The dictator made an impatient gesture for silence. In a flat, abrupt voice he stated: "Veronar, you are an Earthman."

"Once I was an Earthman."

The black flashing eyes probed into him. "Veronar," the Astrarch said, "trouble is coming with Earth. My agents have uncovered a dangerous plot. The leader of it is an engineer named Grimm, who has a Martian wife. The fleet is moving to crush the rebellion." He paused. "Now, do you want the vacation?"

Before those ruthless eyes, Brek Veronar stood silent. Life, he was now certain, depended on his answer. He drew a long, unsteady breath. "No," he said.

Still the Astrarch's searching tension did not relax. "My officers," he said, "have protested against serving with you, against Earth. They are suspicious."

Brek Veronar swallowed. "Grimm and his wife," he whispered hoarsely, "once were friends of mine. I had hoped that it would not be necessary to betray them. But I have received a message from them."

He gulped again, caught his breath. "To prove to your men that I am no longer an Earthman—a ship that they have sent for me will be waiting on April 8th, Earth calendar, in the desert south of the Martian city of Toran."

The white, lax mask of the Astrarch smiled. "I'm glad you told me, Veronar," he said. "You have been very useful—and I like you. Now I call tell you that my agents read the letter in the cigar. The rebel ship was overtaken and destroyed by the space patrol, just a few hours ago."

Brek Veronar swayed to a giddy weakness.

"Entertain no further apprehensions." The Astrarch touched his arm. "You will accompany the fleet, in charge of the autosight. We take off in five hours."

The long black hull of the *Warrior Queen* lifted on flaring reaction tubes, leading the squadron. Other squadrons moved from the bases on Pallas, Vesta, Thule, and Eros. The Second Fleet came plunging sunward from its bases on the Trojan planets. Four weeks later, at the rendezvous just within the orbit of Mars, twenty-nine great vessels had come together.

The armada of the Astrarchy moved down upon Earth.

Joining the dictator in his chartroom, Brek was puzzled. "Still I don't see the reason for such a show of strength," he said. "Why have you gathered three fourths of your space forces to crush a handful of plotters?"

"We have to deal with more than a handful of plotters." Behind the pale mask of the Astrarch's face, Brek could sense a tension of worry. "Millions of Earthmen have labored for years to prepare for this rebellion. Earth has built a space fleet."

Brek was astonished. "A fleet?"

"The parts were manufactured secretly, mostly in underground mills," the Astrarch told him. "The ships were assembled by divers, under the surface of fresh-water lakes. Your old friend, Grimm, is clever and dangerous. We shall have to destroy his fleet before we can bomb the planet into submission."

Steadily, Brek met the Astrarch's eyes. "How many ships?" he asked.

"Six."

"Then we outnumber them five to one." Brek managed a confident smile. "Without considering the further advantage of the autosight. It will be no battle at all."

"Perhaps not," said the Astrarch, "but Grimm is an able man. He has invented a new type reaction tube, in some regards superior to our own." His dark eyes were somber. "It is Earthman against Earthman," he said softly. "And one of you shall perish."

Day after day, the armada dropped Earthward.

The autosight served also as the eyes of the fleet, as well as the fighting brain. In order to give longer base lines for the automatic triangulations, additional achronic-field pick-ups had been installed upon half a dozen ships. Tight achronic beams brought their data to the immense main instrument, on the *Warrior Queen*. The autosight steered every ship, by achronic beam control, and directed the fire of its guns.

The *Warrior Queen* led the fleet. The autosight held the other vessels in accurate line behind her, so that only one circular cross section might be visible to the telescopes of Earth.

The rebel planet was still twenty million miles ahead, and fifty hours at normal deceleration, when the autosight discovered the enemy fleet.

Brek Veronar sat at the curving control table.

Behind him, in the dim-lit vastness of the armored room, bulked the main instrument. Banked thousands of green-painted cases—the intricate cells of the mechanical brain—whirred with geodesic analyzers and integrators. The achronic-field pick-ups—sense organs of the brain—were housed in insignificant black boxes. And the web of achronic transmission beams—instantaneous, ultrashort, nonelectromagnetic waves of the subelectronic order—the nerve fibers that joined the busy cells—was quite invisible.

Before Brek stood the twenty-foot cube of the stereoscreen, through which the brain communicated its findings. The cube was black, now, with the crystal blackness of space. Earth, in it, made a long misty crescent of wavering crimson splendor. The moon was a smaller scimitar, blue with the dazzle of its artificial atmosphere.

Brek touched intricate controls. Th moon slipped out of the cube. Earth grew—and turned. So far had the autosight conquered time and space. It showed the planet's sunward side.

Earth filled the cube, incredibly real. The vast white disk of one low-pressure area lay upon the Pacific's glinting blue. Another, blotting out the winter brown of North America, reached to the bright cap of the arctic.

Softly, in the dim room, a gong clanged. Numerals of white fire flickered against the image in the cube. An arrow of red flame pointed. At its point was a tiny fleck of black.

The gong throbbed again, and another black mote came up out of the clouds. A third followed. Presently there were six. Watching, Brek Veronar felt a little stir of involuntary pride, a dim numbness of regret.

Those six vessels were the mighty children of Tony Grimm and Elora, the fighting strength of Earth. Brek felt an aching tenseness in his throat, and tears stung his eyes. It was too bad that they had to be destroyed.

Tony would be aboard one of those ships. Brek wondered how he would look, after twenty years. Did his freckles still show? Had he grown stout? Did concentration still plow little furrows between his blue eyes?

Elora—would she be with him? Brek knew she would. His mind saw the Martian girl, slim and vivid and intense as ever. He tried to thrust away the image. Time must have changed her. Probably she looked worn from the years of toil and danger; her dark eyes must have lost their sparkle.

Brek had to forget that those six little blots represented the lives of Tony and Elora, and the independence of the Earth. They were only six little lumps of matter, six targets for the autosight.

He watched them, rising, swinging around the huge, luminous curve of the planet. They were only six mathematical points, tracing world lines through the continuum, making a geodesic pattern for the analyzers to unravel and the integrators to project against the future—

The gong throbbed again.

Tense with abrupt apprehension, Brek caught up a telephone.

"Give me the Astrarch. . . . An urgent report. . . . No, the admiral won't do. . . . Gorro, the autosight has picked up the Earth's fleet . . . Yes, only six ships, just taking off from the sunward face. But there is one alarming thing."

Brek Veronar was hoarse, breathless. "Already, behind the planet, they have formed a cruising line. The axis extends exactly in our direction. That means that they know our precise position, before they have come into telescopic view. That suggests that Tony Grimm has invented an autosight of his own!"

Strained hours dragged by. The Astrarch's fleet decelerated, to circle and bombard the mother world, after the battle was done. The Earth ships came out at full normal acceleration.

"They must stop," the Astrarch said. "That is our advantage. If they go by us at any great velocity, we'll have the planet bombed into submission before they can return. They must turn back—and then we'll pick them off."

Puzzlingly, however, the Earth fleet kept up acceleration, and a slow apprehension grew in the heart of Brek Veronar. There was but one explanation. The Earthmen were staking the life of their planet on one brief encounter.

As if certain of victory!

The hour of battle neared. Tight achronic beams relayed telephoned orders from the Astrarch's chartroom, and the fleet deployed into battle formation—into the shape of an immense bowl, so that every possible gun could be trained upon the enemy.

The hour—and the instant!

Startling in the huge dim space that housed the autosight, crackling out above the whirring of the achron-integrator, the speaker that was the great brain's voice counted off the minutes.

"Minus four—"

The autosight was set, the pick-ups tuned, the director relays tested, a thousand details checked. By the control table, Brek Veronar tried to relax. His part was done.

A space battle was a conflict of machines. Humans beings were too puny, too slow, even to comprehend the play of the titanic forces they had set loose. Brek tried to remember that he was the autosight's inventor; he fought an oppression of helpless dread.

"Minus three—"

Sodium bombs filled the void ahead with vast silver plumes and streamers—for the autosight removed the need of telescopic eyes, and enabled ships to fight from deep smoke screens.

"Minus two—"

The two fleets came together at a relative velocity of twelve hundred thousand miles an hour. Maximum useful range of twenty-inch guns, even with the autosight, was only twenty thousand miles in free space.

Which meant, Brek realized, that the battle could last just two minutes. In that brief time lay the destinies of Astrarchy and Earth—and Tony Grimm's and Elora's and his own.

"Minus one—"

The sodium screens made little puffs and trails of silver in the great black cube. The six Earth ships were visible behind them, through the magic of the achronic-field pick-ups, now spaced in a close ring, ready for action.

Brek Veronar looked down at the jeweled chronometer on his wrist—a gift from the Astrarch. Listening to the rising hum of the achron-integrators, he caught his breath, tensed instinctively.

"Zero!"

The *Warrior Queen* began quivering to her great guns, a salvo of four firing every half-second. Brek breathed again, watched the chronometer. That was all he had to do. And in two minutes—

The vessel shuddered, and the lights went out. Sirens wailed, and air valves clanged. The lights came on, went off again. And abruptly the cube of the stereoscreen was dark. The achron-integrators clattered and stopped.

The guns ceased to thud.

"Power!" Brek gasped into a telephone. "Give me power! Emergency! The autosight has stopped and—"

But the telephone was dead.

There were no more hits. Smothered in darkness, the great room remained very silent. After an eternal time, feeble emergency lights came on. Brek looked again at his chronometer, and knew that the battle was ended.

But who was the victor?

He tried to hope that the battle had been won before some last chance broadside crippled the flagship—until the Astrarch came stumbling into the room, looking dazed and pale.

"Crushed," he muttered. "You failed me, Veronar."

"What are the losses?" whispered Brek.

"Everything." The shaken ruler dropped wearily at the control table. "Your achronic beams are dead. Five ships remain able to report defeat by radio. Two of them hope to make repairs.

"The *Queen* is disabled. Reaction batteries shot away, and main power plant dead. Repair is hopeless. And our present orbit will carry us far too close to the sun. None of our ships able to undertake rescue. We'll be baked alive."

His perfumed dark head sank hopelessly. "In those two minutes, the Astrarchy was destroyed." His hollow, smoldering eyes lifted resentfully to Brek. "Just two minutes!" He crushed a soft white fist against the table. "If time could be recaptured—"

"How were we beaten?" demanded Brek. "I can't understand!"

"Marksmanship," said the tired Astrarch. "Tony Grimm has something better than your autosight. He shot us to pieces before we could find the range." His face was a pale mask of bitterness. "If my agents had employed him, twenty years ago, instead of you—" He bit blood from his lip. "But the past cannot be changed."

Brek was staring at the huge, silent bulk of the autosight. "Perhaps"—he whispered—"it can be!"

Trembling, the Astrarch rose to clutch his arm. "You spoke of that before," gasped the agitated ruler. "Then I wouldn't listen. But now—try anything you can, Veronar. To save us from roasting alive, at perihelion. Do you really think—" The Astrarch shook his pale head. "I'm the madman," he whispered. "To speak of changing even two minutes of the past!" His hollow eyes clung to Brek. "Though you have done amazing things, Veronar."

The Earthman continued to stare at his huge creation. "The autosight itself brought me one clue, before the battle," he breathed slowly. "The detector fields caught a beam of Tony Grimm's, and analyzed the frequencies. He's using achronic radiation a whole octave higher than anything I've tried. That must be the way to the sensitivity and penetration I have hoped for."

Hope flickered in the Astrarch's eyes. "You believe you can save us? How?"

"If the high-frequency beam can search out the determiner factors," Brek told him, "it might be possible to alter them, with a sufficiently powerful field. Remember that we deal with probabilities, not with absolutes. And that small factors can determine vast results.

"The pick-ups will have to be rebuilt. And we'll have to have power. Power to project the tracer fields. And a river of power—if we can trace out a decisive factor and attempt to change it. But the power plants are dead."

"Rebuild your pick-ups," the Astrarch told him. "And you'll have power—if I have to march every man aboard into the conversion furnaces, for fuel."

Calm again, and confident, the short man surveyed the tall, gaunt Earthman with wondering eyes.

"You're a strange individual, Veronar," he said. "Fighting time and destiny to crush the planet of your birth! It isn't strange that men call you the Renegade."

Silent for a moment, Brek shook his haggard head. "I don't want to be baked alive," he said at last. "Give me power— and we'll fight that battle again."

The wreck dropped sunward. A score of expert technicians toiled, under Brek's expert direction, to reconstruct the achronic pick-ups. And a hundred men labored, beneath the ruthless eye of the Astrarch himself, to repair the damaged atomic converters.

They had crossed the orbit of Venus, when the autosight came back to humming life. The Astrarch was standing beside Brek, at the curved control table. The shadow of doubt had returned to his reddened, sleepless eyes. "Now," he demanded, "what can you do about the battle?"

"Nothing, directly," Brek admitted. "First we must search the past. We must find the factor that caused Tony Grimm to invent a better autosight than mine. With the high-frequency field—and the full power of the ship's converters, if need be—we must reverse the factor. Then the battle should have a different outcome."

The achron-integrators whirred, as Brek manipulated the controls, and the huge black cube began to flicker with the passage of ghostly images. Symbols of colored fire flashed and vanished within it.

"Well?" anxiously rasped the Astrarch.

"It works!" Brek assured him. "The tracer fields are following all the world lines that intersected at the battle, back across the months and years. The analyzers will isolate the smallest—and hence most easily altered—essential factor."

The Astrarch gripped his shoulder. "There—in the cube—yourself!"

The ghostly shape of the Earthman flickered out, and came again. A hundred times, Brek Veronar glimpsed himself in the cube. Usually the scene was the great arsenal laboratory, at Astrophon. Always he was differently garbed, always younger.

Then the background shifted. Brek caught his breath as he recognized glimpses of barren, stony, ocher-colored hills, and low, yellow adobe buildings. He gasped to see a freckled, red-haired youth and a slim, tanned, dark-eyed girl.

"That's on Mars!" he whispered. "At Toran. He's Tony Grimm. And she's Elora Ronee—the Martian girl we loved."

The racing flicker abruptly stopped, upon one frozen tableau. A bench on the dusty campus, against a low adobe wall. Elora Ronee, with a pile of books propped on her knees to support pen and paper. Her dark eyes were staring away across the campus, and her sun-brown face looked tense and troubled.

In the huge dim room aboard the wrecked warship, a gong throbbed softly. A red arrow flamed in the cube, pointing down at the note on the girl's knee. Cryptic symbols flashed above it. And Brek realized that the humming of the achron-integrators had stopped.

"What's this?" rasped the anxious Astrarch. "A schoolgirl writing a note—what has she to do with a space battle?"

Brek scanned the fiery symbols. "She was deciding the battle—that day twenty years ago!" His voice rang with elation. "You see, she had a date to go dancing in Toran with Tony Grimm that night. But her father was giving a special lecture on the new theories of achronic force. Tony broke the date, to attend the lecture."

As Brek watched the motionless image in the cube his voice turned a little husky. "Elora was angry—that was before she knew Tony very well. I had asked her for a date. And, at the moment you see, she has just written a note, to say that she would go dancing with me."

Brek gulped. "But she is undecided, you see. Because she loves Tony. A very little would make her tear up the note to me, and write another to Tony, to say that she would go to the lecture with him."

The Astrarch stared cadaverously. "But how could that decide the battle?"

"In the past that we have lived," Brek told him, "Elora sent the note to me. I went dancing with her, and missed the lecture. Tony attended it—and got the germ idea that finally caused his autosight to be better than mine.

"But, if she had written to Tony instead, he would have offered, out of contrition, to cut the lecture—so the analyzers indicate. I should have attended the lecture in Tony's place, and my autosight would have been superior in the end."

The Astrarch's waxen head nodded slowly. "But—can you really change the past?"

Brek paused for a moment, solemnly. "We have all the power of the ship's converters," he said at last. "We have the high-frequency achronic field, as a lever through which to apply it. Surely, with the millions of kilowatts to spend, we can stimulate a few cells in a schoolgirl's brain. We shall see."

His long, pale fingers moved swiftly over the control keys. At last, deliberately, he touched a green button. The converters whispered again through the silent ship. The achron-integrators whirred again. Beyond, giant transformers began to whine.

And that still tableau came to sudden life.

Elora Ronee tore up the note that began, "Dear Bill—" Brek and the Astrarch leaned forward, as her trembling fingers swiftly wrote: "Dear Tony—I'm so sorry that I was angry. May I come with you to father's lecture? Tonight—"

The image faded.

"Minus four—"

The metallic rasp of the speaker brought Brek Veronar to himself with a start. Could he have been dozing—with contact just four minutes away? He shook himself. He had a queer, unpleasant feeling—as if he had forgotten a nightmare dream in which the battle was fought and lost.

He rubbed his eyes, scanned the control board. The autosight was set, the pick-ups were tuned, the director relays tested. His part was done. He tried to relax the puzzling tension in him.

"Minus three—"

Sodium bombs filled the void ahead with vast silver plumes and streamers. Staring into the black cube of the screen, Brek found once more the six tiny black motes of Tony Grimm's ships. He couldn't help an uneasy shake of his head.

Was Tony mad? Why didn't he veer aside, delay the contact? Scattered in space, his ships could harry the Astrarchy's commerce, and interrupt bombardment of the Earth. But, in a head-on battle, they were doomed.

Brek listened to the quiet hum of the achron-integrators. Under these conditions, the new autosight gave an accuracy of fire of forty percent. Even if Tony's gunnery was perfect, the odds were still two to one against him.

"Minus two—"

Two minutes! Brek looked down at the jeweled chronometer on his wrist. For a moment he had an odd feeling that the design was unfamiliar. Strange, when he had worn it for twenty years.

The dial blurred a little. He remembered the day that Tony and Elora gave it to him—the day he left the university to come to Astrophon. It was too nice a gift. Neither of them had much money.

He wondered if Tony had ever guessed his love for Elora. Probably it was better that she had always declined his attentions. No shadow of jealousy had ever come over their friendship.

"Minus one—"

This wouldn't do! Half angrily, Brek jerked his eyes back to the screen. Still, however, in the silvery sodium clouds, he saw the faces of Tony and Elora. Still he couldn't forget the oddly unfamiliar pressure of the chronometer on his wrist—it was like the soft touch of Elora's fingers, when she had fastened it there.

Suddenly the black flecks in the screen were not targets any more. Brek caught a long gasping breath. After all, he was an Earthman. After twenty years in the Astrarch's generous pay, this timepiece was still his most precious possession.

His gray eyes narrowed grimly. Without the autosight, the Astrarch's fleet would be utterly blind in the sodium clouds. Given any sort of achronic range finder, Tony Grimm could wipe it out.

Brek's gaunt body trembled. Death, he knew, would be the sure penalty. In the battle or afterward—it didn't matter. He knew that he would accept it without regret.

"Zero!"

The achron-integrators were whirring busily, and the *Warrior Queen* quivered to the first salvo of her guns. Then

Brek's clenched fists came down on the carefully set keyboard. The autosight stopped humming. The guns ceased to fire.

Brek picked up the Astrach's telephone. "I've stopped the autosight." His voice was quiet and low. "It is quite impossible to set it again in two minutes."

The telephone clicked and was dead.

The vessel shuddered and the lights went out. Sirens wailed. Air valves clanged. The lights came on, went off again. Presently, there were no more hits. Smothered in darkness, the great room remained very silent.

The tiny racing tick of the chronometer was the only sound.

After an eternal time, feeble emergency lights came on. The Astrarch came stumbling into the room, looking dazed and pale.

A group of spacemen followed him. Their stricken, angry faces made an odd contrast with their gay uniforms. Before their vengeful hatred, Brek felt cold and ill. But the Astrarch stopped their ominous advance.

"The Earthman has doomed himself as well," the shaken ruler told them. "There's not much more that you can do. And certainly no haste about it."

He left them muttering at the door and came slowly to Brek.

"Crushed," he whispered. "You destroyed me, Veronar." A trembling hand wiped at the pale waxen mask of his face. "Everything is lost. The *Queen* disabled. None of our ships able to undertake the rescue. We'll be baked alive."

His hollow eyes stared dully at Brek. "In those two minutes, you destroyed the Astrarchy." His voice seemed merely tired, strangely without bitterness. "Just two minutes," he murmured wearily. "If time could be recaptured—"

"Yes," Brek said, "I stopped the autosight." He lifted his gaunt shoulders defiantly, and met the menacing stares of the spacemen. "And they can do nothing about it?"

"Can you?" Hope flickered in the Astrarch's eyes.

"Once you told me, Veronar, that the past could be changed. Then I wouldn't listen. But now—try anything you can. You might be able to save yourself from the unpleasantness that my men are planning."

Looking at the muttering men, Brek shook his head. "I was mistaken," he said deliberately. "I failed to take account of the two-way nature of time. But the future, I see now, is as real as the past. Aside from the direction of entropy change and the flow of consciousness, future and past cannot be distinguished.

"The future determines the past, as much as the past does the future. It is possible to trace out the determiner factors, and even, with sufficient power, to cause a local deflection of the geodesics. But world lines are fixed in the future, as rigidly as in the past. However the factors are rearranged, the end result will always be the same."

The Astrarch's waxen face was ruthless. "Then, Veronar, you are doomed."

Slowly, Brek smiled. "Don't call me Veronar," he said softly. "I remembered, just in time, that I am William Webster, Earthman. You can kill me in any way you please. But the defeat of the Astrarchy and the new freedom of Earth are fixed in time—forever."

# POSTPAID TO PARADISE *Argosy*
## June

## by Robert Arthur (1909-1969)

*Robert Arthur (Robert A. Feder) is a neglected writer of sf and fantasy, best known as a television and radio producer and scriptwriter. This is unfortunate, because he produced a number of excellent stories, many of them outside the sf magazines. In the science fiction field his reputation resides with his "Murchison Morks" series of which this story was the first.*

*"Postpaid to Paradise" has an interesting publishing history, since it was reprinted by* The Magazine of Fantasy and Science Fiction *in 1950 and, in spite of its non-original status, was selected for inclusion in the first* Best From F & SF.

(Nowadays, of course, with the vast increase in the number of science fiction writers, I am not surprised that there are so many I haven't met—or having met them, that they don't stick in my aging mind. It bothers me, though, that I never met some of the old-timers. I never met Robert Arthur, for instance, but I was always particularly fond of his stories. I.A.)

It was Hobby Week at the Club, and Malcolm was displaying his stamp collection.

"Now take these triangulars," he said. "Their value is not definitely known, since they've never been sold as a unit. But they make up the rarest and most interesting complete set known to philatelists. They—"

"I once had a set of stamps that was even rarer and more

65

interesting," Murchison Morks interrupted, his voice melancholy. Morks is a small, wispy man who usually sits by the fireplace and smokes his pipe, silently contemplating the coals. I do not believe he particularly cares for Malcolm, who is our only millionaire and likes what he owns to be better than what anybody else owns.

"You own a set of stamps *rarer* than my triangulars?" Malcolm asked incredulously, a dark tinge of annoyance creeping into his ruddy cheeks.

"Not own, no." Morks shook his head in gentle correction. "Owned."

"Oh!" Malcolm snorted. "I suppose they got burned? Or stolen?"

"No"—and Morks uttered a sigh—"I used them. For postage, I mean. Before I realized their utter uniqueness."

Malcolm gnawed at his lip.

"This set of stamps," he said with great positiveness, laying a possessive hand on the glass covering the triangular bits of paper, "cost the life of at least one man."

"Mine," Morks replied, "cost me my best friend."

"Cost you the *life* of your best friend?" Malcolm demanded.

Morks shook his head, his face expressing a reflective sadness, as if in his mind he were living again a bit of the past that it still hurt him to remember.

"I don't know," he answered the philatelist. "I really don't. I suspect not. I honestly think that Harry Norris—that was my friend—at this moment is a dozen times happier than any man here. And when I reflect that but for a bit of timidity on my part I might be with him—

"But I had better tell you the whole story," he said more briskly, "so you can fully understand."

I am not a stamp collector myself [he began, with a pleasant nod toward Malcolm] but my father was. He died some years ago, and among other things he left me his collection.

It was not a particularly good one—he had leaned more toward picturesqueness in his items than toward rarity or value—and when I sold it, I hardly got enough for it to repay me for the trouble I went to in having it appraised.

I even thought for a time of keeping it; for some of his collection, particularly those stamps from tropical countries that featured exotic birds and beasts, were highly decorative.

But in the end I sold them all—except one set of five

which the dealer refused to take, because he said they were forgeries.

Forgeries! If he had only guessed.

But naturally I took his word for it. I assumed he knew. Especially since the five stamps differed considerably from any I had ever seen before, and had not even been pasted into my father's album. Instead, they had been loose in an envelope tucked in at the rear of the book.

But forgeries or not, they were both interesting and attractive. The five were in differing denominations: ten cents, fifty cents, one dollar, three dollars, and five dollars.

All were unused, in mint condition—that's the term, isn't it, Malcolm?—and in the gayest of colors; vermillion and ultramarine, emerald and yellow, orange and azure, chocolate and ivory, black and gold.

And since they were all large—their size was roughly four times that of the current airmail stamps, with which you are all familiar—the scenes they showed had great vividness and reality.

In particular the three-dollar one, portraying the native girl with the platter of fruit on her head—

However, that's getting ahead of my story. Let me say simply that, thinking they were forgeries, I put them away in my desk and forgot about them.

I found them again one night, quite by accident, when I was rummaging around in the back of a drawer, looking for an envelope in which to post a letter I had just written to my best friend, Harry Norris. Harry was at the time living in Boston.

It so happened that the only envelope I could find was the one in which I had been keeping those stamps of my father's. I emptied them out, addressed the envelope, and then, after I had sealed the letter inside, found my attention attracted to those five strange stamps.

I have mentioned that they were all large and rectangular: almost the size of baggage labels, rather than of conventional postage stamps. But then, of course, these were not conventional postage stamps.

Across the top of them was a line in bold print: FEDERATED STATES OF EL DORADO. Then, on either side, about the center, the denomination. And at the bottom, another line, *Rapid Post.*

Being unfamiliar with such things, I had assumed when first I found them that El Dorado was one of these small Indian states, or perhaps it was in Central America someplace. Rapid Post, I judged, would probably correspond to our own airmail.

Since the denominations were in cents and dollars, I rather leaned to the Latin American theory: there are a lot of little countries down there that I'm always getting confused, like San Salvador and Colombia. But until that moment I had never really given the matter much thought.

Now, staring at them, I began to wonder whether that dealer had known his business. They were done so well, the engraving executed with such superb verve, the colors so bold and attractive, that it hardly seemed likely any forger could have gotten them up.

It is true the subjects they depicted were far from usual. The ten-cent value, for instance, pictured a unicorn standing erect, head up, spiral horn pointing skyward, mane flowing, the very breathing image of life.

It was almost impossible to look at it without *knowing* that the artist had worked with a real unicorn for a model. Except, of course, that there aren't any unicorns any more.

The fifty-center showed Neptune, trident held aloft, riding a pair of harnessed dolphins through a foaming surf. It was just as real as the first.

The one-dollar value depicted Pan playing on his pipes, with a Greek temple in the background, and three fauns dancing on the grass. Looking at it, I could almost hear the music he was making.

I'm not exaggerating in the least. I must admit I was a little puzzled that a tropical country should be putting Pan on one of its stamps, for I thought he was purely a Greek monopoly. But when I moved on to the three-dollar stamp, I forgot all about him.

I probably can't put into words quite the impression that stamp made upon me—and upon Harry Norris, later.

The central figure was a girl; I believe I spoke of that.

A native girl, against a background of tropical flowers, a girl of about sixteen, I should say, just blossomed into womanhood, smiling a little secret smile that managed to combine the utter innocence of girlhood with all the inherited wisdom of a woman.

Or am I making myself clear? Not very? Well, no matter. Let it go at that. I'll only add that on her head, native fashion, she was carrying a great flat platter piled high with fruit of every kind you can imagine; and that platter, together with some flowers at her feet, was her only attire.

I looked at her for quite a long time, before I examined the last of the set—the five-dollar value.

This one was relatively uninteresting, by comparison—just a map. It showed several small islands set down in an expanse of water labeled, in neat letters, *Sea of El Dorado*. I assumed that the islands represented the Federated States of El Dorado itself, and that the little dot on the largest, marked by the word Nirvana, was the capital of the country.

Then an idea occurred to me. Harry had a nephew who collected stamps. Just for the fun of it, I might put one of those El Dorado forgeries—if they were forgeries—on my letter to Harry, along with the regular stamp, and see whether it wouldn't go through the post office. If it did, Harry's nephew might get a rarity, a foreign stamp with an American cancellation.

It was a silly idea, but it was late at night and finding the stamps had put me in a gay mood. I promptly licked the ten-cent El Dorado, pasted it onto the corner of Harry's letter, and then got up to hunt a regulation stamp to put with it.

The search took me into my bedroom, where I found the necessary postage in the wallet I had left in my coat. While I was gone, I left the letter itself lying in plain sight on my desk.

And when I got back into the library, the letter was gone.

I don't need to say I was puzzled. There wasn't any place it could have gone to. There wasn't anybody who could have taken it. The window was open, but it was a penthouse window overlooking twenty floors of empty space, and nobody had come in through it.

Nor was there any breeze that might have blown the envelope to the floor. I looked. In fact, I looked everywhere, growing steadily more puzzled.

And then, as I was about to give up, my phone began ringing.

It was Harry Norris, calling me from Boston. His voice, as he said hello, was a little strained. I quickly found out why.

Three minutes before, as he was getting ready for bed, the letter I had just finished giving up for lost had come swooping in his window, hung for a moment in midair as he stared at it, and then fluttered to the floor.

The next afternoon, Harry Norris arrived in New York. I had promised him over the phone, after explaining about the

El Dorado stamp on the letter, not to touch the others except to put them safely away.

It was obvious that the stamp was responsible for what had happened. In some manner it had carried that letter from my library straight to Harry Norris' feet in an estimated time of three minutes, or at an average rate of approximately five thousand miles an hour.

It was a thought to stagger the imagination. Certainly it staggered mine.

Harry arrived just at lunch time, and over lunch I told him all I knew; just what I've told you now. He was disappointed at the meagerness of my information. But I couldn't add a thing to the facts we already knew, and those facts spoke for themselves.

Basically, they reduced to this: I had put the El Dorado stamp on Harry's letter, and promptly that letter had delivered itself to him with no intermediary processes whatever.

"No, that's not quite right!" Harry burst out. "Look. I brought the letter with me. And—"

He held it out to me, and I saw I had been wrong. There *had* been an intermediary process of some kind, for the stamp was canceled. Yes, and the envelope was postmarked, too, in a clearly legible, pale purple ink.

*Federated States of El Dorado,* the postmark said. It was circular, like our own; and in the center of the circle, where the time of cancellation usually is, was just the word *Thursday*.

"Today is Thursday," Harry remarked. "It was after midnight when you put the stamp on the letter?"

"Just after," I told him. "Seems queer these El Dorado people pay no attention to the hour and the minute, doesn't it?"

"Only proves they're a tropical country," Harry suggested. "Time means little or nothing in the tropics, you know. But what I was getting at, the Thursday postmark goes to show El Dorado is probably down in Central America, as you suggested. If it were in India, or the Orient, it would have been marked Wednesday, wouldn't it? On account of the time difference?"

"Or would it have been Friday?" I asked, rather doubtfully, not knowing much about those things. "In any case we can find out easily enough. We've just to look in the atlas. I don't know why I didn't think of it before."

Harry brightened.

"Of course," he said. "Where do you keep yours?"

But it turned out I hadn't any atlas in the house—not even a small one. So we phoned downtown to one of the big bookstores to send up their latest and largest atlas. And while we waited for it we examined the letter again and speculated upon the method by which it had been transmitted.

"Rapid post!" Harry explained. "I should say so! It beats airmail all hollow. Why, if that letter not only traveled from here to Boston between the time you missed it and it fell at my feet, but actually went all the way to Central America, was canceled and postmarked, and *then* went on to Boston, its average speed must have been—"

We did a little rough calculation and hit upon two thousand miles a minute as a probable speed. When we'd done that, we looked at each other.

"Good Lord!" Harry gasped. "The Federated States of El Dorado may be a tropical country, but they've really hit upon something new in this thing! I wonder why we haven't heard about it before?"

"May be keeping it a secret," I suggested. "No, that won't do, because I've had the stamps for several years, and of course, my father had them before that."

"I tell you, there's something queer here," Harry suggested, darkly. "Where are those others you told me about? I think we ought to make a few tests with them while we're waiting for that atlas."

With that I brought out the four remaining unused stamps, and handed them to him. Now Harry, among other things, was a rather good artist; and his whistle at the workmanship was appreciative. He examined each with care, but it was— I'd thought it would be—the three-dollar value that really caught his eye. The one with the native girl on it, you remember.

"Lord!" Harry said aloud. "What a beauty!"

Presently, however, Harry put that one aside and finished examining the others. Then he turned to me.

"The thing I can't get over," he commented, "is the *life-likeness* of the figures. You know what I'd suspect if I didn't know better? I'd suspect these stamps were never engraved at all. I'd believe that the plates they came from were prepared from photographs."

"From photographs!" I exclaimed; and Harry nodded.

"Of course, you know and I know they can't have been," he added. "Unicorns and Neptunes and Pans aren't running around to be photographed, these days. But that's the feeling they give me."

I confessed that I had had the same feeling. But since we both agreed on the impossibility of its being so, we dismissed that phase of the matter and went back again to the problem of the method used in transporting the letter.

"You say you were out of the room when it vanished," Harry remarked. "That means you didn't see it go. You don't actually know what happened when you put that stamp on and turned your back, do you?"

I agreed that was so, and Harry sat in thoughtful silence. At last he looked up.

"*I* think," he said, "we ought to find out by using one of these other stamps to mail something with."

Why that hadn't occurred to me before I can't imagine. As soon as Harry said it, I recognized the rightness of the idea. The only thing was to decide what to send, and to whom.

That held us up for several minutes. There wasn't anybody else either of us cared to have know about this just now; and we couldn't send anything to each other very well, being both there together.

"I'll tell you!" Harry exclaimed at last. "We'll send something to El Dorado itself!"

I agreed to that readily enough, but how it came about that we decided to send, not a letter, but Thomas à Becket, my aged and ailing Siamese cat, I can't remember.

I do know that I told myself it would be a kind way to dispose of the creature. Transmission through space at the terrific velocity of one hundred and twenty thousand miles an hour would surely put him out of his sufferings, quickly and painlessly.

Thomas à Becket was asleep under the couch, breathing asthmatically and with difficulty. I found a cardboard box the right size and we punched some air holes in it. Then I gathered up Thomas and placed him in the container. He opened rheumy old eyes, gazed at me vaguely, and relapsed into slumber again. With a pang I put the lid on and we tied the box.

"Now," Harry said thoughtfully, "there's the question of how to address him, of course. However, any address will do for our purpose."

He took up a pen and wrote with rapidity. *Mr. Henry Smith, 711 Elysian Fields Avenue, Nirvana, Federated*

*States of El Dorado.* And beneath that he added, *Perishable! Handle With Care!*

"But—" I began. Harry cut me off.

"No," he said, "of course I don't know of any such address. I just made it up. But the post-office people won't know that, will they?"

"But what will happen when—" I began again, and again he had had the answer before I'd finished the question.

"It'll go to the dead letter office, I expect," he told me. "And if he *is* dead, they'll dispose of him. If he's alive, I've no doubt they'll take good care of him. From the stamps I've gotten a notion living is easy there."

That silenced my questions, and Harry picked up a stamp—the fifty-cent value—licked it, and placed it firmly on the box. Then he withdrew his hand and stepped back beside me.

Intently, we watched the parcel.

For a moment, nothing whatever happened.

And then, just as disappointment was gathering on Harry Norris' countenance, the box holding Thomas à Becket rose slowly into the air, turned like a compass needle, and began to drift with increasing speed toward the open window.

By the time it reached the window, it was moving with racehorse velocity. It shot through and into the open. We rushed to the window and saw it moving upward in a westerly direction, above the Manhattan skyline.

And then, as we stared, it began to be vague in outline, misty; and an instant later had vanished entirely. Because of its speed, I suggested, the same way a rifle bullet is invisible.

But Harry had another idea. He shook his head as we stepped back toward the center of the room.

"No," he began, "I don't think that's the answer. I have a notion—"

What his notion was I never did find out. Because just then he stopped speaking, with his mouth still open, and I saw him stiffen. He was looking past me, and I turned to see what had affected him so.

Outside the window was the package we had just seen vanish. It hung there for a moment, then moved slowly into the room, gave a little swoop, and settled lightly onto the table from which, not two minutes before, it had left.

Harry and I rushed over to it, and our eyes must have bugged out a bit.

Because the package was all properly canceled and postmarked, just as the letter had been. With the addition that across the corner, in large purple letters, somebody had stamped, RETURN TO SENDER. NO SUCH PERSON AT THIS ADDRESS.

"Well!" Harry said at last. It wasn't exactly adequate, but it was all either of us could think of. Then, inside the box, Thomas à Becket let out a squall.

I cut the cords and lifted the lid. Thomas à Becket leaped out with an animation he had not shown in years.

There was no denying it. Instead of killing him, his trip to El Dorado, brief as it was, had done him good. He looked five years younger.

Harry Norris was turning the box over in his hands, perplexed.

"What I can't get over," he remarked, "is that there really *is* such an address as 711 Elysian Fields Avenue. I swear I just made it up."

"There's more to it than that," I reminded him. "The very fact that the package came back. We didn't put any return address on it."

"So we didn't," Harry agreed. "Yet they knew just where to return it, didn't they?"

He pondered for a moment longer. Then he put the box down.

"I'm beginning to think," he said, an odd expression on his face, "that there is more to this than we realize. A great deal more. I suspect the whole truth is a lot more exciting than we have any notion. As for this Federated States of El Dorado, I have a theory—"

But he didn't tell me what his theory was. Instead, that three-dollar chocolate-and-ivory stamp caught his eye again.

"Jove!" he whispered, more to himself than to me—he was given occasionally to these archaic ejaculations—"she's beautiful. Heavenly! With a model like that an artist might paint—"

"He might forget to paint, too," I put in. Harry nodded.

"He might indeed," he agreed. "Though I think he'd be inspired in the end to work he'd never on earth have dreamed of doing, otherwise." His gaze at the stamp was almost hungry. "This girl," he declared, "is the one I've been waiting all my life to find. To meet her I'd give—I'd give— Well, almost anything."

"I'm afraid you'd have to go to El Dorado to do that," I suggested flippantly, and Harry started.

"So I would! And I'm perfectly willing to do it, too. Listen! These stamps suggest this El Dorado place must be rather fascinating. What do you say we both pay it a visit? We neither of us have any ties to keep us, and—"

"Go there just so you can meet the girl who was the model for that stamp?" I demanded.

"Why not? Can you think of a better reason?" he asked me. "I can give you more. For one thing, the climate. Look how much better the cat is. His little excursion took years off his age. Must be a highly healthful place. Maybe it'll make a young man of you again. And besides—"

But he didn't have to go on. I was already convinced.

"All right," I agreed. "We'll take the first boat. But when we get there, how will we—"

"By logic," Harry shot back. "Purely by logic. The girl must have posed for an artist, mustn't she? And the postmaster general of El Dorado must know who the artist is, mustn't he? We'll go straight to the postmaster general. He'll direct us to the artist. The artist will give us her name and address. Could anything be simpler?"

I hadn't realized how easy it would be. Now some of his impatience was getting into my own blood.

"Maybe we won't have to take a boat," I suggested. "Maybe there's a plane service. That would save—"

"Boat!" Harry Norris snorted, stalking back and forth across the room and waving his hands. "Plane! You can take boats and planes if you want to. I've got a better idea. I'm going to El Dorado by mail!"

Until I saw how beautifully simple his idea was, I was a bit stunned. But he quickly pointed out that Thomas à Becket had made the trip, and come back, without injury. If a cat could do it, a man could.

There wasn't a thing in the way except the choice of a destination. It would be rather wasted effort to go, only to be sent back ignominiously for want of proper addressing.

"I have that figured out too," Harry told me promptly when I voiced the matter. "The first person I'd go to see anyway when I got there would be the postmaster general. *He* must exist, certainly. And mail addressed to him would be the easiest of all to deliver. So why not kill two birds with one stone by posting myself to his office?"

That answered all my objections. It was as sound and sensible a plan as I'd ever heard.

"Why," Harry Norris added with rising excitement, "I may

be having dinner with the girl tonight! Wine and pome-
granates beneath a gold-washed moon, with Pan piping in
the shadows and nymphs dancing on the velvet green!"

"But"—I felt I had to prepare him for possible disappointment—"suppose she's married by now?"

He shook his head.

"She won't be. I have a feeling. Just a feeling. Now to
settle the details. We've got three stamps left—nine dollars'
worth altogether. That should be enough. I'm a bit lighter;
you've been taking on weight lately, I see. Four dollars
should carry me—the one and the three. That leaves the
five-dollar for you.

"As for the address, we'll write that on tags and tie them
to our wrists. You have tags, haven't you? Yes, here's a couple in this drawer. Now give me that pen and ink. Something
like this ought to do very well . . ."

He wrote, then held the tags out to me. They were just
alike. *Office of the Postmaster General,* they said. *Nirvana,
Federated States of El Dorado. Perishable. Handle With
Care.*

"Now," he said, "we'll each tie one to our wrist—"

But I drew back. Somehow I couldn't quite nerve myself to
it. Delightful as the prospects he had painted of the place, the
idea of posting myself into the unknown, the way I had sent
off Thomas à Becket, did something queer to me.

I told him I would join him. I would take the first boat, or
plane, and meet him there, say at the principal hotel.

Harry was disappointed, but he was too impatient by now
to argue.

"Well," he agreed, "all right. But if for any reason you
can't get a boat or plane, you'll use that last stamp to join
me?"

I promised faithfully that I would. With that he held out
his right wrist and I tied a tag about it. Then he took up the
one-dollar stamp, moistened it, and applied it to the tag. He
had the three-dollar one in his hand when the doorbell rang.

"In a minute," he was saying, "or maybe in less, I shall
probably be in the fairest land man's combined imagination
has ever been able to picture."

"Wait!" I called, and hurried out to answer the bell. I don't
know whether he heard me or not. He was just lifting that
second stamp to his tongue to moisten it when I turned away,
and that was the last I ever saw of him.

When I came back, with the package in my hands—the

ring had been the messenger from the bookshop, with the atlas we had ordered—Harry Norris was gone.

Thomas à Becket was sitting up and staring toward the window. The curtains were still fluttering. I hurried over. But Norris was not in sight.

Well, I thought, he must have put on that stamp he had in his hand, not knowing I'd left the room. I could see him, in my mind's eye, that very moment being deposited on his feet in the office of an astonished postmaster general.

Then it occurred to me I might as well find out just where the Federated States of El Dorado were, after all. So I ripped the paper off the large volume the bookstore had sent and began to leaf through it.

When I had finished, I sat in silence for a while. From time to time I glanced at that unused tag, and that uncanceled stamp still lying on my desk. Then I made my decision.

I got up and fetched Harry's bag. It was summer, luckily, and he had brought mostly light clothing. To it I added anything of mine I thought he might be able to use, including a carton of cigarettes, and pen and ink on the chance he might want to write me.

As an afterthought I added a small Bible—just in case.

Then I strapped the bag shut and affixed the tag to it. I wrote *Harry Norris* above the address, pasted that last El Dorado stamp to it, and waited.

In a moment the bag rose in the air, floated to the window, out, and began to speed away.

It would reach there, I figured, before Harry had had time to leave the postmaster general's office, and I hoped he might send me a postcard or something by way of acknowledgment. But he didn't. Perhaps he couldn't.

. . . At this point Morks stopped, as if he had finished his story. But unnoticed Malcolm had left our little group for a moment. Now he came pushing back into it with a large atlas-gazeteer in his hands.

"So that's what became of your set of rarities!" he said, with a scarcely veiled sneer. "Very interesting and entertaining. But there's one point I want to clear up. The stamps were issued by the Federated States of El Dorado, you say. Well, I've just been looking through this atlas, and there's no such place on earth."

Morks looked at him, his melancholy countenance calm.

"I know it," he said. "That's why, after glancing through my own atlas that day, I didn't keep my promise to Harry Norris and use that last stamp to join him. I'm sorry now. When I think of how Harry must be enjoying himself there—

"But it's no good regretting what I did or didn't do. I couldn't help it. The truth is that my nerve failed me, just for a moment then, when I discovered there *was* no such place as the Federated States of El Dorado—on earth, I mean."

And sadly he shook his head.

"I've often wished I knew where my father got those stamps," he murmured, almost to himself; then fell into a meditative silence.

# COVENTRY* *Astounding Science Fiction*
July

## by Robert A. Heinlein

"Coventry" is a sequel to "If This Goes On . . ." (ASF, February, 1940) and with the addition of "Misfit" (see Volume One) was published as *Revolt in 2100* in 1953 by Shasta, one of the early specialist science fiction publishers. The present selection is perhaps Heinlein's finest statement of his position on, and commitment to, individualism, privacy, and the necessity to *earn* liberty. It can also be read as an indictment of synthetic contemporary Western civilization.

(Although Bob and I have been good friends for forty years now, whe don't see eye-to-eye politically. I, for instance, am suspicious of any doctrine that tells us we must *earn* liberty. Who decides when we have earned it and who has the right to withhold it if we haven't earned it? It bothers me.

I'm also suspicious of those who equate liberty with "small government," meaning less interference from Washington over the details of our life. I don't believe there can be less interference; just a change of interference. If Washington bows out, then it is the local bully on the block who will take over, and I'd rather have Washington. Every once in a while through history, places have tried "small government" and replaced a tyrannical central power with local "self-help." It's called "feudalism" and it's also called "dark ages" and I don't want it. —But I must say Bob preaches his point of view charmingly. I.A.)

* See note following end of Introduction.

# INTO THE DARKNESS

*Astonishing Stories*

June

## by Ross Rocklynne (1913-        )

> *One of the best of the "second rank" writers of
> the late thirties and forties, Ross Rocklynne (real
> name Ross L. Rocklin), has been a neglected figure
> in science fiction, largely because he produced very
> little long fiction. The best of his work, including
> stories like "Jackdaw" (1942), "Jaywalker" (1950),
> and "Time Wants a Skeleton" can be found in his
> two Ace Books collections* The Men and the Mirror
> *and* The Sun Destroyers, *both 1973. He has con-
> tinued to write and has produced some interesting
> work in recent years, especially "Ching Witch" in*
> Again Dangerous Visions *(1972) and "Randy-Tandy
> Man" in* Universe 3.
>
> *"Into the Darkness" is a remarkable story, very
> different from the "usual" sf of 1940—with a little
> polishing, it would find little difficulty fitting in to
> the so-called "New Wave" of the 1960s. As Terry
> Carr reminds us, this story was written in 1934, but
> none of the editors of the day would touch it until
> Fred Pohl published it in* Astonishing.

(I'm not sure how you define "New Wave," a name given
to stories that appeared in the 1960s except to say that they
were characterized by writing that was experimental and different and by tales that broke new ground.

Well, what about 1940? Who ever heard about "New
Wave" then? I remember that in the April, 1940 *Astonishing
Stories,* I published a story called "The Callistan Menace,"
the second story I ever wrote and it was Old Wave; it was
Ancient Wave; it was Antediluvian Wave.

Yet one issue later, one little issue, in the June, 1940 *Astonishing* Ross Rocklynne published "Into the Darkness."
What do you make of it? It never slips. It stays inside the

minds of creatures and life and conditions altogether different from ours. It breaks new ground; it is experimental and different. The style and literary gloss may not be quite as high and polished as was the writing of the 1960s, but "Into the Darkness" is surely New Wave a quarter-century before its time. Fred Pohl was the editor who accepted it. Not surprising. I.A.)

## I. Birth of "Darkness"

Out in space, on the lip of the farthest galaxy, and betwixt two star clusters, there came into being a luminiferous globe that radiated for light-years around. A life had been born!

It became aware of light; one of its visions had become activated. First it saw the innumerable suns and nebulae whose radiated energy now fed it. Beyond that it saw a dense, impenetrable darkness.

The darkness intrigued it. It could understand the stars, but the darkness it could not. The babe probed outward several light-years and met only lightlessness. It probed farther, and farther, but there was no light. Only after its visions could not delve deeper did it give up, but a strange seed had been sown; that there was light on the far edge of the darkness became its innate conviction.

Wonders never seemed to cease parading themselves before this newly born. It became aware of another personality hovering near, an energy creature thirty millions of miles across. At its core hung a globe of subtly glowing green light one million miles in diameter.

He explored this being with his vision, and it remained still during his inspection. He felt strange forces plucking at him, forces that filled him to overflowing with peacefulness. At once, he discovered a system of energy waves having marvelous possibilities.

"Who are you?" these waves were able to inquire of that other life.

Softly soothing, he received answer.

"I am your mother."

"You mean—?"

"You are my son—my creation. I shall call you—

Darkness. Lie here and grow, Darkness, and when you are many times larger, I will come again."

She had vanished, swallowed untraceably by a vast spiral nebula—a cloud of swiftly twisting stardust.

He lay motionless, strange thoughts flowing. Mostly he wondered about the sea of lightlessness lapping the shore of this galaxy in which he had been born. Sometime later, he wondered about life, what life was, and its purpose.

"When *she* comes again, I shall ask her," he mused. "Darkness, she called me—Darkness!"

His thoughts swung back to the darkness.

For five million years he bathed himself in the rays that permeate space. He grew. He was ten million miles in diameter.

His mother came; he saw her hurtling toward him from a far distance. She stopped close.

"You are much larger, Darkness. You grow faster than the other newly born." He detected pride in her transmitted thoughts.

"I have been lying here, thinking," he said. "I have been wondering, and I have come to guess at many things. There are others, like you and myself."

"There are thousands of others. I am going to take you to them. Have you tried propellents?"

"I have not tried, but I shall." There was a silence. "I have discovered the propellents," said Darkness, puzzled, "but they will not move me."

She seemed amused. "That is one thing you do not know, Darkness. You are inhabiting the seventeenth band of hyperspace; propellents will not work there. See if you can expand."

All these were new things, but instinctively he felt himself expand to twice his original size.

"Good. I am going to snap you into the first band. . . . There. Try your propellents."

He tried them, and, to his intense delight, the flaring lights that were the stars fled past. So great was his exhilaration that he worked up a speed that placed him several light-years from his mother.

She drew up beside him. "For one so young, you have speed. I shall be proud of you. I feel, Darkness," and there was wistfulness in her tone, "that you will be different from the others."

She searched his memory swirls. "But try not to be too different."

Puzzled at this, he gazed at her, but she turned away. "Come."

He followed her down the aisles formed by the stars, as she accommodated her pace to his.

They stopped at the sixth galaxy from the abyss of lightlessness. He discerned thousands of shapes that were his kind moving swiftly past and around him. These, then, were his people.

She pointed them out to him. "You will know them by their vibrations, and the varying shades of the colored globes of light at their centers."

She ran off a great list of names which he had no trouble in impressing on his memory swirls.

"Radiant, Vibrant, Swift, Milky, Incandescent, Great Power, Sun-eater, Light-year. . . ."

"Come, I am going to present you to Oldster."

They whirled off to a space seven light-years distant. They stopped, just outside the galaxy. There was a peculiar snap in his consciousness.

"Oldster has isolated himself in the sixth band of hyperspace," said his mother.

Where before he had seen nothing save inky space, dotted with masses of flaming, tortured matter, he now saw an energy creature whose aura fairly radiated old age. And the immense purple globe which hung at his core lacked a certain vital luster which Darkness had instinctively linked with his own youth and boundless energy.

His mother caught the old being's attention, and Darkness felt his thought-rays contact them.

"Oh, it's you, Sparkle," the old being's kindly thoughts said. "And who is it with you?"

Darkness saw his mother, Sparkle, shoot off streams of crystalline light.

"This is my first son."

The newly born felt Oldster's thought rays going through his memory swirls.

"And you have named him Darkness," said Oldster slowly. "Because he has wondered about it." His visions withdrew, half-absently. "He is so young, and yet he is a thinker; already he thinks about life."

For long and long Oldster bent a penetrating gaze upon him. Abruptly, his vision rays swung away and centered on a tiny, isolated group of stars. There was a heavy, dragging silence.

"Darkness," Oldster said finally, "your thoughts are useless." The thoughts now seemed to come from an immeasurable distance, or an infinitely tired mind. "You are young, Darkness. Do not think so much—so much that the happiness of life is destroyed in the over-estimation of it. When you wish, you may come to see me. I shall be in the sixth band for many millions of years."

Abruptly, Oldster vanished. He had snapped both mother and son back in the first band.

She fixed her vision on him. "Darkness, what he says is true—every word. Play for a while—there are innumerable things to do. And once in great intervals, if you wish, go to see Oldster; but for a long time do not bother him with your questions."

"I will try," answered Darkness, in sudden decision.

## II. Cosmic Children

Darkness played. He played for many millions of years. With playmates of his own age, he roamed through and through the endless numbers of galaxies that composed the universe. From one end to another he dashed in a reckless obedience to Oldster's command.

He explored the surfaces of stars, often disrupting them into fragments, sending scalding geysers of belching flame millions of miles into space. He followed his companions into the swirling depths of the green-hued nebulae that hung in intergalactic space. But to disturb these mighty creations of nature was impossible. Majestically they rolled around and around, or coiled into spirals, or at times condensed into matter that formed beautiful, hot suns.

Energy to feed on was rampant here, but so densely and widely was it distributed that he and his comrades could not even dream of absorbing more than a trillionth part of it in all their lives.

He learned the mysteries of the forty-seven bands of hyperspace. He learned to snap into them or out again into the first or true band at will. He knew the delights of blackness impenetrable in the fifteenth band, of a queerly illusory multiple existence in the twenty-third, and an equally strange sensation of speeding away from himself in an opposite direction in the thirty-first, and of the forty-seventh, where all space turned into a nightmarish concoction of cubistic suns and galaxies.

Incomprehensible were those forty-seven bands. They were coexistent in space, yet they were separated from each other by a means which no one had ever discovered. In each band were unmistakable signs that it was the same universe. Darkness only knew that each band was one of forty-seven subtly differing faces which the universe possessed, and the powers of his mind experienced no difficulty in allowing him to cross the unseen bridges which spanned the gulfs between them.

And he made no attempts toward finding the solution—he was determined to cease thinking, for the time being at least. He was content to play, and to draw as much pleasure and excitement as he could from every new possibility of amusement.

But the end of all *that* came, as he had suspected it would. He played, and loved all this, until. . . .

He had come to his fifty-millionth year, still a youth. The purple globe at his core could have swallowed a sun a million miles in diameter, and his whole body could have displaced fifty suns of that size. For a period of a hundred thousand years he lay asleep in the seventh band, where a soft, colorless light pervaded the universe.

He awoke, and was about to transfer himself to the first band and rejoin the children of Radiant, Light-year, Great Power and all those others.

He stopped, almost dumbfounded, for a sudden, overwhelming antipathy for companionship had come over him. He discovered, indeed, that he never wanted to join his friends again. While he had slept, a metamorphosis had come about, and he was as alienated from his playmates as if he had never known them.

What had caused it? Something. Perhaps, long before his years, he had passed into the adult stage of mind. Now he was rebelling against the friendships which meant nothing more than futile play.

Play! Bouncing huge suns around like rubber balls, and then tearing them up into solar systems; chasing one another up the scale through the forty-seven bands, and back again; darting about in the immense spaces between galaxies, rendering themselves invisible by expanding to ten times normal size.

He did not want to play, and he never wanted to see his

friends again. He did not hate them, but he was intolerant of the characteristics which bade them to disport among the stars for eternity.

He was not mature in size, but he felt he had become an adult, while they were still children—tossing suns the length of a galaxy, and then hurling small bits of materialized energy around them to form planets; then just as likely to hurl huger masses to disrupt the planetary systems they so painstakingly made.

He had felt it all along—this superiority. He had manifested it by besting them in every form of play they conceived. They generally bungled everything, more apt to explode a star into small fragments than to whirl it until centrifugal force threw off planets.

"I have become an adult in mind, if not in body; I am at the point where I must accumulate wisdom, and perhaps sorrow," he thought whimsically. "I will see Oldster, and ask him my questions—the questions I have thus far kept in the background of my thoughts. But," he added thoughtfully, "I have a feeling that even his wisdom will fail to enlighten me. Nevertheless, there must be answers. What is life? Why is it? And there must be—another universe beyond the darkness that hems this one in."

Darkness reluctantly turned and made a slow trail across that galaxy and into the next, where he discovered those young energy creatures with whom it would be impossible to enjoy himself again.

He drew up, and absently translated his time standard to one corresponding with theirs, a rate of consciousness at which they could observe the six planets whirling around a small, white-hot sun as separate bodies, and not mere rings of light.

They were gathered in numbers of some hundreds around this sun, and Darkness hovered on the outskirts of the crowd, watching them moodily.

One of the young purple lights, Cosmic by name, threw a mass of matter a short distance into space, reached out with a tractor ray and drew it in. He swung it 'round and 'round on the tip of that ray, gradually forming ever-decreasing circles. To endow the planet with a velocity that would hurl it unerringly between the two outermost planetary orbits required a delicate sense of compensatory adjustment between the factors of mass, velocity, and solar attraction.

When Cosmic had got the lump of matter down to an an-

gular velocity that was uniform, Darkness knew an irritation
he had never succeeded in suppressing. An intuition, which
had unfailingly proved itself accurate, told him that anything
but creating an orbit for that planet was likely to ensue.

"Cosmic." He contacted the planet-maker's thought rays.
"Cosmic, the velocity you have generated is too great. The
whole system will break up."

"Oh, Darkness." Cosmic threw a vision on him. "Come on,
join us. You say the speed is wrong? Never; you are! I've calculated everything to a fine point."

"To the wrong point," insisted Darkness stubbornly. "Undoubtedly, your estimation of the planet's mass is the factor
which makes your equation incorrect. Lower the velocity.
You'll see."

Cosmic continued to swing his lump of matter, but stared
curiously at Darkness.

"What's the matter with you?" he inquired. "You don't
sound just right. What does it matter if I do calculate wrong,
and disturb the system's equilibrium? We'll very probably
break up the whole thing later, anyway."

A flash of passion came over Darkness. "That's the trouble," he said fiercely. "It doesn't matter to any of you. You
will always be children. You will always be playing. Careful
construction, joyous destruction—that is the creed on which
you base your lives. Don't you feel as if you'd like, sometime,
to quit playing, and do something—worthwhile?"

As if they had discovered a strangely different set of laws
governing an alien galaxy, the hundreds of youths, greens and
purples, stared at Darkness.

Cosmic continued swinging the planet he had made
through space, but he was plainly puzzled. "What's wrong
with you, Darkness? What else is there to do except to roam
the galaxies, and make suns? I can't think of a single living
thing that might be called more worthwhile."

"What good is playing?" answered Darkness. "What good
is making a solar system? If you made one, and then, perhaps, vitalized it with life, that would be worthwhile! Or
think, think! About yourself, about life, why it is, and what it
means in the scheme of things! Or," and he trembled a little,
"try discovering what lies beyond the veil of lightlessness
which surrounds the universe."

The hundreds of youths looked at the darkness.

Cosmic stared anxiously at him. "Are you crazy? We all
know there's nothing beyond. Everything that is is right here

in the universe. That blackness is just empty, and it stretches away from here forever."

"Where did you get that information?" Darkness inquired scornfully. "You don't know that. Nobody does. But I am going to know! I awoke from sleep a short while ago, and I couldn't bear the thought of play. I wanted to do something substantial. So I am going into the darkness."

He turned his gaze hungrily on the deep abyss hemming in the stars. There were thousands of years, even under its lower time-standard, in which awe dominated the gathering. In his astonishment at such an unheard-of intention, Cosmic entirely forgot his circling planet. It lessened in velocity, and then tore loose from the tractor ray that had become weak, in a tangent to the circle it had been performing.

It sped toward that solar system, and entered between the orbits of the outmost planets. Solar gravitation seized it, the lone planet took up an erratic orbit, and then the whole system had settled into complete stability, with seven planets where there had been six.

"You see," said Darkness, with a note of unsteady mirth, "if you had used your intended speed, the system would have coalesced. The speed of the planet dropped, and then escaped you. Some blind chance sent it in the right direction. It was purely an accident. Now throw in a second sun, and watch the system break up. That has always amused you." His aura quivered. "Goodbye, friends."

### III. Oldster

He was gone from their sight forever. He had snapped into the sixth band.

He ranged back to the spot where Oldster should have been. He was not.

"Probably in some other band," thought Darkness, and went through all the others, excepting the fifteenth, where resided a complete lack of light. With a feeling akin to awe, since Oldster was apparently in none of them, he went into the fifteenth, and called out.

There was a period of silence. Then Oldster answered, in his thoughts a cadence of infinite weariness.

"Yes, my son; who calls me?"

"It is I, Darkness, whom Sparkle presented to you nearly fifty million years ago." Hesitating, an unexplainable feeling, as of sadness unquenchable, came to him.

"I looked for you in the sixth," he went on in a rush of words, "but did not expect to find you here, isolated, with no light to see by."

"I am tired of seeing, my son. I have lived too long. I have tired of thinking and of seeing. I am sad."

Darkness hung motionless, hardly daring to interrupt the strange thought of this incredible ancient. He ventured timidly, "It is just that I am tired of playing, Oldster, tired of doing nothing. I should like to accomplish something of some use. Therefore, I have come to you, to ask you three questions, the answers to which I must know."

Oldster stirred restlessly. "Ask your questions."

"I am curious about life." Oldster's visitor hesitated nervously, and then went on. "It has a purpose, I know, and I want to know that purpose. That is my first question."

"But why, Darkness? What makes you think life *has* a purpose, an ultimate purpose?"

"I don't know," came the answer, and for the first time Darkness was startled with the knowledge that he really didn't! "But there must be some purpose!" he cried.

"How can you say 'must'? Oh, Darkness, you have clothed life in garments far too rich for its ordinary character! You have given it the sacred aspect of meaning! There is no meaning to it. Once upon a time the spark of life fired a blob of common energy with consciousness of its existence. From that, by some obscure evolutionary process, we came. That is all. We are born. We live, and grow, and then we die! After that, there is nothing! Nothing!"

Something in Darkness shuddered violently, and then rebelliilously. But his thoughts were quiet and tense. "I won't believe that! You are telling me that life is only meant for death, then. Why—why, if that were so, why should there be life? No, Oldster! I feel that there must be something which justifies my existence."

Was it pity that came flowing along with Oldster's thoughts? "You will never believe me. I knew it. All my ancient wisdom could not change you, and perhaps it is just as well. Yet you may spend a lifetime in learning what I have told you."

His thoughts withdrew, absently, and then returned.

"Your other questions, Darkness."

For a long time Darkness did not answer. He was of half a mind to leave Oldster, and leave it to his own experiences to solve his other problems. His resentment was hotter than a dwarf sun, for a moment. But it cooled and though he was beginning to doubt the wisdom to which Oldster laid claim, he continued with his questioning.

"What is the use of the globe of purple light which forever remains at my center, and even returns, no matter how far I hurl it from me?"

Such a wave of mingled agitation and sadness passed from the old being that Darkness shuddered. Oldster turned on him with extraordinary fierceness. "Do not learn *that* secret! I will not tell you! What might I not have spared myself had I not sought and found the answer to that riddle! I was a thinker, Darkness, like you! Darkness, if you value— Come, Darkness," he went on in a singularly broken manner, "your remaining question." His thought rays switched back and forth with an uncommon sign of utter chaos of mind.

Then they centered on Darkness again. "I know your other query, Darkness. I know, knew when first Sparkle brought you to me, eons ago.

"What is beyond the darkness? That has occupied your mind since your creation. What lies on the fringe of the lightless section by which this universe is bounded?

"I do not know, Darkness. Nor does anyone know."

"But you *must* believe there is something beyond," cried Darkness.

"Darkness, in the dim past of our race, beings of your caliber have tried—five of them I remember in my time, billions of years ago. But, they never came back. They left the universe, hurling themselves into that awful void, and they never came back."

"How do you know they didn't reach that foreign universe?" asked Darkness breathlessly.

"Because they didn't come back," answered Oldster, simply. "If they could have gotten across, at least one or two of them would have returned. They never reached that universe. Why? All the energy they were able to accumulate for that staggering voyage was exhausted. And they dissipated— died—in the energiless emptiness of the darkness."

"There must be a way to cross!" said Darkness violently. "There must be a way to gather energy for the crossing! Oldster, you are destroying my life-dream! I have wanted to cross. I want to find the edge of the darkness. I want to find life there—perhaps then I will find the meaning of all life!"

"Find the—" began Oldster pityingly, then stoppped, realizing the futility of completing the sentence.

"It is a pity you are not like the others, Darkness. Perhaps they understand that it is as purposeful to lie sleeping in the seventh band as to discover the riddle of the darkness. They are truly happy, you are not. Always, my son, you overestimate the worth of life."

"Am I wrong in doing so?"

"No. Think as you will, and think that life is high. There is no harm. Dream your dream of great life, and dream your dream of another universe. There is joy even in the sadness of unattainment."

Again that long silence, and again the smoldering flame of resentment in Darkness' mind. This time there was no quenching of that flame. It burned fiercely.

"I will not dream!" said Darkness furiously. "When first my visions became activated, they rested on the darkness, and my newborn thought-swirls wondered about the darkness, and knew that something lay beyond it!

"And whether or not I die in that void, I am going into it!"

Abruptly, irately, he snapped from the fifteenth band into the first, but before he had time to use his propellents, he saw Oldster, a giant body of intense, swirling energies of pure light, materialize before him.

"Darkness, stop!" and Oldster's thoughts were unsteady. "Darkness," he went on, as the younger energy creature stared spellbound, "I had vowed to myself never to leave the band of lightlessness. I have come from it, a moment, for— you!

"You will die. You will dissipate in the void! You will never cross it, if it can be crossed, with the limited energy your body contains!"

He seized Darkness' thought-swirls in tight bands of energy.

"Darkness, there is knowledge that I possess. Receive it!"

With newborn wonder, Darkness erased consciousness. The mighty accumulated knowledge of Oldster sped into him in a swift flow, a great tide of space lore no other being had ever possessed.

The inflow ceased, and as from an immeasurably distant space came Oldster's parting words:

"Darkness, farewell! Use your knowledge, use it to further your dream. Use it to cross the darkness."

Again fully conscious, Darkness knew that Oldster had gone again into the fifteenth band of utter lightlessness, in his vain attempt at peace.

He hung tensely motionless in the first band, exploring the knowledge that now was his. At the portent of one particular portion of it, he trembled.

In wildest exhilaration, he thrust out his propellents, dashing at full speed to his mother.

He hung before her.

"Mother, I am going into the darkness!"

There was a silence, pregnant with her sorrow. "Yes, I know. It was destined when first you were born. For that I named you Darkness." A restless quiver of sparks left her. Her gaze sad and loving. She said, "Farewell, Darkness, my son."

She wrenched herself from true space, and he was alone. The thought stabbed him. He was alone—alone as Oldster.

Struggling against the vast depression that overwhelmed him, he slowly started on his way to the very farthest edge of the universe, for there lay the Great Energy.

Absently he drifted across the galaxies, the brilliant denizens of the cosmos, lying quiescent on their eternal black beds. He drew a small sun into him, and converted it into energy for the long flight.

And suddenly afar off he saw his innumerable former companions. A cold mirth seized him. Playing! The folly of children, the aimlessness of stars!

He sped away from them, and slowly increased his velocity, the thousands of galaxies flashing away behind. His speed mounted, a frightful acceleration carrying him toward his goal.

## IV. Beyond Light

It took him seven millions of years to cross the universe, going at the tremendous velocity he had attained. And he was in a galaxy whose far flung suns hung out into the darkness, were themselves traveling into the darkness at the comparatively slow pace of several thousand miles a second.

Instantaneously, his vision rested on an immense star, a star so immense that he felt himself unconsciously expand in an effort to rival it. So titanic was its mass that it drew all light rays save the short ultraviolet back into it.

It was hot, an inconceivable mass of matter a billion miles across. Like an evil, sentient monster of the skies it hung, dominating the tiny suns of this galaxy that were perhaps its children, to Darkness flooding the heavens with ultraviolet light from its great expanse of writhing, coiling, belching sur face; and mingled with that light was a radiation of energy so virulent that it ate its way painfully into his very brain.

Still another radiation impinged on him, an energy which, were he to possess its source, would activate his propellents to such an extent that his velocity would pale any to which his race had attained in all its long history!—would hurl him into the darkness at such an unthinkable rate that the universe would be gone in the infinitesimal part of a second!

But how hopeless seemed the task of rending it from that giant of the universe! The source of that energy, he knew with knowledge that was sure, was matter, matter so incomparably dense, its electrons crowding each other till they touched, that even that furiously molten star could not destroy it.

He spurred back several millions of miles, and stared at it. Suddenly he knew fear, a cold fear. He felt that the sun was animate, that it knew he was waiting there, that it was prepared to resist his pitiable onslaughts. And as if in support of his fears, he felt rays of such intense repelling power, such alive, painful malignancy that he almost threw away his mad intentions of splitting it.

"I have eaten suns before," he told himself, with the air of one arguing against himself. "I can at least split that one open, and extract the morsel that lies in its interior."

He drew into him as many of the surrounding suns as he was able, converting them into pure energy. He ceased at last, for no longer could his body, a giant complexity of swarming intense fields sixty millions of miles across, assimilate more.

Then, with all the acceleration he could muster, he dashed headlong at the celestial monster.

It grew and expanded, filling all the skies until he could no longer see anything but it. He drew near its surface. Rays of fearful potency smote him until he convulsed in the whiplash agony of it. A frightful velocity, he contacted the heaving surface, and—made a tiny dent some millions of miles in depth.

He strove to push forward, but streams of energy repelled him, energy that flung him away from the star in acceleration.

He stoppped his backward flight, fighting his torment, and threw himself upon the star again. It repulsed him with an uncanny likeness to a living thing. Again and again he went through the agonizing process, to be as often thrust back.

He could not account for those repelling rays, which seemed to operate in direct contrariness to the star's obviously great gravitational field, nor did he try to account for them. There were mysteries in space which even Oldster had never been able to solve.

But there was a new awe in him. He hung in space, spent and quivering.

"It is *almost* alive," he thought, and then adopted new tactics. Rushing at the giant, he skimmed over and through its surface in titanic spirals, until he had swept it entirely free of raging, incandescent gases. Before the star could replenish its surface, he spiraled it again, clinging to it until he could no longer resist the repelling forces, or the burning rays which impinged upon him.

The star now lay in the heavens diminished by a tenth of its former bulk. Darkness, hardly able to keep himself together, retired a distance from it and discarded excess energy.

He went back to the star.

Churning seas of pure light flickered fitfully across. Now and then there were belchings of matter bursting within itself.

Darkness began again. He charged, head on. He contacted, bored millions of miles, and was thrown back with mounting velocity. Hurtling back into space, Darkness finally knew that all these tactics would in the last analysis prove useless. His glance roving, it came to rest on a dense, redly glowing sun. For a moment it meant nothing, and then he knew, knew that here at last lay the solution.

He plucked that dying star from its place, and swinging it in huge circles on the tip of a tractor ray, flung it with the utmost of his savage force at the gargantuan star.

Fiercely, he watched the smaller sun appproach its parent. Closer, closer, and then—they collided! A titanic explosion ripped space, sending out wave after wave of cosmic rays, causing an inferno of venomous, raging flames that extended far into the skies, licking it in a fury of utter abandon. The mighty sun split wide open, exhibiting a violet hot, gaping maw more than a billion miles wide.

Darkness activated his propellents, and dropped into the awful cavity until he was far beneath its rim, and had approached the center of the star where lay that mass of matter which was the source of the Great Energy. To his sight, it was invisible, save as a blank area of nothingness, since light rays of no wavelength whatsoever could leave it.

Darkness wrapped himself exotically around the sphere, and at the same time the two halves of the giant star fell together, imprisoning him at its core.

This possibility he had not overlooked. With concentrated knots of force, he ate away the merest portion of the surface of the sphere, and absorbed it in him. He was amazed at the metamorphosis. He became aware of a vigor so infinite that he felt nothing could withstand him.

Slowly, he began to expand. He was inexorable. The star could not stop him; it gave. It cracked, great gaping cracks which parted with displays of blinding light and pure heat. He continued to grow, pushing outward.

With the sphere of Great Energy, which was no more than ten million miles across, in his grasp, he continued inflation. A terrific blast of malignant energy ripped at him; cracks millions of miles in length appeared, cosmic displays of pure energy flared. After that, the gargantua gave way before Darkness so readily that he had split it up into separate parts before he ever knew it.

He then became aware that he was in the center of thousands of large and small pieces of the star that were shooting away from him in all directions, forming new suns that would chart individual orbits for themselves.

He had conquered. He hung motionless, grasping the sphere of Great Energy at his center, along with the mystic globe of purple light.

He swung his vision on the darkness, and looked at it in fascination for a long time. Then, without a last look at the universe of his birth, he activated his propellents with the nameless Great Energy, and plunged into that dark well.

All light, save that he created, vanished. He was hemmed in on all sides by the vastness of empty space. Exaltation, coupled with an awareness of the infinite power in his grasp, took hold of his thoughts and made them soar. His acceleration was minimum rather than maximum, yet in a brief space of his time standard he traversed uncountable billions of light-years.

Darkness ahead, and darkness behind, and darkness all around—that had been his dream. It had been his dream all through his life, even during those formless years in which he had played, in obedience to Oldster's admonishment. Always there had been the thought—what lies at the other end of the darkness? Now he was in the darkness, and a joy such as he had never known claimed him. He was on the way! Would he find another universe, a universe which had bred the same kind of life as he had known? He could not think otherwise.

His acceleration was incredible! Yet he knew that he was using a minimum of power. He began to step it up, swiftly increasing even the vast velocity which he had attained. Where lay that other universe? He could not know, and he had chosen no single direction in which to leave his own universe. There had been no choice of direction. Any line stretching into the vault of the darkness might have ended in that alien universe. . . .

Not until a million years had elapsed did his emotions subside. Then there were other thoughts. He began to feel a dreadful fright, a fright that grew on him as he left his universe farther behind. He was hurtling into the darkness that none before him had crossed, and few had dared to try crossing, at a velocity which he finally realized he could attain, but not comprehend. Mind could not think it, thoughts could not say it!

And—he was alone! *Alone!* An icy hand clutched at him. He had never known the true meaning of that word. There were none of his friends near, nor his mother, nor great-brained Oldster—there was no living thing within innumerable light-centuries. *He* was the only life in the void!

Thus, for almost exactly ninety millions of years he wondered and thought, first about life, then the edge of the darkness, and lastly the mysterious energy field eternally at his core. He found the answer to two, and perhaps, in the end, the other.

Ever, each infinitesimal second that elapsed, his visions were probing hundreds of light-years ahead, seeking the first sign of that universe he believed in; but no, all was darkness so dense it seemed to possess mass.

The monotony became agony. A colossal loneliness began to tear at him. He wanted to do anything, even play, or slice huge stars up into planets. But there was only one escape from the phantasmal horror of the unending ebon path. Now and anon he seized the globe of light with a tractor ray and hurled it into the curtain of darkness behind him at terrific velocity.

It sped away under the momentum imparted to it until sight of it was lost. But always, though millions of years

might elapse, it returned, attached to him by invisible strings
of energy. It was part of him, it defied penetration of its
secret, and it would never leave him, until, perhaps, of itself
it revealed its true purpose.

Infinite numbers of light-years, so infinite that if written a
sheet as broad as the universe would have been required,
reeled behind.

Eighty millions of years passed. Darkness had not been as
old as that when he had gone into the void for which he had
been named. Fear that he had been wrong took a stronger
foothold in his thoughts. But now he knew that he would
never go back.

Long before the eighty-nine-millionth year came, he had
exhausted all sources of amusement. Sometimes he expanded or contracted to incredible sizes. Sometimes he automatically went through the motions of traversing the
forty-seven bands. He felt the click in his consciousness
which told him that if there had been hyperspace in the
darkness, he would have been transported into it. But how
could there be different kinds of darkness? He strongly
doubted the existence of hyperspace here, for only matter
could occasion the dimensional disturbances which obtained
in his universe.

But with the eighty-nine-millionth year came the end of his
pilgrimage. It came abruptly. For one tiny space of time, his
visions contacted a stream of light, light that was left as the
outward trail of a celestial body. Darkness' body, fifty millions of miles in girth, involuntarily contracted to half its size.
Energy streamed together and formed molten blobs of flaring
matter that sped from him in the chaotic emotions of the moment.

A wave of shuddering thankfulness shook him, and his
thoughts rioted sobbingly in his memory swirls.

"Oldster, Oldster, if only your great brain could know
this. . . ."

Uncontrollably inflating and deflating, he tore onward,
shearing vast quantities of energy from the tight matter at his
core, converting it into propellent power that drove him at a
velocity that was more than unthinkable, toward the universe
from whence had come that light-giving body.

## V. The Colored Globes

In the ninety-millionth year a dim spot of light rushed at him, and, as he hurtled onward, the spot of light grew, and expanded, and broke up into tinier lights, tinier lights that in turn broke up into their components—until the darkness was blotted out, giving way to the dazzling, beautiful radiance of an egg shaped universe.

He was out of the darkness; he had discovered its edge. Instinctively, he lessened his velocity to a fraction of its former self, and then, as if some mightier will than his had overcome him, he lost consciousness, and sped unknowingly, at steady speed, through the outlying fringe of the outer galaxy, through it, through its brothers, until, unconscious, he was in the midst of that alien galactic system.

First he made a rigid tour of inspection, flying about from star to star, tearing them wantonly apart, as if each and every atom belonged solely to him. The galaxies, the suns, the very elements of construction, all were the same as he knew them. All nature, he decided, was probably alike, in this universe, or in that one.

But was there life?

An abrupt wave of restlessness, of unease, passed over him. He felt unhappy, and unsated. He looked about on the stars, great giants, dwarfs fiercely burning, other hulks of matter cooled to black, forbidding cinders, intergalactic nebulae wreathing unpurposefully about, assuming weird and beautiful formations over periods of thousands of years. He, Darkness, had come to them, had crossed the great gap of nothing, but they were unaffected by this unbelievable feat, went swinging on their courses knowing nothing of him. He felt small, without meaning. Such thoughts seemed the very apostasy of sense, but there they were—he could not shake them off. It was with a growing feeling of disillusionment that he drifted through the countless galaxies and nebulae that unrolled before him, in search of life.

And his quest was rewarded. From afar off, the beating flow of the life-energy came. He drove toward its source, thirty or forty light-years, and hung in its presence.

The being was a green-light, that one of the two classes in which Darkness had divided the life he knew. He himself was a purple-light, containing at his core a globe of pure light, the purpose of which had been one of the major problems of his existence.

The green-light, when she saw him, came to a stop. They stared at each other.

Finally she spoke, and there was wonder and doubt in her thoughts.

"Who are you? You seem—alien."

"You will hardly believe me," Darkness replied, now trembling with a sensation which, inexplicably, could not be defined by the fact that he was in converse with a being of another universe. "But I am alien. I do not belong to this universe."

"But that seems quite impossible. Perhaps you are from another space, beyond the forty-seventh. But that is more impossible!" She eyed him with growing puzzlement and awe.

"I am from no other space," said Darkness somberly. "I am from another universe beyond the darkness."

"From beyond the darkness?" she said faintly, and then she involuntarily contracted. Abruptly she turned her visions on the darkness. For a long, long time she stared at it, and then she returned her vision rays to Darkness.

"So you have crossed the darkness," she whispered. "They used to tell me that that was the most impossible thing it was possible to dream of—to cross that terrible section of lightlessness. No one could cross, they said, because there was nothing on the other side. But I never believed, purple-light, I never believed them. And there have been times when I have desperately wanted to traverse it myself. But there were tales of beings who had gone into it, and never returned. . . . And you have crossed it!"

A shower of crystalline sparks fled from her. So evident was the sudden hero worship carried on her thought waves, that Darkness felt a wild rise in spirits. And suddenly he was able to define the never before experienced emotions which had enwrapped him when first this green-light spoke.

"Green-light, I have journeyed a distance the length of which I cannot think to you, seeking the riddle of the darkness. But perhaps there was something else I was seeking, something to fill a vacant part of me. I know now what it was. A mate, green-light, a thinker. And you are that thinker, that friend with whom I can journey, voyaging from universe to universe, finding the secrets of all that is. Look! The Great Energy which alone made it possible for me to cross the darkness, has been barely tapped!"

Imperceptibly she drew away. There was an unexplainable wariness that seemed half sorrow in her thoughts.

"You are a thinker," he exclaimed. "Will you come with me?"

She stared at him, and he felt she possessed a natural wisdom he could never hope to accumulate. There was a strange shrinkage of his spirits. What was that she was saying?

"Darkness," she said gently, "you would do well to turn and leave me, a green-light, forever. You are a purple-light, I a green. Green-light and purple-light—is that all you have thought about the two types of life? Then you must know that beyond the difference in color, there is another: the greens have a knowledge not vouchsafed the purples, until it is . . . too late. For your own sake, then, I ask you to leave me forever."

He looked at her puzzled. Then slowly, "That is an impossible request, now that I have found you. You are what I need," he insisted.

"But don't you understand?" she cried. "I know something you have not even guessed at! Darkness—leave me!"

He became bewildered. What was she driving at? What was it she knew that he could not know? For a moment he hesitated. Far down in him a voice was bidding him to do as she asked, and quickly. But another voice, that of a growing emotion he could not name, bid him stay; for she was the complement of himself, the half of him that would make him complete. And the second voice was stronger.

"I am not going," he said firmly, and the force of his thoughts left no doubt to the unshakable quality of his decision.

She spoke faintly, as if some outside will had overcome her. "No, Darkness, now you are not going; it is too late! Learn the secret of the purple globe!"

Abruptly, she wrenched herself into a hyperspace, and all his doubts and fears were erased as she disappeared. He followed her delightedly up the scale, catching sight of her in one band just as she vanished into the next.

And so they came to the forty-seventh, where all matter, its largest and smallest components, assumed the shapes of unchangeable cubes; even he and the green-light appeared as cubes, gigantic cubes millions of miles in extent, a geometric figure they could never hope to distort.

Darkness watched her expectantly. Perhaps she would now start a game of chopping chunks off these cubed suns, and swing them around as planets. Well, he would be willing to do that for a while, in her curious mood of playfulness, but after that they must settle down to discovering possible galactic systems beyond this one.

As he looked at her she vanished.

"Hmm, probably gone down the scale," thought Darkness, and he dropped through the lower bands. He found her in none.

"Darkness . . . try the . . . forty-eighth. . . ." Her thought came faintly.

"The forty-eighth!" he cried in astonishment. At the same time, there was a seething of his memory-swirls as if the knowledge of his life were being arranged to fit some new fact, a strange alchemy of the mind by which he came to know that there *was* a forty-eighth.

Now he knew, as he had always known, that there was a forty-eighth. He snapped himself into it.

Energy became rampant in a ceaseless shifting about him. A strange energy, reminding him of nothing so much as the beating flow of an energy creature approaching him from a near distance. His vision sought out the green-light.

She was facing him somberly, yet with a queerly detached arrogance. His mind was suddenly choked with the freezing sensation that he was face to face with horror.

"I have never been here before," he whispered faintly.

He thought he detected pity in her, but it was overwhelmed by the feeling that she was under the influence of an outside will that could not know pity.

Yet she said, "I am sadder than ever before. But too late. You are my mate, and this is the band of—life!"

Abruptly while he stared, she receded, and he could not follow, save with his visions. Presently, as if an hypnotist had clamped his mind, she herself disapppeared, all that he saw of her being the green globe of light she carried. He saw nothing else, knew nothing else. It became his whole universe, his whole life. A peacefulness, complete and uncorroded by vain striving, settled on him like stardust.

The green globe of light dimmed, became smaller, until it was less than a pinpoint, surrounded by an infinity of colorless white energy.

Then, so abruptly it was in the nature of a shock, he came from his torpor, and was conscious. Far off he still saw the green globe of light, but it was growing in size, approaching—approaching a purple globe of light that in turn raced toward it at high velocity.

"It is my own light," he thought, startled. "I must have unwittingly hurled it forth when she settled that hypnotic influence over me. No matter. It will come back."

But would it come back? Green globe of light was expanding in apparent size, approaching purple which, in turn, dwindled toward it at increasing speed.

"At that rate," he thought in panic, "they will collide. Then how will my light come back to me?"

He watched intently, a poignantly cold feeling clutching at him. Closer . . . closer. He quivered. Green globe and purple globe had crashed.

They met in a blinding crescendo of light that brightened space for light-years around. A huge mistiness of light formed into a sphere, in the center of which hung a brilliant ball. The misty light slowly subsided until it had been absorbed into the brighter light that remained as motionless as Darkness himself. Then it commenced pulsating with a strange, rhythmic regularity.

Something about that pulsing stirred ancient memories, something that said, "You, too, were once no more than that pulsing ball."

Thoughts immense in scope, to him, tumbled in his mind.

"That globe is life," he thought starkly. "The green-light and I have created life. That was her meaning, when she said this was the band of life. Its activating energy flows rampant here.

"That is the secret of the purple globe; with the green globe it creates life. And I had never known the forty-eighth band until she made it known to me!

"The purpose of life—to create life." The thought of that took fire in his brain. For one brief, intoxicating moment he thought that he had solved the last and most baffling of his mighty problems.

As with all other moments of exaltation he had known, disillusionment followed swiftly after. To what end was that? The process continued on and on, and what came of it? Was creation of life the only use of life? A meaningless circle! He recalled Oldster's words of the past, and horror claimed him.

"Life, my life," he whispered dully. "A dead sun and life—one of equal importance with the other. That is unbelievable!" he burst out.

He was aware of the green-light hovering near; yes, she possessed a central light, while his was gone!

She looked at him sorrowfully. "Darkness, if only you had listened to me!"

Blankly, he returned her gaze. "Why is it that you have a light, while I have none?"

"A provision of whatever it was that created us, endows the green-lights with the ability to replace their lights three times. Each merging of a purple and green light may result in the creation of one or several newly born. Thus the number born over-balances the number of deaths. When my fourth light has gone, as it will some day, I know, I too, will die."

"You mean, I will—die?"

"Soon."

Darkness shuddered, caught halfway between an emotion of blind anger and mental agony. "There is death everywhere," he whispered, "and everything is futile!"

"Perhaps," she said softly, her grief carrying poignantly to him. "Darkness, do not be sad. Darkness, death does indeed come to all, but that does not say that life is of no significance.

"Far past in the gone ages of our race, we were pitiful, tiny blobs of energy which crept along at less than light speed. An energy creature of that time knew nothing of any but the first and forty-eighth bands of hyperspace. The rest he could not conceive of as being existent. He was ignorant, possessing elementary means of absorbing energy for life. For countless billions of years he never knew there was an edge to the universe. He could not conceive an edge.

"He was weak, but he gained in strength. Slowly, he evolved, and intelligence entered his mind.

"Always, he discovered things he had been formerly unable to conceive in his mind, and even now there are things that lie beyond the mind; one of them is the end of all space. And the greatest is, why life exists. Both are something we cannot conceive, but in time evolution of mental powers will allow us to conceive them, even as we conceived the existence of hyperspace, and those other things. Dimly, so dimly, even now I can see some reason, but it slips the mind. But Darkness! All of matter is destined to break down to an unchanging state of maximum entropy; it is life, and life alone, that builds in an upward direction. So . . . faith!"

She was gone. She had sown what comfort she could.

Her words shot Darkness full of the wild fire of hope. That

was the answer! Vague and promissory it was, but no one could arrive nearer to the solution than that. For a moment he was suffused with the blissful thought that the last of his problems was disposed of.

Then, in one awful space of time, the green-light's philosophy was gone from his memory as if it had never been uttered. He felt the pangs of an unassailable weariness, as if life energies were seeping away.

Haggardly, he put into effect one driving thought. With lagging power, he shot from the fatal band of life . . . and death . . . down the scale. Something unnameable, perhaps some natal memory, made him pause for the merest second in the seventeenth band. Afar off, he saw the green-light and her newly born. They had left the highest band, come to the band where propellents became useless. So it had been at his own birth.

He paused no more and dropped to the true band, pursuing a slow course across the star-beds of this universe, until he at last emerged on its ragged shore. He went on into the darkness, until hundreds of light-years separated him from the universe his people had never known existed.

## VI. Dissipation

He stopped and looked back at the lens of misty radiance. "I have not even discovered the edge of the darkness," he thought. "It stretched out and around. That galactic system and my own are just pinpoints of light, sticking up, vast distances apart, through an unlimited ebon cloth. They are so small in the darkness they barely have the one dimension of existence!"

He went on his way, slowly, wearily, as if the power to activate his propellents were diminishing. There came a time, in his slow, desperate striving after the great velocity he had known in crossing the lightless section, when that universe, that pinpoint sticking up, became as a pinpoint to his sight.

He stopped, took one longing look at it, and accelerated until it was lost to view.

"I am alone again," he thought vaguely. "I am more alone than Oldster ever was. How did he escape death from the green-lights? Perhaps he discovered their terrible secret, and fled before they could wreak their havoc on him. He was a lover of wisdom, and he did not want to die. Now he is living, and he is alone, marooning himself in the lightless band, striving not to think. He could make himself die, but he is afraid to, even though he is so tired of life, and of thinking his endless thoughts.

"I will die. But no . . . ! Ah, yes, I will."

He grew bewildered. He thought, or tried to think, of what came after death. Why, there would be nothing! He would not be there, and without him nothing else could exist!

"I would not be there, and therefore there would be nothing," he thought starkly. "Oh, that is inconceivable. Death! Why, forever after I died, I would be—dead!"

He strove to alleviate the awfulness of the eternal unconsciousness. "I was nothing once, that is true; why cannot that time come again? But it is unthinkable. I feel as if I am the center of everything, the cause, the focal point, and even the foundation."

For some time this thought gave him a kind of gloating satisfaction. Death was indeed not so bad, when one could thus drag to oblivion the very things which had sponsored his life. But at length reason supplanted dreams. He sighed. "And that is vanity!"

Again he felt the ineffably horrible sensation of an incapacity to activate his propellents the full measure, and an inability to keep himself down to normal size. His memory swirls were pulsating, and striving, sometimes, to obliterate themselves.

Everything seemed meaningless. His very drop into the darkness, at slow acceleration, was without purpose.

"I could not reach either universe now," he commented to himself, "because I am dying. Poor Mother! Poor Oldster! They will not even know I crossed. That seems the greatest sorrow—to do a great thing, and not be able to tell of it. Why did they not tell me of the central lights? With Oldster, it was fear that I should come to the same deathless end as he. With Mother—she obeyed an instinct as deeply rooted as space. There must be perpetuation of life.

"Why? Was the green-light right? Is there some tangible purpose to life which we are unable to perceive? But where is my gain, if I have to die to bring to ultimate fruition that purpose? I suppose Oldster knew the truth. Life just is, had an accidental birth, and exists haphazardly, like a star, or an electron.

"But, knowing these things, why do I not immediately give way to the expanding forces within me? Ah, I do not know!"

Convulsively he applied his mind to the continuance of life within his insistently expanding body. For a while he gloried in the small increase of his fading vigor.

"Making solar systems!" his mind took up the thread of a lost thought. "Happy sons of Radiant, Incandecsent, Great Power, and all the others!"

He concentrated on the sudden thought that struck him. He was dying, of that he was well aware, but he was dying without doing anything. What had he actually done, in this life of his?

"But what can I do? I am alone," he thought vaguely. Then, "I could make a planet, and I could put the life germ on it. Oldster taught me that."

Suddenly he was afraid he would die before he created this planet. He set his mind to it, and began to strip from the sphere of tight matter vast quantities of energy, then condensed it to form matter more attenuated. With lagging power, he formed mass after mass of matter, ranging all through the ninety-eight elements that he knew.

Fifty thousand years saw the planet's first stage of completion. It had become a tiny sphere some fifteen thousand miles in diameter. With a heat ray he then boiled it, and with another ray cooled its crust, at the same time forming oceans and continents on its surface. Both water and land, he knew, were necessary to life which was bound by nature of its construction to the surface of a planet.

Then came the final, completing touch. No other being had ever deliberately done what Darkness did then. Carefully, he created an infinitesimal splash of life-perpetuating protoplasm; he dropped it aimlessly into a tiny wrinkle on the planet's surface.

He looked at the finished work, the most perfect planet he or his playmates had ever created, with satisfaction, notwithstanding the dull pain of weariness that throbbed through the complex energy fields of his body.

Then he took the planet up in a tractor ray, and swung it around and around, as he now so vividly recalled doing in his childhood. He gave it a swift angular velocity, and then shot it off at a tangent, in a direction along the line of which he was reasonably sure lay his own universe. He watched it with dulling visions. It receded into the darkness that would surround it for ages, and then it was a pinpoint, and then nothing.

"It is gone," he said, somehow wretchedly lonely because

of that, "but it will reach the universe; perhaps for millions of years it will traverse the galaxies unmolested. Then a sun will reach out and claim it. There will be life upon it, life that will grow until it is intelligent, and will say it has a soul, and purpose in existing."

Nor did the ironic humor of the ultimate swift and speedy death of even that type of life, once it had begun existence, escape him. Perhaps for one or ten million years it would flourish, and then even it would be gone—once upon a time nothing and then nothing again.

He felt a sensation that brought blankness nearer, a sensation of expansion, but now he made no further attempts to prolong a life which was, in effect, already dead. There was a heave within him, as if some subconscious force were deliberately attempting to tear him apart.

He told himself that he was no longer afraid. "I am simply going into another darkness—but it will be a much longer journey than the other."

Like a protecting cloak, he drew in his vision rays about him, away from the ebon emptiness. He drifted, expanding through the vast, interuniversal space.

The last expansion came, the expansion that dissipated his memory swirls. A vast compact sphere of living drew itself out until Darkness was only free energy distributed over light-years of space.

And death, in that last moment, seemed suddenly to be a far greater and more astounding occurrence than birth had ever seemed.

# DARK MISSION

*Astounding Science Fiction*
July

## by Lester del Rey (1915-    )

*Many people believe that July was a special
month in the history of* Astounding Science Fiction
*because so many excellent and influential stories
seemed to fill that issue during the Golden Age.
Heinlein's "Coventry" dominated the July, 1940
ASF and may have been partially responsible for
the relative neglect of this fine story of tragedy and
sacrifice. It was first reprinted in del Rey's 1948
collection from Prime Press . . . And Some Were
Human, one of the pioneer single-author collections
in science fiction.*

(Lester del Rey always reminds me of Harlan Ellison; or,
rather, vice versa, since I've known Lester much longer. He's
another one of the brotherhood who goes back forty years
with me. —Astonishing how many of us have survived and
are still active. Maybe science fiction has a preservative effect.

In any case, Lester, like Harlan, is short, and loud, and
quarrelsome and prickly. And, as in the case of Harlan, if
you can make your way through the prickles and stay
alive—by no means certain—you'll find Lester is soft as
mush underneath and will do anything for you. A true, trusty
friend who will give you anything but a kind word.

And he's an excellent cook. If you've never eaten a Pass-
over meal that he's cooked, you haven't truly lived.—I.A.)

The rays of the Sun lanced down over the tops of the trees
and into the clearing, revealing a scene of chaos and havoc.

Yesterday there had been a wooden frame house there, but now only pieces of it remained. One wall had been broken away, as by an explosion, and lay on the ground in fragments; the roof was crushed in, as if some giant had stepped on it and passed on.

But the cause of the damage was still there, lying on the ruins of the house. A tangled mass of buckled girders and metal plates lay mixed with a litter of laboratory equipment that had been neatly arranged in one room of the house, and parts of a strange engine lay at one side. Beyond was a tube that might have been a rocket. The great metal object that lay across the broken roof now only hinted at the sleek cylinder it had once been, but a trained observer might have guessed that it was the wreck of a rocketship. From the former laboratory, flames were licking up at the metal hull, and slowly spreading toward the rest of the house.

In the clearing, two figures lay outstretched, of similar size and build, but otherwise unlike. One was of a dark man of middle age, completely naked, with a face cut and battered beyond all recognition. The odd angle of the head was unmistakable proof that his neck was broken. The other man might have been a brawny sea viking of earlier days, both from his size and appearance, but his face revealed something finer and of a higher culture. He was fully clothed, and the slow movement of his chest showed that there was still life in him. Beside him, there was a broken beam from the roof, a few spots of blood on it. There was more blood on the man's head, but the cut was minor, and he was only stunned.

Now he stirred uneasily and groped uncertainly to his feet, shaking his head and fingering the cut on his scalp. His eyes traveled slowly across the clearing and to the ruins that were burning merrily. The corpse claimed his next attention, and he turned it over to examine the neck. He knit his brows and shook his head savagely, trying to call back the memories that eluded him.

They would not come. He recognized what his eyes saw, but his mind produced no words to describe them, and the past was missing. His first memory was of waking to find his head pounding with an ache that was almost unbearable. Without surprise, he studied the rocket and saw that it had come down on the house, out of control, but it evoked no pictures in his mind, and he gave up. He might have been in the rocket or the house at the time; he had no way of telling which. Probably the naked man had been asleep at the time in the house.

Something prickled gently in the back of his mind, growing stronger and urging him to do something. He must not waste time here, but must fulfill some vital mission. What mission? For a second, he almost had it, and then it was gone again, leaving only the compelling urge that must be obeyed. He shrugged and started away from the ruins toward the little trail that showed through the trees.

Then another impulse called him back to the corpse, and he obeyed it because he knew of nothing else to do. Acting without conscious volition, he tugged at the corpse, found it strangely heavy, and dragged it toward the house. The flames were everywhere now, but he found a place where the heat was not too great and pulled the corpse over a pile of combustibles.

With the secondary impulse satisfied, the first urge returned, and he set off down the trail, moving slowly. The shoes hurt his feet, and his legs were leaden, but he kept on grimly, while a series of questions went around his head in circles. Who was he, where, and why?

Whoever had lived in the house, himself or the corpse, had obviously chosen the spot for privacy; the trail seemed to go on through the woods endlessly, and he saw no signs of houses along it. He clumped on mechanically, wondering if there was no end, until a row of crossed poles bearing wires caught his eye. Ahead, he made out a broad highway, with vehicles speeding along it in both directions, and hastened forward, hoping to meet someone.

Luck was with him. Pulled up at the side of the road was one of the vehicles, and a man was doing something at the front end of the car. Rough words carried back to him suggesting anger. He grinned suddenly and hastened toward the car, his eyes riveted on the man's head. A tense feeling shot through his brain and left, just as he reached the machine.

"Need help?" The words slipped out unconsciously, and now other words came pouring into his head, along with ideas and knowledge that had not been there before. But the sight of the man, or whatever had restored that section of his memory, had brought back no personal knowledge, and that seemed wrong somehow. The driving impulse he felt was still unexplained.

The man had looked up at his words, and relief shot over the sweating face. "Help's the one thing I need," he replied gratefully. "I been fussing with this blasted contraption darned near an hour, and nobody's even stopped to ask, so far. Know anything about it?"

"Um-m-m." The stranger, as he was calling himself for want of a better name, tested the wires himself, vaguely troubled at the simplicity of the engine. He gave up and went around to the other side, lifting the hood and inspecting the design. Then sureness came to him as he reached for the tool kit. "Probably the . . . um . . . timing pins," he said.

It was. A few minutes later the engine purred softly and the driver turned to the stranger. "O. K. now, I guess. Good thing you came along; worst part of the road and not a repair shop for miles. Where you going?"

"I—" The stranger caught himself. "The big city," he said, for want of a better destination.

"Hop in, then. I'm going to Elizabeth, right on your way. Glad to have you along; gets so a man talks to himself on these long drives, unless he has something to do. Smoke?"

"Thank you, no. I never do." He watched the other light up, feeling uncomfortable about it. The smell of the smoke, when it reached him, was nauseating, as were the odor of gasoline and the man's own personal effluvium, but he pushed them out of his mind as much as possible. "Have you heard or read anything about a rocketship of some kind?"

"Sure. Oglethorpe's, you mean? I been reading what the papers had to say about it." The drummer took his eyes off the road for a second, and his beady little eyes gleamed. "I been wondering a long time why some of these big-shot financiers don't back up the rockets, and finally Oglethorpe does. Boy, now maybe we'll find out something about this Mars business."

The stranger grinned mechanically. "What does his ship look like?"

"Picture of it in the *Scoop*, front page. Find it back of the seat, there. Yeah, that's it. Wonder what the Martians look like?"

"Hard to guess," the stranger answered. Even rough halftones of the picture showed that it was not the ship that had crashed, but radically different. "No word of other rockets?"

"Nope, not that I know of. You know, I kinda feel maybe the Martians might look like us. Sure." He took the other's skepticism for granted without looking around. "Wrote a story about that once, for one of these science-fiction magazines, but they sent it back. I figured out maybe a long time ago there was a civilization on Earth—Atlantis, maybe—and they went over and settled on Mars. Only Atlantis sunk on them, and there they were, stranded. I figured maybe one day they came back, sort of lost out for a while, but popped up again and started civilization humming. Not bad, eh?"

"Clever," the stranger admitted. "But it sounds vaguely familiar. Suppose we said instead there was a war between the mother world and Mars that wrecked both civilizations, instead of your Atlantis sinking. Wouldn't that be more logical?"

"Maybe, I dunno. Might try it, though mostly they seem to want freaks— Darned fool, passing on a hill!" He leaned out to shake a pudgy fist, then came back to his rambling account. "Read one the other day with two races, one like octopuses, the others twenty feet tall and all blue."

Memory pricked tantalizingly and came almost to the surface. Blue— Then it was gone again, leaving only a troubled feeling. The stranger frowned and settled down in the seat, answering in monosyllables to the other's monologue, and watching the patchwork of country and cities slip by.

"There's Elizabeth. Any particular place you want me to drop you?"

The stranger stirred from the half-coma induced by the cutting ache in his head, and looked about. "Any place," he answered. Then the urge in the back of his mind grabbed at him again, and he changed it. "Some doctor's office."

That made sense, of course. Perhaps the impulse had been only the logical desire to seek medical aid, all along. But it was still there, clamoring for expression, and he doubted the logic of anything connected with it. The call for aid could not explain the sense of disaster that accompanied it. As the car stopped before a house with a doctor's shingle, his pulse was hammering with frenzied urgency.

"Here we are." The drummer reached out toward the door hangle, almost brushing one of the other's hands. The stranger jerked it back savagely, avoiding contact by a narrow margin, and a cold chill ran up his back and quivered its way down again. If that hand had touched him— The half-opened door closed again, but left one fact impressed on him. Under no conditions must he suffer another to make a direct contact with his body, lest something horrible should happen! Another crazy angle, unconnected with the others, but too strong for disobedience.

He climbed out, muttering his thanks, and made up the walk toward the office of Dr. Lanahan, hours 12:00 to 4:00.

The doctor was an old man, with the seamed and rugged good-nature of the general practitioner, and his office fitted him. There was a row of medical books along one wall, a glass-doored cabinet containing various medicaments, and a clutter of medical instruments. He listened to the stranger's account quietly, smiling encouragement at times, and tapping the desk with his pencil.

"Amnesia, of course," he agreed, finally. "Rather peculiar in some respects, but most cases of that are individual. When the brain is injured, its actions are usually unpredictable. Have you considered the possibility of hallucinations in connection with those impulses you mention?"

"Yes." He had considered it from all angles, and rejected the solutions as too feeble. "If they were ordinary impulses, I'd agree with you. But they're far deeper than that, and there's a good reason for them, somewhere. I'm sure of that."

"Hm-m-m." The doctor tapped his pencil again and considered. The stranger sat staring at the base of his neck, and the tense feeling in his head returned, as it had been when he first met the drummer. Something rolled around in his mind and quieted. "And you have nothing on you in the way of identification?"

"Uh!" The stranger grunted, feeling foolish, and reached into his pockets. "I hadn't thought of that." He brought out a package of cigarettes, a stained handkerchief, glasses, odds and ends that meant nothing to him, and finally a wallet stuffed with bills. The doctor seized on that and ran through its contents quickly.

"Evidently you had money. . . . Hm-m-m, no identification card, except for the letters. L.H. Ah, here we are; a calling card." He passed it over, along with the wallet, and smiled in self-satisfaction. "Evidently you're a fellow physician, Dr. Lurton Haines. Does that recall anything?"

"Nothing." It was good to have a name, in a way, but that was his only response to the sight of the card. And why was he carrying glasses and cigarettes for which he had no earthly use?

The doctor was hunting through his pile of books, and finally came up with a dirty red volume. "Who's Who," he explained. "Let's see. Hm-m-m! Here we are. 'Lurton R. Haines, M.D.' Odd, I thought you were younger than that. Work along cancer research. No relatives mentioned. The

address is evidently that of the house you remember first—
'Surrey Road, Danesville.' Want to see it?"

He passed the volume over, and the stranger or
Haines—scanned it carefully, but got no more out of it than
the other's summary, except for the fact that he was forty-
two years old. He put the book back on the desk, and
reached for his wallet, laying a bill on the pad where the
other could reach it.

"Thank you, Dr. Lanahan." There was obviously nothing
more the doctor could do for him, and the odor of the little
room and the doctor was stifling him; apparently he was allergic to the smell of other men. "Never mind the cut on the
head—it's purely superficial."

"But—"

Haines shrugged and mustered a smile, reached for the
door, and made for the outside again. The urge was gone
now, replaced by a vast sense of gloom, and he knew that his
mission had ended in failure.

They knew so little about healing, though they tried so
hard. The entire field of medicine ran through Haines' mind
now, with all its startling successes and hopeless failures, and
he knew that even his own problem was beyond their ability.
And the knowledge, like the sudden return of speech, was a
mystery; it had come rushing into his mind while he stared at
the doctor, at the end of the sudden tenseness, and a numb-
ing sense of failure had accompanied it. Strangely, it was
not the knowledge of a specialist in cancer research, but such
common methods as a general practitioner might use.

One solution suggested itself, but it was too fantastic for
belief. The existence of telepaths was suspected, but not ones
who could steal whole pages of knowledge from the mind of
another, merely by looking at him. No, that was more illogical than the sudden wakening of isolated fields of memory by
the sight of the two men.

He stopped at a corner, weary under the load of despon-
dency he was carrying, and mulled it over dully. A newsboy
approached hopefully. *"Time* a' *News* out!" the boy sing-
songed his wares. *"Scoop* 'n' *Juhnal!* Read awl about the big
train wreck! Paper, mister?"

Haines shrugged dully. "No paper!"

"Blonde found moidehed in bathtub," the boy insinuated.
"Mahs rocket account!" The man must have an Achilles' heel
somewhere.

But the garbled jargon only half registered on Haines' ears. He started across the street, rubbing his temples, before the second driving impulse caught at him and sent him back remorselessly to the paper boy. He found some small change in his pocket, dropped a nickel on the pile of papers, disregarding the boy's hand, and picked up a copy of the *Scoop*. "Screwball," the boy decided aloud, and dived for the nickel.

The picture was no longer on the front page of the tabloid, but Haines located the account with some effort. "Mars Rocket Take-off Wednesday," said the headline in conservative twenty-four-point type, and there was three-quarters of a column under it. "Man's first flight to Mars will not be delayed, James Oglethorpe told reporters here today. Undismayed by the skepticism of the scientist, the financier is going ahead with his plans, and expects his men to take off for Mars Wednesday, June 8, as scheduled. Construction had been completed, and the rocket machine is now undergoing tests."

Haines scanned down the page, noting the salient facts. The writer had kept his tongue in his cheek, but under the faintly mocking words there was the information he wanted. The rocket might work; man was at last on his way toward the conquests of the planets. There was no mention of another rocket. Obviously then, that one must have been built in secret in a futile effort to beat Oglethorpe's model.

But that was unimportant. The important thing was that he must stop the flight! Above all else, man must not make that trip! There was no sanity to it, and yet somehow it was beyond mere sanity. It was his duty to prevent any such voyage, and that duty was not to be questioned.

He returned quickly to the newsboy, reached out to touch his shoulder, and felt his hand jerk back to avoid the touch. The boy seemed to sense it, though, for he turned quickly. "Paper?" he began brightly before recognizing the stranger. "Oh, it's you. Watcha want?"

"Where can I find a train to New York?" Haines pulled a quarter from his pocket and tossed it on the pile of papers.

The boy's eyes brightened again.

"Four blocks down, turn right, and keep going till you come to the station. Can't miss it. Thanks, mister."

The discovery of the telephone book as a source of information was Haines' single major triumph, and the fact that the first Oglethorpe he tried was a colored street cleaner failed to take the edge off it. Now he trudged uptown, counting the numbers that made no sense to him; apparently the only system was one of arithmetical progression, irrespective of streets.

His shoulders were drooping, and the lines of pain around his eyes had finally succeeded in drawing his brows together. A coughing spell hit him, torturing his lungs for long minutes, and then passed. That was a new development, as was the pressure around his heart. And everywhere was the irritating aroma of men, gasoline, and tobacco, a stale mixture that he could not escape. He thrust his hands deeper into his pockets to avoid chance contact with someone on the street, and crossed over toward the building that bore the number for which he was searching.

Another man was entering the elevator, and he followed mechanically, relieved that he would not have to plod up the stairs. "Oglethorpe?" he asked the operator, uncertainly.

"Fourth floor, Room 405." The boy slid the gate open, pointing, and Haines stepped out and into the chromium-trimmed reception room. There were half a dozen doors leading from it, but he spotted the one marked "James H. Oglethorpe, Private," and slouched forward.

"Were you expected, sir?" The girl popped up in his face, one hand on the gate that barred his way. Her face was a study in frustration, which probably explained the sharpness of her tone. She delivered an Horatius-guarding-the-bridge formula. "Mr. Oglethorpe is busy now."

"Lunch," Haines answered curtly. He had already noticed that men talked more freely over food.

She flipped a little book in her hand and stared at it. "There's no record here of a luncheon engagement, Mr.—"

"Haines. Dr. Lurton Haines." He grinned wryly, wiggling a twenty-dollar bill casually in one hand. Money was apparently the one disease to which nobody was immune. Her eyes dropped to it, and hesitation entered her voice as she consulted her book.

"Of course, Mr. Oglethorpe might have made it some time ago and forgotten to tell me—" She caught his slight nod, and followed the bill to the corner of the desk. "Just have a seat, and I'll speak to Mr. Oglethorpe."

She came out of the office a few minutes later, and winked quickly. "He'd forgotten," she told Haines, "but it's all right now. He'll be right out, Dr. Haines. It's lucky he's having lunch late today."

James Oglethorpe was a younger man than Haines had expected, though his interest in rocketry might have been some clue to that. He came out of his office, pushing a Homburg down on curly black hair, and raked the other with his eyes. "Dr. Haines?" he asked, thrusting out a large hand. "Seems we have a luncheon engagement."

Haines rose quickly and bowed before the other had a chance to grasp his hand. Appparently Oglethorp did not notice, for he went on smoothly. "Easy to forget these telephone engagements, sometimes. Aren't you the cancer man? One of your friends was in a few months ago for a contribution to your work."

They were in the elevator then, and Haines waited until it opened and they headed for the lunchroom in the building before answering. "I'm not looking for money this time, however. It's the rocket you're financing that interests me. I think it may work."

"It will, though you're one of the few that believes it." Caution, doubt, and interest were mingled on Oglethorpe's face. He ordered before turning back to Haines. "Want to go along? If you do, there's still room for a physician in the crew."

"No, nothing like that. Toast and milk only, please—" Haines had no idea of how to broach the subject, with nothing concrete to back up his statements. Looking at the set of the other's jaw and the general bulldog attitude of the man, he gave up hope and only continued because he had to. He fell back on imagination, wondering how much of it was true.

"Another rocket made that trip, Mr. Oglethorpe, and returned. But the pilot was dying before he landed. I can show you the wreck of his machine, though there's not much left after the fire—perhaps not enough to prove it was a rocketship. Somewhere out on Mars there's something man should never find. It's—"

"Ghosts?" suggested Oglethorpe, brusquely.

"Death! I'm asking you—"

Again Oglethorpe interrupted. "Don't. There was a man in to see me yesterday who claimed he'd been there—offered to show me the wreck of *his* machine. A letter this morning explained that the Martians had visited the writer and threatened all manner of things. I'm not calling you a liar, Dr. Haines, but I've heard too many of those stories; whoever told you this one was either a crank or a horror-monger. I can show you a stack of letters that range from astrology to zombies, all explaining why I can't go, and some offer photographs for proof."

"Suppose I said I'd made the trip in that rocket?" The card in the wallet said he was Haines, and the wallet had been in the suit he was wearing; but there had also been the glasses and cigarettes for which he had no use.

Oglethorpe twisted his lips, either in disgust or amusement. "You're an intelligent man, Dr. Haines; let's assume I am, also. It may sound ridiculous to you, but the only reason I had for making the fortune I'm credited with was to build that ship, and it's taken more work and time than the layman would believe. If a green ant, seven feet high, walked into my office and threatened Armageddon, I'd still go."

Even the impossible impulse recognized the impossible. Oglethorpe was a man who did things first and worried about them when the mood hit him—and there was nothing moody about him. The conversation turned to everyday matters and Haines let it drift as it would, finally dragging out into silence.

At least, he was wiser by one thing: he knew the location of the rocket ground and the set-up of guards around it—something even the newspapermen had failed to learn, since all pictures and information had come through Oglethorpe. There could no longer be any question of his ability to gain desired information by some hazy telepathic process. Either he was a mental freak, or the accident had done things to him that should have been surprising but weren't.

Haines had taken a cab from the airport, giving instructions that caused the driver to lift his eyebrows; but money was still all-powerful. Now they were slipping through country even more desolate than the woods around Haines' house, and the end of the road came into view, with a rutted muddy trail leading off, marked by the tires of the trucks Oglethrope had used for his freighting. The cab stopped there.

"This the place?" the driver asked uncertainly.

"It is." Haines added a bill to what had already been paid and dismissed him. Then he dragged his way out to the dirt road and followed it, stopping for rest frequently. His ears were humming loudly now, and each separate little vertebra of his back protested at his going on. But there was no turning back; he had tried that at the airport and found the urge strong enough to combat his weakening will.

"Only a little rest!" he muttered thickly, but the force in

his head lifted his leaden feet and sent them marching toward the rocket camp. Above him the gray clouds passed over the Moon, and he looked up at Mars shining in the sky. Words from the lower part of the drummer's vocabulary came into his throat, but the effort of saying them was more than the red planet merited. He plowed on in silence.

Mars had moved over several degrees in the sky when he first sighted the camp, lying in a long, narrow valley. At one end were the shacks of the workmen, at the other a big structure that housed the rocket from chance prying eyes. Haines stopped to cough out part of his lungs, and his breath was husky and labored as he worked his way down.

The guards should be strung out along the edge of the valley. Oglethorpe was taking no chances with the cranks who had written him letters and denounced him as a godless fool leading his men to death. Rockets at best were fragile things, and only a few men would be needed to ruin the machine once it was discovered. Haines ran over the guards' positions, and skirted through the underbrush, watching for periods when the Moon was darkened. Once he almost tripped an alarm, but missed it in time.

Beyond there was no shrubbery, but his suit was almost the shade of the ground in the moonlight, and by lying still between dark spells, he crawled forward toward the rocket shed, undetected. He noticed the distance of the houses and the outlying guards and nodded to himself; they should be safe from any explosion.

The coast looked clear. Then, in the shadow of the building, a tiny red spark gleamed and subsided slowly; a man was there, smoking a cigarette. By straining his eyes, Haines made out the long barrel of a rifle against the building. This guard must be an added precaution, unknown to Oglethorpe.

A sudden rift in the thickening clouds came, and Haines slid himself flat against the ground, puzzling over the new complication. For a second he considered turning back, but realized that he could not—his path now was clearly defined, and he had no choice but to follow it. As the Moon slid out of sight again, he came to his feet quietly and moved toward the figure waiting there.

"Hello!" His voice was soft, designed to reach the man at the building but not the guards behind the outskirts. "Hello, there. Can I come forward? Special inspector from Oglethorpe."

A beam of light lanced out from the shadow, blinding him,

and he walked forward at the best pace he could muster. The light might reveal him to the other guards, but he doubted it; their attention was directed outward, away from the buildings.

"Come ahead," the answer came finally. "How'd you get past the others?" The voice was suspicious, but not unusually so. The rifle, Haines saw, was directed at his midsection, and he stopped a few feet away, where the other could watch him.

"Jimmy Durham knew I was coming," he told the guard. According to the information he had stolen from Oglethorpe's mind, Durham was in charge of the guards. "He told me he hadn't had time to notify you, but I took a chance."

"Hm-m-m. Guess it's all right, since they let you through; but you can't leave here until somebody identifies you. Keep your hands up." The guard came forward cautiously to feel for concealed weapons. Haines held his hands up out of the other's reach, where there was no danger of a direct skin to skin contact. "O.K., seems all right. What's your business here?"

"General inspection; the boss got word there might be a little trouble brewing and sent me here to make sure guard was being kept, and to warn you. All locked up here?"

"Nope. A lock wouldn't do much good on this shack; that's why I'm here. Want I should signal Jimmy to come and identify you so you can go?"

"Don't bother." Conditions were apparently ideal, except for one thing. But he would not murder the guard! There must be some other way, without adding that to the work he was forced to do. "I'm in no hurry, now that I've seen everything. Have a smoke?"

"Just threw one away. 'Smatter, no matches? Here."

Haines rubbed one against the friction surface of the box and lit the cigarette gingerly. The raw smoke stung against his burning throat, but he controlled the cough, and blew it out again; in the dark, the guard could not see his eyes watering, nor the grimaces he made. He was waging a bitter fight with himself against the impulse that had ordered the smoke to distract the guard's attention, and he knew he was failing. "Thanks!"

One of the guard's hands met his, reaching for the box. The next second the man's throat was between the stranger's hands, and he was staggering back, struggling to tear away and cry for help. Surprise confused his efforts for the split second necessary, and one of Haines' hands came free and out, then chopped down sharply to strike the guard's neck with the edge of the palm. A low grunt gurgled out, and the figure went limp.

Impulse had conquered again! The guard was dead, his neck broken by the sharp blow. Haines leaned against the building, catching his breath and fighting back the desire to lose his stomach's contents. When some control came back, he picked up the guard's flashlight, and turned into the building. In the darkness, the outlines of the great rocketship were barely visible.

With fumbling fingers Haines groped forward to the hull, then struck a match and shaded it in his hands until he could make out the airport, standing open. Too much light might show through a window and attract attention.

Inside, he threw the low power of the flashlight on and moved forward, down the catwalk and toward the rear where the power machinery would be housed. It had been simple, after all, and only the quick work of destruction still remained.

He traced the control valves easily, running an eye over the uncovered walls and searching out the pipes that led from them. From the little apparatus he saw, this ship was obviously inferior to the one that had crashed, yet it had taken years to build and drained Oglethorpe's money almost to the limit. Once destroyed, it might take men ten more years to replace it; two was the minimum, and in those two years—

The thought slipped from him, but some memories were coming back. He saw himself in a small metal room, fighting against the inexorable exhaustion of fuel, and losing. Then there had been a final burst from the rockets, and the ship had dropped sickeningly through the atmosphere. He had barely had time to get to the air locks before the crash. Miraculously, as the ship's fall was cushioned by the house, he had been thrown free into the lower branches of a tree, to catch, and lose momentum before striking Earth.

The man who had been in the house had fared worse; he had been thrown out with the wrecked wall, already dead. Roughly, the stranger remembered a hasty transfer of clothing from the corpse, and then the beam had dropped on him, shutting out his memory in blackness. So he was not Haines, after all, but someone from the rocket, and his story to Oglethorpe had been basically true.

Haines—he still thought of himself under that name— caught himself as his knees gave under him, and hauled himself up by the aid of a protruding bar. There was work to be done; after that, what happened to his own failing body was another matter. It seemed now that from his awakening he had expected to meet death before another day, and had been careless of the fact.

He ran his eyes around the rocket room again, until he came to a tool kit that lay invitingly open with a large wrench sticking up from it. That would serve to open the valves. The flashlight lay on the floor where he had dropped it, and he kicked it around with his foot to point at the wall, groping out for the wrench. His fingers were stiff as they clasped around the handle.

And, in the beam of light, he noticed his hand for the first time in hours. Dark-blue veins rose high on the flesh that was marked with a faint pale-blue. He considered it dully, thrusting out his other hand and examining it; there, too, was the blue flush, and on his palms, as he turned them upward, the same color showed. Blue!

The last of his memory flashed through his brain in a roaring wave, bringing a slow tide of pictures with it. With one part of his mind, he was working on the valves with the wrench, while the other considered the knowledge that had returned to him. He saw the streets of a delicate, fairy city, half deserted, and as he seemed to watch, a man staggered out of a doorway, clutching at his throat with blue hands, to fall writhing to the ground! The people passed on quickly, avoiding contact with the corpse, fearful even to touch each other.

Everywhere, death reached out for the people. The planet was riddled with it. It lay on the skin of an infected person, to be picked up by the touch of another, and passed on to still more. In the air, a few seconds sufficed to kill the germs, but new ones were being sent out from the pores of the skin, so that there were always a few active ones lurking there. On contact, the disease began an insidious conquest, until, after months without a sign, it suddenly attacked the body housing it, turned it blue, and brought death in a few painful hours.

Some claimed it was the result of an experiment that had gone beyond control, others that it had dropped as a spore from space. Whatever it was, there was no cure for it on Mars. Only the legends that spoke of a race of their people on the mother world of Earth offered any faint hope, and to that they had turned when there was no other chance.

He saw himself undergoing examinations that finally resulted in his being chosen to go in the rocket they were building feverishly. He had been picked because his powers of telepathy were unusual, even to the mental science of Mars; the few remaining weeks had been used in developing that power systematically, and implanting in his head the duties that he must perform, so long as a vestige of life remained to him.

Haines watched the first of the liquid from the fuel pipes splash out, and dropped the wrench. Old León Dagh had doubted his ability to draw knowledge by telepathy from a race of a different culture, he reflected; too bad the old man had died without knowing of the success his methods had met, even though the mission had been a failure, due to man's feeble knowledge of the curative sciences. Now his one task was to prevent the race of this world from dying in the same manner.

He pulled himself to his feet and went staggering down the catwalk, muttering disconnected sentences. The blue of his skin was darker now, and he had to force himself across the space from the ship to the door of the building, grimly commanding his failing muscles, to the guard's body that still lay where he had left it.

Most of the strength left him was useless against the pull of this heavier planet and the torture movement had become. He tried to drag the corpse behind him, then fell on hands and knees and backed toward the ship, using one arm and his teeth on the collar to pull it after him. He was swimming in a world that was bordering on unconsciousness, now, and once darkness claimed him; he came out of it to find himself inside the rocket, still dragging his burden, the implanted impulses stronger than his will.

Bit by bit, he dragged his burden behind him down the catwalk, until the engine room was reached, and he could drop it on the floor, where the liquid fuel had made a thin film. The air was heavy with vapors, and chilled by the evaporation, but he was only partly conscious of that. Only a spark was needed now, and his last duty would be finished.

Inevitably, a few of the dead on Mars would be left unburned, where men might find the last of that unfortunate race, and the germs would still live within them. Earthmen must not face that. Until such a time as the last Martian had crumbled to dust and released the plague into the air to be destroyed, the race of Earth must remain within the confines of its own atmosphere, and safe.

There was only himself and the corpse he had touched left here to carry possible germs, and the ship to carry the men to other sources of infection; all that was easily remedied.

The stranger from Mars groped in his pocket for the guard's match box, smiling faintly. Just before the final darkness swept over him, he drew one of the matches from the box and scraped it across the friction surface. Flame danced from the point and outward—

# IT

Unknown

August

## by Theodore Sturgeon (1918-     )

*Ted Sturgeon is as good a writer of fantasy as he is of science fiction. For evidence, the reader is directed to stories like* The Dreaming Jewels, *"The Professor's Teddy-Bear," "Bianca's Hands," "A God In the Garden," and "Talent."*

*Although he is considered to be a master of portraying human relationships and the complexities of the emotion called love, Sturgeon can also chill. Witness this story—simply one of the finest horror tales of all time.*

(When Marty says "one of the finest horror tales of all time" he's not just whistling Dixie. The trouble with horror tales is that most of them don't horrify you. Nothing by Lovecraft ever horrified me for instance because he labored so hard over the atmosphere and spent so much time *telling* you it was horrible, that you grew bored. Not so here. If you've never read this before, read it now, and it will be a long time before you can look garbage in the face again.

Theodore Sturgeon is very adept at prickling your mind and spine and yet, like so many horror experts, he neither looks nor sounds it. Of course, he's not young anymore. (Who is, other than myself?) But when he was young, he could have posed for anyone wanting to draw a pixie. No retouching necessary. And to this day his voice is soft and winning. You have to keep these gentle people away from the typewriter if you don't want grue. Robert Bloch is, and Fredric Brown was, just the same—I.A.)

125

It walked in the woods.

It was never born. It existed. Under the pine needles the fires burn, deep and smokeless in the mold. In heat and in darkness and decay there is growth. There is life and there is growth. It grew, but it was not alive. It walked unbreathing through the woods, and thought and saw and was hideous and strong, and it was not born and it did not live. It grew and moved about without living.

It crawled out of the darkness and hot damp mold into the cool of a morning. It was huge. It was lumped and crusted with its own hateful substances, and pieces of it dropped off as it went its way, dropped off and lay writhing, and stilled, and sank putrescent into the forest loam.

It had no mercy, no laughter, no beauty. It had strength and great intelligence. And—perhaps it could not be destroyed. It crawled out of its mound in the wood and lay pulsing in the sunlight for a long moment. Patches of it shone wetly in the golden glow, parts of it were nubbled and flaked. And whose dead bones had given it the form of a man?

It scrabbled painfully with its half-formed hands, beating the ground and the bole of a tree. It rolled and lifted itself up on its crumbling elbows, and it tore up a great handful of herbs and shredded them against its chest, and it paused and gazed at the gray-green juices with intelligent calm. It wavered to its feet, and seized a young sapling and destroyed it, folding the slender trunk back on itself again and again, watching attentively the useless, fibered splinters. And it snatched up a fear-frozen field-creature, crushing it slowly, letting blood and pulpy flesh and fur ooze from between its fingers, run down and rot on the forearms.

It began searching.

Kimbo drifted through the tall grasses like a puff of dust, his bushy tail curled tightly over his back and his long jaws agape. He ran with an easy lope, loving his freedom and the power of his flanks and furry shoulders. His tongue lolled listlessly over his lips. His lips were black and serrated, and each tiny pointed liplet swayed with his doggy gallop. Kimbo was all dog, all healthy animal.

He leaped high over a boulder and landed with a startled yelp as a long-eared cony shot from its hiding place under the rock. Kimbo hurtled after it, grunting with each great thrust of his legs. The rabbit bounced just ahead of him, keeping its distance, its ears flattened on its curving back and its little legs nibbling away at distance hungrily. It stopped, and Kimbo pounced, and the rabbit shot away at a tangent and popped into a hollow log. Kimbo yelped again and rushed snuffling at the log, and knowing his failure, curvetted but once around the stump and ran on into the forest. The thing that watched from the wood raised its crusted arms and waited for Kimbo.

Kimbo sensed it there, standing dead-still by the path. To him it was a bulk which smelled of carrion not fit to roll in, and he snuffled distastefully and ran to pass it.

The thing let him come abreast and dropped a heavy twisted fist on him. Kimbo saw it coming and curled up tight as he ran, and the hand clipped stunningly on his rump, sending him rolling and yipping down the slope. Kimbo straddled to his feet, shook his head, shook his body with a deep growl, came back to the silent thing with green murder in his eyes. He walked stiffly, straight-legged, his tail as low as his lowered head and a ruff of fury round his neck. The thing raised its arms again, waited.

Kimbo slowed, then flipped himself through the air at the monster's throat. His jaws closed on it; his teeth clicked together through a mass of filth, and he fell choking and snarling at its feet. The thing leaned down and struck twice, and after the dog's back was broken, it sat beside him and began to tear him apart.

"Be back in an hour or so," said Alton Drew, picking up his rifle from the corner behind the wood box. His brother laughed.

"Old Kimbo 'bout runs your life, Alton," he said.

"Ah, I know the ol' devil," said Alton. "When I whistle for him for half an hour and he don't show up, he's in a jam or he's treed something wuth shootin' at. The ol' son of a gun calls me by not answerin'."

Cory Crew shoved a full glass of milk over to his nine-year-old daughter and smiled. "You think as much o' that houn' dog o' yours as I do of Babe here."

Babe slid off her chair and ran to her uncle. "Gonna catch me the bad fella, Uncle Alton?" she shrilled. The "bad fella" was Cory's invention—the one who lurked in corners ready to pounce on little girls who chased the chickens and played around mowing machines and hurled green apples with a powerful young arm at the sides of the hogs, to hear the synchronized thud and grunt; little girls who swore with an

Austrian accent like an ex-hired man they had had; who dug caves in haystacks till they tipped over, and kept pet crawfish in tomorrow's milk cans, and rode work horses to a lather in the night pasture.

"Get back here and keep away from Uncle Alton's gun!" said Cory. "If you see the bad fella, Alton, chase him back here. He has a date with Babe here for that stunt of hers last night." The preceding evening, Babe had kind-heartedly poured pepper on the cows' salt block.

"Don't worry, kiddo," grinned her uncle, "I'll bring you the bad fella's hide if he don't get me first."

Alton Drew walked up the path toward the wood, thinking about Babe. She was a phenomenon—a pampered farm child. Ah well—she had to be. They'd both loved Clissa Drew, and she'd married Cory, and they had to love Clissa's child. Funny thing, love. Alton was a man's man, and thought things out that way; and his reaction to love was a strong and frightened one. He knew what love was because he felt it still for his brother's wife and would feel it as long as he lived for Babe. It led him through his life, and yet he embarrassed himself by thinking of it. Loving a dog was an easy thing, because you and the old devil could love one another completely without talking about it. The smell of gunsmoke and wet fur in the rain were perfume enough for Alton Drew, a grunt of satisfaction and the scream of something hunted and hit were poetry enough. They weren't like love for a human, that choked his throat so he could not say words he could not have thought of anyway. So Alton loved his dog Kimbo and his Winchester for all to see, and let his love for his brother's women, Clissa and Babe, eat at him quietly and unmentioned.

His quick eyes saw the fresh indentations in the soft earth behind the boulder, which showed where Kimbo had turned and leaped with a single surge, chasing the rabbit. Ignoring the tracks, he looked for the nearest place where a rabbit might hide, and strolled over to the stump. Kimbo had been there, he saw, and had been there too late. "You're an ol' fool," muttered Alton. "Y' can't catch a cony by chasin' it. You want to cross him up some way." He gave a peculiar trilling whistle, sure that Kimbo was digging frantically under some nearby stump for a rabbit that was three counties away by now. No answer. A little puzzled, Alton went back to the path. "He never done this before," he said softly.

He cocked his .32-40 and cradled it. At the county fair someone had once said of Alton Drew that he could shoot at a handful of corn and peas thrown in the air and hit only the corn. Once he split a bullet on the blade of a knife and put two candles out. He had no need to fear anything that could be shot at. That's what he believed.

The thing in the woods looked curiously down at what it had done to Kimbo, and tried to moan the way Kimbo had before he died. It stood a minute storing away facts in its foul, unemotional mind. Blood was warm. The sunlight was warm. Things that moved and bore fur had a muscle to force the thick liquid through tiny tubes in their bodies. The liquid coagulated after a time. The liquid on rooted green things was thinner and the loss of a limb did not mean loss of life. It was very interesting, but the thing, the mold with a mind, was not pleased. Neither was it displeased. Its accidental urge was a thirst for knowledge, and it was only—interested.

It was growing late, and the sun reddened and rested awhile on the hilly horizon, teaching the clouds to be inverted flames. The thing threw up its head suddenly, noticing the dusk. Night was ever a strange thing, even for those of us who have known it in life. It would have been frightening for the monster had it been capable of fright, but it could only be curious; it could only reason from what it had observed.

What was happening? It was getting harder to see. Why? It threw its shapeless head from side to side. It was true—things were dim, and growing dimmer. Things were changing shape, taking on a new and darker color. What did the creatures it had crushed and torn apart see? How did they see? The larger one, the one that had attacked, had used two organs in its head. That must have been it, because after the thing had torn off two of the dog's legs it had struck at the hairy muzzle; and the dog, seeing the blow coming, had dropped folds of skin over the organs—closed its eyes. Ergo, the dog saw with its eyes. But then after the dog was dead, and its body still, repeated blows had had no effect on the eyes. They remained open and staring. The logical conclusion was, then, that a being that had ceased to live and breathe and move about lost the use of its eyes. It must be that to lose sight was, conversely, to die. Dead things did not walk about. They lay down and did not move. Therefore the thing in the wood concluded that it must be dead, and so it lay down by the path, not far away from Kimbo's scattered body, lay down and believed itself dead.

Alton Drew came up through the dusk to the wood. He was frankly worried. He whistled again, and then called, and there was still no response, and he said again, "The ol' flea-bus never done this before," and shook his heavy head. It was past milking time, and Cory would need him. "Kimbo!" he roared. The cry echoed through the shadows, and Alton flipped on the safety catch of his rifle and put the butt on the ground beside the path. Leaning on it, he took off his cap and scratched the back of his head, wondering. The rifle butt sank into what he thought was soft earth; he staggered and stepped into the chest of the thing that lay beside the path. His foot went up to the ankle in its yielding rottenness, and he swore and jumped back.

*"Whew!* Somp'n sure dead as hell there! Ugh!" He swabbed at his boot with a handful of leaves while the monster lay in the growing blackness with the edges of the deep footprint in its chest sliding into it, filling it up. It lay there regarding him dimly out of its muddy eyes, thinking it was dead because of the darkness, watching the articulation of Alton Drew's joints, wondering at this new uncautious creature.

Alton cleaned the butt of his gun with more leaves and went on up the path, whistling anxiously for Kimbo.

Clissa Drew stood in the door of the milk shed, very lovely in red-checked gingham and a blue apron. Her hair was clean yellow, parted in the middle and stretched tautly back to a heavy braided knot. "Cory! Alton!" she called a little sharply.

"Well?" Cory responded gruffly from the barn, where he was stripping off the Ayrshire. The dwindling streams of milk plopped pleasantly into the froth of a full pail.

"I've called and called," said Clissa. "Supper's cold, and Babe won't eat until you come. Why—where's Alton?"

Cory grunted, heaved the stool out of the way, threw over the stanchion lock and slapped the Ayrshire on the rump. The cow backed and filled like a towboat, clattered down the line and out into the barnyard. "Ain't back yet."

"Not back?" Clissa came in and stood beside him as he sat by the next cow, put his forehead against the warm flank. "But, Cory, he said he'd—"

"Yeh, yeh, I know. He said he'd be back fer the milkin'. I heard him. Well, he ain't."

"And you have to— Oh, Cory, I'll help you finish up. Alton would be back if he could. Maybe he's—"

"Maybe he's treed a blue jay," snapped her husband. "Him an' that damn dog," He gestured hugely with one hand while the other went on milking. "I got twenty-six head o' cows to milk. I got pigs to feed an' chickens to put to bed. I got to toss hay for the mare and turn the team out. I got harness to mend and a wire down in the night pasture. I got wood to split an' carry." He milked for a moment in silence, chewing on his lip. Clissa stood twisting her hands together, trying to think of something to stem the tide. It wasn't the first time Alton's hunting had interfered with the chores. "So I got to go ahead with it. I can't interfere with Alton's spoorin'.' Every damn time that hound o' his smells out a squirrel I go without my supper. I'm gettin' sick and—"

"Oh, I'll help you!" said Clissa. She was thinking of the spring, when Kimbo had held four hundred pounds of raging black bear at bay until Alton could put a bullet in its brain, the time Babe had found a bearcub and started to carry it home, and had fallen into a freshet, cutting her head. You can't hate a dog that has saved your child for you, she thought.

"You'll do nothin' of the kind!" Cory growled. "Get back to the house. You'll find work enough there. I'll be along when I can. Dammit, Clissa, don't cry! I didn't mean to— Oh, shucks!" He got up and put his arms around her. "I'm wrought up," he said. "Go on now. I'd no call to speak that way to you. I'm sorry. Go back to Babe. I'll put a stop to this for good tonight. I've had enough. There's work here for four farmers an' all we've got is me an' that . . . that huntsman.

"Go on now, Clissa."

"All right," she said into his shoulder. "But, Cory, hear him out first when he comes back. He might be unable to come back. He might be unable to come back this time. Maybe he . . . he—"

"Ain't nothin' kin hurt my brother that a bullet will hit. He can take care of himself. He's got no excuse good enough this time. Go on, now. Make the kid eat."

Clissa went back to the house, her young face furrowed. If Cory quarreled with Alton now and drove him away, what with the drought and the creamery about to close and all, they just couldn't manage. Hiring a man was out of the question. Cory'd have to work himself to death, and he just wouldn't be able to make it. No one man could. She sighed and went into the house. It was seven o'clock, and the milk-ing not done yet. Oh, why did Alton have to—

Babe was in bed at nine when Clissa heard Cory in the shed, slinging the wire cutters into a corner. "Alton back yet?" they both said at once as Cory stepped into the kitchen; and as she shook her head he clumped over to the stove, and lifting a lid, spat into the coals. "Come to bed," he said.

She laid down her stitching and looked at his broad back. He was twenty-eight, and he walked and acted like a man ten years older, and looked like a man five years younger. "I'll be up in a while," Clissa said.

Cory glanced at the corner behind the wood box where Al-ton's rifle usually stood, then made an unspellable, disgusted sound and sat down to take off his heavy muddy shoes.

"It's after nine," Clissa volunteered timidly. Cory said nothing, reaching for house slippers.

"Cory, you're not going to—"

"Not going to what?"

"Oh, nothing. I just thought that maybe Alton—"

"Alton," Cory flared. "The dog goes hunting field mice. Al-ton goes hunting the dog. Now you want me to go hunting Alton. That's what you want?"

"I just— He was never this late before."

"I won't do it! Go out lookin' for him at nine o'clock in the night? I'll be damned! He has no call to use us so, Clissa."

Clissa said nothing. She went to the stove, peered into the wash boiler, set aside at the back of the range. When she turned around, Cory had his shoes and coat on again.

"I knew you'd go," she said. Her voice smiled though she did not.

"I'll be back durned soon," said Cory. "I don't reckon he's strayed far. It is late. I ain't feared for him, but—" He broke his 12-gauge shotgun, looked through the barrels, slipped two shells in the breech and a box of them into his pocket. "Don't wait up," he said over his shoulder as he went out.

"I won't," Clissa replied to the closed door, and went back to her stitching by the lamp.

The path up the slope to the wood was very dark when Cory went up it, peering and calling. The air was chill and quiet, and a fetid odor of mold hung in it. Cory blew the taste of it out through impatient nostrils, drew it in again with the next breath, and swore. "Nonsense," he muttered. "Houn' dawg. Huntin', at ten in th' night, too. Alton!" he bel-lowed. "Alton Drew!" Echoes answered him, and he entered the wood. The huddled thing he passed in the dark heard him and felt the vibrations of his footsteps and did not move because it thought it was dead.

Cory strode on, looking around and ahead and not down since his feet knew the path.

"Alton!"

"That you, Cory?"

Cory Drew froze. That corner of the wood was thickly set and as dark as a burial vault. The voice he heard was choked, quiet, penetrating.

"Alton?"

"I found Kimbo, Cory."

"Where the hell have you been?" shouted Cory furiously. He disliked this pitch-darkness; he was afraid at the tense hopelessness of Alton's voice, and he mistrusted his ability to stay angry at his brother.

"I called him, Cory. I whistled at him, an' the ol' devil didn't answer."

"I can say the same for you, you . . . you louse. Why weren't you to milkin'? Where are you? You caught in a trap?"

"The houn' never missed answerin' me before, you know," said the tight, monotonous voice from the darkness.

"Alton! What the devil's the matter with you? What do I care if your mutt didn't answer? Where—"

"I guess because he ain't never died before," said Alton, refusing to be interrupted.

"You *what?*" Cory clicked his lips together twice and then said, "Alton, you turned crazy? What's that you say?"

"Kimbo's dead."

"Kim . . . oh! Oh!" Cory was seeing that picture again in his mind— Babe sprawled unconscious in the freshet, and Kimbo raging and snapping against a monster bear, holding her back until Alton could get there. "What happened, Alton?" he asked more quietly.

"I aim to find out. Someone tore him up."

*"Tore him up?"*

"There ain't a bit of him left tacked together, Cory. Every damn joint in his body tore apart. Guts out of him."

"Good God! Bear, you reckon?"

"No bear, nor nothin' on four legs. He's all here. None of him's been et. Whoever done it just killed him an'—tore him up."

"Good God!" Cory said again. "Who could've—" There

was a long silence, then. "Come 'long home," he said almost gently. "There's no call for you to set up by him all night."

"I'll set. I aim to be here at sunup, an' I'm going to start trackin', an' I'm goin' to keep trackin' till I find the one done this job on Kimbo."

"You're drunk or crazy, Alton."

"I ain't drunk. You can think what you like about the rest of it. I'm stickin' here."

"We got a farm back yonder. Remember? I ain't going to milk twenty-six head o' cows again in the mornin' like I did jest now, Alton."

"Somebody's got to. I can't be there. I guess you'll just have to, Cory."

"You dirty scum!" Cory screamed. "You'll come back with me now or I'll know why!"

Alton's voice was still tight, half-sleepy. "Don't you come no nearer, bud."

Cory kept moving toward Alton's voice.

"I said"—the voice was very quiet now—"*stop where you are.*" Cory kept coming. A sharp click told of the release of the .32-40's safety. Cory stopped.

"You got your gun on me, Alton?" Cory whispered.

"Thass right, bud. You ain't a-trompin' up these tracks for me. I need 'em at sunup."

A full minute passed, and the only sound in the blackness was that of Cory's pained breathing. Finally:

"I got my gun, too, Alton. Come home."

"You can't see to shoot me."

"We're even on that."

"We ain't. I know just where you stand, Cory. I been here four hours."

"My gun scatters."

"My gun kills."

Without another word Cory Drew turned on his heel and stamped back to the farm.

Black and liquidescent it lay in the blackness, not alive, not understanding death, believing itself dead. Things that were alive saw and moved about. Things that were not alive could do neither. It rested its muddy gaze on the line of trees at the crest of the rise, and deep within it thoughts trickled wetly. It lay huddled, dividing its newfound facts, dissecting them as it had dissected live things when there was light, comparing, concluding, pigeonholing.

The trees at the top of the slope could just be seen, as their trunks were a fraction of a shade lighter than the dark sky behind them. At length they, too, disappeared, and for a moment sky and trees were a monotone. The thing knew it was dead now, and like many a being before it, it wondered how long it must stay like this. And then the sky beyond the trees grew a little lighter. That was a manifestly impossible occurrence, thought the thing, but it could see it and it must be so. Did dead things live again? That was curious. What about dismembered dead things? It would wait and see.

The sun came hand over hand up a beam of light. A bird somewhere made a high yawning peep, and as an owl killed a shrew, a skunk pounced on another, so that the night shift deaths and those of the day could go on without cessation. Two flowers nodded archly to each other, comparing their pretty clothes. A dragon-fly nymph decided it was tired of looking serious and cracked its back open, to crawl out and dry gauzily. The first golden ray sheared down between the trees, through the grasses, passed over the mass in the shadowed bushes. "I am alive again," thought the thing that could not possibly live. "I am alive, for I see clearly." It stood up on its thick legs, up into the golden glow. In a little while the wet flakes that had grown during the night dried in the sun, and when it took its first steps, they cracked off and a small shower of them fell away. It walked up the slope to find Kimbo, to see if he, too, was alive again.

Babe let the sun come into her room by opening her eyes. Uncle Alton was gone—that was the first thing that ran through her head. Dad had come home last night and had shouted at mother for an hour. Alton was plumb crazy. He'd turned a gun on his own brother. If Alton ever came ten feet into Cory's land, Cory would fill him so full of holes, he'd look like a tumbleweed. Alton was lazy, shiftless, selfish, and one or two other things of questionable taste but undoubted vividness. Babe knew her father. Uncle Alton would never be safe in this county.

She bounced out of bed in the enviable way of the very young, and ran to the window. Cory was trudging down to the night pasture with two bridles over his arm, to get the team. There were kitchen noises from downstairs.

Babe ducked her head in the washbowl and shook off the water like a terrier before she toweled. Trailing clean shirt and dungarees, she went to the head of the stairs, slid into the shirt, and began her morning ritual with the trousers. One step down was a step through the right leg. One more, and she was into the left. Then, bouncing step by step on both feet, buttoning one button per step, she reached the bottom fully dressed and ran into the kitchen.

"Didn't Uncle Alton come back a-tall, Mum?"

"Morning, Babe. No, dear." Clissa was too quiet, smiling too much Babe thought shrewdly. Wasn't happy.

"Where'd he go, Mum?"

"We don't know, Babe. Sit down and eat your breakfast."

"What's a misbegotten, Mum?" the Babe asked suddenly. Her mother nearly dropped the dish she was drying. "Babe! You must never say that again!"

"Oh. Well, why is Uncle Alton, then?"

"Why is he what?"

Babe's mouth muscled around an outsize spoonful of oatmeal. "A misbe—"

"Babe!"

"All right, Mum," said Babe with her mouth full. "Well, why?"

"I told Cory not to shout last night," Clissa said half to herself.

"Well, whatever it means, he isn't," said Babe with finality. "Did he go hunting again?"

"He went to look for Kimbo, darling."

"Kimbo? Oh Mummy, is Kimbo gone, too? Didn't he come back either?"

"No dear. Oh, please, Babe, stop asking questions!"

"All right. Where do you think they went?"

"Into the north woods. Be quiet."

Babe gulped away at her breakfast. An idea struck her; and as she thought of it she ate slower and slower, and cast more and more glances at her mother from under the lashes of her tilted eyes. It would be awful if daddy did anything to Uncle Alton. Someone ought to warn him.

Babe was halfway to the woods when Alton's .32-40 sent echoes giggling up and down the valley.

Cory was in the south thirty, riding a cultivator and cussing at the team of grays when he heard the gun. "Hoa," he called to the horses, and sat a moment to listen to the sound. "One-two-three. Four," he counted. "Saw someone, blasted away at him. Had a chance to take aim and give him another, careful. My God!" He threw up the cultivator points and steered the team into the shade of three oaks. He hobbled the gelding with swift tosses of a spare strap, and headed for the woods. "Alton a killer," he murmured, and doubled back to the house for his gun. Clissa was standing just outside the door.

"Get shells!" he snapped and flung into the house. Clissa followed him. He was strapping his hunting knife on before she could get a box off the shelf. "Cory—"

"Hear that gun, did you? Alton's off his nut. He don't waste lead. He shot at someone just then, and he wasn't fixin' to shoot pa'tridges when I saw him last. He was out to get a man. Gimme my gun."

"Cory, Babe—"

"You keep her here. Oh, God, this is a helluva mess. I can't stand much more." Cory ran out the door.

Clissa caught his arm: "Cory I'm trying to tell you. Babe isn't here. I've called, and she isn't here."

Cory's heavy, young-old face tautened. "Babe— Where did you last see her?"

"Breakfast." Clissa was crying now.

"She say where she was going?"

"No. She asked a lot of questions about Alton and where he'd gone."

"Did you say?"

Clissa's eyes widened, and she nodded, biting the back of her hand.

"You shouldn't ha' done that, Clissa," he gritted, and ran toward the woods, Clissa looking after him, and in that moment she could have killed herself.

Cory ran with his head up, straining with his legs and lungs and eyes at the long path. He puffed up the slope to the woods, agonized for breath after the forty-five minutes' heavy going. He couldn't even notice the damp smell of mold in the air.

He caught a movement in a thicket to his right, and dropped. Struggling to keep his breath, he crept forward until he could see clearly. There was something in there, all right. Something black, keeping still. Cory relaxed his legs and torso completely to make it easier for his heart to pump some strength back into them, and slowly raised the 12-gauge until it bore on the thing hidden in the thicket.

"Come out!" Cory said when he could speak.

Nothing happened.

"Come out or by God I'll shoot!" rasped Cory.

There was a long moment of silence, and his finger tightened on the trigger.

"You asked for it," he said, and as he fired, the thing leaped sideways into the open, screaming.

It was a thin little man dressed in sepulchral black, and bearing the rosiest baby-face Cory had ever seen. The face was twisted with fright and pain. The man scrambled to his feet and hopped up and down saying over and over, "Oh, my hand. Don't shoot again! Oh, my hand. Don't shoot again!" He stopped after a bit, when Cory had climbed to his feet, and he regarded the farmer out of sad china-blue eyes. "You shot me," he said reproachfully, holding up a little bloody hand. "Oh, my goodness."

Cory said, "Now, who the hell are you?"

The man immediately became hysterical, mouthing such a flood of broken sentences that Cory stepped back a pace and half-raised his gun in self-defense. It seemed to consist mostly of "I lost my papers," and "I didn't do it," and "It was horrible. Horrible. Horrible," and "The dead man," and "Oh, don't shoot again."

Cory tried twice to ask him a question, and then he stepped over and knocked the man down. He lay on the ground writhing and moaning and blubbering and putting his bloody hand to his mouth where Cory had hit him.

"Now what's going on around here?"

The man rolled over and sat up. "I didn't do it!" he sobbed. "I didn't. I was walking along and I heard the gun and I heard some swearing and an awful scream and I went over there and peeped and I saw the dead man and I ran away and you came and I hid and you shot me and—"

*"Shut up!"* The man did, as if a switch had been thrown. "Now," said Cory, pointing along the path, "you say there's a dead man up there?"

The man nodded and began crying in earnest. Cory helped him up. "Follow this path back to my farmhouse," he said. "Tell my wife to fix up your hand. *Don't* tell her anything else. And wait there until I come. Hear?"

"Yes. Thank you. Oh, thank you. *Snff.*"

"Go on now." Cory gave him a gentle shove in the right direction and went alone, in cold fear, up the path to the spot where he had found Alton the night before.

He found him here now, too, and Kimbo. Kimbo and Alton had spent several years together in the deepest friendship; they had hunted and fought and slept together, and the lives they owed each other were finished now. They were dead together.

It was terrible that they died the same way. Cory Drew was a strong man, but he gasped and fainted dead away when he saw what the thing of the mold had done to his brother and his brother's dog.

The little man in black hurried down the path, whimpering and holding his injured hand as if he rather wished he could limp with it. After a while the whimper faded away, and the hurried stride changed to a walk as the gibbering terror of the last hour receded. He drew two deep breaths, said: "My goodness!" and felt almost normal. He bound a linen handkerchief around his wrist, but the hand kept bleeding. He tried the elbow, and that made it hurt. So he stuffed the handkerchief back in his pocket and simply waved the hand stupidly in the air until the blood clotted. He did not see the great moist horror that clumped along behind him, although his nostrils crinkled with its foulness.

The monster had three holes close together on its chest, and one hole in the middle of its slimy forehead. It had three close-set pits in its back and one on the back of its head. These marks were where Alton Drew's bullets had struck and passed through. Half of the monster's shapeless face was sloughed away, and there was a deep indentation on its shoulder. This was what Alton Drew's gun butt had done after he clubbed it and struck at the thing that would not lie down after he put his four bullets through it. When these things happened the monster was not hurt or angry. It only wondered why Alton Drew acted that way. Now it followed the little man without hurrying at all, matching his stride step by step and dropping little particles of muck behind it.

The little man went on out of the wood and stood with his back against a big tree at the forest's edge, and he thought. Enough had happened to him here. What good would it do to stay and face a horrible murder inquest, just to continue this silly, vague search? There was supposed to be the ruin of an old, old hunting lodge deep in this wood somewhere, and perhaps it would hold the evidence he wanted. But it was a vague report—vague enough to be forgotten without regret. It would be the height of foolishness to stay for all the hicktown red tape that would follow that ghastly affair back in the wood. Ergo, it would be ridiculous to follow that farmer's advice, to go to his house and wait for him. He would go back to town.

The monster was leaning against the other side of the big tree.

The little man snuffled disgustedly at a sudden overpowering odor of rot. He reached for his handkerchief, fumbled and dropped it. As he bent to pick it up, the monster's arm *whuffed* heavily in the air where his head had been —a blow that would certainly have removed that baby-face protuberance. The man stood up and would have put the handkerchief to his nose had it not been so bloody. The creature behind the tree lifted its arm again just as the little man tossed the handkerchief away and stepped out into the field, heading across country to the distant highway that would take him back to town. The monster pounced on the handkerchief, picked it up, studied it, tore it across several times and inspected the tattered edges. Then it gazed vacantly at the disappearing figure of the little man, and finding him no longer interesting, turned back into the woods.

Babe broke into a trot at the sound of the shots. It was important to warn Uncle Alton about what her father had said, but it was more interesting to find out what he had bagged. Oh, he'd bagged it, all right. Uncle Alton never fired without killing. This was about the first time she had ever heard him blast away like that. Must be a bear, she thought excitedly, tripping over a root, sprawling, rolling to her feet again, without noticing the tumble. She'd love to have another bearskin in her room. Where would she put it? Maybe they could line it and she could have it for a blanket. Uncle Alton could sit on it and read to her in the evening— Oh, no. No. Not with this trouble between him and dad. Oh, if she could only do something! She tried to run faster, worried and anticipating, but she was out of breath and went more slowly instead.

At the top of the rise by the edge of the woods she stopped and looked back. Far down in the valley lay the south thirty. She scanned it carefully, looking for her father. The new furrows and the old were sharply defined, and her keen eyes saw immediately that Cory had left the line with the cultivator and had angled the team over to the shade trees without finishing his row. That wasn't like him. She could see the team now, and Cory's pale-blue denim was nowhere in sight. She giggled lightly to herself as she thought of the way she would

fool her father. And the little sound of laughter drowned out,
for her, the sound of Alton's hoarse dying scream.

She reached and crossed the path and slid through the
brush beside it. The shots came from up around here somewhere. She stopped and listened several times, and then suddenly heard something coming toward her, fast. She ducked
under cover, terrified, and a little baby-faced man in black,
his blue eyes wide with horror, crashed blindly past her, the
leather case he carried catching on the branches. It spun a
moment and then fell right in front of her. The man never
missed it.

Babe lay there for a long moment and then picked up the
case and faded into the woods. Things were happening too
fast for her. She wanted Uncle Alton, but she dared not call.
She stopped again and strained her ears. Back toward the
edge of the wood she heard her father's voice, and another's—probably the man who had dropped the briefcase.
She dared not go over there. Filled with enjoyable terror, she
thought hard, then snapped her fingers in triumph. She and
Alton had played Injun many times up here; they had a
whole repertoire of secret signals. She had practiced bird calls
until oho knew them better than the birds themselves. What
would it be? Ah—blue jay. She threw back her head and by
some youthful alchemy produced a nerve-shattering screech
that would have done justice to any jay that ever flew. She
repeated it, and then twice more.

The response was immediate—the call of a blue jay, four
times, spaced two and two. Babe nodded to herself happily.
That was the signal that they were to meet immediately at
The Place. The Place was a hideout that he had discovered
and shared with her, and not another soul knew of it; an
angle of rock beside a stream not far away. It wasn't exactly
a cave, but almost. Enough so to be entrancing. Babe trotted
happily away toward the brook. She had just known that
Uncle Alton would remember the call of the blue jay, and
what it meant.

In the tree that arched over Alton's scattered body perched
a large jay bird, preening itself and shining in the sun. Quite
unconscious of the presence of death, hardly noticing the
Babe's realistic cry, it screamed again four times, two and
two.

It took Cory more than a moment to recover himself from
what he had seen. He turned away from it and leaned weakly

against a pine, panting. Alton. That was Alton lying there, in—parts.

"God! God, God, God—"

Gradually his strength returned, and he forced himself to turn again. Stepping carefully, he bent and picked up the .32-40. Its barrel was bright and clean, but the butt and stock were smeared with some kind of stinking rottenness. Where had he seen the stuff before? Somewhere—no matter. He cleaned it off absently, throwing the befouled bandanna away afterward. Through his mind ran Alton's words—was that only last night?—"*I'm goin' to start trackin'. An' I'm goin' to keep trackin' till I find the one done this job on Kimbo.*"

Cory searched shrinkingly until he found Alton's box of shells. The box was wet and sticky. That made it—better, somehow. A bullet wet with Alton's blood was the right thing to use. He went away a short distance, circled around till he found heavy footprints, then came back.

"I'm a-trackin' for you, bud," he whispered thickly, and began. Through the brush he followed its wavering spoor, amazed at the amount of filthy mold about, gradually associating it with the thing that had killed his brother. There was nothing in the world for him any more but hate and doggedness. Cursing himself for not getting Alton home last night, he followed the tracks to the edge of the woods. They led him to a big tree there, and there he saw something else—the footprints of the little city man. Nearby lay some tattered scraps of linen, and—what was that?

Another set of prints—small ones. Small, stub-toed ones.

"Babe!"

No answer. The wind sighed. Somewhere a blue jay called.

Babe stopped and turned when she heard her father's voice, faint with distance, piercing.

"Listen at him holler," she crooned delightedly. "Gee, he sounds mad." She sent a jay bird's call disrespectfully back to him and hurried to The Place.

It consisted of a mammoth boulder beside the brook. Some upheaval in the glacial age had cleft it, cutting out a huge V-shaped chunk. The widest part of the cleft was at the water's edge, and the narrowest was hidden by bushes. It made a little ceilingless room, rough and uneven and full of pot-holes and cavelets inside, and yet with quite a level floor. The open end was at the water's edge.

Babe parted the bushes and peered down the cleft.

"Uncle Alton!" she called softly. There was no answer. Oh,

well, he'd be along. She scrambled in and slid down to the
floor.

She loved it here. It was shaded and cool, and the chattering stream filled it with shifting golden lights and laughing
gurgles. She called again, on principle, and then perched on
an outcropping to wait. It was only then she realized that she
still carried the little man's briefcase.

She turned it over a couple of times and then opened it. It
was divided in the middle by a leather wall. On one side were
a few papers in a large yellow envelope, and on the other
some sandwiches, a candy bar, and an apple. With a youngster's complacent acceptance of manna from heaven, Babe
fell to. She saved one sandwich for Alton, mainly because she
didn't like its highly spiced bologna. The rest made quite a
feast.

She was a little worried when Alton hadn't arrived, even
after she had consumed the apple core. She got up and tried
to skim some flat pebbles across the rolling brook, and she
stood on her hands, and she tried to think of a story to tell
herself, and she tried just waiting. Finally, in desperation,
she turned again to the briefcase, took out the papers, curled
up by the rocky wall and began to read them. It was something to do, anyway.

There was an old newspaper clipping that told about
strange wills that people had left. An old lady had once left a
lot of money to whoever would make the trip from the
Earth to the Moon and back. Another had financed a home
for cats whose masters and mistresses had died. A man left
thousands of dollars to the first person who could solve a certain mathematical problem and prove his solution. But one
item was blue-penciled. It was:

> One of the strangest of wills still in force is that
> of Thaddeus M. Kirk, who died in 1920. It appears
> that he built an elaborate mausoleum with burial
> vaults for all the remains of his family. He collect-
> ed and removed caskets from all over the country
> to fill the designated niches. Kirk was the last of his
> line; there were no relatives when he died. His will
> stated that the mausoleum was to be kept in repair
> permanently, and that a certain sum was to be set
> aside as a reward for whoever could produce the
> body of his grandfather, Roger Kirk, whose niche is

still empty. Anyone finding this body is eligible to
receive a substantial fortune.

Babe yawned vaguely over this, but kept on reading because there was nothing else to do. Next was a thick sheet of
business correspondence, bearing the letterhead of a firm of
lawyers. The body of it ran:

> In regard to your query regarding the will of
> Thaddeus Kirk, we are authorized to state that his
> grandfather was a man about five feet, five inches,
> whose left arm had been broken and who had a tri-
> angular silver plate set into his skull. There is no in-
> formation as to the whereabouts of his death. He
> disappeared and was declared legally dead after the
> lapse of fourteen years.
> The amount of the reward as stated in the will,
> plus accrued interest, now amounts to a fraction
> over sixty-two thousand dollars. This will be paid to
> anyone who produces the remains, providing that
> said remains answer descriptions kept in our private
> files.

There was more, but Babe was bored. She went on to the
little black notebook. There was nothing in it but penciled
and highly abbreviated records of visits to libraries; quota-
tions from books with titles like "History of Angelina and
Tyler Counties" and "Kirk Family History." Babe threw that
aside, too. Where could Uncle Alton be?

She began to sing tunelessly, "Tumalumalum tum, ta ta
ta," pretending to dance a minuet with flowing skirts like a
girl she had seen in the movies. A rustle of the bushes at the
entrance to The Place stopped her. She peeped upward, saw
them being thrust aside. Quickly she ran to a tiny cul-de-sac
in the rock wall, just big enough for her to hide in. She
giggled at the thought of how surprised Uncle Alton would
be when she jumped out at him.

She heard the newcomer come shuffling down the steep
slope of the crevice and land heavily on the floor. There was
something about the sound— What was it? It occurred to her
that though it was a hard job for a big man like Uncle Alton
to get through the little opening in the bushes, she could hear
no heavy breathing. She heard no breathing at all!

Babe peeped out into the main cave and squealed in utmost horror. Standing there was, not Uncle Alton, but a massive caricature of a man: a huge thing like an irregular mud doll, clumsily made. It quivered and parts of it glistened and parts of it were dried and crumbly. Half of the lower part of its face was gone, giving it a lopsided look. It had no perceptible mouth or nose, and its eyes were crooked, one higher than the other, both a dingy brown with no whites at all. It stood quite still looking at her, its only movement a seedy unalive quivering.

It wondered about the queer little noise Babe had made.

Babe crept far back against a little pocket of stone, her brain running round and round in tiny circles of agony. She opened her mouth to cry out, and could not. Her eyes bulged and her face flamed with the strangling effort, and the two golden ropes of her braided hair twitched and twitched as she hunted hopelessly for a way out. If only she were out in the open—or in the wedge-shaped half-cave where the thing was—or home in bed!

The thing clumped toward her, expressionless, moving with a slow inevitability that was the sheer crux of horror. Babe lay wide-eyed and frozen, mounting pressure of terror stilling her lungs, making her heart shake the whole world. The monster came to the mouth of the little pocket, tried to walk to her and was stopped by the sides. It was such a narrow little fissure, and it was all Babe could do to get it. The thing from the wood stood straining against the rock at its shoulders, pressing harder and harder to get to Babe. She sat up slowly, so near to the thing that its odor was almost thick enough to see, and a wild hope burst through her voiceless fear. It couldn't get in! It couldn't get in because it was too big!

The substance of its feet spread slowly under the tremendous strain and at its shoulder appeared a slight crack. It widened as the monster unfeelingly crushed itself against the rock, and suddenly a large piece of the shoulder came away and the being twisted slushily three feet farther in. It lay quietly with its muddy eyes fixed on her, and then brought one thick arm up over its head and reached.

Babe scrambled in the inch farther she had believed impossible, and the filthy clubbed hand stroked down her back, leaving a trail of muck on the blue denim of the shirt she wore. The monster surged suddenly and, lying full length now, gained that last precious inch. A black hand seized one of her braids, and for Babe the lights went out.

When she came to, she was dangling by her hair from that

same crusted paw. The thing held her high, so that her face and its featureless head were not more than a foot apart. It gazed at her with a mild curiosity in its eyes, and it swung her slowly back and forth. The agony of her pulled hair did what fear could not do—gave her a voice. She screamed. She opened her mouth and puffed up her powerful young lungs, and she sounded off. She held her throat in the position of the first scream, and her chest labored and pumped more air through the frozen throat. Shrill and monotonous and infinitely piercing, her screams.

The thing did not mind. It held her as she was, and watched. When it had learned all it could from this phenomenon, it dropped her jarringly, and looked around the half-cave, ignoring the stunned and huddled Babe. It reached over and picked up the leather briefcase and tore it twice across as if it were tissue. It saw the sandwich Babe had left, picked it up, crushed it, dropped it.

Babe opened her eyes, saw that she was free, and just as the thing turned back to her she dove between its legs and out into the shallow pool in front of the rock, paddled across and hit the other bank screaming. A vicious little light of fury burned in her; she picked up a grapefruit-sized stone and hurled it with all her frenzied might. It flew low and fast, and struck squashily on the monster's ankle. The thing was just taking a step toward the water; the stone caught it off balance, and its unpracticed equilibrium could not save it. It tottered for a long, silent moment at the edge and then splashed into the stream. Without a second look Babe ran shrieking away.

Cory Drew was following the little gobs of mold that somehow indicated the path of the murderer, and he was nearby when he first heard her scream. He broke into a run, dropping his shotgun and holding the .32-40 ready to fire. He ran with such deadly panic in his heart that he ran right past the huge cleft rock and was a hundred yards past it before she burst out through the pool and ran up the bank. He had to run hard and fast to catch her, because anything behind her was that faceless horror in the cave, and she was living for the one idea of getting away from there. He caught her in his arms and swung her to him, and she screamed on and on and on.

Babe didn't see Cory at all, even when he held her and quieted her.

The monster lay in the water. It neither liked nor disliked this new element. It rested on the bottom, its massive head a foot beneath the surface, and it curiously considered the facts that it had garnered. There was the little humming noise of Babe's voice that sent the monster questing into the cave. There was the black material of the briefcase that resisted so much more than green things when he tore it. There was the little two-legged one who sang and brought him near, and who screamed when he came. There was this new cold moving thing he had fallen into. It was washing his body away. That had never happened before. That was interesting. The monster decided to stay and observe this new thing. It felt no urge to save itself; it could only be curious.

The brook came laughing down out of its spring, ran down from its source beckoning to the sunbeams and embracing freshets and helpful brooklets. It shouted and played with streaming little roots, and nudged the minnows and pollywogs about in its tiny backwaters. It was a happy brook. When it came to the pool by the cloven rock it found the monster there, and plucked at it. It soaked the foul substances and smoothed and melted the molds, and the waters below the thing eddied darkly with its diluted matter. It was a thorough brook. It washed all it touched, persistently. Where it found filth, it removed filth; and if there was layer on layer of foulness, then layer by foul layer it was removed. It was a good brook. It did not mind the poison of the monster, but took it up and thinned it and spread it in little rings round rocks downstream, and let it drift to the rootlets of water plants, that they might grow greener and lovelier. And the monster melted.

"I am smaller," the thing thought. "That is interesting. I could not move now. And now this part of me which thinks is going, too. It will stop in just a moment, and drift away with the rest of the body. It will stop thinking and I will stop being, and that, too, is a very interesting thing."

So the monster melted and dirtied the water, and the water was clean again, washing and washing the skeleton that the monster had left. It was not very big, and there was a badly healed knot on the left arm. The sunlight flickered on the triangular silver plate set into the pale skull, and the skeleton was very clean now. The brook laughed about it for an age.

They found the skeleton, six grim-lipped men who came to find a killer. No one had believed Babe, when she told her

story days later. It had to be days later because Babe had
screamed for seven hours without stopping, and had lain like
a dead child for a day. No one believed her at all, because
her story was all about the bad fella, and they knew that the
bad fella was simply a thing that her father had made up to
frighten her with. But it was through her that the skeleton
was found, and so the men at the bank sent a check to the
Drews for more money than they had ever dreamed about. It
was old Roger Kirk, sure enough, that skeleton, though it was
found five miles from where he had died and sank into the
forest floor where the hot molds builded around his skeleton
and emerged—a monster.

So the Drews had a new barn and fine new livestock and
they hired four men. But they didn't have Alton. And they
didn't have Kimbo. And Babe screams at night and has
grown very thin.

# VAULT OF THE BEAST

*Astounding Science Fiction*

August

## by A. E. van Vogt (1912-        )

*The shape-changer is among the most fearsome creatures in the canon of science fiction and fantasy. Here, A. E. van Vogt, one of the brightest stars of the 1940s, presents a most unusual shape-changer— a robot. "The Tower" which holds the key to the defeat of the Beast is one of the most memorable edifices in science fiction and rightly captured the imagination of the readers of* Astounding. *This was one of the most talked about and written about stories in the magazine's history, both because of its qualities as fiction and its very strange mathematics. There was never an ultimate prime number like this one!*

(I saw science fiction through John Campbell's eyes during the magic years of 1938 to 1942, when I was learning how to write under that great editor's tutelage. Each month I would come to his office and each month he would tell me of the great stories he had received and my mouth would water and my heart would yearn to be able to duplicate such marvels and have John speak of *me* and *my* stories that way.

And in those years there was no question at all which writers John admired most and which absolutely bestrode the field like colossi. They were Robert Heinlein and A. E. van Vogt. How fortunate those two were. Never again will the field be bestridden like that. It's now too large for any one or two writers to set the pace. But while it lasted it was those two on one side and everyone else on the other. I.A.)

The creature crept. It whimpered from fear and pain, a thing, slobbering sound horrible to hear. Shapeless, formless thing yet changing shape and form with every jerky movement.

It crept along the corridor of the space freighter, fighting the terrible urge of its elements to take the shape of its surroundings. A gray blob of disintegrating stuff, it crept, it cascaded, it rolled, flowed, dissolved, every movement an agony of struggle against the abnormal need to become a stable shape.

Any shape! The hard, chilled-blue metal wall of the Earthbound freighter, the thick, rubbery floor. The floor was easy to fight. It wasn't like the metal that pulled and pulled. It would be easy to become metal for all eternity.

But something prevented it. An implanted purpose. A purpose that drummed from electron to electron, vibrated from atom to atom with an unvarying intensity that was like a special pain: *Find the greatest mathematical mind in the solar system, and bring it to the vault of the Martian ultimate metal. The Great One must be freed! The prime number time lock must be opened!*

That was the purpose that hummed with unrelenting agony through its elements. That was the thought that had been seared into its fundamental consciousness by the great and evil minds that had created it.

There was movement at the far end of the corridor. A door opened. Footsteps sounded. A man whistling to himself. With a metallic hiss, almost a sigh, the creature dissolved, looking momentarily like diluted mercury. Then it turned brown like the floor. It became the floor, a slightly thicker stretch of dark-brown rubber spread out for yards.

It was ecstasy just to lie there, to be flat and to have shape, and to be so nearly dead that there was no pain. Death was so sweet, so utterly desirable. And life such an unbearable torment of agony, such a throbbing, piercing nightmare of anguished convulsion. If only the life that was approaching would pass swiftly. If the life stopped, it would pull it into shape. Life could do that. Life was stronger than metal, stronger than anything. The approaching life meant torture, struggle, pain.

The creature tensed its now flat, grotesque body—the body that could develop muscles of steel—and waited in terror for the death struggle.

Spacecraftsman Parelli whistled happily as he strode along

the gleaming corridor that led from the engine room. He had just received a wireless from the hospital. His wife was doing well, and it was a boy. Eight pounds, the radiogram had said. He suppressed a desire to whoop and dance. A boy. Life sure was good.

Pain came to the thing on the floor. Primeval pain that sucked through its elements like acid burning, burning. The brown floor shuddered in every atom as Parelli strode over it. The aching urge to pull toward him, to take his shape. The thing fought its horrible desire, fought with anguish and shivering dread, more consciously now that it could think with Parelli's brain. A ripple of floor rolled after the man.

Fighting didn't help. The ripple grew into a blob that momentarily seemed to become a human head. Gray, hellish nightmare of demoniac shape. The creature hissed metallically in terror, then collapsed palpitating, slobbering with fear and pain and hate as Parelli strode on rapidly—too rapidly for its creeping pace.

The thin, horrible sound died; the thing dissolved into brown floor, and lay quiescent yet quivering in every atom from its unquenchable, uncontrollable urge to live—live in spite of pain, in spite of abysmal terror and primordial longing for stable shape. To live and fulfill the purpose of its lusting and malignant creators.

Thirty feet up the corridor, Parelli stopped. He jerked his mind from its thoughts of child and wife. He spun on his heels, and stared uncertainly along the passageway from the engine room.

"Now, what the devil was that?" he pondered aloud.

A sound—a queer, faint yet unmistakably horrid sound was echoing and re-echoing through his consciousness. A shiver ran the length of his spine. That sound—that devilish sound.

He stood there, a tall, magnificently muscled man, stripped to the waist, sweating from the heat generated by the rockets that were decelerating the craft after its meteoric flight from Mars. Shuddering, he clenched his fists, and walked slowly back the way he had come.

The creature throbbed with the pull of him, a gnawing, writhing, tormenting struggle that pierced into the deeps of every restless, agitated cell, stabbing agonizingly along the alien nervous system; and then became terrifyingly aware of the inevitable, the irresistible need to take the shape of the life.

Parelli stopped uncertainly. The floor moved under him, a visible wave that reared brown and horrible before his incredulous eyes and grew into a bulbous, slobbering, hissing mass. A venomous demon head reared on twisted, half-human shoulders. Gnarled hands on apelike, malformed arms clawed at his face with insenate rate—and changed even as they tore at him.

"Good God!" Parelli bellowed.

The hands, the arms that clutched him grew more normal, more human, brown, muscular. The face assumed familiar lines, sprouted a nose, eyes, a red gash of mouth. The body was suddenly his own, trousers and all, sweat and all.

"—God!" his image echoed; and pawed at him with letching fingers and an impossible strength.

Gasping, Parelli fought free, then launched one crushing blow straight into the distorted face. A drooling scream of agony came from the thing. It turned and ran, dissolving as it ran, fighting dissolution, uttering strange half-human cries.

And, struggling against horror, Parelli chased it, his knees weak and trembling from sheer funk and incredulity. His arm reached out and plucked at the disintegrating trousers. A piece came away in his hand, a cold, slimy, writhing lump like wet clay.

The feel of it was too much. His gorge rising in disgust, he faltered in his stride. He heard the pilot shouting ahead:

"What's the matter?"

Parelli saw the open door of the storeroom. With a gasp, he dived in, came out a moment later, wild-eyed, an ato-gun in his fingers. He saw the pilot, standing with staring, horrified brown eyes, white face and rigid body, facing one of the great windows.

"There it is!" the man cried.

A gray blob was dissolving into the edge of the glass, becoming glass. Parelli rushed forward, ato-gun poised. A ripple went through the glass, darkening it; and then, briefly, he caught a glimpse of a blob emerging on the other side of the glass into the cold of space.

The officer stood gaping beside him; the two of them watched the gray, shapeless mass creep out of sight along the side of the rushing freight liner.

Parelli sprang to life. "I got a piece of it!" he gasped. "Flung it down on the floor of the storeroom."

It was Lieutenant Morton who found it. A tiny section of floor reared up, and then grew amazingly large as it tried to expand into human shape. Parelli with distorted, crazy eyes scooped it up in a shovel. It hissed; it nearly became a part of the metal shovel, but couldn't because Parelli was so close. Changing, fighting for shape, it slobbered and hissed as Parelli staggered with it behind his superior officer. He was laughing hysterically. "I touched it," he kept saying, "I touched it."

A large blister of metal on the outside of the space freighter stirred into sluggish life, as the ship tore into the Earth's atmosphere. The metal walls of the freighter grew red, then white-hot, but the creature, unaffected, continued its slow transformation into gray mass. Vague thought came to the thing, realization that it was time to act.

Suddenly, it was floating free of the ship, falling slowly, heavily, as if somehow the gravitation of Earth had no serious effect upon it. A minute distortion in its electrons started it falling faster, as in some alien way it suddenly became more allergic to gravity.

The Earth was green below; and in the dim distance a gorgeous and tremendous city of spires and massive buildings glittered in the sinking sun. The thing slowed, and drifted like a falling leaf in a breeze toward the still-distant Earth. It landed in an arroyo beside a bridge at the outskirts of the city.

A man walked over the bridge with quick, nervous steps. He would have been amazed, if he had looked back, to see a replica of himself climb from the ditch to the road, and start walking briskly after him.

*Find the—greatest mathematician!*

It was an hour later; and the pain of the throbbing thought was a dull, continuous ache in the creature's brain, as it walked along the crowded street. There were other pains, too. The pain of fighting the pull of the pushing, hurrying mass of humanity that swarmed by with unseeing eyes. But it was easier to think, easier to hold form now that it had the brain and body of a man.

*Find—mathematician!*

"Why?" asked the man's brain of the thing; and the whole body shook with startled shock at such heretical questioning. The brown eyes darted in fright from side to side, as if expecting instant and terrible doom. The face dissolved a little in that brief moment of mental chaos, became successively the man with the hooked nose who swung by, the tanned face of the tall woman who was looking into the shop window, the—

With a second gasp, the creature pulled its mind back from fear, and fought to readjust its face to that of the smooth-shaven young man who sauntered idly in from a side street. The young man glanced at him, looked away, then glanced back again startled. The creature echoed the thought in the man's brain: "Who the devil is that? Where have I seen that fellow before?"

Half a dozen women in a group approached. The creature shrank aside as they passed, its face twisted with the agony of the urge to become woman. Its brown suit turned just the faintest shade of blue, the color of the nearest dress, as it momentarily lost control of its outer atoms. Its mind hummed with the chatter of clothes and "My dear, didn't she look dreadful in that awful hat?"

There was a solid cluster of giant buildings ahead. The thing shook its human head consciously. So many buildings meant metal; and the forces that held metal together would pull and pull at its human shape. The creature comprehended the reason for this with the understanding of the slight man in a dark suit who wandered by dully. The slight man was a clerk; the thing caught his thought. He was thinking enviously of his boss who was Jim Brender, of the financial firm of J. P. Brender & Co.

The overtones of that thought struck along the vibrating elements of the creature. It turned abruptly and followed Lawrence Pearson, bookkeeper. If people ever paid attention to other people on the street, they would have been amazed after a moment to see two Lawrence Pearsons proceeding down the street, one some fifty feet behind the other. The second Lawrence Pearson had learned from the mind of the first that Jim Brender was a Harvard graduate in mathematics, finance and political economy, the latest of a long line of financial geniuses, thirty years old, and the head of the tremendously wealthy J. P. Brender & Co. Jim Brender had just married the most beautiful girl in the world; and this was the reason for Lawrence Pearson's discontent with life.

"Here I'm thirty, too," his thoughts echoed in the creature's mind, "and I've got nothing. He's got everything—everything while all I've got to look forward to is the same old boarding house till the end of time."

It was getting dark as the two crossed the river. The creature quickened its pace, striding forward with aggressive alertness that Lawrence Pearson in the flesh could never have managed. Some glimmering of its terrible purpose communicated itself in that last instant to the victim. The slight man turned; and let out a faint squawk as those steel-muscled fingers jerked at his throat, a single, fearful snap.

The creature's brain went black with dizziness as the brain of Lawrence Pearson crashed into the night of death. Gasping whimpering, fighting dissolution, it finally gained control of itself. With one sweeping movement, it caught the dead body and flung it over the cement railing. There was a splash below, then a sound of gurgling water.

The thing that was now Lawrence Pearson walked on hurriedly, then more slowly till it came to a large, rambling brick house. It looked anxiously at the number, suddenly uncertain if it had remembered rightly. Hesitantly, it opened the door.

A streamer of yellow light splashed out, and laughter vibrated in the thing's sensitive ears. There was the same hum of many thoughts and many brains, as there had been in the street. The creature fought against the inflow of thought that threatened to crowd out the mind of Lawrence Pearson. A little dazed by the struggle, it found itself in a large, bright hall, which looked through a door into a room where a dozen people were sitting around a dining table.

"Oh, it's you, Mr. Pearson," said the landlady from the head of the table. She was a sharp-nosed, thin-mouthed woman at whom the creature stared with brief intentness. From her mind, a thought had come. She had a son who was a mathematics teacher in a high school. The creature shrugged. In one penetrating glance, the truth throbbed along the intricate atomic structure of its body. This woman's son was as much of an intellectual lightweight as his mother.

"You're just in time," she said incuriously. "Sarah, bring Mr. Pearson's plate."

"Thank you, but I'm not feeling hungry," the creature replied; and its human brain vibrated to the first silent, ironic laughter that it had ever known. "I think I'll just lie down."

All night long it lay on the bed of Lawrence Pearson, bright-eyed, alert, becoming more and more aware of itself. It thought:

"I'm a machine, without a brain of my own. I use the brains of other people, but somehow my creators made it possible for me to be more than just an echo. I use people's brains to carry out my purpose."

It pondered about those creators, and felt a surge of panic sweeping along its alien system, darkening its human mind. There was a vague physiological memory of pain unutterable, and of tearing chemical action that was frightening.

The creature rose at dawn, and walked the streets till half past nine. At that hour, it approached the imposing marble entrance of J. P. Brender & Co. Inside, it sank down in the comfortable chair initialed L. P.; and began painstakingly to work at the books Lawrence Pearson had put away the night before.

At ten o'clock, a tall young man in a dark suit entered the arched hallway and walked briskly through the row after row of offices. He smiled with easy confidence to every side. The thing did not need the chorus of "Good morning, Mr. Brender" to know that its prey had arrived.

Terrible in its slow-won self-confidence, it rose with a lithe, graceful movement that would have been impossible to the real Lawrence Pearson, and walked briskly to the washroom. A moment later, the very image of Jim Brender emerged from the door and walked with easy confidence to the door of the private office which Jim Brender had entered a few minutes before.

The thing knocked and walked in—and simultaneously became aware of three things: The first was that it had found the mind after which it had been sent. The second was that its image mind was incapable of imitating the finer subtleties of the razor-sharp brain of the young man who was staring up from dark-gray eyes that were a little startled. And the third was the large metal bas-relief that hung on the wall.

With a shock that almost brought chaos, it felt the overpowering tug of that metal. And in one flash it knew that this was ultimate metal, product of the fine craft of the ancient Martians, whose metal cities, loaded with treasures of furniture, art and machinery, were slowly being dug up by enterprising human beings from the sands under which they had been buried for thirty or fifty million years.

The ultimate metal! The metal that no heat would even warm, that no diamond or other cutting device, could scratch, never duplicated by human beings, as mysterious as the *ieis* force which the Martians made from apparent nothingness.

All these thoughts crowded the creature's brain, as it explored the memory cells of Jim Brender. With an effort that was a special pain, the thing wrenched its mind from the metal, and fastened its eyes on Jim Brender. It caught the full flood of the wonder in his mind, as he stood up.

"Good lord," said Jim Brender, "who are you?"

"My name's Jim Brender," said the thing, conscious of grim amusement, conscious, too, that it was progress for it to be able to feel such an emotion.

The real Jim Brender had recovered himself. "Sit down, sit down," he said heartily. "This is the most amazing coincidence I've ever seen."

He went over to the mirror that made one panel of the left wall. He stared, first at himself, then at the creature. "Amazing," he said. "Absolutely amazing."

"Mr. Brender," said the creature, "I saw your picture in the paper, and I thought our astounding resemblance would make you listen, where otherwise you might pay no attention. I have recently returned from Mars, and I am here to persuade you to come back to Mars with me."

"That," said Jim Brender, "is impossible."

"Wait," the creature said, "until I have told you why. Have you ever heard of the Tower of the Beast?"

"The Tower of the Beast!" Jim Brender repeated slowly. He went around his desk and pushed a button.

A voice from an ornamental box said: "Yes, Mr. Brender?"

"Dave, get me all the data on the Tower of the Beast and the lengendary city of Li in which it is supposed to exist."

"Don't need to look it up," came the crisp reply. "Most Martian histories refer to it as the beast that fell from the sky when Mars was young—some terrible warning connected with it—the beast was unconscious when found—said to be the result of its falling out of sub-space. Martians read its mind; and were so horrified by its subconscious intentions they tried to kill it, but couldn't. So they built a huge vault, about fifteen hundred feet in diameter and a mile high—and the beast, apparently of these dimensions, was locked in. Several attempts have been made to find the city of Li, but without success. Generally believed to be a myth. That's all, Jim."

"Thank you!" Jim Brender clicked off the connection, and turned to his visitor. "Well?"

"It is not a myth. I know where the Tower of the Beast is; and I also know that the beast is still alive."

"Now, see here," said Brender good-humoredly, "I'm intrigued by your resemblance to me; and as a matter of fact I'd like Pamela—my wife—to see you. How about coming over to dinner? But don't, for Heaven's sake, expect me to believe such a story. The beast, if there is such a thing, fell from the sky when Mars was young. There are some authorities who maintain that the Martian race died out a hundred million years ago, though twenty-five million is the conservative estimate. The only things remaining of their civilization are their constructions of ultimate metal. Fortunately, toward the end they built almost everything from that indestructible metal."

"Let me tell you about the Tower of the Beast," said the thing quietly. "It is a tower of gigantic size, but only a hundred feet or so projected above the sand when I saw it. The whole top is a door, and that door is geared to a time lock, which in turn has been integrated along a line of *ieis* to the ultimate prime number."

Jim Brender stared; and the thing caught his startled thought, the first uncertainty, and the beginning of belief.

"Ultimate prime number!" Brender ejaculated. "What do you mean?" He caught himself. "I know of course that a prime number is a number divisible only by itself and by one."

He snatched at a book from the little wall library beside his desk, and rippled through it. "The largest known prime is—ah, here it is—is 230584300921393951. Some others, according to this authority, are 77843839397, 182521213001, and 78875943472201."

He frowned. "That makes the whole thing ridiculous. The ultimate prime would be an indefinite number." He smiled at the thing. "If there is a beast, and it is locked up in a vault of ultimate metal, the door of which is geared to a time lock, integrated along a line of *ieis* to the ultimate prime number— then the beast is caught. Nothing in the world can free it."

"To the contrary," said the creature. "I have been assured by the beast that it is within the scope of human mathematics to solve the problem, but that what is required is a born mathematical mind, equipped with all the mathematical training that Earth science can afford. You are that man."

"You expect me to release this evil creature—even if I could perform this miracle of mathematics."

"Evil nothing!" snapped the thing. "That ridiculous fear of the unknown which made the Martians imprison it has resulted in a very grave wrong. The beast is a scientist from another space, accidentally caught in one of his experiments. I say 'his' when of course I do not know whether this race has a sexual differentiation."

"You actually talked with the beast?"

"It communicated with me by mental telepathy."

"It has been proven that thoughts cannot penetrate ultimate metal."

"What do humans know about telepathy? They cannot even communicate with each other except under special conditions." The creature spoke contemptuously.

"That's right. And if your story is true, then this is a matter for the Council."

"This is a matter for two men, you and I. Have you forgotten that the vault of the beast is the central tower of the great city of Li—billions of dollars' worth of treasure in furniture, art and machinery? The beast demands release from its prison before it will permit anyone to mine that treasure. You can release it. We can share the treasure."

"Let me ask you a question," said Jim Brender. "What is your real name?"

"P-Pierce Lawrence!" the creature stammered. For the moment, it could think of no greater variation of the name of its first victim than reversing the two words, with a slight change on "Pearson." Its thoughts darkened with confusion as the voice of Brender pounded:

"On what ship did you come from Mars?"

"O-on *F 4961*," the thing stammered chaotically, fury adding to the confused state of its mind. It fought for control, felt itself slipping, suddenly felt the pull of the ultimate metal that made up the bas-relief on the wall, and knew by that tug that it was dangerously near dissolution.

"That would be a freighter," said Jim Brender. He pressed a button. "Carltons, find out if the *F 4961* had a passenger or person aboard, named Pierce Lawrence. How long will it take?"

"About a minute, sir."

"You see," said Jim Brender, leaning back, "this is mere formality. If you were on that ship, then I shall be compelled to give serious attention to your statements. You can understand, of course, that I could not possibly go into a thing like this blindly. I—"

The buzzer rang. "Yes?" said Jim Brender.

"Only the crew of two was on the *F 4961* when it landed yesterday. No such person as Pierce Lawrence was aboard."

"Thank you." Jim Brender stood up. He said coldly, "Good-bye, Mr. Lawrence. I cannot imagine what you hoped to gain by this ridiculous story. However, it has been most intriguing, and the problem you presented was very ingenious indeed—"

The buzzer was ringing. "What is it?"

"Mr. Gorson to see you, sir."

"Very well, send him right in."

The thing had greater control of its brain now, and it saw in Brender's mind that Gorson was a financial magnate, whose business ranked with the Brender firm. It saw other things, too, things that made it walk out of the private office, out of the building, and wait patiently until Mr. Gorson emerged from the imposing entrance. A few minutes later, there were two Mr. Gorsons walking down the street.

Mr. Gorson was a vigorous man in his early fifties. He had lived a clean, active life; and the hard memories of many climates and several planets were stored away in his brain. The thing caught the alertness of this man on its sensitive elements, and followed him warily, respectfully, not quite decided whether it would act.

It thought: "I've come a long way from the primitive life that couldn't hold its shape. My creators, in designing me, gave to me powers of learning, developing. It is easier to fight dissolution, easier to be human. In handling this man, I must remember that my strength is invincible when properly used."

With minute care, it explored in the mind of its intended victim the exact route of his walk to his office. There was the entrance to a large building clearly etched on his mind. Then a long, marble corridor, into an automatic elevator up to the eighth floor, along a short corridor with two doors. One door led to the private entrance of the man's private office. The other to a storeroom used by the janitor. Gorson had looked into the place on various occasions; and there was in his mind, among other things, the memory of a large chest—

The thing waited in the storeroom till the unsuspecting Gorson was past the door. The door creaked. Gorson turned, his eyes widening. He didn't have a chance. A fist of solid steel smashed his face to a pulp, knocking the bones back into his brain.

This time, the creature did not make the mistake of keeping its mind tuned to that of its victim. It caught him viciously as he fell, forcing its steel fist back to a semblance of human flesh. With furious speed, it stuffed the bulky and athletic form into a large chest, and clamped the lid down tight.

Alertly, it emerged from the storeroom, entered the private office of Mr. Gorson, and sat down before the gleaming desk of oak. The man who responded to the pressing of a button saw John Gorson sitting there, and heard John Gorson say:

"Crispins, I want you to start selling these stocks through the secret channels right away. Sell until I tell you to stop, even if you think it's crazy. I have information of something big on."

Crispins glanced down the row after row of stock names; and his eyes grew wider and wider. "Good lord, man!" he gasped finally, with that familiarity which is the right of a trusted adviser, "these are all the gilt-edged stocks. Your whole fortune can't swing a deal like this."

"I told you I'm not in this alone."

"But it's against the law to break the market," the man protested.

"Crispins, you heard what I said. I'm leaving the office. Don't try to get in touch with me. I'll call you."

The thing that was John Gorson stood up, paying no attention to the bewildered thoughts that flowed from Crispins. It went out of the door by which it had entered. As it emerged from the building, it was thinking: "All I've got to do is kill half a dozen financial giants, start their stocks selling, and then—"

By one o'clock it was over. The exchange didn't close till three, but at one o'clock the news was flashed on the New York tickers. In London, where it was getting dark, the papers brought out an extra. In Hankow and Shanghai, a dazzling new day was breaking as the newsboys ran along the streets in the shadows of skyscrapers, and shouted that J. P. Brender & Co. had assigned; and that there was to be an investigation—

"We are facing," said the chairman of the investigation committee, in his opening address the following morning, "one of the most astounding coincidences in all history. An ancient and respected firm, with world-wide affiliations and branches, with investments in more than a thousand companies of every description, is struck bankrupt by an unexpected crash in every stock in which the firm was interested. It will require months to take evidence on the responsibility for the short-selling which brought about this disaster. In the meantime, I see no reason, regrettable as the action must be to all the old friends of the late J. P. Brender, and of his son, why the demands of the creditors should not be met, and the properties liquidated through auction sales and such other methods as may be deemed proper and legal—"

"Really, I don't blame her," said the first woman, as they wandered through the spacious rooms of the Brenders' Chinese palace. "I have no doubt she does love Jim Brender, but no one could seriously expect her to remain married to him *now*. She's a woman of the world, and it's utterly impossible to expect her to live with a man who's going to be a mere pilot or space hand or something on a Martian spaceship—"

Commander Hughes of Interplanetary Spaceways entered the office of his employer truculently. He was a small man, but extremely wiry; and the thing that was Louis Dyer gazed at him tensely, conscious of the force and power of this man.

Hughes began: "You have my report on this Brender case?"

The thing twirled the mustache of Louis Dyer nervously; then picked up a small folder, and read out loud:

"Dangerous for psychological reasons . . . to employ Brender. . . . So many blows in succession. Loss of wealth, position and wife. . . . No normal man could remain normal under . . . circumstances. Take him into office . . . befriend him . . . give him a sinecure, or position where his undoubted great ability . . . but not on a spaceship, where the utmost hardiness, both mental, moral, spiritual and physical is required—"

Hughes interrupted: "Those are exactly the points which I am stressing. I knew you would see what I meant, Louis."

"Of course, I see," said the creature, smiling in grim amusement, for it was feeling very superior these days. "Your thoughts, your ideas, your codes and your methods are stamped irrevocably on your brain and"—it added hastily—"you have never left me in doubt as to where you stand. However, in this case I must insist. Jim Brender will not take an ordinary position offered by his friends. And it is ridiculous to ask him to subordinate himself to men to whom he is in every way superior. He has commanded his own space yacht; he knows more about the mathematical end of the work than our whole staff put together; and that is no reflection on our staff. He knows the hardships connected with space flying, and believes that it is exactly what he needs. I, therefore, command you, for the first time in our long association, Peter, to put him on space freighter *F 4961* in the place of Spacecraftsman Parelli who collapsed into a nervous breakdown after that curious affair with the creature from space, as Lieutenant Morton described it— By the way, did you find the . . . er . . . sample of that creature yet?"

"No, sir, it vanished the day you came in to look at it. We've searched the place high and low—queerest stuff you ever saw. Goes through glass as easy as light; you'd think it was some form of light-stuff—scares me, too. A pure sympodial development—actually more adaptable to environment than anything hitherto discovered; and that's putting it mildly. I tell you, sir— But see here, you can't steer me off the Brender case like that."

"Peter, I don't understand your attitude. This is the first time I've interferred with your end of the work and—"

"I'll resign," groaned that sorely beset man.

The thing stifled a smile. "Peter, you've built up the staff of Spaceways. It's your child, your creation; you can't give it up, you know you can't—"

The words hissed softly into alarm; for into Hughes' brain had flashed the first real intention of resigning. Just hearing of his accomplishments and the story of his beloved job brought such a rush of memories, such a realization of how tremendous an outrage was this threatened interference. In one mental leap, the creature saw what this man's resignation would mean: The discontent of the men; the swift perception of the situation by Jim Brender; and his refusal to accept the job. There was only one way out—that Brender would get to the ship without finding out what had happened. Once on it, he must carry through with one trip to Mars; and that was all that was needed.

The thing pondered the possibility of imitating Hughes' body; then agonizingly realized that it was hopeless. Both Louis Dyer and Hughes must be around until the last minute.

"But, Peter, listen!" the creature began chaotically. Then it said, "Damn!" for it was very human in its mentality; and the realization that Hughes took its words as a sign of weakness was maddening. Uncertainty descended like a black cloud over its brain.

"I'll tell Brender when he arrives in five minutes how I feel about all this!" Hughes snapped; and the creature knew that the worst had happened. "If you forbid me to tell him then I resign. I— Good God, man, your face!"

Confusion and horror came to the creature simultaneously. It knew abruptly that its face had dissolved before the threatened ruin of its plans. It fought for control, leaped to its feet, seeing the incredible danger. The large office just beyond the frosted glass door—Hughes' first outcry would bring help—

With a half sob, it sought to force its arm into an imitation of a metal fist, but there was no metal in the room to pull it into shape. There was only the solid maple desk. With a harsh cry, the creature leaped completely over the desk, and sought to bury a pointed shaft of stick into Hughes' throat.

Hughes cursed in amazement, and caught at the stick with furious strength. There was sudden commotion in the outer office, raised voices, running feet—

It was quite accidental the way it happened. The surface cars swayed to a stop, drawing up side by side as the red light blinked on ahead. Jim Brender glanced at the next car.

A girl and a man sat in the rear of the long, shiny, streamlined affair, and the girl was desperately striving to crouch down out of his sight, striving with equal desperation not to be too obvious in her intention. Realizing that she was seen, she smiled brilliantly, and leaned out of the window.

"Hello, Jim, how's everything?"

"Hello, Pamela!" Jim Brender's fingers tightened on the steering wheel till the knuckles showed white, as he tried to keep his voice steady. He couldn't help adding: "When does the divorce become final?"

"I get my papers tomorrow," she said, "but I suppose you won't get yours till you return from your first trip. Leaving today, aren't you?"

"In about fifteen minutes." He hesitated. "When is the wedding?"

The rather plump, white-faced man who had not participated in the conversation so far, leaned forward.

"Next week," he said. He put his fingers possessively over Pamela's hand. "I wanted it tomorrow but Pamela wouldn't—er, good-bye."

His last words were hastily spoken, as the traffic lights switched, and the cars rolled on, separating at the first corner.

The rest of the drive to the spaceport was a blur. He hadn't expected the wedding to take place so soon. Hadn't, when he came right down to it, expected it to take place at all. Like a fool, he had hoped blindly—

Not that it was Pamela's fault. Her training, her very life made this the only possible course of action for her. But— *one week!* The spaceship would be one fourth of the long trip to Mars—

He parked his car. As he paused beside the runway that led to the open door of *F 4961*—a huge globe of shining metal, three hundred feet in diameter—he saw a man running toward him. Then he recognized Hughes.

The thing that was Hughes approached, fighting for calmness. The whole world was a flame of cross-pulling forces. It shrank from the thoughts of the people milling about in the office it had just left. Everything had gone wrong. It had never intended to do what it now had to do. It had intended to spend most of the trip to Mars as a blister of metal on the outer shield of the ship. With an effort, it controlled its funk, its terror, its brain.

"We're leaving right away," it said.

Brender looked amazed. "But that means I'll have to figure out a new orbit under the most difficult—"

"Exactly," the creature interrupted. "I've been hearing a lot about your marvelous mathematical ability. It's time the words were proved by deeds."

Jim Brender shrugged. "I have no objection. But how is it that you're coming along?"

"I always go with a new man."

It sounded reasonable. Brender climbed the runway, closely followed by Hughes. The powerful pull of the metal was the first real pain the creature had known for days. For a long month, it would now have to fight the metal, fight to retain the shape of Hughes—and carry on a thousand duties at the same time.

That first stabbing pain tore along its elements, and smashed the confidence that days of being human had built up. And then, as it followed Brender through the door, it heard a shout behind it. It looked back hastily. People were streaming out of several doors, running toward the ship.

Brender was several yards along the corridor. With a hiss that was almost a sob, the creature leaped inside, and pulled the lever that clicked the great door shut.

There was an emergency lever that controlled the antigravity plates. With one jerk, the creature pulled the heavy lever hard over. There was a sensation of lightness and a sense of falling.

Through the great plate window, the creature caught a flashing glimpse of the field below, swarming with people. White faces turning upward, arm waving. Then the scene grew remote, as a thunder of rockets vibrated through the ship.

"I hope," said Brender, as Hughes entered the control room, "you wanted me to start the rockets."

"Yes," the thing replied, and felt brief panic at the chaos in its brain, the tendency of its tongue to blur. "I'm leaving the mathematical end entirely in your hands."

It didn't dare to stay so near the heavy metal engines, even with Brender's body there to help it keep its human shape. Hurriedly, it started up the corridor. The best place would be the insulated bedroom—

Abruptly, it stopped in its headlong walk, teetered for an instant on tiptoes. From the control room it had just left, a thought was trickling—a thought from Brender's brain. The creature almost dissolved in terror as it reailzed that Brender was sitting at the radio, answering an insistent call from Earth.

It burst into the control room, and braked to a halt, its eyes widening with humanlike dismay. Brender whirled from before the radio with a single twisting step. In his fingers, he held a revolver. In his mind, the creature read a dawning comprehension of the whole truth. Brender cried:

"You're the . . . thing that came to my office, and talked about prime numbers and the vault of the beast."

He took a step to one side to cover an open doorway that led down another corridor. The movement brought the telescreen into the vision of the creature. In the screen was the image of the real Hughes. Simultaneously, Hughes saw the thing.

"Brender," he bellowed, "it's the monster that Morton and Parelli saw on their trip from Mars. It doesn't react to heat or any chemicals, but we never tried bullets. Shoot, you fool!"

It was too much, there was too much metal, too much confusion. With a whimpering cry, the creature dissolved. The pull of the metal twisted it horribly into thick half metal; the struggle to be human left it a malignant structure of bulbous head, with one eye half gone, and two snakelike arms attached to the half metal of the body.

Instinctively, it fought closer to Brender, letting the pull of his body make it more human. The half metal became flesh-like stuff that sought to return to its human shape.

"Listen, Brender!" Hughes' voice came urgently. "The fuel vats in the engine room are made of ultimate metal. One of them is empty. We caught a part of this thing once before, and it couldn't get out of the small jar of ultimate metal. If you could drive it into the vat while it's lost control of itself, as it seems to do very easily—"

"I'll see what lead can do!" Brender rapped in a brittle voice.

*Bang!* The half-human creature screamed from its half-formed slit of mouth, and retreated, its legs dissolving into gray dough.

"It hurts, doesn't it?" Brender ground out. "Get over into the engine room, you damned thing, into the vat!"

"Go on, go on!" Hughes was screaming from the tele-screen.

Brender fired again. The creature made a horrible slobbering sound, and retreated once more. But it was bigger again, more human; and in one caricature hand a caricature of Brender's revolver was growing.

It raised the unfinished, unformed gun. There was an explosion, and a shriek from the thing. The revolver fell, a shapeless, tattered blob, to the floor. The little gray mass of it scrambled frantically toward the parent body, and attached itself like some monstrous canker to the right foot.

And then, for the first time, the mighty and evil brains that had created the thing, sought to dominate their robot. Furious, yet conscious that the game must be carefully played, the Controller forced the terrified and utterly beaten thing to its will. Scream after agonized scream rent the air, as the change was forced upon the unstable elements. In an instant, the thing stood in the shape of Brender, but instead of a revolver, there grew from one browned, powerful hand a pencil of shining metal. Mirror bright, it glittered in every facet like some incredible gem.

The metal glowed ever so faintly, an unearthly radiance. And where the radio had been, and the screen with Hughes' face on it, there was a gaping hole. Desperately, Brender pumped bullets into the body before him, but though the shape trembled, it stared at him now, unaffected. The shining weapon swung toward him.

"When you are quite finished," it said, "perhaps we can talk."

It spoke so mildly that Brender, tensing to meet death, lowered his gun in amazement. The thing went on:

"Do not be alarmed. This which you hear and see is a robot, designed by us to cope with your space and number world. Several of us are working here under the most difficult conditions to maintain this connection, so I must be brief.

"We exist in a time world immeasurably more slow than your own. By a system of synchronization, we have geared a number of these spaces in such fashion that, though one of our days is millions of your years, we can communicate. Our purpose is to free our colleague, Kalorn, from the Martian vault. Kalorn was caught accidentally in a time warp of his own making and precipitated onto the planet you know as Mars. The Martians, needlessly fearing his great size, constructed a most diabolical prison, and we need your knowledge of the mathematics peculiar to your space and number world—and to it alone—in order to free him."

The calm voice continued, earnest but not offensively so, insistent but friendly. He regretted that their robot had killed human beings. In greater detail, he explained that every space was constructed on a different numbers system, some all negative, some all positive, some a mixture of the two, the whole an infinite variety, and every mathematic interwoven into the very fabric of the space it ruled.

*Ieis* force was not really mysterious. It was simply a flow from one space to another, the result of a difference in potential. This flow, however, was one of the universal forces, which only one other force could affect, the one he had used a few minutes before. Ultimate metal was *actually* ultimate.

In their space they had a similar metal, built up from negative atoms. He could see from Brender's mind that the Martians had known nothing about minus numbers, so that they must have built it up from ordinary atoms. It could be done that way, too, though not so easily. He finished:

"The problem narrows down to this: Your mathematics must tell us how, with our universal force, we can short-circuit the ultimate prime number—that is, factor it—so that the door will open any time. You may ask how a prime can be factored when it is divisible only by itself and by one.

That problem is, for your system, solvable only by your mathematics. Will you do it?"

Brender realized with a start that he was still holding his revolver. He tossed it aside. His nerves were calm as he said:

"Everything you have said sounds reasonable and honest. If you were desirous of making trouble, it would be the simplest thing in the world to send as many of your kind as you wished. Of course, the whole affair must be placed before the Council—"

"Then it is hopeless—the Council could not possibly accede—"

"And you expect me to do what you do not believe the highest governmental authority in the System would do?" Brender exclaimed.

"It is inherent in the nature of a democracy that it cannot gamble with the lives of its citizens. We have such a government here; and its members have already informed us that, in a similar condition, they would not consider releasing an unknown beast upon their people. Individuals, however, can gamble where governments must not. You have agreed that our argument is logical. What system do men follow if not that of logic?"

The Controller, through its robot, watched Brender's thoughts alertly. It saw doubt and uncertainty, opposed by a very human desire to help, based upon the logical conviction that it was safe. Probing his mind, it saw swiftly that it was unwise, in dealing with men, to trust too much to logic. It pressed on:

"To an individual we can offer—everything. In a minute, with your permission, we shall transfer this ship to Mars; not in thirty days, but in thirty seconds. The knowledge of how this is done will remain with you. Arrived at Mars, you will find yourself the only living person who knows the whereabouts of the ancient city of Li, of which the vault of the beast is the central tower. In this city will be found literally billions of dollars' worth of treasure made of ultimate metal; and according to the laws of Earth, fifty percent will be yours. Your fortune re-established, you will be able to return to Earth this very day, and reclaim your former wife, and your position. Poor silly child, she loves you still, but the iron conventions and training of her youth leave her no alternative. If she were older, she would have the character to defy

those conventions. You must save her from herself. Will you
do it?"

Brender was as white as a sheet, his hands clenching and
unclencing. Malevolently, the thing watched the flaming
thought sweeping through his brain—the memory of a pudgy
white hand closing over Pamela's fingers, watched the reaction of Brender to its words, those words that expressed exactly what he had always thought. Brender looked up with
tortured eyes.

"Yes," he said, "I'll do what I can."


A bleak range of mountains fell away into a valley of
reddish gray sand. The thin winds of Mars blew a mist of
sand against the building.                    •

*Such* a building! At a distance, it had looked merely big. A
bare hundred feet projected above the desert, a hundred feet
of length and *fifteen hundred feet of diameter*. Literally thousands of feet must extend beneath the restless ocean of sand
to make the perfect balance of form, the graceful flow, the
fairylike beauty, which the long-dead Martians demanded of
all their constructions, however massive. Brender felt suddenly small and insignificant as the rockets of his spacesuit
pounded him along a few feet above the sand toward that incredible building.

At close range the ugliness of sheer size was miraculously
lost in the wealth of the decorative. Columns and pilasters
assembled in groups and clusters, broke up the façades,
gathered and dispersed again restlessly. The flat surfaces of
wall and roof melted into a wealth of ornaments and imitation stucco work, vanished and broke into a play of light and
shade.

The creature floated beside Brender; and its Controller
said: "I see that you have been giving considerable thought to
the problem, but this robot seems incapable of following abstract thoughts, so I have no means of knowing the source of
your speculations. I see however that you seem to be satisfied."

"I think I've got the answer," said Brender, "but first I
wish to see the time lock. Let's climb."

They rose into the sky, dipping over the lip of the building.
Brender saw a vast flat expanse; and in the center— He
caught his breath!

The meager light from the distant sun of Mars shone down
on a structure located at what seemed the exact center of the

great door. The structure was about fifty feet high, and seemed nothing less than a series of quadrants coming together at the center, which was a metal arrow pointing straight up.

The arrow head was not solid metal. Rather it was as if the metal had divided in two parts, then curved together again. But not quite together. About a foot separated the two sections of metal. But that foot was bridged by a vague, thin, green flame of *ieis* force.

"The time lock!" Brender nodded. "I thought it would be something like that, though I expected it would be bigger, more substantial."

"Do not be deceived by its fragile appearance," answered the thing. "Theoretically, the strength of ultimate metal is infinite; and the *ieis* force can only be affected by the universal I have mentioned. Exactly what the effect will be, it is impossible to say as it involves the temporary derangement of the whole number system upon which that particular area of space is built. But now tell us what to do."

"Very well." Brender eased himself onto a bank of sand, and cut off his antigravity plates. He lay on his back, and stared thoughtfully into the blue-black sky. For the time being all doubts, worries and fears were gone from him, forced out by sheer will power. He began to explain:

"The Martian mathematic, like that of Euclid and Pythagoras, was based on endless magnitude. Minus numbers were beyond their philosophy. On Earth, however, beginning with Descartes, an analytical mathematic was evolved. Magnitude and perceivable dimensions were replaced by that of variable relation-values between positions in space.

"For the Martians, there was only one number between 1 and 3. Actually, the totality of such numbers is an infinite aggregate. And with the introduction of the idea of the square root of minus one—or *i*—and the complex numbers, mathematics definitely ceased to be a simple thing of magnitude, perceivable in pictures. Only the intellectual step from the infinitely small quantity to the lower limit of every possible finite magnitude brought out the conception of a variable number which oscillated beneath any assignable number that was not zero.

"The prime number, being a conception of pure magnitude, had no reality in *real* mathematics, but in this case was rigidly bound up with the reality of the *ieis* force. The Martians knew *ieis* as a pale-green flow about a foot in length and developing say a thousand horsepower. (It was actually 12.171 inches and 1021.23 horsepower, but that was unimportant.) The power produced never varied, the length never varied, from year end to year end, for tens of thousands of years. The Martians took the length as their basis of measurement, and called it one 'el'; they took the power as their basis of power and called it one 'rb.' And because of the absolute invariability of the flow they knew it was eternal.

"They knew furthermore that nothing could be eternal without being prime; their whole mathematic was based on numbers which could be factored, that is, disintegrated, destroyed, rendered less than they had been; and numbers which could not be factored, disintegrated, or divided into smaller groups.

"Any number which could be factored was incapable of being infinite. Contrariwise, the infinite number must be prime.

"Therefore, they built a lock and integrated it along a line of *ieis*, to operate when the *ieis* ceased to flow—which would be at the end of Time, provided it was not interfered with. To prevent interference, they buried the motivating mechanism of the flow in ultimate metal, which could not be destroyed or corroded in any way. According to their mathematic, that settled it."

"But you have the answer," said the voice of the thing eagerly.

"Simply this: The Martians set a value on the flow of one 'rb.' If you interfere with that flow to no matter what small degree, you no longer have an 'rb.' You have something less. The flow, which is a universal, becomes automatically less than a universal, less than infinite. The prime number ceases to be prime. Let us suppose that you interfere with it to the extent of *infinity minus one*. You will then have a number divisible by two. As a matter of fact, the number, like most large numbers, will immediately break into thousands of pieces, i.e., it will be divisible by tens of thousands of smaller numbers. If the present time falls anywhere near one of these breaks, the door would open then. In other words, the door will open immediately if you can so interfere with the flow that one of the factors occurs in immediate time."

"That is very clear," said the Controller with satisfaction and the image of Brender was smiling triumphantly. "We shall now use this robot to manufacture a universal; and Kalorn shall be free very shortly." He laughed aloud. "The poor robit is protesting violently at the thought of being destroyed, but after all it is only a machine, and not a very good one at that. Besides, it is interfering with my proper reception of your thoughts. Listen to it scream, as I twist it into shape."

The cold-blooded words chilled Brender, pulled him from the heights of his abstract thought. Because of the prolonged intensity of his thinking, he saw with sharp clarity something that had escaped him before.

"Just a minute," he said. "How is it that the robot, introduced from your world, is living at the same time rate as I am, whereas Kalorn continues to live at your time rate?"

"A very good question." The face of the robot was twisted into a triumphant sneer, as the Controller continued. "Because, my dear Brender, you have been duped. It is true that Kalorn is living in our time rate, but that was due to a shortcoming in our machine. The machine which Kalorn built, while large enough to transport him, was not large enough in its adaptive mechanism to adapt him to each new space as he entered it. With the result that he was transported but not adapted. It was possible of course for us, his helpers, to transport such a small thing as the robot, though we have no more idea of the machine's construction than you have.

"In short, we can use what there is of the machine, but the secret of its construction is locked in the insides of our own particular ultimate metal, and in the brain of Kalorn. Its invention by Kalorn was one of those accidents which, by the law of averages, will not be repeated in millions of our years. Now that you have provided us with the method of bringing Kalorn back, we shall be able to build innumerable interspace machines. Our purpose is to control all spaces, all worlds— particularly those which are inhabited. We intend to be absolute rulers of the entire Universe."

The ironic voice ended; and Brender lay in his prone position the prey of horror. The horror was twofold, partly due to the Controller's monstrous plan, and partly due to the thought that was pulsing in his brain. He groaned, as he realized that warning thought must be ticking away on the automatic receiving brain of the robot. "Wait," his thought was saying, "that adds a new factor. Time—"

There was a scream from the creature as it was forcibly dissolved. The scream choked to a sob, then silence. An intricate machine of shining metal lay there on that great gray-brown expanse of sand and ultimate metal.

The metal glowed; and then the machine was floating in the air. It rose to the top of the arrow, and settled over the green flame of *ieis*.

Brender jerked on his antigravity screen, and leaped to his feet. The violent action carried him some hundred feet into the air. His rockets sputtered into staccato fire, and he clamped his teeth against the pain of acceleration.

Below him, the great door began to turn, to unscrew, faster and faster, till it was like a flywheel. Sand flew in all directions in a miniature storm.

At top acceleration, Brender darted to one side.

Just in time. First, the robot machine was flung off that tremendous wheel by sheer centrifugal power. Then the door came off, and, spinning now at an incredible rate, hurtled straight into the air, and vanished into space.

A puff of black dust came floating up out of the blackness of the vault. Suppressing his horror, yet perspiring from awful relief, he rocketed to where the robot had fallen into the sand.

Instead of glistening metal, a time-dulled piece of junk lay there. The dull metal flowed sluggishly and assumed a quasi-human shape. The flesh remained gray and in little rolls as if it were ready to fall apart from old age. The thing tried to stand up on wrinkled, horrible legs, but finally lay still. Its lips moved, mumbled:

"I caught your warning thought, but I didn't let them know. Now, Kalorn is dead. They realized the truth as it was happening. End of Time came—"

It faltered into silence, and Brender went on: "Yes, end of Time came when the flow became momentarily less than eternal—came at the factor point which occurred a few minutes ago."

"I was . . . only partly . . . within its . . . influence, Kalorn all the way. . . . Even if they're lucky . . . will be years before . . . they invent another machine . . . and one of their years is billions . . . of yours. . . . I didn't tell them. . . . I caught your thought . . . and kept it . . . from them—"

"But why did you do it? Why?"

"Because they were hurting me. They were going to destroy me. Because . . . I liked . . . being human. I was . . . somebody!"

The flesh dissolved. It flowed slowly into a pool of lavalike gray. The lava crinkled, split into dry, brittle pieces. Brender touched one of the pieces. It crumbled into a fine powder of gray dust. He gazed out across that grim, deserted valley of sand, and said aloud, pityingly:

"Poor Frankenstein."

He turned toward the distant spaceship, toward the swift trip to Earth. As he climbed out of the ship a few minutes later, one of the first persons he saw was Pamela.

She flew into his arms. "Oh, Jim, Jim," she sobbed. "What a fool I've been. When I heard what had happened, and realized you were in danger, I— Oh, Jim!"

Later, he would tell her about their new fortune.

# THE IMPOSSIBLE HIGHWAY

*Thrilling Wonder Stories*

August

## by Oscar J. Friend (1897-1963)

*Oscar J. Friend was one of the pioneer literary agents in the sf field, directing the briefly influential Otis Kline Literary Agency. He was also an editor of some note, editing* Thrilling Wonder Stories *and its companion magazine* Startling Stories *from 1941–1944. In addition, he was a competent to good writer, and his stories appeared (often under pseudonyms) in a wide variety of pulp markets.*

*"The Impossible Highway" is a superior example of the kind of enigmatic story that so entralled the science fiction readers of the 40s.*

(Martin brought this story to my attention. I could have sworn there wasn't a story in the 1930s and 1940s I wasn't familiar with, but either I missed this issue of TWS, which doesn't seem likely, or I am softening as I approach early middle age.

In any case I read it fresh now and it brought back my youth. We had never heard of flying saucers then, but there is always this vague yearning for mysterious and all-powerful beings from beyond, even if their doings on Earth are not clear. This story is an example of the kind of thing that stirred what Sam Moskowitz called "the sense of wonder." We may have learned too much and grown too sophisticated to be impressed by this kind of story any longer, but to some extent that's our loss.—I.A.)

Dr. Albert Nelson looked at his young assistant, Robert Mackensie, and scowled.

176

"So this was just what I needed!" he snapped. "Leave my laboratory and take a walking tour with you in the Ozarks. Lovely vacation. Bah!"

"But, Doctor," Mackensie protested mildly, "you did need a vacation. I can't help it if we had an accident." A grin crept over his youthful face. "Besides, it's kind of funny—two erudite scientists helpless as babes in the woods!"

But Dr. Nelson could not see the humor in the situation. They were lost—lost deep in the Ozark Mountains, their compass hopelessly smashed. And that annoyed him no end.

For Dr. Nelson was an orderly soul. He had always been a logical thinker. He had a mathematical mind that clicked like a machine. No loose ends existed for him. That was why he made such an excellent biologist. He traced everything to its source and pigeonholed it permanently within his brain before letting go of it.

To Dr. Nelson, two plus two equaled four, and he had to get that answer before he quit. Every positive had a negative, every cause an effect. There was never any unfinished research work in his laboratory, no litter of paper on his desk, no clutter of stuff in is mind. He repudiated everything which did not have a logical explanation. He had no patience with unfinished symphonies, lady-and-tiger stories, enigmas, or unsolved mysteries. Quite a definite, positive chap.

That's why he was peeved and exasperated when he and Mackensie came upon the end of the road. It wasn't the cumulative effect of the facts that they were lost, that their compass had accidentally been broken, that they had been pushing on since early morning and it was three o'clock in the afternoon now, that they were weary and scratched up and hungry and thirsty. None of this. It was the inexplicable fact of the road itself.

"What is that ahead of us?" Dr. Nelson panted as his keen eyes caught sight of a shining, white expanse through the trees and underbrush. They had been climbing steadily for the past hour, seeking a high spot from which they might survey the surrounding terrain and get their bearings. "An expanse of water, or the sky?"

Mackensie puffed on ahead. His young voice floated back in eager accents.

"It's a road, Doctor! A concrete highway! Thank God, we can find our way back to civilization now."

It was a road, all right. Nelson wrinkled his brows in thought as he quickened his pace to overtake his companion.

But what was a concrete road doing here in the heart of a wild country which sane white men never even trod on foot? How could there be a cement highway up here in these mountains where there weren't even country side roads, where only wild game lived and an occasional blue jay raised his raucous voice or a lone turkey buzzard wheeled in solitary splendor overhead? And there was something else.

There was nothing peculiar about the concrete slab itself. It was a quite normal specimen of the engineer's and road builder's art. Twenty feet wide, fully eight inches thick, it stretched suddenly away before the two men in a properly graded, sweet white expanse that curved through the pines and elms and cedars and dipped gracefully out of sight over the brow of a slope.

No, it wasn't the construction or condition of the road; it was the very fact of its sudden presence here. Dr. Nelson became aware of the fact that he had used the adverb "suddenly" twice in as many seconds in thinking of this thoroughfare. That described the thing. Abruptly—just like that—the road began, its near end as squarely chopped off and finished as the shoulders running along the side edges of the best-behaved highways. In the midst of a primordial wilderness the road just suddenly began.

There was no evidence that it was intended to continue in this direction. No blazed trees, no surveyor's marks, no grading, no sand or gravel or lumber piles, no machinery, no tools, no barricade, no road marker, no detour sign. Nothing. Not even a dirt road, trail, or footpath leading in any direction from the end of the concrete slab. Simply a wild and untrammeled hillside in the heart of uncharted mountains, and there, as abruptly as a pistol shot—the near end of a gleaming highway!

The incongruity of it must have finally struck Mackensie in spite of his relief, for the young biologist was standing just short of the end of the paving and staring around him in perplexity as Nelson joined him. His bright blue eyes met the steady brown eyes of the older man, and his face twisted quizzically. He wagged his hands helplessly.

"Why doesn't it go on?" he asked. "Can it be an abandoned project?"

"Who ever heard of even an abandoned trail that didn't lead at least to a house or a shack?" snorted Nelson irritably.

"Can it be a test stretch of road?" suggested Mackensie.

Wordlessly, Dr. Nelson pointed at the road's unsullied surface. There wasn't a drop of oil, a tire mark, a clamp of caked dirt from a hoof, a footprint—anything, to mar the slab's virgin purity. And yet the road, beginning here in the thick of the forest, curved out of sight before them as though it led on forever, an important artery of transportation.

"It's a senseless riddle!" snapped Nelson. "And I detest riddles."

"Well, although it begins spontaneously, Doctor, it seems to lead somewhere," Mackensie said. "At least, it will lead us back to civilization. We can solve its mystery at the other end. Are you too tired to go on?"

"No. No," repeated Nelson irritably, frowning along the road. But he felt a vague reluctance to set foot on the slab. Why, he did not know. He hesitated, mopped his perspiring brow with a handkerchief, and gazed around at the deep woods through which they had come. Then he shrugged and stepped up on the end of the road.

Mackensie stepped up beside him and set off along the paving in a swinging stride. Perforce, Nelson fell in step, and they marched together in silence. For a brief space there was no sound at all save the rhythmic tramping of their boots and the occasional slithering noises which came from Nelson's knapsack. This was the little green lizard the biologist had captured some time before noon.

"Always the indefatigable scientist," Mackensie had observed when Nelson had adroitly caught the little reptile sunning itself on a rock and had popped it into an emptied sandwich box to study later.

Now, the noise of the little lizard was the only sound outside themselves which kept them company. It was the queer significance of this that caused Nelson to put his hand on Mackensie's arm and stop suddenly.

"Why are we stopping?" asked the younger man in surprise. "This beats tearing our way through brambles and underbrush by a house and farm."

"Listen," said Nelson.

Mackensie did so tensely. All around was utter silence. There wasn't even a breath of wind stirring the leaves on the trees.

"I don't hear anything," he said.

"That's just it," commented Nelson. "Not even the buzz of an insect—not a bird in the sky—not a rustle in the thickets alongside the road. What became of the blue jays and the

gnats that kept us company and annoyed us before we
reached this road?"

Mackensie's blue eyes looked startled. Nelson turned to
stare along the section of road they had already traversed. It
stretched there for twenty yards, white and spotless save for
the faint markings of their own recent passage. It was as
though they stood alone in a dead and lifeless world. No, it
wasn't like that exactly. All around them was the evidence of
floral life, but a life in arrested motion. That was it—a Tech-
nicolor, three-dimensional still—a rigid, frozen world in
which only they themselves had the power of motion. It was
uncanny.

"Not a bug crawling across the road," whispered Mackensie in awe. "Not even a distant sound to indicate that anything or anybody is on this planet. But I have a queer sort of
feeling deep inside me that—that the forces of life are surging all about us. Doctor, I feel as though this very road is
quivering and teeming with life even as it lies rigid beneath
our feet. What in God's name is all this?"

Nelson lowered his gaze to the area about his feet. Mackensie was right. There was a psychic sort of hum or quiver to
the concrete, to the very air about them, and yet everything
was so still and silent. Slowly an odd impression upon the
perturbed scientist.

It was as though his eyes penetrated the fraction of an inch
below the smooth surface of the concrete slab. He felt, rather
than saw, that this was an incredible highway of life, that billions and billions of living entities had trod this way before
him in endless, teeming throngs.

"Come on," said Nelson in a muffled voice. "Let's go on."

It was around the next curve, where the forest thinned
away and the road appeared to wind majestically across a
series of plateaus on top of the world, that they came upon
the first variation to the smooth progress of the road. This
was a concrete pedestal about waist high on the left-hand
shoulder of the highway, an integral part of the concrete itself. It was as though the road had paused and flung up a
sort of pseudopodium at its edge.

On top of this slim pedestal was a cube of what appeared
to be quartz glass. At least it was crystal of some sort, faintly
iridescent and sparkling under the rays of the afternoon sun.
As they approached, they saw that it was a hollow cube
which enclosed a powerful binocular microscope. Its twin
eye-pieces, capped against the weather, protruded outside the

case. On the flaring top of the pedestal, just below the glass
cube and easily discernible without stopping or squinting, was
a bronze plate containing raised letters. The inscription was
in English.

Both men halted in amazement at the further incongruity
of this. A fine microscope mounted like a museum display in
a wilderness which contained only a deserted concrete highway! What did it mean?

"My God!" murmured Mackensie. "Look! Read it, Dr.
Nelson." Together they stared at the dark but clearly legible
plaque.

## UNIVERSAL LIFE SPORTS—PAN-COSMIC

> These minute cellular specimens are the tiniest evolved
> seeds of that phenomenon called life, whether floral or
> faunal, which are self-contained and practically im-
> mortal. They are propelled throughout the universe on
> beams of light. Peculiarly deathless, they settle like a
> fungoid mold upon the most barren and arid planet and
> father all forms of living matter. Their primary origin is
> unknown.

Nelson whipped the caps from the binocular eyepieces and
glued his eyes to the lenses. He was conscious of a queer sort
of magnetic thrill as he touched the glass-encased instrument.
The crystal cabinet scintillated and glowed as though endowed with a life force of its own. It was impossible to adjust
the controls of the microscope since they were within the
glass shell, but this proved needless.

On the field before his eyes, perfectly adjusted, was a typical stained glass slide similar to thousands the biologist had
examined. There, immobile, deathless, changeless, were
hundreds of tiny gray cells which resembled the various fern
molds he had studied more than once, and yet they were different. They were cellular; they were undoubtedly bacteria—
but they had a sharply distinct rim or shell which might well
have been impervious to the darkness and cold and cosmic
rays of outer space. Certainly, Dr. Nelson had never seen
their exact like before.

After a careful study, he raised his head, stepped aside,
and motioned Mackensie to look. The young man did so.

"Good heavens, Doctor," he murmured. "They don't even
take the stain the least bit. They reject it completely, standing
out like dots against a field of pale pink."

"Precisely," Nelson agreed, frowning thoughtfully. "And you notice that they are motionless, inert—as though arrested by magic in the midst of their activity."

"Yes," nodded Mackensie, still looking. "Doubtless they are dead."

"I wonder," said Nelson.

"I can't understand it," pursued Mackensie. "Even the most minute organisms would show at least molecular motion."

"Let's go on," said Nelson, recapping the eyepieces. "I see another pedestal a few yards beyond, on the opposite side of this infernal road."

Mackensie was the first to reach the second queer pedestal with its faintly glowing and pulsing glass case enclosing another microscope. He was already peering through the eyepieces when Nelson read the bronze plaque below the crystal case.

## LEPTOTHRIX—A GENUS OF THE FAMILY CHLAMYDOBACTERIACEAE

One of the earliest forms of cellular life on this planet, dating from archaeozoic rocks at least one billion years old. Filamental in form, with unbranched segments, it reproduces by fission from one end only. Walls of filaments are of iron deposited around the living cells by accretion. Man and beast are fueled by plants which consume earth elements and build up by chlorophyl sun power, but LEPTOTHRIX literally eats iron. Most veins of iron ore have been built by the action of this bacterium.

When Mackensie, dazed and uncertain, removed his eyes from the microscope, Nelson looked. He recognized the specimens instantly. And these bacteria were caught in an immobile net, frozen rigid as statues in the midst of life. When he looked up, Mackensie was already running on to the next pedestal twenty or thirty feet beyond. Nelson followed more slowly.

"Algae!" cried out Mackensie.

Nelson read the bronze plaque and then stared at the familiar blue-green strands of the primitive water plant which becomes visible to the naked eye as the greenish scum on stagnant pond water. And once again he noted the frozen and arrested condition of the specimens.

"Plankton!" shouted Mackensie next, reaching the fourth

pedestal. "Good Lord, Doctor, this is like—like going through an open-air penny arcade of bacteriology." He smiled.

That was precisely what Nelson was thinking. He still hadn't solved the enigma of the road itself. The additional mystery of high-powered microscopes mounted here in the open in queer crystal cases he thrust to the background of his mind to be explained in due and proper course. It was, as Mackensie said, like a laboratory of the gods. Almost fearfully Nelson looked up at the sky as though he half expected the head and shoulders of some superscientist to materialize from behind a fleecy cloud. But nothing happened. It was still three o'clock in the afternoon. Nothing lived or moved save the two men and the confined little lizard.

One thing was significant to the methodical Nelson as he plodded along this weird and unaccountable highway. There had been no unnecessary or haphazard placements of specimens. Everything was in logical and chronological order as far as he could determine. The trend was precisely and steadily upward in the mighty cycle of life.

Coming into view before them, lining the highway like trees in a park, were crystal specimen cases of varying sizes and shapes. No longer did a microscope accompany each exhibit. Life specimens now were in forms discernible to the naked eye. A distinct line of cleavage between plant and animal life had come into being, both being carried forward in faithful progression. And in each case every specimen was perfectly preserved and apparently lifeless.

The entire array of crystal cases pulsed and glowed in the sun with an eerie life of their own.

Up through the ages ran this bizarre story of life. Through the day of the fossils, the fern forests, the primordial piscine life of the sea, the first conifers, the first reptiles, the age of gigantic reptilian mammals—along the ladder of life they marched, seeing actual specimens no man, presumably, had seen before. It was like a tour through a marvelous combination of laboratory, botanical garden, aquarium, and the Smithsonian Institution.

The two biologists forgot their hunger, their thirst, their weariness. They lost all track of time, although it must have been hours and hours that they marched along this corridor of still life. It was like looking at color plates in a three-dimensional magazine of the future, or like gazing at stereopticon enlargements of the screen of life. And the sun hung brilliantly in the sky at three o'clock in the afternoon.

The written matter on the various bronze plaques—which was always there, regardless of the size of the display cabinet or the nature of its contents—would have composed a complete and unique thumbnail history of the surging course of that tenacious, fragile, but indestructible thing called life. Nelson began to regret that he had not copied down each one of them, realizing as he did so that it would have been impossible. He wouldn't have had enough paper if his knapsack had been full of nothing else.

Mackensie began to mourn that he hadn't brought a camera with him. Some of the specimens were such as man, in filling in the gaps of life's history, had never even imagined. The main enigma still unsolved, Nelson pushed onward with a mounting fever which amazed him. He felt, without analysis, that he was being drawn onward by the hand of destiny, approaching a climax, a height, a fate that was inexorable.

The same fire must have imbued Mackensie, for the young man now marveled at the Gargantuan panorama, at the magnetic oddity of the crystal cases, at the puzzling thought and speculation of how this *outré* museum came to be, at the impossible fact that time stood still.

And then they came to the first empty display case. It was a little cabinet, and they paused to read the bronze plaque. They had long since passed into a comparatively modern era, reaching a stage of presentation which encompassed flora and fauna as it now existed. Primitive man had already appeared, and his image was in properly spaced and graded cabinets.

Nelson had got a start at his view of the first shaggy brute which was definitely the long-sought missing link between man and the lower animals. A queer and repulsive thing to the esthete, Nelson the biologist almost worshiped before the lifelike mammal. From there on the story of mankind was written graphically for the two amazed travelers to read.

But here was the first vacant case. Conscious of great annoyance, Nelson read the bronze plaque.

## LACERTA VIRIDIS

This green lizard is a specimen of the small, four-legged reptile with tapering tail which, along with related families, form the suborder of all the LACERTILIA with the exception of geckos and chameleons, which see.

The biologist raised his eyes. But the case, pulsing and glowing with its faintly bluish-green sheen, unharmed and unbroken, was empty. There simply was nothing within it.

"That's funny," mused Mackensie aloud, as Nelson thoughtfully examined the crystal case which, in this instance, resembled a bell jar. "That's the first gap in all the series."

"Yes," almost growled Nelson as he tugged at the knob of the bell jar. To his surprise, he was able to remove it. Then he saw at the base of the jar, on the flaring ledge of the pedestal, the little wheel which controlled the air-exhausting and sealing apparatus.

He accidentally placed one hand on the spot which had been covered by the bell jar, and instantly he lost all feeling in the member. It was as though his entire hand, from the wrist down, was nothing but a lump of insensate matter. Hastily he snatched it back. At once life and feeling returned.

"What's the matter?" asked Mackensie quickly in professional interest. "Hot?"

"No," answered Nelson, replacing the bell jar carefully. "Just—nothing at all. No feeling. My hand went completely dead."

"Is it all right now?"

"Quite. There must be something about these magnetic pulsations that blanket and cut off the life force without destroying life."

"Then, if that's so, all those—those specimens we have seen are alive? Alive but dormant?"

"I wonder," said Nelson.

Mackensie shuddered silently.

"Come on," he said. "Let's go. I think I see a mountain lion yonder."

Knitting his brows in irritation at this minor break in this colossal display of specimens, Nelson followed on. The scampering, rattling, slithering sound of the little lizard in the lunchbox in his knapsack was like the annoying impulse scurrying around in his brain. They passed the chameleon, the specimens of wild game and small fauna, and reached the spot where the depicted story of this era of plant life was resumed.

Here, perhaps a couple of hundred yards on from the empty lizard case, Nelson halted in the fashion of a man who has firmly made up his mind. Mackensie looked at him in astonishment.

"Come," said Nelson. "We're going back."

"Back?" echoed the younger man incredulously. "Where? Why?"

"Only as far as the *Lacerta Viridis* case. I've got to. I've just got to. I can't go on."

"But—but, can we go—back?" whispered Mackensie.

This was a startling thought. Nelson had never considered such a possibility.

"Will we have time?" pursued his assistant biologist. "Night may overtake us as it is before we come to the end of this road."

For answer, Nelson pointed at the sun. It hung in the bright sky precisely at the three o'clock position.

"Come," ordered Nelson.

Obediently, almost like a man under the power of hypnosis, Mackensie turned and started back along the highway. Nelson paced him. It was as though they breasted a strong and resistant tide, as though they fought a steady and powerful wind. Nelson felt like a man in a dream, almost overpowered with a lethargy he could not understand. Only his indomitable will forced them both onward. And still nothing moved or lived along the entire ghastly highway save the two men, walking in the warm sunlight.

Slowly they retraced their steps and drew up before the empty lizard case.

"Well, we're here," panted Mackensie. "Now what?"

For answer Nelson removed his knapsack in a methodical fashion and took out the lunchbox. Pinioning the little lizard swiftly by the nape of the neck, he removed the bell jar and placed the squirming reptile on the pedestal.

Instantly the creature went rigid. Nelson withdrew his numbed hand and stared at the specimen. In lifelike manner the lizard rested on its four tiny feet, body half-coiled, head uplifted, beady little eyes glittering as it stared at nothing.

Primly Nelson covered it with the bell jar and turned the wheel to seal the vacuum. A faint hum resulted from within the base of the pedestal and then died into nothingness. The god of science accepting an offering. When Mackensie tried to lift the bell jar he found it immovable.

The two men stared at each other.

"At least, it is a passable specimen," observed Nelson. "It is similar to the Old World species. Let's go now."

With a quicker step he led the way. All annoyance over the empty case had vanished.

It must have been hours later, and God only knew how

many curving miles, when they reached the second and final empty specimen case.

"Look!" cried Mackensie in heartfelt relief. "We are coming to the end of the road!"

Nelson had lost interest in the road. The mighty story of life which had unfolded had swept him up and on in an irresistible surge. It was with a start that he came back to a realization of his surroundings and focused his attention on the distance.

Mackensie was right. About a hundred yards on, ending in a thicket of trees on a downward slope, was the end of the road.

Just as it started, so the road ended—abruptly, inexplicably. Not far from its termination was a specimen case which appeared to be about three feet tall upon its low pedestal. But Nelson was more interested in the seven-foot case opposite him.

## TWENTIETH-CENTURY MAN

This specimen of the warm-blooded biped mammal with the developing brainpan and thyroidal glands represents man at the physical peak of his evolution. As has been pointed out through the various case histories, animal and plant life, having come far from a common origin, differing principally in the matter of an atom of magnesium in chlorophyl structure instead of an atom of iron in the hemoglobin of blood, have now passed their separate evolution goals. From this point on, their parallel paths converge, finally uniting once more in a common structure which approaches the apex of mental development.

Dr. Nelson raised his eyes from the bronze plaque. The pulsating hollow cube was empty. There was no specimen. Instead, there was only a door of beveled glass which swung out over the road on invisible hinges, as if inviting a weary sojourner to enter and rest—for eternity.

The biologist frowned in utter exasperation. Why, of all specimen cases should this one be empty? He pulled restlessly at one ear as he turned to stare along the road. He was annoyed again, disappointed, to note there were no more specimen cases save the one three-foot case at the very end of the way.

The story was almost told. Past hundreds of thousands of

crystal cases they had walked for endless hours—only to find
this most important case, as far as mankind was concerned,
empty. Somehow, Nelson could not go on and leave it thus.
His methodical nature seemed to be driving him onward with
inexorable logic. His gaze fell upon his companion.

"Mackensie," he said in a queer voice. "Mackensie, come
here."

The younger man paled and shrank away.

"No," he cried out, intuitively guessing the other's purpose.
"No! You are mad, Doctor. Let's get away from this hellish
thing. I . . ."

He ended in a cry of stark terror as Nelson pounced upon
him. The biologist was twenty years older than Mackensie,
but he was also the larger man physically. Mackensie had no
chance against him. The struggle was as short as its meaning
was horrible. In a matter of seconds, Nelson had his victim
helpless.

"No!" screamed Mackensie, horror dawning in his eyes.
"Dr. Nelson, you mustn't! You can't do this! You . . ."

He ended in shrill scream after scream of fainting madness
as Nelson lifted him erect and carried him to the ajar door of
the crystal cabinet.

"It is painless," murmured Nelson gently. "I know. *And
why is the case empty*, if not for one of us? Answer me
that!"

But Mackensie was past answering anything. He was passing into a state of cataleptic horror.

Like a man in a dream, like a puppet controlled by extra-
terrestrial strings, Nelson shifted his burden dexterously
around to face him and then, balancing himself carefully, he
thrust the body of his companion squarely and smoothly into
the empty crystal case. The change that took place was
miraculous, instantaneous. The texture of Mackensie's body
became like marble. Remaining erect, he rocked back against
the rear of the cabinet and then forward like a tottering
statue.

Nelson quickly pulled the heavy crystal door around, literally closing it in the set face of his companion. With a soft
*whoosh* of air, the beveled edges of the door fitted smoothly
into the beveled crystal frame—and the last case had its perfect specimen.

The biologist was trembling as he stared into the glazed
eyes of his former laboratory assistant. Then he sighed, mop-

ping his brow, and glanced at the sun. It was three o'clock in the afternoon.

Turning slowly, as though loath to part company with the man who had made this incredible journey with him, Nelson strode on to the end of the road.

Reaching that last case, he paused to study the specimen within. Almost in the shade of the thickening trees, the pulsating aura of the case was faintly phosphorescent. But it was the nature of the specimen that fascinated the biologist.

Squat, scarcely three feet tall, pallid and sickly brownish in tinge, the thing looked more like an overgrown mushroom than anything else. A mushroom with a bulging dome that was a horrible caricature of a human head. A pair of enormous orifices denoted what may have been meant for eyes. The mouth was nothing but a seam or a weal which indicated where a mouth once had been. The thing was sexless and stood upon three rootlike feet. At last Nelson brought himself to read the bronze plaque.

## THYROIDICUS—PLANT MAN

The final evolution of mammalian life upon this planet. Composed principally of a fibrous brain tissue and a free iodine-producing organism which is the development of what was formerly man's iodine plant, the thyroid gland located in the throat, this creature has neither blood nor chlorophyl.

Like LEPTOTHRIX, this form of life has learned at long last to assimilate its food directly from the elements, transmuting it instantly and releasing free energy. THYROIDICUS, the ultimate goal of physical evolution, is practically all brain. The next stage of evolution, inevitably, crosses the boundary of animate existance, and life becomes purely spiritual.

That was all. The story was told. The end of the road was reached—abruptly. No blazed trees, no surveyor's marks, no grading, no material piles, no machinery, no tools, no barricades, no detour sign. Not even a dirt road, a trail, or a footpath leading in any direction from the end of the concrete slab.

Simply a wild and untrammeled hillside in the heart of uncharted mountains, and the road which had begun as suddenly as a pistol shot led nowhere and ended as precipitantly.

Dr. Nelson was a methodical and orderly soul. Ironically

so, he realized grimly. He hadn't been able to help himself. His cold logic had been tapped to the $n$th degree.

He thoughtfully turned and stared back along the way he had come. He felt that vague and incomprehensible tremble of vibrant life flowing onward in the road beneath his feet. Now there was not an empty case, not a broken thread in the two lines of specimen cases which stretched off into the illimitable distance there. The record was complete.

What record? Just what was this incredible scientific display? That it was not of Earth he was now firmly convinced. Was it a time trap or a gigantic trophy corridor of some superhunter from beyond the stars?

The doctor shrugged his shoulders as he gave up the enigma. He stepped off the near end of the Impossible Highway, relieved to feel the more prosaic sod and grass beneath his feet. He turned once more to look back on the concrete slab.

The highway had disappeared. There was nothing beyond but the tangled underbrush of the wilderness. The sun was sinking redly behind the western mountains.

# QUIETUS

*Astounding Science Fiction*
September

## by Ross Rocklynne (1913-    )

> *One of the best of the "second rank" writers of the late thirties and forties, Ross Rocklynne (real name Ross L. Rocklin), has been a neglected figure in science fiction, largely because he produced very little long fiction. The best of his work, including stories like "Jackdaw" (1942), "Jaywalker" (1950), and "Time Wants a Skeleton" can be found in his two Ace Books collections* The Men and the Mirror *and* The Sun Destroyers, *both 1973. He has continued to write and has produced some interesting work in recent years, especially "Ching Witch" in* Again Dangerous Visions *(1972) and "Randy-Tandy Man" in* Universe 3.*
> "Quietus" is a lovely and tragic story about the difficulty of making life and death decisions, and the relative meaning of "intelligence."*

(What an issue this one was. It contained this story and "Blowups Happen" which follows, and it also contained the first installment of A. E. van Vogt's "Slan" which may very well be the best first installment of any s.f. serial ever written. It's no wonder that the second story I sold to Campbell, "Homo Sol," which also appeared in this issue, sank without a trace.

I have always remembered Ross Rocklynne's stories with affection. He wrote a series of detective-adventure stories in which pursuer and pursued fell into a trap and had to rescue themselves by using a scientific principle. "The Men and the Mirror" was the best of these.—I.A.)

191

The creatures from Alcon saw from the first that Earth, as a planet, was practically dead; dead in the sense that it had given birth to life, and was responsible, indirectly, for its almost complete extinction.

"This type of planet is the most distressing," said Tark, absently smoothing down the brilliantly colored feathers of his left wing. "I can stand the dark, barren worlds which never have, and probably never will, hold life. But these that have been killed by some celestial catastrophe! Think of what great things might have come from their inhabitants."

As he spoke thus to his mate, Vascar, he was marking down in a book the position of this planet, its general appearance from space, and the number and kind of satellites it supported.

Vascar, sitting at the controls, both her claws and her vestigial hands at work, guided the spherical ship at slowly decreasing speed toward the planet Earth. A thousand miles above it, she set the craft into an orbital motion, and then proceeded to study the planet, Tark setting the account into his book, for later insertion into the Astronomical Archives of Alcon.

"Evidently," mused Vascar, her brilliant, unblinking eyes looking at the planet through a transparent section above the control board, "some large meteor, or an errant asteroid— that seems most likely—must have struck this specimen a terrible blow. Look at those great, gaping cracks that run from pole to pole, Tark. It looks as if volcanic eruptions are still taking place, too. At any rate, the whole planet seems entirely denuded—except for that single, short strip of green we saw as we came in."

Tark nodded. He was truly a bird, for in the evolutionary race on his planet, distant uncounted light years, his stock had won out over the others. His wings were short, true, and in another thousand years would be too short for flight, save in a dense atmosphere; but his head was large, and his eyes, red, small, set close together, showed intelligence and a kind benevolence. He and Vascar had left Alcon, their planet, a good many years ago; but they were on their way back now. Their outward-bound trip had taken them many light years north of the Solar System; but on the way back, they had decided to make it one of the stop-off points in their zigzag course. Probably their greatest interest in all this long cruise was in the discovery of planets—they were indeed few. And that pleasure might even be secondary to the discovery of life. To find a planet that had almost entirely died was, conversely, distressing. Their interest in the planet Earth was, because of this, a wistful one.

The ship made the slow circuit of Earth—the planet was a hodge-podge of tumbled, churned mountains; of abysmal, frightfully long cracks exuding unholy vapors; of volcanoes that threw their fires and hot liquid rocks far into the sky; of vast oceans disturbed from the ocean bed by cataclysmic eruptions. And of life they saw nothing save a single strip of green perhaps a thousand miles long, a hundred wide, in the Western Hemisphere.

"I don't think we'll find intelligent life, though," Tark said pessimistically. "This planet was given a terrific blow—I wouldn't be surprised if her rotation period was cut down considerably in a single instant. Such a charge would be unsupportable. Whole cities would literally be snapped away from their foundations—churned, ground to dust. The intelligent creatures who built them would die by the millions—the billions—in that holocaust; and whatever destruction was left incomplete would be finished up by the appearance of volcanoes and faults in the crust of the planet."

Vascar reminded him, "Remember, where there's vegetation, even as little as evidenced by that single strip down there, there must be some kind of animal life."

Tark ruffled his wings in a shrug. "I doubt it. The plants would get all the carbon dioxide they needed from volcanoes—animal life wouldn't have to exist. Still, let's take a look. Don't worry, I'm hoping there's intelligent life, too. If there is, it will doubtless need some help if it is to survive. Which ties in with our aims, for that is our principal purpose on this expedition—to discover intelligent life, and, wherever possible, to give it what help we can, if it needs help."

Vascar's vestigial hands worked the controls, and the ship dropped leisurely downward toward the green strip.

A rabbit darted out of the underbrush—Tommy leaped at it with the speed and dexterity of a thoroughly wild animal. His powerful hands wrapped around the creature—its struggles ceased as its vertebra was snapped. Tommy squatted, tore the skin off the creature, and proceeded to eat great mouthfuls of the still warm flesh.

Blacky cawed harshly, squawked, and his untidy form came flashing down through the air to land precariously on Tommy's shoulder. Tommy went on eating, while the crow fluttered its wings, smoothed them out, and settled down to a restless somnolence. The quiet of the scrub forest, save for the cries and sounds of movement of birds and small animals moving through the forest, settled down about Tommy as he ate. "Tommy" was what he called himself. A long time ago, he remembered, there used to be a great many people in the world—perhaps a hundred—many of whom, and particularly two people whom he had called Mom and Pop, had called him by that name. They were gone now, and the others with them. Exactly where they went, Tommy did not know. But the world had rocked one night—it was the night Tommy ran away from home, with Blacky riding on his shoulder—and when Tommy came out of the cave where he had been sleeping, all was in flames, and the city on the horizon had fallen so that it was nothing but a huge pile of dust—but in the end it had not mattered to Tommy. Of course, he was lonesome, terrified, at first, but he got over that. He continued to live, eating, drinking, sleeping, walking endlessly; and Blacky, his talking crow, was good company. Blacky was smart. He could speak every word that Tommy knew, and a good many others that he didn't. Tommy was not Blacky's first owner.

But though he had been happy, the last year had brought the recurrence of a strange feeling that had plagued him off and on, but never so strongly as now. A strange, terrible hunger was settling on him. Hunger? He knew this sensation. He had forthwith slain a wild dog, and eaten of the meat. He saw then that it was not a hunger of the belly. It was a hunger of the mind, and it was all the worse because he could not know what it was. He had come to his feet, restless, looking into the tangled depths of the second growth forest.

"Hungry," he had said, and his shoulders shook and tears coursed out of his eyes, and he sat down on the ground and sobbed without trying to stop himself, for he had never been told that to weep was unmanly. What was it he wanted?

He had everything there was all to himself. Southward in winter, northward in summer, eating of berries and small animals as he went, and Blacky to talk to and Blacky to talk the same words back at him. This was the natural life—he had lived it ever since the world went bang. But still he cried, and felt a panic growing in his stomach, and he didn't know what it was he was afraid of, or longed for, whichever it was. He was twenty-one years old. Tears were natural to him, to be indulged in whenever he felt like it. Before the world went bang—there were some things he remembered—the creature whom he called Mom generally put her arms around him and merely said, "It's all right, Tommy, it's all right."

So on that occasion, he arose from the ground and said, "It's all right, Tommy, it's all right."

Blacky, he with the split tongue, said harshly, as was his wont, "It's all right, Tommy, it's all right! I tell you, the price of wheat is going down!"

Blacky, the smartest crow anybody had—why did he say that? There wasn't anybody else, and there weren't any more crows—helped a lot. He not only knew all the words and sentences that Tommy knew, but he knew others that Tommy could never understand because he didn't know where they came from, or what they referred to. And in addition to all that, Blacky had the ability to anticipate what Tommy said, and frequently took whole words and sentences right out of Tommy's mouth.

Tommy finished eating his rabbit, and threw the skin aside, and sat quite still, a peculiarly blank look in his eyes. The strange hunger was on him again. He looked off across the lush plain of grasses that stretched away, searching into the distance, toward where the sun was setting. He looked to left and right. He drew himself softly to his feet, and peered into the shadows of the forest behind him. His heavily bearded lips began to tremble, and the tears started from his eyes again. He turned and stumbled from the forest, blinded.

Blacky clutched at Tommy's broad shoulder, and rode him, and a split second before Tommy, said, "It's all right, Tommy, it's all right."

Tommy said the words angrily to himself, and blinked the tears away.

He was a little bit tired. The sun was setting, and night would soon come. But it wasn't that that made him tired. It was a weariness of the mind, a feeling of futility, for, whatever it was he wanted, he could never, never find it, because he would not know where he should look for it.

His bare foot trampled on something wet—he stopped and looked at the ground. He stooped and picked up the skin of a recently killed rabbit. He turned it over and over in his hands, frowning. This was not an animal he had killed, certainly—the skin had been taken off in a different way. Someone else—no! But his shoulders began to shake with a wild excitement. Someone else? No, it couldn't be! There was no one—there could be no one—could there? The skin dropped from his nerveless fingers as he saw a single footprint not far ahead of him. He stooped over it, examining, and knew again that he had not done this, either. And certainly it could be no other animal than a man!

It was a small footprint at which he stared, as if a child, or an under-sized man, might have stepped in the soft humus. Suddenly he raised his head. He had definitely heard the crackling of a twig, not more than forty feet away, certainly. His eyes stared ahead through the gathering dusk. Something looking back at him? Yes! Something there in the bushes that was not an animal!

"No noise, Blacky," he whispered, and forgot Blacky's general response to that command.

"No noise, Blacky!" the big, ugly bird blasted out. "No noise, Blacky! Well, fer cryin' out loud!"

Blacky uttered a scared squawk as Tommy leaped ahead, a snarl contorting his features, and flapped from his master's shoulder. For several minutes Tommy ran after the vanishing figure, with all the strength and agility of his singularly powerful legs. But whoever—or whatever—it was that fled him, outdistanced him easily, and Tommy had to stop at last, panting. Then he stooped, and picked up a handful of pebbles and hurled them at the squawking bird. A single tail feather fell to earth as Blacky swooped away.

"Told you not to make noise," Tommy snarled, and the tears started to run again. The hunger was starting up in his mind again, too! He sat down on a log, and put his chin in his palms, while his tears flowed. Blacky came flapping through the air, almost like a shadow—it was getting dark. The bird tentatively settled on his shoulder, cautiously flapped away again and then came back.

Tommy turned his head and looked at it bitterly, and then turned away, and groaned.

"It's all your fault, Blacky!"

"It's all your fault," the bird said. "Oh, Tommy, I could spank you! I get so exasperated!"

Sitting there, Tommy tried to learn exactly what he had seen. He had been sure it was a human figure, just like himself, only different. Different! It had been smaller, had seemed to possess a slender grace—it was impossible! Every time he thought of it, the hunger in his mind raged!

He jumped to his feet, his fists clenched. This hunger had been in him too long! He must find out what caused it—he must find her—why did the word *her* come to his mind? Suddenly, he was flooded with a host of childhood remembrances.

"It was a girl!" he gasped. "Oh, Tommy must want a girl!"

The thought was so utterly new that it left him stunned; but the thought grew. He must find her, if it took him all the rest of his life! His chest deepened, his muscles swelled, and a new light came into his blue eyes. Southward in winter, northward in summer—eating—sleeping—truly, there was nothing in such a life. Now he felt the strength of a purpose swelling up in him. He threw himself to the ground and slept; and Blacky flapped to the limb of a tree, inserted his head beneath a wing, and slept also. Perhaps, in the last ten or fifteen years, he also had wanted a mate, but probably he had long ago given up hope—for, it seemed, there were no more crows left in the world. Anyway, Blacky was very old, perhaps twice as old as Tommy; he was merely content to live.

Tark and Vascar sent their spherical ship lightly plummeting above the green strip—it proved to be vegetation, just as they had supposed. Either one or the other kept constant watch of the ground below—they discovered nothing that might conceivably be classed as intelligent life. Insects they found, and decided that they worked entirely by instinct; small animals, rabbits, squirrels, rats, raccoons, otters, opossums, and large animals, deer, horses, sheep, cattle, pigs, dogs, they found to be just that—animals, and nothing more.

"Looks as if it was all killed off, Vascar," said Tark, "and not so long ago at that, judging by the fact that this forest must have grown entirely in the last few years."

Vascar agreed; she suggested they put the ship down for a few days and rest.

"It would be wonderful if we could find intelligent life after all," she said wistfully. "Think what a great triumph it would be if we were the ones to start the last members of that race on the upward trail again. Anyway," she added, "I think this atmosphere is dense enough for us to fly in."

He laughed—a trilling sound. "You've been looking for such an atmosphere for years. But I think you're right about this one. Put the ship down there, Vascar—looks like a good spot."

For five days Tommy followed the trail of the girl with a grim determination. He knew now that it was a woman; perhaps—indeed, very probably—the only one left alive. He had only the vaguest of ideas of why he wanted her—he thought it was for human companionship, that alone. At any rate, he felt that this terrible hunger in him—he could give it no other word—would be allayed when he caught up with her.

She was fleeing him, and staying just near enough to him to make him continue the chase, he knew that with a fierce exultation. And somehow her actions seemed right and proper. Twice he had seen her, once on the crest of a ridge, once as she swam a river. Both times she had easily outdistanced him. But by cross-hatching, he picked up her trail again—a bent twig or weed, a footprint, the skin of a dead rabbit.

Once, at night, he had the impression that she crept up close, and looked at him curiously, perhaps with the same great longing that he felt. He could not be sure. But he knew that very soon now she would be his—and perhaps she would be glad of it.

Once he heard a terrible moaning, high up in the air. He looked upward. Blacky uttered a surprised squawk. A large, spherical thing was darting overhead.

"I wonder what that is," Blacky squawked.

"I wonder what that is," said Tommy, feeling a faint fear. "There ain't nothin' like that in the yard."

He watched as the spaceship disappeared from sight. Then, with the unquestioning attitude of the savage, he dismissed the matter from his mind, and took up his tantalizing trail again.

"Better watch out, Tommy," the bird cawed.

"Better watch out, Tommy," Tommy muttered to himself. He only vaguely heard Blacky—Blacky always anticipated what Tommy was going to say, because he had known Tommy so long.

The river was wide, swirling, muddy, primeval in its surge of resistless strength. Tommy stood on the bank, and looked out over the waters—suddenly his breath soughed from his lungs.

"It's her!" he gasped. "It's her, Blacky! She's drownin'!"

No time to waste in thought—a figure truly struggled against the push of the treacherous waters, seemingly went under. Tommy dived cleanly, and Blacky spread his wings at the last instant and escaped a bath. He saw his master disappear beneath the swirling waters, saw him emerge, strike out with singularly powerful arms, slightly upstream, fighting every inch of the way. Blacky hovered over the waters, cawing frantically, and screaming.

"Tommy, I could spank you! I could spank you! I get so exasperated! You wait till your father comes home!"

A log was coming downstream. Tommy saw it coming, but knew he'd escape it. He struck out, paid no more attention to it. The log came down with a rush, and would have missed him had it not suddenly swung broadside on. It clipped the swimming man on the side of the head. Tommy went under, threshing feebly, barely conscious, his limbs like leaden bars. That seemed to go on for a very long time. He seemed to be breathing water. Then something grabbed hold of his long black hair—

When he awoke, he was lying on his back, and he was staring into her eyes. Something in Tommy's stomach fell out—perhaps the hunger was going. He came to his feet, staring at her, his eyes blazing. She stood only about twenty feet away from him. There was something pleasing about her, the slimness of her arms, the roundness of her hips, the strangeness of her body, her large, startled, timid eyes, the mass of ebon hair that fell below her hips. He started toward her. She gazed at him as if in a trance.

Blacky came flapping mournfully across the river. He was making no sound, but the girl must have been frightened as he landed on Tommy's shoulder. She tensed, and was away like a rabbit. Tommy went after her in long, loping bounds, but his foot caught in a tangle of dead grass, and he plummeted head foremost to the ground.

The other vanished over a rise of ground.

He arose again, and knew no disappointment that he had again lost her. He knew now that it was only her timidity, the timidity of a wild creature, that made her flee him. He started off again, for now that he knew what the hunger was, it seemed worse than ever.

The air of this planet was deliciously breathable, and was the nearest thing to their own atmosphere that Tark and Vascar had encountered.

Vascar ruffled her brilliant plumage, and spread her wings, flapping them. Tark watched her, as she laughed at him in her own way, and then made a few short, running jumps and took off. She spiraled, called down to him.

"Come on up. The air's fine, Tark."

*Ross Rocklynne*

Tark considered. "All right," he conceded, "but wait until I get a couple of guns."

"I can't imagine why," Vascar called down; but nevertheless, as they rose higher and higher above the second growth forest, each had a belt strapped loosely around the neck, carrying a weapon similar to a pistol.

"I can't help but hope we run into some kind of intelligent life," said Vascar. "This is really a lovely planet. In time the volcanoes will die down, and vegetation will spread all over. It's a shame that the planet has to go to waste."

"We could stay and colonize it," Tark suggested rakishly.

"Oh, not I. I like Alcon too well for that, and the sooner we get back there, the better—Look! Tark! Down there!"

Tark looked, caught sight of a medium large animal moving through the underbrush. He dropped a little lower. And then rose again.

"It's nothing," he said. "An animal, somewhat larger than the majority we've seen, probably the last of its kind. From the looks of it, I'd say it wasn't particularly pleasant on the eyes. Its skin shows—Oh, now I see what you mean, Vascar!"

This time he was really interested as he dropped lower, and a strange excitement throbbed through his veins. Could it be that they were going to discover intelligent life after all—perhaps the last of its kind?

It was indeed an exciting sight the two bird-creatures from another planet saw. They flapped slowly above and a number of yards behind the unsuspecting upright beast that moved swiftly through the forest, a black creature not unlike themselves in general structure riding its shoulder.

"It must mean intelligence!" Vascar whispered excitedly, her brilliant red eyes glowing with interest. "One of the first requisites of intelligent creatures is to put animals lower in the scale of evolution to work as beasts of burden and transportation."

"Wait awhile," cautioned Tark, "before you make any irrational conclusions. After all, there are creatures of different species which live together in friendship. Perhaps the creature which looks so much like us keeps the other's skin and hair free of vermin. And perhaps the other way around, too."

"I don't think so," insisted his mate. "Tark, the bird-creature is riding the shoulder of the beast. Perhaps that means its race is so old, and has used this means of transportation so long, that its wings have atrophied. That would almost cer-

tainly mean intelligence. It's talking now—you can hear it.
It's probably telling its beast to stop—there, it has stopped!"

"It's voice is not so melodious," said Tark dryly.

She looked at him reprovingly; the tips of their flapping
wings were almost touching.

"That isn't like you, Tark. You know very well that one of
our rules is not to place intelligence on creatures who seem
like ourselves, and neglect others while we do so. Its harsh
voice proves nothing—to one of its race, if there are any left,
its voice may be pleasing in the extreme. At any rate, it ordered the large beast of burden to stop—you saw that."

"Well, perhaps," conceded Tark.

They continued to wing their slow way after the perplexing
duo, following slightly behind, skimming the tops of the trees.
They saw the white beast stop, and place its paws on its hips.
Vascar, listening very closely, because she was anxious to
gain proof of her contention, heard the bird-creature say,

"Now what, Blacky?" and also the featherless beast repeat
the same words: "Now what, Blacky?"

"There's your proof," said Vascar excitedly. "Evidently the
white beast is highly imitative. Did you hear it repeat what its
master said?"

Tark said uneasily, "I wouldn't jump to conclusions, just
from a hasty survey like this. I admit that, so far, all the
proof points to the bird. It seems truly intelligent; or at least
more intelligent than the other. But you must bear in mind
that we are naturally prejudiced in favor of the bird—it may
not be intelligent at all. As I said, they may merely be friends
in the sense that animals of different species are friends."

Vascar made a scornful sound.

"Well, let's get goin', Blacky," she heard the bird say; and
heard the white, upright beast repeat the strange, alien words.
The white beast started off again, traveling very stealthily,
making not the least amount of noise. Again Vascar called
this quality to the attention of her skeptical mate—such
stealth was the mark of the animal, certainly not of the intelligent creature.

"We should be certain of it now," she insisted. "I think we
ought to get in touch with the bird. Remember, Tark, that
our primary purpose on this expedition is to give what help
we can to the intelligent races of the planets we visit. What
creature could be more in need of help than the bird-creature
down there? It is evidently the last of its kind. At least, we

could make the effort of saving it from a life of sheer boredom; it would probably leap at the chance to hold converse with intelligent creatures. Certainly it gets no pleasure from the company of dumb beasts."

But Tark shook his handsome, red-plumed head worriedly.

"I would prefer," he said uneasily, "first to investigate the creature you are so sure is a beast of burden. There is a chance—though, I admit, a farfetched one—that it is the intelligent creature, and not the other."

But Vascar did not hear him. All her feminine instincts had gone out in pity to the seemingly intelligent bird that rode Tommy's broad shoulder. And so intent were she and Tark on the duo, that they did not see, less than a hundred yards ahead, that another creature, smaller in form, more graceful, but indubitably the same species as the whiteskinned, unfeathered beast, was slinking softly through the underbrush, now and anon casting indecisive glances behind her toward him who pursued her. He was out of sight, but she could hear—

Tommy slunk ahead, his breath coming fast; for the trail was very strong, and his keen ears picked up the sounds of footsteps ahead. The chase was surely over—his terrible hunger about to end! He felt wildly exhilarated. Instincts were telling him much that his experience could not. He and this girl were the last of mankind. Something told him that now mankind would rise again—yet he did not know why. He slunk ahead, Blacky on his shoulder, all unaware of the two brilliantly colored denizens of another planet who followed above and behind him. But Blacky was not so easy of mind. His neck feathers were standing erect. Nervousness made him raise his wings up from his body—perhaps he heard the soft swish of large-winged creatures, beating the air behind, and though all birds of prey had been dead these last fifteen years, the old fear rose up.

Tommy glued himself to a tree, on the edge of a clearing. His breath escaped from his lungs as he caught a glimpse of a white, unclothed figure. It was she! She was looking back at him. She was tired of running. She was ready, glad to give up. Tommy experienced a dizzy elation. He stepped forth into the clearing, and slowly, very slowly, holding her large, dark eyes with his, started toward her. The slightest swift motion, the slightest untoward sound, and she would be gone. Her whole body was poised on the balls of her feet. She was not at all sure whether she should be afraid of him or not.

Behind him, the two feathered creatures from another planet settled slowly into a tree, and watched. Blacky certainly did not hear them come to rest—what he must have noticed was that the beat of wings, nagging at the back of his mind, had disappeared. It was enough.

"No noise, Blacky!" the bird screamed affrightedly, and flung himself into the air and forward, a bundle of ebon feathers with tattered wings outspread, as it darted across the clearing. For the third time, it was Blacky who scared her, for again she was gone, and had lost herself to sight even before Tommy could move.

"Come back!" Tommy shouted ragingly. "I ain't gonna hurt you!" He ran after her full speed, tears streaming down his face, tears of rage and heartbreak at the same time. But already he knew it was useless! He stopped suddenly, on the edge of the clearing, and sobbing to himself, caught sight of Blacky, high above the ground, cawing piercingly, warningly. Tommy stooped and picked up a handful of pebbles. With deadly, murderous intent he threw them at the bird. It soared and swooped in the air—twice it was hit glancingly.

"It's all your fault, Blacky!" Tommy raged. He picked up a rock the size of his fist. He started to throw it, but did not. A tiny, sharp sound bit through the air. Tommy pitched forward. He did not make the slightest twitching motion to show that he had bridged the gap between life and death. He did not know that Blacky swooped down and landed on his chest; and then flung himself upward, crying, "Oh, Tommy, I could spank you!" He did not see the girl come into the clearing and stoop over him; and did not see the tears that began to gush from her eyes, or hear the sobs that racked her body. But Tark saw.

Tark wrested the weapon from Vascar with a trill of rage.

"Why did you do that?" he cried. He threw the weapon from him as far as it would go. "You've done a terrible thing, Vascar!"

Vascar looked at him in amazement. "It was only a beast, Tark," she protested. "It was trying to kill its master! Surely, you saw it. It was trying to kill the intelligent bird-creature, the last of its kind on the planet."

But Tark pointed with horror at the two unfeathered beasts, one bent over the body of the other. "But they were mates! You have killed their species! The female is grieving for its mate, Vascar. You have done a terrible thing!"

But Vascar shook her head crossly. "I'm sorry I did it then," she said acidly. "I suppose it was perfectly in keeping with our aim on this expedition to let the dumb beast kill its master! That isn't like you at all, Tark! Come, let us see if the intelligent creature will not make friends with us."

And she flapped away toward the cawing crow. When Blacky saw Vascar coming toward him, he wheeled and darted away.

Tark took one last look at the female bending over the male. He saw her raise her head, and saw the tears in her eyes, and heard the sobs that shook her. Then, in a rising, inchoate series of bewildering emotions, he turned his eyes away, and hurriedly flapped after Vascar. And all that day they pursued Blacky. They circled him, they cornered him; and Vascar tried to speak to him in friendly tones, all to no avail. It only cawed, and darted away, and spoke volumes of disappointingly incomprehensible words.

When dark came, Vascar alighted in a tree beside the strangely quiet Tark.

"I suppose it's no use," she said sadly. "Either it is terribly afraid of us, or it is not as intelligent as we supposed it was, or else it has become mentally deranged in these last years of loneliness. I guess we might as well leave now, Tark; let the poor creature have its planet to itself. Shall we stop by and see if we can help the female beast whose mate we shot?"

Tark slowly looked at her, his red eyes luminous in the gathering dusk. "No," he said briefly. "Let us go, Vascar."

The spaceship of the creatures from Alcon left the dead planet Earth. It darted out into space. Tark sat at the controls. The ship went faster and faster. And still faster. Fled at ever-increasing speed beyond the solar system and into the wastes of interstellar space. And still farther, until the star that gave heat to Earth was not even visible.

Yet even this terrible velocity was not enough for Tark. Vascar looked at him strangely.

"We're not in that much of a hurry to get home, are we, Tark?"

"No," Tark said in a low, terrible voice; but still he urged the ship to greater and greater speed, though he knew it was useless. He could run away from the thing that happened on the planet Earth; but he could never, never outrun his mind, though he passionately wished he could.

# BLOWUPS HAPPEN*

*Astounding Science Fiction*

September

## by Robert A. Heinlein

> Here is one of the earliest stories of the possibility of an accident at a nuclear power plant, one of several that would grace the pages of the scence fiction magazines in advance of the explosion of the first atomic device. Its emphasis on the *pressure* involved in working in such a plant anticipated Lester del Rey's classic "Nerves," published in 1942.

(In my opinion, this was one of the best stories Robert Heinlein ever wrote. It was an example of how he, more than any other science fiction writer in the business could anticipate the future. This was published less than a year after the discovery of fission so it must have been written only months after the discovery, and two years *before* the Manhattan Project began. Bob, of course, didn't get all the details right. It's not just uranium we use—he left out the graphite, cadmium, heavy water, things like that. Also nuclear fission reactors *can't* explode. However, he *did* spot danger, long before anyone else did, and he *did* suggest a solution, which is only now beginning to be a practical one for handling all kinds of dangerous technologies.—I.A.)

* See note following end of Introduction.

# STRANGE PLAYFELLOW

*Super Science Stories*

September

## by Isaac Asimov (1920-    )

*I'm writing this introduction all by myself because I suspect Marty won't touch my stories with a ten-foot pole.*

*In any case, my early notoriety was based on three things: my story "Nightfall," my "Foundation series" and my "positronic robot series." My own feeling is that the last of these, with the "three laws of robotics" was most influential actually. And, as it happened, I started it first.*

*"Strange Playfellow," the first of the positronic robot series, was written in May, 1939, and John Campbell rejected it promptly. I did not manage to sell it till nearly a year later, when Fred Pohl took it.*

*I had called the story "Robbie" but Fred, an inveterate title-changer, made it "Strange Playfellow" to my indignation. I restored the name to "Robbie" when it appeared as the lead story in "I, Robot" in 1950, and it has kept that title ever since. "Strange Playfellow" was used only in this one case in the magazine, but I keep it here to maintain historical accuracy.*

*It is also here in its magazine version for the same reason. I polished it somewhat before it appeared in the book, but never mind. Let it be here as the 19-year-old-I-was wrote it.*

*By the way, you won't find the three laws of robotics here. I hadn't worked them out yet. You'll get a vague reference to the first law, though, if you look for it.—I.A.*

206

"Ninety-eight—ninety-nine—one hundred."

Gloria withdrew her chubby little forearm from before her eyes and stood for a moment, wrinkling her nose and blinking in the sunlight. Then, she gazed about her and withdrew a few cautious steps from the tree against which she had been leaning.

She craned her neck to investigate the possibilities of a clump of bushes. The quiet was profound except for the incessant buzzing of insects and the occasional chirrup of some hardy bird, braving the midday sun.

Gloria pouted, "I'll bet he went inside the house, and I've told him a million times that that's not fair." With tiny lips pressed together tightly and a severe frown crinkling her forehead, she moved determinedly toward the two-story building on the other side of the fence.

Too late, she heard a rustling sound behind her, followed by the distinctive and rhythmic clump-clump of Robbie's heavy feet. She whirled about to see her traitorous companion emerge from hiding and make for the "home" tree at full speed.

Gloria shrieked in dismay. "Wait, Robbie! That wasn't fair, Robbie! You promised you wouldn't run before I found you." Her little feet could make no headway at all against Robbie's giant strides. Then, within ten feet of "home," Robbie's pace suddenly slowed to the merest of crawls, and Gloria with one final burst of wild speed touched the welcome bark of "home" first.

Gleefully, she turned on the faithful Robbie. "Robbie can't run," she shouted at the top of her eight-year-old voice. "I can beat him any day. He's a terrible runner!"

Robbie didn't answer—because he couldn't. In spite of all science could do, it was still impossible to equip robots with phonographic attachments of sufficient complexity—not without sacrificing mobility. Consequently, he contented himself with snatching her up in the air and whirling her about till she begged to be put down again.

"Anyway, Robbie, it's my turn to hide now," she insisted seriously, "because you've got longer legs and you promised not to run till I found you."

Robbie nodded his head and obediently faced the tree. A thin, metal film descended over his glowing eyes and from within his body came a steady metallic clicking—for all the world like a metronome counting off the seconds.

"Don't peek now—and don't skip any numbers," and Gloria scurried for cover.

At the hundredth second, up went the eyelids, and the glowing red of Robbie's eyes swept the prospect. They rested for a moment on a bit of colorful gingham that protruded from behind a boulder. Thereupon one tentacle slapped against his gleaming metal chest with a resounding clang and another pointed straight at the boulder. Gloria emerged sulkily.

"You peeked!" she exclaimed with gross unfairness. "Besides I'm tired of playing hide-and-seek. I want a ride."

But Robbie was hurt at the unjust accusation, so he seated himself carefully and shook his head ponderously from side to side.

Gloria changed her tone to one of gentle coaxing immediately. "Come on, Robbie. I didn't mean it about the peeking. Give me a ride. If you don't, I'm going to cry," and her face twisted into an appalling position.

Hard-hearted Robbie paid scant attention to this dreadful prospect, and Gloria found it necessary to play her trump card.

"If you don't," she exclaimed warmly, "I won't tell you any more fairy tales, so there!"

Robbie gave in immediately and unconditionally and nodded his head vigorously until the metal of his neck hummed. Carefully, he raised the little girl and placed her on his broad, flat shoulders.

Gloria's threatened tears vanished immediately and she crowed with delight. Robbie's metal skin, kept at the constant temperature of seventy degrees by the high resistance coils within, felt nice and comfortable, and the beautifully loud sound her shoes made as they bumped rhythmically against his chest was enchanting.

"I knew you'd let me ride for the fairy tales, Robbie," she giggled. "I knew it. She grasped him about the head and began bouncing up and down.

"Faster, Robbie, faster," and the robot increased his speed until the vibration forced out Gloria's happy laughter in convulsive jerks. Clear across the field he sped, to the patch of tall grass on the other side, where he stopped with a suddenness that evoked a shriek from his flushed rider, and tumbled her onto the soft, natural carpet.

Gloria gasped and panted and gave voice to intermittent whispered exclamations of "That was nice!"

Robbie waited until she had caught her breath and then lifted a tentacle with which he gently pulled her hair—a sign that he wished her attention.

"What do you want, Robbie," she asked roguishly, pretending an artless perplexity that fooled the wise Robbie not at all. He only pulled one golden curl the harder.

"Oh, I know! You want a story." Robbie nodded rapidly. "Which one?" Robbie curled one tentacular finger into a semi-circle. "But I've told you Cinderella a million times. Aren't you tired of it?" The semi-circle persisted.

"Oh, well." Gloria composed herself, ran over the details of the tale in her mind, and began.

"Are you ready? Well—once upon a time there was a beautiful little girl whose name was Ella. And she had a terribly cruel step-mother and two very ugly and very cruel step-sisters and—"

Gloria was reaching the very climax of the tale when the interruption came.

"Gloria!"

"Mama's calling me," said Gloria, not quite happily. "Carry me back to the house, Robbie."

Robbie obeyed with alacrity. Gloria's mother was a source of uneasiness to him.

"I've shouted myself hoarse, Gloria," Mrs. Weston said severely. "Where were you?"

"I was with Robbie," quavered Gloria. "I was telling him Cinderella, and I forgot it was dinnertime."

"Well, it's a pity Robbie forgot, too." Then, as if that reminded her of the robot's presence, she whirled toward him. "You may go, Robbie. She doesn't need you now." Then, brutally, "And don't come back till I call you."

Robbie turned to go, but hesitated as Gloria cried out in his defense. "Let him stay, Mama, please let him stay. I want to finish Cinderella for him."

"Gloria!"

"Honest and truly, Mama, he'll stay so quiet, you won't even know he's here. Won't you, Robbie?"

Robbie nodded his massive head up and down once, in manifest fear of the woman before him.

"Gloria, if you don't stop this at once, you shan't see Robbie for a whole week."

The girl's eyes fell. "All right! But Cinderella is his favorite story!"

The robot left with a disconsolate step and Gloria choked back a sob.

George Weston wasn't pleased when his wife walked in. After ten years of married life, he still was so unutterably foolish as to love her, and there was no question that he was always glad to see her—still Sunday afternoons just after dinner were sacred to him and his idea of solid comfort was to be left in utter solitude for two or three hours. Consequently, he fixed his eye firmly on the latest report of the Douglas expedition to the moon (which looked as if it might actually succeed) and pretended she wasn't there.

Mrs. Weston waited patiently for two minutes, then impatiently for two more, and finally broke the silence.

"George!"

"Hmpph!"

"George, I say! Will you put down that paper and look at me?"

The paper rustled to the floor and Weston turned a weary face toward his wife, "What is it, dear?"

"You know what it is, George. It's Gloria and that terrible machine."

"What terrible machine?"

"Now don't pretend you don't know what I'm talking about. It's that robot Gloria calls Robbie. He doesn't leave her for a moment."

"Well, why should he? He's not supposed to. And he certainly isn't a terrible machine. He's the best darn robot money can buy and Lord knows he set me back half a year's income. He's worth it, too—darn sight cleverer, he is, than half my office staff."

He made a move to pick up the paper again, but his wife was quicker and snatched it away.

"You listen to me, George. I won't have my daughter entrusted to a machine—and I don't care how clever it is. A child just isn't made to be guarded by a thing of metal."

"Dear! A robot is infinitely more to be trusted than a human nursemaid. Robbie was constructed for only one purpose—to be the companion of a little child. His entire 'mentality' has been created for the purpose. He just can't help being faithful and loving and kind. He's a machine—made so."

"Yes, but something might go wrong. Some—some—" Mrs. Weston was a bit hazy about the insides of a robot—"some little jigger will come loose and the awful thing will go berserk and—and—" She couldn't bring herself to complete the quite obvious thought.

"Nonsense," Weston denied. "You're jumping at shadows, Grace. Pretend Robbie's a dog. I've seen hundreds of children no less crazy about their pets."

"A dog is different. George, we must get rid of that horrible thing. You can easily sell it back to the company."

"That's out, Grace, and I don't want to hear of it again. You'd better stop reading 'Frankenstein'—if that's what you've been doing."

And with that he walked out of the room in a huff.

And yet he loved his wife—and what was worse, his wife knew it. George Weston, after all, was only a man, and his wife made full use of every art and wile which a clumsier and more scrupulous sex has learned from time immemorial to fear.

Ten times in the ensuing week, he would cry, "Robbie stays—and that's final!" and each time it was weaker and accompanied by a louder and more agonized groan.

Came the day, at last, when Weston approached his daughter guiltily and suggested a "beautiful" visivox show in the village.

Gloria clapped her hands happily. "Can Robbie go?"

"No, dear," and how his conscience did twinge, "they won't allow robots at the visivox—and besides you can tell him all about it when you get home." He stumbled over the last few words and decided within himself that he made a terribly poor liar.

Gloria came back from town bubbling over with enthusiasm, for the visivox had been a gorgeous spectacle indeed, and the antics of the famous comic, Francis Frin, amid the fierce "leopard-men of the Moon" had evoked delightfully hysterical bursts of laughter.

She ran into the house joyfully and stopped suddenly at the sight of a beautiful collie which regarded her out of serious brown eyes as it wagged its tail on the porch.

"Oh, what a nice dog." Gloria approached cautiously and patted it. "Is it for me, Daddy?"

Weston cleared his throat miserably and wondered whether the substitution would do any good. "Yes, dear!"

"Oh—! Thank you very much, Daddy." Then, turning precipitously, she ran down the basement steps, shouting as she went, "Oh Robbie! Come and see what Daddy's brought me, Robbie!"

In a minute she returned, a frightened little girl. "Mama, Robbie isn't in his room. Where is he?" There was no answer, and George Weston coughed and suddenly seemed to be extremely interested in an aimlessly drifting cloud. Gloria's voice quavered on the verge of tears. "Where's Robbie, Mama?"

Mrs. Weston sat down and drew her daughter gently to her. "Don't feel bad, Gloria. Robbie has gone away."

"Gone away? Where? Where's he gone away, Mama?"

"No one knows, darling. He just walked away. We've looked and we've looked and we've looked for him, but we can't find him."

"You mean I'll never see him again?" Her eyes were round in horror.

"We may find him some day, and meanwhile, you can play with your nice new doggie. Look at him! His name is Lightning and he can—"

But Gloria's eyelids had overflowed. "I don't want the nasty dog—I want Robbie. I want you to find me Robbie." Her feelings became too deep for words, and she spluttered into a shrill wail.

Her mother groaned in defeat and left Gloria to her sorrow.

"Let her have her cry out," she told her husband. "Childish griefs are never lasting. In a few days, she'll forget that awful robot ever existed."

But time proved Mrs. Weston a bit too optimistic. To be sure, Gloria ceased crying, but she ceased smiling too, and the passing days seemed but to increase the inner hurt. Gradually, her attitude of passive unhappiness wore Mrs. Weston down, and all that kept her from yielding was the impossibility of admitting defeat to her husband.

Then, one evening, she flounced into the living room, sat down, folded her arms and looked boiling mad.

Her husband stretched his neck in order to see her over his newspaper, "What now, Grace?"

"It's that child, George. I had to send back the dog today. Gloria positively couldn't stand the sight of him. She's driving me into a nervous breakdown."

Weston laid down the paper and a hopeful gleam entered his eye. "Maybe—maybe we ought to get Robbie back. It might be done, you know. I can get in touch with—"

"No!" she replied grimly. "I won't hear of it. We're not giving up that easily. My child shall not be brought up by a robot if it takes years to break her of it. What Gloria needs is a change of environment. We're going to take her to New York."

"Oh, Lord," groaned the lesser half, "back to the frying pavements."

"You'll have to," was the unshaken response. "Gloria has lost five pounds in the last month and my little girl's health is more important to me than your comfort."

"It's a pity you didn't think of your little girl's health before you deprived her of her pet robot," he muttered—but to himself.

Gloria displayed immediate signs of improvement when told of the impending trip to the city. She began to smile, and to eat with something of her former appetite.

Mrs. Weston lost no opportunity to triumph over her still skeptical husband.

"You see, George, she chatters away as if she hadn't a care in the world. It's just as I told you—all we need to do is substitute other interests."

"Hmpph," was the skeptical response. "I hope so."

In high good-humor, the family drove down to the airport and entered the waiting liner.

"Come, Gloria," called Mrs. Weston, "I've saved you a seat near the window so you can watch the scenery."

"Yes, Mama," was Gloria's unenthusiastic rejoinder. She turned to her mother with a sudden mysterious air of secret knowledge.

"I know why we're going to the city, Mama."

"Do you?" Mrs. Weston was puzzled. "Why, dear?"

"You didn't tell me because you wanted it to be a surprise, but I know." For a moment she was lost in admiration at her own acute penetration, and then she laughed gaily. "We're going to New York so we can find Robbie, aren't we?"

Mrs. Weston maintained her composure, but she found her temper rather bent.

"Maybe," she retorted tartly. "Now sit and be still, for heaven's sake."

New York City, in this good year of 1982, is quite a place for an eight-year-old girl. Gloria's parents made the most of it.

Gloria was taken to the top of the half-mile-tall Roosevelt Building, to gaze down in awe upon the jagged panorama of rooftops, far off to where they blended into the fields of Long Island and New Jersey. They visited the zoos where Gloria stared in delicious fright at the "real live lion" (rather disappointed that the keepers fed him raw steaks, instead of human beings, as she had expected), and asked insistently and peremptorily to see "the whale."

The various museums came in for their share of attention, together with the parks and the beaches and the aquarium.

She was taken halfway up the Hudson in an excursion steamer fitted out in the delicious old-fashioned style of the "gay twenties." She traveled into the stratosphere on an exhibition trip, where the sky turned deep purple and the stars came out and the misty earth below looked like a huge concave bowl. Down under the waters of the Long Island Sound, she was taken in a glass-walled sub-sea vessel, where in a green and wavering world, quaint and curious sea-things ogled her and wiggled slowly to and fro.

In fact, when the month had nearly sped the Westons were convinced that everything conceivable had been done to take Gloria's mind once and for all off the departed Robbie—but they were not quite sure they had succeeded.

It was the episode at the Museum of Science and Industry, though, that finally convinced Mrs. Weston. She was standing totally absorbed in the exploits of a powerful electro-magnet when she suddenly became aware of the fact that Gloria was no longer with her. Initial panic gave way to calm decision and, enlisting the aid of three attendants, the Westons began a careful search.

Gloria's disappearance was simply enough explained. A huge sign on the third floor said, "This Way to see the Talking Robot." Having spelled it out to herself and having noticed that her parents did not seem to wish to move in the proper direction, she determined to see it for herself.

The "Talking Robot" as a scientific achievement left much to be desired. It sprawled its unwieldy mass of wires and coils through twenty-five square yards, and every robotical function had been subordinated to the vital attribute of speech. It worked—and was in this respect quite a victory—but as yet, it could translate only the simpler and more concrete thoughts into words. Certainly, it was not half so clever as Robbie in Gloria's opinion.

Gloria watched it silently for a while, waiting for the two or three who watched with her to depart. Then, when she stood there alone for the moment, she asked hurriedly, "Have you seen Robbie, Mr. Robot, sir?" She was not quite sure how polite one must be to a robot that could talk.

There was an oily whir of gears, and a metallically tim-bered voice boomed out in words that lacked accent and in-tonation, "Who—is—Robbie?"

"He's a robot, Mr. Robot, sir. Just like you, you know, only he can't talk, of course."

"A—robot—like—me?"

"Yes, Mr. Robot, sir."

But the talking robot's only response to this was an erratic splutter and occasional incoherent sound. The conception of other robots like him had stalled his "thinking" engine, for he had not the mental complexity to grasp the idea.

Gloria was still waiting, with carefully concealed impa-tience, for the machine's answer when she heard the cry be-hind her of "There she is," and recognized that cry as her mother's.

"What are you doing here, you bad girl?" cried Mrs. Wes-ton, anxiety dissolving at once into anger. "Do you know you frightened your Mama and Daddy almost to death? Why did you run away?"

"I only came to see the talking robot, Mama. I thought he might know where Robbie was because they're both robots." And then, as the thought of Robbie was brought forcefully home to her, she burst into a sudden storm of tears. "And oh, Mama, I do want to see Robbie again. I miss him like any-thing."

Her mother gave forth a strangled cry, more than half a sob, and cried to her husband, "Come home, George. This is more than I can stand."

That night, George Weston left on a mysterious errand, and the next morning he approached his wife with something that looked suspiciously like smug complacence.

"I've got an idea, Grace."

"About what?" was the gloomy, uninterested query.

"About Gloria."

"Well, go ahead. I might as well listen to you. Nothing I've done seems to have been any good. But remember, I will not consent to buying back that awful robot."

"Of course not. That's understood. However, here's what I've been thinking. The whole trouble with Gloria is that she thinks of Robbie as a person and not as a machine. Naturally, she can't forget him. Now if we managed to con-vince her that Robbie was nothing more than a mess of steel and copper in the form of sheets and wires with electricity its juice of life, how long would this aberration last?"

Mrs. Weston frowned in thought. "It sounds good, but how are you going to do it?"

"Simple. Where do you suppose I was last night? I persuaded old Finmark of the Finmark Robot Corporation to arrange for a complete tour of his premises tomorrow. The three of us will go, and by the time we're through, Gloria will have it drilled into her that a robot is not alive."

His wife's eyes widened. "Why, George, how did you manage to think of that?" There was a gleam of determination in Mrs. Weston's eye. "Gloria is not going to miss a step of the process. We'll settle this once and for all!"

Mr. Struthers was a conscientious General Manager and naturally inclined to be a bit talkative. The combination resulted in a tour that was fully explained—perhaps even overabundantly explained—at every step. In spite of this, Mrs. Weston was not bored. Indeed, she stopped him several times and begged him to repeat his statements in simpler language so that Gloria might understand. Under the influence of this appreciation of his narrative powers, Mr. Struthers explained genially and became even more communicative—if possible.

Weston, himself, displayed an odd impatience, nevertheless—an almost angry impatience.

"Pardon me, Struthers," he broke in suddenly, in the midst of a lecture on the photo-electric cell, "I understand you have a section of the factory where only robot labor is employed?"

"Eh? Oh, yes! Yes, indeed!" He smiled at Mrs. Weston. "A vicious circle in a way—robots creating more robots. However we don't intend to make a general practice of it. You see," he tapped his pince-nez on one palm, "the robot—"

"Yes, yes, Struthers—may we see it? It would be a most interesting experience."

"Yes! Yes, of course." Mr. Struthers replaced his pince-nez in one convulsive movement and gave vent to a soft cough of discomfiture. "Follow me, please."

He was comparatively quiet, while leading the three through a long corridor and down a flight of stairs. Then, when they had entered a large well-lit room that buzzed with metallic activity, the sluices opened and the flood of explanation poured forth again.

"There you are," he said in part, and with quite a bit of pride in his voice. "Robots only! Five men act as overseers and they don't even stay in the room. In five years, ever since we began this project, not a single accident has occurred. Of course, very few robots here are intelligent—"

The General Manager's voice had long died to a rather soothing murmur in Gloria's ears. The whole trip seemed rather dull and pointless to her, though there were many robots in sight. None was even remotely like Robbie and she surveyed them all with open contempt.

Her glance fell upon six or seven robots busily engaged about a round table halfway across the room. Her eyes widened in incredulous surprise. One of the robots looked like—looked like—

"Robbie!" Her shriek pierced the air, and one of the robots about the table faltered and dropped the tool he was holding. Gloria went almost mad with joy. Squeezing through the railing before either parent could stop her, she dropped lightly to the floor a few feet below and ran toward her Robbie, arms waving and hair flying.

And the three horrified adults, as they stood frozen in their tracks, saw what the excited little girl did not see—a huge, lumbering tractor rolling blindly down its track.

It took a split second for Weston to come to his senses, but that split second meant everything, for Gloria could not be overtaken. Although Weston vaulted the railing in a wild attempt, he knew it was hopeless. Mr. Struthers signalled wildly to the overseers to stop the tractor, but the overseers were only human and it took time to act.

Robbie acted immediately and with precision.

With metal legs eating up the space between himself and his little mistress, he charged down from the opposite direction. Everything then happened at once. With one sweep of an arm, Robbie snatched up Gloria, slackening his speed not one iota, and consequently knocking every bit of breath out of her. Weston, not quite comprehending all that was happening, felt rather than saw Robbie brush past him, and he came to a sudden, bewildered halt. The tractor intersected Gloria's path half a second after Robbie, rolled on ten feet farther and came to a grinding, long-drawn-out halt.

Gloria finally regained her breath, submitted to a series of passionate hugs on the part of both parents, and turned eagerly toward Robbie. As far as she was concerned, nothing had happened except that she had found her robot.

Mrs. Weston regained her composure rather quickly, aided by a sudden suspicion that struck her. She turned to her husband, and, despite her disheveled and undignified appearance, managed to look quite formidable. "You engineered this, didn't you?"

George Weston swabbed at a hot, perspiring forehead with his handkerchief. His hand was none too steady, and his lips curved with a tremulous and exceedingly weak smile. "But Grace, I had no idea the reunion would be so violent."

Weston watched her keenly and ventured a further remark, "Anyway, you can't deny Robbie has saved her life. You can't send him away now."

His wife thought it over. It was a bit difficult to keep up her anger. She turned toward Gloria and Robbie and watched them abstractedly for a moment. Gloria had a grip about the robot's neck that would have asphyxiated any creature but one of metal, and was prattling nonsense in half-hysterical frenzy. Robbie's chrome-steel arms (capable of bending a bar of steel two inches in diameter into a pretzel) wound about the little girl gently and lovingly, and his eyes glowed a deep, deep red.

Mrs. Weston's anger faded still further and she became almost genial.

"Well," she breathed at last, smiling in spite of herself. "I guess Robbie can stay with us until he rusts, for all I care."

# THE WARRIOR RACE

*Astounding Science Fiction*

October

## by L. Sprague de Camp (1907-    )

*L. Sprague de Camp was one of the first prolific
science fiction and fantasy writers to branch out
into nonfiction in a major way, one of his earliest
efforts being* Lost Continents *(1952). "The Warrior
Race" appeared in* The Wheels of If, *one of the
earliest collections of sf (most of the stories are
fantasies) to be published by a major figure from
within the genre (Shasta, 1949).*

(Since Sprague is my oldest friend in science fiction, it isn't
surprising that in some cases I know the genesis of some of
his stories. Sprague is the best amateur historian in science
fiction. What he doesn't know about ancient engineering or
ancient warfare, for instance, isn't known to anyone but professional specialists in the field.

It so happens that ancient Sparta had an extremely rigid
war-centered society, with its aristocratic warriors held to an
ascetic, incorruptible life. At the time of the Persian and,
later, the Peloponnesian War, they came out of their shell
and some of their leaders came to be in positions of authority. And what happened to them—Pausania, Lysander—was
precisely what happened to the Centaurians in this story.
Sprague was retelling history (my favorite trick, too).

Of course, Sprague points the moral at the end perhaps
more explicitly than was necessary but that's not really
Sprague. It was John Campbell, I'm certain.—I.A.)

They were serious these days, the young men who gathered
in Prof. Tadeusz Lechon's room to drink his mighty tea and

set up propositions for him to knock down. Between relief
that the war was over without their having come to harm personally, and apprehension for the future, and some indignation at the prospect of foreign rule, there was not much room
left for undergraduate exuberance and orneriness. Something
was going to happen to them, they thought.

"Whatever it is," said Tadeusz Lechon, "it is not cow-
ardice, I am sure." He moved his large bald head forward to
a cup of tea the color of an old boot, his big gold-plated earrings bobbling. He sucked noisily, watching Frederick Merrian.

Fred Merrian, a sandy-haired sophomore with squirrel
teeth, looked grateful but still defiant. He was in civilian
clothes. Baldwin Dowling, the co-ed's dream, was in a very
new U. S. Army uniform. The uniform was so new because,
by the time Dowling had reached his unit in Los Angeles, the
war was over, and he had been told to return home, free, on
anything he liked. He had taken the next 'plane back to
Philadelphia.

Lechon continued: "It is rather an example of the conviction of most thoughtful young men, that human problems
*must* have a solution. Those problems being what they are,
one cannot prove that any of them has *no* solution, the way
Abel proved the problem of solving quintic equations alge-
braically impossible. So they try one idea after another, these
young men; it may be Adrenalism or Anarcho-Communism
or Neo-Paganism. In your case it was non-resistance. Perhaps
it is well that they do—"

"But—" said Fred Merrian.

Lechon stopped the waiting flood of impassioned argument
with a wave. "We have been over all this before. Some day
you will tire of Centaurian rule, and join some other movement with equally impractical ideals. Our Centaurian is nos-
ing around the campus. He may visit us. Suppose we let
Baldwin tell us what he has learned about them."

"Yeah, what are they like?" asked Merrian.

"Much like other people," said Baldwin Dowling. "They're
pretty big. I guess the original group of colonists that went to
Proxima Centauri were a pretty tall bunch. They have a
funny manner, though; sort of as if they ran by clockwork.
You don't get palsy with a Bozo."

Arthur Hsi smiled his idiotic smile. His name was really
Hsi A-tsz, and he was not at all idiotic. "I came halfway

around the world so I could study away from the Bozos. Not far enough, it seems."

Dowling asked: "Heard anything from China?"

"Bozos are busy, trying to make everything sternly efficient and incorruptible, like themselves. May be the greatest fighters on earth, but don't know China. My father writes—"

"Shh!" hissed Lechon, his big red face alert. Then he relaxed. "I thought it was our Centaurian." There was an uncomfortable pause; nobody had much enthusiasm left for chatter, even if the superman failed to appear. Finally Lechon took it up: "Everybody I talk to says what an impossible thing it was, that war. But if you read your history, gentlemen, you will see that it was nothing new. In 1241 the Hungarians never dreamed the Mongols had things like divisional organization and wig-wig signals. So they were swamped. Our government never dreamed the Centaurians had an oxidizing ray, and airplanes with fifteen-centimeter armor. So we were swamped. You follow me? The tune is always different, but the notes stay much the same."

He broke off again, listening. A brisk step approached. Somebody knocked. The history professor said to come in. The Centaurian came.

"My name," he said in a metallic voice, "is Juggins." He was about thirty, with a lantern jaw, high cheekbones, and outstanding ears. He wore the odd plum-colored uniform of the Centaurians: descendants of those hardy souls who had colonized a planet of Proxima Centauri, had fought a three-generation battle against hostile environment and more hostile natives, and had finally swarmed back to earth fifty-odd years ago. Australia had been turned over to them, and their science had made this second most useless continent the world's most productive area. Their terrible stay on the other planet had made them something more and something less than men. Now they ruled the earth.

"Hello, Mr. Jug—" began Dowling. The Centaurian cut him off: "You will not use 'mister' in speaking to a Centaurian. I am Juggins."

"Will you sit down?" invited Lechon.

"I will." The Bozo folded his long legs, sat, and waited for somebody to say something.

Somebody finally did. Dowling asked: "How do you like Philly?"

"You mean Philadelphia?"

"Yeah, sure."

"Then kindly say so. I don't like it at all. It's dirty, corrupt, and inefficient. But we shall fix that. You will do well to cooperate with us. We shall give you a much healthier life than you have ever known." He got this out with some difficulty, as if saying more than one sentence at a time made him self-conscious.

Even Dowling, who, though a native, was not bothered by an excess of local pride, was taken aback by such candor. He murmured: "You guys don't pull any punches."

"I think I grasp the meaning of your slang expression. We are taught to tell the truth." He made telling the truth sound like a most unattractive occupation.

Hsi spoke up: "I hope you do something about the water system. This morning when I turned on the faucet, I got a live eel, a size twelve rubber, and about a cubic meter of chlorine gas before the water came through."

The Bozo stared at him coldly. "Young man, that is an unpardonable exaggeration. A rubber could not possibly pass through the waterpipes."

"He is juckink," said Lechon helplessly, the stress of conflicting emotions bringing out his Polish accent.

Juggins shifted his glare. "I understand. That's what you call a ˈoke, is it? Very funny."

"Have a cigarette," suggested Dowling.

"We never use the filthy weed. It's unhealthy."

"Some tea, then," sighed Lechon.

"Hmm. It *is* a drug."

"Oh, I would not say that, Juggins. It does contain caffein, which is a stimulant, but most foods have one or more things like that in them."

"Very well, if you'll make it weak. And no sugar."

Hsi poured, and added some very hot water. The Bozo stirred it suspiciously. He looked up to say: "I want you, and everybody in the University, to look on me as a kind of father. There's no sense in your taking a hostile attitude, because you can't change conditions. If you will cooperate—Gaw!" He was staring popeyed at his spoon.

The lower half of the spoon had melted all at once and run down into a puddle of molten metal at the bottom of the cup.

"You stirred too hard," said Hsi.

"I—" said Juggins. He glared from face to face. Then he carefully put down his cup, laid the unmelted half of the spoon in the saucer, rose, and stalked out.

Lechon mopped his red forehead. "That was terrible, Arthur! You shouldn't play jokes on him. He might have us all shot."

Hsi let a long-suppressed giggle escape. "Maybe so. But I had that Wood's-metal spoon handy, and it was too good to miss."

"Is he real?" asked Merrian.

"Yeah," said Dowling. "A lot of people have wondered if the Bozos weren't robots or something. But they're real people; reproduced in the normal fashion and everything. They're a new kind of man, I guess."

"No," said Lechon. "Read your history, gentleman. The warrior race. The latest example of what can be done with men by intensive training and discipline. The Spartans and the Osmanli Turks did it in their time. Our Centaurian is more like a Spartan Peer than a Turkish Janissary. Lycurgus would know our father Juggins for a true Spartiate at once . . ."

He went on. The three undergraduates listened with one ear. Merrian was in the throes of a soul-search. Was force an evil when used against creatures like these?

Dowling and Hsi, not introspective idealists, were concerned with the recasting of their personal plans. Dowling guessed that there would still be local Philadelphia politics to get into when he finished his course, Bozos or no Bozos. There'd have to be go-betweens between the supermen and their subjects.

Hsi was thinking of the soft job in the Sino-American Transport Co. that his father would shoe-horn him into when he finished college. If he could, by hard work and family influence, worm his way to the Directorate, there were some big deals he had in mind . . . There would be the omnipresent and allegedly incorruptible Bozos. But that incorruptibility was, to his mind, still only alleged.

Class reunions, like weddings and funerals, bring together a lot of people who would not ordinarily cross the street to speak to one another. So when the class of '09 broke up after the formalities, Hsi and Dowling and Merrian drifted together and wandered off to a restaurant to compare biographies.

Baldwin Dowling had filled out a bit, though he still had the wavy black hair and flashing smile. He had acquired a wife and one child. Arthur Hsi looked much the same, but had acquired a wife and six children. Fred Merrian had lost most of his sandy hair, and had received in exchange two wives, two divorces, and a thin feverish look.

Hsi had just come from a trip to Australia, and was full of it. "It's a wonderful place. Everything goes just like clockwork. No tips, no bribes. No fun, either. Every Bozo is a soldier of some sort, even the ones who run elevators and sell dog-biscuit."

Fred Merrian showed signs of building up argumentative back-pressure. "You mean you approve of them?" he snapped.

Hsi looked stupidly amused. "I wouldn't say that, Fred. But we have to get along with them. The Sino-American Transport Company is a huge organization, with subsidiaries all over the Pacific: hotels and airlines and whale-hatcheries and things. So we must get along with them. What have you been doing the last ten years?"

Merrian looked bitter. "I'm trying to make a living as a writer. But I won't write the sort of trash the cheap magazines buy, so—" He shrugged.

"What about you, Baldwin? I seem to hear about you in politics."

Dowling said: "Yeah, maybe you have. I'm the official mediator for the city of Philadelphia. When one of my—ah—flock gets into trouble with the Bozos, I try to get him out."

"You look prosperous," said Hsi.

"I haven't done so badly." Dowling's smile had a trace of leer. "Sort of like a tribune of the people, as Professor Lechon explained it to me."

"Lechon?" said Hsi. "Is he still here?"

"Yep, and still dishing out the love-life of the ancient Parthians." He noted Merrian's expression, and said: "Fred no doubt thinks I'm a raw renegade. But as you said, the Bozos are here, and we've got to get along with them. By the way, I met a man who knows you; Cass Young. Said your Chinese business methods had nearly driven him crazy."

"What didn't he like?"

"Oh, the way you never mean exactly what you say, and act hurt when some sucker objects to it. And the—ah—dryness of the Oriental palm, as he expressed it. Oh, remember the Bozo Juggins? The first administrator of the University of Pennsylvania? He's still here; administrator for the whole metropolitan area."

"Really?" said Hsi. "By the way, did Mr. Young tell you what he had been seeing me about?"

"No."

"Well, I want to talk to you about it." Hsi looked questioningly at Fred Merrian. Merrian looked at his watch, and reluctantly took his leave.

"Too bad," said Dowling. "He's the most decent and upright guy I know. But he isn't practical." He lowered his voice. "I could swear he was mixed up in some anti-Bozo movement."

"That would account for the hungry-wolf look," said Hsi. "Do you know about such movements?"

"I know a lot of things I don't let on. But what's this deal you have in mind?"

"I say nothing about a deal." Hsi paused to giggle. "But I see I can't fool you, Baldwin. You know the Morehouse project?"

"The mailing-tube unification plan? Yeah."

"Well, Sino-American controls the Philadelphia-Baltimore tube, as perhaps you don't know. And the tubes from Boston to Miami can't be unified without the Philadephia-Baltimore link, obviously. But we don't want to sell our stock in the link outright."

"What, then?"

"If exchange of stock could be arranged—some good friends of ours already hold 45 per cent of the stock in the new Boston-Miami company—it would give us a strong voice in the affairs of the new company."

"In other words, majority control?"

"I would not say that. A strong voice."

Dowling grinned. "Don't try to kid me into thinking these 'good friends' aren't Sino-American dummies. How much stock of the new company do you want? Six per cent?"

"Seven and a fraction would look better."

"I get you. But you know how we do things here. The Bozos have their fingers in everything. If you make anything, they grab it; if you lose, that's your hard luck. All the disadvantages of socialism without the advantages. And it's as much as your life's worth to try to hush one of them up. Still, I *might* be able to handle Juggins."

Hsi giggled. "So they are still incorruptible here, eh? How much of that 'healthier life' they promised have you gotten?"

"Well," said Dowling dubiously, "they did clean things up somewhat."

"Have you a new water system yet?"

"No, though they've been talk—"

*Boom!* Far off across the Schuylkill, a yellow flash tore the night sky. Other explosions followed in quick succession. Broken glass tinkled. Hsi and Dowling gripped their table. Dowling muttered: "The fools!"

"A revolution?" asked Hsi.

"That's what *they* think." The faint tapping of gunfire became audible.

A pair of hard-looking men in uniform appeared in the doorway. Dowling murmured: "Watchdogs." He did not have to describe these police, whose list of virtues stopped after bravery and loyalty to their masters, the warrior race.

There was nothing to do but sit and listen. When the noise abated, Dowling went over to one of the watchdogs and spoke in a low voice.

The watchdog said: "Didn't recognize you, Mr. Dowling. I guess you can go home, and take your friend."

As the two men left the restaurant, Hsi was conscious of the hostile glares of the other customers. Outside, Dowling grinned wryly. "Nobody likes special privilege, except when he's the guy who's got it. We're walking."

"But your car—" wailed Hsi, a completely unathletic person.

"I'm leaving it here. If we tried to drive, the watchdogs would shoot first and ask questions afterwards. If we see anybody, we raise our hands and walk slowly."

Off to the northeast, the sky was red. A lot of houses in North Philadelphia had been set afire by the oxidizers . . .

Hsi and Dowling spent the next day at the latter's home, without news of any kind. Edna Dowling tried to pump Hsi on the subject of ancient Chinese art. Arthur Hsi grinned foolishly, and spread his hands. "But Mrs. Dowling, I don't know anything about art. I'm a businessman!"

The next morning a newspaper did arrive over the ticker. It told of outbreaks, and their suppression, in Philadelphia, New York, Detroit, St. Louis . . .

Baldwin Dowling was shown into Juggins' office. The Centaurian looked much the same, except that his hair was turning prematurely gray.

"Hello, Juggins," said Dowling. Then he sniffed. He sniffed again. There was an unmistakable smell of tobacco smoke.

Dowling looked accusingly at Juggins. Juggins looked back, at first blankly, then uncomfortably. "What is it?" he barked.

Dowling grinned easily. "Don't worry, Juggins. I won't—"

"You will kindly mind your own business!"

"What are you sore about? I didn't say anything. And I have every intention of minding my own business. That's what I came here about." He explained about the stock exchange proposed by Hsi. He put the most favorable interpretation on it. But Juggins was not fooled.

Juggins thoughtfully studied the ornate penholder that marred the Spartan simplicity of his office. He said: "Your plan may be sound. But if my superiors heard of it, they might take a—an excessively rigid view." Silence. "I try to be fair. Haven't I always been fair with the Philadelphians?"

"Of course, Juggins. And it's about time we showed our gratitude, don't you think?"

"Of course we Centaurians aren't swayed by material considerations."

"Sure. Utterly incorruptible. But it would make me happy if I could show my appreciation. I'm not one of you selfless supermen, you know."

"What had you in mind?"

Dowling told him. Juggins took a deep breath, pursed his lips, and nodded somberly. He kept his eyes on the penholder.

"By the way," said Dowling, "now that that's settled, there's another little favor you might do for me. I believe one of the people you captured in the recent uprising was an old classmate named Frederick Merrian."

"What about him?"

"What are the Centaurians' plans for disposing of the rebels?"

"The leaders will be shot, and the others blinded. I don't think your Merrian was a leader; I'd recognize his name if he were."

"For old times' sake, I wondered if you couldn't do something for Merrian."

"Is he an intimate friend of yours?" Juggins looked at Dowling keenly.

"No; I've seen him only occasionally since we finished college. He means well, but he goes off on crazy tangents."

"I don't know what I could do. I couldn't have him turned loose."

"You don't have to. Put in a death certificate for him. Say

he died of natural causes. Then substitute for him one of the regular prisoners in the Lancaster prison farm. They're dying all the time anyway."

"I'll see."

When Dowling picked up Arthur Hsi, his grin answered the Transport Director's question before it was asked.

"I offered him a hundred thousand, and he took it without argument."

Hsi whistled. "I was authorized to pay ten times that much! Our Bozo doesn't know his own value yet."

"Maybe it's the first real bribe he's taken."

"Really? Well, we don't put him wise to what he could have got, eh? He'll learn soon enough."

Fred Merrian shambled into the visitors' room, looking beaten but brightened a bit at the sight of Dowling, Hsi, and Dr. Lechon.

He sat down, then looked puzzled. "How come the guard went out? They don't do that ordinarily."

Dowling grinned. "He's not supposed to hear what we've got to say." He explained the plan for shifting Merrian to the Lancaster farm under a new name.

"Then—then I'm going to keep my eyes? Oh—"

"Now, now, don't break down, Fred."

They got the overwrought writer calmed. He said: "I still don't understand why the uprising failed. You have no idea how careful we were. We thought of *everything*."

Dowling said: "Guess you just didn't have the stuff. As long as the Bozos have a large and well-armed corps of watchdogs—" He shrugged.

"You mean it's hopeless?"

"Uh-huh. Knowing you, Fred, I know you'll find that a hard thing to reconcile yourself to."

"I'll never be reconciled to it. There must be *something*."

"I'm afraid not."

"I am not too sure," said Lechon. "Armed uprising, no. With the complicated weapons used nowadays, civilians can do little. It is like trying to stop a—a buzz-saw with your bare hands. But there are other possibilities."

"What?" asked the three younger men together.

"Read your history, gentlemen. Read your history." And that was all they could get out of him.

"I'm not worrying," said Juggins. "We can trust each other." He leaned back in his chair and sucked on a cigar. He coughed a bit, and said: "Damn, I keep forgetting that one doesn't inhale these things." He had taken to the American fashion of men's earrings.

Dowling smiled. "You mean, we'll *have* to."

"You might put it that way, yes. What's the proposal this time?"

Arthur Hsi explained: "You know the Atlantic City project Sino-American is trying to promote? Our subsidiary is all ready to set up."

"Yes."

"Well, first, there's a Society for Preservation of Ancient Monuments objecting. Say if we modernize Atlantic City we'll ruin it. Say Hotel Traymore has been there three hundred years and it would be sacrilege to tear it down."

Juggins waved his cigar. "I can shoot a few of this Society. That'll shut them up."

"Oh, no," said Hsi, shocked. "Cause all kinds of trouble. People would boycott the project."

"Well, what do you want me to do then?"

"If you could have some of these old ruins moved, as a government project—"

"Hmm. That would cost money."

"Perhaps my company could see its way to sharing the expense."

Juggins still frowned. "My superior, the Centaurian MacWhirtle, would have to approve. I think he's suspicious of me."

Dowling broke in: "Is MacWhirtle married?"

"Yes, but his wife's back in Australia. Why?"

"I just had an idea. Go on, Arthur."

Hsi continued: "Then there's the matter of financing improvement company. We thought we could have it issue some common stock, some non-cumulative preferred. Sino-American could buy most of former; public latter. You and MacWhirtle would have a chance at former also, before it was put on market."

Juggins frowned again. "I seem to remember some rule against non-cumulative preferred. Though I never knew why."

Hsi explained: "This wouldn't be called non-cumulative; some fancy name, but would mean same thing. You sell so much non-cumulative to public, and hold common. Then year comes along, you tell preferred stockholders, conditions are very bad, can't pay any dividends at all, on common *or* preferred. Then next year you say conditions are better. You pay preferred stockholders their regular seven percent—for that year only. You pay yourself regular dividend on common, plus the common stock dividend you didn't pay previous year, *plus* seven percent preferred stock dividend you didn't pay previous year also. It's wonderful."

"I see," said Juggins. "I see why there's a rule against it. But I suppose that sort of thing is necessary in modern finance."

"Oh, absolutely," said Dowling.

"I try to be fair," said Juggins. "Some of my fellow Centaurians lean over backward. I think they do more harm than good."

"Sure," said Dowling. "And do you suppose we could meet MacWhirtle? Socially, I mean."

Dowling dialed his wrist-phone. "Helen? This is Baldwin. . . . Yep, the old political wizard himself. Doing anything next weekend? . . . No, no. It's a party. . . . In New York. . . . Uh-huh, got a Bozo for you to waggle your alabaster torso at . . . Yep, a very big shot indeed. It's all very discreet, understand. . . . No, no, I will not! I've told you I'm very well satisfied with the woman I have. Love her, in fact. This is business. Right. See you Saturday."

The Centaurian MacWhirtle was a smaller and older edition of Juggins. Although his manner still retained most of the clockwork stiffness of the uncontaminated Bozo, it was evident he was under a strain of some kind.

"Sit down!" he barked.

Dowling sat.

MacWhirtle leaned forward. "I understand you're—you and that Chinaman Hsi are—are willing to let me have some common stock in the Atlantic City Improvement Company below the price it'll be offered the public at."

"Yep." Dowling grinned. "Reminds me, can my friend Osborn have his secretarial job back?"

"Why? What do you know about Osborn?"

"He was fired for using a preposition to end a sentence *with*. If we're offering the stock to the public *at*—"

The Bozo purpled. "I'll do what I—why you insolent—" The sentence died in sputters, while Dowling mentally kicked himself for breaking his long-standing rule never to joke with a Bozo.

MacWhirtle calmed himself enough to ask for more details about the stock. Dowling explained.

MacWhirtle looked intently at his fingernails. He said, barely audibly: "I could use force, but she'd hate me—" He realized that Dowling was listening to him, and yelled: "Get out! I won't have men spying on my private—"

Dowling, annoyed but not discouraged, got up to leave. MacWhirtle shouted: "Sit down, you silly ass! I didn't mean it seriously. I admit I've got to have money. You said. . . ."

Dowling walked from the hotel where he had met MacWhirtle to the Penn Station. It was after four, and the only time of day or night when New York's streets are almost deserted. MacWhirtle had shown a bargaining ability incongruous with the financial innocence expected of a true Bozo.

On West 35th he approached a group of men. He recognized the uniform of the watchdogs. One of the national police saw him, whipped out a pistol, and fired. Dowling dived down a set of basement steps. He yelled up: "What the hell's the matter with you?"

There were mutterings in the dark. A deep voice addressed the world at large: "The first open window gets a bullet through it. Go back to bed, all of you." Then the owner of the voice appeared, rocking a bulbous body along on huge flat feet.

The watchdog flashed a light at Dowling's face, and said: "Glory be, if it isn't Mr. Dowling, the Philadelphia mediator! Come out, Mr. Dowling. I'm sorry one of the boys got nervous and took a shot at you. You see—some of them Bozos was took sick, and we was helping them. Naturally we didn't want nobody to see them in that condition."

"You'd have been a hell of a lot sorrier if he'd hit me," grumbled Dowling. He followed the watchdog down to the knot. The three Bozos were sick, all right. The reek of regurgitated alcohol implied the nature of their sickness.

One of the other watchdogs was muttering: "So these are the supermen, who never have any fun, eh? Well, well. Well, well."

Weathered granite disintegrates, but it takes time. Dowling, as he helped Arthur Hsi to spin their web, reflected that he was getting a paunch. People might refer to him as a "rising young man" still, but without unduly stressing the "young." His daughter was in high school. He was not altogether pleased to observe that she was turning into a beauty. He'd have to keep her out of sight of the Bozos with whom he was in constant contact.

Hsi complained: "If we cut a few more Bozos in on this space-port deal, Sino-American might just as well sell out its American holdings and go back to China."

Dowling grinned. "We've got 'em where we want 'em, haven't we?"

"Oh, yes. They follow our—suggestions—like little lambs. But—"

Dowling's wrist-phone rang. Juggins' voice said hoarsely: "Dowling! A terrible thing has happened! MacWhirtle has just shot Solovyov!"

"Killed him?"

"Yes!"

Dowling whistled. Solovyov was Administrator for all of North America. Juggins continued: "It was a quarrel over— you remember that girl, that Miss Helen Kistler, whom you introduced to MacWhirtle last year? It was a quarrel over her!"

"What'll happen?"

"I don't know, but Australia will come down on us. They'll send investigators. God knows what they won't do."

"Well," soothed Dowling. "We'll just have to stick together. Pass the word along to the others."

Australia came down on them all right. In a week the Middle Atlantic States swarmed with Bozo investigators, stiff, grim, and arrogant. The plain citizens, whose hatred for their masters had become a bit dulled with familiarity, awoke to find their newspapers plastered with drastic new decrees—to "tighten up the incredibly lax moral standards prevailing in North America." "Absolute prohibition of intoxicating liquors." "No married women shall work for pay." "*No smoking in public places, the same to include public thoroughfares, hotels, restaurants. . . .*"

Baldwin Dowling entered Juggins' office—the Philadelphia Administrator now had a huge one with rugs in which one practically sank ankle-deep. Juggins and five other local Bozos were facing one of the investigators, a small waspish man.

"Get over there with the others," snarled the little man, evidently mistaking Dowling for another Centaurian. The investigator continued his tirade: "And here I find you fallen into the slime of corruption and depravity! Tea! Coffee! Tobacco! *Liquor! Women! Bribery!* Centaurians, eh? Rotten, filthy, weaklings! You're coming with me now. We're taking a special plane to Australia, where you shall stand trial for enough corruption and immorality to hang a continent. Don't worry about packing; you won't need anything but a coffin. Come on!"

He strode to the door and yanked it open. The six Bozos, looking dazed, started to file out. The frightful discipline of their childhood still told.

Dowling caught Juggins' eye. Juggins returned his look dully. Dowling muttered: "Going to let him get away with it?"

"What do you mean?"

"You're bigger'n he is."

Light slowly dawned. Juggins faced his small tormentor. The other Bozos stopped and faced him too.

"Well?" barked the little man. It did not seem to have occurred to him for an instant that his order might be disobeyed.

The six moved toward him. He looked puzzled, then incredulous, then furious, then alarmed. He reached for his pocket. The Bozos rolled over him in a wave. A gun went off, once. The Bozos untangled themselves. The investigator lay with half his face shot off.

"What now?" panted Juggins. "What'll they do when they hear of this? Where can we go? What's that?"

"That" was the noise of an angry mob, flowing along the street outside and smashing things for no reason other than that it was angry.

The Bozos raced downstairs, Dowling after them.

A dozen watchdogs lounged around the entrance of the building. The mob kept clear of them, though none of them had a weapon out.

"Why don't you shoot?" yelled one of the Bozos to the commander of the police.

The watchdog yawned ostentatiously. "Because, Jack, we don't like not being able to smoke in public no more'n they do." And he turned his back on the Centaurian.

That was all the encouragement the mob needed. But by the time they reached the portals, the six Bozos were not there. They had departed for the rear exit with an audible swish.

Baldwin Dowling, prudently keeping out of the mob's way, dialed his wrist-phone. "Hey, Arthur! Juggins and his friends killed the investigator, and skipped! It looks like maybe they've cracked. I'll try to raise New York, and see if I can start a rumpus there. They're a pushover! See if you can find out what's doing in China! I've got to organize an interim government for Philly. Boy, oh boy!"

A telephone call to New York informed Dowling that a mob had formed there—several mobs, in fact—and that the Centaurians had fled or been lynched. Their leader, the new New York Administrator, had been dead drunk, and had failed to give orders at the critical time. . . .

The New York mob, like the Philadelphia mob, was not actuated by noble motives of daring all for freedom. They were rioting because they had been forbidden to smoke in public.

The same four men who had met in Professor Lechon's rooms in the University of Pennsylvania dormitories, so many years ago, met there again. Fred Merrian was tanned and husky, but subdued. The treatment at the Lancaster camp had almost killed him, but ended by hardening him.

He said: "The latest radio news is that the Second Garrison Corps is retreating through Russia."

"Uh-huh," said Dowling. "When they pulled them out of Europe to use against us, Europe went whoosh."

"Isn't it wonderful?" said Merrian. "It'll be a cleaner, finer world when we've gotten rid of them." He looked at his watch. "I've got to run. Everybody I ever knew wants to pinch me to see if I'm real."

When he had gone, Tadeusz Lechon (he was quite old now) said: "I didn't want to disillusion him again. You know how he is. It won't be a cleaner, finer world. It'll be the same old world, with rascals like you two running it."

"*If* we get rid of them," said Dowling. "They still hold Australia and most of southern Asia. It looks like years of war to me. And if we get rid of the Bozos, a lot of countries will be ruled by watchdogs, who won't be much improvement."

Arthur Hsi asked: "Why did they fold up so easily? One man with machine-gun could have dispersed that mob here last month."

Dowling said: "The Bozos didn't have the guts, and the watchdogs didn't want to. So there wasn't anybody to use the machine-gun. But it still seems goofy. Professor Lechon. Why could they beat us twenty years ago, and we beat them now, when they're at least as strong as they were then and we're very much weaker."

Lechon smiled: "Read your history, gentlemen. The same thing happened to the Spartans, remember, when Epaminondas beat them. Why? They were a warrior race, too. Being such, they were unfitted to live among civilized people. Civilized people are always more or less corrupt. The warrior race has a rigid discipline and an inhumanly high standard of conduct. As long as they keep to themselves they are invincible. When they mix with civilized people, they are corrupted by the contact.

"When a people that have never known a disease are exposed to it, it ravages them fearfully, because they have acquired no immunity to it. We, being slightly corrupt to begin with, have an immunity to corruption, just as if it were a bacterial disease. The Centaurians had no such protection. When exposed to temptation, from being much higher morally than we are, they fell much lower.

"The same thing happened to them as to the Spartans. When their government called on them to go to war to preserve its rule over the earth, most of them were too busy grafting off the civilized people to obey. So the Centaurian government found itself with the most powerful military machine on earth, but only a fraction of the men needed to man it. And many of those they did call home were rotten with dissipation, or were thoroughly unreliable watchdogs whose loyalty to their masters had turned to contempt.

"Aristotle said something on the subject a long time ago, in his *Politics*. If I remember the quotation rightly, it ran:

'Militaristic states are apt to survive only so long as they remain at war, while they go to ruin as soon as they have finished making their conquests. Peace causes their metal to decay; and the fault lies with a social system which does not teach its soldiers what to make of their lives when they are off duty.'

"All of which will not bring back the people the Centaurians killed, or give eyes back to those they blinded. Aristotle's statement, if true, is no ground for complacency. We have a grim time ahead of us yet.

"But to a historian like me it is interesting, from a long-range point of view. And it is somewhat comforting to know that my species' faults, however deplorable, do in fact afford it a certain protection.

"Read your history, gentlemen. The tune is always different, but the notes, as I once remarked, are always the same."

# FAREWELL TO THE MASTER

*Astounding Science Fiction*

October

## by Harry Bates (1900-      )

*Best known as the first editor of* Astounding Stories *(1930-33), Harry Bates was famous with science
fiction readers as the author of the "Hawk Carse"
series about the adventures of an interstellar adven-
turer that was published under the name "Anthony
Gilmore." These stories, most of which Bates wrote
with D. W. Hall, were quite popular and were later
collected as* Space Hawk *(1952). Another exceptional story from this period was "A Matter of
Size." (*Astounding Stories, *1934).*

*But Bates's real fame rests on this wonderful
story, which provided the basis for the film* The
Day the Earth Stood Still *(1951). The film version,
which starred Michael Rennie and Patricia Neal,
was one of the best of the Fifties attempts to bring
science fiction to the screen, even though it did not
faithfully follow the story. The story is also one of
the first to portray mankind as inferior to aliens, especially in moral terms, and it anticipated similar
messages from other, more famous writers, including Arthur C. Clarke's* Childhood's End *(1953).*

(It is always frustrating for an author, I imagine, to be
known for a single story. And for the reader who yearns for
other stories equally good. You have no idea how I feared
that fate after "Nightfall" and how delighted I was when my
"Foundation" stories caught on. Considering how much I
loved this story, I was *so* frustrated when Lester del Rey and
I were both commissioned to write memorial essays for John
Campbell after his death and it was Lester, *not* I, who
thought of entitling it "Farewell to the Master." I could have
chewed nails.—I.A.)

# I

From his perch high on the ladder above the museum floor, Cliff Sutherland studied carefully each line and shadow of the great robot, then turned and looked thoughtfully down at the rush of visitors come from all over the solar system to see Gnut and the traveler for themselves and to hear once again their amazing, tragic story.

He himself had come to feel an almost proprietary interest in the exhibit, and with some reason. He had been the only free-lance picture reporter on the Capitol grounds when the visitors from the Unknown had arrived, and had obtained the first professional shots of the ship. He had witnessed at close hand every event of the next mad few days. He had thereafter photographed many times the eight-foot robot, the ship, and the beautiful slain ambassador, Klaatu, and his imposing tomb out in the center of the Tidal Basin, and, such was the continuing news value of the event to the billions of persons throughout habitable space, he was there now once more to get still other shots and, if possible, a new "angle."

This time he was after a picture which showed Gnut as weird and menacing. The shots he had taken the day before had not given quite the effect he wanted, and he hoped to get it today; but the light was not yet right and he had to wait for the afternoon to wane a little.

The last of the crowd admitted in the present group hurried in, exclaiming at the great pure green curves of the mysterious time-space traveler, then completely forgetting the ship at sight of the awesome figure and great head of the giant Gnut. Hinged robots of crude man-like appearance were familiar enough, but never had Earthling eyes lain on one like this. For Gnut had almost exactly the shape of a man—a giant, but a man—with greenish metal for man's covering flesh, and greenish metal for man's bulging muscles. Except for a loin cloth, he was nude. He stood like the powerful god of the machine of some undreamed-of scientific civilization, on his face a look of sullen, brooding thought. Those who looked at him did not make jests or idle remarks, and those nearest him usually did not speak at all. His strange, internally illuminated red eyes were so set that every observer felt they were fixed on himself alone, and he engendered a feeling that he might at any moment step forward in anger and perform unimaginable deeds.

A slight rustling sound came from speakers hidden in the

ceiling above, and at once the noises of the crowd lessened. The recorded lecture was about to be given. Cliff sighed. He knew the thing by heart; had even been present when the recording was made, and met the speaker, a young chap named Stillwell.

"Ladies and gentlemen," began a clear and well-modulated voice—but Cliff was no longer attending. The shadows in the hollows of Gnut's face and figure were deeper; it was almost time for his shot. He picked up and examined the proofs of the pictures he had taken the day before and compared them critically with the subject.

As he looked a wrinkle came to his brow. He had not noticed it before, but now, suddenly, he had the feeling that since yesterday something about Gnut was changed. The pose before him was the identical one in the photographs, every detail on comparison seemed the same, but nevertheless the feeling persisted. He took up his viewing glass and more carefully compared subject and photographs, line by line. And then he saw that there was a difference.

With sudden excitement, Cliff snapped two pictures at different exposures. He knew he should wait a little and take others, but he was so sure he had stumbled on an important mystery that he had to get going, and quickly folding his accessory equipment he descended the ladder and made his way out. Twenty minutes later, consumed with curiosity, he was developing the new shots in his hotel bedroom.

What Cliff saw when he compared the negatives taken yesterday and today caused his scalp to tingle. Here was a slant indeed! And apparently no one but he knew! Still, what he had discovered, though it would have made the front page of every paper in the solar system, was after all only a lead. The story, what really had happened, he knew no better than anyone else. It must be his job to find out.

And that meant he would have to secrete himself in the building and stay there all night. That very night; there was still time for him to get back before closing. He would take a small, very fast infrared camera that could see in the dark, and he would get the real picture and the story.

He snatched up the little camera, grabbed an aircab and hurried back to the museum. The place was filled with another section of the ever-present queue, and the lecture was just ending. He thanked Heaven that his arrangement with the museum permitted him to go in and out at will.

He had already decided what to do. First he made his way to the "floating" guard and asked a single question, and anticipation broadened on his face as he heard the expected answer. The second thing was to find a spot where he would be safe from the eyes of the men who would close the floor for the night. There was only one possible place, the laboratory set up behind the ship. Boldly he showed his press credentials to the second guard, stationed at the partitioned passageway leading to it, stating that he had come to interview the scientists; and in a moment was at the laboratory door.

He had been there a number of times and knew the room well. It was a large area roughly partitioned off for the work of the scientists engaged in breaking their way into the ship, and full of a confusion of massive and heavy objects—electric and hot-air ovens, carboys of chemicals, asbestos sheeting, compressors, basins, ladles, a microscope, and a great deal of smaller equipment common to a metallurgical laboratory. Three white-smocked men were deeply engrossed in an experiment at the far end. Cliff, waiting a good moment, slipped inside and hid himself under a table half buried with supplies. He felt reasonably safe from detection there. Very soon now the scientists would be going home for the night.

From beyond the ship he could hear another section of the waiting queue filing in—the last, he hoped, of the day. He settled himself as comfortably as he could. In a moment the lecture would begin. He had to smile when he thought of one thing the recording would say.

Then there it was again—the clear, trained voice of the chap Stillwell. The foot scrapings and whispers of the crowd died away, and Cliff could hear every word in spite of the great bulk of the ship lying interposed.

"Ladies and gentlemen," began the familiar words, "the Smithsonian Institution welcomes you to its new Interplanetary Wing and to the marvelous exhibits at this moment before you."

A slight pause. "All of you must know by now something of what happened here three months ago, if indeed you did not see it for yourself in the telescreen," the voice went on. "The few facts are briefly told. A little after 5:00 p.m. on September 16th, visitors to Washington thronged the grounds outside this building in their usual numbers and no doubt with their usual thoughts. The day was warm and fair. A stream of people was leaving the main entrance of the museum just outside in the direction you are facing. This wing, of course, was not here at that time. Everyone was homeward bound, tired no doubt from hours on their feet, seeing the exhibits of the museum and visiting the many buildings on the grounds nearby. And then it happened.

"On the area just to your right, just as it is now, appeared the time-space traveler. It appeared in the blink of an eye. It did not come down from the sky; dozens of witnesses swear to that; it just appeared. One moment it was not here, the next it was. It appeared on the very spot it now rests on.

"The people nearest the ship were stricken with panic and ran back with cries and screams. Excitement spread out over Washington in a tidal wave., Radio, television, and newspapermen rushed here at once. Police formed a wide cordon around the ship, and army units appeared and trained guns and ray projectors on it. The direst calamity was feared.

"For it was recognized from the very beginning that this was no spaceship from anywhere in the solar system. Every child knew that only two spaceships had ever been built on Earth, and none at all on any of the other planets and satellites; and of those two, one had been destroyed when it was pulled into the sun, and the other had just been reported safely arrived on Mars. Then, the ones made here had a shell of a strong aluminum alloy, while this one, as you see, is of an unknown greenish metal.

"The ship appeared and just sat here. No one emerged, and there was no sign that it contained life of any kind. That, as much as any single thing, caused excitement to sky-rocket. Who, or what, was inside? Were the visitors hostile or friendly? Where did the ship come from? How did it arrive so suddenly right on this spot without dropping from the sky?

"For two days the ship rested here, just as you now see it, without motion or sign that it contained life. Long before the end of that time the scientists had explained that it was not so much a spaceship as a space-time traveler, because only such a ship could arrive as this one did—materialize. They pointed out that such a traveler, while theoretically understandable to us Earthmen, was far beyond attempt at our present state of knowledge, and that this one, activated by relativity principles, might well have come from the far corner of the Universe, from a distance which light itself would require millions of years to cross.

"When this opinion was disseminated, public tension grew until it was almost intolerable. Where had the traveler come from? Who were its occupants? Why had they come to Earth? Above all, why did they not show themselves? Were they perhaps preparing some terrible weapon of destruction?

"And where was the ship's entrance port? Men who dared go look reported that none could be found. No slightest break or crack marred the perfect smoothness of the ship's curving ovoid surface. And a delegation of high-ranking officials who visited the ship could not, by knocking, elicit from its occupants any sign that they had been heard.

"At last, after exactly two days, in full view of tens of thousands of persons assembled and standing well back, and under the muzzles of scores of the army's most powerful guns and ray projectors, an opening appeared in the wall of the ship, and a ramp slid down, and out stepped a man, godlike in appearance and human in form, closely followed by a giant robot. And when they touched the ground the ramp slid back and the entrance closed as before."

"It was immediately apparent to all the assembled thousands that the stranger was friendly. The first thing he did was to raise his right arm high in the universal gesture of peace; but it was not that which impressed those nearest so much as the expression on his face, which radiated kindness, wisdom, the purest nobility. In his delicately tinted robe he looked like a benign god.

"At once, waiting for this appearance, a large committee of high-ranking government officials and army officers advanced to greet the visitor. With graciousness and dignity the man pointed to himself, then to his robot companion, and said in perfect English with a peculiar accent, 'I am Klaatu,' or a name that sounded like that, 'and this is Gnut.' The names were not well understood at the time, but the sight-and-sound film of the television men caught them and they became known to everyone subsequently.

"And then occurred the thing which shall always be to the shame of the human race. From a treetop a hundred yards away came a wink of violet light and Klaatu fell. The assembled multitude stood for a moment stunned, not comprehending what had happened. Gnut, a little behind his master and to one side, slowly turned his body a little toward him, moved his head twice, and stood still, in exactly the position you now see him.

"Then followed pandemonium. The police pulled the slayer of Klaatu out of the tree. They found him mentally unbalanced; he kept crying that the devil had come to kill everyone on Earth. He was taken away, and Klaatu, although obviously dead, was rushed to the nearest hospital to see if anything could be done to revive him. Confused and frightened crowds milled about the Capitol grounds the rest of the afternoon and much of that night. The ship remained as silent and motionless as before. And Gnut, too, never moved from the position he had come to rest in.

"Gnut never moved again. He remained exactly as you see him all that night and for the ensuing days. When the mausoleum in the Tidal Basin was built, Klaatu's burial services took place where you are standing now, attended by the highest functionaries of all the great countries of the world. It was not only the most appropriate but the safest thing to do, for if there should be other living creatures in the traveler, as seemed possible at that time, they had to be impressed by the sincere sorrow of us Earthmen at what had happened. If Gnut was still alive, or perhaps I had better say functionable, there was no sign. He stood as you see him during the entire ceremony. He stood so while his master was floated out to the mausoleum and given to the centuries with the tragically short sight-and-sound record of his historic visit. And he stood so afterward, day after day, night after night, in fair weather and in rain, never moving or showing by any slightest sign that he was aware of what had gone on.

"After the interment, this wing was built out from the museum to cover the traveler and Gnut. Nothing else could very well have been done, it was learned, for both Gnut and the ship were far too heavy to be moved safely by any means at hand.

"You have heard about the efforts of our metallurgists since then to break into the ship, and of their complete failure. Behind the ship now, as you can see from either end, a partitioned workroom has been set up where the attempt still goes on. So far its wonderful greenish metal has proved inviolable. Not only are they unable to get in, but they cannot even find the exact place from which Klaatu and Gnut emerged. The chalk marks you see are the best approximation.

"Many people have feared that Gnut was only temporarily deranged, and that on return to function might be dangerous, so the scientists have completely destroyed all chance of that. The greenish metal of which he is made seemed to be the same as that of the ship and could no more be attacked, they found, nor could they find any way to penetrate to his internals; but they had other means. They sent electrical currents of tremendous voltages and amperages through him. They applied terrific heat to all parts of his metal shell. They immersed him for days in gases and acids and strongly corroding solutions, and they have bombarded him with every known kind of ray. You need have no fear of him now. He cannot possibly have retained the ability to function in any way.

"But—a word of caution. The officials of the government know that visitors will not show any disrespect in this building. It may be that the unknown and unthinkably powerful civilization from which Klaatu and Gnut came may send other emissaries to see what happened to them. Whether or not they do, not one of us must be found amiss in our attitude. None of us could very well anticipate what happened, and we all are immeasurably sorry, but we are still in a sense responsible, and must do what we can to avoid possible retaliations.

"You will be allowed to remain five minutes longer, and then, when the gong sounds, you will please leave promptly. The robot attendants along the wall will answer any questions you may have.

"Look well, for before you stand stark symbols of the achievement, mystery, and frailty of the human race."

The recorded voice ceased speaking. Cliff, carefully moving his cramped limbs, broke out in a wide smile. If they knew what he knew!

For his photographs told a slightly different story from that of the lecturer. In yesterday's a line of the figured floor showed clearly at the outer edge of the robot's near foot; in today's, *that line was covered*. Gnut had moved!

Or been moved, though this was very unlikely. Where were the derrick and other evidence of such activity? It could hardly have been done in one night, and all signs so quickly concealed. And why should it be done at all?

Still, to make sure, he had asked the guard. He could almost remember verbatim his answer:

"No, Gnut has neither moved nor been moved since the death of his master. A special point was made of keeping him in the position he assumed at Klaatu's death. The floor was built in under him, and the scientists who completed his derangement erected their apparatus around him, just as he stands. You need have no fears."

Cliff smiled again. He did not have any fears.

Not yet.

## II

A moment later the big gong above the entrance doors rang the closing hour, and immediately following it a voice from the speakers called out, "Five o'clock, ladies and gentlemen. Closing time, ladies and gentlemen."

The three scientists, as if surprised it was so late, hurriedly washed their hands, changed to their street clothes and disappeared down the partitioned corridor, oblivious of the young picture man hidden under the table. The slide and scrape of the feet on the exhibition floor rapidly dwindled, until at last there were only the steps of the two guards walking from one point to another, making sure everything was all right for the night. For just a moment one of them glanced in the doorway of the laboratory, then he joined the other at the entrance. Then the great metal doors clanged to, and there was silence.

Cliff waited several minutes, then carefully poked his way out from under the table. As he straightened up, a faint tinkling crash sounded at the floor by his feet. Carefully stooping, he found the shattered remains of a thin glass pipette. He had knocked it off the table.

That caused him to realize something he had not thought of before: A Gnut who had moved might be a Gnut who could see and hear—and really be dangerous. He would have to be very careful.

He looked about him. The room was bounded at the ends by two fiber partitions which at the inner ends followed close under the curving bottom of the ship. The inner side of the room was the ship itself, and the outer was the southern wall of the wing. There were four large high windows. The only entrance was by way of the passage.

Without moving, from his knowledge of the building, he made his plan. The wing was connected with the western end of the museum by a doorway, never used, and extended westward toward the Washington Monument. The ship lay nearest the southern wall, and Gnut stood out in front of it, not far from the northeast corner and at the opposite end of the room from the entrance of the building and the passageway leading to the laboratory. By retracing his steps he would come out on the floor at the point farthest removed from the robot. This was just what he wanted, for on the other side of the entrance, on a low platform, stood a paneled table containing the lecture apparatus, and this table was the only object in the room which afforded a place for him to lie concealed while watching what might go on. The only other objects on the floor were the six manlike robot attendants in fixed stations along the northern wall, placed there to answer visitors' questions. He would have to gain the table.

He turned and began cautiously tiptoeing out of the laboratory and down the passageway. It was already dark there, for what light still entered the exhibition hall was shut off by the great bulk of the ship. He reached the end of the room without making a sound. Very carefully he edged forward and peered around the bottom of the ship at Gnut.

He had a momentary shock. The robot's eyes were right on him!—or so it seemed. Was that only the effect of the set of his eyes, he wondered, or was he already discovered? The position of Gnut's head did not seem to have changed, at any rate. Probably everything was all right, but he wished he did not have to cross that end of the room with the feeling that the robot's eyes were following him.

He drew back and sat down and waited. It would have to be totally dark before he essayed the trip to the table.

He waited a full hour, until the faint beams from the lamps on the grounds outside began to make the room seem to grow lighter; then he got up and peeped around the ship once more. The robot's eyes seemed to pierce right at him as before, only now, due no doubt to the darkness, the strange internal illumination seemed much brighter. This was a chilling thing. Did Gnut know he was there? What were the thoughts of the robot? What *could* be the thoughts of a man-made machine, even so wonderful a one as Gnut?

It was time for the cross, so Cliff slung his camera around on his back, went down on his hands and knees, and carefully moved to the edge of the entrance hall. There he fitted himself as closely as he could into the angle made by it with the floor and started inching ahead. Never pausing, not risking a glance at Gnut's unnerving red eyes, moving an inch at a time, he snaked along. He took ten minutes to cross the space of a hundred feet, and he was wet with perspiration when his fingers at last touched the one-foot rise of the platform on which the table stood. Still slowly, silently as a shadow, he made his way over the edge and melted behind the protection of the table. At last he was there.

He relaxed for a moment, then, anxious to know whether he had been seen, carefully turned and looked around the side of the table.

Gnut's eyes were now full on him! Or so it seemed. Against the general darkness, the robot loomed a mysterious and still darker shadow that, for all his being a hundred and fifty feet away, seemed to dominate the room. Cliff could not tell whether the position of his body was changed or not.

But if Gnut were looking at him, he at least did nothing else. Not by the slightest motion that Cliff could discern did he appear to move. His position was the one he had maintained these last three months, in the darkness, in the rain, and this last week in the museum.

Cliff made up his mind not to give away to fear. He became conscious of his own body. The cautious trip had taken something out of him—his knees and elbows burned and his trousers were no doubt ruined. But these were little things if what he hoped for came to pass. If Gnut so much as moved, and he could catch him with his infrared camera, he would have a story that would buy him fifty suits of clothes. And if on top of that he could learn the purpose of Gnut's moving—provided there was a purpose—that would be a story that would set the world on its ears.

He settled down to a period of waiting; there was no telling when Gnut would move, if indeed he would move that night. Cliff's eyes had long been adjusted to the dark and he could make out the larger objects well enough. From time to time he peered out at the robot—peered long and hard, till his outlines wavered and he seemed to move, and he had to blink and rest his eyes to be sure it was only his imagination.

Again the minute hand of his watch crept around the dial. The inactivity made Cliff careless, and for longer and longer periods he kept his head back out of sight behind the table. And so it was that when Gnut did move he was scared almost out of his wits. Dull and a little bored, he suddenly found the robot out on the floor, halfway in his direction.

But that was not the most frightening thing. It was that when he did see Gnut he did not catch him moving! He was stopped as still as a cat in the middle of stalking a mouse. His eyes were now much brighter, and there was no remaining doubt about their direction: he was looking right at Cliff!

Scarcely breathing, half hypnotized, Cliff looked back. His thoughts tumbled. What was the robot's intention? Why had he stopped so still? Was he being stalked? How could he move with such silence?

In the heavy darkness Gnut's eyes moved nearer. Slowly but in perfect rhythm the almost imperceptible sound of his footsteps beat on Cliff's ears. Cliff, usually resourceful enough, was this time caught flatfooted. Frozen with fear, utterly incapable of fleeing, he lay where he was while the metal monster with the fiery eyes came on.

For a moment Cliff all but fainted, and when he recovered, there was Gnut towering over him, legs almost within reach. He was bending slightly, burning his terrible eyes right into his own!

Too late to try to think of running now. Trembling like any cornered mouse, Cliff waited for the blow that would crush him. For an eternity, it seemed, Gnut scrutinized him without moving. For each second of that eternity Cliff expected annihilation, sudden, quick, complete. And then suddenly and unexpectedly it was over. Gnut's body straightened and he stepped back. He turned. And then, with the almost jerkless rhythm which only he among robots possessed, he started back toward the place from which he came.

Cliff could hardly believe he had been spared. Gnut could have crushed him like a worm—and he had only turned around and gone back. Why? It could not be supposed that a robot was capable of human considerations.

Gnut went straight to the other end of the traveler. At a certain place he stopped and made a curious succession of sounds. At once Cliff saw an opening, blacker than the gloom of the building, appear in the ship's side, and it was followed by a slight sliding sound as a ramp slid out and met the floor. Gnut walked up the ramp and, stooping a little, disappeared inside the ship.

Then, for the first time, Cliff remembered the picture he had come to get. Gnut had moved, but he had not caught him! But at least now, whatever opportunies there might be later, he could get the shot of the ramp connecting with the opened door; so he twisted his camera into position, set it for the proper exposure, and took a shot.

A long time passed and Gnut did not come out. What could he be doing inside? Cliff wondered. Some of his courage returned to him and he toyed with the idea of creeping forward and peeping through the port, but he found he had not the courage for that. Gnut had spared him, at least for the time, but there was no telling how far his tolerance would go.

An hour passed, then another, Gnut was doing something inside the ship, but what. Cliff could not imagine. If the robot had been a human being, he knew he would have sneaked a look, but as it was, he was too much of an unknown quantity. Even the simplest of Earth's robots under certain circumstances were inexplicable things; what, then, of this one, come from an unknown and even unthinkable civilization, by far the most wonderful construction ever seen—what superhuman powers might he not possess? All that the scientists of Earth could do had not served to derange him. Acid, heat, rays, terrific crushing blows—he had withstood them all; even his finish had been unmarred. He might be able to see perfectly in the dark. And right where he was, he might be able to hear or in some way sense the least change in Cliff's position.

More time passed, and then, some time after two o'clock in the morning, a simple homely thing happened, but a thing so unexpected that for a moment it quite destroyed Cliff's equilibrium. Suddenly, through the dark and silent building, there was a faint whir of wings, soon followed by the piercing, sweet voice of a bird. A mockingbird. Somewhere in the gloom above his head. Clear and full throated were its notes; a dozen little songs it sang, one after the other without pause between—short insistent calls, twirrings, coaxings, cooings— the spring love song of perhaps the finest singer in the world. Then, as suddenly as it began, the voice was silent.

If an invading army had poured out of the traveler, Cliff would have been less surprised. The month was December; even in Florida the mockingbirds had not yet begun their song. How had one gotten into that tight, gloomy museum? How and why was it singing there?

He waited, full of curiosity. Then suddenly he was aware of Gnut, standing just outside the port of the ship. He stood quite still, his glowing eyes turned squarely in Cliff's direction. For a moment the hush in the museum seemed to deepen; then it was broken by a soft thud on the floor near where Cliff was lying.

He wondered. The light in Gnut's eyes changed, and he started his almost jerkless walk in Cliff's direction. When only a little away, the robot stopped, bent over, and picked something from the floor. For some time he stood without motion and looked at a little object he held in his hand. Cliff knew, though he could not see, that it was the mockingbird. Its body, for he was sure that it had lost its song forever. Gnut then turned, and without a glance at Cliff, walked back to the ship and again went inside.

Hours passed while Cliff waited for some sequel to this surprising happening. Perhaps it was because of his curiosity that his fear of the robot began to lessen. Surely if the mechanism was unfriendly, if he intended him any harm, he would have finished him before, when he had such a perfect opportunity. Cliff began to nerve himself for a quick look inside the port. And a picture; he must remember the picture. He kept forgetting the very reason he was there.

It was in the deeper darkness of the false dawn when he got sufficient courage and made the start. He took off his shoes, and in his stockinged feet, his shoes tied together and slung over his shoulder, he moved stiffly but rapidly to a position behind the nearest of the six robot attendants stationed along the wall, then paused for some sign which might indicate that Gnut knew he had moved. Hearing none, he slipped along behind the next robot attendant and paused again. Bolder now, he made in one spurt all the distance to the farthest one, the sixth, fixed just opposite the port of the ship. There he met with a disappointment. No light that he could detect was visible within; there was only darkness and the all-permeating silence. Still, he had better get the picture. He raised his camera, focused it on the dark opening, and gave the film a comparatively long exposure. Then he stood there, at a loss what to do next.

As he paused, a peculiar series of muffled noises reached his ears, apparently from within the ship. Animal noises—first scrapings and pantings, punctuated by several sharp clicks, then deep, rough snarls, interrupted by more scrapings and pantings, as if a struggle of some kind were going on. Then suddenly, before Cliff could even decide to run back to the table, a low, wide, dark shape bounded out of the port and immediately turned and grew to the height of a man. A terrible fear swept over Cliff, even before he knew what the shape was.

In the next second Gnut appeared in the port and stepped unhesitatingly down the ramp toward the shape. As he advanced it backed slowly away for a few feet; but then it stood its ground, and thick arms rose from its sides and began a loud drumming on its chest, while from its throat came a deep roar of defiance. Only one creature in the world beat its chest and made a sound like that. The shape was a gorilla!

And a huge one!

Gnut kept advancing, and when close, charged forward and grappled with the beast. Cliff would not have guessed that Gnut could move so fast. In the darkness he could not see the details of what happened; all he knew was that the two great shapes, the titanic metal Gnut and the squat but terrifically strong gorilla, merged for a moment with silence on the robot's part and terrible, deep, indescribable roars on the other's; then the two separated, and it was as if the gorilla had been flung back and away.

The animal at once rose to its full height and roared deafeningly. Gnut advanced. They closed again, and the separation of before was repeated. The robot continued inexorably, and now the gorilla began to fall back down the building. Suddenly the beast darted at a manlike shape against the wall, and with one rapid side movement dashed the fifth robot attendant to the floor and decapitated it.

Tense with fear, Cliff crouched behind his own robot attendant. He thanked Heaven that Gnut was between him and the gorilla and was continuing his advance. The gorilla backed farther, darted suddenly at the next robot in the row, and with strength almost unbelievable picked it from its roots and hurled it at Gnut. With a sharp metallic clang, robot hit robot, and the one of Earth bounced off to one side and rolled to a stop.

Cliff cursed himself for it afterward, but again he completely forgot the picture. The gorilla kept falling back down the building, demolishing with terrific bursts of rage every robot attendant that he passed and throwing the pieces at the implacable Gnut. Soon they arrived opposite the table, and Cliff now thanked his stars he had come away. There followed a brief silence. Cliff could not make out what was going on, but he imagined that the gorilla had at last reached the corner of the wing and was trapped.

If he was, it was only for a moment. The silence was suddenly shattered by a terrific roar, and the thick, squat shape of the animal came bounding toward Cliff. He came all the way back and turned just between Cliff and the port of the ship. Cliff prayed frantically for Gnut to come back quickly, for there was now only the last remaining robot attendant between him and the madly dangerous brute. Out of the dimness Gnut did appear. The gorilla rose to its full height and again beat its chest and roared its challenge.

And then occurred a curious thing. It fell on all fours and slowly rolled over on its side, as if weak or hurt. Then panting, making frightening noises, it forced itself again to its feet and faced the oncoming Gnut. As it waited, its eye was caught by the last robot attendant and perhaps Cliff, shrunk close behind it. With a surge of terrible destructive rage, the gorilla waddled sideward toward Cliff, but this time, even through his panic, he saw that the animal moved with difficulty, again apparently sick or severely wounded. He jumped back just in time; the gorilla pulled out the last robot attendant and hurled it violently at Gnut, missing him narrowly.

That was its last effort. The weakness caught it again; it dropped heavily on one side, rocked back and forth a few times, and fell to twitching. Then it lay still and did not move again.

The first faint pale light of the dawn was seeping into the room. From the corner where he had taken refuge, Cliff watched closely the great robot. It seemed to him that he behaved very queerly. He stood over the dead gorilla, looking down at him with what in a human would be called sadness. Cliff saw this clearly; Gnut's heavy greenish features bore a thoughtful, grieving expression new to his experience. For some moments he stood so, then as might a father with his sick child, he leaned over, lifted the great animal in his metal arms and carried it tenderly within the ship.

Cliff flew back to the table, suddenly fearful of yet other dangerous and inexplicable happenings. It struck him that he might be safer in the laboratory, and with trembling knees he made his way there and hid in one of the big ovens. He prayed for full daylight. His thoughts were chaos. Rapidly, one after another, his mind churned up the amazing events of the night, but all was mystery; it seemed there could be no rational explanation for them. That mockingbird. The gorilla. Gnut's sad expression and his tenderness. What could account for a fantastic melange like that!

Gradually full daylight did come. A long time passed. At last he began to believe he might yet get out of that place of mystery and danger alive. At 8:30 there were noises at the entrance, and the good sound of human voices came to his ears. He stepped out of the oven and tiptoed to the passage-way.

The noises stopped suddenly and there was a frightened exclamation and then the sound of running feet, and then silence. Stealthily Cliff sneaked down the narrow way and peeped fearfully around the ship.

There Gnut was in his accustomed place, in the identical pose he had taken at the death of his master, brooding sullenly and alone over a space traveler once again closed tight and a room that was a shambles. The entrance doors stood open and, heart in his mouth, Cliff ran out.

A few minutes later, safe in his hotel room, completely done in, he sat down for a second and almost at once fell asleep. Later, still in his clothes and still asleep, he staggered over to the bed. He did not wake up till midafternoon.

## III

Cliff awoke slowly, at first not realizing that the images tumbling in his head were real memories and not a fantastic dream. It was recollection of the pictures which brought him to his feet. Hastily he set about developing the film in his camera.

Then in his hands were proof that the events of the night were real. Both shots turned out well. The first showed clearly the ramp leading up to the port as he had dimly discerned it from his position behind the table. The second, of the open port as snapped from in front, was a disappointment, for a blank wall just back of the opening cut off all view of the interior. That would account for the fact that no light had escaped from the ship while Gnut was inside. Assuming Gnut required light for whatever he did.

Cliff looked at the negatives and was ashamed of himself. What a rotten picture man he was to come back with two ridiculous shots like these! He had had a score of opportunities to get real ones—shots of Gnut in action—Gnut's fight with the gorilla—even Gnut holding the mockingbird—spine-chilling stuff!—and all he had brought back was two stills of a doorway. Oh, sure, they were valuable, but he was a grade A ass.

And to top this brilliant performance, he had fallen asleep!

Well, he'd better get out on the street and find out what was doing.

Quickly he showered, shaved, and changed his clothes, and

soon was entering a nearby restaurant patronized by other picture and newsmen. Sitting alone at the lunch bar, he spotted a friend and competitor.

"Well, what do you think?" asked his friend when he took the stool at his side.

"I don't think anything until I've had breakfast," Cliff answered.

"Then haven't you heard?"

"Heard what?" fended Cliff, who knew very well what was coming.

"You're a fine picture man," was the other's remark. "When something really big happens, you are asleep in bed." But then he told him what had been discovered that morning in the museum, and of the world-wide excitement at the news. Cliff did three things at once, successfully—gobbled a substantial breakfast, kept thanking his stars that nothing new had transpired, and showed continuous surprise. Still chewing he got up and hurried over to the building.

Outside, balked at the door, was a large crowd of the curious, but Cliff had no trouble gaining admittance when he showed his press credentials. Gnut and the ship stood just as he had left them, but the floor had been cleaned up and the pieces of the demolished robot attendants were lined up in one place along the wall. Several other competitor friends of his were there.

"I was away; missed the whole thing," he said to one of them—Gus. "What's supposed to be the explanation for what happened?"

"Ask something easy," was the answer. "Nobody knows. It's thought maybe something came out of the ship, maybe another robot like Gnut. Say—where have you been?"

"Asleep."

"Better catch up. Several billion bipeds are scared stiff. Revenge for the death of Klaatu. Earth about to be invaded."

"But that's—"

"Oh, I know it's all crazy, but that's the story they're being fed; it sells news. But there's a new angle just turned up, very surprising. Come here."

He led Cliff to the table where stood a knot of people looking with great interest at several objects guarded by a technician. Gus pointed to a long slide on which were mounted a number of short dark-brown hairs.

"Those hairs came off a large male gorilla," Gus said with

a certain hard-boiled casualness. "Most of them were found among the sweepings of the floor this morning. The rest were found on the robot attendants."

Cliff tried to look astounded. Gus pointed to a test tube partly filled with a light amber fluid.

"And that's blood, diluted—gorilla blood. It was found on Gnut's arms."

"Good Heaven!" Cliff managed to exclaim. "And there's no explanation?"

"Not even a theory. It's your big chance, wonder boy."

Cliff broke away from Gus, unable to maintain his act any longer. He couldn't decide what to do about his story. The press services would bid heavily for it—with all his pictures—but that would take further action out of his hands. In the back of his mind he wanted to stay in the wing again that night, but—well, he simply was afraid. He'd had a pretty stiff dose, and he wanted very much to remain alive.

He walked over and looked a long time at Gnut. No one would ever have guessed that he had moved, or that there had rested on his greenish metal face a look of sadness. Those weird eyes! Cliff wondered if they were really looking at him, as they seemed, recognizing him as the bold intruder of last night. Of what unknown stuff were they made—those materials placed in his eye sockets by one branch of the race of man which all the science of his own could not even serve to disfunction? What was Gnut thinking? What could be the thoughts of a robot—a mechanism of metal poured out of man's clay crucibles? Was he angry at him? Cliff thought not. Gnut had had him at his mercy—and had walked away.

Dared he stay again?

Cliff thought perhaps he did.

He walked about the room, thinking it over. He felt sure Gnut would move again. A Mikton ray gun would protect him from another gorilla—or fifty of them. He did not yet have the real story. He had come back with two miserable architectural stills!

He might have known from the first that he would stay. At dusk that night, armed with his camera and a small Mikton gun, he lay once more under the table of supplies in the laboratory and heard the metal doors of the wing clang to for the night.

This time he would get the story—and the pictures.

If only no guard was posted inside!

## IV

Cliff listened hard for a long time for any sound which might tell him that a guard had been left, but the silence within the wing remained unbroken. He was thankful for that—but not quite completely. The gathering darkness and the realization that he was now irrevocably committed made the thought of a companion not altogether unpleasant.

About an hour after it reached maximum darkness he took off his shoes, tied them together and slung them around his neck, down his back, and stole quietly down the passageway to where it opened into the exhibition area. All seemed as it had been the preceding night. Gnut looked an ominous, indistinct shadow at the far end of the room, his glowing red eyes again seemingly right on the spot from which Cliff peeped out. As on the previous night, but even more carefully, Cliff went down on his stomach in the angle of the wall and slowly snaked across to the low platform on which stood the table. Once in its shelter, he fixed his shoes so that they straddled one shoulder, and brought his camera and gun holster around, ready on his breast. This time, he told himself, he would get pictures.

He settled down to wait, keeping Gnut in full sight every minute. His vision reached maximum adjustment to the darkness. Eventually he began to feel lonely and a little afraid. Gnut's red-glowing eyes were getting on his nerves; he had to keep assuring himself that the robot would not harm him. He had little doubt but that he himself was being watched.

Hours slowly passed. From time to time he heard slight noises at the entrance, on the outside—a guard, perhaps, or maybe curious visitors.

At about nine o'clock he saw Gnut move. First his head alone; it turned so that the eyes burned stronger in the direction where Cliff lay. For a moment that was all; then the dark metal form stirred slightly and began moving forward—straight toward himself. Cliff had thought he would not be afraid—much—but now his heart stood still. What would happen this time?

With amazing silence, Gnut drew nearer, until he towered an ominous shadow over the spot where Cliff lay. For a long time his red eyes burned down on the prone man. Cliff trembled all over; this was worse than the first time. Without having planned it, he found himself speaking to the creature.

·

"You would not hurt me," he pleaded. "I was only curious to see what's going on. It's my job. Can you understand me? I would not harm or bother you. I . . . I couldn't if I wanted to! Please!"

The robot never moved, and Cliff could not guess whether his words had been understood or even heard. When he felt he could not bear the suspense any longer, Gnut reached out and took something from a drawer of the table, or perhaps he put something back in; then he stepped back, turned, and retraced his steps. Cliff was safe! Again the robot had spared him!

Beginning then, Cliff lost much of his fear. He felt sure now that this Gnut would do him no harm. Twice he had had him in his power, and each time he had only looked and quietly moved away. Cliff could not imagine what Gnut had done in the drawer of the table. He watched with the greatest curiosity to see what would happen next.

As on the night before, the robot went straight to the end of the ship and made the peculiar sequence of sounds that opened the port, and when the ramp slid out he went inside. After that Cliff was alone in the darkness for a very long time, probably two hours. Not a sound came from the ship.

Cliff knew he should sneak up to the port and peep inside, but he could not quite bring himself to do it. With his gun he could handle another gorilla, but if Gnut caught him it might be the end. Momentarily he expected something fantastic to happen—he knew not what; maybe the mockingbird's sweet song again, maybe a gorilla, maybe—anything. What did at last happen once more caught him with complete surprise.

He heard a sudden muffled sound, then words—human words—every one familiar.

"Gentlemen," was the first, and then there was a very slight pause. "The Smithsonian Institution welcomes you to its new Interplanetary Wing and to the marvelous exhibits at this moment before you."

It was the recorded voice of Stillwell! But it was not coming through the speakers overhead, but much muted, from within the ship.

After a slight pause it went on:

"All of you must . . . must—" Here it stammered and came to a stop. Cliff's hair bristled. That stammering was not in the lecture!

For just a moment there was silence; then came a scream,

a hoarse man's scream, muffled, from somewhere within the heart of the ship; and it was followed by muted gasps and cries, as of a man in great fright or distress.

Every nerve tight, Cliff watched the port. He heard a thudding noise within the ship, then out the door flew the shadow of what was surely a human being. Gasping and half stumbling, he ran straight down the room in Cliff's direction. When twenty feet away, the great shadow of Gnut followed him out of the port.

Cliff watched, breathless. The man—it was Stillwell, he saw now—came straight for the table behind which Cliff himself lay, as if to get behind it, but when only a few feet away, his knees buckled and he fell to the floor. Suddenly Gnut was standing over him, but Stillwell did not seem to be aware of it. He appeared very ill, but kept making spasmodic futile efforts to creep on to the protection of the table.

Gnut did not move, so Cliff was emboldened to speak.

"What's the matter, Stillwell?" he asked. "Can I help? Don't be afraid. I'm Cliff Sutherland; you know, the picture man."

Without showing the least surprise at finding Cliff there, and clutching at his presence like a drowning man would a straw, Stillwell gasped out:

"Help me! Gnut . . . Gnut—" He seemed unable to go on.

"Gnut what?" asked Cliff. Very conscious of the fire-eyed robot looming above, and afraid even to move out to the man, Cliff added reassuringly: "Gnut won't hurt you. I'm sure he won't. He doesn't hurt me. What's the matter? What can I do?"

With a sudden accession of energy, Stillwell rose on his elbows.

"Where am I?" he asked.

"In the Interplanetary Wing," Cliff answered. "Don't you know?"

Only Stillwell's hard breathing was heard for a moment. Then hoarsely, weakly, he asked:

"How did I get here?"

"I don't know," said Cliff.

"I was making a lecture recording," Stillwell said, "when suddenly I found myself here . . . or I mean in there—"

He broke off and showed a return of his terror.

"Then what?" asked Cliff gently.

"I was in that box—and there, above me, was Gnut, the

robot. Gnut! But they made Gnut harmless! He's never moved!"

"Steady, now," said Cliff. "I don't think Gnut will hurt you."

Stillwell fell back on the floor.

"I'm very weak," he gasped. "Something—Will you get a doctor?"

He was utterly unaware that towering above him, eyes boring down at him through the darkness, was the robot he feared so greatly.

As Cliff hesitated, at a loss what to do, the man's breath began coming in short gasps, as regular as the ticking of a clock. Cliff dared to move out to him, but no act on his part could have helped the man now. His gasps weakened and became spasmodic, then suddenly he was completely silent and still. Cliff felt for his heart, then looked up to the eyes in the shadow above.

"He is dead," he whispered.

The robot seemed to understand, or at least to hear. He bent forward and regarded the still figure.

"What is it, Gnut?" Cliff asked the robot suddenly. "What are you doing? Can I help you in any way? Somehow I don't believe you are unfriendly, and I don't believe you killed this man. But what happened? Can you understand me? Can you speak? What is it you're trying to do?"

Gnut made no sound or motion, but only looked at the still figure at his feet. In the robot's face, now so close, Cliff saw the look of sad contemplation.

Gnut stood so several minutes; then he bent lower, took the limp form carefully—even gently, Cliff thought—in his mighty arms, and carried him to the place along the wall where lay the dismembered pieces of the robot attendants. Carefully he laid him by their side. Then he went back into the ship.

Without fear now, Cliff stole along the wall of the room. He had gotten almost as far as the shattered figures on the floor when he suddenly stopped motionless. Gnut was emerging again.

He was bearing a shape that looked like another body, a larger one. He held it in one arm and placed it carefully by the body of Stillwell. In the hand of his other arm he held something that Cliff could not make out, and this he placed at the side of the body he had just put down. Then he went to the ship and returned once more with a shape which he laid gently by the others; and when this last trip was over he looked down at them all for a moment, then turned slowly back to the ship and stood motionless, as if in deep thought, by the ramp.

Cliff restrained his curiosity as long as he could, then slipped forward and bent over the objects Gnut had placed there. First in the row was the body of Stillwell, as he expected, and next was the great shapeless furry mass of a dead gorilla—the one of last night. By the gorilla lay the object the robot had carried in his free hand—the little body of the mockingbird. These last two had remained in the ship all night, and Gnut, for all his surprising gentleness in handling them, was only cleaning house. But there was a fourth body whose history he did not know. He moved closer and bent very low to look.

What he saw made him catch his breath. Impossible!—he thought; there was some confusion in his directions; he brought his face back, close to the first body. Then his blood ran cold. The first body was that of Stillwell, but the last in the row was Stillwell, too; there were two bodies of Stillwell, both exactly alike, both dead.

Cliff backed away with a cry, and then panic took him and he ran down the room away from Gnut and yelled and beat wildly on the door. There was a noise on the outside.

"Let me out!" he yelled in terror. "Let me out! Let me out! Oh, hurry!"

A crack opened between the two doors and he forced his way through like a wild animal and ran far out on the lawn. A belated couple on a nearby path stared at him with amazement, and this brought some sense to his head and he slowed down and came to a stop. Back at the building, everything looked as usual, and in spite of his terror, Gnut was not chasing him.

He was still in his stockinged feet. Breathing heavily, he sat down on the wet grass and put on his shoes; then he stood and looked at the building, trying to pull himself together. What an incredible melange! The dead Stillwell, the dead gorilla, and the dead mockingbird—all dying before his eyes. And then that last frightening thing, the second dead Stillwell whom he had *not* seen die. And Gnut's strange gentleness, and the sad expression he had twice seen on his face.

As he looked, the grounds about the building came to life. Several people collected at the door of the wing, above sounded the siren of a police copter, then in the distance another, and from all sides people came running, a few at first, then more and more. The police planes landed on the lawn just outside the door of the wing, and he thought he could see the officers peeping inside. Then suddenly the lights of the wing flooded on. In control of himself now, Cliff went back.

He entered. He had left Gnut standing in thought at the side of the ramp, but now he was again in his old familiar pose in the usual place, as if he had never moved. The ship's door was closed, and the ramp gone. But the bodies, the four strangely assorted bodies, were still lying by the demolished robot attendants where he had left them in the dark.

He was startled by a cry behind his back. A uniformed museum guard was pointing at him.

"This is the man!" the guard shouted. "When I opened the door this man forced his way out and ran like the devil!"

The police officers converged on Cliff.

"Who are you? What is all this?" one of them asked him roughly.

"I'm Cliff Sutherland, picture reporter," Cliff answered calmly. "And I was the one who was inside here and ran away, as the guard says."

"What were you doing?" the officer asked, eyeing him. "And where did these bodies come from?"

"Gentlemen, I'd tell you gladly—only business first," Cliff answered. "There's been some fantastic goings on in this room, and I saw them and have the story, but"—he smiled—"I must decline to answer without advice of counsel until I've sold my story to one of the news syndicates. You know how it is. If you'd allow me the use of the radio in your plane—just for a moment, gentlemen—you'll have the whole story right afterward—say in half an hour, when the television men broadcast it. Meanwhile, believe me, there's nothing for you to do, and there'll be no loss by the delay."

The officer who had asked the questions blinked, and one of the others, quicker to react and certainly not a gentleman, stepped toward Cliff with clenched fists. Cliff disarmed him by handing him his press credentials. He glanced at them rapidly and put them in his pocket.

By now half a hundred people were there, and among them were two members of a syndicate crew whom he knew, arrived by copter. The police growled, but they let him whisper in their ear and then go out under escort to the crew's plane. There, by radio, in five minutes, Cliff made a deal which would bring him more money than he had ever before earned in a year. After that he turned over all his pictures and negatives to the crew and gave them the story, and they lost not one second in spinning back to their office with the flash.

More and more people arrived, and the police cleared the building. Ten minutes later a big crew of radio and television men forced their way in, sent there by the syndicate with which he had dealt. And then a few minutes later, under the glaring lights set up by the operators and standing close by the ship and not far from Gnut—he refused to stand underneath him—Cliff gave his story to the cameras and microphones, which in a fraction of a second shot it to every corner of the solar system.

Immediately afterward the police took him to jail. On general principles and because they were pretty blooming mad.

## V

Cliff stayed in jail all that night—until eight o'clock the next morning, when the syndicate finally succeeded in digging up a lawyer and got him out. And then, when at last he was leaving, a Federal man caught him by the wrist.

"You're wanted for further questioning over at the Continental Bureau of Investigation," the agent told him. Cliff went along willingly.

Fully thirty-five high-ranking Federal officials and "big names" were waiting for him in an imposing conference room—one of the president's secretaries, the undersecretary of state, the underminister of defense, scientists, a colonel, executives, department heads, and ranking "C" men. Old gray-mustached Sanders, chief of the CBI, was presiding.

They made him tell his story all over again, and then, in parts, all over once more—not because they did not believe him, but because they kept hoping to elicit some fact which would cast significant light on the mystery of Gnut's behavior and the happenings of the last three nights. Patiently Cliff racked his brains for every detail.

Chief Sanders asked most of the questions. After more than an hour, when Cliff thought they had finished, Sanders asked him several more, all involving his personal opinions of what had transpired.

"Do you think Gnut was deranged in any way by the

acids, rays, heat, and so forth applied to him by the scientists?"

"I saw no evidence of it."

"Do you think he can see?"

"I'm sure he can see, or else has other powers which are equivalent."

"Do you think he can hear?"

"Yes, sir. That time when I whispered to him that Stillwell was dead, he bent lower, as if to see for himself. I would not be surprised if he also understood what I said."

"At no time did he speak, except those sounds he made to open the ship?"

"Not one word, in English or any other language. Not one sound with his mouth."

"In your opinion, has his strength been impaired in any way by our treatment?" asked one of the scientists.

"I have told you how easily he handled the gorilla. He attacked the animal and threw it back, after which it retreated all the way down the building, afraid of him."

"How would you explain the fact that our autopsies disclosed no mortal wound, no cause of death, in any of the bodies—gorilla, mockingbird, or the two identical Stillwells?"—this from a medical officer.

"I can't."

"You think Gnut is dangerous?"—from Sanders.

"Potentially very dangerous."

"Yet you say you have the feeling he is not hostile."

"To me, I meant. I do have that feeling, and I'm afraid that I can't give any good reason for it, except the way he spared me twice when he had me in his power. I think maybe the gentle way he handled the bodies had something to do with it, and maybe the sad, thoughtful look I twice caught on his face."

"Would you risk staying in the building alone another night?"

"Not for anything." There were smiles.

"Did you get any pictures of what happened last night?"

"No, sir." Cliff, with an effort, held on to his composure, but he was swept by a wave of shame. A man hitherto silent rescued him by saying:

"A while ago you used the word 'purposive' in connection with Gnut's actions. Can you explain that a little?"

"Yes, that was one of the things that struck me: Gnut never seems to waste a motion. He can move with surprising speed when he wants to; I saw that when he attacked the gorilla; but most other times he walks around as if methodically completing some simple task. And that reminds me of a peculiar thing: at times he gets into one position, any position, maybe half bent over, and stays there for minutes at a time. It's as if his scale of time values was eccentric, compared to ours; some things he does surprisingly fast, and others surprisingly slow. This might account for his long periods of immobility."

"That's very interesting," said one of the scientists. "How would you account for the fact that he recently moves only at night?"

"I think he's doing something he wants no one to see, and the night is the only time he is alone."

"But he went ahead even after finding you there."

"I know. But I have no other explanation, unless he considered me harmless or unable to stop him—which was certainly the case."

"Before you arrived, we were considering encasing him in a large block of glasstex. Do you think he would permit it?"

"I don't know. Probably he would; he stood for the acids and rays and heat. But it had better be done in the daytime; night seems to be the time he moves."

"But he moved in the daytime when he emerged from the traveler with Klaatu."

"I know."

That seemed to be all they could think of to ask him. Sanders slapped his hand on the table.

"Well, I guess that's all Mr. Sutherland," he said. "Thank you for your help, and let me congratulate you for a very foolish, stubborn, brave young man—young businessman." He smiled very faintly. "You are free to go now, but it may be that I'll have to call you back later. We'll see."

"May I remain while you decide about that glasstex?" Cliff asked. "As long as I'm here I'd like to have the tip."

"The decision has already been made—the tip's yours. The pouring will be started at once."

"Thank you, sir," said Cliff—and calmly asked more: "And will you be so kind as to authorize me to be present outside the building tonight? Just outside. I've a feeling something's going to happen."

"You want still another scoop, I see," said Sanders not

unkindly, "then you'll let the police wait while you transact your business."

"Not again, sir. If anything happens, they'll get it at once."

The chief hesitated. "I don't know," he said. "I'll tell you what. All the news services will want men there, and we can't have that; but if you can arrange to represent them all yourself, it's a go. Nothing's going to happen, but your reports will help calm the hysterical ones. Let me know."

Cliff thanked him and hurried out and phoned his syndicate the tip—free—then told them Sanders' proposal. Ten minutes later they called him back, said all was arranged, and told him to catch some sleep. They would cover the pouring. With light heart, Cliff hurried over to the museum. The place was surrounded by thousands of the curious, held far back by a strong cordon of police. For once he could not get through; he was recognized, and the police were still sore. But he did not care much; he suddenly felt very tired and needed that nap. He went back to his hotel, left a call, and went to bed.

He had been asleep only a few minutes when his phone rang. Eyes shut, he answered it. It was one of the boys at the syndicate, with peculiar news. Stillwell had just reported, very much alive—the real Stillwell. The two dead ones were some kind of copies; he couldn't imagine how to explain them. He had no brothers.

For a moment Cliff came fully awake, then he went back to bed. Nothing was fantastic any more.

## VI

At four o'clock, much refreshed and with an infrared viewing magnifier slung over his shoulder, Cliff passed through the cordon and entered the door of the wing. He had been expected and there was no trouble. As his eyes fell on Gnut, an odd feeling went through him, and for some obscure reason he was almost sorry for the giant robot.

Gnut stood exactly as he had always stood, the right foot advanced a little, and the same brooding expression on his face; but now there was something more. He was solidly encased in a huge block of transparent glasstex. From the floor on which he stood to the top of his full eight feet, and from there on up for an equal distance, and for about eight feet to the left, right, back, and front, he was immured in a water-clear prison which confined every inch of his surface and would prevent the slightest twitch of even his amazing muscles.

It was absurd, no doubt, to feel sorry for a robot, a man-made mechanism, but Cliff had come to think of him as being really alive, as a human is alive. He showed purpose and will; he performed complicated and resourceful acts; his face had twice clearly shown the emotion of sadness, and several times what appeared to be deep thought; he had been ruthless with the gorilla, and gentle with the mockingbird and the other two bodies, and he had twice refrained from crushing Cliff when there seemed every reason that he might. Cliff did not doubt for a minute that he was still alive, whatever that "alive" might mean.

But outside were waiting the radio and television men; he had work to do. He turned and went to them and all got busy.

An hour later Cliff sat alone about fifteen feet above the ground in a big tree which, located just across the walk from the building, commanded through a window a clear view of the upper part of Gnut's body. Strapped to the limbs about him were three instruments—his infrared viewing magnifier, a radio mike, and an infrared television eye with sound pickup. The first, the viewing magnifier, would allow him to see in the dark with his own eyes, as if by daylight, a magnified image of the robot, and the others would pick up any sights and sounds, including his own remarks, and transmit them to the several broadcast studios which would fling them millions of miles in all directions through space. Never before had a picture man had such an important assignment, probably—certainly not one who forgot to take pictures. But now that was forgotten, and Cliff was quite proud, and ready.

Far back in a great circle stood a multitude of the curious—and the fearful. Would the plastic glasstex hold Gnut? If it did not, would he come out thirsting for revenge? Would unimaginable beings come out of the traveler and release him, and perhaps exact revenge? Millions at their receivers were jittery; those in the distance hoped nothing awful would happen, yet they hoped something would, and they were prepared to run.

In carefully selected spots not far from Cliff on all sides were mobile ray batteries manned by army units, and in a hollow in back of him, well to his right, there was stationed a huge tank with a large gun. Every weapon was trained on the door of the wing. A row of smaller, faster tanks stood ready fifty yards directly north. Their ray projectors were aimed at the door, but not their guns. The grounds about the building contained only one spot—the hollow where the great tank was—where, by close calculation, a shell directed at the doorway would not cause damage and loss of life to some part of the sprawling capital.

Dusk fell; out streamed the last of the army officers, politicians, and other privileged ones; the great metal doors of the wing clanged to and were locked for the night. Soon Cliff was alone, except for the watchers at their weapons scattered around him.

Hours passed. The moon came out. From time to time Cliff reported to the studio crew that all was quiet. His unaided eyes could now see nothing of Gnut but the two faint red points of his eyes, but through the magnifier he stood out as clearly as if in daylight from an apparent distance of only ten feet. Except for his eyes, there was no evidence that he was anything but dead and unfunctionable metal.

Another hour passed. Now and again Cliff thumbed the levels of his tiny radio-television watch—only a few seconds at a time because of its limited battery. The air was full of Gnut and his own face and his own name, and once the tiny screen showed the tree in which he was then sitting and even, minutely, himself. Powerful infrared long-distance television pickups were even then focused on him from nearby points of vantage. It gave him a funny feeling.

Then, suddenly, Cliff saw something and quickly bent his eye to the viewing magnifier. Gnut's eyes were moving; at least the intensity of the light emanating from them varied. It was as if two tiny red flashlights were turned from side to side, their beams at each motion crossing Cliff's eyes.

Thrilling, Cliff signaled the studios, cut in his pickups, and described the phenomenon. Millions resonated to the excitement in his voice. Could Gnut conceivably break out of that terrible prison?

Minutes passed, the eye flashes continued, but Cliff could discern no movement or attempted movement of the robot's body. In brief snatches he described what he saw. Gnut was clearly alive; there could be no doubt he was straining against the transparent prison in which he had at last been locked fast; but unless he could crack it, no motion should show.

Cliff took his eye from the magnifier—and started. His

unaided eye, looking at Gnut shrouded in darkness, saw an astonishing thing not yet visible through his instrument. A faint red glow was spreading over the robot's body. With trembling fingers he readjusted the lens of the television eye, but even as he did so the glow grew in intensity. It looked as if Gnut's body were being heated to incandescence!

He described it in excited fragments, for it took most of his attention to keep correcting the lens. Gnut passed from a figure of dull red to one brighter and brighter, clearly glowing now even through the magnifier. And then he moved! Unmistakably he moved!

He had within himself somehow the means to raise his own body temperature, and was exploiting the one limitation of the plastic in which he was locked. For glasstex, Cliff now remembered, was a thermoplastic material, one that set by cooling and conversely would soften again with heat. Gnut was melting his way out!

In three-word snatches, Cliff described this. The robot became cherry-red, the sharp edges of the icelike block rounded, and the whole structure began to sag. The process accelerated. The robot's body moved more widely. The plastic lowered to the crown of his head, then to his neck, then his waist, which was as far as Cliff could see. His body was free! And then, still cherry-red, he moved forward out of sight!

Cliff strained eyes and ears, but caught nothing but the distant roar of the watchers beyond the police lines and a few low, sharp commands from the batteries posted around him. They, too, had heard, and perhaps seen by telescreen, and were waiting.

Several minutes passed. There was a sharp, ringing crack; the great metal doors of the wing flew open, and out stepped the metal giant, glowing no longer. He stood stockstill, and his red eyes pierced from side to side through the darkness.

Voices out in the dark barked orders and in a twinkling Gnut was bathed in narrow crisscrossing rays of sizzling, colored light. Behind him the metal doors began to melt, but his great green body showed no change at all. Then the world seemed to come to an end; there was a deafening roar, everything before Cliff seemed to explode in smoke and chaos, his tree whipped to one side so that he was nearly thrown out. Pieces of debris rained down. The tank gun had spoken, and Gnut, he was sure, had been hit.

Cliff held on tight and peered into the haze. As it cleared he made out a stirring among the debris at the door, and then dimly but unmistakably he saw the great form of Gnut rise to his feet. He got up slowly, turned toward the tank, and suddenly darted toward it in a wide arc. The big gun swung in an attempt to cover him, but the robot side-stepped and then was upon it. As the crew scattered, he destroyed its breech with one blow of his fist, and then he turned and looked right at Cliff.

He moved toward him, and in a moment was under the tree. Cliff climbed higher. Gnut put his two arms around the tree and gave a lifting push, and the tree tore out at the roots and fell crashing to its side. Before Cliff could scramble away, the robot had lifted him in his metal hands.

Cliff thought his time had come, but strange things were yet in store for him that night. Gnut did not hurt him. He looked at him from arm's length for a moment, then lifted him to a sitting position on his shoulders, legs straddling his neck. Then, holding one ankle, he turned and without hesitation started down the path which led westward away from the building.

Cliff rode helpless. Out over the lawns he saw the muzzles of the scattered field pieces move as he moved, Gnut—and himself—their one focus. But they did not fire. Gnut, by placing him on his shoulders, had secured himself against that—Cliff hoped.

The robot bore straight toward the Tidal Basin. Most of the field pieces throbbed slowly after. Far back, Cliff saw a dark tide of confusion roll into the cleared area—the police lines had broken. Ahead, the ring thinned rapidly off to the sides; then, from all directions but the front, the tide rolled in until individual shouts and cries could be made out. It came to a stop about fifty yards off, and few people ventured nearer.

Gnut paid them no attention, and he no more noticed his burden than he might a fly. His neck and shoulders made Cliff a seat hard as steel, but with the difference that their underlying muscles with each movement flexed, just as would those of a human being. To Cliff, this metal musculature became a vivid wonder.

Straight as the flight of a bee, over paths, across lawns and through thin rows of trees Gnut bore the young man, the roar of thousands of people following close. Above droned copters and darting planes, among them police cars with their nerve-shattering sirens. Just ahead lay the still waters of the Tidal Basin, and in its midst the simple marble tomb of the slain ambassador, Klaatu, gleaming black and cold in the light of the dozen searchlights always trained on it at night. Was this a rendezvous with the dead?

Without an instant's hesitation, Gnut strode down the bank and entered the water. It rose to his knees, then waist, until Cliff's feet were under. Straight through the dark waters for the tomb of Klaatu the robot made his inevitable way.

The dark square mass of gleaming marble rose higher as they neared it. Gnut's body began emerging from the water as the bottom shelved upward, until his dripping feet took the first of the rising pyramid of steps. In a moment they were at the top, on the narrow platform in the middle of which rested the simple oblong tomb.

Stark in the blinding searchlights, the giant robot walked once around it, then, bending, he braced himself and gave a mighty push against the top. The marble cracked; the thick cover slipped askew and broke with a loud noise on the far side. Gnut went to his knees and looked within, bringing Cliff well up over the edge.

Inside, in sharp shadow against the converging light beams, lay a transparent plastic coffin, thick walled and sealed against the centuries, and containing all that was mortal of Klaatu, unspoken visitor from the great Unknown. He lay as if asleep, on his face the look of godlike nobility that had caused some of the ignorant to believe him divine. He wore the robe he had arrived in. There were no faded flowers, no jewelry, no ornaments; they would have seemed profane. At the foot of the coffin lay the small sealed box, also of transparent plastic, which contained all of Earth's records of his visit—a description of the events attending his arrival, pictures of Gnut and the traveler, and the little roll of sight-and-sound film which had caught for all time his few brief motions and words.

Cliff sat very still, wishing he could see the face of the robot. Gnut, too, did not move from his position of reverent contemplation—not for a long time. There on the brilliantly lighted pyramid, under the eyes of a fearful, tumultuous multitude, Gnut paid final respect to his beautiful and adored master.

Suddenly, then, it was over. Gnut reached out and took the

little box of records, rose to his feet and started down the steps.

Back through the water, straight back to the building, across lawns and paths as before, he made his irresistible way. Before him the chaotic ring of people melted away, behind they followed as close as they dared, trampling each other in their efforts to keep him in sight. There are no television records of his return. Every pickup was damaged on the way to the tomb.

As they drew near the building, Cliff saw that the tank's projectile had made a hole twenty feet wide extending from the roof to the ground. The door still stood open, and Gnut, hardly varying his almost jerkless rhythm, made his way over the debris and went straight for the port end of the ship. Cliff wondered if he would be set free.

He was. The robot set him down and pointed toward the door; then, turning, he made the sounds that opened the ship. The ramp slid down and he entered.

Then Cliff did the mad, courageous thing which made him famous for a generation. Just as the ramp started sliding back in he skipped over it and himself entered the ship. The port closed.

## VII

It was pitch dark, and the silence was absolute. Cliff did not move. He felt that Gnut was close, just ahead, and it was so.

His hard metal hand took him by the waist, pulled him against his cold side, and carried him somewhere ahead. Hidden lamps suddenly bathed the surroundings with bluish light.

He set Cliff down and stood looking at him. The young man already regretted his rash action, but the robot, except for his always unfathomable eyes, did not seem angry. He pointed to a stool in one corner of the room. Cliff quickly obeyed this time and sat meekly, for a while not even venturing to look around.

He saw he was in a small laboratory of some kind. Complicated metal and plastic apparatus lined the walls and filled several small tables; he could not recognize or guess the function of a single piece. Dominating the center of the room was a long metal table on whose top lay a large box, much like a coffin on the outside, connected by many wires to a complicated apparatus at the far end. From close above spread a cone of bright light from a many-tubed lamp.

One thing, half covered on a nearby table, did look familiar—and very much out of place. From where he sat it seemed to be a briefcase—an ordinary Earthman's briefcase. He wondered.

Gnut paid him no attention, but at once, with the narrow edge of a thick tool, sliced the lid off the little box of records. He lifted out the strip of sight-and-sound film and spent fully half an hour adjusting it within the apparatus at the end of the big table. Cliff watched, fascinated, wondering at the skill with which the robot used his tough metal fingers. This done, Gnut worked for a long time over some accessory apparatus on an adjoining table. Then he paused thoughtfully a moment and pushed inward a long rod.

A voice came out of the coffinlike box—the voice of the slain ambassador.

"I am Klaatu," it said, "and this is Gnut."

From the recording!—flashed through Cliff's mind. The first and only words the ambassador had spoken. But, then, in the very next second he saw that it was not so. There was a man in the box! The man stirred and sat up, and Cliff saw the living face of Klaatu!

Klaatu appeared somewhat surprised and spoke quickly in an unknown tongue to Gnut—and Gnut, for the first time in Cliff's experience, spoke himself in answer. The robot's syllables tumbled out as if born of human emotion, and the expression on Klaatu's face changed from surprise to wonder. They talked for several minutes. Klaatu, apparently fatigued, then began to lie down, but stopped midway, for he saw Cliff. Gnut spoke again, at length. Klaatu beckoned Cliff with his hand, and he went to him.

"Gnut has told me everything," he said in a low, gentle voice, then looked at Cliff for a moment in silence, on his face a faint, tired smile.

Cliff had a hundred questions to ask, but for a moment hardly dared open his mouth.

"But you," he began at last—very respectfully, but with an escaping excitement—"you are not the Klaatu that was in the tomb?"

The man's smile faded and he shook his head.

"No." He turned to the towering Gnut and said something in his own tongue, and at his words the metal features of the robot twisted as if with pain. Then he turned back to Cliff. "I am dying," he announced simply, as if repeating his words for the Earthman. Again to his face came the faint, tired smile.

Cliff's tongue was locked. He just stared, hoping for light. Klaatu seemed to read his mind.

"I see you don't understand," he said. "Although unlike us, Gnut has great powers. When the wing was built and the lectures began, there came to him a striking inspiration. Acting on it at once, in the night, he assembled this apparatus . . . and now he has made me again, from my voice, as recorded by your people. As you must know, a given body makes a characteristic sound. He constructed an apparatus which reversed the recording process, and from the given sound made the characteristic body."

Cliff gasped. So that was it!

"But you needn't die!" Cliff exclaimed suddenly, eagerly. "Your voice recording was taken when you stepped out of the ship, while you were well! You must let me take you to a hospital! Our doctors are very skillful!"

Hardly perceptibly, Klaatu shook his head.

"You still don't understand," he said slowly and more faintly. "Your recording had imperfections. Perhaps very slight ones, but they doom the product. All of Gnut's experiments died in a few minutes, he tells me . . . and so must I."

Suddenly, then, Cliff understood the origin of the "experiments." He remembered that on the day the wing was opened a Smithsonian official had lost a briefcase containing film strips recording the speech of various world fauna. There, on that table, was a briefcase! And the Stillwells must have been made from strips kept in the table drawer!

But his heart was heavy. He did not want this stranger to die. Slowly there dawned on him an important idea. He explained it with growing excitement.

"You say the recording was imperfect, and of course it was. But the cause of that lay in the use of an imperfect recording apparatus. So if Gnut, in his reversal of the process, had used exactly the same pieces of apparatus that your voice was recorded with, the imperfections could be studied, canceled out, and you'd live, and not die!"

As the last words left his lips, Gnut whipped around like a cat and gripped him tight. A truly human excitement was shining in the metal muscles of his face.

"Get me that apparatus!" he ordered—in clear and perfect

English! He started pushing Cliff toward the door, but Klaatu raised his hand.

"There is no hurry," Klaatu said gently; "it is too late for me. What is your name, young man?"

Cliff told him.

"Stay with me to the end," he asked. Klaatu closed his eyes and rested; then, smiling just a little, but not opening his eyes, he added: "And don't be sad, for I shall now perhaps live again . . . and it will be due to you. There is no pain—" His voice was rapidly growing weaker. Cliff, for all the questions he had, could only look on, dumb. Again Klaatu seemed to be aware of his thoughts.

"I know," he said feebly, "I know. We have so much to ask each other. About your civilization . . . and Gnut's—"

"And yours," said Cliff.

"And Gnut's," said the gentle voice again. "Perhaps . . . some day . . . perhaps I will be back—"

He lay without moving. He lay so for a long time, and at last Cliff knew that he was dead. Tears came to his eyes; in only these few minutes he had come to love this man. He looked at Gnut. The robot knew, too, that he was dead, but no tears filled his red-lighted eyes; they were fixed on Cliff, and for once the young man knew what was in his mind.

"Gnut," he announced earnestly, as if taking a sacred oath, "I'll get the original apparatus. I'll get it. Every piece of it, the exact same things."

Without a word, Gnut conducted him to the port. He made the sounds that unlocked it. As it opened, a noisy crowd of Earthmen outside trampled each other in a sudden scramble to get out of the building. The wing was lighted. Cliff stepped down the ramp.

The next two hours always in Cliff's memory had a dreamlike quality. It was as if that mysterious laboratory with the peacefully sleeping dead man was the real and central part of his life, and his scene with the noisy men with whom he talked a gross and barbaric interlude. He stood not far from the ramp. He told only part of his story. He was believed. He waited quietly while all the pressure which the highest officials in the land could exert was directed toward obtaining for him the appartus the robot had demanded.

When it arrived, he carried it to the floor of the little vestibule behind the port. Gnut was there, as if waiting. In his arms he held the slender body of the second Klaatu. Tenderly he passed him out to Cliff, who took him without a word, as if all this had been arranged. It seemed to be the parting.

Of all the things Cliff had wanted to say to Klaatu, one remained imperatively present in his mind. Now, as the green metal robot stood framed in the great green ship, he seized his chance.

"Gnut," he said earnestly, holding carefully the limp body in his arms, "you must do one thing for me. Listen carefully. I want you to tell your master—the master yet to come—that what happened to the first Klaatu was an accident, for which all Earth is immeasurably sorry. Will you do that?"

"I have known it," the robot answered gently.

"But will you promise to tell your master—just those words—as soon as he is arrived?"

"You misunderstand," said Gnut, still gently, and quietly spoke four more words. As Cliff heard them a mist passed over his eyes and his body went numb.

As he recovered and his eyes came back to focus he saw the great ship disappear. It just suddenly was not there any more. He fell back a step or two. In his ears, like great bells, rang Gnut's last words. Never, never was he to disclose them till the day he came to die.

"You misunderstand," the mighty robot had said. "I am the master."

# BUTYL AND THE BREATHER

*Astounding Science Fiction*

October

## by Theodore Sturgeon

*Sequels are almost invariably disappointing. The fire and drive that produced the first story is extremely difficult to replicate and the reader's expectations are usually too high to satisfy. This story, which is a sequel to Sturgeon's first published work ("Ether Breather"—see Volume One of this series), is one of the rare exceptions.*

(I was still not old enough to vote in 1940—in those days voting age was 21. All the great writers whom I was envying and worshipping and trying to emulate were older than I was, and to my dazzled eyes *much* older. I suppose that was, in part, a bit of self-protection on my part. It excused their superiority to me and saved me from unbearable humiliation. And yet Ted Sturgeon, who was burning up the sf track in this year was only 22 years old in 1940. It's a lucky thing 22 seemed quite mature to me at the time, or I might have crawled into a hole and pulled it in after me. —I.A.)

I was still melancholic about chasing the Ether Breather out of the ken of man, the day I got that bright idea of bringing the Breather back. I should have let it stay in idea form. I should not have gone to see Berbelot about it. I also should have stayed in bed. I've got brains, but no sense. I went to see Berbelot.

He wasn't glad to see me, which he did through the televisor in his foyer. Quite a gadget, that foyer. I knew that it was an elevator to take guests up to his quarters in the mansion, the "House that Perfume Built." I hadn't known till now that it was also a highly efficient bouncing mechanism. I had no sooner passed my hand over the sensitized plate that served as a doorbell when his face appeared on the screen. He said "Hmph! Hamilton!" and next thing I knew the foyer's walls had extended and pinned me tight. I was turned upside down, shaken twice, and then dropped on my ear outside the house. I think he designed that bouncer just for me. He was a nice old boy, but, man, how he could hang on to a grouch. A whole year, this one had lasted. Just because I had been tactless with the Breather.

I got up and dusted myself off and swore I'd never bother the irascible old heel again. And then I hunted a drugstore to call him up. That's the way it was. Berbelot was a peculiar duck. His respect for me meant more than anger against him could make up for. He was the only man I ever met that ever made me sorry for anything.

I went into the visiphone booth and pressed my identification tab against the resilient panel on the phone. That made a record of the call so I could be billed for it. Then I dialed Berbelot. I got his bun-faced valet.

"I want to speak to Mr. Berbelot, Cogan."

"Mr. Berbelot is out, Mr. Hamilton."

"So!" I snapped, my voice rising. "You're the one who tossed me out just now with that salesman mangler on your doorstep! I'll macerate you, you subatomic idiot!"

"Oh . . . I . . . I didn't, Mr. Hamilton, really. I—"

"Then if you didn't Berbelot did. If he did, he's home. Incidentally, I saw him in the viewplate. Enough of the chit-chat, doughface. Tell him I want to speak to him."

"B-but he won't speak to you, Mr. Hamilton. He gave strict orders a year ago."

"Tell him I've thought of a way to get in touch with the Ether Breather again. Go on. He won't fire you, you crumb from the breadline. He'll kiss you on both cheeks. Snap into it!"

The screen went vacant as he moved away, and I heard Berbelot's voice—"I thought I told you"—and then the bumble of Cogan's, and then "WHAT!" from the old man, and another short bumble that was interrupted by Berbelot's sliding to a stop in front of the transmitter. "Hamilton," he said sternly into the visiplate, "if this is a joke of yours . . . if you think you can worm your way into my confidence with . . . if you dare to lead me on some wild-goose cha . . . if you—"

"If you'll give me a chance, King of Stink," I said, knowing that if I got him really mad he'd listen to me, being the type that got speechless with rage, "I'll give you the dope. I have an idea that I think will bring the Breather back, but it's up to you to carry it out. You have the apparatus."

"Come up," he whispered, his wattles quivering. "But I warn you, if you dare to take this liberty on a bluff, I shall most certainly have you pried loose from your esophagus."

"Comin' up!" I said. "By the way, when I get into that foyer again, please be sure which button you push."

"Don't worry," he growled, "I have a dingus up here that is quite as efficient. It throws people from the sixtieth floor. Do come up." The screen darkened. I sighed and started for the "House that Perfume Built."

The elevator glided to a stop that made my stomach feel puffy, and I stepped out. Berbelot was standing in front of it looking suspicious as a pawnbroker. I held out my hand with some remark about how swell it was to see him again, and he just stared at it. When I thought he was going to forego the honor of shaking it, he put his hand into mine, withdrew it quickly, looked at it, and wiped it carefully on his jacket. Without his saying a word I gathered that he wasn't glad to see me, that he thought I was an undesirable and unsanitary character, and that he didn't trust me.

"Did I ever tell you," I said as calmly as I could, "that I am terribly sorry about what happened?"

Berbelot said, "I knew a man who said that after he murdered somebody. They burned him anyway."

I thought that was very nice. "Do you want to find out about my idea or not?" I gritted. "I don't have to stay here to be insulted."

"I realize that. You're insulted everywhere, I imagine. Well, what's your idea?"

I saw Cogan hovering over the old man's shoulder and threw my hat at him. Since Berbelot apparently found it difficult to be hospitable, I saved him the trouble of inviting me to sit down by sitting down.

"Berbelot," I said, when I had one of his best cigarettes fuming as nicely as he was, "you're being unreasonable. But I have you interested, and as long as that lasts you'll be sociable. Sit down. I am about to be Socratic. It may take a little while."

"I suffer." He sat down. "I suffer exceedingly." He paused, and then added pensively, "I never thought I could be so irritated by anyone who bored me. Go ahead, Hamilton."

I closed my eyes and counted ten. Berbelot could manufacture more printable invective than anyone I ever met.

"Question one," I said. "What is the nature of the creature you dubbed Ether Breather?"

"Why, it's a . . . well, apparently a combination of etheric forces, living in and around us. It's as if the air in this room were a thinking animal. What are you—"

"I'll ask questions. Now, will you grant it intelligence?"

"Of course. A peculiar kind, though. It seems to be motivated by a childish desire to have fun—mostly at some poor human's expense."

"But its reactions were reasonable, weren't they?"

"Yes, although exaggerated. It reached us through color television; that was its only medium of expression. And it raised particular hell with the programs—a cosmic practical joker, quite uninhibited, altogether unafraid of any consequences to itself. And then when you, you blockhead, told it that it had hurt someone's feelings and that it ought to get off the air, it apologized and was never heard from again. Again an exaggerated reaction. But what has that got to do with—"

"Everything. Look; you made it laugh easily. You made it ashamed of itself easily. It cried easily. If you really want to get in touch with it again, you just have to go on from there."

Berbelot pressed a concealed button and the lights took on a greenish cast. He always claimed a man thought more clearly under a green light. "I'll admit that that particular thought sequence has escaped me," he nodded, "since I do not have a mind which is led astray by illogical obscurities. But in all justice to you—not that you deserve anything approaching a compliment—I think you have something there. I suppose that is as far as you have gone, though. I've spent hours on the problem. I've called that creature for days on end on a directional polychrome wave. I've apologized to it and pleaded with it and begged it and told it funny stories and practically asked it to put its invisible feet out of my television receiver so I could kiss them. And never a whisper have I had. No, Hamilton; the Ether Breather is definitely miffed, peeved, and not at home. And it's all your fault."

"Once," I said dreamily, "I knew a woman whose husband went astray. She knew where he was, and sent him message after message. She begged and she pleaded and she wept into visiphones. It didn't get her anywhere. Then she got a bright idea. She sent him a tele-facsimile letter, written on her very best stationery. It described in great detail the nineteen different kinds of heel she thought he was."

"I don't know what this has to do with the Breather, but what happened?" asked Berbelot.

"Why, he got sore. He got so sore he dropped everything and ran home to take a poke at her!"

"Ah," said Berbelot. "And the Breather laughs easily, and you think it would—"

"It would," I nodded, "get angry easily, if we could find the right way to do it."

Berbelot rubbed his long hands together and beamed. "You're a hot-headed fool, Hamilton, and I'm convinced that your genius is a happy accident quite unattached to your hypothetical mind. But I must congratulate you for the idea. In other words, you think if we get the Breather sore enough, it will try to get even, and contact us some way or other? I'll be darned!"

"Thought you'd like it," I said.

"Well, come on," he said testily. "What are we waiting for? Let's go down to the laboratory!" Suddenly he stopped. "Er . . . Hamilton . . . this story of yours. Did that man poke his wife after he got home?"

"I dunno," I said blankly. "I just made up the story to illustrate my point. Could be."

"Hm-m-m. If the Breather decided to . . . I mean, it's a big creature, you know, and we have no idea—"

"Oh, never mind that," I laughed, "the Breather can't get past a television screen!"

Which only goes to show you how little I knew about the Ether Breather.

I was amazed by Berbelot's laboratory museum. Did you know that in the old days more than two hundred years ago, they used electrically powered sets with a ground glass, fluorescent screen built right into the end of huge cathode tubes? Imagine. And before that, they used a revolving disk with holes punctured spirally, as a scanning mechanism! They had the beginnings of frequency modulation, though. But their sets were so crude, incredible as it may seem, that atmospheric disturbances caused interference in reception! Berbelot had copies of all these old and laughable attempts at broadcasting and receiving devices.

"All right, all right," he snapped, elbow-deep in one of the first polychrome transmitters, "you've been here before. Come over here and give me a hand. You're gawking like a castor bean farmer."

I went over and followed his directions as he spot-welded, relayed, and wound a coil or two of hair-fine wire. "My gosh," I marveled, "how did you ever learn so much about television, Berbelot? I imagine it must have used up a little of your spare time to make a fortune in the perfume business."

He laughed. "I'll tell you, Hamilton," he said. "Television and perfumery are very much alike. You know yourself that no such lovely women ever walk the Earth as you see every day in the news broadcasts. For the last eighty years, since the Duval shade selector was introduced, television has given flawless complexions to all the ladies that come over the air, and bull-shoulders to all the men. It's all very phony, but it's nice to look at. Perfumery is the same proposition. A woman who smelled like a rose petal naturally would undoubtedly have something the matter with her. But science gets to work on what has been termed, through the ages, as 'B.O.' My interest in esthetically deluding the masses led me to both sciences."

"Very ingenious," I said, "but it isn't going to help you to make the Breather sore."

"My dear boy," he said, "don't be obtuse. Oh, turn down the nitrogen jets a trifle—that's it." He skillfully spotted seven leads into the video-circuit of the polychrome wave generator. "You see," he went on, running the leads over to a box control with five push buttons and a rheostat set into it, "the Breather requires very special handling. It knows us and how our minds work, or it could never have thought, for instance, of having our secretary of state recite risqué verse over the air, the first time that official used color television. Now, you are noteworthy for your spontaneity. How would you go about angering this puff of etheric wind?"

"Well, I'd . . . I'd tell it it was a dirty so-and-so. I'd insult it. I'd say it was a sissy and dare it to fight. I . . . I'd—"

"That's what I thought," said Berbelot unkindly. "You'd cuss it out in your own foul idiom, forgetting that it has no pride to take down, and, as far as we know, no colleagues, communities, enamoratae, or fellows to gossip to. No, Hamilton, we can't insult it. It can insult us because it knows what we are and how we think, but we know nothing of it."

"How else can you get a being sore, then, when you can't hold it up to ridicule or censure before itself or its fellow creatures?"

"By doing something to it personally that it won't like."

"Yeah—take a poke at it. Kick it in its vibrations. Stick a knife into its multiple personality."

Berbelot laughed. "To change the subject, for no apparent reason," he said, "have you ever run across my *Vierge Folle?*"

"A new perfume? Why, no."

Berbelot crossed the room and came back with a handful of tiny vials. "Here."

I sniffed. It was a marvelously delicate scent. It was subtle, smooth, calling up a mental picture of the veins in fine ivory. "Mmm. Nice."

"Try this one," he said. I did. It was fainter than the other; I had to draw in a lot of it before I detected the sweet, faint odor. "It's called *Casuiste*," said Berbelot. "Now try this one. It's much fainter, you'll have to really stretch to get it at all."

"Nice business," I grinned. "Making the poor unsuspecting male get inside the circle of the vixen's arms before he's under her spell." I'd been reading some of his ad proofs. He chuckled. "That's about the idea. Here."

Berbelot handed me the vial and I expelled all the air in my lungs, hung my nose over the lip of the tube and let the air in with a roar. Next thing I knew I was strangling, staggering, swearing and letting go murderous rights and lefts at empty air. I thought I was going to die and I wished I could. When I blinked the tears out of my eyes, Berbelot was nowhere to be seen. I raged around the laboratory and finally saw him whisk around behind a massive old photoelectric transmitter. With a shriek I rushed him. He got practically inside the machine and I began taking it apart, with the firm conviction that I would keep on taking things apart long after I reached him. Luckily for him there were four thick busbars between us. He crouched behind them giggling until I reached a red-eyed state of wheezing impotence.

"Come out!" I gasped. "You ape-faced arthritic, come out of there and I'll hit you so hard you'll throttle on your shoelaces!"

"That," he said instructively, "was a quadruple quintessence of musk." He grinned. "Skunk." He looked at me and laughed outright. "Super-skunk."

I wrenched ineffectually at the bars. "A poor thing, but your very own, I'll bet," I said. "I am going to stick your arm so far down your neck you'll digest your fingernails."

"Mad, aren't you?"

"Huh?"

"I said, you're sore. I didn't cuss you out, or hold you up to ridicule, or anything, and look how mad you are!"

I began to see the light. Make the Breather angry by—
"What are you gibbering about?"

He took out a white handkerchief and waved it as he unwrapped his own body from the viscera of the old-fashioned transmitter. I had to grin. What can you do with a man like that?

"O.K.," I said. "Peace, brother. But I'd suggest you treat the Breather better than you just treated me. And how in blazes you expect to get a smell like that through a polychrome transmitter is a little beyond me."

"It isn't simple," he said, "but I think it can be done. Do you know anything about the wave theory of perception?"

"Not a helluva lot," I said. "Something about a sort of spectrum arrangement of the vibrations of sensory perception, isn't it?"

"Mmm . . . yes. Thought waves are of high-frequency, and although ether-borne, not of an electromagnetic character. So also are the allied vibrations, taste and smell. Sound, too."

"Wait a minute! Sound is a purely physical vibration of air particles against our auditory apparatus."

"Of course—from the source of the sound *to* that apparatus. But from the inner ear to the hearing center in the brain, it is translated into a wave of the spectrum group I'm talking about. So with touch and sight."

"I begin to see what you're driving at. But how can you reach the Breather with these waves—providing you can produce and transmit them?"

"Oh, I can do that. Simply a matter of stepping up high-frequency emanations."

"You seem pretty confident that the Breather will be affected by the same waves that influence our senses."

"I wouldn't use the same waves. That's why I brought up the spectrum theory. Now look; we'll take thought waves of the purely internal psyche . . . the messages that relay brain impulses to different brain centers. Pure thought, with no action; pure imagery. These are of a certain wave length. We'll call it 1000. Now, take the frequencies of smell, touch and sight waves. They're 780, 850, and 960 respectively. Now, how did we contact the Ether Breather?"

"By the polychrome wave."

"That's right."

"And you mean that the ratio—"

Berbelot nodded. "The ratio between the Breather's thought waves and its sensory vibrations must be the same as that between ours."

"Why must it be?"

"Because its mental reactions are the same, as I told you before—only exaggerated. It reasons as we do, more or less. Its mental set-up corresponds with ours."

"Doggone," I said admiringly, "it's all so simple when you're told how to do it. You mean, then, to discover the ratio between what is to me a pain in the neck, and what it would be to the Breather."

"That's it. But it won't be a pain in the neck."

"Where will it be, then?"

"You're tuning in the wrong frequency," he chuckled. "I'm going to make him suffer the best way I know how, and—my business is perfumery."

"Ah," I breathed.

"Now, I'm going to cook up something really pretty. I'm going to turn out a stench that will make the Breather's illimitable edges curl!"

"From the smell of the essence of ancient egg you just gassed me with," I said, "it ought to be pretty."

"It will be. Let's see; for a base we'll use butyl mercaptan. Something sweet, and something sour—"

"—something borrowed and something blue."

"Don't be a silly romanticist." He was busy at his chemical bench. "I'll scorch a little pork fat and . . . ah. Attar of roses."

For a moment he was quiet, carefully measuring drops of liquid into a sealed exciter. Then he flipped the switch and came over to me. "It'll be ready in a jiffy. Let's rig up the transmitter."

We did as we had done before, a year ago. We maneuvered the transmitting cells of the polychrome transmitter over and above a receiver. It would send to Berbelot's country place eight hundred miles away by a directional beam, and return the signal by wire. If the Breather interfered, it would show up on the receiver. When we had done it before, we had had the odd experience of holding a conversation with our own images on the screen.

"Now I'll distill my *odeur d'ordure*," he said, "and when it's run through, you can be my guinea pig."

"Not on your life, Berbelot," I said, backing away. He grinned and went about fixing his still. It was a beautiful little glass affair, and he worked entirely under a huge bell jar in transferring it from the exciter. Butyl and burned meat and attar of roses. My gosh.

In half an hour it was ready—a dusty-brown colloid, just a few drops in the retort. "Come on, Hamilton," said Berbelot, "just a little sniff. I want to give you a preview."

"Uh-uh!" I snorted. "Here—wait."

I gave a buzz on the buzzer, and in a couple of seconds Cogan, Berbelot's valet, popped in. Cogan's face always reminded me, for some reason, of a smorgasbord tray.

"Did you bring your nose?" I asked, leading him over to the chemical bench.

"Yessir."

"Well"—I slid back the little panel in the neck of the retort, standing at arm's length—"stick it in there."

"Oh, but I—" He looked plaintively toward Berbelot, who smiled.

"Well . . . oh!" The "Well" was diffidence, and the "Oh" was when I grabbed him by the collar and stuck his face in the warm fumes.

Cogan went limp and stiffened so fast that he didn't move. He rose slowly, as if the power of that mighty stench was lifting him by the jawbone, turned around twice with his eyes streaming, and headed for the door. He walked lightly and slowly on the balls of his feet, with his arms bent and half raised, like a somnambulist. He walked smack into the doorpost, squeaked, said "oh . . . my . . . goodness—" faintly, and disappeared into the corridor.

"Well," said Berbelot pensively. "I really think that that stuff smells bad."

"Seems as though," I grinned. "I . . . oh, boy!" I ran to the retort and closed the slide. "Good gosh! Did we give him a concentrated shot of *that?*"

"*You* did."

It permeated the room, and of all malodorous effluvia, it was the most noisome. It was rotten celery, than which there is no more sickening smell in nature. It was rancid butter. It was bread-mold. It was garlic garnishing fermented Limburger. It was decay. It was things running around on six legs, mashed. It was awful.

"Berbelot," I gasped, "you don't want to kill the Breather."

"It won't kill him. He just won't like it."

"Check. *Whew!*" I mopped my face. "Now how are you going to get it up to the Ether Breather?"

"Well, we'll use the olfactometer on it," he said.

"What's that?"

"Trade gadget. I knocked it together years ago. Without it I wouldn't have made a cent in this business." He led me over to a stand on which was an enormously complicated machine, all glittering relays and electratomic bridges. "Good heavens!" I said. "What does it do—play music?"

"Maybe you wondered why I could reel off so much about the wave theory of sensory perception," he said. "Look—see these dials? And this sensitized knob?"

"Yeah?"

"That fist size, faceted knob has each of its twelve hundred and two sides coated with a different chemical reagent, very sensitive. I drop it into a smell—"

"You *what?*"

"You heard me. An odor is an emanation of gases from the smellable specimen, constituting a loss of mass of about one fifty-billionth in a year, more or less, depending on the strength of the odor and the consistency of the emanating body. Now, I expose this knob to our Cogan-crusher"—he walked over to the retort with the knob in his hand, trailing its cable, and slid the panel back a bit—"and the gas touches every surface. Each reacts if it can. The results are collected, returned to the olfactometer, translated into a number on the big dial."

"And that is—"

"The ratio I spoke to you about. See . . . the dial reads just 786. With the frequency of abstract thought set arbitrarily at one thousand, we have a ratio between this smell and thought."

"Take it easy, Berbelot. I'm a layman."

He smiled. "That gives us an equation to work with. 786 is to 1000 as $x$ is to our polychrome wave."

"Isn't that a little like mixing liquor?" I said. "One set of figures is in thought vibrations, the other in radio waves."

"Ratios are like that," he reminded me. "I can have one-third as many apples as you have oranges, no matter how many or how few oranges you have."

"I consider myself stood in the corner," I said. "By golly, with that gadget, no wonder your perfumes are practically a monopoly nowadays. Would it be giving away a trade secret to tell me what went into that *Doux Rêves* of yours? How on earth did you figure out that odor? It'll make a ninety-year-old woman put on lipstick and a centenarian buy spats."

He laughed. "Sure, I'll tell you. *Doux Rêves* is 789.783 on that dial, which happens to be the smell of a rich juicy steak! But they don't associate it with steak when they buy it—at three hundred an ounce. It just smells like something desirable."

"Berbelot, you're chiseling the public."

"Mmmm-hm. That's why I pay half a billion in income tax every year. Get over on that bench."

"In front of the receiver? What are you going to do?"

"Oh, I'll have to be over here by the transmitter. I've got to adjust a carrier wave that will have the right ratio to the polychrome wave. Don't turn on the receiver yet."

I sat down. This amazing man was about to pull something unheard of. I didn't feel comfortable about it, either. How could he be so confident? He didn't know much about the Breather, any more than I did. He was acting like a man in perfect control of everything—which he was—who didn't have to worry about taking a rap for what he was about to do. Well, he built that smell, didn't he? I didn't. I could always blame him for it, even if I was the instigator. I remember wondering if I'd be able to convince the Ether Breather of that, in case the Breather got tough. Oh, well.

"O.K., Hamilton. Turn her on!"

I did so, and a few seconds later the transmitting floods clicked on. From the suspended bank of cells came a hum as soft as their soft glow. The screen flickered and cleared, and I saw myself in it, almost as if I were looking into a mirror, except that my image was not reversed. "O.K., Berbelot."

"Right. Here goes a shot of Berbelot's *Essence of Evil!*"

I heard a switch click and then the faint grate of a rheostat. I stared at my image and my image stared back, and Berbelot came and stood where he could see me. It was only later that I remembered noticing that he was careful to stand out of range of the transmitter. The image didn't change—each tiny movement was mine, each facial twist, each—

"Look!" snapped Berbelot, and faded back to his switchboard again.

For a moment I didn't notice anything in particular, and then I saw it, too. The smallest possible twitching of the nostrils. A sudden little movement of the head. And then a just audible sniffing through the speaker. As suddenly the movement stopped.

"You got something that time, Berbelot," I yelped, "but it seems to have gone away again. The image is true."

"Splendid!" said the old man. He clicked off the transmitter and the receiving screen glowed blankly. "Now listen. I only gave it about as much as we got a few minutes ago when you left the slide open. This time I'm going to give it what you gave poor Cogan!"

"My gosh! What am I supposed to do?"

"Sit tight! If and when the Breather starts kicking, give it right back to him. Don't admit that we did it to coax him back, or, being what he . . . it . . . is, he'll just get coy and disappear again."

"I think you're right. Want me to get him real mad, then?"

"For a while. Then we'll sign off and go to work on him tomorrow. After a bit we'll tell him the whole story; he'll think it's funny. Having fun seems to be his reason for living—if you can call that supercosmic existence living. Then he'll be appeased. Y'know Hamilton, if we get him running errands for us he might make us a nice piece of change. We could buy up an advertising agency and have him blank out all competition with his typically wise-guy sort of interference, for instance."

"You think of everything! All right, let's go!"

The floods and cells lit up again, and in a few seconds I was staring at myself in the screen. It made me feel a little queasy. There I was looking at myself, looking at myself, looking at myself, as it were. It dizzied me.

The rheostat twirled over, and an auxiliary somewhere deep in the complicated transmitter moaned quietly. For about five minutes I strained my eyes, but not by the slightest sign did my image show that it sensed anything off-color.

"Are you sure your gadgets are working all right?" I asked Berbelot.

"Absolutely. Nothing yet? I'll be darned. Wait. A little more juice here, and I think I can build that smell up a—"

"What goes on here?" roared the speaker.

I stared. I was still seated, but my image was rising slowly. One odd thing about it—when it had been my true image, it showed me from the waist up. As it rose from the bench in the picture, it had no legs. Apparently the Breather could only distort just those waves that were transmitted. A weird sight.

I'd never have known that as my face. It was twisted, and furious, and altogether unpleasant.

"Are you doing that, punk?" it asked me.

"Wh-what?"

"Don't be like that," whispered Berbelot. He was off to one side, staring entranced and exultant into the receiver. "Give'm hell, Ham!" I drew a deep breath. "Am I doing what, and who's a punk?" I asked the receiver pugnaciously.

"That stink, and you are."

"Yeah, I'm doing it, and who are you to call me one?"

"Well, cut it out, and who do I look like?"

"I wish you boys would have one conversation at a time," said Berbelot.

"None of your lip, pantywaist," I told the Breather, "or I'll come out there and plaster your shadow with substance."

"Wise guy, huh? Why, you insignificant nematode!"

"You etheric regurgitation!"

"You little quadridimensional stinkpot!"

"You faceless, formless, fightless phantasm!" I was beginning to enjoy this.

"Listen, mug, if you don't stop that business of smelling up my environment I'll strain you through a sheet of plate glass."

"Try it and I'll knock you so flat you'll call a plane a convex hemisphere."

"If you had the guts that God gave a goose, you'd come up here and fight me."

"If you weren't about as dangerous as a moth on a battle cruiser, you'd come down here and fight."

"Touché," said Berbelot.

"Oh, yeah?" said the Breather.

"Yeah."

"Cliché," said Berbelot.

"I don't like your face," said the Breather.

"Take it off then."

"Not as long as I can insult you by making you look at it."

"It's more of a face to brag about than you got."

"Why, you hair-mantled, flint-hurling, aboriginal anthropophagus!"

Berbelot clicked off both transmitter and receiver. It was only then that I realized the Breather had made me see red. I was in the laboratory, on my feet, all set to take a swing at a thousand-dollar television set.

"What'd you do that for?" I snapped, turning on Berbelot.

"Easy, lad, easy!" he laughed. "The Breather's had enough, in the first place. In the second place, he was quoting Carlyle, an ancient seventeenth or eighteenth century author. You ran him plumb out of originality. You did fine!"

"Thanks," I said, wiping my fevered brow. "Think he was sore?"

"I gathered as much. We'll work on him in the morning. I'm going to leave the smell on—just a suggestion of it, so he won't forget us."

"Don't you think he'll start messing up commercial programs again?"

"No. He knows where the trouble is coming from. He's too sore just now to think of anything but that source. He might think of the commercials later on, but if there's any danger of that we'll wise him up and laugh the whole thing off."

"Darned if you don't get me into the doggonedest things," I said wonderingly.

He chuckled, and slapped me on the back. "Go on upstairs and get Cogan to feed you. I'll be along soon; I have some work to do. You're spending the night here, my boy."

I thanked him and went upstairs. I should have gone home.

I was dog tired, but before I thought of going to bed I had some figuring to do. It had been a delicious meal, though from the way Cogan acted I thought dark thoughts about arsenic in the coffee and or a knife in the back. But the room he had shown me to was a beauty. Berbelot, as I should have expected, was as good at decorating as he was at anything else. The place was finished in chrome and gray and black, the whole thing centering around a huge mirror at one end. Building a room around a mirror is the most complimentary thing a host can do in a guest room.

It was a fascinating mirror, too. It wasn't exactly silvered—it was of a dull gray sheen, like rough-finished stainless steel. And whether it was metal or glass I couldn't tell. It gave a beautiful image—deep and true, and accentuating natural color. Probably something he "knocked together" himself.

I walked up and down absently, thinking about Berbelot and the Breather. They had a lot in common. No one could tell exactly what they were, or how great, or how powerful. Thinking about the Breather's series of cracks at me, I realized that he, or it, had spoken exactly in my idiom. Berbelot did that, too. And yet I knew that both of them could have completely swamped me with dialectical trickery.

My shadow caught my eye and I amused myself for a moment by making shadows on the wall opposite the mirror. A

bird—a cat—a funny face. I'd done it ever since I was a kid
and the thing fascinated me. I was pretty good at it. I wandered around the room making shadow pictures on the wall
and thinking about the Breather and Berbelot, and then
found myself looking into that deep mirror.

"Hi!" I said to my reflection.

It looked out at me placidly. Not a bad-looking guy, in a
pair of Berbelot's cellusilk pajamas and that cocky expression.
That was quite a mirror. What was it that made a guy look
different? The color trick? Not entirely. Let's see. I stuck out
my tongue and so did my reflection. I thumbed my nose, and
turned cold inside. I knew now what it was.

The image was—not reversed.

I stood there with my right arm up, my right thumb to my
nose. The reflection's right arm—the one toward my left,
since it was facing me—was raised, and it thumbed its nose. I
was white as a sheet.

Was I bats? Did I have a mental hangover from seeing that
unreversed image in the television set downstairs?

"This is awful," I said.

It couldn't be a mirror. Not even Berbelot could build a—
or was it a mirror? A—a television screen? Couldn't be—not
with the depth it had. It was almost as if I were standing in
front of a glass cabinet, looking at me inside. The image was
three dimensional. I suddenly decided I had been thumbing
my nose long enough. This must be some trick of that old
devil's, I thought. No wonder he didn't have dinner with me.
He was rigging up this gadget while I was eating. If it *was* a
television screen—and I'd never heard of one like this—then
that thing in there wasn't me—it was the Ether Breather. I
listened carefully, and sure enough, heard the hum of transmitting cells. What a gag! There were cells somewhere hidden
in this room sending my image away and returning it by
wire! But that screen—

My reflection suddenly set its legs apart and put its hands
on its hips. "What are you looking at?" it asked me.

"N-nothing," I said as sarcastically as I could while my
teeth were chattering. "The Breather again, huh?"

"That's right. My, but you're ugly."

"Mind your tongue!" I said sharply. "I can switch you off,
you know."

"Heh!" he jeered. "I don't have to be afraid of that any
more, thanks to a trick you just showed me."

"Yeah? You can't kid me, bud. You're just some amoral cosmic ray's little accident."

"I warn you, don't get tough with me."

"I'll do what I please. You couldn't pull your finger out of a tub of lard," I euphemized.

He sighed. "O.K. You asked for it."

And then I had to live through the worst thing that any poor mortal in the history of the world ever experienced. It's one thing to have an argument with yourself in the mirror. It's something entirely different to have your reflection reach out a leg, kick down the mirror with a shattering crash, walk up to you and belt you in the mouth a couple of times before it smears you on the carpet with a terrific right hook. That's what happened to me. Just that, so help me, Hannah.

I lay there on the rug looking up at me, which had just socked I, and I said "Whooie!" and went to sleep.

I've no idea how long I lay there. When light glimmered into my jarred brain again, Berbelot was kneeling beside me chafing my wrists. The beautiful mirror—or whatever the devil it was—was in some thousand-odd pieces on the floor, and I had gone to about as many pieces psychically. I finally realized that Berbelot was saying something.

"Hamilton! What happened? What happened? Do you realize you just busted thirty thousand dollars' worth of apparatus? What's the matter with you . . . are you sick?"

I rolled over and sat up, then went hand over hand up Berbelot until I was standing beside him. My head felt like a fur-lined ball of fire and every time my heart beat it blinded me.

"What did you wreck that receiver for?" Berbelot said irascibly.

"Me wreck it? Me didn't wreck it . . . I wrecked it," I said groggily. "I was standing in front of the mirror when who should kick it down and poke me but myself"—I shook my head and let the pain of it shake my carcass—"Ow! *Whew.* I was just—"

"Stop it!" Berbelot snapped.

Almost suddenly I recovered. "Receiver . . . what do you mean receiver?"

Berbelot was hopping mad. "The new job," he shouted, pointing at the debris. "My first three-dimensional television receiver!"

"Three . . . what are you talking about, man?"

He calmed down the way he invariably did when he was

asked a question about television. "It's a box of tiny projectors," he said. "They're set . . . studded . . . inside that closet affair behind the screen you just broke. The combined beams from them give a three-dimensional, or stereoscopic, effect. And now you've gone and wrecked my screen," he wailed. "Why were you ever born? Why must I suffer so because of you? Why——"

"Wait a minute, Pop—hold on there. I didn't bust your precious screen."

"You just said you did."

"Mmm-mm. So help me. It was the Breather. I had a little argument with him and he kicked down the screen and came out and beat the stern off me."

"What?" Berbelot was really shocked this time. "You're a gibbering maniac! That was your own image! You were broadcast and your image reproduced there!"

"You're a muddy-headed old stink-merchant!" I bellowed. "I suppose I kicked down your mirror, put three teeth on hinges, and then knocked myself colder'n a cake of carbonice just for a chance to lie to you!"

"This is what comes of getting an overgrown cretin to help out in an experiment," moaned Berbelot. "Don't try my patience any more, Hamilton!"

"*Your* patience? What the hell was that new-fangled set doing in this room anyway?"

He grinned weakly. "Oh—that. Well, I just wanted to have some fun with you. After you left I tuned in on the Breather and told him to stand by; I'd put him in touch with . . . with the guy that was smelling up his world."

"You old crumb! Fun! You wanted me to argue with that misplaced gamma-particle all night, hey? Why, I ought to . . . I think I will at that!" And I grabbed him by the neck.

"Allow *me*," said a voice behind us, and we were seized, each by a shoulder. Then our heads were cracked violently together and we found ourselves groveling at the feet of my spittin' image. Berbelot looked up at my erstwhile reflection in silent awe.

"Where were you?" I growled.

"In the corner," he said, throwing a thumb over his shoulder. "You're a pretty-looking pair, I must say."

"Berbelot," I said, "meet your Ether Breather. Now I'm going to stand on your face until you eat the shoes off my feet, because you called me a liar."

Berbelot said, "Well, I'm damned!"

The Breather remarked quietly, "You two better explain yourselves in a hysterical hurry. Otherwise I shall most certainly take you apart and put you together again, alternating the pieces."

"Oh, we were just trying to get in contact with you again."

"What for?"

"We were interested in you. We talked to you a year or so ago and then you disappeared. We wanted to talk to you again." In spite of my anger at him I found something else to admire Berbelot for. He had remembered the Breather's peculiar childishness and was using it just when somebody had to do something, quickly.

"But you told me to stop interfering!" Presto—the creature was already plaintive, on the amicable defensive. Its mutability was amazing.

"He told you," Berbelot snorted, indicating me, where I rolled and moaned over my twice-bruised sconce. "I didn't."

"Don't you speak for each other, then? We do."

"You—singular and plural—are a homogeneous being. All humanity is not blessed with my particularly affable nature."

"Why you old narcissist!" I snorted, and lunged at him. For every inch of my lunge the Breather calmly kicked me back a foot. I did some more moaning.

"You mean you are my friend and he is not?" said the Breather, staring at me coldly as one does at a roach which is going to be stepped on if and when it moves out from the wall.

"Oh, I wouldn't go so far as to say that," said Berbelot kindly.

I had an inspiration which, for all I know, saved my life. "You said you learned from me how to come out of the television set!" I blurted.

"True. I should be grateful for that, I suppose. I shall not tear you in little pieces." He turned to Berbelot. "I heard your call, of course, but being told once was enough for me. I did not understand. When I say anything I generally mean it. Humans are not understandable, but they are very funny."

The scientist in Berbelot popped up. "What was that you said about Hamilton showing you how to come out of the set?"

"Oh, I was watching him from the screen over there. I am sorry I broke it. He was walking around the room making pictures on the walls with shadows. That's what I am doing now."

"Shadow pictures?"

"Certainly. I am a creature living in five dimensions and aware of four, just as you live in four dimensions and are aware of three. He made three-dimensional shadows that were projected on a two-dimensional surface. I am making four dimensional pictures that are being projected in three dimensions."

Berbelot frowned. "On what surface?"

"On that of your fourth dimension, of course."

"Our fourth. Hm-m-m . . . with what light source?"

"A five-dimensional one just as your sun, for instance, has four."

"How many dimensions are there altogether?"

"How high is up?" twinkled the Breather.

"Could I project myself into your world?"

"I don't know. Maybe . . . maybe not. Are you going to stop making that awful smell?" he said suddenly.

"Of course! We only made it to get you angry enough to come to us for a talk. We didn't mean anything by it."

"Oh!" squealed the Ether Breather delightedly. "A joke! Fun!"

"Told you he'd take it well," murmured Berbelot.

"Yeah . . . suppose he hadn't? You're a rat, Berbelot. You made darn sure that if someone had to take a rap for this aeration here, it wouldn't be you. Nice guy." There was a strained silence for a while, and then I grinned. "Aw, hell, you had it doped out, Berbelot. Shake. I'd have done the same if I had the brains."

"He isn't bad at all, is he?" asked the Breather in surprise, staring at me.

"Well, is everything all right now, Breather? Do you feel that you're welcome to come any time you wish?"

"Yes . . . yes, I think so. But I won't come this way again. I can only take form in that lovely new three-dimensional machine of yours, and I have to break a screen to get out. I am sorry. I'll talk to you any time, though. And may I do something for you sometime?"

"Why should you?" I piped up glumly.

"Oh, think of the *fun* we'll have!"

"Would you really like to do something for us?"

"Oh, yes. Please."

"Can you direct that interference of yours into any radio frequency at any time?"

"Sure."

"Now look. We are going to start a company to advertise certain products. There are other companies in the same business. Will you leave our programs strictly alone and have all the fun you want with our competitors?"

"I'd love that!"

"That will be splendid!"

"Berbelot, we're rich!"

"You're rich," he corrected gleefully, "I'm richer!"

# THE EXALTED

*Astounding Science Fiction*
November

## by L. Sprague de Camp (1907-    )

*During his long and productive career, L. Sprague de Camp frequently worked within a series format. He has developed at least five series: the Viagens Interplanetarias stories, of which the best known is "The Queen of Zamba"; the Poseidonis stories, most of which have been collected as* The Tritonian Ring; *the Harold Shea tales (written with the late Fletcher Pratt), two of which comprise* The Incomplete Enchanter; *the Gavagan's Bar stories, also written with Pratt and collected as* Tales From Gavagan's Bar; *and the least known—the Johnny Black stories about a bear too smart for his own good.*

*"The Exalted" is the last (there were four) of these stories and the funniest.*

(Next to John Campbell, L. Sprague de Camp was my father figure in science fiction. He was the first of the authors to accept me as a social equal and to invite me to his home—where I promptly fell in love, platonically, with his beautiful wife. We were at the Philadelphia Navy Yard together—along with Bob Heinlein—during World War II. We are now fellow-members of the Trap-Door Spiders—along with Lester del Rey. In all that time, his friendship has never wavered and he has always been kind and affectionate and I have admired and loved everything he has ever written—his nonfiction even more than his fiction. In fact, my nonfiction style began as a conscious imitation of his.—I.A.)

The storklike man with the gray goatee shuffled the twelve black billets about on the tabletop. "Try it again," he said.

The undergraduate sighed. "O. K., Professor Methuen." He looked apprehensively at Johnny Black, sitting across the table with one claw on the button of the stop clock. Johnny returned the look impassively through the spectacles perched on his yellowish muzzle.

"Go," said Ira Methuen.

Johnny depressed the button. The undergraduate started the second run of his wiggly-block test. The twelve billets formed a kind of three-dimensional jigsaw puzzle; when assembled they would make a cube. But the block had originally been sawn apart on wavy, irregular lines, so that the twelve billets had to be put together just so.

The undergraduate fiddled with the billets, trying this one and that one against one he held in his hand. The clock ticked round. In four minutes he had all but one in place. This one, a corner piece, simply would not fit. The undergraduate wiggled it and pushed it. He looked at it closely and tried again. But its maladjustment remained.

The undergraduate gave up. "What's the trick?" he asked.

Methuen reversed the billet end for end. It fitted.

"Oh, heck," said the undergraduate. "I could have gotten it if it hadn't been for Johnny."

Instead of being annoyed, Johnny Black twitched his mouth in a bear's equivalent of a grin. Methuen asked the student why.

"He distracts me somehow. I know he's friendly and all that, but . . . it's this way, sort of. Here I come to Yale to get to be a psychologist. I hear all about testing animals, chimps and bears and such. And when I get here I find a bear testing *me*. It's kind of upsetting."

"That's all right," said Methuen. "Just what we wanted. We're after, not your wiggly-block score by itself, but the effect of Johnny's presence on people taking the test. We're getting Johnny's distraction factor—his ability to distract people. We're also getting the distraction factor of a lot of other things, such as various sounds and smells. I didn't tell you sooner because the knowledge might have affected your performance."

"I see. Do I still get my five bucks?"

"Of course. Good day, Kitchell. Come on, Johnny; we've just got time to make Psychobiology 100. We'll clean up the stuff later."

On the way out of Methuen's office, Johnny asked: "Hey, boss! Do you feer any effec' yet?"

"Not a bit," said Methuen. "I think my original theory was right: that the electrical resistance of the gaps between human neurons is already as low as it can be, so the Methuen injections won't have any appreciable effect on a human being. Sorry, Johnny, but I'm afraid your boss won't become any great genius as a result of trying a dose of his own medicine."

The Methuen treatment had raised Johnny's intelligence from that of a normal black bear to that of—or more exactly to the equivalent of that of—a human being. It had enabled him to carry out those spectacular coups in the Virgin Islands and the Central Park Zoo. It had also worked on a number of other animals in the said zoo, with regrettable results.

Johnny grumbled in his urso-American accent: "Stirr, I don't sink it is smart to teach a crass when you are furr of zat stuff. You never know—"

But they had arrived. The class comprised a handful of grave graduate students, on whom Johnny's distraction factor had little effect.

Ira Methuen was not a good lecturer. He put in too many uh's and er's, and tended to mumble. Besides, Psychobiology 100 was an elementary survey, and Johnny was pretty well up in the field himself. So he settled himself to a view of the Grove Street Cemetery across the street, and to melancholy reflections on the short life span of his species compared with that of men.

*"Ouch!"*

R. H. Wimpus, B.S., '68, jerked his backbone from its normally nonchalant arc into a quivering reflex curve. His eyes were wide with mute indignation.

Methuen was saying: "—whereupon it was discovered that the . . . uh . . . paralysis of the pes resulting from excision of the corresponding motor area of the cortex was much more lasting among the Simiidae than among the other catarrhine primates; that it was more lasting among these than among the platyrrhines—Mr. Wimpus?"

"Nothing," said Wimpus. "I'm sorry."

"And that the platyrrhines, in turn, suffered more than the lemuroids and tarsioids. When—"

*"Unh!"* Another graduate student jerked upright. While

Methuen paused with his mouth open, a third man picked a small object off the floor and held it up.

"Really, gentlemen," said Methuen, "I thought you'd outgrown such amusements as shooting rubber bands at each other. As I was saying when—"

Wimpus gave another grunt and jerk. He glared about him. Methuen tried to get his lecture going again. But, as rubber bands from nowhere continued to sting the necks and ears of the listeners, the classroom organization visibly disintegrated like a lump of sugar in a cup of weak tea.

Johnny had put on his spectacles and was peering about the room. But he was no more successful than the others in locating the source of the bombardment.

He slid off his chair and shuffled over to the light switch. The daylight through the windows left the rear end of the classroom dark. As soon as the lights went on, the source of the elastics was obvious. A couple of the graduates pounced on a small wooden box on the shelf beside the projector.

The box gave out a faint whir, and spat rubber bands through a slit, one every few seconds. They brought it up and opened it on Methuen's lecture table. Inside was a mass of machinery apparently made of the parts of a couple of alarm clocks and a lot of hand-whittled wooden cams and things.

"My, my," said Methuen. "A most ingenious contraption, isn't it?"

The machine ran down with a click. While they were still examining it, the bell rang.

Methuen looked out the window. A September rain was coming up. Ira Methuen pulled on his topcoat and his rubbers and took his umbrella from the corner. He never wore a hat. He went out and headed down Prospect Street, Johnny padding behind.

"Hi!" said a young man, a fat young man in need of a haircut. "Got any news for us, Professor Methuen?"

"I'm afraid not, Bruce," replied Methuen. "Unless you call Ford's giant mouse news."

"What? What giant mouse?"

"Dr. Ford has produced a three-hundred-pound mouse by orthogonal mutation. He had to alter its morphological characteristics—"

"Its *what?*"

"Its shape, to you. He had to alter it to make it possible for it to live—"

"Where? Where is it?"

"Osborn Labs. If—" But Bruce Inglehart was gone up the hill toward the science buildings. Methuen continued: "With no war on, and New Haven as dead a town as it always has been, they have to come to us for news, I suppose. Come on, Johnny. Getting garrulous in my old age."

A passing dog went crazy at the sight of Johnny, snarling and yelping. Johnny ignored it. They entered Woodbridge Hall.

Dr. Wendell Cook, president of Yale University, had Methuen sent in at once. Johnny, excluded from the sanctum, went up to the president's secretary. He stood up and put his paws on her desk. He leered—you have to see a bear leer to know how it is done—and said: "How about it, kid?"

Miss Prescott, an unmistakable Boston spinster, smiled at him. "Suttinly, Johnny. Just a moment." She finished typing a letter, opened a drawer, and took out a copy of Hecht's "Fantazius Mallare." This she gave Johnny. He curled up on the floor, adjusted his glasses, and read.

After a while he looked up, saying: "Miss Prescott, I am halfway srough zis, and I stirr don't see why zey cawr it obscene. I sink it is just durr. Can't you get me a *rearry* dirty book?"

"Well, really, Johnny, I don't run a pornography shop, you know. Most people find that quite strong enough."

Johnny sighed. "Peopre get excited over ze funnies' sings."

Meanwhile, Methuen was closeted with Cook and Dalrymple, the prospective endower, in another of those interminable and indecisive conferences. R. Hanscom Dalrymple looked like a statue that the sculptor had never gotten around to finishing. The only expression the steel chairman ever allowed himself was a canny, secretive smile. Cook and Methuen had a feeling he was playing them on the end of a long and well-knit fish line made of U.S. Federal Reserve notes. It was not because he wasn't willing to part with the damned endowment, but because he enjoyed the sensation of power over these oh-so-educated men. And in the actual world, one doesn't lose one's temper and tell Croesus what to do with his loot. One says: "Yes, Mr. Dalrymple. My, my, that *is* a brilliant suggestion, Mr. Dalrymple! Why didn't we think of it ourselves?" Cook and Methuen were both old hands at this game. Methuen, though otherwise he considered Wendell Cook a pompous ass, admired the president's endowment-snagging ability. After all, wasn't Yale University named af-

ter a retired merchant on the basis of a gift of five hundred
and sixty-two pounds twelve shillings?

"Say, Dr. Cook," said Dalrymple, "why don't you come
over to the Taft and have lunch on me for a change? You,
too, Professor Methuen."

The academics murmured their delight and pulled on their
rubbers. On the way out Dalrymple paused to scratch Johnny
behind the ears. Johnny put his book away, keeping the title
on the cover out of sight, and restrained himself from snapping at the steel man's hand. Dalrymple meant well enough,
but Johnny did not like people to take such liberties with his
person.

So three men and a bear slopped down College Street.
Cook paused now and then, ignoring the sprinkle, to make
studied gestures toward one or another of the units of the
great soufflé of Georgian and Collegiate Gothic architecture.
He explained this and that. Dalrymple merely smiled his
blank little smile.

Johnny, plodding behind, was the first to notice that passing undergraduates were pausing to stare at the president's
feet. The word "feet" is meant literally. For Cook's rubbers
were rapidly changing into a pair of enormous pink bare feet.

Cook himself was quite unconscious of it, until quite a
group of undergraduates had collected. These gave forth the
catarrhal snorts of men trying unsuccessfully not to laugh. By
the time Cook had followed their stares and looked down, the
metamorphosis was complete. That he should be startled was
only natural. The feet were startling enough. His face gradually matched the feet in redness, making a cheerful note of
color in the gray landscape.

R. Hanscom Dalrymple lost his reserve for once. His howls
did nothing to save prexy's now-apoplectic face. Cook finally
stooped and pulled off the rubbers. It transpired that the feet
had been painted on the outside of the rubbers and covered
over with lampblack. The rain had washed the lampblack off.

Wendell Cook resumed his walk to the Hotel Taft in
gloomy silence. He held the offensive rubbers between thumb
and finger as if they were something unclean and loathsome.
He wondered who had done this dastardly deed. There hadn't
been any undergraduates in his office for some days, but you
never wanted to underestimate the ingenuity of undergraduates. He noticed that Ira Methuen was wearing rubbers of the
same size and make as his own. But he put suspicion in that
direction out of his mind before it had fully formed. Cer-

tainly Methuen wouldn't play practical jokes with Dalrymple around, when he'd be the head of the new Department of Biophysics when—if—Dalrymple came through with the endowment.

The next man to suspect that the Yale campus was undergoing a severe pixilation was John Dugan, the tall thin one of the two campus cops. He was passing Christ Church—which is so veddy high-church Episcopal that they refer to Charles I of England as St. Charles the Martyr—on his way to his lair in Phelps Tower. A still small voice spoke in his ear: "Beware, John Dugan! Your sins will find you out!"

Dugan jumped and looked around. The voice repeated its message. There was nobody within fifty feet of Dugan. Moreover, he could not think of any really serious sins he had committed lately. The only people in sight were a few undergraduates and Professor Methuen's educated black bear, trailing after his boss as usual. There was nothing for John Dugan to suspect but his own sanity.

R. Hanscom Dalrymple was a bit surprised at the grim earnestness of the professors in putting away their respective shares of the James Pierpont dinner. They were staying the eternal gnaw of hunger that afflicts those who depend on a college commissary for sustenance. Many of them suspected a conspiracy among college cooks to see that the razor edge wasn't taken off students' and instructors' intellects by overfeeding. They knew that conditions were much the same in most colleges.

Dalrymple sipped his coffee and looked at his notes. Presently Cook would get up and say a few pleasant nothings. Then he would announce Dalrymple's endowment, which was to be spent in building a Dalrymple Biophysical Laboratory and setting up a new department. Everybody would applaud and agree that biophysics had floated in the void between the domains of the departments of zoology, psychology, and the physiological sciences long enough. Then Dalrymple would get up and clear his throat and say—though in much more dignified language: "Shucks, fellas, it really isn't nothing."

Dr. Wendell Cook duly got up, beamed out over the ranked shirt fronts, and said his pleasant nothings. The professors exchanged nervous looks when he showed signs of going off into his favorite oration, there-is-no-conflict-between-science-and-religion. They had heard it before.

He was well launched into Version 3A of this homily, when he began to turn blue in the face. It was not the dark purplish-gray called loosely "blue" that appears on the faces of stranglees, but a bright, cheerful cobalt. Now, such a color is all very well in a painting of a ship sailing under a clear blue sky, or in the uniform of a movie-theater doorman. But it is distinctly out of place in the face of a college president. Or so felt the professors. They leaned this way and that, their boiled shirts bulging, popping and gaping as they did so, and whispered.

Cook frowned and continued. He was observed to sniff the air as if he smelled something. Those at the speakers' table detected a slight smell of acetone. But that seemed hardly an adequate explanation of the robin's-egg hue of their prexy's face. The color was now quite solid on the face proper. It ran up into the area where Cook's hair would have been if he had had some. His collar showed a trace of it, too.

Cook, on his part, had no idea of why the members of his audience were swaying in their seats like saplings in a gale and whispering. He thought it very rude of them. But his frowns had no effect. So presently he cut Version 3A short. He announced the endowment in concise, businesslike terms, and paused to the expected thunder of applause.

There was none. To be exact, there was a feeble patter that nobody in his right mind would call a thunder of anything.

Cook looked at R. Hanscom Dalrymple, hoping that the steel man would not be insulted. Dalrymple's face showed nothing. Cook assumed that this was part of his general reserve. The truth was that Dalrymple was too curious about the blue face to notice the lack of applause. When Cook introduced him to the audience, it took him some seconds to pull himself together.

He started rather lamely: "Gentlemen and members of the Yale faculty . . . uh . . . I mean, of course, you're *all* gentlemen . . . I am reminded of a story about the poultry farmer who got married—I mean, I'm not reminded of *that* story, but the one about the divinity student who died and went to—" Here Dalrymple caught the eye of the dean of the divinity school. He tacked again: "Maybe I'd . . . uh . . . better tell the one about the Scotchman who got lost on his way home and—"

It was not a bad story, as such things go. But it got practically no laughter. Instead, the professors began swaying, like a roomful of boiled-shirted Eastern ascetics at their prayers, and whispering again.

Dalrymple could put two and two together. He leaned over and hissed into Cook's ear: "Is there anything wrong with me?"

"Yes, your face has turned green."

"Green?"

"Bright green. Like grass. Nice young grass."

"Well, you might like to know that yours is blue."

Both men felt their faces. There was no doubt; they were masked with coatings of some sort of paint, still wet.

Dalrymple whispered: "What kind of gag is this?"

"I don't know. Better finish your speech."

Dalrymple tried. But his thoughts were scattered beyond recovery. He made a few remarks about how glad he was to be there amid the elms and ivy and traditions of old Eli, and sat down. His face looked rougher-hewn than ever. If a joke had been played on him—well, he hadn't signed any checks yet.

The lieutenant governor of the State of Connecticut was next on the list. Cook shot a question at him. He mumbled: "But if I'm going to turn a funny color when I get up—"

The question of whether his honor should speak was never satisfactorily settled. For at that moment a thing appeared on one end of the speakers' table. It was a beast the size of a St. Bernard. It looked rather the way a common bat would look if, instead of wings, it had arms with disk-shaped pads on the ends of the fingers. Its eyes were as big around as luncheon plates.

There was commotion. The speaker sitting nearest the thing fell over backward. The lieutenant governor crossed himself. An English zoölogist put on his glasses and said: "By Jove, a spectral tarsier! But a bit large, what?"

A natural-sized tarsier would fit in your hand comfortably, and is rather cute if a bit spooky. But a tarsier the size of this one is not the kind of thing one can glance at and then go on reading the adventures of Alley Oop. It breaks one's train of thought. It disconcerts one. It may give one the screaming meemies.

This tarsier walked gravely down the twenty feet of table. The diners were too busy going away from there to observe that it upset no tumblers and kicked no ashtrays about; that it was, in fact, slightly transparent. At the other end of the table it vanished.

Johnny Black's curiosity wrestled with his better judgment. His curiosity told him that all these odd happenings had taken place in the presence of Ira Methuen. Therefore, Ira Methuen was at least a promising suspect. "So what?" said his better judgment. "He's the only man you have a real affection for. If you learned that he was the pixie in the case, you wouldn't expose him, would you? Better keep your muzzle out of this."

But in the end his curiosity won, as usual. The wonder was that his better judgment kept on trying.

He got hold of Bruce Inglehart. The young reporter had a reputation for discretion.

Johnny explained: "He gave himserf ze Messuen treatment—you know, ze spinar injection—to see what it would do to a man. Zat was a week ago. Should have worked by now. But he says it had no effec'. Maybe not. But day after ze dose, awr zese sings start happening. Very eraborate jokes. Kind a crazy scientific genius would do. If it's him, I mus' stop him before he makes rear troubre. You wirr he'p me?"

"Sure, Johnny. Shake on it."

Johnny extended his paw.

It was two nights later that Durfee Hall caught fire. Yale had been discussing the erasure of this singularly ugly and useless building for forty years. It had been vacant for some time, except for the bursar's office in the basement.

About ten o'clock an undergraduate noticed little red tongues of flame crawling up the roof. He gave the alarm at once. The New Haven fire department was not to be blamed for the fact that the fire spread as fast as if the building had been soaked in kerosene. By the time they, and about a thousand spectators, had arrived, the whole center of the building was going up with a fine roar and crackle. The assistant bursar bravely dashed into the building and reappeared with an armful of papers, which later turned out to be a pile of quite useless examination forms. The fire department squirted enough water onto the burning section to put out Mount Vesuvius. Some of them climbed ladders at the ends of the building to chop holes in the roof.

The water seemed to have no effect. So the fire department called for some more apparatus, connected up more hoses, and squirted more water. The undergraduates yelled:

"Rah, rah, fire department! Rah, rah, fire! Go get 'em, department! Hold that line, fire!"

Johnny Black bumped into Bruce Inglehart, who was dodging about in the crowd with a pad and pencil, trying to get information for his New Haven *Courier*. Inglehart asked Johnny whether he knew anything.

Johnny, in his deliberate manner, said: "I know one sing. Zat is ze firs' hetress fire I have seen."

Inglehart looked at Johnny, then at the conflagration. "My gosh!" he said. "We ought to feel the radiation here, oughtn't we? Heatless fire is right. Another superscientific joke, you suppose?"

"We can rook around," said Johnny. Turning their backs on the conflagration, they began searching among the shrubbery and railings along Elm Street.

"Woof!" said Johnny. "Come here, Bruce!"

In a patch of shadow stood Professor Ira Methuen and a tripod whereon was mounted a motion-picture projector. It took Johnny a second to distinguish which was which.

Methuen seemed uneasily poised on the verge of flight. He said:

"Why, hello, Johnny, why aren't you asleep? I just found this . . . uh . . . this projector—"

Johnny, thinking fast, slapped the projector with his paw. Methuen caught it as it toppled. Its whir ceased. At the same instant the fire went out, vanished utterly. The roar and crackle still came from the place where the fire had been. But there was no fire. There was not even a burned place in the roof, off which gallons of water were still pouring. The fire department looked at one another foolishly.

While Johnny's and Inglehart's pupils were still expanding in the sudden darkness, Methuen and his projector vanished. They got a glimpse of him galloping around the College Street corner, lugging the tripod. They ran after him. A few undergraduates ran after Johnny and Inglehart, being moved by the instinct that makes dogs chase automobiles.

They caught sight of Methuen, lost him, and caught sight of him again. Inglehart was not built for running, and Johnny's eyesight was an affair of limited objectives. Johnny opened up when it became evident that Methuen was heading for the old Phelps mansion, where he, Johnny, and several unmarried instructors lived. Everybody in the house had gone to see the fire. Methuen dashed in the front door three jumps ahead of Johnny and slammed it in the bear's face.

Johnny padded around in the dark with the idea of attacking a window. But while he was making up his mind, something happened to the front steps under him. They became slicker than the smoothest ice. Down the steps went Johnny, *bump-bump-bump.*

Johnny picked himself up in no pleasant mood. So this was the sort of treatment he got from the one man— But then, he reflected, if Methuen was really crazy, you couldn't blame him.

Some of the undergraduates caught up with them. These crowded toward the mansion—until their feet went out from under them as if they were wearing invisible roller skates. They tried to get up, and fell again, sliding down the slight grade of the crown of the road into heaps in the gutter. They retired on hands and knees, their clothes showing large holes.

A police car drove up and tried to stop. Apparently neither brakes nor tires would hold. It skidded about, banged against the curb once, and finally stopped down the street beyond the slippery zone. The cop—he was a fairly important cop, a captain—got out and charged the mansion.

He fell down, too. He tried to keep going on hands and knees. But every time he applied a horizontal component of force to a hand or knee, the hand or knee simply slid backward. The sight reminded Johnny of the efforts of those garter snakes to crawl on the smooth concrete floor of the Central Park Zoo monkey house.

When the police captain gave up and tried to retreat, the laws of friction came back on. But when he stood up, all his clothes below the waist, except his shoes, disintegrated into a cloud of textile fibers.

"My word!" said the English zoölogist, who had just arrived. "Just like one of those Etruscan statues, don't you know!"

The police captain bawled at Bruce Inglehart: "Hey, you, for gossakes gimmie a handkerchief!"

"What's the matter; got a cold?" asked Inglehart innocently.

"No, you dope! You know what I want it for!"

Inglehart suggested that a better idea would be for the captain to use his coat as an apron. While the captain was knotting the sleeves behind his back, Inglehart and Johnny explained their version of the situation to him.

"Hm-m-m," said the captain. "We don't want nobody to get hurt, or the place to get damaged. But suppose he's got a death ray or sumpm?"

"I don't sink so," said Johnny. "He has not hurt anybody. Jus' prayed jokes."

The captain thought for a few seconds of ringing up headquarters and having them send an emergency truck. But the credit for overpowering a dangerous maniac singlehanded was too tempting. He said: "How'll we get into the place, if he can make everything so slippery?"

They thought. Johnny said: "Can you get one of zose sings wiss a wood stick and a rubber cup on end?"

The captain frowned. Johnny made motions. Inglehart said: "Oh, you mean the plumber's friend! Sure. You wait. I'll get one. See if you can find a key to the place."

The assault on Methuen's stronghold was made on all fours. The captain, in front, jammed the end of the plumber's friend against the rise of the lowest front step. If Methuen could abolish friction, he had not discovered how to get rid of barometric pressure. The rubber cup held, and the cop pulled himself, Inglehart, and Johnny after him. By using the instrument on successive steps, they mounted them. Then the captain anchored them to the front door and pulled them up to it. He hauled himself to his feet by the door handle, and opened the door with a key borrowed from Dr. Wendell Cook.

At one window, Methuen crouched behind a thing like a surveyor's transit. He swiveled the thing toward them, and made adjustments. The captain and Inglehart, feeling their shoes grip the floor, gathered themselves to jump. But Methuen got the contraption going, and their feet went out from under them.

Johnny used his head. He was standing next to the door. He lay down, braced his hind feet against the door frame, and kicked out. His body whizzed across the frictionless floor and bowled over Methuen and his contraption.

The professor offered no more resistance. He seemed more amused than anything, despite the lump that was growing on his forehead. He said: "My, my, you fellows *are* persistent. I suppose you're going to take me off to some asylum. I thought you and you"—he indicated Ingelhart and Johnny—"were friends of mine. Oh, well, it doesn't matter."

The captain growled: "What did you do to my pants?"

"Simple. My telelubricator here neutralizes the interatomic bonds on the surface of any solid on which the beam falls. So the surface, to a depth of a few molecules, is put in the condition of a supercooled liquid as long as the beam is focused on it. Since the liquid form of any compound will wet the solid form, you have perfect lubrication."

"But my pants—"

"They were held together by friction between the fibers, weren't they? And I have a lot more inventions like that. My soft-speaker and my three-dimensional projector, for instance, are—"

Inglehart interrupted: "Is that how you made that phony fire, and that whatchamacallit that scared the people at the dinner? With a three-dimensional projector?"

"Yes, of course, though, to be exact, it took two projectors at right angles, and a phonograph and amplifier to give the sound effect. It was amusing, wasn't it?"

"But," wailed Johnny, "why do you *do* zese sings? You trying to ruin your career?"

Methuen shrugged. "It doesn't matter. Nothing matters. Johnny, as you'd know if you were in my . . . uh . . . condition. And now, gentlemen, where do you want me to go? Wherever it is, I'll find something amusing there."

Dr. Wendell Cook visited Ira Methuen on the first day of his incarceration in the New Haven Hospital. In ordinary conversation Methuen seemed sane enough, and quite agreeable. He readily admitted that he had been the one responsible for the jokes. He explained: "I painted your and Dalrymple's face with a high-powered needle sprayer I invented. It's a most amusing little thing. Fits in your hand and discharges through a ring on your finger. With your thumb you can regulate the amount of acetone mixed in with the water, which in turn controls the surface tension and therefore the point at which the needle spray breaks up into droplets. I made the spray break up just before it reached your face. You were a sight, Cook, especially when you found out what was wrong with you. You looked almost as funny as the day I painted those feet on my rubbers and substituted them for yours. You react so beautifully to having your dignity pricked. You always were a pompous ass, you know."

Cook puffed out his cheeks and controlled himself. After all, the poor man was mad. These absurd outbursts about Cook's pompousness proved it. He said sadly: "Dalrymple's leaving tomorrow night. He was most displeased about the face-painting episode, and when he found that you were under observation, he told me that no useful purpose would be served by his remaining here. I'm afraid that's the end of our endowment. Unless you can pull yourself together and tell us what's happened to you and how to cure it."

Ira Methuen laughed. "Pull myself togehter? I am all in one piece, I assure you. And I've told you what's the matter with me, as you put it. I gave myself my own treatment. As for curing it, I wouldn't tell you how even if I knew. I wouldn't give up my present condition for anything. I at last realize that nothing really matters, including endowments. I shall be taken care of, and I will devote myself to amusing myself as I see fit."

Johnny had been haunting Cook's office all day. He way-laid the president when the latter returned from the hospital.

Cook told Johnny what had happened. He said: "He seems to be completely irresponsible. We'll have to get in touch with his son, and have a guardian appointed. And we'll have to do something about you, Johnny."

Johnny didn't relish the prospect of the "something." He knew he had no legal status other than that of a tamed wild animal. The fact that Methuen technically owned him was his only protection if somebody took a notion to shoot him during bear-hunting season. And he was not enthusiastic about Ralph Methuen. Ralph was a very average young school-teacher without his father's scientific acumen or whimsical humor. Finding Johnny on his hands, his reaction would be to give Johnny to a zoo or something.

He put his paws on Miss Prescott's desk and asked: "Hey, good-rooking, wirr you cawr up Bruce Ingrehart at ze *Courier?*"

"Johnny," said the president's secretary, "you get fresher every day."

"Ze bad infruence of ze undergraduates. Wirr you cawr Mr. Ingrehart, beautifur?" Miss Prescott, who was not, did so.

Bruce Inglehart arrived at the Phelps mansion to find Johnny taking a shower. Johnny was also making a horrible bawling noise. *"Waaaaa!"* he howled. *"Hoooooooo! Yrrrrrrr! Waaaaaaa!"*

"Whatcha doing?" yelled Inglehart.

"Taking a bass," replied Johnny. *"Wuuuuuuh!"*

"Are you sick?"

"No. Jus' singing in bass. People sing whire taking bass; why shouldn't I? *Yaaaaaaaaaaa!"*

"Well, for Pete's sake don't. It sounds like you were having your throat cut. What's the idea of these bath towels spread all over the floor?"

"I show you." Johnny came out of the shower, lay down on the bath towels, and rolled. When he was more or less dry, he scooped the towels up in his forepaws and hove them into a corner. Neatness was not one of Johnny's strong points.

He told Inglehart about the Methuen situation. "Rook here, Bruce," he said, "I sink I can fix him, but you wirr have to he'p me."

"O. K. Count me in."

*Pop!*

The orderly looked up from his paper. But none of the buttons showed a light. So, presumably, none of the patients wanted attention. He went back to his reading.

*Pop!*

It sounded a little like a breaking light bulb. The orderly sighed, put away his paper, and began prowling. As he approached the room of the mad professor, No. 14, he noticed a smell of limburger.

*Pop!*

There was no doubt that the noise came from No. 14. The orderly stuck his head in.

At one side of the room sat Ira Methuen. He held a contraption made of a length of glass rod and assorted wires. At the other side of the room, on the floor, lay a number of crumbs of cheese. A cockroach scuttled out of the shadows and made for the crumbs. Methuen sighted along his glass rod and pressed a button. *Pop!* A flash, and there was no more cockroach.

Methuen swung the rod toward the orderly. "Stand back, sir! I'm Buck Rogers, and this is my disintegrator!"

"Hey," said the orderly feebly. The old goof might be crazy, but after what happened to the roach— He ducked out and summoned a squad of interns.

But the interns had no trouble with Methuen. He tossed the contraption on the bed, saying: "If I thought it mattered, I'd raise a hell of a stink about cockroaches in a supposedly sanitary hospital."

One of the interns protested: "But I'm sure there aren't any here."

"What do you call that?" asked Methuen dryly, pointing at the shattered remains of one of his victims.

"It must have been attracted in from the outside by the smell of that cheese. *Phew!* Judson, clean up the floor. What *is* this, professor?" He picked up the rod and the flashlight battery attached to it.

Methuen waved a deprecating hand. "Nothing important. Just a little gadget I thought up. By applying the right e.m.f. to pure crown glass, it's possible to raise its index of refraction to a remarkable degree. The result is that light striking the glass is so slowed up that it takes weeks to pass through it in the ordinary manner. The light that is thus trapped can be released by making a small spark near the glass. So I simply lay the rod on the window sill all afternoon to soak up sunlight, a part of which is released by making a spark with that button. Thus I can shoot an hour's accumulated light-energy out the front end of the rod in a very small fraction of a second. Natuarlly when this beam hits an opaque object, it raises its temperature. So I've been amusing myself by luring the roaches in here and exploding them. You may have the thing; its charge is about exhausted."

The intern was stern. "That's a dangerous weapon. We can't let you play with things like that."

"Oh, can't you? Not that it matters, but I'm only staying here because I'm taken care of. I can walk out any time I like."

"No you can't, professor. You're under a temporary commitment for observation."

"That's all right, son. I still say I can walk out whenever I feel like it. I just don't care much whether I do or not." With which Methuen began tuning the radio by his bed, ignoring the interns.

Exactly twelve hours later, at 10 A.M., Ira Methuen's room in the hospital was found to be vacant. A search of the hospital failed to locate him. The only clue to his disappearance was the fact that his radio had been disemboweled. Tubes, wires, and condensers lay in untidy heaps on the floor.

The New Haven police cars received instructions to look for a tall, thin man with gray hair and goatee, probably armed with death rays, disintegrators, and all the other advanced weapons of fact and fiction.

For hours they scoured the city with screaming sirens. They finally located the menacing madman, sitting placidly on a park bench three blocks from the hospital and reading a newspaper. Far from resisting, he grinned at them and looked at his watch. "Three hours and forty-eight minutes. Not bad, boys, not bad, considering how carefully I hid myself."

One of the cops pounced on a bulge in Methuen's pocket. The bulge was made by another wire contraption. Methuen shrugged. "My hyperbolic solenoid. Gives you a conical magnetic field, and enables you to manipulate ferrous objects at a distance. I picked the lock of the door to the elevators with it."

When Bruce Inglehart arrived at the hospital about four, he was told Methuen was asleep. That was amended to the statement that Methuen was getting up, and could see a visitor in a few minutes. He found Methuen in a dressing gown.

Methuen said: "Hello, Bruce. They had me wrapped up in a wet sheet, like a mummy. It's swell for naps; relaxes you. I told 'em they could do it whenever they liked. I think they were annoyed about my getting out."

Inglehart was slightly embarrassed.

Methuen said: "Don't worry; I'm not mad at you. I realize that nothing matters, including resentments. And I've had a most amusing time here. Just watch them fizz the next time I escape."

"But don't you care about your future?" said Inglehart. "They'll transfer you to a padded cell at Middletown—"

Methuen waved a hand. "That doesn't bother me. I'll have fun there, too."

"But how about Johnny Black, and Dalrymple's endowment?"

"I don't give a damn what happens to them."

Here the orderly stuck his head in the door briefly to check up on this unpredictable patient. The hospital, being shorthanded, was unable to keep a continuous watch on him.

Methuen continued: "Not that I don't like Johnny. But when you get a real sense of proportion, like mine, you realize that humanity is nothing but a sort of skin disease on a ball of dirt, and that no effort beyond subsistence, shelter, and casual amusement is worthwhile. The State of Connecticut is willing to provide the first two for me, so I shall devote myself to the third. What's that you have there?"

Inglehart thought. *They're right; he's become a childishly irresponsible scientific genius.* Keeping his back to the door, the reporter brought out his family heirloom: a big silver pocket flask dating back to the fabulous prohibition period. His aunt Martha had left it to him, and he himself expected to will it to a museum.

THE EXALTED 315

"Apricot brandy," he murmured. Johnny had tipped him off to Methuen's tastes.

"Now, Bruce, that's something sensible. Why didn't you bring it out sooner, instead of making futile appeals to my sense of duty?"

The flask was empty. Ira Methuen sprawled in his chair. Now and then he passed a hand across his forehead. He said: "I can't believe it. I can't believe that I felt that way half an hour ago. O Lord, what have I done?"

"Plenty," said Inglehart.

Methuen was not acting at all drunk. He was full of sober remorse.

"I remember everything—those inventions that popped out of my mind, everything. But I didn't care. How did you know alcohol would counteract the Methuen injection?"

"Johnny figured it out. He looked up its effects, and discovered that in massive doses it coagulates the proteins in the nerve cells. He guessed it would lower their conductivity to counteract the increased conductivity through the gaps between them that your treatment causes."

"So," said Methuen, "when I'm sober I'm drunk, and when I'm drunk I'm sober. But what'll we do about the endowment—my new department and the laboratory and everything?"

"I don't know. Dalrymple's leaving tonight; he had to stay over a day on account of some trustee business. And they won't let you out for a while yet, even when they know about the alcohol counter-treatment. Better think of something quick, because the visiting period is pretty near up."

Methuen thought. He said: "I remember how all those inventions work, though I couldn't possibly invent any more of them unless I went back to the other condition." He shuddered. "There's the soft-speaker, for instance—"

"What's that?"

"It's like a loud-speaker, only it doesn't speak loudly. It throws a supersonic beam, modulated by the human voice to give the effect of audible sound-frequencies when it hits the human ear. Since you can throw a supersonic beam almost as accurately as you can throw a light beam, you can turn the soft-speaker on a person, who will then hear a still small voice in his ear apparently coming from nowhere. I tried it on Dugan one day. It worked. Could you do anything with that?"

"I don't know. Maybe."

"I hope you can. This is terrible. I thought I was perfectly sane and rational. Maybe I was— Maybe nothing *is* important. But I don't feel that way now, and I don't want to feel that way again—"

The omnipresent ivy, of which Yale is so proud, affords splendid handholds for climbing. Bruce Inglehart, keeping an eye peeled for campus cops, swarmed up the big tower at the corner of Bingham Hall. Below, in the dark, Johnny waited.

Presently the end of a clothesline came dangling down. Johnny inserted the hook in the end of the rope ladder into the loop in the end of the line. Inglehart hauled the ladder up and secured it, wishing that he and Johnny could change bodies for a while. That climb up the ivy had scared him and winded him badly. But he could climb ivy and Johnny couldn't.

The ladder creaked under Johnny's five hundred pounds. A few minutes later it slid slowly, jerkily up the wall, like a giant centipede. Then Inglehart, Johnny, ladder, and all were on top of the tower.

Inglehart got out the soft-speaker and trained the telescopic sight on the window of Dalrymple's room in the Taft, across the intersection of College and Chapel Streets. He found the yellow rectangle of light. He could see into about half the room. His heart skipped a few beats until a stocky figure moved into his field of vision. Dalrymple had not yet left. But he was packing a couple of suitcases.

Inglehart slipped the transmitter clip around his neck, so that the transmitter nestled against his larynx. The next time Dalrymple appeared, Inglehart focused the crosshairs on the steel man's head. He spoke: "Hanscom Dalrymple!" He saw the man stop suddenly. He repeated: "Hanscom Dalrymple!"

"Huh?" said Dalrymple. "Who the hell are you? Where the hell are you?" Inglehart could not hear him, of course, but he could guess.

Inglehart said, in a solemn tones: "I am your conscience."

By now Dalrymple's agitation was evident even at that distance. Inglehart continued: "Who squeezed out all the common stockholders of Hephaestus Steel in that phony reorganization?" Pause. "You did, Hanscom Dalrymple!

"Who bribed a United States senator to swing the vote for a higher steel tariff, with fifty thousand dollars and a promise of fifty thousand more, which was never paid?" Pause. "You did, Hanscom Dalrymple!

"Who promised Wendell Cook the money for a new biophysics building, and then let his greed get the better of him and backed out on the thin excuse that the man who was to have headed the new department had had a nervous breakdown?" Pause, while Inglehart reflected that "nervous breakdown" was merely a nice way of saying "gone nuts." "You did, Hanscom Dalrymple!

"Do you know what'll happen to you if you don't atone, Dalrymple? You'll be reincarnated as a spider, and probably caught by a wasp and used as live fodder for her larvæ. How will you like that, *heh-heh?*

"What can you do to atone? Don't be a sap. Call up Cook. Tell him you've changed your mind, and are renewing your offer!" Pause. "Well, what are you waiting for? Tell him you're not only renewing it, but doubling it!" Pause. "Tell him—"

But at this point Dalrymple moved swiftly to the telephone. Inglehart said, "Ah, that's better, Dalrymple," and shut off the machine.

Johnny asked: "How did you know awr zose sings about him?"

"I got his belief in reincarnation out of his obit down at the shop. And one of our rewrite men who used to work in Washington says everybody down there knows about the other things. Only you can't print a thing like that unless you have evidence to back it up."

They lowered the rope ladder and reversed the process by which they had come up. They gathered up their stuff and started for the Phelps mansion. But as they rounded the corner of Bingham they almost ran into a familiar storklike figure. Methuen was just setting up another contraption at the corner of Welch.

"Hello," he said.

Man and bear gaped at him. Inlgehart asked: "Did you escape again?"

"Uh-huh. When I sobered up and got my point of view back. It was easy, even though they'd taken my radio away. I invented a hypnotizer, using a light bulb and a rheostat made of wire from my mattress, and hypnotized the orderly into giving me his uniform and opening the doors for me. My, my, that *was* amusing."

"What are you doing now?" Inglehart became aware that Johnny's black pelt had melted off into the darkness.

"This? Oh, I dropped around home and knocked together an improved soft-speaker. This one'll work through masonry walls. I'm going to put all the undergraduates to sleep and tell 'em they're monkeys. When they wake up, it will be most amusing to see them running around on all fours and scratching and climbing the chandeliers. They're practically monkeys to begin with, so it shouldn't be difficult."

"But you can't, professor! Johnny and I just went to a lot of trouble getting Dalrymple to renew his offer. You don't want to let us down, do you?"

"What you and Johnny do doesn't matter to me in the slightest. Nothing matters. I'm going to have my fun. And don't try to interfere, Bruce." Methuen pointed another glass rod at Inglehart's middle. "You're a nice young fellow, and it would be too bad if I had to let you have three hours' accumulation of sun-ray energy all at once."

"But this afternoon you said—"

"I know what I said this afternoon. I was drunk and back in my old state of mind, full of responsibility and conscientiousness and such bunk. I'll never touch the stuff again if it has that effect on me. Only a man who has received the Methuen treatment can appreciate the futility of all human effort."

Methuen shrank back into the shadows as a couple of undergraduates passed. Then he resumed work on his contraption, using one hand and keeping Inglehart covered with the other. Inglehart, not knowing what else to do, asked him questions about the machine. Methuen responded with a string of technical jargon. Inglehart wondered desperately what to do. He was not an outstandingly brave young man, especially in the face of a gun or its equivalent. Methuen's bony hand never wavered. He made the adjustments on his machine mostly by feel.

"Now," he said, "that ought to be about right. This contains a tonic metronome that will send them a note of frequency of 349 cycles a second, with 68.4 pulses of sound a minute. This, for various technical reasons, has the maximum hypnotic effect. From here I can rake the colleges along College Street—" He made a final adjustment. "This will be the most amusing joke yet. And the cream of it is that, since Connecticut is determined to consider me insane, they can't do anything to me for it! Here goes, Bruce—*Phew*, has somebody started a still here, or what? I've been smelling and tasting alcohol for the last five minutes—*ouch!*"

The glass rod gave one dazzling flash, and then Johnny's hairy black body catapulted out of the darkness. Down went Ira Methuen, all the wind knocked out of him.

"Quick, Bruce!" barked Johnny. "Pick up zat needre sprayer I dropped. Unscrew ze container on ze bottom. Don't spirr it. Zen come here and pour it down his sroat!"

This was done, with Johnny holding Methuen's jaws apart with his claws, like Sampson slaying the lion, only conversely.

They waited a few minutes for the alcohol to take effect, listening for sounds that they had been discovered. But the colleges were silent save for the occasional tick of a typewriter.

Johnny explained: "I ran home and got ze needre sprayer from his room. Zen I got Webb, ze research assistant in bi-physics, to ret me in ze raboratory for ze arcohor. Zen I try to sneak up and squirt a spray in his mouse whire he talks. I get some in, but I don't get ze sprayer adjusted right, and ze spray hit him before it breaks up, and stings him. I don't have fingers, you know. So we have to use what ze books cawr brute force."

Methuen began to show signs of normalcy. As without his glass rod he was just a harmless old professor, Johnny let him up. His words tumbled out: "I'm so glad you did, Johnny—you saved my reputation, maybe my life. Those fatheads at the hospital wouldn't believe I had to be kept full of alcohol, so, of course, I sobered up and went crazy again—maybe they'll believe now. Come on; let's get back there quickly. If they haven't discovered my absence, they might be willing to keep this last escape quiet. When they let me out, I'll work on a permanent cure for the Methuen treatment. I'll find it, if I don't die of stomach ulcers from all the alcohol I'll have to drink."

Johnny waddled up Temple Street to his home, feeling rather smug about his ability as a fixer. Maybe Methuen, sober, was right about the futility of it all. But if such a philosophy led to the upsetting of Johnny's pleasant existence, Johnny preferred Methuen drunk.

He was glad Methuen would soon be well and coming home. Methuen was the only man he had any sentimental regard for. But as long as Methuen was shut up, Johnny was going to take advantage of that fact. When he reached the

Phelps mansion, instead of going directly in, he thrust a fore-
leg around behind the hedge next to the wall. It came out
with a huge slab of chewing tobacco. Johnny bit off about
half the slab, thrust the rest back in its cache, and went in,
drooling happily a little at each step. Why not?

# OLD MAN MULLIGAN

Astounding Science Fiction

December

## by P. Schuyler Miller (1912-1974)

*Although he had a master's degree in chemistry, P. Schuyler Miller's first love was archaeology, a passion that found its way into several of his best sf stories. He began to publish in the 1930s, with stories like "The Chrysalis" (1936), the justly famous "The Sands of Time" (1937), and "Spawn" (1939). Best known as the long-time book reviewer (1951-1975) for* Astounding/Analog, *There his "The Reference Library" became an institution, he published only two books in the field:* Genus Homo *(1950, a revision of a 1941 story), a novel written in collaboration with L. Sprague de Camp; and an excellent collection,* The Titan *(1952). Please. Won't someone bring these two fine books back into print?*

(I met Schuyler Miller now and then at science fiction conventions. He was gentle, rational, and a comer. So it seemed to me. He had begun writing in 1931 and one of his early stories "Tetrahedra of Space" transfixed me in my pre-teen days. He was a regular in John Campbell's stable in the first three or four years of that editor's incumbency and then, during World War II, Schuyler stopped writing. He spent the rest of his science fiction life as Campbell's book reviewer and the kindest and least impassioned reviewer there was. I was always sorry he had stopped writing though.

"Old Man Mulligan" was perhaps his most popular story and it's easy to see why. The rest may be cops and robbers but Mulligan is a work of genius. There's a Neanderthal that's a Neanderthal. "Old Man Mulligan" is at one end; Lester del Rey's "The Day Is Done" is at the other and L. Sprague de Camp's "The Gnarly Man" is somewhere in between. —I.A.)

Davis stopped under the glowlamp to light a cigarette. Ten feet away the mist clamped down, swallowing all but the pale cone of light in which he stood, the hulking shape of Top-Sergeant Gibbon casting its gorilla's shadow beside his own. The fishy reek of Venus's shallow sea and the stench of discarded garbage in Laxa's narrow alleys got in a man's throat and made his mouth taste like rotten cabbage. He'd be glad to breathe canned air again, and see the stars hanging like diamond spangles against space. There wasn't a planet in the System, outside of Earth, fit for a man to live on—and Venus was the worst of the lot.

Down the street a door swung open, silhouetting two wavering shapes against a blur of yellow lamplight. The yowl of maudlin voices spilled out after them, with one raucous bellow rising above the rest:

"I was bo-o-orn a hunnerd thousan' years ago-o-o,
   An' there's nothin' in the world that I dunno-o-o;
   I seen Peter, Paul an' Moses . . ."

The door slammed, shutting it off, but Davis was already grinding his cigarette under his heel and the sergeant's boots were scuffing restlessly on the cobbled street. They knew that voice of old. Mulligan! And when Mulligan sang that song there'd be hell to pay in a matter of minutes!

Gibbon's hairy fist smashed into the door. Gun in hand, Davis stepped after him into the barroom. Over the heads of the cutthroat crew that packed the place the patrolman's eyes went unerringly to the source of trouble. Mulligan was standing on the bar, spraddle-legged, his favorite oaken staff gripped threateningly in one huge fist and his beet-red face thrust forward like an angry ape's. His little red eyes peered furiously out from under massive eaves of bone and his bun-shaped skull shone like a china doorknob. His back was hunched, his shirt was open on a barrel chest, and an empty bottle swung at the end of his long left arm.

"Who called me that?" he bellowed.

There was a party of slummers in a wall booth—a blonde girl and three pale, sleek youths in faultless formal dress. One, with a smear of mustache and horn-rimmed spectacles, was pretty far gone. His face was as red as Mulligan's as he wavered to his feet.

"S'a lie!" he shouted. "S'a damn lie! He—nobody's that old!"

Davis's gun snapped up. The drunken fool! But he was too late. Mulligan's arms swung like striking snakes. The bottle smashed on the wall above the youngster's head. His legs slid out from under him and he sat down hard just as the oaken staff bored a hole through the flimsy partition beside his ear.

Things happened then. The girl was on her feet, slim, white-faced, scarlet-lipped, wound in a sheath of silver. Her escorts were struggling with their chairs. And from somewhere behind their booth came the *sput* of a silenced gun. A dripping red line slashed across Mulligan's receding jaw. And in the same instant Gibbon shouted, David spun instinctively, and the world went out in a splash of fire.

That same hoarse voice wormed its way into Davis's dreams and made him wince. It brought back memories that started chariots of fire careening around inside his skull:

"... I seen Peter, Paul an' Moses
Playing 'ring-around-the-roses
Aaaan' I'll lick the guy who claims that it ain't so!

"I'm the guy that got ol' Sampson's whiskers curled;
I helped Joe an' Adolf divvy up the world,
An' I led the gang to cover
When George Washington came over
With the A.E.F. to see their game was spoiled!

"I taught Solomon to say his A-B-C's;
I helped Brigham Young invent Limburger cheese;
An' I ran the plane for Lindy
On his trans-Atlantic shindy,
While Chris Columbus whistled for a breeze!"

It was all he could endure. He pulled himself up on his rubber legs and held his splitting head in both hands and yelled *"Shuddup!"* Then he opened his eyes.

He saw bare gray rock and gray sky, and a curtain of gray mist that blanketed it all. It was drizzling, and he was stark naked, with little dribbles of tipid water running down his spine and dripping off the end of his nose. He saw Mulligan, a hundred yards away at the edge of the gray sea that lapped and gurgled horridly against the wet, gray rocks. The old man was as bare and pink as a skinned monkey, hunkered down puzzling over a clam.

Mulligan's monkey-face twisted toward him. It grinned, and the old man brought his fist down with a whack on the rock in front of him. Clam juice spurted and Mulligan began painstakingly to slurp up the mess out of his cupped palm.

Behind him Davis heard the noises of someone being sick. It was the very drunk young man of the barroom. In nothing but spectacles and a mustache he looked even less impressive than he had in a boiled shirt and a red sash. He was a little knock-kneed and his belly bulged more than it should have at his age. Davis patted his own taut abdomen approvingly and strode masterfully to investigate.

They were on a lump of rock that stuck up out of the steaming, stinking waters of Venus's mud-hole of a sea. From the marks on the rock they'd have six or eight feet to themselves at high tide. And there'd be things that would want to eat them.

He counted noses. Six, with Mulligan. Gibbon was sitting up in a puddle, staring ruefully at his bare toes. There was a bullet hole through the biceps of his right arm and a bloody gash in the clipped hair of his round skull. The two kids who had been with Goggles and the girl were still out. And they were all as naked as the day they were born, if you excepted the fur on Gibbon's chest and the toothbrush under Goggles' nose.

Old Man Mulligan came paddling over the rocks toward them. He was sober now and looked as harmless as a kitten. Davis felt his official temper rising.

"You got us into this mess, Mulligan," he snarled. "Now get us out of it!"

Mulligan's long face wrinkled in a toothless grin. "You look pretty good without pants, Cap," he observed. "I remember one time down in Nubia we run into a tribe that didn't wear nothing at all—but could they fight! Pharaoh, he says to me, 'Mike' he says—that was short for whatever it was those Egyptians used to call me—'Mike, you train me a couple thousan' of them cannibals an' we'll wipe ol' Hubble-Bubble an' his damn' Hittites right off the map!" So I picked me a brigade of the biggest an' barest an' blackest bucks I could find an' put 'em through the ol' West Point stuff. Then we got over in there back of Carchemish, an' damn' if the lot of 'em didn't get homesick an' light out for Nubia! Left me with my pants down, so to speak, so I hopped a ship for Mycenae an' got mixed up in a war they was havin' over a babe called Helena. Redhead, she was." His little eyes had a faraway look. "Geez, Cap—them was the days!"

Davis found his shoulder muscles sagging. You couldn't

bawl Mulligan out. Tougher men than he had tried. "You damned old liar!" he snapped. "Can't you drop that phoney past of yours long enough to think about the mess we're in?"

The red glint came into Mulligan's eyes again and the chin he didn't have jammed forward and set. "They was too many of 'em," he complained. "I'd of handled 'em, only the barkeep took me from behind with a full bottle." He fingered the back of his hairless skull. "Look—I got a bump like a egg."

"Never mind your bump!" There was more in this than met the eye. Mulligan's ruckuses usually landed him in jail or the hospital, not on a rock in the middle of the ocean. "Who shot you—and why?"

"Oh—him? That was one of Slip Hanlan's boys. I got him with a chair while Slip an' the rest was busy with the girl."

"What about the girl? What happened to her? How did we get here?" It was the young man with the mustache. He had come up silently in his bare feet, and the others were with him. "What happened to the girl?" he repeated. "Where is she?"

"Her?" Mulligan seemed surprised that anyone should be interested. "Hanlan got her." He chuckled. "She's got guts, that babe! Blacked Slip's eye for him an' damn near took the ear off one of his monkeys with a bottle. They had to put a bag over her head an' tie her up like a bale of weeds. That was when the barkeep slugged me. You was already out, Cap—you an' the Sarge both."

Davis heard Gibbon's growl and intervened hastily. "Who is this girl?" he demanded. "What does Slip Hanlan want with her—and why did he dump us here?"

One of the pale young men answered. "She's my cousin—Anne Bradshaw. Her father's Regent, you know. I—I guess they just figured she'd be worth a lot of money, so they kidnapped her."

The Regent's daughter! The kid was right—she would bring anything Hanlan wanted to ask—but the System wouldn't hold the man who kidnapped her after she was back in her father's hands, nor the man who failed to return her after the ransom was paid. Every man in the Space Patrol would be personally pledged to blow the guts out of the man who laid hands on Anne Bradshaw—and Slip Hanlan was ordinarily a smart guy. Too smart to stick his neck out—unless he had an absolutely sure thing.

"What were you punks doing in that dump, anyway?" he

asked. "Haven't you got sense enough to keep a woman out of a dive like that? Hell—you might have run into some lug who didn't know who she is and was too hopped up to care!"

"Captain Davis." It was Goggles again. "Perhaps I can explain. I am at the University—professor of anthropology there—and these two young men are my students. There was a dance at the University Club and Miss Bradshaw herself insisted on our taking her to the place. We must find her, at once!"

He looked like the kind of daisy the government would import for their pet boarding school at Laxa. All on a very high plane—no rough competitive sports, no engineering, nothing practical: the young of Laxa's Brass Hats had to have culture, so the pedigreed cream of Earth's Ph.D.'s was shipped to Venus to teach them. What the planet needed, Davis reflected grimly, was a military academy with a major in pioneering. Because the first generation on Venus had had a tough time keeping alive, they wanted everything to be silk and sugar for their offspring. The only trouble with that was that human beings had a toehold on less than two percent of the planet's surface, and the days of pioneering had a couple of generations yet to run.

"Look, boss." Gibbon's face was glum and he seemed self-conscious in his nakedness. "The way I see it there's got to be politics mixed up in this business. Any other way Slip'd be drizzly to try it. It's been fixed at headquarters that the whole thing'll be hushed up when he brings the girl back. The Patrol won't even know she was missing—or the professor here, or these young punks. Only Mulligan mixed in and we showed up. So they ferried us out here where we'd be out of their way, and no questions asked. Somebody'll come past with a boat when it's all over and be very much surprised to find us here. Then we'll be told just what we're supposed to know and how unfortunate it'd be to have other ideas about things.

"Only we won't be alive. Not in winter, and without clothes. Slip Hanlan's foxy that way!"

The girl's cousin, young Bradshaw, pushed forward. His face was flushed. "I don't believe it!" he cried. "Uncle Arthur would never stoop to anything like that."

Davis patted his thin shoulder. "Take it easy," he advised. "Even if the Sergeant's right, that doesn't mean your uncle is mixed up in it. There are powers behind him, here and on Earth, with their own strings to pull and their own reasons for pulling them. It could be pretty smart to pick up his daughter and keep him worried about her instead of about other things that may be brewing. If nothing happens to her, he'll play along for the good of the colony. That's how politics works."

He turned to Mulligan. The old man was down on his hunkers again, pulling shellfish off the rocks and sucking them out of their shells with gusto. "Mike," he called, "come back here. You know more about Venus than any man on it. My father told me so. Where are we, and how do we get out of here?"

Mulligan's face wrinkled perplexedly. "I been here," he admitted. "There's a lot of these little islands off the coast where the main ridge of the Skyscrapers runs into the ocean. I was here once with Morgan, back in the old days, fishin' for sea serpents."

"Sea serpents?" It was the second boy. "You mean here, in these waters—around us?"

The old man nodded. "Yeah. It's pretty deep here. There's plenty room for 'em to get real big, like they used to be back on Earth. Why, I remember—"

"You forget it!" Davis told him. "Do you mean that we're stuck here?"

"I wouldn't say that," the old man protested. "You better leave me puzzle it over a bit. We got to wait for high tide, anyway."

They left him opening clams and sought shelter under a ledge where they could hug their knees and steam in a little less discomfort. Winter on Venus was predominantly wet and windy. It was hot, the air was soakingly humid, and the rain was like cold soup, but the rock-shelter made them feel a little more like men.

The Professor had given up trying to see through his glasses and was peering owlishly over them. "Can we trust this man?" he wanted to know. "What can he do?"

Davis shrugged. "He can do all anyone can," he replied. "Old Man Mulligan's the biggest puzzle on Venus. He's been around as long as anyone living can remember. He was here with Morgan on the first exploring trip, if you believe the records. He hasn't changed a bit in two men's lifetimes, and I seriously doubt that he'll change in mine or yours. He knows Venus better than any man in the system, and if he says he can get us off, he's got a way of doing it. Am I right, Gibbon?"

"Yeah!" The sergeant had been packing lichens over the

hole in his arm. "That song of his was the first thing I heard when I stepped out of the transport thirty years ago. He was drunk and whalin' the bejasus out of some dope that called him a liar, and I had to get three other cops to help me put him in a cell. Then I had to hear him tell about Moses and Pharaoh's daughter, and how he'd been a priest over in a place called Midian and this Moses married his daughter. He's got daughters all over the system, if you believe half he says."

"Fantastic!" The Professor was on the verge of exploding. "No man can have lived since the days of Moses. Four thousand years! It's absurd! I happen to be an anthropologist, and I know!"

"He lays claim to a hundred thousand, if I remember," Davis said dryly. "I know for a fact he was alive eighty years ago, when my father came out here, and the records give him nearly twice that. He knows a lot about history, too, if he does get it garbled up sometimes. There must be a hell of a lot in your head to get twisted if you've lived a hundred thousand years!"

The Professor stared at him accusingly over his glasses. "Be serious!" he snapped. "You're an educated man; you know as well as I do that no man can live a thousand years, let alone a hundred thousand. It's ridiculous! I'll admit there is something peculiar about the man—the shape of his head for one thing, and his posture, and that brow-ridge. He definitely represents a very primitive type. Almost Neanderthaloid, I would say. A throwback, I presume. Where is he now?"

The second boy, Wilson, was at the far end of the shelter. "He's been hammering at a big rock," he reported, "and now he's knocking little pieces off it with another stone. Look—about those clams. If we're marooned here, shouldn't we be doing something to conserve them? I mean, they're all we have to eat, and they won't last long if Mulligan goes on wolfing them down like that!"

It was growing colder as night drew on. Venus never got really cold, even now, near the Pole and in the dead of "winter," but night in the rainy season could be as dismal an affair as you'd ask for. Davis tried to remember how the tides were running. The shallow sea and submerged coastline made them freakish and irregular, even though Venus had only the sun to produce them. Getting to his feet he peered out to sea. There was a definite strong current setting past the end of the island and rocks he had seen well above water a half hour before were buried in phosphorescent spume. The tide was rising.

He scrambled painfully down over the ledges to where the old man squatted. In the open the rising wind caught him and he shivered with the sudden chill. He heard other feet padding behind him and saw that Gibbon and the Professor were following him.

Mulligan had found a vein of flint in the limestone of which the island was made. He had half a dozen big chunks of the stuff on the ground beside him and was knocking fist-sized spalls off them with a lump of waterworn quartzite. He had about a dozen of them, and as the men approached began to work them down to shape with deft, quick raps of his hammer-stone, flaking off smaller chips all round their edge. Pretty soon he had a spear-shaped blade, flat on one side and rounded on the other, with an uneven cutting edge and a rounded base. He laid it down and started on another. The Professor nudged Davis excitedly.

"The Mousterian technique," he whispered. "Indubitable! Extraordinary!"

Davis cleared his throat apologetically. He felt like an ass, standing here in the rain watching an old man play caveman, but he had a feeling that he was intruding on something important.

"Mulligan," he said, "the tide's rising. Hadn't we better do something pretty soon?"

The old man looked up at him. "I am," he answered. "I'm makin' knives an' spears for the lot of us. There's things comin' in with the tide that'd make one nip of the Sergeant or you an' use the Professor for a toothpick. If I was you, I'd get them punks out lookin' for somethin' I can use for handles. It ain't always convenient to get real close to critters like them."

"Do you claim that you are one hundred thousand years old?" The professor's voice nearly cracked.

Mulligan ducked his head sheepishly. "I guess mebbe that's a little strong," he admitted, "but it fits good in the song. Last time I figured it out for a feller that knew about things like that it came out about thirty thousand. Might be five or ten thousand off one way or the other, he thought. There was a long time there I didn't have no inclination to keep track of stuff like that, an' it was pretty hard to catch up. Even in Sumer they wasn't much good at big numbers, an' this was way before that—before they come down out of the hills, even."

Davis turned away as he saw the professor's jaw beginning to drop. The damned old liar! He rounded up Gibbon and the two boys, and they began to search for long, straight staves of driftwood which might serve as spear shafts. They found only three which were long enough and strong enough to be of any use. The continent must be fairly close, Davis reflected, to get any green wood out here at all. Maybe Mulligan knew what he was doing, after all.

They still had an hour's half-light left, Davis estimated. The dense Venusian atmosphere strung twilight out into what was practically a diurnal season. They found Mulligan up to his armpits in the surf, his enormous nose nearly in the water prodding and poking with a notched and pointed stick. As they reached the water's edge he jabbed viciously at the general neighborhood of his feet and plunged after the harpoon to come up coughing and spewing salt water, with something leggy and shapeless squirming on the end of his stick.

Davis watched with interest and the Professor with what bordered on despair as the old man planted his bare feet on the thing's lashing tectacles and proceeded to slice it up with his flint knife. Presently he had several long strips of tough leathery tissue with which he lashed his spearheads firmly into the cleft ends of the shafts they had found. Inasmuch as Gibbon's right arm was useless, Davis decided that he would have to be their reserve. To the tune of the sergeant's grumbling the five men returned to their shelter to watch and wait.

Mulligan did not join them. He was making a weapon for himself—a wicked-looking tooth of chipped flint half as long as his forearm, with the butt rounded for a grip. The professor called it a fist-axe and went into a profound sulk because evidence and science were growing more and more at odds with every moment.

It was fast growing darker. Mulligan's squat frame was barely visible against the pallid phosphorescence of the sea, perched on the end of a spine of rock that thrust out into deep water. Davis wondered how long it would be before the tide flooded them out and forced them to take refuge on the exposed crown of the island, at the mercy of winds and rain and every famished sea monster that came that way. Grimly he watched the glowing line of surf lap higher and higher. It was almost up to Mulligan's dangling legs when he let out a piercing yell and vanished.

They went pelting down the rocks, spears in hand, to the promontory where Mulligan had been. Waist deep in the rising water, the old man was jumping up and down like a maniac, waving his arms and hooting like a demented ape. Then a hundred feet beyond, Davis saw something rise sluggishly to the surface. The old man saw it too. He retreated toward shore, still yelling and waving his arms frantically. Then it rose again!

It was like Leviathan of the legends. It rose out of the sea like a billowing wave, washed over with creamy spume—a colossal turtle's carapace, studded and ribbed and grown over with barnacles and clinging weeds—an armored, vast-eyed head with sneering beak, set on a wrinkled neck—huge, curving flippers that hooked and scrabbled at the sloping rock. The black bubbles of its lidless eyes stared at the little bandy-legged creature who danced tauntingly before it. A wave broke over its back, hiding it, and then it appeared again, much closer, and began to move ponderously toward the shore, its snaking dragon's head thrust evilly forward.

Mulligan came scrambling over the rocks toward them, shouting at them in some unknown tongue. With a yell to the others Davis began the same insane dance, drawing the thing's attention, luring it ashore. The hooked beak and staring eyes rose out of the foam at their very feet. It lunged at the little group on the rock's summit, fell short, and before it could recover the old man leaped.

He twisted like a cat in midair and came down astride of the monster's wrinkled neck. Flat on his belly, legs locked around that barrel of muscle, he drove his fist-axe into the creature's throat. Blood spurted like black oil into the burning sea. His whole arm was buried in the gaping wound he had torn. The monster writhed and twisted, striving vainly to reach him. Its flippers churned the sea. It was turning—heading for deeper water!

Gibbon, empty-handed, went over the side of the rock. He came up flailing madly with his good arm, found footing and dashed at the thing's head, turning it. As it snapped at him he leaped back, and then Davis and the others were beside him. Young Bradshaw's spear glanced harmlessly off the monster's armored head and vanished into the sea. The professor's eyes were gleaming strangely behind his spectacles. He danced down the slippery ledge under the sea-thing's very beak, and rising on tiptoe planted his spear deep in the giant turtle's staring eye.

The thing recoiled, nearly hurling Mulligan from his perch, then lunged viciously. The edge of its carapace caught the professor, spinning him aside, and its beak gaped before Davis's startled eyes. Before it could close he drove his spear deep down that reeking gullet and flung himself out of its path. Its horny jaws closed on the shaft, clipping it like a twig, then the Wilson boy darted in and drove his weapon into its other eye and through into the brain beyond.

The gigantic jaws gaped wide. Black blood poured out of them. The scrabbling flippers sagged and the monster surged forward on the beach, its long neck writhing blindly. Then Mulligan's blade reached home and the life gushed out of the great beast in a steaming stream, leaving it inert on the rocks with the tide lapping against its vast, curving shell.

The old man clambered to his feet and stood looking them over. They were a bloody, draggled crew—but they had won! He grinned approvingly and waved an arm up the beach.

"Get the knives," he ordered. "We got work to do."

Thigh-deep in blood and foam the six men hacked and pried at the giant carcass, hewing away the muscles which held the bowl-shaped carapace, separating the ribs and cutting through the giant spinal column. The sea was red around them, and beyond the first line of breakers they could see black, misshapen forms rising and falling with the surge of the waves. Ghouls, drawn by the taste of death. And, Davis reflected, a living wall between them and the mainland.

The tide had nearly reached the high-water mark when they finally lifted the edge of the great shell and tipped it over into the sea. It floated low in the water, with a bloody soup slopping around inside it, and Davis's stomach turned over as he realized that this was to be their ferry to the mainland.

A rocky point, which had been a ridge when the day began, ran into the sea at the tip of the island. At Mulligan's direction they dragged the huge shell away from the carcass—and away from the ravening creatures of the deep that had scented its blood nad were waiting for the tide to float it out to them. Young Wilson had kept his spear, and the professor's had been dragged out of the ruin of the turtle's eye after it collapsed. Mulligan's fist-axe was their only other weapon. And the thrash and bellow of monstrous life out there in the darkness told them what they might expect before their crazy coracle reached shore.

While Mulligan busied himself with the sea-thing's tangled

entrails, cutting long strips of gut and twisting it into a kind of cord which he wrapped around his waist, the others bailed out what they could of the mess inside the shell and gingerly took their places on its slippery bottom. Davis and the old man were last. Slowly they edged the great bowl along the rocks and out into the current that swirled past the point. As the tide caught it, they tumbled in and crouched with the others in the bottom. It rocked drunkenly with the force of their shove, grated for a moment on a submerged rock, then swung ponderously around and was loose.

Every other wave, it seemed, broke into the sluggish craft. Gibbon and the boys bailed furiously with their hands. Davis took Wilson's spear and stationed himself at what had been the tail end of the oval shell. The professor, using his weapon as a staff, crouched unsteadily in the middle, and Mulligan, still gripping his spike of flint, squatted in the bow, his long toes gripping the slimy ladder made by the creature's ribs.

The old man's restless eyes sighted the first danger. At his grunt Davis raised himself as far as he dared. Ten yards away the thing broke water. It had a snout like a crocodile and a streamlined, glistening body that slipped effortlessly through the waves. It rolled over, showing a gleaming belly, and dove. Ten seconds slipped by—twenty—a minute, and Davis let himself drop back. Then at his very elbow the monster rose again. Two tiny red eyes, buried in slits in the glistening flesh, glared down at him. A snout edged with tiny, saw-edged teeth grinned at him. And with all his strength he drove his heavy spear into the soft, pouched throat beneath that narrow jaw.

The great thing rose like a breaching whale—up and up and up until it seemed to stand on its tail in midair. Then with a crash that nearly swamped the shell it fell back. Davis hung on grimly with both hands and watched the sea spin past. Off to the left the creature rose again. Its outline was barely visible against the pale phosphorescence of the water. Something stout and stubby, with bristling fins, had fastened itself savagely to its dangling lower jaw.

Suddenly the sea about them was alive. The taint of fresh blood was in the waves, and the death-watch gathered. A vast, scaly something rose almost under the shell, tipping it, and hurled Davis back into the human tangle in the bottom. Water poured over them, and out of the murk a spined and wattled head peered down at them. Mulligan yelled defiance, brandishing his fist-axe like a war club. Another wave caught

Davis in the face and bowled him over. Over the bellow of
the sea beasts the sergeant's voice rose in a howl of anguish:

"Bail, damn you! We'll be under!"

They bailed—Gibbon with his one good arm, the others
with both hands, splashing bloody water out a little faster
than it vomited in. The professor's spear was somewhere underfoot, swashing back and forth in the reeking bilge, and
Mulligan still clung like a limpet to his perch. Off in the night
another of the sea monsters grumbled, and Davis's fingers
closed on the floating spear.

He straightened up, straddling the knobby column of bone
that ran from stem to stern of their drunken craft—the
turtle's spine. His eyes fell on Mulligan, silhouetted against
the pallid glow of the sea, and a tingling chill ran down his
spine. The old man's head was drawn down between his
scarred shoulders, his chinless face thrust out, tasting the
wind. His broad back was curved like a crouching wolf's, his
bandy legs drawn up under him, his long arms dangling. He
was like a great, hairless ape of the night, carved out of ebony
and set there for a figurehead to ward off demons. His great
bald head swung suddenly toward the men, and Davis
thought he caught a glint of greenish fire in the little eyes before it turned away.

The minutes passed by over them, and the hours. How
long it was Davis could not tell. The wind had fallen and the
sea was more quiet. There was an oily swell that rocked their
cranky craft like a cradle, up and down, back and forth. The
professor was sick and the two boys crouched miserably together in the bottom. Hour after hour passed, while Davis
watched vainly for some glint of dawn in the sky and Old
Man Mulligan squatted silent and inscrutable in the bow,
peering ahead into the darkness.

They were the sea's toy, tossed where it willed, at the
mercy of unknown, uncharted currents. If the tide had turned
they might be drifting away from land, out into the unmap-
ped, unfathomed, mist-wrapped waste that covered half of
Venus. Five men, naked in the night with the cold rain slat-
ting down across their backs and the slap and whisper of the
phosphorescent waves the only sound in the world. Five men,
Davis thought—and Mulligan.

He closed his eyes and listened. Very far away, he thought,
he could hear a sullen roar as of surf against rocky ledges.
Perhaps the tide was carrying them back to the island. It

might be land. He strained his ears, but it was gone, and Mulligan had not stirred.

Suddenly the old man was on his feet, his legs braced, his head thrust forward like a scenting hound's. He was unwinding the rope of twisted gut from his waist and running it through his gnarled fingers, tightening it, forming a noose. Cautiously Davis got to his feet. It was lighter now. Past the old man's tense shape he saw the arch of a glistening dome—another of the great turtles. Mulligan crouched lower, and with a cry to Gibbon Davis hurled himself back into the stern as the old man's noose settled over the monster's head.

Their weight in the stern was all that saved the shell from going over. As the rope tightened the front of the carapace plowed deep into the waves. Davis was hanging to the rim with both hands; Gibbon had him around the waist, and the others were sprawled on the bottom. One by one they scrambled to join the two Patrolmen. Like five naked apes they perched on the edge of the great shell, balancing the pull of the runaway monster. Both feet planted against an arching rib, Old Man Mulligan was lying back with all his weight, the rope tight around his waist. The muscles stood out like oak roots on his arms and back. They were on their way at last, but where they were going only the Almighty—or the turtle—knew.

At a word from Davis, young Bradshaw slipped down from his perch and went to give Mulligan a hand. He was the lightest of them, and the old man could not stand the strain alone much longer. Side by side, like charioteers of old, they stood and rode the sea—the gnarled, brown body and the slim white one, outlined in the brightening day.

There was no doubt—ahead there came the roar of surf. Mulligan shouted back at them but his voice was whipped away in the wind. Then with a crash that hurled them headlong into the sea the shell struck. It split like a gourd and went down sucking them after it. Savagely Davis fought his way to the surface. Gibbon was clinging to a rock, just clear of the water. Wilson's head bobbed up between them, and the boy struck out vigorously to join the sergeant. But of Mulligan and young Bradshaw there was no trace.

The mist was lifting. There were rocks all around them, jagged and black, with the waves breaking angrily over them. Then out of the gloom came a hail:

"Ho-o-o o-o!"

A second voice joined the first "Ho-o o-o-o! Da-a-avis!"

Gibbon answered with a strangled bellow, and then Davis saw them. The cliffs were close, steep and frowning, with the sea smashing against them. Mulligan and the boy were clinging to a long, rocky spit that ran out from a little cove at their base. Davis took a long breath and let the sea carry him in.

Mulligan's hand closed over his wrist and dragged him to safety on the reef. Out in the welter of foam he saw Gibbon's clipped head and young Wilson's sleek one. The sergeant was forging ahead vigorously in spite of his wounded arm. A few minutes later they were all together—all but the Professor.

A step at a time, feeling their way through the surf that broke over the reef, they edged their way shoreward. It was Gibbon who saw the missing man, lying in the wash of the waves. His glasses were gone and there was a great bruise on his forehead, but when they dragged him up on the little beach he stirred feebly and opened his eyes.

Watching Gibbon drain the water out of the bedraggled teacher, Davis wondered what came next. They were naked, famished, marooned miles from the nearest settlement. There might be a way over the circle of cliffs, but beyond was the unexplored wilderness of the Skyscrapers, peaks that dwarfed many of Earth's proudest ranges, and beyond them the jungle. Venus was no Eden.

He studied Mulligan, busy over the professor. The old man was the only one of them who didn't seem out of place. Those cruel scars and massive muscles spoke of battles with nature more terrible than anything they had yet gone through. What was the truth about him?

Gibbon limped over, hugging his hurt arm. "The prof took quite a beating, Boss," he observed sourly. "We better stay here a while." He scowled. "We won't get any place barefoot, without anything in our bellies."

"You'd oughta have feet like mine." It was Mulligan. The old man's soles were like black horn. "I been goin' barefoot every chance I get, ever since I can remember. Shoes is crampin' if you was brought up free-footed like me."

"We weren't," Davis pointed out acidly. "We've got to get back and start on Hanlan's trail before he puts over whatever trick he has up his sleeve, but without shoes we won't make a mile a day over those mountains. What's more, we'll starve at that pace."

The old man chuckled. "You'll get shoes," he said. "Nor you won't starve. I been here before, remember, an' if I hadn't I could still keep goin' any place that'll grow worms. Tell those two punks they got to find a little pile of sand, up above high water. When they got it, yell."

In less then ten minutes Bradshaw let out a whoop. Almost simultaneously Wilson called from further down the beach. Each had a low mound about eight feet in diameter, heaped up in the sand. Mulligan went at the first like a terrier in a rat-hole. Sand flew for a minute; then he swung back on his heels and held up a dirty yellow object about a foot long.

"Turtle eggs," he explained. "There's a string of these little beaches along the coast where they come to lay. The one we rode in was likely headed for this one, but we scared her off."

There were twelve eggs in the nest Bradshaw had found, and ten in Wilson's. Mulligan made himself another crude stone knife with which he carefully cut a circle out of an egg, just short of the end, big enough to push a foot through. The leathery shell made a crude but effective moccasin, and the egg itself went a long way toward satisfying their hunger.

They spent the night huddled together under the cliffs, wet and miserable. What wood they could find was too waterlogged to burn, even if they had had any way of lighting a fire. As the first gray light began to filter through the clouds they gulped down a breakfast of raw turtle eggs, pulled on their clumsy shoes, and set out to explore the circuit of the cliffs. The professor seemed himself again, and Mulligan was as chipper as a youngster. Gibbon's arm was paining him, and Davis fashioned a sling out of strands of seaweed, but there was nothing more he could do.

Davis had been planning a conference in which every contingency would be brought up and disposed of, and a plan of action worked out. He never had the opportunity to suggest one. Before he could protest, Mulligan went at the cliffs like a squirrel, his seaweed basket of eggs bobbing merrily on his back. They could only follow.

The old man was thoroughly at home. He trotted along with the thin drizzle of rain cascading down his backbone, uncomplaining and sure-footed as a goat. The others were less fortunate. After struggling painfully up a precipitous slope, clinging to the rock with tooth and nail, they would reach the top and find him squatting on a hand's breadth of level ground, only to have him swing tirelessly to his feet and disappear into some chasm or up a steepling crag.

When at last they came down out of the mountains into the jungle it was worse. There was no trail. Mulligan seemed

to flow through the underbrush where the others had to fight
their way step by step through a wall of thorns and tangled
vines. Nevertheless, it was Mulligan who kept them alive. The
six-foot staff he had provided for himself was like a magic
wand. With it he probed seemingly bottomless morasses or
made a bridge from root to root where black ooze crawling
with venomous life was the only floor to the jungle. With it
he knocked down small animals which they learned to eat
raw, and on it he strung poisonous looking fungi which nevertheless filled their stomachs. With it, once, he fought off a
snarling, yellow cat-like thing which contested their way.

Once, even, the old man found a tree whose inner bark
was dry and tindery, and all that night they crowded gratefully around the little fire he made by rubbing a stick of dry
wood in a wooden groove. By morning the crude friction
device was soaked and their fuel gone. They got stiffly to
their feet and stumbled on, cold and empty, following the old
man's great splayed footprints in the mud.

They had spent a night at sea in the shell and a night on
the beach. They spent a night in the mountains and three
more in the forest. A little light was still filtering down
through the giant tree-ferns when they suddenly came upon
Mulligan, flat on his face in the mud at the edge of a clearing.

Davis was bringing up the rear. He nearly fell over the
professor, who was lying in the middle of the trail peering
near-sightedly ahead. On hands and knees he made his way
to where Mulligan and the sergeant were lying. Gibbon
pointed wordlessly.

There was a house in the clearing. It was the familiar pill-
box of the Venusian trader, a rambling affair of concrete
without windows or any other unnecessary openings which
would afford an entrance for the unpleasantly persistent
fauna of the jungle.

"Hanlan!" the sergeant muttered through his teeth.

Hanlan? Then Mulligan had known all along where they
were. He had brought them here deliberately, naked and
unarmed, where they could only sit and fume at their helplessness. Red spots danced before Davis's eyes. He'd been
playing second fiddle long enough!

"Sergeant Gibbon," he snapped, "we're taking over. I'll
reconnoiter. Stay here until I signal you. If Hanlan is here, he
won't be expecting us. We have the advantage of surprise,
and we'll have to use it."

Beside them in the mud old Mulligan chuckled. "You ain't got a badge any more Cap'n," he pointed out slyly. "You ain't even got a uniform. Mebbe Slip won't reconnize you."

Davis ignored him. "Hanlan may not be here," he went on. "We have only Mulligan's word that it's his hideout. But if it is his, and I don't come back, you're in command. Understand?"

"Sure, Boss." Gibbon saluted awkwardly. "Only I don't see what we can do about it if he puts up an argument."

Well inside the forest, Davis made a circuit of the clearing. Someone was evidently in the place, for a good-sized launch was tied up inside a breakwater where the jungle met an arm of the sea. For safety's sake, he removed some of the engine's vitals and watched them disappear in a dozen feet of turgid water.

A series of terraces rose steeply behind the hut, and a quick examination showed him no easy road over them. The place was set in a sort of niche in the hillside and would probably be entirely invisible to patrol boats unless they ventured into the unknown waters of the fjord on which it faced. It was an ideal hideout.

If Hanlan had tele-cells set, there was no evidence of it. When he made sure that there were none of the scanning eyes in evidence anywhere on the hut's interior, Davis made bold to scurry up close to its walls. He located the radiation plate of the cooling system, at the end opposite the single door. It was hot, proving that there was someone inside.

There might be spying devices in the door frame, invisible from a distance, and he kept away from that. The rest of the walls he went over foot by foot. There was a ventilator on the roof, but it had a stout grating across it and in any case was barely big enough to admit a man's head, let alone his body. If Slip Hanlon wanted to stay inside till doomsday there was nothing Davis could do about it.

He went back to the radiation plate. If the hut was built on the usual plan, the conditioner would be in a booth in the little storeroom which was in the rear of most such shacks. The chances were good that nobody ever went into the place unless something went wrong. He studied the plate carefully. The metal grid of cooling fins was set flush with the wall, but the concrete was stained and crumbling around its edges, and in one place there was a good-sized crack. If only he had some sort of tool!

He remembered the launch. Fifteen minutes later he was

hard at work, chipping away at the concrete. It was soft and fell away easily. Soon he was able to get the end of a steel bar under the edge of the plate. He heaved with all his strength and the thing yielded a little. He heaved again. Inside the hut something spanged and the plate came out a good two inches.

Whoever had set the conditioner up had been careless. The bolts which held the plate were loose enough for Davis to get a wrench in through the slit and remove them completely. This gave him enough room to push an arm through and grope around for the couplings of the heat exhaust tubes. He found them at once because they were hot, and it took much poking and swearing before he had them loose from the radiation plate, and had lowered it gently to the ground.

He listened. Everything was dark and still inside except for the liquid chuckle of the refrigeration fluid in the pipes of the conditioner. Using wads of wet leaves to protect his hands, he bent the tubes aside as far as they would go. With a chisel from the yacht's tool kit he slid back the tongue of the lock on the cabinet door. It swung noiselessly open. With a wriggle he went through the hole, grazing the hot tubes painfully and scraping a patch of skin off his hip.

The storeroom was dark, but there was a crack of light under the door leading to the other part of the hut. He tiptoed toward it, one fist closed tightly around a man-sized wrench. Then something clipped him neatly behind the left ear and he went down with a thud.

His legs were hobbled and his arms tied behind his back when he came to. A wad of metallic tasting cloth was jammed into his mouth. He struggled and commented violently through the gag. A small hand slapped him smartly on the jaw.

"Shut up!" a woman's voice hissed.

Twenty years later in life Davis might have been in danger of apoplexy. "Gug ga gu!" he gargled. "Ge goe gow! Gu-gu!"

A small, cold circle pressed purposefully into his naked stomach. He knew the feeling. She had a gun.

"Be quiet!" she whispered. "They'll be in here any minute! Get under that bed at once or I'll knock you out again and put you there."

He submitted meekly to being rolled under a small iron cot that stood against one wall. She dropped a blanket over the side to hide him and switched on the lights. He twisted his wrists tentatively. She'd done a good job, but maybe not good enough. By dint of much writhing he was able to bring one eye close to a hole in the blanket. What he saw made his jaws clamp down hard on his gag.

It was the girl in the bar-room, Anne Bradshaw. It would be, he thought. Her silver gown was rumpled, and the skirt had been torn off knee-high, revealing a pair of entirely satisfactory legs. She was fiddling with her hair. With a glance toward the bed, she turned her back and rummaged for a moment under her skirt. Davis's eyes hardened when he saw the gun in her hand—small but businesslike. Chances were that it threw the new high-velocity slug that bowled a man over like a cannonball.

There was a brisk knock on the door. Stooping, the girl slid the little gun across the floor and under the bed. A key rattled in the lock and two men stepped into the room.

The smaller of the two was Slip Hanlan. Every man in the Patrol knew his face and record. He was sleek and dark, with a ratty little mustache. He had a long red scratch down one cheek which might have been made by an enameled fingernail. The man with him was the standard slugger: burly, empty faced, thoroughly overdressed in imitation of his leader.

At Hanlan's gesture the gun-lug closed the door and leaned against it. The gang leader looked the girl over coolly from head to toe and she stared calmly back at him, eye to eye. Straining furiously at his bonds, with the little gun lying under his very nose, Davis watched apprehensively.

"We have visitors." Hanlan was going to be silky about it. "Know anything about 'em? It wouldn't be nice to have 'em trying to bust in where they're not wanted."

The girl stared at him, blank faced. "What do you mean?" she inquired.

His smile was very like a snarl. "I mean that if any snooping sons of crump-worms interfere with our little conference it might be embarrassing for you. Regent's Daughter Surprised with Gang Boss. Debutante in Jungle Rendezvous. That stuff. It'll stink!"

She sat down on the bed and crossed her long legs calmly. "There were friends with me who know what really happened. The Patrol knows by now. Probably they're getting ready to give you the going over you deserve! They've wanted to get something on you for a long time. I'll enjoy watching them!"

Hanlan's little laugh was nasty. "Whoever it is out there is lying low," he told her. "The Patrol don't act like that. As for those monkeys you were with, they're keeping cool where nobody'll bother 'em until I say so."

The strands of twisted cloth with which Davis's hands were tied yielded so suddenly that he nearly rammed his elbow into the wall behind him. He pulled the gag out of his mouth and unfastened the hobbles on his legs, then cautiously picked up the little gun. It was loaded.

"Plug." Hanlan jerked a thumb at the lug by the door. "Get outside and tell the boys to keep an eye open. Old Bradshaw may have put a scout on the babe here, but it won't do him any good. I'm calling the play from here on."

"Are you really?" Anne Bradshaw's voice dripped icicles. "And what is the play, as you see it?"

Hanlan's nasty little smile vanished. "I'm sick of being kicked around by stuffed shirts," he snapped. "Twenty years ago every one of 'em was doing what I've done, an' getting rich on it. They were pioneers an' I'm a criminal. They're rich an' have fancy mansions, an' I have to hide out in a stinking shack. They've killed and thieved and cut the government's throat, and they're respected for it. Well—I'm joining 'em!"

"What do I have to do with that?" There was a satin-smooth note in the girl's voice that made Davis suspicious.

"You're my ticket," Hanlan sneered. "Right now there's a bill on the Regent's desk. It's had the vote of all the Council and all he's got to do is put his name to it. It leases the government development on the West Continent to the Dobermann Colonization Association for ninety-nine Earth years. The Association has to build roads and houses, and provide transportation for good, able-bodied, honest settlers who want to come out and be big shots in a new world. They're all members of the Association, and if they're still alive after ten years they can sell out or sign up for another ten. If a man don't stick out his time he pays cash for every day he's used the land and every mouthful of food he's put in his belly up to the time he quits. The government goes his bond when it picks him to come out here and sells the Association the idea he's a good risk. If he can't pay up, or won't, his holdings go to the Association outright, on account of the trouble and money it's put into him. It's legal and it's respectable. Only—if the regent should somehow get the idea that Felix Dobermann, the millionaire promoter, is also Slip Hanlan, he might let his own respectability run away with his common sense.

"That's where you come in. While he's reading that bill over an' reaching for his pen he'll be remembering where his daughter is, and how long you've been here, and the kind of stink the papers will make if they hear about it. He'll remember that Slip Hanlan never backtracks on his sayso and that you're okay unless something happens to that bill. If it was crooked he might hold out, but it's legal and it's got big men behind it. Bigger than he is, maybe. So he'll figure what he don't know is none of his business and maybe Felix Dobermann is just as good as any other man with the same money and the same friends. He'll sign—and ten minutes after he does you'll be on your way home. Simple, ain't it?"

Anne Bradshaw began to laugh. It was silvery, taunting laughter, but there was nothing hysterical about it. She was just very, very much amused about something, and from what Davis could see of Slip Hanlan's face the gangster didn't like it much.

"So that's it!" she gasped. "Slip Hanlan—a social climber. Trying to buy into the white coat circle. I suppose Felix Dobermann would be trying to buy himself a seat on the Council after a while. Maybe he'd like to be regent, after the big boys got to know what a square guy he is. It's funny!"

Davis saw Slip Hanlan's lips curl in a snarl of fury. No dame laughed at him! He slipped back the safety catch on the little gun. Then something crashed into the back of the shack with a shock that brought flakes of concrete rattling down from the ceiling.

It was a privilege to watch Hanlan draw. There were guns in both hands before he had turned. As he reached the door a second blow shook the hut. A long crack opened in the rear wall and more fragments of concrete dusted down.

The door burst open in his face. It was the slugger, Plug. The man's eyes were popping. "Gees, Slip," he cried, "they're rollin' rocks down on us! Whatta we do?"

There was no silk in Hanlan's snarl now. "Get out there with the Manton and cut their guts out! Use hot stuff on 'em. If they want to play, we'll play with 'em!"

As the door closed behind them Davis was crawling out from under the bed. The girl confronted him, face white, blue eyes blazing. "You meddling fool!" she snapped. "Can't you play detective somewhere else?"

Another boulder struck the rear of the hut with terrific

force. Davis remembered the steeply mounting ledges behind the clearing. Gibbon was using a potent weapon, but against a Manton rapid-fire gun with explosive bullets five naked men would be like babies. Why hadn't the fool stayed put!

What was left of the girl's skirt after she had bound him was on the bed. He twisted it around his middle in a kind of kilt and cautiously tested the door. It was unlocked. He eased It open.

There were three men with Hanlan in the outer room. A frantic pounding began on the outside door. One of the three pulled it open. A man crumpled on his face on the floor. Something whizzed past Davis's head and stuck singing in the wall behind him. It was a long sliver of wood, smeared with some black stuff that smelled like dead fish. As they rolled the man over he saw a second dart buried in his throat.

A man whimpered as another blow rocked the hut. "Whatta we do, Slip?" he wailed. "They got poison on them darts. They got Plug an' Benny too. Whatta we do?"

"We sit tight!" Hanlan snarled. "They can't get us by rollin' rocks. Blowguns won't shoot through concrete. We can wait as long as they can, an' when old Bradshaw gets wise to himself he'll call 'em off!"

"Will he?" Davis stepped out into the room, his gun ready. "Those are my men out there, Hanlan. The men you left sitting on a rock in the middle of the ocean. The regent has nothing to do with them. Open that door."

There was an ugly glint in Hanlan's eyes. It changed suddenly as something dropped over Davis's head, binding his arms to his side. A slim leg tangled with his and he went down with the girl on top of him.

Propped against the wall with his wrists wired together and his legs doubled behind him, Davis watched furiously as Hanlan and the girl faced it out across the little room. She had the gun now, and Hanlan seemed distinctly uncomfortable.

"You talk like a politician, Mr. Hanlan—or is it Dobermann?" she said coolly, "but you don't think like one. Who really planned your little deal for you? Who taught you the pretty speech you made just now? My father has been very curious about that ever since he heard that your precious association was lobbying for a land grant. He wants settlers on Venus, but he doesn't want them exploited, you see. And he's not interested in figureheads. He likes to get to the bottom of things, and so do I."

Hanlan eyed her sullenly. The nose of the little gun was

leveled at the fancy silver buckle on his belt. He said nothing.

"The naked gentleman was telling the truth," the girl told him. "I'm perfectly able to take care of myself without calling in the Boy Heroes. I came here of my own free will, to see just what your game was and how you were going to play it. I want to know who is playing it with you."

"What does it get me?" Hanlan demanded. "I been paid well to keep my mouth shut about that. Why should I spill it to you."

"That's a good question," the girl admitted. "You're really a businessman. You've lost two men, you know. You can't leave this place until someone calls off that blowgun squad." She lifted one slim foot and unfastened a silver rosette from her shoulder; tossed it to the gangster. "That little gadget has been buzzing over since you picked me up," she told him. "There's a Coast Patrol cruiser offshore now, listening to it and waiting for me to signal them in. There'll be a kidnapping charge against you. Our gallant hero here may want to add a charge of *lese majesté* unless you give him back his badge and uniform. Tell me what I want to know and we'll all walk out of here together like old friends."

An oily smile had crept over Hanlan's face. He flipped the little transmitter lightly in the air and caught it again. "Clever, ain't you?" he jeered. "The boat that brought you here was screened against gadgets like this. This shack is screened. Nobody's heard it, and nobody's going to."

Davis thought the gun wavered a little in the girl's hand. His own patience was exhausted. "Stop your crazy chatter and untie me," he growled. "I have men out there who can handle him if you haven't. The Patrol knows how to deal with lugs like him. Now we've got something we can prove on him, there'll be a hundred rats squealing about other things we've known for years but couldn't prove. That's what his kind is like. You won't have to worry about Mister Slip Hanlan Dobermann!"

Anne Bradshaw's eyes blazed. "I expected that of you!" she cried. "The way you blundered into this affair in the beginning was typical of you high and mighty tin horn policemen. You got what you deserved, and I'm glad of it! The Venus government is handling this business in its own way, and that happens to be my way. The Space Patrol will have nothing whatever to do with it!"

Davis wriggled into a sitting position. The maneuver brought his bound wrists against an angular bit of steel that had been digging into his shoulder for the past several minutes. It was apparently a bit of the skeleton of the shack, and it was firmly anchored where it would do the most good.

"When I do get out of here we'll see who handles this case how!" he retorted. "If you think the Patrol or the Triplanetary Commission is going to stand by and see a lot of fatheaded politicians exploit some poor half-starved imbeciles who'll sign anything for a chance at a decent living, you're mistaken. I know too much. My men know too much. Maybe Hanlan and his lugs won't be the only ones we lock up!"

The girl turned her back on him with a jerk. She was fairly quivering with anger. "Mr. Hanlan," she said. "You're looking for a chance to be respectable. All right, you can have it. For the information we want you can be Felix Dobermann. We want settlers here, and the people who can hurt them are the crooked politicians, not nobodies like you. Tell me who is back of this deal and we'll forget I ever left Laxa. We'll forget there ever was a Slip Hanlan. I think you can make sure that the news doesn't slip out in any other way."

Hanlan's jaw sagged. His beady eyes scanned the girl incredulously. "What are you drivin' at?" he demanded.

She never answered, because at that moment one of Hanlan's gunmen let out an anguished yelp and batted at his neck. A new sound impressed itself on Davis—a shrill, humming whine that grew louder every minute. Hanlan himself ducked violently and began to wave his arms like a madman. Then Davis saw them—a little cloud like a wisp of black smoke, streaming through the ventilator grille above his head. Midges!

He sawed furiously at the wires that bound him. Midges had made their life miserable in the jungle. Their bite was sheer torment, and men had been killed by them. Mulligan had found a plant whose odor kept them off, but the cure was about as bad as the complaint.

The room was full of the little demons. The four men were stamping, swatting, stumbling blindly around in what must have been an agony. Then the first of the midges found Davis. Its bite was like a hot needle, pouring vitriol into his veins. Through the tears that filled his eyes he saw Anne Bradshaw, backed against the door with an arm over her eyes, the gun pointed waveringly in front of her.

"Keep back!" she cried. "You'll stay here until you answer me—every one of you!"

The wire on Davis's wrists seemed looser. He hooked the

loop under the little point of steel and jerked on it with all his might. A stab of fire under his left ear and another in his thigh spurred him on. The wire broke. Tottering on his bound legs, he snatched the fragment of cloth from his waist and stuffed it into the ventilator, then dove for the safety of the floor just as Hanlan lunged at the girl.

She was blind with the pain of the midge bites. As Hanlan caught her around the waist her little gun went off with a wicked *spat*, bringing a howl of new pain from one of the three gunmen. She came spinning across the room, tripped over Davis's prone form, and fell. Then Hanlan yanked the door open and there was a rush for the open air.

Through half-closed eyes Davis saw Slip Hanlan go down like a rag doll under an enormous club wielded by a monster out of a nightmare. There were five of the things, black and shapeless, plastered from head to foot with dripping, stinking mud and swinging their clubs with a will. Clouds of midges swarmed like smoky haloes around their heads, and there were tufts of leaves growing out of their scalps and behind their ears as though they had taken root and were sprouting.

One of them was fumbling with the wire on his legs. Another was bending over the girl. The door was shut again and the midges were no longer pouring in through the air-intake. Painfully, through one good eye, Davis surveyed the besmeared, one-armed monstrosity which was presumably Top-Sergeant Gibbon.

"Account for yourself!" he barked. "You had orders to stay where you were until I signalled an attack. I gave no signal."

The mud-covered figure snapped to attention. "Yessir! It was Mulligan, sir. I saw 'em whisperin' and then the four of 'em jumped me. By the time I got loose Mulligan and the kids was rollin' rocks down on the shack and the professor was whittlin' himself a blowgun. When he poked a hole in the air filter and began pourin' in some stinkin' stuff as bait for the midges, I figured I might as well lend 'em a hand."

The girl was staring in bewilderment at the mud-covered figure bending over he. "It's Tomkins, Miss Bradshaw," it said apologetically. "Professor Tomkins, from the university. I was with you when—when it happened. Remember?"

That silvery laugh made Davis wince. He distrusted it. "If father could see you now!"

The professor undoubtedly blushed under the mud. "They took our clothes, you know," he told her owlishly. "All of them. But for Captain Davis and Mr. Mulligan we might not be here."

"Not *the* Captain Davis?" She was being acid-sweet. "I've heard so much about you, Captain. I hardly exepcted to meet you so—informally, shall we say?"

Someone had brought in a blanket. Davis draped it around him like a toga and drew himself up with what dignity a badly swollen face left him. She didn't look much better herself, he reflected with satisfaction.

"Bring them in here," he commanded. "All of 'em. We're going to have a showdown!"

They lined up across the end of the little room. Hanlan and his men were swollen and sullen, Gibbon looked sheepish, and the professor and the two boys had dried a little and were beginning to peel. They looked thoroughly embarrassed in spite of the clothes they had managed to find. Only Mulligan and the girl seemed calm.

The old man ambled in after the others, black gobs of mud still dripping from his broad body. "Too bad you got bit, Cap," he said solicitously. "It looked like the best way to smoke 'em out, when the rocks wouldn't fetch 'em." He giggled. "Last time I remember rollin' rocks on anyone was clean back when I was just a cub. The Horse-Eaters was tryin' to take over our caves an' we stood 'em off until our food give out. That was when I got hit on the head. They was a doctor once claimed that might be why I'm so old. I heal quick, like a lizard when you pull his tail off. I dunno how many sets of teeth I had. They just keep on pushin' out an' comin' in again."

"The blowguns were the professor's idea," Gibbon volunteered. "They found some kind of big red snail with poison in it that keeps a man paralyzed for two-three days. Mulligan knew about it. Then the two of 'em kept the door covered while the boys rolled rocks."

Tomkins blushed under his mud. His face, with a disreputable stubble bristling on the chin, was almost clean. "As an anthropologist I have had the opportunity to observe primitive man and study his methods of assault and defense," he explained pedantically.

"Just a moment!" The girl's voice was very quiet but it held a sting. "As representative of the Venus government I happen to be in authority here. These gentlemen will bear me out. And I intend to find out before we leave this room who is really behind the land-grab to which Mr. Hanlan is so naively hitching his wagon. When Mr. Mulligan—interfered—I had made an offer. It is still good."

Davis stared at her aghast. "You'll let that crawling worm get away with this?" he demanded.

She eyed him calmly. "That was my offer," she said. "The government has enough information about Mr. Hanlan to make a very good executive out of him if he chooses to turn his talents and his money to such a worthy project as colonization of the West Continent. I'm sure he will cooperate. If he agrees we will forget about what may have happened in the past few days—all of us. That is an order too. You understand orders, of course, Captain Davis."

A grin spread over Mulligan's long face, cracking its crust of mud. "I got a few scars here some place 'at Slip Hanlan give me onetime," he observed hopefully. "That was quite a while back, when he was just a punk. I'd be willin' to persuade him for you, ma'am."

"Forget it!" Hanlan's swollen face was dark. "It'll be a pleasure to see the slob get it in the neck. Cookson is the one who's behind it. I put up the scrip and he put it through the Council—for half the profits. Only half wasn't enough. If I didn't cut him a bigger piece he was going to let the Regent know about me and get the whole deal turned over to his Department of Immigration, to be handled at government expense until the Council could be sure everything was over the table. That's why I grabbed you—so the Regent would think twice about listening to what he might have to say. You gimme a chance and there won't be any more Slip Hanlan. You have Slip Hanlan's say-so for that!"

Stuffed into pants that were too small for him, Davis sat gloomily in the stern of the Coast Patrol launch that had come at Anne Bradshaw's signal to pick them up. Dimly, through his gloom, he heard Old Man Mulligan's hoarse voice making highly mythical replies to Professor Tomkins' persistent questions. Maybe he was a Neanderthal hangover who had lived out the whole span of human history. Maybe he was Moses' father-in-law and Abraham's bodyguard and Julius Caesar's blacksmith. Maybe he had won the American War and the battle of the Drylands. What difference did it make?

What it boiled down to was that the Space Patrol had been given a going-over by a cocky girl and a doddering old man. It had lost its pants, not to mention its shirt, and it was being ferried back to Laxa by those damned mud-bound landsmen of the Coast Patrol to be the laughing stock of every needle-headed nincompoop in the system!

He'd show 'em yet what the Patrol was! If any living being so much as breathed a word of what had happened he'd blow their pretty little deal wide open! He'd give Slip Hanlan a go-ing-over that would last him as long as he could remember. He'd make old Bradshaw bow and scrape and back water like a crab. He'd get Old Man Mulligan roaring drunk and put him in the Patrol where he'd learn what discipline was like, if he had to drink the old liar silly himself to do it. And as for that girl!

He colored at the flashing smile she threw him. Maybe she could read minds. He hoped so!

He sucked in a long breath of fishy, clammy fog. He'd be glad to smell the tang of canned air again. He'd be glad to get off this hog-wallow of a world and feel peace under him again. He'd be glad to see the stars. Damn glad!

But before he went he'd give that blonde hell-cat something to worry about!